ISBN 978-0-276-44223-0

www.readersdigest.co.uk

The Reader's Digest Association Limited, 11 Westferry Circus, Canary Wharf, London E14 4HE

# of love & life

Three novels selected and condensed
by Reader's Digest

The Reader's Digest Association Limited, London

CONTENTS

Constance
ROSIE THOMAS

If you've never known your real parents how can you truly know who you are? That is the question that has haunted Constance all her life. A foundling left for strangers to find, then adopted into the Thorne family, Constance has never really felt she belonged anywhere. She's spent the years trying to find her identity. Now the time has come to end the search.

Prologue
London, June 1963

THE BOY AND the girl were both sixteen. It was nearly ten o'clock, which meant they would soon have to separate for a night and a whole day.

They crept down the empty street with their arms twined, he shortening his step to match hers and she resting her head on his shoulder. The overhanging plane trees made a tunnel of the pavement. The gardens on either side were dark recesses of rustling leaves, the territory of prowling cats and maybe a rat invading a dustbin. Under one of the trees the boy stopped walking. He hooked his arms round the girl's shoulders and kissed her for the hundredth time. Her mouth felt bruised, but she kissed him back. His hands moved down to cover her breasts.

'Mikey.'

'I love you,' he protested.

'*Mikey*. My dad said ten o'clock. You heard him.'

'We've got ten minutes, then.'

He raised his head and glanced about. There was no one to be seen. He steered her towards the nearest gate. It stood open and a tiled path of coloured triangles and diamonds gleamed faintly in the darkness. No light showed behind the glass door panels, or in any of the windows.

'Mike, we can't,' she murmured, but she came with him anyway.

Behind the hedge she pressed her mouth against his, teasing him with the sly curve of her smile. He answered by stroking his hand upwards from her knee. High up his fingers met the smooth bulge of soft bare flesh above the stocking top. They pressed into the vertical mattress of leaves, their tongues busy.

At first he thought the sound was a cat among the dustbins. It was a high-pitched cry, somewhere between a bleat and a howl. It stopped and then started again.

Kathy moved her head sideways. 'What's that?' she breathed.

'Some old cat.'

The cry came again.

'It's not. Listen, it sounds just like a baby.'

'Don't be soft. Come back here.'

'Leave off. Where *is* it?'

She stooped down, pushed aside the lowest branches of the hedge and felt along the margin of dead leaves and blown litter underneath.

'My God.'

Kathy rocked back, almost tipping over her heels. She was lifting a bag in her two hands, a bag made of brown plastic that was supposed to be leather, with a zip and two upright looped handles. The mouth of the bag gulped open and the cat's cry was much louder.

'Look at this.'

He knelt beside her as she dipped her hands inside.

'Look,' she breathed.

She was holding a small bundle of blanket. Between them they turned the folds aside and touched the baby's tiny head. It was streaked with dark patches and waxy white stuff. Its mouth was open and its eyes screwed shut. Now that they saw that it really was a baby, its crying sounded weak and nearly hopeless.

Mike was amazed. 'What's someone's baby doing out here?'

With the baby cradled against her, Kathy glanced up at him. 'It's abandoned. The mother's left it because she can't keep it. Probably no one knows she's even had it. The poor thing.'

With the tip of her finger, Kathy stroked the baby's cheek. Mike wasn't sure whether *poor thing* meant the baby or its mother.

'What'll we do?'

Kathy answered as she knelt and rocked the bundle. 'We'll have to call the police. And an ambulance. We'll have to knock on someone's door. Big houses like these, probably they've all got phones.' She glanced up at the house, but there were still no lights. 'Next door, there's someone in. Go *on*, then.'

'Just ring their bell, you mean, and say we've found a baby?'

'Yes,' she shouted at him.

A displeased man came to the door in his slippers, and behind him a woman in a nylon housecoat peered into the street. Mike had hardly finished his sentence before the woman brushed past both of them and ran round to the other garden. She reappeared with the brown bag in her hands, and with Kathy still cradling the baby.

'Graham, ring the police and say what's happened. Come in here, love. Let's have a look at the poor mite.'

The two women went into the front room and bent down together. They laid the baby on the cushions of the settee and unwrapped the blanket. The crying had stopped; now it just lay still. Underneath it was dressed in nothing but a tiny yellow cardigan and a dingy piece of towel secured with a safety pin. The woman unpinned the improvised nappy.

'It's a girl,' Kathy whispered. Mike caught a glimpse of a thick purple-grey stump where its bellybutton should be, and quickly looked away.

'What's this?' the woman said. She pointed, and Kathy saw the glint of something pinned to the blanket.

It was a little pendant of marcasites with a rod and a tiny screw fastening for a pierced ear.

'It's an earring.'

As she lifted it, Kathy's eyes filled up with sudden hot tears. Before she said goodbye, before she pushed the bag into the hedge, the baby's mother must have fixed her earring to the blanket as a memento. Perhaps at this very minute she was holding its pair, and crying for her lost daughter. It was the saddest thing Kathy had ever imagined.

The woman touched her shoulder. 'You just don't know, do you? About people's lives?' She hurried away and came back with a folded terry nappy and a white shawl. 'I keep these here for when my Sandra brings her little one round.' Her tongue clicked. 'Baby's cold, isn't she? Out in the night like that. Let's get her wrapped up. I'm going to put the kettle on for a hot-water bottle.'

'I'll hold her while you do it,' Kathy said firmly.

'Slip her inside your cardi. You know, for body warmth.'

'Police ought to be here any minute now,' the man muttered.

He went to the window and looped back the curtain so he could see the street. Before his wife came back with the hot-water bottle, the blue light of a police car was flashing beyond the privet hedge. They heard the shrilling of an ambulance bell and then the room filled up with men in uniforms. One of them took the baby out of Kathy's arms and there was nothing left for her to do but to watch as they prepared to take her away.

'Well done, love,' the ambulance man said to her. 'The nurses will give her a bottle and warm her up and she'll be as right as rain.'

A few minutes later, the ambulance had driven the baby away.

Kathy sat on the sofa, staring at the floor and shivering a little. Mike sat beside her and held her hand, but she didn't seem to notice him.

The brown plastic bag along with the yellow cardigan, the blanket, the damp towel and the single earring lay at the policeman's feet. With a cup of tea balanced on the arm of his chair, he was waiting to take their statements. His partner sat opposite them.

'We were just walking home from the pictures,' Mike said.

'You were walking past and you heard a cry?'

'We weren't walking. We'd stopped.'

'On the pavement?'

'Well, no. We'd gone into next door's garden. Just for a minute. Didn't seem as though there was anyone in.'

The policeman looked at him. 'Let's see. You'd slipped behind the hedge for a kiss and a cuddle?'

Kathy blushed crimson.

Mike said, 'No. Um, yes . . .'

'It's all right, son. It's not against the law. Did you see anyone?'

Kathy and Mike shook their heads. The street had been deserted, they were both sure of that.

'Then we heard this crying. I thought it was a cat.'

'I didn't,' Kathy said. 'I knew what it was, straight off.' She chewed at the corner of her thumb nail. 'Will you find her mother?'

'We'll do our best to get her to come forward. She'll be needing medical attention, for one thing. That baby's no more than a few hours old. But she'll be running the risk of prosecution if she does, and that could mean up to five years in prison, depending on the circumstances. So they don't often change their minds, in my experience.' He put his pen away and looked at his watch. 'That's it, then. Back to work for us. Thanks for the cuppa.'

When Kathy heard it was ten past eleven her hands flew up to her mouth. 'Oh, no. My dad'll kill me,' she gasped.

The policemen gave them a lift home. Kathy's house was nearest and Mike waited in the back of the patrol car as she walked up to her front door with one of the policemen at her shoulder. Even in the dim light of the porch Mike could see how angry her dad was when he opened the door, but the sight of the policeman changed that. After a few words Kathy's dad put his arms round her and led her inside.

She didn't look back, and the door closed behind her.

At the Royal London Hospital, a paediatrician and a nurse finished their examination of the baby. The doctor filled in a form and signed it, then looked up at the nurse.

'We'll be needing a name.'

The nurse glanced at the reports that had come in with the ambulance crew. 'A young couple found her, in a bag under a hedge. In Constance Crescent. I think that's pretty.'

'You can't call a baby Constance Crescent.'

'Constance, I mean.'

The doctor scribbled it down. 'And the surname?'

The nurse glanced at the paperwork again. 'The name of the young girl is Kathleen Merriwether.'

'Constance Merriwether? That's a bit of a mouthful.' But he had already written it in the vacant space on the form.

'If the mother doesn't come forward it'll be a "Baby Constance" picture and story for the local rag,' the nurse said.

The doctor sighed and took off his glasses.

Fed and washed, and dressed in clean clothes, the baby slept in her hospital crib.

Chapter One

NIGHTS ON THE island were rarely silent.

The guttural scraping and grunting and booming that was the frog chorus could rise into a din sufficient to drown out all the other wildlife before fading away into a single disconsolate bleat. The many dogs who ranged the village streets barked incessantly, and in the small hours the roosters started up a brassy call and answer that lasted well into daylight. But towards dawn the world suddenly fell silent.

On this day the sky lightened from pitch-black to a vast grey touched at the eastern rim with green, against which the coconut palms on the crown of the ridge stood out like paper silhouettes. In the waiting hush the light strengthened and the horizon flushed with pink and orange.

In a beautiful place, another lovely day was breaking.

Wayan Tupereme yawned at the door of his house, then shoved his feet into the brown plastic sandals that he had left neatly paired on the step. He made a brief circuit of his garden, nipping off a flower here and there, and by the time he was back at his door it was daylight. A little later he trod quietly down the dusty path beside the thick screen of leathery leaves and twined stems separating his garden from the Englishwoman's, and strolled up to the next-door house. He stooped to place something on the lower step of the deep verandah that ran all the way round the little single-storey house. It was a tiny basket woven from palm fronds and containing some squares of coarse leaf on which were laid an orange flower like a miniature sun, a scatter of scarlet petals and a few grains of rice. Wayan touched his hands to his forehead, then made his way slowly back to his own house.

Ten minutes later, Connie's alarm clock went off. She wasn't used to waking to its shrill beep, and her arm thrashed as she tried to find the button to silence it. She blinked at the time. It was six thirty.

The car would be here to pick her up in half an hour.

'Get going,' she advised herself. She felt apprehensive, but there wasn't time to dwell on that. The car was coming. There was a seven-thirty call.

The bedroom doors opened onto the verandah at the back of the house. As she did every morning, Connie opened them to let the light flood in, and stepped out into the air. It was still cool, with a faint breeze stirring the leaves of the banana palms. There was no pool; she had deliberately chosen not to have one, although the other Europeans who lived in the area all did. There was only the liquid music of water trickling down the rocks a little way off, and the view itself. It took her by surprise and then engrossed her, even after six years.

The house clung to the upper rim of a steep valley. From beneath her feet the ground fell away into the gorge and rose again on the opposite side, densely clothed in a tangle of trees. At the bottom of the cleft lay the river, a wide silver sweep with the morning mist rising from it. The cocks were still crowing, and from the road on the other side of the house came the distant buzz of motorbikes as people headed for work.

Connie smiled at her view, thinking how lucky she was to have all this. On an ordinary day she would have made tea and sat out here, gazing at the green wave until it was time to do something else. But today was not ordinary. The outside world had arrived.

She had laid out the shooting script the night before, her tape-recorder and her laptop and the sheets of music, even her clothes. All she had to do was shower and dress and pack everything into her bag.

At 7 a.m., Connie carried her bag out of the house. The offering placed by Wayan lay in front of the house temple, a little shrine sited at the appropriate corner of the verandah. She nodded her head to acknowledge it, then stepped past. The car was already waiting for her. It was a silver-grey Toyota Land Cruiser, with tinted windows and enough room to seat seven people.

The driver leapt out as she emerged, and hurried to open the rear door for her. '*Selamat pagi*, ma'am,' he said. 'Good morning. All set now?'

Connie knew him quite well. His name was Kadek Daging and he was Wayan's relative by marriage. Usually he worked in his small general store up in the main street of the village, but today he would have left one of his several sons in charge of the shop in order to undertake this important driving assignment for 'the movie company', as he put it. Actually it was less a movie than a trio of expensive thirty-second commercials for an online bank that were being shot on the island. But Connie didn't want to diminish his sense of importance by making the distinction.

She would have shaken his hand, but she took her cue from him and put the palms of her hands together to make a polite bow. 'Good morning, Kadek. Thank you for coming.'

To preserve the formality of the occasion she climbed into the back of the car, even though she would have preferred to sit up front. Kadek jumped smartly into the driver's seat and eased the Toyota out into the stream of scooters and motorcycles.

Once they were established as kings of the village traffic, Kadek asked, 'Ma'am, would you care for a cold drink? A cool towel?'

Normally he would address her as '*Ibu*', as he called all the other European women customers and neighbours. Today, however, they were in a different relationship.

'Thank you,' she said gravely.

There was a cool-box in the foot-well, in which were bottles of water and soft drinks and a couple of rolled hand towels. Connie took out a towel and patted her hands and face with it, although she wasn't hot. Kadek nodded with satisfaction at having done the right thing.

After half an hour's driving, away from the village and following the course of the river to where the valley spread in a series of pale ledges planted with rice, they reached the location.

There were several Toyotas parked in a line, three trucks standing with their doors open, two caravans, a trailer-mounted diesel generator, a couple of pick-ups from which heavy boxes were being unloaded, green awnings set up for shade, and an air of purposeful activity.

Connie looked at her watch. It was seven thirty precisely. The sun was gathering strength, promising a hot day ahead. On the horizon, across the shimmering paddy, the sacred Mount Agung was a pale-blue pyramid.

'Thanks, Kadek.'

He opened the door for her to step out. 'Welcome, ma'am. Anything more for you? I have to collect other film people.'

'Of course. Off you go.'

As Kadek reversed away, Connie shouldered her bag and walked towards the set.

'Hi,' Angela called out, and waved her arm in welcome. Angela was Connie's old friend from London, a producer with the company that was making the commercials.

Connie gave her friend a hug. 'You all right?' she murmured in her ear.

Angela had an unusually expressive set of features. With her back to the location, she made her wasps-invade-the-picnic face. 'Couple of the crew complaining about their hotel. They ran out of beer last night.'

'That all?'

Angela shrugged. 'More or less.'

Connie was relieved to hear it. Usually she worked alone in her studio, either here in Bali or in London, and she rarely came face to face with the agency who commissioned her work, let alone travelled to commercial shoots. But she knew enough about the ad business to be certain that worse things could go wrong on location than the booze being in temporarily short supply. Could, and probably would.

She was anxious, and in Bali that was most unusual. Her life here was calm, pared-down and minimal like the interior of her little house, and in its own uneventful way it was satisfying.

Now, disorientatingly, London had come to her.

She put her arm through Angela's, saying cheerfully, 'So let them drink green tea. Or fresh mango and papaya juice. Be different. This is Bali. Come on, Ange, let's get some breakfast. How's Himself this morning?'

'Fine. In a pretty good mood. Really keen to get rolling.'

Rayner Ingram, the director, was a tall, saturnine man who said little, but when he did speak he made his remarks count. He and Angela worked regularly together. Connie knew that Angela was in love with him. Producer–director relationships weren't exactly uncommon in the business. It was just uncommon for them to have happy endings.

They reached the open flap of the tent, which had a fine net screen across it to keep insects out. Angela gathered the netting in one hand.

'Now's your chance to meet the clients,' she whispered.

Two men were sitting in canvas chairs at a folding table, surrounded by two others and a woman and a circle of cups and plates and cafetieres. Both of them looked up at Connie.

Angela said warmly, 'Simon, Marcus? This is Constance Thorne. Our musical director, of course.'

The older one half got to his feet and held out a big hand. 'Ah, Boom Girl,' he shouted. 'We're honoured. Simon Sheringham.'

Connie smiled at him. 'Hello.'

She hated being called Boom Girl. If it had ever been welcome, it had stopped being so a very long time ago. She had written the Boom music when she was barely twenty. A fluke. A day's work.

'*Boom, boom, baboom ba ba, bababa ba.*' The younger client sang the few bars as he also stood up. 'Hi. Marcus Atkins.'

'Hello.' Connie shook hands with him, and smiled some more.

From farther along the table the ad agency copywriter and art director nodded at her, too cool for introductions. The agency producer was very pretty, Connie noted.

Angela and Rayner were conferring over the schedule of the day's shots.

'I'll just get some coffee,' Connie murmured. As she poured herself a cup, she heard a crackle of walkie-talkies.

'We're on,' the first assistant called to the crew. It was the signal for work to begin. People began shifting towards the set, but there would be several hours of waiting and watching while the rest of the gear was brought in and lights and cameras were set up. If everything went really well the camera would be turning over before the lunch break was called. Connie's gamelan orchestra was listed as the first shot.

When she first arrived in Bali, Connie had been intending to make a short stopover on her way to London from Sydney. The plan had been to take stock of what was left of her life, and let her bewilderment subside a little. It was only a few weeks since Seb had told her that he was in love with a Chinese violinist, and intended to marry her.

At that time Sébastian Bourret was becoming a sought-after conductor. When he made the announcement, sitting on the balcony of their rented flat overlooking Sydney Harbour, Connie had been his lover and partner for more than six years. Their home was nominally in London but Seb travelled so much that they were away more than they were there, and this had suited Connie well. She had her own work, composing music for television and commercials, and as technology developed it was becoming increasingly easy to do that work anywhere in the world.

She wasn't under the illusion that Seb was wildly in love with her, any more than she was with him. But they had much in common, and they were deeply fond of one another.

Then Sébastian really had fallen in love, with the gifted Sung Mae Lin, who was no bigger than a child even though she was almost thirty. Connie was eight years her senior, and Mae Lin unwittingly made her feel too big and the wrong age, and unwanted, and unhappy in a way that was too familiar, however hard she fought against that and the memories that were stirred by it.

None of it was Mae Lin's fault, or Seb's, really, or her own for that matter. It was just one of those things that happened. There had been no alternative for Connie but to withdraw from her own life, as quickly and as gracefully as she could manage it.

Connie's London home was still the apartment that she had shared with Seb. He had made his share of it over to her and she had kept the place, although it was bare of most of the furniture they had chosen and there were few of her possessions set out in it. She liked it better that way; it was easier to slip in and out of an almost empty space. Minimalism was closer to invisibility.

When she arrived in Bali, she'd had no plans. In her raw state she had fled from the big hotels and beaches of the coastal strip close to Denpasar and headed inland. It was here in the village that she first heard gamelan music played live, not for tourists but for the musicians themselves and their friends. This was temple music, and music for festivals, processions and weddings. She had loved the sonorous gongs, and the shimmering notes of metal that fell through the air like drops of clear water.

Angela suddenly appeared at her side, and Connie rapidly gathered her thoughts as she drank the last mouthful of her coffee.

'I'll be on set,' Angela said.

The day's set was the temple at the edge of the rice paddy over which the set dressers were swarming.

Constance consulted her watch, having already looked at it more times this morning than she would normally do in a week. 'The musicians will be here in fifteen minutes or so.'

'Right. Straight to costume and make-up, then.'

The bus carrying the musicians arrived punctually and Connie hurried forward to meet them. Battling with their instruments, a line of six men spilled down the steps. They were not much bigger than their metallophones, big xylophones with keys made of bronze, and considerably smaller than the great gong. They were her friends.

'I am very, very nervous,' Ketut called as soon as he saw her.

Connie held out her hands to him. 'Don't say you don't want to do it?'

Ketut had smooth skin and it gleamed in the bright sunlight like oiled wood. 'Oh, no. We are film stars already in Seminugul. There is no going back. But I am afraid of letting you down, Connie.'

Ketut was one of the most talented musicians she had ever worked with. She had been recording some of his performances with the big ensemble of fifty musicians called the *gamelan gong,* and she counted herself lucky to be able to play percussion with this smaller, less perfectionist group. Connie knew that she was not the best drummer in the world, but she loved the sessions when they played together.

'You won't, Ketut. You don't even have to play if you don't want to; just look as though you are, for the camera.'

The actual music track would be laid down in post-production. This was the music that Connie had been commissioned to produce.

Behind her she could hear the Australian gaffer routinely cursing into his walkie-talkie because someone hadn't brought over a camera dolly. All the musicians were staring into the snake-pit of cables, and at the little temple caught under the brilliant ultra-sunshine of the lights.

'Don't worry, really, don't worry,' she reassured them all. She led them over to the caravan that was being used for male costume and make-up and left them there.

The script called for a Balinese wedding. The temple was dressed up with flowers and baskets of fruit. Over pop-eyed stone statues people had fixed parasols of yellow silk with lavish fringes, and rakish garlands of scarlet and orange blossoms were draped round the necks of stone dragons and snakes. The hot colours seemed to vibrate under the lights.

Eleven o'clock came and went. Connie supervised the unpacking and setting up of the instruments, on the exact spot that the crew indicated. The musicians emerged from make-up, giggling. They had been costumed in sarongs of black and white checks with broad saffron-yellow satin sashes. They wore flowers round their necks, their eyes had been painted and their lips reddened. Their ordinary haircuts, as worn by waiters and teachers and shopkeepers, which is what they were, had been gelled into slick quiffs. Every time they caught a glimpse of each other there was an explosion of laughter. Trying not to laugh herself, Connie shepherded them onto the set.

While the lights were adjusted, she positioned her recording equipment and ran the players through an approximation of the twenty-two seconds of music that would accompany the finished commercial.

'This is really not Balinese wedding music,' Ketut protested.

'I know. Forgive me?'

Angela came across and reassured the musicians that they wouldn't have long to wait. Connie could read the anxiety in her rigid shoulders. The schedule listed the shot of the bridal attendants for completion before the lunch break as well as the gamelan orchestra, and that called for ten little Balinese girls wearing complicated headdresses, who were at present corralled in the female wardrobe caravan. Rayner Ingram was frowning and shaking his head as he looked into the monitor.

But then, suddenly, there was a flurry of action.

'We're going,' the first assistant called. 'Camera rolling.'

Connie gave the signal to Ketut. As if there were no lights, micro-phones, cables or cameras, as if they were doing it for their own pleasure under a bamboo shelter, the little orchestra played her makeshift music. Their faces lit up. The camera on its dolly rolled towards them.

After twenty-two seconds, she gave them the cut signal. Reluctantly the metallophones and kettle gongs pattered into silence.

Rayner and Angela conferred. Then Angela and the first assistant crossed to the agency people and consulted with them. The musicians waited, their eyes fixed on Connie.

'Going again,' came the call.

They did three more takes. Then the first assistant told the musicians, 'That's fine with the orchestra. Director's happy. We're done with you.'

It was Connie they looked to for confirmation. She beamed and applauded. 'Ketut, you were brilliant. All of you. Thank you.'

'I don't know. There were some things,' Ketut began, but the crew were hurrying them and their instruments off the set. Time was money.

Connie and the file of musicians heading back to the caravan passed another procession coming the other way. The bridal attendants were overawed eight-year-old girls cast from the nearby school. Their faces had been painted to resemble dancers' masks, with eyes outlined in thick lines of kohl that swept up at the corners, rouged cheekbones and crimson lips. With tall gilt crowns on their heads and tunic dresses of pale gold tissue, they looked exquisite. Their role was to scatter flower petals in the path of the as-yet-unseen bride as the bridegroom and his supporters waited for her at the temple steps.

Once they had changed into their own clothes, the musicians settled into the service tent, eyeing the handsome Indonesian actor cast as the bridegroom, who was busy with his mobile phone. Connie quietly handed Ketut the fee, in cash, for the orchestra's work.

Out on the set the beautiful Balinese girls scattered flower petals on a strip of crimson carpet. Out of shot, set dressers sprayed the temple garlands with water in an attempt to stop them wilting under the hot sun. Miraculously, the attendants were wrapped after just two takes.

'OK, people, let's have lunch,' called the first assistant.

Within three minutes the service tent was full of ravenous crew. Ketut and the others politely took this influx as a signal to leave. Connie went with them to the bus.

'We play again on Tuesday? You can come?' Ketut asked her.

Tuesday was their regular evening for music.

'Yes, please,' Connie said. It was one of the best times of her week.

She stood and waved as the bus bumped down the rice-paddy track.

In the service tent Angela was asking Tara, the pretty agency producer, what she thought they might do about the British actress who was playing the bride. She had spent the morning confined to her hotel bathroom with a stomach upset.

'I've absolutely *no* idea,' Tara sighed.

On their way out later, Angela said to Connie through clenched teeth, 'If that damned woman says she has "no idea" once more about what is supposed to be her bloody *job,* I'm going to hit her.'

'She's getting a great tan, though,' Connie said, laughing.

In the absence of any bride, the afternoon was given over to the bridegroom and his friends. They marched out of wardrobe splendid in starched white jackets with red headcloths knotted over their foreheads.

It was a complicated reaction shot. The men were supposed to be waiting in profile in a proud, anticipatory little group for the big moment, the first sight of the bride following behind her petal-strewing attendants. Then, as they caught sight of her, the men were to register a sequence of surprise, disbelief and then dismay.

Once the camera had captured all this the view then shifted to the other perspective. The bride's father—an approximate Prince Charles look-alike—was to be kitted out in full morning dress. On his arm would come the bride, dressed in a white meringue wedding dress with a bouquet of pink rosebuds and a dangling silver horseshoe, blonde ringlets framing her face within a froth of veil.

With the establishing shot, Connie's music was to segue into a suggestion of 'Here Comes the Bride', then dip into a minor key to match the surprise and dismay, and end in a clatter of discordant notes. Then, on the screen would appear the bank's logo and the words 'The Right Time and the Right Place. Every Time. Always.' To the accompaniment of a long, reverberating gong-note.

'It's advertising,' Angela said drily.

The day wore on. After five or six takes, Rayner Ingram declared that he was satisfied with the shot. The tropical dusk was beginning to collect at the margins of the paddy, and Mount Agung was a conical smudge of shadow on the far horizon.

'That's it for today, folks,' announced the first assistant.

The crew began dismantling the lights, and Simon Sheringham stood up and yawned. 'Time for a drink, boys and girls,' he said.

'You are so completely right,' Tara drawled.

Angela murmured to Connie, 'Are you joining us for dinner?'

Angela's duties would now shift to hostess and leisure facilitator for the agency and clients, but her eyes were on Rayner Ingram, who was stalking away towards the waiting Toyotas.

'Do you need me?' Connie was thinking of her secluded verandah and the frog chorus, which would sound like a lullaby tonight.

'Well . . . not really,' Angela said.

'Then I think I might just quietly go home.'

An hour later, Connie was sitting on the verandah in her rattan chair. The darkness came with dramatic speed, filling up the gorge and flooding over the palms on the ridge. Dogs barked at the occasional motorbike out on the road, and sometimes she heard a squeak of voices from Wayan Tupereme's house, but mostly there were only the intimate rustlings of wildlife in the vegetation and the conversation of frogs.

Connie ticked off a mental list. After tomorrow, there were two more linked commercials to shoot. It was going to be a hard week's work, but now it was under way her apprehension had faded and she felt stimulated. It was good to have a surge of adrenaline. And then, when it was all over, the agency people and the crew and Angela would disperse, back to the cities, and she would still be here quietly making gamelan music with Ketut and his friends and looking out at her view.

At the same time, the Boom music started running through her head, and stayed there. Damn Simon Sheringham and Marcus Atkins.

It wasn't just the bank clients, though. It was the disorientating effect of finding London in Bali. It stirred her memories and brought them freely floating to the surface of her mind.

Connie's thoughts tracked backwards, all the way down the years to when she was a little girl, to the day after they moved into the new house in Echo Street, London. She was six, her sister Jeanette almost twelve.

On their first night she'd had a terrible nightmare. A faceless man came gliding out of the wardrobe in her unfamiliar bedroom and tried to suffocate her. Her mother rushed in wearing her nightdress, with her hair wound on spiny mesh rollers. Connie was shouting for her father, but Hilda told her that her dad needed his sleep; he had to open the shop at eight o'clock in the morning, like he did every day.

'I don't like this bedroom. It's frightening,' Connie sobbed.

'I've heard quite enough about that.'

Connie had had a fight with Jeanette over who was to get which bedroom. Jeanette had won, as she always did.

Hilda scolded Connie. 'It's a lovely room. You're a lucky little girl. Now go to sleep and let's have no more of this nonsense.'

In the morning, Connie decided to put the spectres of the night behind her. She marched through the house, past Hilda clattering the breakfast dishes, into the garden and all the way to the shed at the far end.

She climbed the wall and made the daring leap to the shed roof, then perched on the ridge. From that vantage point, with its view of the neighbouring gardens, she launched into a long, complicated song that she had made up, bawling it out until Hilda shouted through the kitchen window that she was to stop disturbing the whole neighbourhood.

Now, what Connie recollected most clearly was the importance that the singing and the song had assumed—like a reef in the turbulent currents of daily life. Music was already becoming her resort, in a family with a mother and father who would have had difficulty distinguishing between Handel and Cliff Richard, and a sister who could not hear a note of music. Or any other sound.

In the new front room at Echo Street there was the upright piano that had come with them from their old flat. No one else in the family ever played it and it was badly out of tune, but the instrument had belonged to Connie's father's mother and Tony always insisted that it was a good one, worth a bit of money. Hilda kept it well dusted and used the top as a display shelf for their wedding picture, a photograph of Jeanette as a newborn in layers of pink knitwear, and one of Connie as an older baby, propped up in Jeanette's lap.

As soon as she was old enough to lift the gleaming curved lid for herself, Connie claimed the piano for her own. She loved splaying her hands over the ivory and black keys, linking sequences of notes or hammering out crashing discords. She could sit for an hour at a time, absorbed in her own compositions or in picking out the tunes she heard on the radio. To Connie's ear these first musical experiments sounded festive in the quiet house.

In time, music and musical composition became Connie's profession. Success came early, almost by accident, with the theme music she wrote for a confectionery commercial.

The Boom chocolate-bar tune turned into one of those rare hits that passed out of the realm of mere advertising and drilled into the collective consciousness. For a time the few bars turned into a shorthand trill for anything new and saucy and self-indulgent. The royalties poured in and Connie's small musical world acknowledged her as Boom Girl.

Nowadays the money from her early work had slowed to a trickle, but Connie still earned enough to live on. When she needed more, it was possible to make a rapid sortie from Bali to London and put in some calls to old friends like Angela. Quite often, she could bring the commissions home to Bali and work on them there.

She had no idea how long this arrangement would remain possible, but Connie didn't think about the future very much. The past was more difficult to evade: it was there in her dreams, and just under the skin of consciousness, but in her quiet daily life among the villagers and the gamelan musicians she could contain it.

Now Angela and all the people with her had landed like a spaceship on Connie's remote planet, and they brought London and memories leaking out of the airlocks and caused her to examine her life more critically than she would otherwise have done. As she sat in the warm, scented night, she asked herself unaccustomed questions.

Is this a useful way to live?

Is this what I want?

Am I happy?

That was the hardest question of all. In this beautiful place, living comfortably among friends and making music with them, she had no reason for unhappiness. Except that this island life—for all its sunshine and scent and richness—did not have Bill in it.

Connie had learned to live without him, because there was no alternative. But happiness—that simple resonance with the world that came from being with the man she loved—she didn't have, and never would.

The thought of him, as it always did, sent an electric shock deep into the core of her being. By concentrating hard Connie cut off the flow of thoughts and brought them back to the present. She had work to do, and that was a diversion and a solace as well. She had learned that long ago.

She would do the work and maybe the questions would answer themselves, or at least stop ringing in her ears.

Chapter Two

NOAH HEADED DOWNRIVER, towards the battlements of Tower Bridge. It was the beginning of June, a warm and sunny early evening, and the Embankment was crowded with people leaving work and heading home, or making for bars and cinemas.

Noah had sat with his mother for over an hour. He linked his fingers with hers, rubbing his thumb over the thin skin on the back of her hand. Sometimes she drifted into a doze, then a minute or two later she would be fully awake again, looking into his eyes and smiling.

'Do you want anything, Mum?' he asked, leaning close to her so she could see his face.

She shook her head.

At the end of an hour, she had fallen into a deeper sleep. He slid his hand from beneath hers. He stood up, and kissed her forehead.

'I'll be in tomorrow, same time,' he murmured, for his own benefit rather than hers.

Noah hadn't worked out where he was going; he just wanted to be outside in the fresh air, away from the hospital. He stuck his hands in his pockets and walked more slowly, threading through the crowds.

Under a plane tree, just where the shade from the branches dulled the glitter of dusty cobbles, a performance artist was setting up his pitch. He was wearing a silver robot costume and all the exposed skin of his body was painted to match. As Noah stood watching, with jerky robotic movements the performer tapped a silver metal helmet over his silver-sprayed hair and took a step up onto a plinth. His arms rotated a few degrees and froze in midair. Losing interest, Noah was about to walk on when he noticed the girl standing on the opposite side.

She was watching the metallic man with surprise and delight, as if it was completely new to her. After a moment she took a step closer, then cautiously waved her hand in front of the robot's face. The man gave a reasonably convincing impression of being made of metal.

The girl was laughing now. She reached out a hand with the index finger extended and gently prodded the robot in his metallic middle.

The girl was very pretty, Noah noticed. Her hair was short and spiky, blonde with a greenish tinge that suggested it was dyed. She was quite tall, thin, with long thighs and calves. Her clothes were similar to those worn by all the girls in the passing tide, but at the same time there was something very slightly wrong with them. Her top was flimsy and gathered from a sort of yoke and her jeans were an odd pale colour. Her open-toed shoes were thick-soled and dusty.

Noah experienced a moment's dislocation. His body felt very light and insubstantial, and the plane tree and the metallic man and Tower Bridge seemed to spin round him and the girl. Noah took a breath. The world steadied itself.

He said to her, 'You won't be able to make him move.'

She gave no sign of having heard him.

Disbelief flooded through Noah. It wasn't possible. Maybe it *was* possible; maybe that's why he had noticed her in the first place.

Then she slowly turned her head. It wasn't that she hadn't heard, he realised, rather that she hadn't understood what he was saying.

'Do you speak English?' he asked, smiling.

'Of course. Why not?' she shot back. Her accent sounded Russian.

'I thought you were, you know, perhaps a tourist.'

'No,' she said flatly.

'Ah. Right.' She was making Noah feel a bit of a fool.

As if she sensed this and regretted it, she jerked her chin at the robot man. 'This is clever. Not moving one muscle.'

'Yeah. Sometimes there's a gold man who does it as well. It looks to me like a really hard way of earning money.' The girl looked disappointed, and at once Noah felt sorry that he had diminished the spectacle for her. 'But it is clever, you're right.'

'I was not trying to tease him. I was thinking he cannot be a real man because he is so still, even though I saw him walk up on his step.'

'He won't move, though. That's the point.' Noah was beginning to feel that it was time to steer this conversation forwards. 'Um. Would you like to have a drink? There's a bar just here. We can sit outside . . .'

Suddenly an empty table to one side of the open space looked intensely inviting.

'I have the bicycle with me.' The girl pointed to a bright yellow mountain bike propped against the river wall.

'Nice bike. We can lock it up . . .'

'I do not have a lock.'

'Really? You should have one; someone'll nick a bike like that in five seconds. Look, we'll just park it beside us so we can keep an eye on it. Let's be quick, before someone grabs the table.'

They walked towards it, the girl wheeling her bicycle. He left her sitting at the table, fought his way to the bar for two beers, and was relieved when he got back to find that she was still waiting for him.

'Cheers,' he said as they drank. 'My name's Noah, by the way.'

'I am Roxana.'

'Hello Roxana.' He put out his hand.

Roxana took his fingers, very cautiously, and allowed an infinitesimal squeeze before drawing back again.

'Where are you from? Are you Russian?'

She looked levelly at him. 'I am from Uzbekistan.'

'Are you? Uh, I don't think I even know where that is.'

'It is in Central Asia. We have been independent country since 1991. Our capital is Tashkent. We have borders with Afghanistan, Kazakhstan, Kyrgyzstan, Tajikistan and Turkmenistan.'

Noah raised an eyebrow. 'Thank you. Now I do know. What brings you to England? Are you a student? Your English is really good.'

'Thank you very much. I'm not a student. I'm working here.'

'What do you do?'

Roxana paused. 'I am a dancer.'

Yes, she had the body for it. And explained the studied poise of her head on the long, pale column of her neck.

'Ballet?' She was a bit too tall for that, though.

'No. Not ballet. Modern.' She nodded towards the yellow bicycle. 'I have only just been for, um, a test?'

'Audition?'

'Yes. I have the job, they tell me there and then.' She smiled now.

Noah blinked. 'Congratulations.'

'Thank you. And I should of course ask now about your job but I have to go soon. It's not my bicycle; I have only borrowed it to come to my audition. But in London for two weeks I haven't yet been to see the River Thames, so I came for one hour.'

She pronounced it with a soft *th*, to rhyme with James.

Noah's stomach did something that he associated with a lift dropping very fast. Jesus, he thought. What's happening? Can you fall in love with someone after ten minutes, just because she says *Thames* instead of *Tems?*

'What is your job?' she asked softly.

'I work in IT. For a small publishing company.'

'Near to here?'

'In the West End. I've just been visiting my mother, in the hospital. She's had an operation. She's got cancer.'

Roxana didn't react in the usual way. Her face didn't contract with distress or sympathy and there was no rush of consoling words. Instead she just nodded, quite matter-of-fact. 'Will she recover?'

'Oh yes, I think so.'

'That's good.'

Most people, in his experience, when you told them your mother had cancer, were concerned for you and her, even though they might never have met her. There was a look about Roxana, though, that told him she wasn't unconcerned. He thought she might have heard a lot of stories that were sadder than the illness of a stranger's mother.

Their glasses were empty. 'I have to go,' she said.

He said too quickly, 'No time for one more drink?'

'No. Thank you for this one.'

They both stood up, negotiating the edges of the table. Roxana twisted the handlebars of the yellow bike and prepared to wheel it away.

'Which way are you going?' Noah asked.

'Over there. There is a small bridge.'

'Oh yeah, that's the Millennium Bridge. Known as the Wobbly Bridge, usually. I'll walk that far with you.'

They wove through the crowds together. Noah heard himself giving an overanimated explanation of the footbridge's nickname.

'Would you, um, like to meet up again?' he asked as they crossed the bridge. 'As you don't know London, maybe we could, ah, go on a riverboat.' A big white one was passing directly underneath. Roxana glanced at it. 'Or do something. See a film? Or I could come and see you dance.'

'No,' she said quickly, in a firm voice that meant absolutely not.

At the far end of the bridge she carried the bike down the steps. She looked tired now, and—what? Forlorn. That was it.

'I have to go.' She gestured at the handlebars. 'There will be trouble.'

'Can I have your phone number?'

'I don't have any phone. Not at the moment.'

'Roxana, I'd like to see you again. Is that all right? Won't you tell me where you live?'

She looked in the direction she would be heading as soon as she could get away from him, and Noah knew that she was concealing something.

'I will have a place. In a few days.'

You're getting nowhere, mate, Noah decided. Can't you take a hint?

'Well. I enjoyed talking to you.'

Roxana got on the bike, then stopped. 'You have a telephone?'

'Sure. Yes, of course.' He took a work card out of his wallet and scribbled his mobile number on the back. 'Call me.'

'OK. Goodbye, Noah.'

She tucked the card away, slung her plastic handbag over her shoulder and pedalled uncertainly out into the traffic. He watched until she was out of sight. He was sure he would never see her again and the thought left him entirely disconsolate.

As soon as she was safely round the corner, Roxana peered up at a street sign, then stopped to search in her bag for the street-map book that the man Dylan had lent her. She found where she was now, after some flipping back and forth through the small grey pages, and also where she had come from. She tried to memorise the names and the sequence of the five big roads she needed to follow, but before she had even reached the first junction they had jumbled themselves up in her head.

London was a big place. She couldn't even imagine how far it spread. All these tall buildings and streets and glassy shops. All these people.

She felt very small in the thick of it, as if she were no more than a speck of dust that the wind might suck away. She kept on pedalling, bracing herself against a gust of fear as well as the buffeting of the traffic.

It would turn out fine, she kept telling herself. Why not? She had a job now, at least.

She had got talking to Dylan on her first morning in London, in the café near King's Cross Station. She had spent the previous night in a nearby hotel, in a room that was noisy and dirty and had still cost far more than she budgeted. Her savings and the money her mother's old friend Yakov had loaned her wouldn't go far at this rate.

The thin young man asked her for a light, then slid closer along the red plastic bench. He offered her one of his cigarettes and bought her another cup of coffee. It was nice to talk to someone.

It turned out that Dylan lived in a house where there were cheap rooms to rent. When he asked if she wanted him to find out if the room next to his was free, she said yes, because she had no other ideas. Once she saw the place she didn't want to stay there, not even for one night. But she did stay, because she had no alternative. She promised herself that it was just until she found some work.

Dylan had tried to get inside the room with her, of course he had, but she told him what he could do with himself. He hadn't taken it badly.

She told Dylan that she needed a job and that she was a dancer, not necessarily expecting the two statements to connect. It was true that in Bokhara, where she grew up, Roxana had sometimes gone to classes and then for a whole wonderful term Yakov had helped her and she had studied dance in Tashkent.

But it was not easy to live in Uzbekistan. After her brother was killed in the uprising she made up her mind to leave it behind, every broken street and Russian soldier, all the memories, everything her native country stood for and everything that had happened to her there, and live in England. She would become an English girl.

It had taken a long time to get the money for a holiday flight from Tashkent to Luton, but Roxana had managed it. She didn't plan to be on the return flight.

In London her intention was to find work looking after children. Or if not that, maybe she could be a chambermaid in a big hotel. But she soon found out that without references and papers there was no work with English children. The hotels she walked into all told her that they weren't taking on casuals at the moment.

It was Dylan who came to her rescue again. 'Ye said ye can dance.' His accent was strange. He told her he came from Ireland. 'There's a feller ye can go to see.' He wrote down a name and an address for her, lent her the map book, told her which bus to catch and what time to be there, and advised her not to be late.

On her way out of the house, on a sudden impulse, Roxana borrowed the yellow bike.

It had been in the hallway ever since she came to live there, leaning in the same place among the envelopes that no one picked up. She had not seen anyone touch it, let alone ride it. There was no lock. Maybe someone had just left it at the house and forgotten all about it.

Taking it would save her the bus fares. Buses and tube trains in London cost a lot of money. So she bumped the bicycle down the steps of the house and boldly set off.

At first it was exhilarating to be so free. She flew along in the glittering traffic, the wind of her own speed whistling in her ears and pinning a smile to her face. It was a shame that she ended up getting lost. It meant that she was late for her meeting with Mr Shane at the Cosmos.

Mr Shane was a small, elderly man with quick cold eyes. He looked Roxana up and down as if he was pricing her for sale, and told her that if she was ever late again she could forget working for him. 'This is a quality venue, do you understand me?' he said.

'I understand, yes,' Roxana answered, glancing around her at the tables and the shuttered bar. Before the club opened for the night it looked sordid, but she supposed that it would be different when the lights came up and it was full of people.

'Right. Where are you from and how long have you been here?'

She told him.

'Legal?'

'Yes,' she lied.

Mr Shane sniffed. 'Let's see what you can do, then.'

There wasn't any music and the only audience was Mr Shane, sprawled in a front-row armchair with his mobile phone pressed to his ear. It wasn't difficult to envisage what he wanted, but making her body perform the right sequences wasn't easy at all. Roxana concentrated hard on making it look as though what she was doing came naturally.

At last he held up his hand. 'All right. That'll do. You can start Friday.'

Roxana could hardly believe her luck. 'Friday. Thank you. I—'

'Seven o'clock sharp. Five minutes late and you can go straight home.' He didn't have time for her gratitude. He was already on the phone again, gesturing for her to leave.

She came out of the cavernous dimness of the Cosmos and into the air, breathing deeply with relief. She had a job. She was on her way.

She did get lost on the way back from the river, but not quite as badly as the first time. She was whistling as she pedalled into the street and even the sight of the house, with peeling paint and torn curtains and the rubbish sodden in the basement area, didn't depress her too much. She hauled the bike up the flight of stone steps and leaned it against the broken railings while she groped for the key to the front door.

The flurry of violence was so sudden that she didn't even have time to scream. The bicycle was seized and hauled inside, dragging her with it. One of the pedals bit deep into her shin at the same time as the man grabbed her wrists and forced her up against the wall. The door slammed shut, cutting off her escape route.

'Did I miss something? Did you buy that bike off me? Or did you say to me, "Mr Kemal, I need to borrow a piece of your property"? Or did you just nick it out of here without a word to no one?'

'No,' she said. Her teeth rattled in her head as he shook her.

'No what?'

'I didn't buy it. I didn't ask. I thought it wasn't anyone's.'

'That was a mistake, Russia.'

Roxana lifted her head. The man was plump, black-haired, unshaven. 'I am from Uzbekistan,' she said. 'Not Russia.'

'Like I give a shit.' He twisted her arm and she winced. 'You're not hurt, Russia, not yet. If you take things that don't belong to you, then you'll find out about being hurt. Do you understand what I'm saying?'

'Yes,' she whispered. 'I'm sorry.'

Mr Kemal let go of her arms. 'Upstairs,' he ordered. He followed her, made her unlock her padlocks and kicked open the door of her room so he could take a good look inside.

There wasn't much to see.

On the wall beside her bed she had taped a picture postcard of a tropical beach, which she'd bought from a street vendor in Tashkent. She had fallen in love at first sight with the image of silver sand and blue sea. Apart from that there were her few clothes hanging behind a curtain mounted across one corner, a double gas burner and some tins and packets, a transistor radio, and her Russian–English dictionary lying open beside her plate and cup on the small table.

As he flicked through her belongings the man made a dismissive *tssshhh* through his teeth. 'Didn't you say to me you're not Russian?'

'My father, he came from Novosibirsk. That's Russia. But my mother was Uzbeki and I was born in Bokhara.' Roxana was recovering herself.

To her relief, she understood that he was finished with her. From the doorway he said, 'Keep your thieving hands off my stuff, all right?'

Roxana nodded. She would make every effort to never again come into contact with Mr Kemal, or any of his belongings.

After he had gone she quietly closed the door and secured it from the inside. Then she sat down on the bed, her head bent and her hands loosely hanging between her knees. She could feel blood congealing on her shin and her arm throbbed, but she didn't make the effort to examine her injuries. Once the initial shock and fear had subsided, what Roxana was left with was a feeling of dreary familiarity. Life had a way of repeating itself. To stop the cycle it wasn't enough to be in a different place, even a different continent. You had to be a different person. You had to become a person like, say, the English boy. Noah. Big, and crumpled in a way that meant you were completely certain that you had your rights and that justice was on your side. Roxana wasn't so sure, after all, that she could make this much of a difference in herself.

'That's it, people. We're all through. Good work. Thanks very much, everyone.' The first assistant scissored his arms in the air and the last shot for the third of the online-bank commercials was in the bag.

Connie wasn't sorry that the week to come would not be as ripe with crisis as the one that was just past. The main actress had barely recovered from her stomach upset, and her enfeebled state had led to rescheduling and hours of overage costs, which Angela had had to negotiate with Tara. Relations had become strained.

As Connie made her way to the service tent, one of the riggers whistled at her as he hoisted a grip stand towards the waiting trucks. Inside the tent, Angela was standing with her knuckles tight round a cup of coffee. She looked as if she hadn't slept for a week.

'Ange.' Connie removed the cup from her hand and took her by the shoulders. 'How are you? You look knackered.'

'Oh. You know.' She seemed about to cry.

Connie led Angela outside. The sun had slid behind the cliffs that they had used for the backdrop to the set and the dark rock wall was crowned with a halo of golden light that no lighting cameraman could ever have created. Set-dressers were rolling up an artificial lawn, and the cast were changing in the caravans. The self-important world of the shoot was folding up on itself, shrinking back into the waiting trucks and Toyotas. Tomorrow, when the cast and crew were on their planes home, the clearing would be deserted except for the birds and the bats.

'Look at this,' Angela sighed, as if she was seeing it for the first time.

'Why don't you stay on with me for a few days? Have a holiday.'

'I'm fine,' Angela said. She laughed. 'Completely fine. I've got to start next week on pre-production for a yoghurt commercial. It's really busy at the moment and that's good, isn't it? Can't turn the work down.'

'Angie?' It was Rayner Ingram's voice. Her head turned at once.

'Coming,' she called. 'Con, you'll be there tonight, won't you?' Tonight was the wrap party, traditionally hosted by the production company.

'Yes. Course I will.'

'See you later, then.'

Left alone, Connie sat down on an upturned box and watched the bats dipping for insects. She would feel lonely here next week, when Angela and the others had gone back to London.

Connie found that she was thinking about London as she rarely did, remembering the way that lights reflected in the river on winter's evenings, the catty smell of privet after summer rain, the glittering traffic and the stale whiff of the Underground. She kept the focus deliberately general, excluding places and people for as long as she could.

'I'm going to need that box.' The voice made her jump. She saw it was the rigger who had whistled at her.

'All yours.' Connie smiled at him as she got to her feet. She wasn't sorry to have her train of thought interrupted. In any case it was time to head home to change for the wrap party.

There were more than forty people for dinner. They ate in the garden of the better of the hotels, under lanterns slung in the tree branches.

'This place is a bit of all right,' one of the Australians shouted up the table. 'They've even got beer here.' In the last-night surge of goodwill, the disagreements of the week morphed into jokes.

The actress emerged from her room to join the crew for dinner. Draped in a pashmina against a nonexistent breeze, she was telling everyone who would listen that she had lost nearly a stone.

Tara was wearing a dress that measured about twenty centimetres from neckline to hem. Simon Sheringham's arm rested heavily along the back of her chair, and he regularly clicked his fingers at the waiters to ensure that their two glasses were kept filled. Marcus Atkins and the agency's creative duo sat with their heads close together.

Rayner Ingram naturally took the head of the table. After a successful shoot everyone wanted their piece of the director, and there had been a scramble for the seats closest to him. Connie was relieved to see that he beckoned Angela to the place on his right. She was surprised, as she took her own seat near the other end, by the rigger darting into the next chair.

He extended a large hand. 'Hi. My name's Ed.'

'Connie Thorne.'

'Boom Girl, somebody called you. What's that about?'

She was entirely happy that he didn't know. 'Nothing. History. Let's have a drink.'

'Let's make that our motto.'

The food came and they ate and drank under the lanterns.

Connie learned from Ed that he owned a ski lodge in Thredbo and only took on film work when he needed a cash injection.

'You should come out. I'm heading back for the ski season now.'

'I can't ski.'

He grinned. 'No worries. I'll teach you.'

You could go, Connie told herself. Ed seemed a good, dependable, practical sort of man. Damn, she thought. Why can't it happen?

That question did have an answer, but it wasn't one she was prepared to listen to at this moment.

People were already swaying off in search of further diversions. There were loud splashes and a lot of shouting and laughter from the pool.

'Think about it,' Ed murmured. He took out a marker pen and wrote his email address on her bare arm. 'It's indelible ink, by the way.'

'I will think about it,' she promised, untruthfully.

Connie slipped away from the table and walked over the grass. She was hot and she had drunk more than she was used to, and it was soothing to drift in the dusk under the trees.

Someone rustled over the grass behind her.

'There you are.' To her relief it was not Ed but Angela, and she was carrying a bottle and two glasses. 'Shall we sit here?'

There was a secluded bench with a low light beside it that hollowed an egg-shape of lush greenery out of the darkness. They sat down and Connie obediently took the glass that Angela gave her. They clinked their glasses and drank.

'How is it with you and Rayner?' Connie asked.

Angela exhaled. 'Oh. You noticed?'

'Well. Yes. Probably no one else did, though.'

Angela's smile was a sudden flash in the gloaming. 'He's amazing. We've been working together quite a lot, and we started seeing each other . . . It's difficult because he's still married to Rose and he's very close to his kids, so we're keeping the lid on it, especially on shoots. He's such a talented director; that has to come first a lot of the time.'

Connie did her best to receive this information optimistically. Angela was elated now, probably because Rayner had given her a sign for later. She was revelling in the anticipation of him slipping into her room, locking the door behind him. Connie could remember what all that felt like. But the provisos sounded too ready, and they were ominous.

Not that I'm the one to judge, she thought.

'Don't put his happiness before your own,' was all Connie advised.

'They're the same thing,' Angela breathed.

They sat in silence for a moment.

'Anyway, I wanted to talk about you, not me,' Angela began again. 'About here. And why you stay. Are you hiding from something? Out here. On your own, ever since you split from Seb. Why don't you come back to London? Be with your friends. Don't your family miss you? You've got a . . . sister, haven't you? And that amazing flat. And it's not as though you don't get plenty of work. Honestly. You can't stay out here for ever; you need to come back and . . . connect. Think about it, won't you? Aren't you lonely? Don't you ever think, is this what I really want?'

Angela was warming to her subject. She was happy, and in her benign daze she wished the same for everyone. They had both had quite a lot to drink, Connie allowed. She tilted her glass, then gazed around at the glimmering garden.

'Connie, are you listening?'

'Yep.'

She was wondering which end to pull out of the tangle of Angela's speech. She didn't say that she only asked herself what she really, really wanted when her solitude was compromised.

'I like my life.' It was true, she did.

'But . . . don't you want . . . love, marriage. A family?'

'I'm forty-three.'

'That's not an answer.'

'No, then.'

That silenced Angela for a moment. Eight years younger and in love, she couldn't imagine any woman not wanting those things.

Love Connie did have, and she had come to the conclusion that she always would. Love could exist in a vacuum, with nothing to nourish it, without even a sight of the person involved. It was always there, embedded beneath her skin like an electronic tag, probably sending out its warning signals to everyone within range.

The truth was that Connie had loved Bill Bunting since she was fifteen, and Seb hadn't been the first or even the last attempt she had made to convince herself otherwise. She wasn't going to marry Bill, or even see him, because he was another woman's husband. He wouldn't abandon his wife, and if he had been willing to do so Connie would have had to stop loving him. That was the impossibility of it.

And family . . .

It was significant that even Angela, who had been a friend for more than ten years, had to think twice about whether Connie had a family or not, and what it consisted of.

That was the way Connie preferred it to be.

She turned to look at Angela and started laughing.

'What's funny?'

'Your expression. Angie, I know what you're saying to me, and thank you for being concerned. Your advice is probably good. But I'm happy here, you know. I'm not hiding. And it's very beautiful.'

'Will you think about what I'm saying, though?'

'Yes, I will.'

'It's mostly selfish. I want you to come home so we can see more of each other.'

Connie smiled. 'I'd like that too. But I *am* home.'

Chapter Three

'NEARLY THERE,' Bill said unnecessarily, but in any case Jeanette's head was turned away from him. She seemed to be admiring the bitter green of the hawthorn hedge. Conscious of the bumps in the road, he tried to drive as smoothly as he could so she wouldn't be jarred with pain.

Their house was at the end of a lane, behind a coppice of tall trees. They had lived there for more than twenty years. Noah had grown up in the house, had left for university and then gone to live in London; Jeanette and he were still there. It would be their last home together.

He swung the car past the gateposts and stopped close to the front door. Jeanette did turn her head now, staring past him and up at the house. It had a steep tiled roof with mansard windows that had always made him think of eyes under heavy lids. A purple clematis and a cream climbing rose grew beside the front door, the colours harmonising with the dusty red brick of the house. Bill didn't know the names of the varieties, but Jeanette would. She was a passionate gardener.

He turned off the ignition and the silence enveloped them. He took his wife's hand, letting her fingers rest in his.

Jeanette's eyes were on him now.

'Are you ready to go inside?' he asked.

She nodded.

He helped her out of the car and she leaned on his arm as they made their way. Once they were in the hallway she gestured that she wanted to stop. The parquet floor was warmed by the late sun, the long-case barometer indicated FAIR, and there was a pile of unopened post on the oak table next to the big pot of African violets.

'Good to be home?' Bill asked.

—*Yes*, Jeanette said. —*Thank you*.

Gently he urged her forwards, planning to establish her in her chair beside the French windows so that she could look out at the garden while he made her a cup of tea. She let him lead her, but instead of sinking into her chair she stood and gazed at the room. It looked as it always did.

Her sudden movement startled him.

Jeanette broke away and snatched up a stone paperweight that stood on the glass-topped table. She raised her thin arm above her head and brought it down. There was a crack like a rifle-shot as the glass shattered. Jeanette swung the paperweight a second and a third time and the tabletop shivered into a crystalline sheet.

Appalled, Bill tried to catch her wrists. She threw the paperweight away from her and it thudded and then rolled harmlessly on the rug. She clenched her fists instead and pounded them against Bill's chest. Her mouth gaped and gusts of ragged sobbing shook her body.

Jeanette had been deaf since birth. The sounds she was making now were shapeless bellows of anguish.

He managed to catch her flailing arms and pin them to her sides.

'I know,' he crooned. 'I know, I know.'

She was gasping for breath, tears pouring down her face and dripping from her chin. She was too weak to sustain the paroxysm of rage. It subsided as quickly as it had come, leaving her shuddering in his arms. Bill stood still and held her, smoothing the tufts of her pale hair. He took out his handkerchief and dried her cheeks. At length he was able to steer her towards the chair and she sank down. He brought up the footstool and sat close against her knees.

—*I don't want to die.*

Her words as loose, blurted outbursts. Bill was the only person she trusted to decipher what she said. Even with her son, she preferred to use sign language for almost everything.

'I know,' he told her. 'You aren't going to die yet.'

Jeanette gazed into his face, searching for the truth. —*No?*

'No, you are not,' he said firmly.

The oncologist had told them that she might have six months. It could be rather less, just conceivably more, but six months was what he thought they should allow.

Her head drooped. —*I'm sorry*, she said.

'It doesn't matter. It's a table.' He smiled at her.

—*For being ill. Leaving you and Noah.*

'You haven't left us,' he said. His hands cupped her knees.

The first time he saw Jeanette Thorne was at a student union party. The room was crowded and there was barely enough space for leaping up and down to the punk band. Through a thicket of legs he caught a flicker of her red shoes, platform-soled with a strap across the instep. Then she jumped in the air and the hem of her skirt flipped up to reveal the tender pallor of her bare thighs. He had elbowed his way through the sweaty crowd so he could stand behind her to watch, and ever since that moment he had loved the long blade of her shins and the bluish hollow behind her knees.

That was when they were both twenty-one.

Later that evening he had found himself next to her. He had murmured something into the bell of blonde hair that swung to her shoulders, some banal question about what she thought of the band. She ignored him, and he had been about to creep away, abashed. Then a girl he knew pressed her elbow into his ribs.

'That's Jeanette Thorne. She's in Biological Sciences. She's completely deaf, you know. She does everything, just the same. Amazing, really.'

At that moment Jeanette turned her head and for the first time looked straight into his eyes. It was as if she could see into his head, and read the sexual stirring in him. Words would have been entirely superfluous. Jeanette's mouth merely curved in a smile that transformed the dingy bar into some antechamber to Paradise.

'I am Bill,' he said.

She placed the flat of her right hand over her breastbone and gently inclined her head. A lock of hair fell forwards and revealed the thick plastic aid that curved behind her ear. Bill wanted nothing more than to lean forward and kiss that faulty ear and tuck her hair back into place.

It was only when he came to know Jeanette much better that he understood that her voluptuous body and her mass of blonde hair were at odds with her personality. Jeanette looked wanton, but she was not. She was too determined to be more than just a deaf girl to let even sex distract her for long.

He fell in love with that contradiction.

—*When's Noah coming?* Jeanette asked into the silence.

'He'll be here for dinner.'

—*Will you tell him?*

'I don't exactly know yet.'

Noah would have to be told that his mother's cancer was terminal.

It was a terrible word, that.

They sat with the hurled paperweight on the rug beside them, holding on to each other and looking out into the garden as the sun drifted behind the trees. Permanence had turned into fragility. What had been certain was now a series of questions, neither spoken nor answered.

Later, after Jeanette had gone to bed, Bill and Noah sat in the small, cluttered downstairs room that Bill used as his study.

Bill poured himself a whisky and gave Noah a beer. 'The news about Mum isn't good,' he began tentatively.

'What? What do you mean?' The aggressive edge to Noah's voice suggested that on some level he had feared this and was now intending to contest the information.

'The surgeon who did the operation told us this morning. They found when they reached the tumour site that there was only a part of it they could remove.'

'What does that mean? Is she going to *die*? Is that what you're trying to say?' Noah's voice rose.

With an effort, Bill kept his steady. 'They think it's likely to be about six months.'

'I don't understand. Are they sure? They can't be certain, can they? I mean, you hear of people who've been given a certain amount of time to live and who get better against all the odds?'

Bill said, 'You do hear of that. I don't want to give you false grounds for optimism, but if you can believe that she will get better, maybe that's how it will turn out. I don't know. All I do know is what the specialist told us today. He didn't leave any room for doubt in my mind. I wish he had done. I wish I could say something different to you.'

There was no rejecting this, after all. Noah was beginning to take in what his father's words really meant.

'Poor Mum,' he said at length. 'It's not fair, is it?'

Life had a tendency not to be strictly fair, Bill reflected, although Noah was still too young to appreciate precisely how unfair, how meticulously and even poetically unjust it could be.

Noah said after a while, 'Thanks for telling me straight away. I'd much rather hear than have to guess.'

'Your mother asked me to tell you tonight,' Bill scrupulously pointed out. He didn't believe he should take the credit for courageous honesty when most of his instincts had been to keep the truth from his child for as long as possible.

Noah didn't ask how Jeanette had taken the news. This he would find out directly from his mother; Bill understood that. But there was one more piece of information Bill felt he should convey.

'Mum's afraid that she's letting you down.'

'Me? How come?'

'By dying before you are grown up. Before her job's done, is the way she put it.'

'But I am grown up,' Noah said quietly.

Was the job ever done? Bill wondered. Probably not. Jeanette wasn't quite fifty. No wonder she felt that she was leaving too much undone.

'What happens now?' Noah asked.

'Once she recovers from the hospital and the operation, she won't be too bad for a while. I was thinking, perhaps we could go on a holiday. Jeanette will have to decide about that, though.'

'That sounds like a good idea. And what about you, Dad?'

Bill hadn't yet had time to put the question to himself. Or perhaps had chosen to evade it.

'I want to try to make it as easy as I can for her. Whatever's coming.'

Noah only nodded.

'I need to ask your advice,' Bill continued.

'Go ahead.'

'Should I tell Constance?'

As soon as he uttered her name it seemed to take on a weight of its own, as if it occupied a physical space between them. Noah shifted sideways, away from his father, to make room for it. He rocked his beer bottle on the arm of his chair, studying it with apparent attention.

'Tell her that Mum's ill, you mean? Doesn't she know?'

'I haven't told her.'

And Jeanette certainly would not have done.

Noah shrugged. 'I don't care. I only care about Mum. If she doesn't want Auntie Connie around her, then she doesn't. Simple as.' He tipped the bottle to his mouth.

'Maybe you're right,' Bill said. Half-truths and evasions and unspoken confessions crowded out of history and squeezed into the room with them. Their shadows cut him off from Noah at the moment when he wanted to feel closest to him. Neither of them spoke until Noah sighed and pushed himself to the edge of his chair.

'Dad, I think I'll go up. I'll see you in the morning.'

They both stood up. They hesitated, not having had the kind of adult relationship that involved hugging or shedding of tears. Noah rested his arm awkwardly round his father's shoulders and Bill put his hand to the back of the boy's neck. He inclined his head until their foreheads touched and they shuffled together, a rough two-step of grief.

'We'll manage, Dad,' Noah said.

'Of course we will.'

Roxana was on the stage. She had been nervous when she first started at the Cosmos, but she learned quickly. Two Brazilian girls were the best dancers, which meant that they earned the most money from giving private dances, so she had watched carefully to see what they did. And then she had copied their best tricks into her own routine.

She slid her body up the pole, slowly winding one leg round it, then tipped her head back and arched her spine until only her heel kept her anchored. Then she whipped herself upright again, raised her chin and slid her hands up the pole to stretch farther upwards, up on tiptoe, to her full height. Next she softened all her muscles and sank onto her heels, bending her neck so that her head nodded like a flower on its stalk. From this vulnerable pose she raised her eyes and stared straight into the wall of men who lined the bar.

She would play a game with herself, to see if she could compel one of the customers to take a private dance.

Roxana caught her bottom lip between her teeth and smiled at the man she had chosen. She looked away from him and unhooked the front of her black bodice. When she flicked her glance back again, he was still grinning at her. This one was almost too easy.

She rotated on her pole again, then detached herself for long enough to peel off the bodice. She stood with her naked back to the audience, braced on her high heels, swaying gently to the music. Then she crossed her arms across her front before turning back again, her face lit up with a teasing smile. This dance was almost over.

The girls stripped to their pants on the pole and no further; that was the routine. Nakedness was reserved for the private customers. The spot would blink off and come up on one of the other dancers while Roxana slipped off the stage.

It wasn't difficult work. The nights were long and the other girls were bitchy, but Roxana had done worse jobs. It was quite safe, for one thing. Mr Shane's rule was absolute: customers were never allowed to touch the girls. The law for himself was different, but in the week that she had worked at the Cosmos he hadn't tried anything with her.

With her clothes on again, a short black top over a lace bra, she worked her way through the crowd to the bar. Her customer was one of a group of men in suits with ties pulled open at the neck.

She went straight up to him and said, 'Hello. I am Roxana.'

One of the men said, 'Oi, Dave, yer in, mate.'

'Hello darlin'. Give us a special dance, then.'

She took Dave's hand and wound past the tables to the chairs at the front in their partially screened alcoves. Only Mr Shane, behind the one-way mirrors, could see everything that went on in the booths.

'That will be twenty-five, please,' she murmured in Dave's ear before the dance. Her lips almost touched his skin.

He took a note out of his wallet and waved it in the air before tucking it inside her garter. It was fifty pounds. She gave him his dance, a really good one. It brought small beads of sweat out on his crimson forehead. The folded note crackled minutely against her skin.

And after Dave, two of his friends wanted private dances too. It was a successful night. When it finally ended, Roxana had earned over three hundred pounds.

Most of the girls took taxis home, but Roxana preferred to save her money. A small wad of notes had already accumulated, wrapped in an old T-shirt that she kept under her mattress. She walked towards the night-bus stop with the hood of her outdoor coat pulled over her head.

There were few other people in sight, but they all seemed to be couples hurrying home to burrow together in a warm bed.

Loneliness descended like a black bag dropping over her head.

The house was silent when she let herself in. It was very late. Roxana pressed the timed switch next to the front door and walked quickly up the stairs because the light only stayed on for a few seconds.

Dylan's door was closed. Then she looked at her own and her breath caught. The wood was splintered round the lock. There were splits in the panels where someone had kicked them.

She put out her hand and reluctantly pushed the door open.

Her bed had been tipped over; the mattress lay beneath the frame and the pillow had been slashed. Her clothes lay scattered and shards of plastic and metal from her transistor radio glinted among them.

Roxana knelt beside the mattress and felt for the folded T-shirt. She recovered that, but the envelope of money was gone.

She backed out onto the landing. It was hard to work out which felt less safe now: her ripped-apart room, the shadowed stairwell or the streets outside. Then the light blinked off and left her in darkness.

Roxana shuddered but she made herself keep steady. She felt her way across the landing to Dylan's door and knocked. Softly at first, and then when there was no response she banged with her clenched fist. At last he opened the door and a crack of yellow light shone through.

'Did you do this?' Roxana hissed.

She saw at once that he had not. Dylan looked too thin in his holey vest, too scared and fragile himself.

'Jesus, no. I did not. What d'ye take me for?'

'Who did, then?'

Dylan shook his head. 'Dunno.'

She could have gone back into her room and cleared up the mess and found a way to wedge the door shut, but she knew that however much effort she made it wouldn't be enough to keep the house at bay. Not in her head, anyway.

One thing at a time. Get through this night, first of all.

'All right. Can I sleep with you tonight?'

A flash of eagerness lit up Dylan's face. 'Sure ye can.' He was already reaching for her as she stepped back.

'Not like that. Just let me put my stuff on your floor.'

'Eh? Oh. Right. Well, yeah, I suppose.'

'Help me with my mattress.'

They dragged it into his room and squeezed it into the small floor space. Carefully Roxana unstuck the beach postcard from her wall and brought it with her, placing it next to her torn pillow.

When Dylan turned the light off she lay in the darkness. Her body buzzed with adrenaline. Sleep, she ordered herself. Sleep now, and tomorrow find somewhere else to live.

In his flat in Hammersmith, Noah was yawning and making coffee and playing one of Andy's mixes. Normally at this time on a Sunday morning he would be asleep, but today he was planning to go home again to see Jeanette and Bill. He glanced at the number when his mobile rang, but didn't recognise it.

He knew her voice, though, as soon as she spoke.

'Hello. Is this Noah?'

'*Roxana*. How are you? Where are you?' Now it was happening, he realised how often he had imagined this exchange. Mild fantasies had provided an escape route from worrying about his mother.

'I am . . . I am in a telephone box, near to where I used to be living.'

'Used to be?'

'There is some trouble.'

'Tell me about it.'

An hour later, he was waiting for her at the entrance to the tube station.

Roxana came through the ticket barrier with a cheap tartan suitcase. She looked bruised today, not surprisingly after what she had told him about the break-in. There were circles under her eyes and her hair was greasy and flat, but her mouth was lovelier than he remembered.

They walked through mild summer sunshine back to the flat. Noah carried the suitcase. It wasn't heavy.

He was wondering, now that it was too late, whether he had been too hasty in asking a girl he hardly knew to stay in his flat while she searched for somewhere else to live. But his flatmate Andy had just gone to Barcelona for a week. There was plenty of room, for the next few days at least. Was he really going to say to her, no, I'm afraid I can't help you?

Apparently reading his mind, Roxana said, 'Thank you, Noah. You are kind to do this. I am not going back to that house. It is a bad place.'

'Are you going to tell the police about your money being stolen?'

'Police? No. I don't like to deal with the police.'

She would have her reasons for that, Noah realised. Probably to do with her immigration status.

'How's the dance job working out?' he asked cautiously.

'It is OK.'

When they reached the house she followed him up the communal stairs and stood silently while he fumbled with his keys. Once they were inside she glanced around, then her shoulders slumped with relief.

'It is beautiful,' Roxana said.

Noah knew that it wasn't anything of the kind, but the word gave him a dim picture of what she must have left behind.

'Here's the kitchen, and that's the living room. Bathroom there. This is Andy's room, and this one's mine.' He opened the door. 'You can sleep in here. I'll just dig out some clean sheets and stuff.'

He'd better not put her in Andy's room, he thought. She could sleep in his bed, and he'd camp out in Andy's.

'Thank you,' Roxana said again. 'I am not sure what to have done if you couldn't help me.'

Noah fetched a clean sheet and duvet cover. He bundled up his own linen, relieved that it didn't look too bad. She helped him make the bed.

The room was at the top of the house, under the roof. There were no proper windows, only a skylight over the bed. Roxana looked up into the rectangle of blue. 'I like this. It feels safe here.'

'You're safe. No one's going to break in. There are four giant Kiwis living downstairs. Anyone tries to get in the house they'll be kicked straight into touch.'

Roxana's eyes travelled to him.

'Rugby,' he explained lamely. She laughed for the first time that day. For Noah, it was like a firework going off in his chest.

'Now, what are we going to do?' she asked.

'I have to go in a minute. I'm late already.'

Her eyes widened. 'That is a shame. Where are you going?'

'Home, to see my parents. My mother's out of hospital now, but the news isn't very good. She's only got about six months to live.'

'I am sorry for that. But I thought you said she would get better?'

'I was wrong. I didn't know, then. Are your parents in Uzbekistan?'

'My father and mother are both dead. I have a stepfather still alive, but I don't care for him. He is a bad man.'

'Brothers and sisters?'

'No.'

'Nor me.'

'I had one brother but he was killed,' she said without expression.

'That's really sad. I'm sorry. Was it some kind of accident?'

'In my country there was an uprising, in Andijan, and Niki was shot by soldiers.'

As an only child, Noah could barely imagine the pain of having had a brother and then losing him. He would have liked to offer Roxana some protection, maybe to tell her that he would be her defender from now on, if she would like it, but he couldn't think of a way of saying it that didn't sound either comical or entirely fake.

Instead, he put his hand awkwardly on her arm, above the elbow, where the short sleeve of her top protected her pale skin, and said as simply as he could, 'I'm very sorry, Roxana. It must have been terrible for you. And you must be lonely without him.'

Roxana's eyes had acquired the red-rimmed look that preceded tears.

'Why are you here, in England?' he asked.

She rubbed her nose with the back of her hand and at the same time moved out of his grasp. Noah let his hand fall to his side.

'I am working, earning good money, saving it up when I do not get robbed. I am going to be an English girl.'

She said it with such fervour that he had to laugh.

'Really? Are you sure that's what you want?'

She blinked at him. 'Why not? Where I came from there is no work, people are poor, ignorance is everywhere.'

'I suppose, but Uzbekistan is your home, the culture is yours, the language and traditions. All that has made you what you are, as well as your family, and everything that's happened to you since you were born. Why do you want to turn your back on it? I mean, by making yourself English you'll only be a replica, whereas what you are already is the real thing.'

Roxana unzipped her suitcase. She took out a few clothes and laid them on the bed, then propped a picture postcard of a beach beside the magazines and piled CDs on Noah's table.

In a tone that denied the possibility of contradiction she said, 'I believe that you can be whatever you want.'

Yes, Noah had to concede, Roxana probably could be. He had the impression that there was determination in her, strong as a rib of steel.

He checked his watch. 'I've really got to go,' he sighed. 'I promised my dad I'd be home for Sunday lunch. But I'll be back here this evening. We could maybe go out for a pizza or a drink, and we can talk some more. Shall we do that?'

'I have to go to work this evening.'

'Really? You do a performance on a Sunday night?'

Roxana frowned, obviously trying to come to a decision. Then she said flatly, 'I work in a club, I think I had better tell you. It's called the Cosmos. It opens every night of the week. I am what is called a lap dancer.' She tilted her chin up as she announced this. 'Do you know what this is?'

'Of course I do.' Noah was assailed by a series of images. For a moment he thought it best not to say anything more.

'You are shocked?'

'No,' he managed to say. Shocked wasn't it at all.

'So?'

'I bet you're really good at it.'

Roxana began to laugh. Soon Noah was laughing as well. They laughed until they were both breathless.

'So I'll definitely be coming to see you.'

She turned serious at once. 'No, please, don't do that. I would find it very embarrassing if you were there.'

'Embarrassing? Would you?'

'Of course. When I dance for men I don't know, it doesn't mean anything. But with you, because I like you, it would be different.'

Noah was disarmed. There was such a contradiction in the idea of this girl doing a lap-dance routine in a room full of punters, and at the same time being shy enough not to know where to look as she paid him a mild compliment. She was like no other girl he had ever met, and now they were looking at each other in the equivocal aftermath of her confession and their shared laughter.

'Will you be all right here while I'm out?' he asked. 'I'll give you the spare set of keys.'

She beamed back at him, suddenly full of confidence. 'I am safe here with the men downstairs who play rugby. You told me. All I will do is lie in your bed and go to sleep.'

Noah swallowed hard. 'Good. I'll see you when you come in.'

After he'd gone, Roxana put her clothes neatly aside. Noah's room was tidy, she liked that. She curled up under the duvet and fell asleep.

The garden looked to be at its summer peak, to Noah's uncritical eyes. There were the roses, and tall, pale blue spikes of flowers, some other round, shaggy pink ones, and metallic clumps of silvery leaves spilling on the mown grass. But Jeanette was shaking her head as they made a slow circuit after lunch.

—*There is so much to do.*

'Like pruning the roses?'

Her hand touched his arm. The skin on the back of her hand looked thin, and as finely crinkled as an old leaf. Noah thought that she was ageing and fading before his eyes. He wanted to reach inside her and tear out the black tumour and crush it in his fists, and the fierceness of the impulse balled up in his chest like terrible anger.

She signed again. —*You don't prune this time of year.*

'Whatever.'

—*It's dead-heading. Chopping off dead blooms. Like me.*

'Is that what you are thinking?'

—*I'm still getting used to no next year. But there will be for you and Dad. I think of that. I love you both very much. Do you know?*

'I do know,' he said.

—*Good. Will you remember?*

'I promise. But I don't want to talk like this. We're still here, the three of us. Now is what matters, here, today, not next year or next month.'

Jeanette nodded. —*You are right. But I can't pretend not to have cancer.*

'I didn't mean that.'

—*I know. Tell me about your week?*

'Let's think. Work's OK. Andy's in Barcelona. Oh, and I met a girl.'

—*Did you?* Her face flowered in an eager smile.

But Noah was wondering what possibility there was of any conversation about anything that wouldn't bring them up against a blank wall that had *six months* painted on it in letters higher than a house?

Jeanette wouldn't live to see his wedding. She wasn't going to know her own grandchildren.

Her head was cocked towards him, her eyes on his.

'Her name's Roxana.'

—Unusual.

He talked, and they made another slow circuit of the lawn. He told her about Roxana being robbed, and how she was staying with him while she looked for another place. He kept any mention of her job to a minimum, and then said that her brother had been killed in Andijan. He only vaguely remembered the news stories about the brief popular uprising against a virtual dictatorship.

Jeanette nodded. *—Yes. A massacre. Their government claimed it was only a few. But the international human rights organisations accepted that in the end. President Karimov was supported by the West, until he turned the Americans off their bases out there. Bush needs his allies in Central Asia.*

Noah was impressed, but not surprised that his mother knew so much. Jeanette read everything that came her way, storing up news and comment, fiction and history like bulwarks against her deafness.

—Your Roxana's brother was one of the rebels?

'I think so. She's not "mine". Not yet, anyway, although I'm working on it. Her parents are both dead. Her brother was all she had. How sad is that, to lose your only sibling? The person you grew up with. It must mean Roxana hasn't got any reference left to the little girl she was.'

Jeanette waited. *—Go on?*

Noah faltered. 'I wasn't trying to say anything else, Mum. Not consciously. It must be in my mind, though. You and Connie.'

—Yes. I know. Me and Connie.

He faced her. It meant she could lip-read more easily. 'Dad and I were thinking, Connie would want to know that you're ill.'

—You and Dad?

'Well, yes.'

They resumed their slow walk.

Jeanette's face was suffused with sadness. *—She is my sister.*

'Yes.'

—I should decide what to tell her. And when. Shouldn't I?

'Of course, Mum, if that's what you want.'

Bill strolled across the grass. 'What are you two talking about?'

Noah hesitated. Auntie Connie was rarely mentioned in the family. Or never, now that he thought about it.

—Uzbekistan, Jeanette signed.

'Really?'

—Noah has a new girlfriend who comes from there.

'She's not my girlfriend yet. I've only met her twice.'

Bill smiled easily at him. 'I'll look forward to hearing about her. If and when. Now, does anyone want a cup of tea?'

Chapter Four

THE AFTERNOON HAD reached the point where the light was at its ripest. Connie went out to her chair on the verandah. After the noisy departure of the bank commercial people, peace lapped round her once again. There was no clamour of mobile phones, no crackle of walkie-talkies, and no one was shouting. There was only the trickle of water and the various layers of birdsong.

She sat for a long time, until the tropical twilight swept up from the depths of the gorge. As the sudden darkness fell, she wandered back into the house and poured herself a glass of wine.

She took a long swallow, and set the glass down on her desk as she switched on her computer. It was days since she had checked her emails. Broadband hadn't yet reached the village and she wandered out to the verandah again while the unread messages slowly descended from the ether and filtered into her inbox.

At the screen again Connie clicked through the spam and a couple of emails from London to do with work. Connie flicked her eyes to the sender of the next message. *Bunting*. Her brain had hardly taken it in before her heart was hammering. *Bunting*.

It was only then that she saw the sender wasn't *BBunting*, but *JBunting*. Jeanette.

The last time she had seen her sister was six years ago, after Hilda's funeral. They hadn't spoken since then, nor had they written.

A message from her sister now could only mean that something was wrong. With Noah? With Bill?

Her mouth was dry and her hands shook as she opened the message. It took two readings before the news began to sink in.

There was indeed something very badly wrong.

Dear Connie,

I hope this address still finds you because I want you to hear this news from me, not from anyone else.

I have cancer. I won't go into detail, but after several months of treatment and having our hopes raised and then lowered again, we were told this week that there isn't any more to be done. Six months is the estimate. I am beginning to work out for myself what this means.

It's very hard for Noah. And for Bill. Both of them are full of love and concern for me, and I feel blessed in that.

There it is. I don't want anything, except to know that you know. Love (I mean this . . .)

Jeanette

Connie lowered her face into her hands. The immediate shock made her shiver. Jeanette had always been there: in her silence, in her brave focus on doing and being what she wanted, her influence most powerful—partly because of its very absence—in all Connie's past life.

She lifted her head, reached for her glass and drank the wine.

Her fingers felt uncertain on the keys, like a child's.

She started a new message and typed a single line.

I'll be there as soon as I can get a flight. Connie.

The train from the airport ran past the backs of Victorian terraced houses, irregular like crooked teeth in an overcrowded jaw. Connie watched them sliding past, absorbing the flicker of snapshot images from other people's lives. This couldn't be anywhere but England.

Echo Street was a terrace just like one of these, with a railway line carrying local trains into Liverpool Street, running through a shallow cutting beyond a high fence at the end of the garden.

Connie closed her eyes.

There was lino down the narrow hallway, dark red with paler bluish-pink swirls in it that looked like skimmed milk stirred into stewed plums. The stairs rose steep as a cliff, each tread usually with a sheet of the *Daily Express* folded on it because Hilda had just mopped them yet again. Hilda had a fixation with cleanliness.

In the old flat, Connie and Jeanette had shared a tiny bedroom. But in Echo Street they were to have their own rooms. Jeanette was delighted with hers. She stood in front of the door and signed to Connie: —*My bedroom, mine.*

When Connie looked into the room that was to be hers, she saw a narrow box with a window that looked out onto a brick wall. A tall cupboard was built across one corner. She twisted the handle and saw that the cupboard was empty except for two coat hangers on a hook. In the dim light the hangers looked like two pairs of shoulders that had mislaid their heads and bodies, but that might easily clothe themselves on a dark night and come gliding out of the cupboard in search of little girls.

She ran for the safety of the landing. Jeanette's door stood open a crack, allowing a glimpse of a bigger room where the sun cast a reassuring grid of light and shadow on the floorboards. Jeanette was sitting with her back against the wall, her knees drawn up and her books and magazines laid out beside her. Her fair hair was drawn in one thick plait over her shoulder and she was thoughtfully chewing the end.

It was Connie who started the fight. Overtaken by one of the surges of rage that were her last resort in the unending skirmishes against Jeanette, she launched herself through the doorway and fell on her sister.

'It's not fair. I want the big room. It's not fair.'

Connie yelled and pummelled her fists. Jeanette shouted back, but no words were distinguishable.

At the Joseph Barnes School for the Deaf, the speech therapist had made little progress with helping Jeanette to talk. When she was upset or angry she gave up the attempt to verbalise and lapsed into bellowing.

'You sound like a cow mooing,' Connie screamed.

Jeanette fought harder. Her face swelled close to Connie's as she hooked her fingers in Connie's tangled hair and propelled her backwards until her head smashed against the wall. Connie doubled up like a snake and closed her teeth on Jeanette's upper arm.

The noise brought both parents running, their feet like thunder on the stairs. Tony caught hold of Connie and hoisted her in the air, her arms pinioned and her feet kicking against nothing.

'All right, Con. That's enough. Calm down. Leave your sister alone.'

Connie still wriggled and squawked that it wasn't fair, but the rage was ebbing away. Its departure left her feeling breathless, and confused, and finally soaked in despair. She slumped against Tony's chest, letting out little whimpers of grief. He stroked her hair and rocked her against him. She could hear the steady rhythm of his heart. She didn't know then how finite was the number of those beats.

Jeanette's arm showed a ring of red puncture marks. Hilda pinched the corners of her mouth inwards and went for the first-aid box. She wrung out a hank of cotton wool in a bowl of water clouded with Dettol, and made a performance of disinfecting the tiny wound in front of Connie.

Jeanette's eyes gleamed with the lustre of martyrdom.

'Let go of her,' Hilda said to Tony. He released Connie and Hilda took hold of her by the ear and marched her to the other bedroom.

'You stay in here, my girl,' she said.

Connie sat down, back against the wall and knees drawn up, instinctively copying Jeanette. She sat there until teatime, staring at the closed cupboard door, willing the ghosts to stay where they were.

Connie opened her eyes. The train crept past Battersea Power Station and made a sighing arrival at Victoria. She lifted her small bag and let the surge of passengers carry her off the train and into the thick of London. Only a taxi ride separated her from home. A version of home.

It was three months since she had last been in her apartment. From the front door she could see that there was dust on all the glass surfaces and dead flies speckling the white floor. The air smelt as if it had been hot too many times. Connie walked down the white corridor to her bathroom and turned on the shower. She stripped off her creased clothes and stood under the spray until she felt clean again. Then she wrapped herself in a towel and padded back to the main room.

She stood for a moment at the window that ran the length of one wall, staring out at the view. The apartment was on the top floor and she could see a broad sweep of the city from Canary Wharf tower all the way west to the dome of St Paul's.

Connie's desk faced the view. She stared out at the towers and the brown streets, knowing that she was delaying the moment.

She made herself open the address book that lay next to the telephone, and looked up Jeanette's number. She hadn't committed it to memory; she had hardly ever used it.

They never saw each other, but Jeanette's massive presence was always there like a headland jutting out into the sea. Jeanette was the only person left in the world who knew the same things that Connie knew from long ago, and Connie held her sister's memories furled tight within her in just the same way.

It was *unthinkable* that Jeanette was going to die.

Connie pressed the buttons of the handset. Her heart was thumping as if she were running for her life. She listened to the ringing tone. Another thought rushed in on her.

In a second or two I'll hear his voice.

Because Jeanette wouldn't answer.

If anyone picked up, it would be him.

It was about fifteen years ago, now.

Connie went to a party in a newly completed glass tower in Docklands. One of the advertising agencies was moving out there, with a big fanfare to announce to the known world that a building site east of the City was the new Soho.

She looked past a group of chattering account people and clients, and with a shock saw Bill watching her from across the room.

She put down her glass and went to him.

'You look very beautiful tonight,' he said. There were shadows under his eyes, and he had been drinking.

'Hello, Bill.'

'We don't often run into each other, do we? I am here because I handle the PR account for TotalTime TV. What about you?'

'One of the creative heads at the agency is a friend of mine.'

'Small world. And are you here with anyone?'

'No. I'm not here with anyone.'

They turned to each other, as if there was no one else in the room, as if there was finally no other move they could make but this one.

Bill murmured, 'Connie, can we get out of here?'

'Yes.'

They rode down in the glass-sided lift and walked out into a bull-dozer park. Bill blinked at the desolation.

'If I could magic up a taxi, would you run away with me?'

'We don't need magic; I've got my car,' Connie said. 'Where would you like to go?'

Inside the car, Bill said, 'I don't care where we go. As long as you are with me. I don't care what happens.'

'Yes, you do.'

'Don't pretend to be rational, Con. Don't pretend that what there is between us has ever been rational.'

She was driving an unfamiliar route past hoardings and cranes and what would some day be new roads raised on huge concrete stilts over the razed docklands. She had the strongest sense that they were running away, out of an old world and into a new one that hadn't yet been made. He *had* said the words out loud: *between us.*

What there is. He had acknowledged the existence of a truth, even though he hadn't defined it, and now it couldn't be unsaid. Alarm and joy and longing hammered in her chest.

'I don't know where we're going.'

'Stop the car,' he said roughly.

She turned into a contractors' byway fenced off with tilted sheets of corrugated iron. Her fingers were shaking as she switched off the ignition.

Bill twisted towards her and their mouths met.

This time, as the blood surged in her ears, she knew that there was no way back. Even if she had wanted one.

When they drew apart again, they were both gasping as if they had run a distance too fast.

'Connie,' he said wonderingly. She rubbed her bruised mouth, tasting him on her tongue.

'Where shall we go?' he asked.

'Home,' she answered. Her lack of hesitation should have shocked her, but it did not. Nothing about what was happening was shocking, because of its inevitability. It was wrong, and it was dangerous because of the hurt it would certainly cause, but it didn't take her aback.

They drove back into town, fast, in almost complete silence. When her hand moved to the gear lever Bill's covered it, as if he wanted to make sure that she was real, that she wouldn't escape.

They stumbled into the flat she had lived in back in those days like a pair of wild fugitives.

Bill had never even been here before. He slammed the front door behind them and at once they were in each other's arms. He undressed her as they crossed the hallway. A trail of shoes and clothes marked their passage to the bedroom door.

'Bill . . .' she said, but his hand covered her mouth.

'We'll talk afterwards. Talk for hours if you like. But first this.'

This.

With the man she had loved for almost thirteen years. With the only man she had ever truly loved. With her sister's husband.

At home in Surrey, with Jeanette asleep in their bedroom upstairs, Bill picked up the phone.

'Hello?'

She would have known his voice if she had heard him whispering in an earthquake.

'Bill.'

'Connie,' he said.

He spoke her name as if he were holding her hand.

'I am in London,' she said carefully. 'I want to come and see Jeanette.'

'You know?'

'Yes. She sent me an email.'

She heard him taking in a breath.

'Come tomorrow,' Bill said.

On Saturday mornings Hilda had started taking Jeanette to a special audiology clinic for extra therapy sessions. Mrs Archer, Jeanette's teacher at the Joseph Barnes School for the Deaf, reported that she was an exceptional academic pupil, but she needed more help with her speech if she was to live up to her potential.

So on Saturday mornings Connie went with Tony to the shop. She would sit in Hilda's place in the front seat of the Austin Maxi and Tony would drive them there, turning to wink at her as they eased out of Echo Street and saying, 'Just you and me, eh?'

Thorne's on the Parade was a hardware shop in a row of similarly sized shops on a busy junction. When Tony had unlocked the door and rolled up the heavy shutter that protected the front, Connie helped him to carry out the street stock. Tony shifted the heavy items, the bags of coke, bundles of sticks and metal stepladders, and Connie made a dozen journeys with bunches of galvanised mop buckets, bristly yard brushes and festoons of mop heads like scarecrow wigs. She nudged them into what she judged to be inviting arrangements while Tony put on his brown working coat and wound down the old canopy for the day.

The interior of the shop was a cavern of shelves, with a range of goods from mousetraps to boxes of sugar soap and balls of tarry twine mounted on either side of a high wooden counter. There was a specific, comforting smell of metal polish; paraffin and harsh yellow soap, and Connie had always loved everything about it.

If there were no customers waiting for them at opening-up time, Tony would unfold the *Daily Express*, smooth it out on the counter and say to Connie, 'What kind of assistant are you? Is that kettle not on yet?'

Connie would hurry round to the rear, into a cramped space where a cracked sink and draining board were sagging away from the wall, boil the kettle and make tea the way Tony liked it, in the brown pot with the tannin-enriched interior, two tea bags brewed until dark and then poured into stained mugs. She would carry the mugs through and put them on the counter beside a packet of sugar with a dug-in teaspoon, and they drank it accompanied by two fingers of KitKat each. They never discussed it, but they took their mutual pleasure in this sloppy behaviour because Hilda would never have allowed it at Echo Street.

There was only one stool behind the counter, a high wooden one with the seat polished slippery with use. When she wasn't counting stock lists or tidying shelves, Connie perched on it to read her book or draw pictures. Tony was always on his feet, fetching and wrapping and ringing up sales. Saturday mornings were always busy, as men glumly equipped themselves for a weekend's odd-jobbing and decorating.

At two o'clock, Connie would turn the sign that hung in the glass half of the door from OPEN to CLOSED and they would reverse the morning's procedure with the outside goods.

'That's it then. Until Monday morning,' Tony always said as the shutter unrolled with a shriek of tortured metal.

Connie remembered these uncomplicated hours in the shop with Tony as the very happiest times of her entire childhood.

Then in February 1974, in the darkest week of a bad winter, came the opportunity of piano lessons.

Jeanette's inspiring teacher was by that time becoming an adviser to the whole Thorne family in her efforts to help an unusually able deaf child. Hilda despairingly confided to Mrs Archer that Connie was disruptive at home, aggressive towards her sister, a poor sleeper and was becoming a problem at her mainstream school. Mrs Archer mildly suggested that Hilda might try to make Connie feel that she was special in some way as well as Jeanette, and what was she good at?

'She likes music and singing,' Hilda eventually acknowledged.

'What about channelling that into learning to play an instrument?'

'Our family doesn't go in for music lessons,' Hilda said stiffly. After a glance from Mrs Archer she added, 'We've got a piano.'

'Piano? I'll see if I can come up with a teacher in your area, shall I?'

Not long afterwards, Hilda answered a telephone call that wasn't from her sister Sadie or Tony's brother in South Wales, who were the only people apart from Jeanette's various therapists who normally rang them. It was Mrs Polanski, the piano teacher. She had one spare weekly slot, on Saturday mornings.

Connie had protested at first that she preferred going to the shop with Tony on Saturdays. But in the end, because she liked the idea of learning to play the piano, she agreed.

'I'll have to do without my assistant. It'll be difficult, but I'll manage,' Tony told her.

Piano lessons with Mrs Polanski were a success. Connie knew immediately and instinctively that she was a good teacher. She made everything fun, even C major and D major scales and finger exercises.

'And one, two, three, *play*, my girl,' she would trill as Connie launched into her piece, and she sang the notes to keep her in time and slid her ringed fingers over the backs of Connie's hands to show her the proper positions. Connie practised eagerly every afternoon after school, racing through all the exercises that Mrs Polanski gave her in order to win even more of her liberal praise.

'We will make a concert artiste of you, Constance. Wait and see.'

It was early in May. Constance had been learning the piano for three months and she could play the right-hand part of 'Für Elise' with the proper fingering. She would never have believed that a whole hour could pass so quickly.

She hurried through the rain from the bus stop to Echo Street. As she slid her front-door key into the lock she heard the telephone ringing.

Connie turned the key quickly and almost tripped over the doormat as she catapulted herself inside. As she picked up the phone, the door caught in a gust of wind and slammed shut behind her.

She told the woman caller that Mrs Thorne wasn't at home. This was her daughter. Yes, Mrs Thorne would be back soon. Yes, she would get her to call this number as soon as she came in. The woman was very insistent that Connie fetched a pen and wrote it down. Mrs Thorne was to ask for Sister Evans. As soon as she came home, because it was urgent.

Connie replaced the receiver and sat down at the piano to practise her new scales.

The front door slammed again. Hilda and Jeanette bundled down the hallway. Hilda's umbrella rustled into the recess in the hall stand. Connie let her hands fall into her lap, then stood up and followed her mother and sister into the kitchen.

'There was a telephone call,' she began.

'Let me get in the house, Connie.'

'It's urgent.'

Hilda's eyes flicked to her. 'Well, what is it?'

Connie gave her the number she had written on the cover of the *Radio Times*. Ignoring Connie, Jeanette filled the kettle and put out two mugs and a jar of Nescafé. Hilda went into the front room to make the call, closing the door behind her.

Jeanette poured boiling water, clinked a spoon, unscrewed the lid of the biscuit jar. She sat down at the table and began to read a magazine. Hilda's coffee mug stood on the counter waiting for her to come back.

Connie stared out of the window into the damp passage that separated their house from the next in the terrace. As the minutes passed she slowly became aware of a silence that drew all the oxygen out of the air. The only movement was Jeanette turning the pages of *Woman's Own*.

After what seemed a long time, Connie walked over to the closed door of the front room. She rotated the doorknob, pushed the door open and looked in.

Hilda was sitting in the armchair next to the telephone table. She was white, dry-eyed, frozen. Her eyes moved, settled on Connie as if she had never seen her before.

'Mum?'

Hilda's hands lifted as if to ward her off. Her tongue passed slowly over her lips. 'Tony's gone. He's left us.'

Connie frowned. She knew this wasn't possible. Tony was at the shop, just like always. 'Gone where?'

'Gone,' Hilda repeated.

The telephone began shrilling again. Hilda launched herself at it. 'Sadie? Sadie, he's dead.'

She was gripping the receiver with two hands but she was shaking so much that she could hardly hold it in place.

'Tony's *dead*.'

Connie took two steps backwards. She reached behind her with the flat of her hands, pressed herself against the wall and tried to retreat farther as fragments of her world began to rain down around her.

Suddenly Jeanette was there, in the doorway. Hilda was sobbing.

Jeanette's fingers came up to her lips. —*Speak*, she signed.

Connie stuttered. Her mouth wouldn't form any words.

Isolated in silence and incomprehension, Jeanette turned wild with bewilderment and terror. —*Speak, speak.*

She dug fingers like claws into Connie's arms and shook her until Connie's head banged against the wall.

'It's Dad,' Connie screamed into her contorted face.

The funeral service was held at the crematorium near Thorne's on the Parade. Tony's brother and his wife came from Newport, Sadie's husband Geoff took the day off from his garage business and drove his wife and daughters in from their detached house in Loughton, and some of Tony's old friends and shop owners and customers from the Parade gathered in the colourless room. Hilda and Jeanette and Connie sat in the front row of chairs and listened to a stranger telling the mourners what a devoted husband and loving father Anthony Thorne had been. Connie gazed at the plain coffin under its purple cloth and tried to believe that her father was lying inside it.

She was cold. She had felt either cold or hot ever since last Saturday, when Auntie Sadie and Uncle Geoff had arrived at Echo Street and immediately called the doctor. While he was upstairs with Hilda, their auntie and uncle told Jeanette and Connie that their father had suffered a huge heart attack while he was carrying out the pavement stock. The newsagent had called an ambulance and Tony had been taken to the East London Hospital, but he had not survived the journey.

After the cremation, and the inspection of the flowers laid out in the chilly wind with no grave to make sad sense of them, the mourners were invited back to Echo Street.

Neighbours had made sandwiches and finger rolls and Uncle Geoff had unloaded two heavy, clinking cardboard cartons from the back of his Jaguar. The house quickly filled up with sombre people in dark, unfamiliar clothes who quickly held out their tumblers to a shopkeeper from the Parade as he circulated on Geoff's instructions with a bottle of sherry in one hand and a bottle of whisky in the other.

Hilda sat in the front room, bright spots of colour showing high on her cheeks, and gravely accepted condolences. The cousins, Jackie and Elaine, were seventeen and fifteen. Jackie was already working as a hairdresser, and Elaine would soon be leaving school to go to secretarial college, and like her sister she was accorded semi-adult status. Geoff had given them a glass of sherry each without any questions asked, and somehow Jeanette had taken one too.

The level of talk rose perceptibly as an hour passed. Connie sat awkwardly on the piano stool, holding a glass of orange squash.

'All right, my love?' someone asked her.

'Yes, thank you,' Connie mechanically replied.

After a time Connie noticed that Jeanette and the cousins were missing, and guessed that they had gone upstairs together.

The door to Jeanette's bedroom stood ajar. Jeanette was sitting on her green satin-covered eiderdown with Elaine holding her hand. Jackie was standing in front of her, combing out her hair with long, gentle strokes. Jeanette's eyes were closed with the luxury of this tender grooming.

Connie edged into the room. The cousins glanced over their shoulders at her, then at each other. Nobody spoke.

'Do my hair as well?' Connie asked.

'Yours?' Jackie said.

Connie's scalp prickled; her dark hair seeming to spiral more tightly and thickly. 'Yes. Will you?'

Jackie sighed. 'I don't think I can do much with it.'

Suddenly, Connie was angry. From feeling shivery with cold a flash of heat ran through her, making her face burn.

'You ought to be nice to me as well as Jeanette. My dad's dead, too.'

Elaine's face was flushed and her eyes looked strange. Her thumb massaged the back of Jeanette's hand. 'He wasn't your dad.'

Connie saw that Jeanette's eyes were open now. They were wide, and as blue as the sea.

'What do you mean?'

Jackie shook her head in warning and the comb dropped from her hand. Elaine's flushed face turned darker, meaner.

'You're adopted, aren't you?'

Connie looked from one to the other.

She understood in that moment a mystery that had always been there, nagging like an invisible bruise under the eventless skin of her life, and she knew with perfect certainty that it had been a mystery to her alone.

She bent her head and saw the pale brown of her wrists emerging from the knitted cuffs of her jersey. She felt the dusty twists of her hair, and the narrowness of her shoulders and hips, and then she looked with her dark eyes back at Jeanette, and Jackie and Elaine. They all had pale fine hair, like their mothers', and they had full breasts and hips and round blue eyes.

Jackie had drawn her lower lip between her teeth and Elaine looked hot and angry. Only Jeanette's expression was unchanged; she had heard none of those words of Elaine's that could never be withdrawn or unsaid, but she hadn't needed to.

They were both older, but Bill was the same. He was the same as he always was, and just as necessary to her.

He held his arms out. 'Thank you for coming, Con. I didn't know whether I should tell you. It's been worrying me for a long time.'

Connie lifted her head. He kissed her cheek, lightly and quickly, and then they studied each other's faces. He cupped a shoulder with each hand, then gently released her. She saw that Bill had grown thin. There were lines at the corners of his eyes and mouth, the same signs of age that marked her own, but the hollows in his cheeks were made deeper by the shadows of exhaustion. There was now much more grey than dark brown in his thick hair.

Connie said, 'It's much better that she told me herself. How is she?'

He shook his head. 'Physically? As brave and determined as you would imagine. But she's fighting a battle with herself as much as with the cancer. It's difficult for her to accept what's happening.'

'Where is she?'

'In the garden. She sits out there a lot of the time, communing with her plants. That seems to soothe her in a way that not much else does. How are you, Connie? You look well.'

'I am. But for this.'

'Come and see her.'

Bill led the way through the house. Connie glimpsed a copper trough filled with pots of African violets and an expanse of polished parquet flooring divided into squares by the sun. It was very quiet.

'I'll leave you to talk to her,' Bill said.

The French windows stood open. Jeanette was sitting to one side of the big garden in the shade of a copper beech tree, her head nodding. There was a rug over her knees and a newspaper had slipped to the ground at her feet. Connie walked quickly over the grass, but it seemed to take a long time to cover the few yards to her side. Even in the sunshine it felt as if she were wading against a strong current. Their last parting had been hostile. Neither of them had envisaged a reconciliation.

As soon as Connie's shadow fell on the edge of the newspaper, Jeanette looked up.

—*Here you are.*

'Here I am.'

—*That was quick. All the way from Bali.*

Connie did her best to smile through her shock at her sister's appearance. The last time they met she had been plump and pretty, and now she looked like a woman whose flesh had all seeped away. Her blonde hair, once her shining glory, was a cap of colourless tufts that barely concealed her scalp.

'I came as soon as I got your email. Did I wake you?'

—*No.*

Connie made to kneel down on the grass beside her sister's chair, so that it would be easier for her to lip-read, but Jeanette stopped her.

—*Could you help me up?*

Connie gently put her hands under Jeanette's arms and eased her to her feet. She felt as light as a child.

For a moment they stood uncertainly together, their cheeks not quite touching. Connie tightened her arms round her sister's shoulders. She wanted to find a way to reach beyond words, to leapfrog the impediment that wasn't lodged merely in Jeanette's deafness and to hug her so tightly that nothing could come between them ever again.

'I'm glad to be here,' she began. She stroked her sister's thin hair, just once, very lightly.

—*I wanted to tell you the news myself. I didn't want you to hear from anyone else that I'm going to die. Not even Bill. But I didn't expect you to come straight away like this.*

'Did you *want* me to come?'

Jeanette suddenly smiled. Her teeth looked too big for her mouth, but the lines in her face eased and there was a light in her eyes. —*Yes. You are the only one who remembers everything. That's odd, isn't it?*

'I know,' Connie said. 'I feel the same. All the way in on the train I was thinking about Echo Street. The day we moved in and we fought over the bedrooms. The nightmares I used to have.'

—*So much history.*

Connie nodded. 'I'm so happy to see you,' she said, and it was the truth. Jeanette's hand briefly masked her waxy face. —*Looking like this?*

'Looking anyhow.'

—*Give me your arm. Let's walk.*

'Can you manage? Bill said he'd make us some coffee and bring it out.'

Jeanette looked away. —*Coffee. Like sitting in some waiting room. Drinking coffee. Waiting for your name to be called.*

'Is that how it feels?'

—*Sometimes. Not always.*

They began to walk, a slow shuffle past the flower border. To Connie, used to the coarse brilliance of Balinese vegetation, the blooms looked ghostly pale with petals as fragile as damp tissue, the embodiment of restrained Englishness.

—*Look at my roses.*

'They're very beautiful.'

But Connie didn't want small talk starting to blur these first exchanges of their reunion. There was so much to say, right now, in case they should fall into the old evasions or even hostilities.

'I'd have come long before this, if you had told me that you were ill.'

—*Would you?* Jeanette seemed to be examining the words for layers of meaning. Then she sighed, wearied by the effort. —*I kept expecting to get better.*

Connie asked, 'Do you know for sure that you're not going to?'

—*It's in my spine.*

They took a slow step, then another, walking carefully in their new alignment. If Jeanette had been healthy they would have maintained their distance. Now she was going to die, and the certainty was changing the attitudes of a lifetime.

Connie tried to calculate the combination of defiance and resignation that it must have taken for Jeanette to confess her condition.

Because Jeanette *would* regard it as a confession. For the whole of her life, it had been Jeanette's intention and her satisfaction to do as well as everyone else, and then a bit better than that. She had always wanted to be bigger than her deafness, and to make it incidental that she couldn't hear or speak like other people did.

In that, she had triumphantly succeeded.

So to succumb to cancer might seem, in some guarded corner of Jeanette's being, to be a form of weakness. As would acknowledging it to her sister, with whom she shared everything—and nothing.

What could Connie offer her that might help? All she had was a biting sense of how much had been missed, how much she had failed to make friends with her sister, and how little time they had left to make amends.

'Are you in a lot of pain?'

—*The chemo was awful. I was sick all the time. There won't be any more of that, thank God. I have some good days, now.*

'Is today one?'

—*Yes. Today is one.*

Connie knew that was not just because she was in less pain.

Fifteen slow steps took them to the end of the flowerbed and the point where the lawn ran out into rough grass. Jeanette paused and shaded her eyes with her hand, and at first Connie thought the sun must be too bright for her. Then she saw that her shoulders were shaking. Jeanette was crying.

'Don't cry,' Connie begged.

She realised that she didn't know how to deal with this illness. She had never been ill herself, and had never looked after anyone who was suffering anything more serious than a dose of flu.

Quickly she corrected herself. 'I don't mean that. Cry all you want if that helps. What can I do? Tell me what to do.'

Jeanette sniffed and pressed the heel of her hands into her eyes. —*I don't want to die. You can't do anything about that.*

The obverse of Jeanette's strength had always been anger. Connie could suddenly feel the dry heat of it coming off her thin skin, eating her up like a fever.

—*I am supposed to be brave. It's expected. People want to be able to say, 'She fought all the way. She was so brave.' But I'm not. I don't know how to be. I want to scream and yell. It's not fair that I'm dying. I don't mean just to me. To Bill and Noah as well.*

Connie stared miserably. 'That's what *I* always used to say, not you. That was my refrain, don't you remember? You never complained that life was unfair. You just lived it, made it do what you wanted.'

—*But I can't now. I can't do this.*

'Yes, you can. If anyone can deal with it, it's you. I'll help you.'

—*Will you?*

'If you'll let me,' Connie humbly said.

She caught hold of Jeanette's wrists and held them. For a moment it was as if they were having one of their old fist fights. Then Jeanette's eyes slid over Connie's shoulder towards the house. Connie let go of her.

—*Thank you.*

Connie didn't know whether her offer was accepted or dismissed.

A sudden smile glinted through Jeanette's tears. For an instant, she looked like a girl again. Without turning round, Connie knew that Bill was coming.

—*Here he is.* Jeanette's glance flicked back to Connie. —*I love him. He loves me.* She gave the signs an extra edge of precision, for clarity's sake.

Connie met her sister's gaze. She understood that one of the assurances

Jeanette wanted from her was that she and Bill wouldn't share anything more than memories and kinship, now or ever.

'I know you love each other,' she answered steadily. 'There has never been any doubt about that.'

She held out her arm and Jeanette leaned on it again. They retraced their steps as Bill put down a tray loaded with cups and a coffeepot.

When they reached him, he lowered Jeanette into her chair and tucked the rug over her knees, then folded the crumpled newspaper and laid it aside. He did everything deftly, clearly used to looking after her.

'Next week you'll be making the coffee for me,' he told her.

—*If I have time*, she murmured. —*Busy, busy*.

Bill set up two more folding chairs in the shade of the copper beech tree, and they drew together in a triangle. If anyone had glanced over the hedge they would have looked like any family enjoying a summer's day in a garden flushed with lavender and roses.

The first time Connie met Bill was at Echo Street, in the summer of 1978.

'Who is it tonight? Four Eyes? Or Mr Physics Club?'

Connie despised all Jeanette's followers, as she despised almost everything except music and her tight coterie of like-minded friends. Jeanette whisked her finished shirt off the ironing board and held it up to admire her work. She slipped it on a hanger and took it upstairs with her, not even glancing in Connie's direction.

'Don't call Jeanette's boyfriends rude names,' Hilda warned. 'And don't leave rubbish on the table; you'll make this place look like a tip.'

'It's not rubbish. It's my homework. So who is he?'

Hilda began swabbing the corner of the table with a cloth that smelt of bleach. Her red knuckles jabbed against Connie's wrist.

'He's a new one. You get a boyfriend yourself, you won't want us calling him names.'

Connie gave her a blank stare. *If only you knew*.

Connie was fifteen and she had been having sex with Davy Spencer for the last three months. She didn't really enjoy it, but a lot of the girls in her year fancied him and he played the drums in the best band in their school—although that wasn't saying much.

'What's his name, then?'

'Bill Bunting.'

Connie laughed. 'What is he, some nursery-rhyme character?'

Jeanette came back. Her hair framed her glowing face and hid her hearing aids, her shirt ruffles were crisp and her tight jeans were tucked into soft suede boots. Connie slouched lower in her chair. She was still in her school shirt and scratchy royal-blue synthetic-knit V-necked jumper.

The doorbell rang.

'He's here,' Hilda said, pointing.

Jeanette performed a little pirouette of excitement before giving her hair a last shake and dancing to the door.

Connie deliberately stuck her nose in her English book. She heard his voice, and the busy silence of Jeanette's responses. She didn't look up, even when they both came into the kitchen and Hilda was shaking hands and saying that she was pleased to meet him and he wasn't to mind the mess the place was in because when you were on your own with a family to look after you couldn't always have things looking the way you wanted, could you?

'No,' he said. His voice was distinctive: it sounded as though it had ripples in it. 'It must be difficult. But it looks fine.'

Then she knew that his eyes were on her.

Connie couldn't stop herself glancing up, even though she had meant to ignore all three of them.

She saw immediately that Bill Bunting was worthy of anyone's attention. He had the sort of long, shaggy hair that Connie liked. He was wearing battered jeans, and a not-too-ridiculous shirt. He had dark eyes and one of those curly mouths that always look as if they are about to smile. He was holding Jeanette's hand, without seeming to try to prove anything, but just as if he wanted to keep her close to him.

Connie swallowed.

'Hi, I'm Bill. You must be Connie,' he said.

'I am Constance,' she replied stiffly.

He held his hand out. Hilda was asking him if he wanted a drink, a coffee maybe, or he could have a beer if he wanted one.

In spite of herself, Connie shook his hand.

'What are you reading?' he asked. 'It must be really good.' He did smile now, his mouth curling.

'*Nineteen Eighty-Four*. It's my set book in English.'

'Yes. That's a good book.'

Connie would have liked to ask him why he enjoyed it, because she didn't particularly. It would have been interesting to talk to him, and a fully-fledged fantasy popped into her head in which she and Bill Bunting were sitting at an outdoor table in some exotic but unspecified place, drinking wine and discussing literature and music.

But in reality he was holding her sister's hand and telling Hilda that they couldn't stop, although he'd like to, because he was taking Jeanette for something to eat before they went to hear a new band.

Jeanette was *deaf*. Why was he taking *her* to a gig?

'Go on then, both of you,' Hilda said. 'Have a lovely time.'

Jeanette was almost bouncing with happiness, springing up and down in her little suede boots with the turnover tops. Connie thought that she was looking prettier and sexier than she had ever done before.

'Bye, Constance,' Bill said. She knew that he was gently teasing her for having insisted on her full name, and she couldn't bear to be teased. It took enough concentration to keep the blocks of her life piled up in the right precarious order, without someone threatening to topple them by laughing and making her feel ridiculous. Especially not this Bill Bunting.

Connie wouldn't look at him. She picked up her book again and stared at the grey paragraphs until he and Jeanette departed for their date. Hilda accompanied them to the front door, waved them off and then came back, picked up her cloth and resumed her rubbing.

'What do you want for your tea?' she asked at last, when there was no surface left in the kitchen that could conceivably benefit from further polishing, wiping, sweeping or disinfecting.

Connie shrugged. 'Nothing.'

'You can't eat nothing.'

'Really? Can't I? What makes you think that?'

'I don't want any of your silly sarcasm, my girl.'

Connie gathered up her books and files. 'I might go out.'

'You've got the money for that, have you?'

In fact Connie did; she had a Saturday job in a record shop up in Hackney, although that was more for the chance to admire the new and second-hand vinyl than for the cash it brought in.

She shrugged again and this goaded Hilda enough to make her demand: 'Why can't you be more like your sister?'

Connie let three seconds tick by, deliciously. 'You know why. You should have had another one just like her, if that was what you wanted.'

Hilda's face went tight and dark. Connie strolled out of the kitchen and it was only as she was going up the stairs that Hilda was able to call after her in a loud, harsh voice, 'You've got the devil in you, Connie Thorne. I don't know what you're doing in this house.'

Connie went into her bedroom and closed the door.

Anyway, she thought, I won't *be* in this house for much longer. In a year, or not much more than a year, she would be able to leave school.

She was going to move out and leave Echo Street far behind her, and she was going to find her real mother and father. Once she had found them she could become the person she was born to be, instead of having to be Constance Thorne.

Jeanette tasted two or three sips of her coffee, then replaced her cup on the tray. The saucer rattled. Bill passed her a glass of water instead and she took a brown bottle of pills out of her cardigan pocket and swallowed two capsules, then gave the glass back to Bill. They did all this without a word or a glance, and Connie saw how practised they were at being just the two of them.

Jeanette leaned back in her chair.

—*What about you?* she asked.

Connie said, 'I've been at home, in Bali. Last week I was working on the music for a big commercial shoot.'

The bank clients and Rayner Ingram and Angela seemed already to have fallen into some distant other world. She was startled to think how recent the week's miniature dramas had really been, and how very little they mattered now that she was here.

'That sounds glamorous,' Bill said.

She laughed. 'It does, doesn't it? I had musicians to look after and I enjoyed that. It felt a bit strange, though, seeing London in Bali. I wasn't quite sure which environment was which.'

Jeanette followed all this. Conversations when each person took a turn didn't trouble her, only when everyone was speaking at once.

—*But you said at home. Is Bali your home?*

'Did I say that?'

—*Yes.*

Connie thought about it. 'I've been living there for a while now, so I suppose I do think of it as home.' This wasn't the time or the place to expand on anyone's definition of home.

—*What is it like?* Jeanette leaned forward.

'Beautiful. Hot. Different. Exotic. And that doesn't do it justice.'

—*I would love to have seen it.*

'Would you?' Connie asked. Jeanette had never travelled much, preferring to take villa or hotel holidays with Bill and Noah in Italy or France. A flash of memory came back to her of Bill, in one of their snatched moments during the time long ago when everything hung in the balance between them, calling Connie his wild, wandering girl because she was leaving him to go to Cambodia.

She'd go anywhere, in those days, anywhere in the world that was far enough to try to escape the problem that none of them could solve.

—*Wishful thinking now,* Jeanette signed.

There was a small silence that was waiting for the comfort of words to be dropped into it. Bill rubbed the corner of his jaw with his thumb. A reddish patch in the skin showed that the gesture had become habitual.

Bill hopped up and announced that he was going to go in and make some lunch. As he carried the tray back across the lawn to the house the two women settled themselves again.

'What's Noah doing?' Connie asked.

As when Bill had come out into the garden, Jeanette's face softened and brightened. —*Noah's fine. He's a joy.* She told Connie about Noah's job and his flat and that there might be some new love interest, although they hadn't met her yet. —*He's grown up now. That's one good thing.*

Connie remembered him as a teenager, protective of Jeanette, with a disconcerting physical resemblance to his father.

—*I hope it won't be too hard for him*, Jeanette added.

Her sister's tenderness for the boy moved Connie, and she could imagine the anguish Jeanette felt at the thought of leaving him. But it also touched a place in Connie that she tried to keep covered up. Seeing a mother's love was like pressing on an unhealed wound, an old, deep injury that scabbed over and seemed on the point of disappearing, but broke open when she least expected it and made her wince with pain.

The sudden exposure of it made her push back her chair and drop to her knees. She had to move to ease the hurt so she gathered her sister into her arms, stroking her sparse hair and rocking her as if she were a baby. This time Jeanette didn't resist. Hot, uncalculated words broke out of Connie like fresh blood from beneath the broken scab.

'Jeanette. Jeanette, I'm so sorry. I'm sorry I haven't been here with you. So much in our childhood was wrong. It was nobody's fault, not even Hilda's. I ran away from home and from you. I was full of my own concerns, and I haven't been the sister you wanted or deserved.

'What I did with Bill was bad. But I didn't plan to fall in love with my own sister's husband, you know. Once you were married I should just have kept running, over the horizon, before anything else happened. Bill was in the wrong too, but he's a good man. He loves you. He's not the first or the last husband to make a mistake and regret it ever afterwards.

'I know you don't trust me, why should you? But I'm trying to say I'll do whatever I can now. If you will let me.'

Over the years Connie had taught herself not to cry, but tears came now. They burned her eyes and the green garden blurred.

She didn't even know how much of what she said was intelligible to Jeanette, but she held her and rocked her and slowly Jeanette lifted her arm. She put her hand on Connie's head and stroked her hair, just once.

'It's not too late,' Connie said. 'It's not. It can't be.'

Jeanette made no response.

Silently they held on to each other.

Chapter Five

EVERY EVENING, NOAH came home straight from work instead of going to the gym or stopping off at the pub, in the hope of overlapping with Roxana before she left for the Cosmos. If he was lucky, he would find her still wandering between the bathroom and his bedroom with her hair wrapped in one of his towels, her muscled legs beaded with drops of water from the shower.

'Hi, Noah. Did you have a nice day? What work did you do?'

He took a beer out of the fridge or made himself a mug of tea, and while Roxana perched on the sofa to paint her toenails with silver glitter he told her about providing technical support to editors who could spend days honing a manuscript, somehow manage to lose all their work with a couple of keystrokes, and want him to recover it for them.

'It sounds highly responsible business. You have a good career.'

'Oh, I don't know that it's a career. It's just a job.'

When her hair and toenails were dry she would retreat into his bedroom and put on her street clothes.

'I have to go,' she would sigh.

'What time do you think you will be back?' he asked, and then realised that he sounded like her husband. Or her brother.

She shrugged. 'When the club closes. I will see you tomorrow, Noah, when you come back from work.'

'Right. By the way, you know Andy, my flatmate, is coming back from holiday this evening?'

'Yes. I remember this. I will have to move out. I will find a room, better than the last place.'

'It's fine. I'll just leave a note for Andy, tell him who you are and not to leap up in the night assuming you're a burglar. After tonight I'll be on the sofa until you get sorted.'

She laid her hand on his arm. 'Thank you. I like staying with you, Noah. You have a good heart.'

Roxana's face was close to his, close enough for him to be able to smell the scent of her skin and hair, and the promise of her mouth was suddenly too much for him. He came in closer and kissed her. It was supposed to be an appreciative sort of kiss, casually suggesting that there might be more to come if that happened to be acceptable.

Roxana's reaction was startling. She whipped away from him as if he had seriously assaulted her and her arms came protectively across her chest. She glared at him.

'Whoa. It's all right,' he murmured.

'It is not,' she snapped. 'Perhaps you believe that because I am a lap dancer, I am for anyone? Perhaps now you will offer me some money? Or perhaps you think you let me stay in your flat and I am free?'

He gazed at her in dismay. 'I don't think any of those things. I think you're pretty, and I like you. I've got no reason to believe you dislike me; in fact, you just told me I've got a good heart. We've known each other a couple of weeks. I gave you a very quick kiss. It's what men and women do. At least, they do in London.'

That touched a chord, as he had known it would.

'I see. I am thinking you are the same,' Roxana muttered.

'The same as what?'

'My stepfather. My teacher. Dylan at my other house. Mr Shane.'

Noah was aware that there was a big tangle here that he and Roxana might have to unravel together if they were to go any further. He picked at the nearest thread. 'Mr Shane?'

'He is the man who owns the Cosmos. He likes one of the Brazilian girls, but last night he tried to make some games with me.'

'What did you do?'

'I know how to handle this by now, don't you think? I am pleasant, but he doesn't get me. Perhaps I can't say no for ever, though.'

'Roxy, you have to leave that place. You could get a safe, normal job. Even if it was in a bar, or as a waitress, for the time being.'

'Not for this.' She rubbed her thumb against her bunched fingers.

'Money isn't everything,' he told her pompously.

'Maybe not for you, Mr Noah Bunting.' Roxana made her way to the door. 'But I need to make a good life here in England. I work, I save, and some day I will be somebody.' And with that, she left.

Andy came back from Barcelona, leaving a lava trail of damp and pungent clothing between his room and the washing machine, and Noah moved onto the sofa.

It was 4 a.m. when Roxana returned to the flat in Hammersmith. As soon as she closed the front door with the softest possible click, she knew that Noah was awake.

He was in the kitchen, two hands wrapped round a mug. His hair stood up at the back of his head and he was yawning and blinking. He took a gulp from the mug, looking at Roxana over the rim.

'Do you want some tea?' he asked. He was speaking very quietly, not wanting to risk disturbing Andy.

'Tea? OK, why not?'

He juggled with a tea bag and a mug and the kettle, then handed the mug across to her. They sat down at the kitchen table.

She drank some of her tea, put the mug down and spread her hands flat on the table. Noah matched the gesture and without speaking or looking directly at each other they slid their hands closer until the tips of their middle fingers were just touching. After a moment of this most tenuous connection Noah ventured to raise his hands to cover hers. When he glanced at her face he saw that she was blushing, and the contrast between what she did and what she was like touched him deeply.

Behind her the fridge shuddered and the motor began its low hum. Roxana stirred herself and withdrew her hands from beneath his.

'It is very late.'

'When can we see each other?' he asked.

'We are seeing each other now.'

'You know what I mean.'

She said abruptly, 'Yes. Of course I know.'

'And so?' He might as well be persistent, he thought. You could only get so far with tact and circumspection.

Roxana appeared to consider. 'I would like to be friends.'

For Roxana this was an offer of far greater value than mere sex, because sex was handed over in a transaction or taken in violence. For Noah, it was a brush-off. They misunderstood each other.

He sighed, and then smiled. 'OK. So we will. And now I think it would be best if I take myself off to the sofa.'

They both stood up, bumped into each other as they tried to place their mugs in the sink, stepped quickly back again, turned awkwardly aside. Roxana saw him resignedly ease himself down on the sofa, bend his long legs to fit the shorter space and pull the cover up to his chin. She clicked the light off at the wall and retreated into the bedroom.

She lay down too, but sleep was a long way off. All she could think of was Noah's face, crumpled against the cushions, and the way the tip of his finger had nudged against hers. She was lying in his bed, safe under his roof, with the New Zealand boys who played rugby lined up downstairs like a row of innocent, beefy bodyguards. In the darkness she laughed. Then she kicked off the bedclothes and marched back to the door. She switched the light on again and Noah sat up, blinking at her.

'Come in?' she asked.

He hesitated, but it was an invitation that he was physically incapable of refusing.

Still, he went slowly, knowing that she was offering herself because she felt indebted to him, because he had manoeuvred her into an awkward position. Roxana lay down on her side, her knees drawn up and her hand curled out towards him.

The edge of the mattress gave under his weight. He lay down with his body as far away from hers as possible, then he gently took her hand. She sighed and clasped his in return. Noah looked up and saw that there was grey light creeping round the edges of the skylight blind.

'Close your eyes,' he murmured, stroking the back of her hand with his thumb. 'Everything is all right.'

To his surprise, he fell almost immediately into a deep sleep.

When he woke, the first thing he saw was Roxana's shoulder and the rounded swell of her upper arm. He lay without moving, listening to the sound of her breathing. He heard the water running as Andy took a shower, then a brief snatch of music before the radio was turned down. The smell of burnt toast made Roxana stir. She rolled onto her back and in the pale light he saw her eyes open.

She turned her head towards him, her face still filmed with sleep.

'Hello?' he said.

'Hello, Noah.' Her mouth curved in a smile and they lay looking into the worlds within each other's eyes. Slowly, Noah shifted himself towards her. She didn't move back or try to push him away. Her smile broadened slightly, and then his lips touched hers.

There were some thumps, and finally the door slammed as Andy departed for work.

'What time is it?' Roxana murmured when the kiss ended.

'No idea. Half eight?'

'You have to go to work.'

'I think . . . I think I might pull a sickie.'

Roxana's eyes were dancing. 'What is that?'

'A sickie is when you don't go to work for a whole day. You stay in bed, like this. Doing this . . .' His fingers trailed downwards, found a small round breast.

'I see,' she sighed. Her spine arched, like a stroked cat.

He slid across the remaining inch or so of sheet and suddenly connected with the whole silky length of her body.

Her arms snaked round him and held him tight. 'Now I have you.'

'So you do,' he agreed.

Bill fanned the coals until they glowed, and then stood back to watch the scarlet fade to ash-grey. It was a warm Sunday in July, and therefore, in theory, the perfect opportunity for a family barbecue.

In many ways his marriage to Jeanette had been a conventional one. He had built up a business, a City PR firm that had remained small but was now quite successful, while Jeanette had run their home. Once Noah was old enough for school, with Bill's encouragement Jeanette had built on her undergraduate science degree by taking a postgraduate diploma in plant taxonomy. She had discovered a passion for botany and plant classification. For years she had worked at a botanical garden, with a small team of long-standing colleagues who specialised in plant diversity and conservation techniques. It was stimulating work in an environment where her deafness was not a serious impediment, but it had also left her with enough time to be a regular wife and mother.

Lately, though, Bill had had to take over responsibilities around the house. He thought his cooking was improving, but still a barbecue had seemed the best option for today. Bill had always done the barbecuing.

Noah was coming to lunch, and he had asked if he could bring his new girl. He wanted them to meet her.

Connie was coming too. Jeanette had asked for this, and Connie had accepted the invitation. It was going to be a family party. Bill could count the precedents for this on the fingers of two hands.

Jeanette was sitting in her usual place in the shade of the tree. She was wearing a straw hat, her head bent to deepen the shade over her face, intent on shelling peas into a colander. Bill straightened up to look at her.

It was simple, he thought. They had been married for over twenty-five years. Loyalty and affection and habit took the place of love. Or perhaps at some point in their history, love had become these things. Whichever way it was, when he remembered that next summer she would not be here, he found himself in tears. He often cried these days.

Whereas where Connie was concerned, nothing was simple.

All their long history had been constructed out of negatives: guilt and then denial, pain, then more guilt and absence, and long silence.

And yet still, with the knowledge that soon he would see her, even with his dying wife quietly shelling peas a few feet away from him, Bill was fired up with anticipation as fierce as a boy's.

The coals in the barbecue pan were breaking into surreptitious flames. From his array of barbecuing equipment he selected a metal spray canister and spritzed the flames into submission. When he looked up again, Connie was walking across the grass. She was wearing jeans, flip-flops, a basket slung over her shoulder.

'There was no answer to the bell so I came round the side,' she called.

He met her halfway, kissed her cheek. She was warm, flushed with the sun, and her hair was damp at the nape of her neck.

'Glad you're here,' he said.

Jeanette sat up. Connie turned so she could read her lips.

'How are you? How's the week been?'

—*Good. Quite good today*, Jeanette answered. —*How about you?*

Connie knelt beside the chair and Jeanette leaned forward, pushing back the brim of her hat so their cheeks touched. From her basket Connie produced a row of little gifts: a magazine with an article on plant names, a jar of manuka honey, a ridged wooden cylinder that you were supposed to roll beneath your feet to massage away tension.

Bill watched as they passed the various items back and forth between them. There was no physical resemblance, of course, but their gestures mirrored each other.

'Let me get you a drink, Con. Glass of wine?'

'Please.'

—*Me too*, Jeanette signed.

'Coming up.' Bill carried the colander of shelled peas into the house, tipped them into a pan, and took a bottle of white wine out of the fridge.

He poured wine into three glasses. Jeanette lifted her head and smiled at him. All three raised their glasses in a wordless toast. There were wood pigeons throatily cooing in the tall trees.

Noah and a girl emerged round the side of the house, the same way that Connie had come.

'Hi, here we are. Mum, Dad, this is Roxana.'

Roxana was wearing a denim jacket over a short full skirt that revealed an almost unfeasible length of leg. She looked taken aback by the size of the house and the expanse of the garden.

She shook Jeanette's and then Bill's hand very quickly and stepped back beside Noah.

Noah turned to his aunt. This was not the time to let the faintest wrinkle of uncertainty crease the smooth surface of goodwill. Noah gave her a generous hug and Connie embraced her nephew warmly.

'Hello, Auntie Con,' Noah said.

'Noah. It's so good to see you.' She smiled. He had filled out and lost the accusatory glare of adolescence, and the resemblance to his father had deepened.

He introduced Roxana. Roxana's hand was cool. She gave Connie a quick glance under mascara-heavy lashes.

'You are Noah's aunt, he told me.'

Connie was thinking how striking she was.

'Yes. Jeanette and I are sisters.' It sounded simple enough.

Jeanette stood up. She was the shortest of the group anyway, and so reduced now as to seem hardly bigger than a child, but she commanded attention. She took Roxana firmly by the arm.

'I like your garden very much,' Roxana told her politely, then glanced to Noah for confirmation that she was doing the right thing.

'Mum can follow everything,' Noah told her. 'You'll be surprised. And she can talk. You'll get the hang of it. It's stopping her that's the problem, half the time.'

He grinned and Jeanette shook her head at him. She held on to Roxana's arm and pointed towards the length of the garden. With a sweep of a hand she encompassed her flowerbeds.

—*Come with us*, she beckoned Connie.

Connie took her other side and they began a tour of the borders.

Bill and Noah watched them.

'It's OK that Connie's here, then?' Noah said in a low voice.

'Yes. Your mum wants to see her. I'm glad of that.'

'It still feels a bit weird to me.'

'Everything about dying is weird, isn't it?'

'Yeah. How are you with it?'

'Death?' Bill used a pair of tongs to lift chicken portions out of a marinade, and laid the meat on the barbecue. 'I'm finding the inevitability hard to accept. Just at the moment.'

'I know what you mean. I keep thinking, surely we could do this, or that, and she'll get better. Even though we know she won't. I was asking more about Connie being here, though.'

'I see. Well. Jeanette and Connie predate you, you know. They predate me as well. It's right that they should come back together now, in spite of all the problems in their history. I'm full of admiration for your mother, for having the will to make it happen. And I admire Connie, too.'

Noah put an arm round his father's shoulders. 'You're such a good, good person, Dad, you know?'

Bill laughed briefly. 'You didn't always think that.'

'You know what kids are like.'

'Righteous.'

'A total pain. But I'm a grown man now. I'm not insisting on black or white. I can acknowledge grey. You know, Dad, I love you.'

'Yes,' Bill said, as composedly as he could. He turned a chicken portion, revealing a browned underside. 'I love you too.'

They could say these things to each other now, whereas once it would have seemed impossible. Bill told himself that here was something to hold on to, at the very least. He nodded his head towards the three women, who were just reaching the end of the garden.

'She looks like an interesting girl.'

Noah beamed. 'Roxana is an *amazing* girl,' he said. 'I have never met anyone like her.'

'That's good to hear. Now, how are we doing with this food? Noah, can you go into the house and put the potatoes on?'

Roxana gazed at the tall blue spires and the low misty-blue mounds. She had never been in a garden like this. She had no idea what the flowers were called; she had never even seen most of them. Noah's mother and aunt were making a kind of duet out of telling her about them. They seemed to talk fluently, with only one of them speaking.

'Those are delphiniums. Those, I don't know—Jeanette? Oh yes, it's nepeta.' Jeanette made a low sound and Connie added, 'Catmint, yes.'

'These, um, roses, what a nice colour. What kind are they?'

At least she knew roses. Roxana was trying hard. Her jaw muscles strained with politeness.

The two women conferred. Noah's aunt was quite tall, and interesting to look at. Her plain white shirt with rolled-up sleeves set off her beautiful skin and she was wearing a very thin gold bracelet round her right wrist. Roxana thought she looked very chic. It was difficult to make the same sort of appraisal of Noah's mother, and Roxana knew that that was because she was very ill.

'It's called Buff Beauty,' Connie said.

They began to walk again, slowly.

At the far end of the garden, partly screened by tall bushes and backed by trees, they came to a little green-painted structure with a low door and a pitched roof. Both of the women stopped walking.

Connie said, 'Do you know what I remember?'

Jeanette made a little roof shape by placing her fingers together and then moved her bunched fingertips to her lips and on upwards in an extravagant arc. She was laughing. Connie was laughing too.

'Yes, yes.'

They had forgotten Roxana. There was a ladder leaning against the trunk of one of the trees. Connie ran forwards and seized it, propped it against the side of the hut and clambered up. She perched unsteadily, feet on either side of the roof ridge, struck a pose and then began singing. In a high, loud voice. About a prince, and when he would come to carry her away.

Roxana gaped, thinking that the two of them had perhaps been drinking. She peered back towards the house and saw Noah carrying plates out to the round wooden table, and his father shaking out the folds of a big umbrella.

Jeanette was leaning back against the trunk of a tree, laughing. Connie slithered down the roof and vaulted back down to the grass. She ran to Jeanette and the two of them fell into each other's arms. The noise Jeanette made was loud, a *hoo-hoo* sound against Connie's normal laughter. Then there was a point when they both took a breath and looked into each other's faces.

They weren't laughing any more.

Connie touched her sister's cheek, and then Jeanette's head slowly came forward until it rested against her shoulder. They stood there, swaying a little, arms round each other.

Roxana walked on a few steps, not wanting to intrude on this, and stared over at Noah. He was wiping cutlery and laying it on the checked cloth that had been spread over the table. He looked up and saw her watching him, gave her a wave and then blew a kiss.

After a minute or two the women rejoined her.

Connie said, 'We were just remembering when we were little. We used to have a shed at home, quite like that one. I used to . . . sing.' They were both shaking with laughter again, and Roxana wondered if they were perhaps not drunk but a little bit crazy.

With an effort, Jeanette composed herself. She put her hands together and inclined her head, making such an eloquent apology that Roxana was disarmed. Noah's mother made some more of her quick gestures and his aunt translated them into words.

'What do you think of England?'

'I like it very much,' Roxana answered, choosing the obvious response. She added carefully, 'And Noah has been kind. Now I am looking for a flat to share. There is a room in, what is it, North Ealing? Noah says he will come with me to look at it. London is a big city, and it's very expensive, but I have a job. Perhaps Noah will have told you what work I do?'

Both women casually nodded, careful not to place too much emphasis on knowing about it.

'Are you going to stay in London? Don't you miss home?'

'Not so much. Uzbekistan is a poor country. People work hard, there is some discontent, little freedom to speak.'

Jeanette signed again, and Connie spoke for her. 'Noah told us about your brother. I'm sorry.'

'Thank you,' Roxana said.

She did not want to think about Niki now, although the memories of the Friday Massacre, the images of the main square in Andijan under a rain-heavy sky and the armoured trucks full of men with guns were seldom far from her mind.

Noah's family were kind, like him, Roxana decided. She wished she had a family like this one. But at least she was here, included in the lunch party, just as if she were an English girl. Suddenly she smiled, basking all over again in the white light of freedom and opportunity.

Connie saw the smile. She was thinking, This girl is quite formidable. Jeanette pointed. Bill was waving the barbecue tongs, beckoning them.

'Lunch,' Connie said.

They all sat down under the shade of the big parasol, and there followed an interval of drink-pouring and complicated passing of various dishes of food. Roxana watched covertly to see what Noah did and then copied him. He glanced across and winked at her.

When they all had some of everything, Bill filled Jeanette's glass with wine and Jeanette raised it in Roxana's direction.

'Cheers,' the other three all said.

Roxana put her hand over her heart. '*Za vashe zdorovye.*'

Jeanette ate hardly anything, but she sipped some of her wine and she followed the conversation.

'How's the music biz, Auntie Con?' Noah asked. 'Connie writes music for films and commercials, Roxana. Very big-time.'

Roxana liked Noah's mother and father, but it was Connie who drew her attention. She seemed different from the others, and not just in her appearance. Roxana was very interested to hear what she did.

'Really? What is the work like?'

Connie raised her hands now, laughing and twisting back her dark hair. 'It's a circus. Always has been. But I love it.'

Connie's first job had been at GreenLeaf Music.

On her sixteenth birthday, full of determination to make her escape from Echo Street by finding work in the music business, she had taken a bus and then the tube up to Soho and walked into all the recording studios in the area. The manager at GreenLeaf admitted that they needed a teenager to do odd jobs. They wanted a boy, really, but Connie insisted that she could make better tea and what's more she could start at once. The manager said he'd have to consult his partners, and told her to come back on Monday morning.

That evening there was a family celebration dinner with Uncle Geoff, Auntie Sadie and Elaine in an Italian restaurant.

Once they were seated round the centre table and had ordered their various tagliatelles and saltimboccas, Uncle Geoff said, 'This is a double celebration. We should drink to two fine young women.'

The previous day, Jeanette had learned that she had gained a 2:1 in Biological Sciences. She was the first person in the family to graduate from university. Her cousin Elaine, who worked in a bank, compressed her lips slightly, but she drank the toast with everyone else.

'So, Connie,' Uncle Geoff went on, 'you'll be following in your sister's footsteps, I expect. Which A levels are you going to choose?'

Connie gazed at the red tablecloth and a slice of tiled floor. 'I've got a job,' she said quietly.

'Holiday job? Very good. It's important to get some practice in the real world. It's a harsh climate out there.'

Connie raised her voice. 'It's a real job. In the music business. I'm not going back to school next year.'

Six faces stared at her.

Hilda said sharply, 'Don't talk rubbish. You're staying at school. While you're under my roof, you—'

'I start work on Monday morning. I'm leaving home.'

Hilda laid down her knife. Elaine smiled.

Connie's head swam with sudden elation. The Osteria Antica was lit up with the insanely flickering glow of burning bridges. If she didn't get a job at GreenLeaf Music, she would find a different place to work. She was sharply aware of Bill, across the table, and it was only later that she wondered if she had correctly read admiration in his eyes.

Uncle Geoff's eyes bulged. 'Don't you think, young lady, that after all she has done for you in sixteen years, from the moment she took you in, you owe your mother a debt of gratitude?'

The clamour in the restaurant seemed to die away.

'I will find a way to repay my debts,' Connie said.

Then she stood up and weaved between trolleys and waiters to the cloakroom. When she came out of the cubicle, breathing more calmly and with the elation already draining away like water into sand, leaving her feeling cold and shaken, she found Jeanette standing by the basins.

—Did you mean all that? Jeanette asked.

There was a smell of air freshener, and an echo of dripping taps. 'Yes.'

Their reflections glanced back out of the peach-tinted mirror. Connie caught a glimpse of how different they looked, angel and demon.

—Why do you really want to leave home?

She could hardly tell her sister what had actually precipitated the decision. 'It's time. I want to find out who I really am.'

Jeanette raised an eyebrow.

'Well, I don't know, do I?'

—*No*, Jeanette agreed. She turned to wash her hands, carefully soaping around her diamond ring.

Connie stared at her bent back, wanting to fight her as much as she had done when she was six, and at the same time thinking that love and hate were so close as to be nearly the same thing. Like sisters.

Jeanette stood upright again and shook water from her hands.

—*You've spoiled your own birthday.*

'Yes,' Connie agreed. There was something definitively Thorne family about the disintegration of the evening. They tottered against the clanking roller towel-holder as laughter swept over them.

Connie left Echo Street quietly the following morning, with a rucksack full of clothes, and went to stay at a friend's house. She had a little money saved from her Saturday job, and when she knew the job at GreenLeaf Music was hers, she bought a copy of the *Evening Standard* and went through the accommodation ads until she found a room she reckoned she could just about afford.

At GreenLeaf, she learned how to make herself useful and then indispensable. Eventually she began to get odds and ends of commissioned work that led to writing jingles for commercials, and soon she had a useful little showreel of her work.

Connie lived like this for four years, sharing a dingy flat in Perivale and keeping irregular hours, not seeing the sun often enough and always juggling with work and money. She worked on a retainer for GreenLeaf during the day, and freelanced in the evenings, using the company's studios for her own work.

Then one of the founding partners of GreenLeaf, the amiable but lazy Malcolm Avery, ran a deadline too close. The brief was to write a jingle for the launch of a new chocolate bar called Boom Bar.

Malcolm slumped in his studio chair at six o'clock in the evening, his headphones hanging round his neck like a noose.

'I've got nothing here for the agency and I'm scheduled to meet them at ten tomorrow,' he groaned.

'I'll have a go,' Connie said.

'Go on, then. I'm going home. We'll play them what we've got tomorrow, and promise them the earth in a couple of days' time. See you, Con.'

Connie sat down at the eight-track EMU 2 with a jug of coffee and the brief for the Boom Bar jingle. She worked all night, and in the morning the tune was there.

When Malcolm arrived she played the jingle to him. His face flashed with cunning and then went flat.

'Well, yeah. Not genius, but not bad. I'll chuck it in with the others, mix 'em up, see what the agency thinks. Give me the tape.'

Connie was red-eyed and wired from her sleepless night. Her hand shot out and caught Malcolm by the wrist. 'No. I'm coming to the meeting. I'll play the tape, and make sure everyone knows whose work it is.'

Malcolm laughed. 'Whose brief is it, whose studio is this, who do you work for?'

Somehow, Connie found it within herself to shrug and turn away with the tape in her pocket. 'Suit yourself. I did it in my own time, so it's mine. Go and present whatever you've got.'

She could almost hear Malcolm Avery making calculations. It was an important commission, for a big agency, for a major product launch.

'Oh, what the hell. Come with me if you feel so strongly about it.'

The agency team and the clients all went mad for Connie's tune.

For the first time in her life, Connie found that she was able to call the shots. She agreed to split the commission fee with GreenLeaf, and gleefully put a cheque for £1,000 in her bank. But she made sure when she signed the contract that royalties would come to her alone.

Almost at once, the Boom tune became a huge hit.

By the time she was twenty-three, Connie was living in her own large flat in Belsize Park, with a room in it converted to a studio. In time she formed her own company and employed a manager to run the business side, while she concentrated on writing music. She could spend days at a time shut away in the soundproof studio, working less with live musicians and more via the spiralling trajectories of new technology.

She never wrote another Boom song, although the title stubbornly clung to her, but she was a good composer. Her work won some awards, her showreel gathered depth and range. After the first flood of royalties, her income was steady rather than spectacular, but she had come a long, long way from Echo Street.

Seven years later, when numbers of her friends were marrying and having babies, Connie was certain that neither option was open to her because she was deeply, unwillingly in love with the man who was already married to her sister.

Then one day she went along to the recording of the orchestral music she had written for a television serialisation of *Dombey and Son*. The orchestra was under the baton of Sébastian Bourret.

They edged together, over the space of a year.

Connie liked being with Seb because he was actually as rootless as she felt. Seb was Australian by birth, half Belgian and half South African by parentage. Home for him was wherever he was rehearsing the current ensemble, and Connie fitted well into that structure.

Then came Sung Mae Lin, and the Balinese village house with the verandah and the view became Connie's home.

Noah and Roxana did most of the washing-up. Then they wandered through the house and Noah led her into his old bedroom. Roxana rested her elbows in the deep window embrasure and peered down into the garden. Jeanette and Connie were lying on a rug in the shade of the big tree, seemingly asleep. Bill sat in a deck chair beside them, reading a newspaper.

'Your mother and your auntie are not very like each other.'

Noah leaned behind her and kissed the back of her neck. 'They're not but they are, if you see what I mean. They're not real sisters; Auntie Connie was adopted. I haven't seen her for years. Not since my grandmother's funeral. Mum and Connie really didn't get on.'

'Why is that?' Roxana asked.

'Well. My dad and Connie. They had a sort of relationship. An affair. It must be about fifteen years ago. I was very young and I didn't know much, but my mum was wild. My dad went very quiet and dignified about it, even though you could tell he was massively confused and in pain. He hated hurting my mother. Connie was the loser in the end. She just sort of evaporated. Went to live abroad, and we never saw her. Dad kind of made a point of being exemplary after that, making up for it all. I mean, I don't think it was a penance because I know he loves mum. Once the blood-letting was over there was a silence around it all. Taboo subject, you know. It takes the prospect of someone dying to get anyone to expose it again.'

He looked over Roxana's shoulder at the tranquil scene in the garden. Then he buried his face in the nape of her neck. 'English middle-class silence. Profound deafness has got nothing on the silence of comfortable family dysfunction.' Then he added hotly, his lips against her skin, 'I want my family, the family I *will* have, to talk to each other all the time. No silences.'

Roxana tilted her head and wriggled round to face him. 'Of course. You can have the family you want. You can make it that way.'

He gazed at her. She didn't seem shocked about his father and Connie, although his father's betrayal and his mother's distress was the biggest trauma Noah had had to deal with in his life, up until the present one.

Roxana had lost her mother and father and her only brother and left her whole world behind.

He held her face between his hands and smoothed her broad Asian cheekbones with his thumbs. 'I love you,' he blurted out.

Roxana laughed. 'Is that the truth, or are you saying what men say?'

'It's the truth,' Noah said humbly. 'Do you love me?'

She turned serious. 'Yes. Maybe. That is a difficult question. I want to give a proper answer.'

'Then let's leave it at yes, for the time being,' Noah advised.

Connie opened her eyes as Bill's shadow fell over her. He was holding out a mug of tea. With an effort of will she pushed herself to a sitting position and took it from him.

'How long have I been asleep?'

'Maybe an hour.'

'Where are Noah and Roxana?'

'Upstairs. No, here they are.'

Jeanette stirred. She coughed and sighed, and Bill went to her and helped her to sit up.

'That was a good nap,' he said, holding her against him, and she nodded, still dazed with sleep.

Noah and Roxana chased across the grass and came to a panting standstill in front of them.

'Dad? Mum? We might have to head back quite soon. I'm going to take Rox to North Ealing to look at the room.'

Connie sat more upright. An idea had taken shape.

'Roxana? This might not suit you, but I've got a spare room. It's a big flat, and I'm not there all that often. You'd be welcome to stay.'

Roxana's self-possession finally deserted her. She looked from Noah to his parents, then back at Connie. Jeanette was fully awake now, following the conversation intently.

'With you? In your place?' Roxana stammered.

'Yes. It might not be what you want at all, but until you get your bearings and decide what you really need?'

'Connie?' Bill murmured.

Roxana nodded very quickly. 'Thank you. Yes, please. If you think it would not be a trouble. Thank you.'

Connie wondered, too late, if Jeanette might interpret the offer as an attempt to infiltrate her family, and Jeanette did seem to struggle with herself before she responded. But then she nodded.

—*That's kind of you, Connie. What a good idea.*

Directly to Roxana, Connie added, 'Maybe you and Noah could come back via my place this evening. You could take a look at the room.' She felt suddenly absurdly pleased with the thought of company, of Roxana's company, in her bare white apartment.

'Noah, can we do this?' asked Roxana.

In his easy-going way, Noah said, 'Sure we can. Thanks, Auntie Con.'

Until Roxana saw his parents' house and its garden full of flowers, she thought that Noah's flat in Hammersmith was the most comfortable place in the world. Now Connie unlocked the door to her apartment on the top floor of a tall, anonymously modern building.

'Come in,' Connie said.

Noah and Roxana shuffled in behind her. Their first impression was of a space that opened straight out into the sky, a smoky summer's-evening London sky now fading from amethyst into horizontal bars of grey and rose-pink cloud over tower blocks and trees and church spires. The wall facing the door was an almost complete run of plate glass.

Noah looked about him. The family rift meant that he had never been here before. 'Nice place, Auntie Con,' he murmured.

The room itself was almost empty. There were no ornaments, hardly any furniture. A pair of sofas faced each other across a low table. This emptiness struck Roxana as immensely restful, as well as opulent.

'I'll show you the spare room,' Connie said, clicking on a lamp and creating a pool of pale gold light.

Roxana followed her down a high, pale, empty corridor and they came to a flat door in the bare wall. Connie pushed it open.

The room was unfurnished except for a double bed framed by built-in cupboards and the air smelt faintly stuffy. Connie nudged open an inner door and Roxana saw a small bathroom lined with light-coloured stone. Glass and polished mirrors showed her reflection and Connie's, but otherwise it was completely bare. She frowned.

'Where are your . . . things?' she began, imagining that Connie's talcum powders and face creams must be hidden away somewhere.

'This would be yours. My bedroom's at the other end of the flat, and so is my bathroom.'

Awed, Roxana understood that this amazing apartment must have *two* bathrooms.

'It's very nice,' she whispered.

Noah hovered in the doorway. He didn't look as pleased as Roxana expected. They filed back the way they had come.

'What do you think?' Connie asked.

Roxana's excitement was draining away. How could she possibly, even momentarily, have expected to be able to live here?

'I don't think,' she sighed. 'You see, I don't think I will have money, *enough* money for rent.'

'I don't really need rent. If you wanted, you could just stay here while you decide where you'd like to be.' Connie spoke tentatively, almost as if Roxana were the one offering to do her the favour. 'I'd be glad of some company now and again.' She smiled. 'What do you think?'

Roxana smiled back. 'So I would like to. Thank you.'

Noah frowned. Connie went away and came back with a pair of keys on a metal ring. These she dropped casually into Roxana's pocket.

'We're fixed, then,' she said. 'Come when you're ready. What about a drink now, to celebrate?'

Noah said quickly, 'Thanks, Auntie Con, but we'll be on our way. Work in the morning and all that.' He kissed his aunt lightly on the cheek. 'It's been really good to see you again. And thank you for coming to see Mum. It'll make a difference to her.'

'I'm here. I want to be.'

It was a few days before Roxana stopped feeling like an intruder at Limbeck House, which was the name of the building crowned by Connie's apartment. She half expected, as she tapped in the security code and then rode up in the hushed lift, that some security official would seize her by the shoulder and march her outside again.

But, gradually, she became accustomed to the place. She hung up her few clothes in the cupboard, and stuck her beach postcard right next to the side of the bed. She liked to see the picture when she opened her eyes, although it no longer represented her only idea of Paradise. Where she now found herself came quite close to that.

She smiled as she looked out of her bedroom window at the strange bulging tower that Noah referred to as the Gherkin, and the domes of St Paul's Cathedral bathed bronze by the morning sun. The Cosmos, Mr Shane, her illegal status, what to do next, all of these were just details and she would find a way to deal with them. London was a wonderful place, so wonderful that she would have liked to share the discovery with someone who would understand how far she had already travelled. Most of all, she wished that person could be Niki.

Niki. Roxana's smile faded. It was still hard to come to terms with a world that didn't have her brother in it.

There was always Yakov. She owed him a letter because he had helped her to get here. She thought of him in his curtained room, always reading, with the books piled up to the ceiling and stacked in pyramids on the floor. Yakov had been her mother's friend, but he was well-disposed to Roxana. Maybe she would find an Internet café and send an email message to him.

By the time Roxana got up, Connie had usually gone out, and when she came back from the Cosmos her flatmate was always asleep. Roxana didn't mind at all being alone in the apartment. She unfurled, slowly, like a new leaf.

At first she stayed in her room, watching the clouds and the planes passing her window. She took a long, hot bath and stared at herself in the misted mirrors, not quite recognising the scrubbed, leisurely person who looked back at her.

She left the flat at midday, went to the grocer's store on the corner of the street and bought milk, tomatoes, bread and cheese. Back in Limbeck House, she put the food in the fridge, seeing how lost it looked in the cavernous interior, and wondered what Connie liked to eat.

Later, she ventured beyond the living area to Connie's end of the flat. She peered into the room where Connie spent most of her time when she was at home. From the doorway, she saw a bank of unfamiliar machinery with dozens of sliding keys, a musical keyboard, computer screens. A pair of headphones was hooked over the back of a swivel chair. There was a separate desk covered with papers, a big diary and a telephone. Roxana silently retreated.

The only other door led to Connie's bedroom.

It was tidy. The white bed cover was smooth and flat and there were no scattered clothes. Roxana knew that this was an intrusion but she couldn't help herself. She tiptoed across to take a look into the bathroom. There were tiers of white towels, glass shelves with neat rows of cosmetics, a faint drift of Connie's spicy perfume.

Roxana glided across and opened the nearest cupboard door. Inside, Connie's clothes were ranged on hangers, like so many ghosts of her. Roxana rippled the tips of her fingers over the fabrics. She lifted the sleeve of a dress made of some diaphanous greeny-grey stuff, and buried her face in the fabric as if she could breathe in the essence of the other woman. As if she could make herself into Connie.

Embarrassed by herself, even though there was no one to see her, she dropped the sleeve and closed the cupboard door, turned quickly and retreated to her own room.

The next day, she discovered the Best Little Internet Café on the Planet. It was in a dingy side street that was full of bagged refuse from fast-food restaurants, but the café itself looked inviting. The funny name was printed above the window, in square red letters. Inside were a handful of small wooden tables, with mismatched chairs. At the back, on a raised section of the floor, was a row of terminals. Some young men who looked like Asian students were perched in front of them.

Roxana went inside and ordered a coffee. One of the Asian boys got up from his terminal and paid some money to the owner.

'See you,' the man called after him.

Roxana asked if she could use the terminal that was now free.

'Sure,' the owner answered. 'Half an hour, or one hour?'

She sat down in the still-warm seat. There was a laminated card with printed instructions taped to the tabletop. Roxana read it carefully.

Fumbling with the English keyboard, she chose an Uzbek-language portal offering news and cultural commentary. Obligingly it came straight up, headed by a tourist-brochure picture of four sky-blue tiled majolica domes surmounting four brick minarets. It was the Chor Minor, gatehouse to a ruined madrassa, one of the most famous of the many famous buildings in Roxana's home town of Bokhara.

Roxana blinked at the familiar domes. She needed to feel her distance from the alleys and concrete blocks and the hot white light of Bokhara. Outside the café, taxis reassuringly rumbled in the city street.

A boy was leaning back in the next seat and covertly eyeing her.

'Excuse me?' Roxana said to him, quickly closing the window. 'How do you send email from here?'

Bill mentioned to Connie that Jeanette would like to see her. So she drove down to Surrey one morning, against the flow of traffic, arriving well after Bill had left for work. Apart from Jeanette's cleaner, who hoovered in the distant reaches of the house and laid a tray for coffee, they were on their own.

It would probably be the longest time they had been alone in each other's company, Connie reckoned, since she left Echo Street.

The weather had turned. It was cooler, and there were sharp bursts of rain. Jeanette sat in the room that opened onto the garden, small in her large armchair. She had her mobile that she could use to text for help if it was needed, a small tray with a glass of water and several vials of pills, her book and the newspapers on the low table next to her chair.

—*I am well set up, you see*, Jeanette said.

Connie sat down. 'Do you want to talk?' she asked.

They exchanged a glance of mutual amusement.

Jeanette calmly reached out for her coffee cup, took a sip, replaced it on its saucer and adjusted the teaspoon that lay next to it.

—We could talk about the old days. There are times that only you and I remember now. Only the two us, in all the world.

'I know. I've been conscious of that too. Remember the trains, at Echo Street? I could hear them rumbling through the cutting, when I was waiting to go to sleep and when I woke up in the morning.'

The tip of Jeanette's fingers touched the rim of her ear, then her hand stretched out. The fingertips fluttered, describing the faintest vibration, and the diamond in her engagement ring briefly caught the light.

—I could feel them.

The same experience, Connie thought. Differently perceived.

Talk, she exhorted herself. Before it's too late. Talk about anything, while it's still possible. You've got the words and Jeanette hasn't.

'Remember those Sunday lunches, at Auntie Sadie and Uncle Geoff's?'

They both laughed, recalling the queasy car journey up to the better part of Loughton, to Geoff and Sadie's house. '*Detached*,' Sadie pointed out. Hilda was tense with anxiety and Tony would drum his fingers on the wheel as they waited at traffic lights. When they got there, Jackie and Elaine would scoop Jeanette up and take her off to one of their bedrooms to listen to a record or admire a new pair of shoes. Connie would be left mutely scowling and eavesdropping on the adults' talk.

'Roast beef. Three different veg, in serving dishes,' Connie said.

—Orangeade. Blue glasses.

'Sherry beforehand for Mum and Sadie, beer for the men.'

Sadie and Geoff had divorced after Sadie found out that Geoff was having an affair with his receptionist at the garage.

'How are Elaine and Jackie?'

—The same. Jackie's oldest is a barrister now.

'Really?'

Connie was thinking that families were more alike than they were different. Children grew up. Grandchildren were born, then became lawyers or IT consultants. The woman who had borne her most probably had grandchildren. She'd have framed photographs, similar to the ones of Noah at various ages dotted round this room. Connie hoped that she did, anyway. She wondered if, when the woman looked at her photographs, whether she imagined another child's face among them.

Suddenly she asked, 'What was it like for you, before I came?'

Jeanette signed quickly, laughing. *—Heaven.*

'Was it?'

She shook her head. *—Mum said I'd have a little sister called Constance. Then you were there. In a cot. Black hair, red face.* Jeanette screwed up her eyes, opened her mouth and balled her fists in a swift impression of a howling newborn. —*I wanted you to disappear. But you stayed and stayed.*

'That must have been annoying.'

There were threads of rain stitched across the glass. Connie thought of the fresh air outside, away from the faint smell of illness and the pressure of recollection, but she sat still. It was extraordinary, but Jeanette and she had never discussed their childhood like this.

'Can I ask you something? Before Elaine told me, did you understand about adoption?'

—*Yes.*

'What did you think?'

—*I was angry.*

'Angry?'

Jeanette lifted her head and looked Connie full in the face. —*They didn't want another like me. So they picked you. We were different.*

'We were alike in some things. I was angry as well.'

—*I know that. You were terrible. What were you so cross about?*

'About not being you, of course.'

Jeanette stared, then she started laughing. She laughed so much that she had to wipe the tears from her eyes. —*I see. Yes. That's funny.*

Connie nodded. 'It is. I don't think I ever saw anyone's point of view but my own.' She added, 'Poor Hilda.'

—*Mum would have been touched to hear you say that.*

'Would she?'

—*She was afraid of you.*

'Afraid?

—*You were the unknown. And then you were gone, and a huge success.*

Jeanette's head fell back against the chair cushions. Talking and laughing had tired her. Connie realised how weak she was becoming.

'Are you all right?'

—*Yes.*

The door opened and the large shape of the cleaner appeared.

'Mrs Bunting, love, I'm off now. Your lunch is all ready,' she shouted. 'There's a nice piece of quiche, some tomato salad. You've got your sister here, she'll see you're looked after.'

'I will,' Connie promised.

Connie left when Jeanette's nurse arrived, and said she would come back the next day. When she reached home, Roxana had already gone out, but Connie guessed that she had only just missed her. The flat retained the warmth of another presence.

Roxana had taken to leaving food in the fridge, and yesterday there had been a punnet of strawberries placed on a saucer in the centre of the polished counter, with a note saying *For you*. Today in the same place was a small marguerite bush in a brown plastic pot. A folded piece of kitchen paper had been placed underneath, to protect the counter. Connie smiled, and went in search of a better pot for the plant.

The next morning, Connie knew as soon as she opened her eyes that she wasn't alone in the flat. There wasn't a sound, but she could feel the comforting emanations of another person. She put on her dressing gown and shuffled into the main room. Roxana was standing by the window looking out, but she spun round as soon as Connie appeared.

'Hi. You're up early,' Connie said.

'I did not sleep so well.'

'Would you like some coffee?'

'Yes, please.'

'How was your week?'

'Fine. I have made altogether four hundred and seventy pounds.'

Connie laughed. 'I think that's pretty good.'

She opened a new vacuum pack of espresso coffee. Roxana came and stood by her elbow, watching closely as Connie pressed the ground coffee into the little holder and locked it into place. When she gave her the cup, Roxana took it and sat next to her on a high stool at the counter.

'Thank you for the plant.' Connie stroked the feathery leaves with the tips of her fingers. 'And the strawberries.'

Roxana flushed. 'I am glad you like them.'

Connie splashed some milk into the strong coffee and Roxana did the same. 'What are you doing today?' Connie asked.

'I am going to meet Noah. He says we will see an art gallery.'

'Very Saturday metropolitan.'

'Yes.' Roxana was suddenly beaming. 'Yesterday I did some shopping. The first clothing I have bought in London. Except for stupid things, for working. I'd like to show you. Shall I bring it?'

'I'll come,' Connie said. She followed Roxana along to her bedroom.

There was a Topshop bag on the floor. Roxana reached in and brought out a short blue canvas jacket with oversized buttons. It was very like one that Connie owned. Roxana slipped it on. It suited her.

'Do you think this is nice?'

'I do.'

Carefully Roxana took it off again, smoothing the seams. She took a hanger out of the cupboard. A brown envelope lay on the shelf.

She sighed. 'It cost thirty-five pounds. Is this too much money?'

'No, Roxana, I don't think it's too much. And if it was, so what? It's the money you earned. You can spend it exactly how you like.'

Roxana picked up the envelope and opened it to show Connie a wad of notes. 'After I bought the jacket, I thought that before shopping I should really give you money for rent.'

'Thank you. But I said you didn't have to. If you're here for a while, we can talk about you making a contribution towards the electricity bill, something like that.'

Roxana reflected on this. Whichever way she considered it, however pessimistically, it did not sound as though Connie was telling her to go.

'I think you should put that money in the bank, though.'

'I don't have a bank.'

Connie considered this. Roxana was almost certainly in the country illegally; she had no resources except her dancing and no one to stand up for her except Noah and Connie herself. However tough she might appear to be, she was vulnerable too.

'I can help you with that, if you like.'

Chapter Six

HILDA HAD WANTED A big wedding for Jeanette—*a proper wedding,* was the way she described it.

Jeanette gave the impression that she and Bill would have been happy to slip off to the register office in their ordinary clothes and be back at work the same afternoon. But Connie suspected that Jeanette was actually almost as in love with the full bridal notion as Hilda was.

Connie steered clear of most of the early discussions about arrangements. She knew that Jeanette and Bill had settled on a date, and that a church and a location for the reception had also been chosen. Beyond that she partly chose to be vague because she didn't want to think too much about Bill being her sister's husband anywhere in the near future, and partly it was inevitable anyway because she worked at GreenLeaf Music from the moment the studios opened in the morning until the last person left at night, and the only real contact with Hilda and Jeanette was during Sunday lunches at Echo Street.

She was taken aback, therefore, to realise that over one lunch the bridesmaid's dress was being discussed with the understanding that she was the one who would be wearing it.

'Apricot's a nice warm colour. Yes. But with Connie's complexion, maybe there's too much orange in it? What about a lovely pale blue?'

Connie put down her knife and fork. Bill was sitting directly opposite her at the kitchen table. He flicked a glance at her, then ducked his head again. But not before Connie had seen the curl of his smile.

'I don't want to be a bridesmaid, Jeanette. Thank you, and all that.'

—*Why not?*

'I just don't. Get Jackie or Elaine.'

Hilda clicked her tongue. 'Jackie's due six weeks after the wedding; she can't possibly do it. And Elaine, what will people think if she's Jeanette's bridesmaid and you aren't?'

'They'll probably think how pretty Elaine is, and how lovely she looks in pale blue satin. I'm just not doing it, all right?'

Bill watched her. He wasn't smiling now.

Hilda was all set to pursue the subject to the point of combustion, but Jeanette held up her hand.

—*We'll talk about it.*

These days, Jeanette was very calm and practical.

After the apple pie and ice cream, Connie went out into the garden. She kicked damp leaves off the path and walked the short distance to the shed. A train rattled through the cutting, and as another handful of yellow leaves drifted towards the earth she became aware that Bill had followed her outside. He took out a pack of cigarettes and lit one.

'Can I have one of those?'

He offered her the pack without comment, and struck a match for her. Connie inhaled and watched him through a slice of her hair.

'What will *you* have to wear for this wedding?'

'Lounge suit. Flower of some sort in buttonhole. Sheepish smile.'

'Why?'

'Why? Because I love Jeanette. Because if that's all it takes for us to get married, it's nothing. Even if I have to wear a Tarzan suit I'll do it.'

Shit, shit, Connie thought. I didn't want to hear that. The pain it caused her was like a meat skewer stabbing straight into her heart.

She managed to say, 'I suppose you think that if I love Jeanette too, I should dress up in whatever she wants me to wear on her wedding day?'

'I think you should do what you decide is right, Connie.'

They were standing quite close together. She could see the fine hairs on his wrists and a pulse in his throat just above the line of his collar.

She wanted to confide in him about how she didn't love Jeanette, not the way you were supposed to do when you were sisters, because sometimes she hated her and the rest of the time she felt mostly indifferent. She didn't think he would even be that surprised. Bill had always given her the impression that he understood what went on at Echo Street. But the very idea of mentioning love, and Jeanette and herself, and including Bill in the equation, was much too dangerous.

She said with her teeth clenched, 'I'll do what's right, then. I'll be a bridesmaid if I have to.' But I'll be doing it for you, she silently added.

Before she left Echo Street that afternoon she told Jeanette and Hilda that she'd do it.

'Well, now you're talking sense, thank goodness,' Hilda said. 'Why would any girl not want to be her sister's bridesmaid?'

Jeanette squeezed her arm with unusual warmth. —*Thank you.*

From a swatch of fabrics posted to her by Jeanette she chose a pale gold not-too-shiny satin. She examined the rough sketch that accompanied the material. The dress looked as if it would at least be quite plain, close-fitting, nothing too extreme.

The next thing she heard, she was summoned to a measuring and preliminary fitting. The dressmaker lived somewhere not very accessible, in Bow, and Hilda told Connie that to save time Bill would give her a lift from work. He was going to be in the West End that afternoon, and he could drive her.

Connie walked down the stairs at GreenLeaf. There was a session in progress, and a clash of cymbals and then a ponderous drum roll made the walls vibrate. She saw Bill from above, sitting on the battered sofa.

'Hi,' Connie said.

He stood up at once. 'Hi. Are you ready to leave?'

'Yes, let's go before anyone finds something else for me to do.'

Outside it was smoky and damp. 'That's an interesting place to work,' Bill remarked. 'Are you happy there?'

'Yes. It's really pretty cool, sometimes. Elvis Costello came in the other day with a keyboard player who was doing some work. He sat in reception in exactly the same place as you. Where's your car?'

'On a meter in Wardour Street. Actually, there's been a change of plan. Hilda rang, with a message from Jeanette. There's some drama with her dress; the woman's cut it too big and there's more complicated work to do. Apparently they're going to concentrate on that this evening and start on yours next week. So you and I are surplus to requirements tonight.'

Connie stopped walking and Bill bumped into her. They apologised simultaneously and Connie hesitated.

'Does that mean you've got to go?'

'Not really. I thought we might have a drink,' Bill said. 'You'll pass for eighteen,' he added.

Connie was full of excitement at the legitimate prospect of having Bill all to herself.

'It's only a few *months* off. I'm in pubs all the time.'

'Are you really? Come on, then. There's a place off Regent Street that's quite respectable.'

'What? What do you mean? I don't need *respectable*.'

'Maybe not. But I do.'

They went to a wine bar that was densely furnished with twining plants in wicker baskets. Connie found herself sitting opposite Bill in a ferny alcove, drinking wine and talking, talking as if a cork had been drawn out of her as well as from the bottle. She told him about the flat in Perivale and some of the friends she had made since leaving Echo Street.

'You're very independent, Con.'

'I am, aren't I?'

She gulped some more of her wine, feeling that what she was saying was interesting, and that Bill was very easy to talk to.

'Anyway, who else can you depend on but yourself?'

'Family?' he answered. 'Friends?'

Bill talked a lot, too. She found out things about him that she had never known before. He had elderly parents and he had grown up as an only child in a suburb in the Midlands. His mother had suffered for years from agoraphobia, and rarely left the house.

Connie's eyes widened. 'That's *tragic*. Doesn't she *go anywhere?*'

Bill grinned at her dismay. 'No. And that means my dad doesn't either. But they're not unhappy, Con. There are many worse situations.'

He told her about the PR business he was setting up with two partners. 'You can really make a difference. For instance, we're doing some work for a charity that raises money to buy special wheelchairs for badly disabled children. We've just had a promise from the sports minister that he'll look into putting some government backing into a nationwide series of wheelchair athletics.' He was leaning forward in his seat, full of enthusiasm. 'I love it.'

Connie was dazzled.

'It's not that I'm fixated on making money,' Bill said earnestly. 'But I want to be able to take care of Jeanette, and our children if we have them. That's not very modern sounding, but it's the truth. I know Jeanette could look after herself—of course she can; she's the most determined and capable person I've ever met—but I want to make it so that she doesn't *have* to. I do feel an extra responsibility because she's deaf. Not that we've ever talked about it. She wouldn't want to admit that her deafness makes any difference, and I suppose I've joined her in a kind of conspiracy that it doesn't matter, doesn't really even exist. I've never spoken about this to anyone. Do you mind, Connie?'

'No.'

Yes. But she didn't want him to stop confiding in her.

'It's so good to talk to you. I can tell you that before I asked Jeanette to marry me, I thought very hard. But the deafness and her determination are so much part of the person she is, I can't untangle them. I can't say to myself I love this part of her and if she wasn't that it would be easier for me. She's a whole person and that's the person I'm going to marry, and once I'd worked that out, it was simple. I do love her very much.'

'I know,' she said. Although she did wonder, *So why do you need to say it?* She stared very hard at some drops of wine that had spilt on the varnished wood.

'Well. I shouldn't drive before having something to eat.' He hesitated. 'I wonder—shall we go somewhere and have dinner?'

'Yes, let's do that,' Connie said hastily.

They went to a place a few doors farther down the street. There were red tablecloths and oversized pepper grinders, and they ordered food without Connie paying an instant's attention to what it was going to be.

As they ate they went on talking. It was like a dream to be facing Bill across the red tablecloth, sharing an order of fried potatoes, and at the same time it felt as natural and easy as it had in the wine bar.

This was an evening when nothing could go wrong, whatever she said or did. She was slightly drunk, but it was happiness and not wine that made her feel giddy. Was this what being a couple was like?

She wondered if Jeanette felt like this every day. Probably she did.

She was telling Bill about finding out that she was adopted.

'What did you feel?' he asked.

She thought hard, because she wanted to give him a true answer.

'It was the day of my dad's funeral. That was why Elaine and Jackie were there. It was very bad, because it seemed to cut me off more from him. As if I didn't have the same right as Jeanette and Mum to be sad, to miss him so badly, because I wasn't his and he wasn't really mine. I felt as if I'd been cut out of another picture, a completely different one, and I couldn't blend back into the Echo Street family photograph any longer. It made me realise I probably never had done. In a way, after a while, that was a relief because it explained a lot of things that I'd never understood. Then I started wondering who I really was—Hilda didn't tell me very much—and I made up for the loss of Constance Thorne *and* my dad by making up all kinds of childish fantasies for myself. You know. Princesses and tragedies and stuff like that.'

She took a big swallow of wine. Bill was watching her face, and the sympathetic way he bent towards her made it suddenly seem vital that he shouldn't feel any sorrier for her.

'I don't do that any more. It's probably quite an ordinary story.'

She almost said that the rest of the episode was the strange part. That she was taken into Echo Street, where Jeanette's deafness at the centre of the house sent ripples of silence spreading outwards. Like one absence balancing another, nothing that mattered in the Thorne family was ever openly spoken about, not anger or death or disability or the vast mystery of her adoption. Outbursts of any kind were forbidden. Furniture was dusted, exams were passed, and funerals and weddings were done properly instead. Hilda saw to that, and Connie recognised with a flash of adult understanding that she maintained her rigid ways because she was afraid of the mess of exposure. The only time she had almost collapsed was when Tony died, and with Jeanette's help she had fought her way back from that.

Bill said, 'Have you ever thought about finding your natural mother? It might be easier to know the story than to speculate about it. I read somewhere that adopted children can trace their original families now.'

'I could. Maybe I will.'

He touched her wrist. 'If you don't want to do it on your own, and you might not want to involve Hilda or Jeanette, I'll help you.'

She took these words inside her, wrapping them up with the knowledge that she could come back to them whenever she needed to.

'Thanks,' she said.

Her glass was empty, and so was her plate. Time had telescoped and the dinner was paid for and they were standing up with the table wobbling between them. They walked outside into the fine rain and hesitated, pulling up their coat collars under the shelter of the restaurant awning. Droplets glimmered on the scallops of canvas.

'I'll walk you to the tube,' Bill murmured.

They fell into step, and without thinking about it Connie slipped her hand into his. Their fingers interlaced. She felt as if she had grown a million new nerve endings. Heat ran up her arm and radiated through her body. They were moving as if they were one person. She could feel his breathing in her chest, his words in her head before he uttered them.

'Connie . . .'

They stopped walking. The small side street was deserted. Raindrops slanted into the puddles, splintering the reflected lights. She turned her face up to his and they kissed. The electric shock of it passed through them both and Connie heard his sharp intake of breath. They pressed their bodies closer, fitting shoulder and hip together, arms winding as they kissed more deeply.

'*Connie.*'

With the greatest difficulty Bill stepped back and broke the circuit. He lifted his hands to cup her face, and Connie remembered the contrast between cold rain on her skin and the warmth in his fingers.

'Don't,' he whispered. 'We can't do this.'

She crowded herself against him imploringly, but all he did was drop his hands to her shoulders and gently hold her at arm's length.

'This is not what you want,' he insisted.

'It is. It is.'

It was what he wanted too, she knew that, whatever he might say to try to convince them both otherwise.

'No. With somebody, yes. But not me. You're seventeen, Con. Everything has still got to happen to you. And it will, I know that.' He tried to inject conviction into the words.

Enough has happened already, Connie thought sadly. There were raindrops on her eyelids and lashes. She blinked quickly, and his face blurred. Bill's thumbs smoothed the corners of her mouth, and when he came into focus once more he was smiling at her. Somehow he had made sure of himself again. He was Jeanette's fiancé.

'Come on, or we'll get soaked. Let's go for the tube,' he said. He kissed her forehead, then took her arm and linked it beneath his.

They turned a corner and a crowded bus churned past them. At the end of the street was the mouth of Oxford Circus tube station.

The lights in the ticket hall were very bright. Connie winced and ducked her head, not wanting Bill to see that she was close to tears.

'Have you got a ticket?' he was asking.

'I'm not *twelve*.'

'I know that, Con. I really do.'

She took a breath and lifted her head. 'I'm going home now. Thanks for dinner.' Their eyes met then, and reflected shock and uncertainty and a glimmer of pure madness. Bill blinked.

'What happened back there was my fault,' he muttered. 'I'm sorry.'

Connie marshalled herself. 'It was just a kiss,' she said precisely. 'Nothing to worry about.' Then she flicked him a smile. 'See you,' she said, and turned to the ticket barrier.

She was in love with Bill Bunting.

She had no option but to be nonchalant now. She would have to be nonchalant and sisterly around him for the rest of eternity; her pride depended on it.

Bill stood and watched her go. Her dark head and thin, square shoulders floated down the Central Line escalator and sank out of his sight. It was as if a part of himself had just been torn away.

He wanted to call her back. He wanted to leap over the barrier and chase after her, but he denied the impulse.

Where could it lead, but into pain?

The wedding was predictable, or slightly worse than Connie might have predicted. Her dress was too tight, and the gold satin turned out to be much shinier than it had appeared in the sample. Jeanette was ravishing—happiness transformed her china prettiness into serious beauty. Uncle Geoff walked her up the aisle, and at the altar she turned to Bill and her smile lit up the church. Bill looked proud and pleased. In his speech at the reception he praised Jeanette's lovely bridesmaid and thanked Hilda for her generosity in the same sentence.

After the reception, exactly on schedule, Jeanette changed into her jade-green going-away coat and came out on Bill's arm. The wedding car was waiting for them; some of the technicians from the lab where Jeanette worked had scrawled lipstick messages over the windows, and Bill's friends had tied the usual assortment of junk to the rear bumper.

The door of the car was held open for her. With Bill's arm circling her shoulders, Jeanette searched the crowd of guests for Connie. Catching sight of her, she held up her bouquet and threw it.

Connie's arms stayed stuck at her sides. She couldn't make herself dive for the tumble of petals that would promise her a husband, not Bill. Instead there was a pecking of high heels on the gravel and Elaine's hand shot out. She swung the bouquet upwards, then pressed her flushed face into the flowers.

A laughing Jeanette blew a kiss to Connie, who returned a small wave. She saw Bill as a dark shape but she would not look directly at him. She kept her smile fixed as the doors slammed in a final blizzard of confetti and the car trailed its tin cans over the gravel and away.

There was a party to go to almost every night of the week—the music business took Christmas seriously—but for the first time Connie felt seriously out of key with her new world. However much she drank and danced, she couldn't capture the Christmas spirit. From being pleased with her independence she found herself longing to be loved.

Connie wondered where her real mother was this Christmas, and whether she ever thought about her baby.

One Saturday morning, Connie went to the local library. She looked up Adoption Services and wrote down the information she found there.

During her lunch hour on the following Monday she walked through the crowds of Christmas shoppers and found her way to the General Records Office at St Catherine's House. It was strange to be standing in a queue of coughing people in overcoats, waiting to find out the name of the woman who had given birth to her. Connie wondered if there would be an address. Maybe even a telephone number. How did you begin such a conversation?

When her turn came, she found herself across a wooden counter from a clerk with a birthmark spreading across her neck. Connie concentrated on not staring at the mark while she explained what she wanted.

The clerk said, 'I am afraid we cannot give you access to your file.'

'Why is that?'

'Adopted people born prior to 1975 may only access their records through a counsellor nominated by the Registrar General.'

Connie frowned, trying to make sense of this. The clerk said that she could make an appointment to talk to the approved social worker, if she wished, but there was a waiting list.

'I see,' Connie said. There were several people in the queue behind her. 'Thank you. I'll think.' She turned away from the counter, and fled.

In June, Connie turned eighteen. By the end of the year, Connie was learning the new musical digital technology as rapidly as GreenLeaf took it up. She began mixing and sampling tracks, working up her own compositions after hours on the eight-track in the studio.

Jeanette announced that she was pregnant.

Connie had hardly seen her sister and brother-in-law since their return from honeymoon. They had bought a flat in Stoke Newington and were busy renovating it, and Hilda tended to go over there on Sundays. Jeanette underwent a series of tests, and when the results came back they indicated that the baby was a boy and was highly unlikely to have inherited his mother's deafness. Once this news was confirmed, Jeanette sailed through her pregnancy. Bill sawed skirting boards, sanded floors and put up shelves. Hilda made curtains and covers and knitted piles of blue baby clothes.

Connie worked harder. She claimed to have too little time to go to Stoke Newington or Echo Street, and this was true. But it was also much easier not to have to see Bill in his decorating clothes, unshaven and happy. She also had a boyfriend now, a thin boy called Sam from Newcastle, who was a student at the Royal College of Music.

'Can't you ever bring him home to meet us?' Hilda asked, on one of the rare Sundays when Connie did see the three of them together.

'Yeah, one of these days,' Connie said, knowing that she would not. She liked Sam and he suited her and she was doing everything she could to convince herself that he was what she wanted. And all the time, compared with Bill he was utterly insubstantial.

Bill didn't say anything, and he didn't even look at her. He rubbed one corner of his jaw with his thumb.

Noah was born. Connie went to see him and Jeanette as soon as they came home from the hospital. She had never had much to do with babies and his helplessness and the crimson miniature limbs with their fine down of hair made her cry so suddenly and unexpectedly that she couldn't hide it from Bill and Jeanette.

Jeanette misunderstood.

—*He's fine. We both are. Do you want to hold him?*

'No. I've got to go soon.'

Bill followed her out of the room. 'Seeing him made you think of you, didn't it? When you were that small?'

'Yes. But so what?'

He sighed. 'Connie, you don't have to try to be so hard-boiled all the time. Look, can't I help?'

'Maybe. Not right now,' she said abruptly. It was too difficult to be this close to him and she wished she hadn't come.

She went back to St Catherine's House, and this time she saw a different clerk. She told the woman yes, she did understand that the only way to proceed was by agreeing to talk to a specialist social worker. She made the appointment, and waited for the date to come round.

It was spring again, but the interview room only had a small high window in a gloss-painted wall and no sunlight reached into it. Connie sat and waited while the counsellor fetched her file.

'Here we are,' the woman said. She had introduced herself as Mrs Palmer. Connie stared at the thin buff-coloured folder that Mrs Palmer laid on the desk in front of her. It was odd to think that such an anonymous-looking piece of officialdom contained her personal history.

'I am afraid I'm not allowed to give you direct access to the contents of the file. I can read out the documents to you,' Mrs Palmer explained.

Connie felt a pulse hammering in her head but she forced herself to be calm. 'All right.'

Mrs Palmer took out one slip of paper. 'You were found on the night of June the 17th, 1963. You were taken to the Royal London Hospital, where you were described as being between one and two days old.'

'Found? What does *found* mean?'

'I'm sorry. There's not much information here. Do you know what a foundling is, Constance?'

The word had a Victorian, melodramatic ring to it that was out of place in this utilitarian setting. But she did know what it meant. Stiffly she nodded her head.

Mrs Palmer extracted another flimsy sheet of paper. 'At the Royal London, the medical staff reported that you were healthy on arrival but hungry and dehydrated. You remained at the hospital for two weeks, and were then transferred to St Margaret's Children's Home. From there an adoption order was made, let's see, two months later. Mr and Mrs Anthony Thorne. The order states that you were a foundling.'

Connie had imagined a variety of histories for herself, but this one had never occurred to her.

'Found,' she repeated. 'Is that all?'

'That's usually all there is, in these circumstances.'

'Where was I found?'

Mrs Palmer consulted the first sheet of paper. 'In the garden of number 14 Constance Crescent, London E8. At the hospital you were given the name Constance. That's quite usual. The hospital staff choose what seems appropriate.'

The name of a *street*.

'What do I do next? How can I find out more information?'

Mrs Palmer looked back at her. Connie could see sympathy in her eyes but she didn't want that. She kept her gaze level.

'I'm afraid I don't know. It's difficult, with cases like this. You have to understand that it is a criminal offence to abandon a baby. So the woman might have to face charges. Very rarely do they come forward.'

What circumstances could have driven a woman to make such a decision? An image of tiny Noah Bunting came to her.

'Constance? Are you all right?'

'Yes, thank you. It's a surprise.'

Mrs Palmer gathered the fragments of Connie's history and slid them back into their buff folder. She folded her arms protectively across it.

'If there's anything else I can do?'

Connie felt for the seat of her chair, gripped it and stood up. She held on to the back of it for a second until she was sure that her legs would hold her. Then she said goodbye to Mrs Palmer, turned and walked back down the corridor, then out into the thin April sunshine. Everything looked precisely the same as it had done an hour ago.

Constance Crescent.

The image of herself, a day old, kept separating and then fusing again with that of Noah Bunting, and her mother was a slip of a figure on the margin of her imagination, refusing to come forward. Connie longed to reach out to that woman and hold her, and be held in return, but her hand opened and closed again on nothing.

Holding the A–Z open on her lap, Connie told Bill to take the next left turn. 'Then it's the third on the right,' she said.

They were in an area of medium-sized semi-detached villas and smaller terraced houses, no different from many others in London.

Constance Crescent was a quiet curving street set back from the busier road. There were window boxes on some of the lower sills, brass door knockers and letterboxes, and several had French blue enamel number plates. Number 14 was one of them.

Bill stopped the car. Connie got out and looked around her. There was a privet hedge, recently clipped, separating the garden from the street. A path tiled in red and black diamonds and triangles led to the dark blue front door. The wrought-metal gate stood open.

Bill had got out of the car too, and she was conscious of him standing just behind her.

'It's just a street,' she said.

He didn't ask her what else she had been expecting, although she knew it would have been a fair question. There was nothing here in this patch of urban garden, spruced up with evergreen shrubs, to give her a scrap of information about herself or who had left her here. It had been, she now understood, absurd to believe that it might.

Almost nineteen years ago her mother had walked along this quiet street, carrying a baby in her arms. She had walked away again without her. The connection was too fragile to take any strain, Connie thought.

'Let's go,' she muttered.

Bill put his hand out, didn't quite touch her arm. To both of them, the inch of space between his fingertips and her wrist was charged with unnatural significance. 'Wait. We should talk to whoever lives here.'

He walked up to the blue front door. No one answered.

'They must be out at work. We can come back one evening,' he told her. 'They may have been living here when you were found, or at least know a neighbour who was. Somebody somewhere knows what happened, and all we have to do is ask questions until we find them.'

Connie nodded, without much expectation. She retraced her steps back to Bill's car. She felt stiff and rather cold.

'Let's go and get a coffee,' Bill said. He drove along the curve of the street and Connie watched the houses slide by.

It was just dawning on her that she was not going to find her mother.

There was a coffee shop on the corner, empty in the dead time between the end of the lunch hour and the beginning of children coming home from school. Connie sat looking through the window while Bill fetched two coffees from the counter.

'Thanks for coming with me. I don't think I'd have done even this on my own. But now I know my place of origin, don't I?'

'Does it help to have seen Constance Crescent?'

'Not really.'

'Con, don't you think perhaps you should talk to Hilda? She may be able to give you a lead.'

Connie considered this. 'I don't think I can. She'd be offended, wouldn't she? She'd interpret my wanting to trace my real mother as a criticism of her as an adopted one. I can't imagine our talk going beyond that. It's not really our family thing, is it? Warm and affirming heart-to-hearts, opening up to each other?'

'You're angry, Con.'

'I am not,' she snapped. 'I just want to know who I am.'

His eyes held hers then. 'Don't you already know that? Truly? I think I know who you are. You're what you've made yourself, and will make. Regardless of what or who you were born as.'

Bill's hands lifted, ready to take hers, but then he withdrew them and sheltered them beneath the table, out of danger. They never touched each other, not since the night they had kissed in the rain.

'Does Jeanette know that you've come here with me today?'

She saw his eyes flicker.

'No.'

Connie's decision to trace her mother was private to her, and Bill would respect that, even—maybe especially—where Jeanette was concerned.

'Well. Thank you again,' she murmured.

'We'll come back and talk to the people in the house. That's the next thing to do.'

'Perhaps.' Connie had lost her enthusiasm for detective work. She changed her tone and asked brightly, 'How's Noah?'

Bill smiled. 'He's great. He's sitting up. His favourite game is banging saucepans with a wooden spoon. And how is Sam?'

'Sam is fine, thank you.'

'Good,' Bill said. He began rubbing the skin at the corner of his jaw with the side of his thumb. Connie knew by now that he only did this when he felt unhappy. She was sorry for him, and she was sorry for herself, too, because he was so near to her and familiar and necessary, and also absolutely desirable and equally forbidden.

She reached for her bag. 'Come on,' she said gently. 'I've got to get back to work. They'll be wondering where I've got to.'

Chapter Seven

'HOW IS JEANETTE?' Connie asked Bill on the phone. The previous day, Jeanette had returned to work part-time.

'Not very good,' he told her. 'She was practically transparent with exhaustion when I got her home. She went straight to bed. I couldn't persuade her even to try to eat something. I don't see how she can go back tomorrow, although she insists that she will.'

His voice in her ear was as warm as ever, and as familiar, but there was also a note of imprecision in it.

'I'll be there tomorrow evening,' Connie promised.

Everything else, all their history together, the joy and the long denial, now seemed compacted and whittled down to this single, brittle point of caring between them for Jeanette.

Jeanette was sitting in her chair with a shawl round her shoulders. She was looking out into the garden, with the evening sunlight slanting on spiders' webs. It was a moment before she sensed that Connie was there, but then she turned her head. Her eyes burned in their deep sockets.

—*I had to come home today after just two hours.*

'That must have been tough.'

—*I opened my files. I sat there. My head was useless. Everyone looked at me, then pretended not to. Full of sympathy. Embarrassed, as well. Other people's weakness is embarrassing, isn't it? I felt as if I was already dead.*

'No. You just went back too early after the operation,' Connie soothed.

—*Too early. Too late. They overlap, don't they?* There was a new, mordant edge to her anger at what was overtaking her.

'Try to be a bit patient, Jeanette. You're too harsh on yourself.'

Jeanette regarded her. Her hair was freshly washed, her face made up. Then she jerked her head.

—*I will have to do something else. I can't just sit here. Waiting.*

Bill brought in a bottle of wine and some glasses. From the slope of his shoulders Connie could see his despair.

'It's not waiting, Jan. It's being with us.'

There was a pause.

—*Yes. Of course it is. You're right. I'm sorry.*

Connie stared into the garden, not wanting to risk seeing the look that passed between the two of them. She felt her own spike of anger at the finality ahead.

Bill put a drink into her hand. Jeanette took hers, the finger of wine heavily diluted with water, and sipped at it.

'I think we should have a holiday, instead of worrying about plant taxonomy,' Bill said.

A glorious idea delivered itself to Connie.

'Why don't you both come out and stay with me in Bali?' As soon as the thought came to her she was longing to take Jeanette straight there, to the green wave. 'It's beautiful, and it's warm. My house is comfortable enough. There's a view from the verandah you could look at for ever.'

—*For ever?*

She met her sister's gaze.

She guessed Jeanette would be wondering about moving from her own safe realm into Connie's unknown one, and whether it would be risky to allow her sister and her husband to spend so much time together.

Then, just as clearly, Connie saw her dismiss the questions. They didn't matter any longer. Jeanette's face flowered into a beam of excitement. She held out her hand towards Connie, and they matched their palms together. Affection seemed to flow like a current between them.

—*I'd like that so much.* Then she remembered how weak she had become and turned to Bill. —*Can I? Can we?*

Bill said, 'Of course we can. We'll go as soon as you want.'

It took a week to finalise the arrangements. Connie was to fly out first, to make the house ready, and Jeanette and Bill would follow her two days later.

The night before she left London, she spoke to Angela.

'Sounds a good idea, Connie. Bali will do your sister good.'

'I hope so. I think it will.'

'Email me, let me know how she is, and how you are. By the way—

could you ask Roxana to give me a call? We are setting up a shoot in St Petersburg and I need someone who speaks Russian fluently. It would be to work for a few hours a week, on the phones, finding suppliers out there, that sort of thing. Twenty quid an hour.'

'You know if you hire her she will probably be running the show within a couple of months?'

'Who am I to stand in the way of ambition? Have a good trip.'

'Thanks, Ange.'

A tiny basket made from plaited coconut leaf and containing a few grains of red and white rice, a sliver of lime and a betel leaf lay on the verandah step. The thin white trail of smoke from a burning incense stick drifted in the still air.

Wayan Tupereme prayed for a moment after he had placed the offering. He waved his hand three times, to send the essence of the offering towards God, then padded quietly down the path to his own house. The Englishwoman was back, and now she had guests staying with her. Putu, the taxi driver who had brought them up from Denpasar, was a relative of his wife and she had heard from Putu's wife that the lady who had arrived was very sick.

Wayan was certain that a stay in his village would balance her again.

Connie had moved into the smaller bedroom in her house, to give Jeanette and Bill more space. When she woke up she had to open her eyes before she was able to work out where she was.

She got out of bed and wrapped herself in a sarong. The heat of the coming day was gathered in the corners of the room, waiting to envelop her. She padded across the bare floorboards to fold back the window shutters and immediately the early sun gilded the bare walls.

At first glance the verandah looked deserted. But then a tiny movement caught her eye. Jeanette was sitting in the rocking chair watching a cat-sized yellow-green lizard that was splayed on a corner of the decking.

Connie slid open the screen door and stepped outside. The lizard blinked once, then the creature flowed over the edge of the deck and vanished. Jeanette turned her head. When she saw Connie she pointed to where it had been a second earlier.

'I know. He lives under the boards. If I feel like some company, I feed him. He particularly likes ham and cocktail olives.'

Jeanette smiled.

'How do you feel? Did you sleep?'

Connie was thinking that she looked a bit better than she had done yesterday, although that wasn't saying much. When she met them at the airport, Bill had been pushing Jeanette in an airline wheelchair. Jeanette looked so weak and defeated, Connie was afraid she was going to die there in the midst of the airport's callous scramble of taxis and tour buses.

And now, less than twenty hours later, Jeanette was up, her hair was combed, and she had dressed in a shirt with kindly folds that hid her sharp bones.

—*Better. Thank you,* she answered. —*I was very tired.*

Connie could only admire the depth of her sister's resolve. She pulled a stool across and sat down next to her. They gazed out at the view.

Veils of mist were drawn upwards from the bends of the river. Diaphanous layers silvered the opposite wall of greenery, and where the sun touched them droplets of moisture twinkled with tiny points of light.

Jeanette let her head fall back against the cushions. —*Look at it,* she said. —*It's perfect. And it's so hot.*

Connie was solicitous at once. 'A breeze gets up later. Come inside for now. It's cooler. There's air-con; I'll turn it up.'

—*I like it. I'm usually cold.*

'If you're sure.'

A long moment passed, comfortably silent.

—*So many trees. I don't know half of them.*

'Neither do I. We'll get a book.'

—*Good idea.*

Another moment passed.

—*Connie, I'm so happy we came.*

'I thought the journey was too much for you. I was angry with myself for having suggested you should come out here in the first place.'

Jeanette rolled her head and sighed. —*I threw up all the way. The shame. I hate Bill to see me like that. But I'm all right now I'm here. In this place. It's more beautiful than I imagined.*

'I'm glad you're here,' Connie said.

Jeanette shot her a sudden glance. —*It's a long way from Echo Street.*

The exotic walls of the gorge and the solid sunshine emphasised the physical distance, but Connie shook her head. 'Only in miles. Sitting here with you, I feel as if we could be back there.'

There was another glance. —*Bad or not bad?*

'Neither. Or both. It's what connects us. Echo Street.'

The last time they had been there together, more than five years ago, the rooms were being emptied. Two sweating men hoisted the piano onto a trolley and wheeled it away. Dusty rectangles showed on the bare walls, and the living-room carpet was dimpled with brown-rimmed hollows where the same furniture had stood in the same places for more than thirty years.

That was the day when they had their last, seemingly irrevocable quarrel. The last time they communicated with each other, until Jeanette wrote to tell her sister that she was dying.

Connie bowed her head. The arches of her sister's feet were netted with blue veins, the toes were white, bloodless, and the nails as chalky as if they belonged already to a dead woman. Connie pulled her stool closer and lifted the feet into her lap. She began to massage them, running her thumbs over the ridges, cupping the heels and squeezing the tired ligaments, as if she could rub the life back just by the force of her will and the warmth of her own flesh.

After a moment Jeanette sighed, and her eyes closed.

Later, Jeanette asked, —*What do you do here? Every day?*

Connie had brought out a bowl of salad and a dish of mango and guava, and they ate the simple meal at a table that had been drawn into the deepest shade at the back of the verandah.

Bill sat in the rattan chair next to Jeanette's rocker, checking her from time to time with a glance, but otherwise he was almost silent. Connie had read from the lines in his face precisely how exhausted with nursing and perpetual anxiety he was. To be so close to him, to know his whereabouts and what he was doing every hour, made her skin feel slightly raw. Even in the heat, goose bumps prickled on her arms.

She answered brightly, 'What do I do with my time? You wouldn't believe how busy it can be here. And that's when I'm not working. When I've got a commission I have to lock myself away or it would never get done. There's my orchestra, for instance. That's Tuesdays, for rehearsal. Sometimes we put on a performance. On a normal day if I just call in to the market in the village, it can take half a morning by the time I've greeted everyone I know and asked after the children and grandchildren. I visit my neighbours, the Balinese ones, and they visit me, on a strict turn-by-turn basis. That's not to mention the Europeans, their drinks parties and barbecues and gallery openings . . .'

Bill said, 'That's busy.'

Connie thought, Yes. I am busy, because I need to be. It's the life I've made for myself. She smiled at him. She wanted him to know she had her place in the village. She was not an object for concern, and she was certainly not to be pitied.

'Take today. There's an invitation to go to my neighbour's house, just over here.' She pointed to the thick palm hedge that separated her garden from Wayan Tupereme's house compound. 'Wayan and his family have a big celebration coming soon, and today's party is in preparation for that. All his relatives, the women especially, are coming to the house to help to prepare offerings for the ceremony. The men will be starting to build a roof to provide shade on the day itself. There's a lot of work to be done, but it's a social event too.'

Connie wondered if now was the right time to explain that the big event that was being so elaborately prepared for was the cremation of Wayan's father. The old man had died more than a year ago and was buried in the village cemetery. The most auspicious day had been fixed on months ago, giving the best possible circumstances for the dead man's *atman*, his immortal soul, to continue on its journey to heaven.

She added quickly, 'You're both invited too, of course, as my family. Wayan made a special call, to insist on that. But you are tired . . .'

Jeanette sat up. —*I would like to go to the party. Very much.*

Her sudden eagerness had a feverish glitter. Bill leaned forward to touch her arm, but she waved off the restraint.

—*Why not? We are here. If you will take us, Connie?*

Connie nodded. 'Of course. And they will all want to meet you. They are very curious, always, about new people.'

Jeanette touched her fingers to her mouth in a question, and Connie wondered how she should answer it. It was a difficult concept to sign, but she would do the best she could.

'In Bali, everything is a matter of balance. Each living or inanimate thing is part of an ordered universe. This is called *dharma,* and our personal actions or *karma* must harmonise with our duty to *dharma*. To do this, Balinese Hindus try always to look at the world with regard for others, not themselves. To be old here is a matter for reverence. A new baby is pure and treated almost as a god. For a person to be deaf, or lame, or a stranger, this is also part of the balance of the universe. If a Balinese does not accept these differences, and acknowledge the grace in them, he causes disorder. Or *adharma.*'

Jeanette repeated the words. —*Dharma. Balance.*

'I should explain: this evening marks the beginning of the send-off for my neighbour Wayan's father. The cremation itself is next week, on the most auspicious day.'

Bill's thumb moved to the corner of his mouth. 'We're going to a funeral? A sort of *wake?*'

'Yes. And no, in fact. Of course it is a funeral and it's a sad occasion because the family and friends are saying a final goodbye, but the old man died quite a long time ago.'

Jeanette was following the explanation carefully. —*How long ago?*

'A little more than a year. A big, grand cremation costs a lot of money for the family, and they have to save up for it as well as wait for the auspicious date in the calendar. So the body is temporarily buried, and then when everything is ready they dig it up again in order to cremate it and set the spirit free. It tends to be a wild party.'

Jeanette started to laugh. The surprising sound of it bubbled out of her throat. —*I have to see this, don't I?*

Outside Wayan's house, scooters and cars were parked along the narrow lane, and dozens of pairs of sandals and shoes were lined up at the step. The *bale*, the house pavilion, was overflowing with people. The bamboo pillars that supported the palm-leaf roof were decorated with strips of coloured cloth and the roof itself was swathed in more folds of colour. Most of the men wore white or crimson head-cloths and bright sarongs. The women's long skirts were intricate ikat fabrics and frangipani and hibiscus blossoms were plaited in their hair. Children in their best clothes chased and played between the adults' legs. The effect was of a brilliant moving sea of patterns and faces and smiles.

As the visitors passed through the outer gate into the open compound, Wayan and his wife came forward to greet them. Connie made the introductions, formally, in polite Balinese. Dayu, Wayan's diminutive wife, placed her hands together and bowed to each of them in turn.

'You are welcome,' she said in English. 'Please come to join us.'

The guests were crowding towards the family temple, placed in the most sacred corner of the compound and separated from it by a gate. Connie bowed her head to the people she recognised in the throng.

A priest in white robes was preparing to make the offerings.

Chairs were ranged in a loose row for those who needed them, and without drawing attention to it Wayan made sure that Jeanette found her way to one. The priest lifted a small bronze bell and rang it. At once the talk and laughter died away.

A small group of gamelan musicians were gathered with their instruments in the inner enclosure. One of them struck a long, shivering gong note. It resonated in the warm, damp air.

The musicians began to play. It was sombre temple music, the metallophones with their bamboo resonators laying down a skeletal rhythm that was filled in with the drums and gong-chimes.

The priest was chanting. He lifted and placed the offerings in turn, silver plates of rice cakes garlanded with flowers and bark-frilled bamboo skewers of fruit. The guests mumbled or chanted their prayers, holding a

blossom between their fingers and pressing folded thumbs to their foreheads. The priest's attendant came through the crowd with a clay jug of
tirta, the holy water. Bill was somewhere behind Connie in the crowd,
but she watched Jeanette observing and copying her neighbours. When
Jeanette's turn came she held out her cupped palm for the water as the
others did, sipped three times at it, then dripped the remainder over her
hair. She took a pinch of sticky rice too, and following the grandmother
beside her she pressed a few grains to her forehead and temples.

The tempo of the music changed. It rippled now, faster, like running
water. The prayers were over and people were turning away, laughing
and gossiping again. Connie was struck, as she always was, by the seam-
less way that spiritual and secular life were woven together.

A small group of women had been in one of the enclosed rooms
during the prayers. Now they came out, carrying huge bowls of rice
and baskets of coconut leaves. The working part of the evening was
about to begin. In the centre of a knot of young girls, Connie spotted
Wayan's daughter, Dewi. Her baby son was wrapped in a sky-blue
shawl and tied against her, his smooth brown head just visible.

'Dewi.' Connie smiled and waved.

The girl flashed a smile in return and ducked through the crowd
towards her. Jeanette reached Connie's side at the same time. The grains
of rice were still glued to her tissue-thin skin.

'This is my friend, Dewi,' Connie told her. 'She is Wayan and Dayu's
daughter. And this is their grandson.' She turned to Dewi. 'My sister,'
she said, completing the introduction.

Dewi made her graceful bow, and Jeanette's fingers fluttered close to
the baby's head.

—*Beautiful*, her gesture said, and Dewi smiled proudly. She gestured
in return, *Would you like to hold him?*

Jeanette opened her arms. One hand cupped the baby's head, the
other supported his tiny weight against her breast.

'He's a strong boy,' Connie said to Dewi.

The girl beamed. 'Oh, yes. Like his father.'

There were more people to greet. Wayan's cousin Kadek from the village store came to touch her hand.

'Good evening, *Ibu* Connie.'

Kadek was a relatively wealthy man. He and his brothers and all the
other cousins would be helping to pay for the cremation. Connie had
heard that three other families would also be sending off their relatives
during the same ceremony. It was not unusual for people to club
together to meet the heavy costs.

The women were settling at tables with the bowls of rice and coconut leaves spread between them. Connie went and sat near Dayu, and when Jeanette finally parted with the baby she joined them.

—*That baby. The scent they have. I wish Noah had a son.*

'Maybe he and Roxana will.'

—*Not in my time.* Jeanette's face was smooth. There was no bitterness or anger in it now. She leaned closer. —*Will you do something for me?*

'Of course,' Connie said.

—*If. When. Will you be a grandmother in my place?*

Connie took a breath. 'Yes. I promise. Whatever Noah wants.'

Composedly, Jeanette nodded her head. —*Good. Thank you.*

All around them, women were working. Some of them were scooping up handfuls of rice, coloured bright pink or yellow or pistachio green, and dexterously moulding them into animal shapes. These would be left to dry, then incorporated into the high tiers of offerings on cremation day. The musicians played sweet, liquid music over the frog chorus.

It was almost dark now, and the lights in the compound had come on. Some of the men were carrying in bales of leaves to provide temporary thatch for the open compound. Others were putting up bamboo poles to support the new roof or carry long strings of lights. Connie saw Bill in the middle of one group. He stood head and shoulders taller than the other men, and they were using him as a prop to hold up a pole with one hand and run up a length of cable with the other. He was good at fitting in. It was just one of the reasons why Connie loved him.

Dayu had left the tables to oversee another cohort of women in the kitchen, preparing food for the workers, and now they began to emerge with hot food. It was important for the prestige of the dead man that everything should be of the best quality, and laid on in abundance. The musicians abandoned their instruments and the men put down their tools and cables. The women served them with big, steaming platefuls.

Someone tapped Connie on the shoulder. She turned round to see Ketut. 'Connie, will you play? I think we should not let the people eat without music to help their digestion.'

She beamed at him. 'Ketut, I didn't see you in this crowd.'

'We have missed you. You have been in London, I think?'

'Yes, I have. Jeanette, this is Ketut, my friend and music teacher. Ketut, my sister.'

He bowed. 'You have heard Connie play Balinese music?'

'Jeanette is deaf, Ketut.'

Ketut bowed again in calm acknowledgement.

—*I would like to see you play*, Jeanette signed.

Connie passed this on to Ketut, who darted off through the crowd. He whispered to several people and persuasively patted their arms. A minute later Connie was propelled to the corner where the instruments were set up. An impromptu, giggling group of musicians closed round her. Ketut marshalled them into position.

'Connie, you will play the *wadon*.'

Connie recoiled. The female drum was usually the leader of the ensemble, playing learned patterns that linked to the gong structures but also had to be built up with considerable personal improvisation.

The other musicians were taking up their mallets and Ketut positioned himself in front of his regular instrument, the large gong.

It was too late to back out. Connie swallowed hard.

Ketut took a pinch of rice and laid it on the floor beside the gong stand. The stand was carved in the shape of a giant tortoise, on which according to Balinese mythology the entire world rests. An offering to the spirit of the gong would ensure a harmonious performance.

A second of quiet gathered, then Ketut struck a single note. The powerful reverberation sailed out over the walls of the compound and slowly faded away into the darkness. He gave Connie the conductor's bow of introduction; she obediently settled the drum on its brocaded cushion on her lap and lifted her head.

She struck the drum head with the flat of her left hand, then another beat with her right thumb. She had begun with the certainty that she would forget the sequence, but miraculously the first notes came back to her. Facing her was Bagus, a thin, bespectacled schoolteacher, who had taken the *lanang*, the male drum. His beats interlocked with hers and the metallophones and the gongs and cymbals fell into place.

Connie let herself float away into the music. The pattern of drum beats, *kap pek kap pek kum pung kum pung*, that had started as a rigid imperative suddenly loosened its hold and turned into a platform from which her own pattern launched itself, gathered momentum and soared away. Bagus's drumming was a sinuous thread, confidently rising and knitting with hers, seeming to know where she was heading before she led him there, like the best of lovers. As the splash of the cymbals rose to her lead she knew for sure, here and now, what belonging meant.

The music reached a crescendo, then the sequence unravelled again, simplifying itself down to the last drum beats.

Laughing with exhilaration, Connie looked up at last. She saw Bill at the back of the crowd, his eyes fixed on her.

Ketut struck the last thrilling gong note.

The piece had been a short and simple one, but Wayan and Dayu's guests and even the regular musicians were appreciative. Ketut's ensemble smiled at each other, and Connie formally shook hands with Bagus.

Jeanette was clapping her hands, and her eyes shone. —*How beautiful and graceful. I wish I could have heard it, but I felt the rhythm in here.* She tapped her chest with the flat of her hand.

Bill appeared beside them. Connie pushed her damp hair back from her forehead and grinned at him.

'That', he said simply, 'was the best music I've ever heard.'

'Oh, come on.'

'It was,' he insisted.

Jeanette nodded in agreement, and as she sat between them Connie felt a wave of pride and happiness. Dayu brought a carved wooden dish of fruit and laid it in front of them. The proper gamelan players were taking their seats again.

Fat raindrops slapped on the broad leaves, trickled from the fronds of the roof and drummed on bamboo pipes. For four days it had been thundery, and in the late afternoons swollen masses of cloud had sailed over the gorge and the rice paddies and blotted out the pale blue cone of Mount Agung. Now the rain had finally come.

Jeanette spent most of the days reclining in the rocker. She studied the book of trees that Connie had brought back from the European bookshop in the village. Connie usually sat with her, while Bill sometimes went out with Wayan and his brothers and cousins to help build the *wadah*. This was a bamboo cremation tower, with the tortoise and two dragon-snakes at the bottom, representing the universe. Successive tiers rose to a height of thirty feet, to a little pagoda that stood for heaven. When it was ready, the structure, with a symbol of the old man's body in the *bale* within it, would be carried by his male descendants through the village to the cremation ground. For now, work had stopped.

Connie and Jeanette looked out through a curtain of falling water.

—*It takes a long time. Getting ready for the cremation.*

'Months.'

—*I like that. The proper rituals. Everyone doing their part.*

'It's seen as part of a natural cycle. Grief and the work going on. The body is only a container. The better the ceremony, the more likely that the spirit eventually becomes one of the deified ancestors.'

Jeanette's head fell back. —*I didn't know it took so long just to die.*

'Does it seem so long?'

—*Yes. I thought death came quick in the Thorne family.*

'It seemed that way,' Connie agreed.

She had been away with Seb.

Sébastian Bourret with the Sydney Symphony had been a big event in Hobart, Tasmania. Seb had been irritable after the rehearsals and performances, and had wanted to get as far away from the music world as he could. On the spur of the moment they rented a motorhome intended for backpackers, and drove out to Cradle Mountain Park. For five days Seb fished in the lakes while Connie read, and in the evenings she grilled the fish he caught over an open fire. They went for walks and spoke to no one, and Connie thought that they were happy.

On their way back through Hobart, Seb picked up a message that was waiting for him. He studied it for a moment, then turned to Connie.

'It's for you,' he said quietly. 'I'm afraid it's bad news.'

Bill and Jeanette had failed to reach her in London or in Sydney, and as a last resort had tried Seb's management company.

Connie learned that her adopted mother had died one night, alone at Echo Street, of a cerebral haemorrhage. The funeral was taking place more or less as she stood trying to take in the news on the opposite side of the world.

'Hilda is dead,' Connie repeated, disbelieving.

Seb had never even met her. He took Connie in his arms to comfort her. 'I'm so sorry,' he said.

Connie didn't cry, but her eyes burned and she felt that there was a tourniquet round her throat, coming close to strangling her. In a voice quite unlike her own she whispered, 'I never felt that she was my mother, even when I didn't know that she wasn't. I don't think she ever convinced herself that I could be her daughter. It makes it harder to believe that she's gone, because now it's too late.'

The funeral was over; there was no reason to hurry home to London.

When she did get back, Jeanette was already clearing out the house in Echo Street before selling it.

Jeanette opened the door to her. The smell of the old house flooded into Connie's face. The past was like a vapour, spiralling into the chambers of her head. They stood and looked at each other.

—*You're here.*

'I would have come before now, Jeanette. Given the chance.'

—*I couldn't postpone the funeral until you turned up.*

'That was your decision to make, of course.'

Two overalled men edged out of the kitchen doorway, hauling Hilda's old refrigerator between them. Connie remembered the day in 1969 when they moved into the house, when Tony and another set of removals men had carried in their belongings from the old flat, and the new rooms had seemed big enough to echo with emptiness.

To get out of the way of the removers, she angled past Jeanette and climbed the stairs.

Her old bedroom was already empty. The corner cupboard stood open. Connie rested her fingers on the old-fashioned latch, trying to recall exactly why the enclosed space had frightened her so badly.

Jeanette had followed her. Now she stood framed in the doorway, her plump body held as taut as a wire. Connie turned.

—*Bill's not here*, Jeanette signed, as if Connie might have come up the stairs in search of him.

You are so bloody difficult, Connie thought. Why can't you let it go, just for today? Anger inflated like a balloon inside her. She said coldly, 'Hilda has just died. Can't we be civil to each other?'

Jeanette seemed to rear up. —*Civil? Was what you did civil?*

'No. It was wrong. We know that. But it's over. It was over years and years ago.' That's all true, Connie thought. But I think of Bill every day. Does that make me guilty, still?

The balloon of anger collapsed again. The sound of heavy furniture being shifted came up the stairs.

She began again. 'Today's not about what happened between Bill and me. It's about Hilda, and you and me, and what's left in this house. If you can't see that, shall we try to do what we've come here for? Then I'll go.'

Jeanette lifted her chin. —*You think you can run away. You always did.*

'Jeanette. For Christ's sake. Shut up and stop attacking. I'm not your enemy, I never was.'

—*You are shouting.*

It was true, she was. Connie rubbed her face with her hands.

It became very important to make Jeanette understand what she was trying to say. She took two steps across the room and caught hold of her.

'I didn't think Mum would just go and die like this. It's a shock. I still thought there would be plenty of time for the three of us to work out the . . . the resentments. They were always there, weren't they, long, long before Bill? Isn't that right? That must be what you feel too?'

Jeanette's flesh was solid under her hands. She was angry too, Connie could feel the heat of it.

—*Resentment?*

'Yes. Couldn't we talk about it?'

—*Talk changes nothing.*

Jeanette made a twist, away from Connie, then beckoned. Connie followed her into Hilda's bedroom.

The place where the divan base had rested was outlined in grey furry dust. The dressing table with the triple mirror was gone, and the bedside tables. Connie looked at what had once been familiar, and wondered how a person's absence could be so tangible.

A pyramid of cardboard boxes stood in the middle of the floor. Some of Hilda's clothes had been packed into them.

—*Do you want any of this?*

'No. But thank you.'

—*There is something else. It's yours*, she added. She pointed out to the landing, where the square trap giving access into the roof space stood open. —*It was up there.*

A smaller cardboard box stood a little apart from the others. It had once contained tins of corned beef. Connie stooped down. She pulled aside the tape that had been used to seal it, grown brittle with age, and opened the flaps. Inside the box, under some folded paper, she found an old brown leatherette shopping bag. It had looped handles, and the plastic material was torn around the rivets to reveal yellowed padding.

'What's this?' she asked, although she already knew. Her heart was banging like a drum.

—*You had better look.*

Inside the bag, folded up together, lay a knitted baby's blanket and a tiny yellow cardigan. As Connie unfolded the cardigan, an ordinary cheap brown envelope fell out. Her hands were shaking as she opened the envelope's flap. Into her uncertain hand an earring fell.

It was a little pendant of marcasites with a rod and a screw fastening for a pierced ear. Connie closed her fist on it.

'These things are mine. They belong to *me*.' She stared into Jeanette's eyes. 'Why didn't Hilda give them to me?'

Jeanette shrugged. —*I suppose because you didn't need them. Mum gave you a home, a new family. Why would you want those things?*

'Why? *Why*? Because these are mine. *This* is my identity.'

Jeanette looked incredulous. —*An identity from someone who put you in a bag and left you under a hedge? You were lucky that Mum and Dad took you in. Even though you were what you were.*

'What I was?' Connie asked, dangerously.

—*Not one of us.*

Not creamy-skinned, plump, blonde, like Hilda and Sadie and their three pretty daughters. Different. Unidentified. Unidentifiable.

The divide had always been there.

Not spoken of, never, of course not. But scrawny little Constance Thorne had always been different, with her loud voice and her singing, her tight hair and her skin a shade darker than anyone else's in the street.

Connie had learned to accept that she would never know her birth mother and father. There were tests, of course, modern ones, that would indicate exactly what mixture of blood ran in her veins. But no test, however elaborate, would tell her who she really was.

She folded the blanket, awkwardly because her hand was still closed on the earring. She tucked it and the cardigan away inside the bag.

'Why did Hilda *want* to adopt a foundling?'

Jeanette's face suddenly blazed with fury. She grabbed Connie by the shoulders and shook her. —*Why? Why do you think? Because of me. Deaf. Deaf. Deaf. They didn't want another like me, did they? And with one deaf-and-dumb kid in the family, they weren't going to get given a nice new pink baby. They were only going to get one like you.*

Connie breathed in sharply. It was like being children again, fighting and scratching, trying to damage each other by any means.

—*And what did you do in return? Tried to take my husband.*

'I didn't try to take Bill from you. I made the mistake of loving him. I regret what I did.'

—*You are a liar.*

Connie pulled away from her. She had to get away, out of the room before one of them hit out. She snatched up the bag, made sure of its contents, and ran down the steep stairs past the gaping removals men.

She heard Jeanette's yell. —*Running away.*

The front door stood open. She ran out and slammed it behind her.

Leaving Echo Street for the last time.

Chapter Eight

'ROX? CAN YOU hear me? Where are you?'

Noah was calling Roxana on her new mobile. She had left the offices of Angela's production company, and was on her way to the bus stop.

'I am in the street, Noah. I am going to the Cosmos, I can't be late.'

She had done three hours on the telephone in Angela's office, talking in Russian to unimportant officials in the Russian Film Institute who would eventually open the doors to conversations with the more senior officials who had the power to grant the production company the permits they needed to film in St Petersburg. Angela seemed pleased with her.

'When can I see you?' Noah asked.

'I am not sure. On Saturday?'

'That's four days' time.'

'I know that. What can I do?'

Noah sighed. 'You can let me pick you up from the club tonight.'

'No. I don't want you to see me in that place. You don't understand why, but I don't want it.'

'I do understand. Sort of. But—'

'Noah, here is my bus. I will call you tomorrow.' She chirped a kiss to him. As the bus doors opened she skipped inside and inserted herself into a just-vacated seat.

Roxana couldn't help smiling. She kept counting them up, as if the wonders of her life might otherwise be snatched away. She had two jobs, one of them in the *film business*. She had an English boyfriend who called her more often than she needed to hear from him, a proper bank account with money in it, a mobile phone, an Oyster card, and a place to live that made her feel as if she was in a movie. She was a London girl.

It was a quiet night at the Cosmos, which was always harder than when it was busy. Roxana worked the pole as enthusiastically as she could. She locked eyes with each of the men in turn but she couldn't make a single one of them pay for a private dance. Towards the end of the interminable evening, Mr Shane sent for Roxana to come to his office.

He took his cigar out of his mouth and exhaled a swirl of dirty blue smoke. 'Shut the door. Come here.'

Roxana took one small step forwards.

'Here,' he said, indicating with the cigar. 'That's better. Well now. Hmm.' His manicured hands twitched her lace top away. He put the cigar back in his mouth, reached up and deftly unhooked her bra.

Roxana looked straight over his bald head. She wouldn't give him the satisfaction of reacting.

Casually he fondled her. 'Do you enjoy your job here?'

'It is a job.'

'Like to keep it, would you?'

Now his hands slid over her breasts and insinuatingly over her hips. There was no doubt what Mr Shane had in mind. The same thing as her stepfather. Always the same. Hatred stabbed through her.

'Oh yes, please.'

'Take that thing off,' he ordered.

Roxana smiled at him now. She reached behind her, undoing her miniskirt with deliberately slow movements as Mr Shane waited. She slid the skirt down over her hips, to her knees. Then she raised her leg, as if she was about to step out of the garment. The man's eyes travelled down the length of her thigh and calf, down to the stiletto heel of her shoe.

Roxana let her skirt drop. She jack-knifed her knee to her chest, then used the momentum to stamp her foot hard into his crotch.

There was a liquid gasp, like a bubble of air escaping from a blocked drain. As Mr Shane doubled up into his own lap, Roxana grabbed her skirt and ran for the door.

In the cubbyhole that the dancers used as a dressing room, she collected up her belongings and stuffed them into her bag. She put on her outdoor coat and hurried up the customers' stairs to the ground floor.

Roxana knew that this was her last ever moment inside the Cosmos Club. She felt no regrets. She elbowed her way out through the crowd before Mr Shane could send anyone to catch her and repay her for stamping on him. The night air tasted cool and fresh.

Noah had been waiting only a few minutes. He saw her erupt from the club, the light briefly catching her blonde crop. He also saw that she was laughing. Roxana slowed her pace and strolled away down the street, her stilettos click-clicking and her bag swinging from her shoulder. He jumped out of the car and ran to catch up with her.

Roxana heard the hurrying footsteps, then an arm caught hers. She wheeled round, two hands grasping her bag with the intention of using it to batter her attacker rather than to secure it.

'Hey. Hey, Roxana, it's me.'

'Noah, what are you doing here?'

'Picking you up from work.'

'I said not to.'

'Not inside the club. Nothing wrong with waiting outside, is there?'

'No, I suppose. Anyway, there is no argument. I won't be going back there again. I don't have a job any more.'

'Why's that?'

'I kicked my boss in the testicles.'

'What for?'

Roxana shrugged. 'The usual reason.'

Noah shouted, 'What? What did he do to you? I'm going to go in there and do worse than just kick him in the balls; I'll tear them off and stuff them down his throat.'

'Thank you for the idea, but you don't need to. I have looked after myself already.'

Noah wound his arms round her and kissed her. 'That was why you were laughing, when you came out of there?'

'If you knew Mr Shane, you would be laughing too.'

'Come on, let's go. I'm taking you back to Auntie Con's place.'

With their arms round each other and Roxana's head tipped on Noah's shoulder, they retraced their steps to the car. A few late-night pedestrians passed by, and Roxana remembered the night when she was leaving the Cosmos and felt lonely because all the world seemed to be made of couples hurrying home to bed together. To anyone looking at her it would seem that she had joined the lucky people, and yet now she was here she knew the world was still a precarious place where you could lose your job in a flash of anger.

The man was there again, waiting in reception with his laptop case. He sat with one leg crossed over the other, the shiny toe of his loafer gently tapping the air. Once he turned back the immaculate blue cuff of his shirt with his little finger and glanced at his thin gold watch. He caught Roxana's eye again through the glass door of the office where she was working, raised one eyebrow by a millimetre, and flashed a smile back at her. This was his second visit to Oyster Films, and Roxana had been aware of him right from the start because he kept looking at her.

He was handsome. He looked rich, too. She wondered who he was.

'Mr Antonelli?'

The unfriendly girl who was the boss's PA had come downstairs. The man got up and followed her out of Roxana's sight.

Roxana went back to work. Angela had asked her to obtain the details of several Russian companies who might supply catering on location in St Petersburg, and to compare their quotes. In the back of her mind, as she tallied the boring figures, was worry about money and finding a new job. Working a few hours a week for Oyster Films was fine, but it paid next to nothing. Money was what counted, in the end.

She did everything that Angela might possibly want, but at half past six there was nothing left to deal with. Noah was playing football tonight for his office team, and the prospect of an empty evening ahead of her was unfamiliar and slightly unwelcome. Roxana put on her jacket with the large buttons and went out into reception. The lift doors slid open and Mr Antonelli emerged.

He smiled. 'Hello. Finished for today?' He held open the street door.

When she began walking, he fell into step beside her.

'How long have you been working at the company?' he asked in a companionable way, as if they already knew and liked each other.

'Not so long. But it is a good job. I like it very much.'

He gave her a glance. 'Are you a producer?'

'No, in fact. I am, er, a translator.'

He looked impressed. 'Is that so? What languages?'

'Russian. I am from Uzbekistan, but now I live in London.'

'Of course.' Mr Antonelli nodded. They reached the end of the street and he glanced at his thin gold watch again. 'I have an hour before my next appointment. Would you like to have a drink?'

Roxana considered it. Mr Antonelli was obviously important. Maybe he could be a useful person to know.

'Thank you,' she said. 'That would be very nice.'

He seemed to know his way around. He briskly steered her towards a place she had often passed but had never thought of going in to.

The bar was flooded with soft golden light. Wall mirrors reflected the backs of the women's smooth blonde heads and the shoulders of men in City suits. There were waitresses in black uniforms, and low music playing. Mr Antonelli steered them to a table in a little alcove. Roxana blinked as a glass of champagne materialised in front of her.

'I am Cesare Antonelli.' He took a card from his wallet and slid it across to her. Underneath his name it said *Film Director*, with an address in Rome.

'My name is Roxana.'

'How do you do?' Cesare Antonelli clinked his glass to hers. He leaned back against the leather seating. 'So, Roxana. Do you do some acting, or modelling perhaps, as well as translating? You look as if you might.'

Her attention sharpened. This could be an opportunity much bigger than making phone calls to Russian caterers.

'Not at the moment.' She smiled. 'But I am interested, of course.'

'And you are a good dancer; that is always useful.'

She stared at him. A flush rose from her throat to her cheeks.

Cesare lightly gestured. 'I was at the Cosmos Club with some Japanese business associates, after a long evening, you know what it can be like, and I saw you dance. You were really very good.'

Roxana was embarrassed. She had been thinking that Mr Antonelli recognised her talent, but it was only that he had seen her pole dancing.

'I don't work at that place any longer,' she said coolly. 'I am concentrating on Oyster Films and my work in the movie and advertising business. Are you going to direct a picture for them, perhaps?'

He said that he was setting up an Anglo-Italian co-production deal for a big feature film, which he would be directing, and he had been visiting Oyster Films to see if they might be a suitable partner.

'But they are not really in the big league, you know. They are mostly commercials and small stuff. Nice people, but I don't think I am going to be able to make it work with them, very unfortunately.'

In answer to his questions she told him about Noah and, without quite mentioning Connie, about living in her beautiful apartment, making it all sound as though she had lived in London for a long time.

When they had finished the champagne, Cesare said that he had to go and meet an associate to discuss some business over dinner. He hesitated, then added that if Roxana didn't think that would be too boring, she could perhaps join them. His colleague might be a useful contact for her.

Roxana was thinking the same thing.

They took a taxi to a restaurant. Cesare's associate was waiting at a table for two, but it was quickly re-laid for three. The man was called Philip. He was younger than Cesare and his clothes were scruffier. He told Roxana that he was a photographer. Fashion, glamour, he said airily.

An understanding arose that Roxana would do some unspecified work in the area of business that he and Cesare dealt in. She would need some publicity photographs, but Philip could help her with that.

They encouraged her to order food from the big, tasselled menu. When it came it was delicious, with soft, glistening meat and small puddles of unctuous sauces. She ate everything. Cesare and Philip had similar dishes but took only a few mouthfuls. As the talked, they drank wine followed by whisky with a lot of ice in short, chunky glasses. Roxana drank quite a lot too. She sank into a honeyed daze of optimism.

Of course she could be an actress, or a model.

After a while, the food and the drinks and the series of espressos that followed were all finished. They were out in the twinkly night, and Cesare hailed a taxi. Both men insisted that they couldn't let her go home unescorted. Roxana confidently gave the driver the address of Limbeck House. When they reached her building, to her faint dismay they got out and Cesare paid the fare and the cab drove off. They were talking about coming up with her for a final nightcap.

Roxana hesitated, but they had bought her dinner.

They took the lift to the top floor. Once they were in the big white room the two men strolled to the window and gazed out at the city.

'Nice place,' Cesare said.

'Live here on your own, do you?' Philip wanted to know.

'I have a flatmate. She is away tonight.' As soon as she said it, she cursed her stupidity. She should have said she would be back any minute.

They asked for whisky. Cesare examined the music stacked on the top of Connie's grand piano.

'Are you a musician, too?' he asked.

'No.' Roxana searched through the cupboards. She knew that Connie kept drink somewhere, but she couldn't remember where she had seen it. She didn't like the way Philip was wandering about picking up Connie's possessions and putting them down again.

He saw her watching him and grinned at her. Very casually, he produced a little camera from the pocket of his jacket. 'Now we're here, shall we take a few pictures?'

'Perhaps it is too late for that,' she said.

'It's early. Isn't it, Cesare?'

Roxana closed the door of the last cupboard with a snap. 'I am sorry that I don't have whisky.'

Philip studied her through half-closed eyes. 'What have you got?'

A shiver of apprehension passed through her, followed by a dull sense of familiarity, disappointment and absolute recognition.

Model, indeed. Actress, ha ha.

'Nothing. It's time for you both to go.'

Philip came at her. 'Come on, darling. A nice picture or two. On that lovely sofa, eh?'

'No. If you don't leave I will have to call for the police.'

Her hand stretched out to the telephone. Philip caught her wrist and Roxana squirmed in his grasp, trying to bring her knee into his groin. Is this all that is ever going to happen to me? she wondered.

Cesare dashed forward. He looked genuinely distressed. 'Now, now. Don't spoil a beautiful evening. Stop that, Philip. If the lady doesn't want you to take her picture, you can't force her.'

Philip let go, reluctantly.

'There we are. All friends again,' Cesare smiled. 'And Roxana is quite right. It's late, and past everyone's bedtime.'

She breathed again. 'Thank you,' she said.

'I'll just use the bathroom before you throw us out,' Philip muttered.

Roxana silently pointed along the corridor.

While he was out of the room Cesare apologised for him. He hoped very much that Roxana hadn't been upset.

'I am all right. Thank you,' she said stiffly.

There was no more talk of opportunities in the film business.

When Philip reappeared his coat was done up, and he stood by the front door without coming back into the main room.

Cesare kissed her on the cheek. 'Goodbye, Roxana,' he said.

Roxana locked the door after them, and slid the chain into place. She let her head fall against the heavy door, her shoulders sagging in relief.

Jeanette slept better than she had done for months. The heat was soporific. It drew some of the pain out of her.

The pace of the village matched her invalid rhythms. Dewi would come to call, and sit drinking tea for an hour at a time with her baby shawled against her chest while Jeanette rocked in her chair. Sometimes Jeanette would make a slow walk to the market with Connie, and sit on a stallholder's plastic stool while Connie tested the mangoes for ripeness.

Jeanette went with Dayu once or twice to the village temple with an offering, and came back with the symbolic grains of rice pressed to her temples. She said that for almost the first time since she had fallen ill, she didn't feel that the whole world was racing ahead and leaving her like a piece of broken machinery at the side of the road.

The wet weather persisted. One afternoon Connie looked into the bedroom while Jeanette was taking a rest. Bill had come from the opposite direction with the same intention.

He stood close behind Connie, looking over her shoulder as if they were a mother and father checking on a sleeping child. It was as if with the progression of the disease they had become Jeanette's parents, Connie thought. They fed her, and encouraged her with affectionate words, and watched over her. Only they weren't proudly watching her grow up. They were bringing her towards death.

She turned abruptly, almost collided with Bill. As always, her skin felt minutely sensitive to his nearness. They were only six inches apart.

Gently, he cupped her face in his hands. He kissed her forehead and then involuntarily they folded together, listening to one another's breathing and the steady drumming of the rain.

Connie wondered how it was that you could love one person so much, for so many years, and yet have so few shared memories. So little to sustain you. Except for those few months when neither of them had been able to stop themselves, everything between them—chains of days, months and years—had been made up of absence.

Bill traced the line of her cheekbones. The palms of his hands were warm. She thought how much she wanted to kiss him. She wanted it so badly that she felt dizzy, and she asked herself how desire could sprout so nakedly and unashamedly out of the desert of Jeanette's illness.

Tears gathered and ran out of the corners of her eyes. Bill trapped them with his thumbs and then touched his mouth to her wet skin.

'Don't cry,' he said. 'I can't bear it if you cry.'

Connie made a sound in her throat that wasn't a word or—not quite—a murmur of pure pain. She turned her head to escape his scrutiny, then pulled herself out of his arms.

'I'm going out,' she managed to say. 'I'm going for a walk.'

She pulled on a nylon jacket and ran into the rain.

Her intention had been to shut out all the thoughts of Bill, hurrying away from him yet again and closing up her mind as if she were preparing the defences against a tidal wave. But the wave smashed through the barriers and swept her away.

She was submerged in memories.

Bill and Connie saw each other at Christmases and birthdays, marking the milestones of the years. Without ever speaking of it, they had tacitly agreed never to hug each other like a brother- and sister-in-law, because they knew such an embrace would never be fraternal. They never even allowed their hands to touch.

Then came Noah's tenth birthday. There was a football party, with Bill acting as referee for twenty boys who ran up and down the garden. In the kitchen, Connie helped Hilda to lay out plates of sausages and bowls of crisps. At the end of the game the boys chased into the house.

These days Jeanette didn't enjoy parties or crowds, and she was white in the face with the strain of communicating with children who didn't understand her signs. Noah was boisterous and he pushed past his mother to get to the table. In doing so, he knocked a big bowl of sliced fruit off the counter and onto the tiled floor. Chunks of pineapple and chips of broken china flew up into the air. Jeanette swung round in mute, boiling anger. Up to her ankles in fruit and unable or unwilling to strike out at Noah, she raised her hand at Bill as if to hit him.

A flash of loathing passed between them.

Connie saw it. A terrible, wild excitement shot through her.

Bill caught his wife by the wrist and gently steered her away from the mess. Hilda dashed forwards with a cloth and a bucket and the boys cheered and began to stuff food into their mouths. A minute later Bill was telling knock-knock jokes and Jeanette was triumphantly bearing the birthday cake to Noah at the head of the table.

Connie sang 'Happy Birthday', then hurried away. All marriages go through dark patches, she told herself. In any case, whatever was happening between the two of them did not, *must not*, mean anything to her.

Then, a month later, she went to a party given by the advertising agency that was relocating to Docklands.

From across the room, through a sea of faces and dislocated talk, she saw Bill. She walked towards him, knowing that she should turn and run, because if she didn't it would be too late.

But that night, the will and the determination to keep on running finally deserted her.

Bill had been drinking, but he was clear in his mind. His marriage was a shaky edifice and the woman who came towards him was solid reality. She was light and warmth and food and water to him. To hold her at arm's length tonight would have been to ask his heart to stop beating.

They left the party. As soon as they had taken a single step out of the room, there was no going back. Every evasive action that they had both taken over the years now seemed to have been leading to this moment.

Instead of extricating herself and sending him home to Jeanette, Connie took Bill to her flat in Belsize Park.

All Bill's careful structures of duty and responsibility were burning down, and he let them blaze and then collapse into ashes.

They stumbled into the refuge of her flat, and the heat of passion melted and fused them.

He said, 'I want you. I can't sleepwalk through one more day.'

'I have been so lonely without you,' she whispered.

'I've been like a machine. But without you, everything's starting to break down and run out of power.'

He undressed her, there in the hallway. She pulled off his clothes, just as greedy as he was. Reckless, laughing, they scattered a trail of discarded shoes and shirts behind them.

There were no miracles, but Bill's presence in her bed, in her body, closed a circle. Connie felt for a brief few moments that she wasn't searching the landscape for signposts or trying to decipher a mysterious language. For the first time in her life she was at home, where she belonged, in a place that wasn't defined by time or history.

Afterwards she held him against her.

'Why tonight?' Connie whispered.

'Because I can't go on persuading myself that what's true is not. And you?'

'Truth and reality aren't necessarily compatible, are they? The truth, if I'm going to admit it, is that I fell in love with you the minute you walked into Echo Street on your first date with Jeanette. Before I even saw you. As soon as I heard your voice.'

He smiled. 'Look. You're blushing.' His finger touched her cheek.

'We're talking about truth, remember? It's often embarrassing. Reality is that you are Jeanette's husband. But tonight the truth is that I still love you and you are here with me. I don't care about tomorrow.'

His mouth moved over her face. 'And do you remember the wet night just before the wedding, when we kissed on the way to the tube?'

'Oh, yes.'

'That was a shock. You were supposed to be just a kid.'

'I was seventeen.'

'And then I took you out to find Constance Crescent, that empty street that didn't tell your story. You wanted so much to find where you came from, and I wanted to tell you that it mattered much less than where you were going. I don't know if it was then that I realised it, or if it came to me more gradually, but I was beginning to suspect that I might have married the wrong sister. I told myself that it was absurd, plain wrong. But I couldn't escape the conviction. It was there.

'It wasn't that I didn't love Jeanette, because I did. I do. And Noah. But how many variations of love are there? I kept seeing you and wanting to know you more. I was certain that if I could get close enough to you, if you would allow me to, then I would find—I don't know—*yes, I do*—the love of my life. I'm making this sound so narcissistic, I'm sorry. All I can do is try to tell you the truth. I know that your truth is likely to be different. Jeanette's will be totally other, God knows.'

Connie tried to interrupt, to tell him that she knew what he was trying to say and that it was the same for her, but he gently put his fingers to her mouth. She understood how much he needed to talk.

'You seemed opaque. But inside here'—he touched his fist to her forehead—'I knew you were as clear as spring water. It's a matter of contrasts. You see, Jeanette is the opposite of you. On the outside, she is translucent. Her pale skin. That smile. But I made the classic bloke's mistake of confusing looks with character. Jeanette's inside is your outside. It's dark. Of course she's angry; that's understood. It's her anger that gives her the will to shape her life the way she wants it. That's all right it's admirable. It's just the silence, Con. It's the *silence* I can't bear.'

He tightened his arms, as if she might try to escape from him. His face was hidden in her hair but she could hear the grief in his voice.

'Not the deafness. That's only external. I mean the real silence.'

'I know,' Connie said.

Echo Street had bred that deeper silence. It was rooted in the cultivation of appearances, the fear of exposure, the pin-neat, net-curtained, buttoned-lip and averted-glance rebuttal of the unwieldy and passionate world, as invented by Hilda and upheld by Jeanette.

After Tony died, those standards had gone so much against the grain for Connie that she had run away as soon as she was old enough.

'At Noah's birthday party. You saw what happened when he smashed the bowl.'

'Yes.'

'You or I would have yelled at him. But that's not what Jeanette does. Her only outlet is me. Everything is channelled through me.'

'It looked for a second as though you hated each other.'

'We do, sometimes. I don't want to be a lifeline, Connie. All I can be is a man.' There was a break in his voice that she had never heard before. She couldn't see Bill's face, but she was sure that he was close to tears.

In all the time she had known him, she had never felt that he needed her or that she could help him, instead of the other way round. The wash of tenderness that came with the recognition was as powerful as desire. She hadn't guessed that it was possible to love someone so much.

Connie walked back through the village, calculating that Jeanette would be awake by now.

She found Bill and Jeanette sitting in their accustomed places on the verandah. The low sun had emerged into a broad band of pistachio-green sky, and the margins of the banana palm leaves were glinting gold. Steam gently rose where the sun struck the thick-knit vegetation and the frogs were clearing their throats for a long night.

Jeanette pointed, beyond the greenery, over towards Wayan's house.

The upper storeys of the thirty-foot-high cremation tower constructed over the past weeks were shuddering and tipping sideways. Jeanette's hands flew to her mouth as the whole edifice threatened to topple over. There was an echo of shouting before it righted itself again.

'Don't worry,' Connie said. 'Now they are decorating the *wadah*, ready for tomorrow.'

As the dusk gathered, Wayan emerged from his house compound. Two bamboo poles, one tall and one short, were planted beside the entrance. From the shorter one hung a bird woven from bamboo and decorated with coloured feathers, and from the taller a coconut-oil lamp covered with a white cloth.

The bird was the watchman and the lamp was kept alight to guide his father's soul back to its home. It would burn until the cremation was over.

At midday Wayan unhooked the coconut-oil lamp from the pole at his gate. The lane was so packed with people he could hardly turn.

'The whole neighbourhood is here,' Connie said.

'It's like a huge party,' Bill said.

'That's just what it is. A send-off for the spirit.'

A big group of laughing young men pushed by. They wore long tunics with yellow sashes, and headcloths knotted round their foreheads.

Jeanette's eyes glittered as she watched.

In the middle of the lane towered the *wadah*. It was decorated now to the tip of the highest tier with a mass of coloured streamers, tinsel and branches and garlands of flowers, and on the back of it a grotesque painted mask bared its fangs over the heads of the crowd. The monster had huge paper wings on bamboo frames that flapped and creaked.

Bill pointed. 'Look!'

Out of the house compound came a group of relatives, carrying an object wrapped in white cloth. Hands grabbed it and hoisted it onto a shelf within the level of the tower that represented the world of men.

'That's not the body?' Bill muttered.

'An effigy. The real body's been buried in the ground all these months, so it's impure and can't be brought to the house. They'll have dug it up and it'll be waiting in the cemetery.'

The tower shook as two boys scrambled up it. They wedged themselves among the decorations and waved to the cheering crowd. There was a fresh burst of shouting and laughing and farther down the lane the throng parted. A pair of horns was all that was visible at first, but then a larger-than-life carving of a black bull appeared, standing tall on four splayed legs and borne on a platform of bamboo poles by yet more of the dead man's family and neighbours.

A loose procession began to form. At the head of the line, a young cousin lifted the coconut-oil lamp to guide the spirit to its destination. The bull came lurching and capering to the front. The rows of women in their gold and best brocades came next, balancing silver dishes heaped with rice cakes and fruit and flowers on their heads. Dayu and Dewi were carrying bamboo poles speared with carved pineapples and papayas.

A long white cloth was unfurled over everyone's heads. A mass of people rushed underneath it, reaching up to grab a handful of the cloth. Connie explained to Bill and Jeanette that the cloth was for everyone who couldn't carry the tower itself to share in bearing the dead man's remains to cremation. At the tail end of the procession, the strongest men were straining to lift the poles supporting the tower onto their shoulders.

The bull sarcophagus, the pyramids of multicoloured offerings, the cloth, the tower and the hubbub of supporters began the journey through the village. The procession moved slowly enough for Jeanette to keep pace without difficulty because the bull kept wheeling away from the route and making feints into the crowd. The bearers capered and spun in circles to confuse the spirit, so it would never be able to find its way back to the house and haunt the family.

Jeanette clapped. —*So remember, twice round the roundabout on the way to the cemetery for me*, she ordered Bill.

He caught her hand and kissed the knuckles.

As they came to the cemetery, they could see three more towers bobbing over the low roofs of the houses. Wayan's family procession merged with the other three funerals and hundreds of people surged towards the cremation ground.

Bill and Connie guided Jeanette away from the mob.

—*What happens now?*

Connie pointed.

In a quiet corner under the shade of a huge tree, the robed priests were waiting in a circle of musicians and dancers. The bull and the *wadah* were manoeuvred into place.

The musicians began to play. As the chains of notes swelled against an expectant hush, the people pressed round a pavilion hung with plain white draperies. The bull was carried into its shelter and set down, with a collective groan of relief from the bearers. At the side, on a low platform, a bundle wrapped in white cloths lay waiting.

The music grew louder and the whole crowd surged three times round the pavilion. Wooden cages were opened and chickens flapped and squawked to freedom, with dozens of pairs of hands waving them off in the auspicious direction.

There was a roar from the crowd. The hinged back was torn off the bull as the body was snatched up from its resting place. As it was manhandled to the sarcophagus, the cloths fell back to reveal a little heap of bones and hair and leather skin.

Bill put his arm out to shield Jeanette but she shook her head. She was watching intently.

The family piled the remains into the belly of the bull. More people tore the shrouded effigy from the shelf within the tower and crammed it in alongside the real bones. A jingling skeleton of human form made from pierced coins was thrown in on top. The priest poured holy water from an earthenware jar, then smashed the jar to fragments.

Now Wayan and Kadek and the other men packed kindling and logs into the space that was left and the two boys reluctantly jumped from their perch in the *wadah*.

The stench of kerosene was momentarily overpowering.

Wayan stepped forward with a blazing torch. Flames leapt in a sheet and tore a long *aaaaah* from the throats of the crowd. The *wadah* was torched, causing the monster's paper and bamboo wings to arch and swoop just once as the heat rose, as if the creature would take flight from the fire. Flames licked from the snakes and serpents twining at the base and up towards the pagoda roofs of heaven.

Connie and Bill and Jeanette sank down, huddled together against the trunk of a tree, mesmerised by the blaze and showers of sparks that shot over the treetops. The other pyres were blazing too and the cremation ground became a nether world of drifting smoke, gyrating dancers and milling soot-blackened faces split into white smiles of elation.

The priest shouted mantras at the sky. Processions of women laid their offerings in the flames as the bull, the tower and the bones were gradually consumed. It took a long time for everything to be burned.

Jeanette's eyes followed the smoke up into the sky. —*Just bones. Dry bones on the blaze and the spirit set free. I like that.*

'So do I,' Bill murmured.

The smouldering ashes were finally doused with jars of water, and children raked through them with sticks to collect the coins. The families had been kneeling on the grass to pray, but now they brought urns and scooped up the ashes. Carrying the filled urns between them they began to leave in slow groups, walking through the twilight. Bill and Connie and Jeanette followed them back into the lane.

Wayan's immediate family climbed into a line of waiting cars.

—*Where are they going?* Jeanette asked.

Connie said, 'They are taking the ashes down to the sea. They'll wade with them into the water, and then the tide will carry them away. The body has been reduced to its five elements, earth, water, fire, air and space, and the spirit has started on its journey. It's over.'

Jeanette surprised them with her smile. —*The sea, you said? I'd like to go and see the sea, before we leave.*

'I know a place,' Connie answered. 'We can go there. It's on the way to the airport.'

In two days' time, Bill and Jeanette would be flying back to London.

Connie made a picnic, and the airport taxi driver took them down a winding road that turned away from the high-rise hotels and cheap shopping malls that blighted most of the coastal strip.

The beach was a thumbnail curve of silver-grey sand overhung by coconut palms, and the midday sea was a sheet of sapphire scalloped with foam where the tiny waves tipped over into the sand.

They paddled along the water's edge, but after only a hundred yards Jeanette was tired.

Bill spread out a blanket in the shade of the nearest clump of trees and Jeanette lay down, propping her head on one hand. A jet crossed in front of them, on a direct line to the airport.

—*Will we really be in England tomorrow? I don't want to leave this place.*

Bill and Connie glanced at each other. They were expert collaborators now in giving Jeanette whatever she wanted.

'You don't have to. You could stay,' Connie said at once.

Jeanette shook her head. —*It's time to go home. I miss Noah.*

She stretched out her arms and sifted warm sand through her fingers. She had given up pretending to eat, but Connie and Bill peeled fruit and drank white wine out of the cool-box.

As Connie watched her, she wished with all her heart that it were possible to step out of the past, and the deep parallel grooves the three of them had worn, separately and in their pairs.

Connie and Jeanette, Bill and Jeanette, Bill and Connie.

She knelt down in the sand, and took her sister in her arms. Jeanette let her head rest on her shoulder. 'I love you,' Connie said.

She had to strain to catch the blurred syllables of the answer.

—*Do you? I haven't always been loveable.*

'I love you now. And I always will.'

—*I love you too.* Her breath was warm on Connie's cheek.

Bill lay down on the other side of Jeanette. He folded himself against her spine, knees pressed into the crook of her knees. As they would have lain for a lifetime of nights, Connie thought. They cradled Jeanette between them. Connie felt the ancient scabs of jealousy as if they were peeling off her skin and drifting like the flakes of soot.

'I'm sorry,' she breathed.

—*I am sorry, too. But I am so happy that the three of us are here.*

Bill looked up into the clear sky. It was harder to speak than he could have imagined, and he was the one who had long ago railed to Connie about the damage of silence.

He wanted to tell Jeanette that he loved her, and honoured her, but there would be enough time and privacy for that. He wished he could have told Connie out loud that he held her in his heart, then and now and always, but he believed she knew it without his words.

Through the band of colourless, shimmering air between blue sky and sea, another plane roared towards Denpasar. The airport was waiting, already full of people.

Jeanette watched the diminishing arrow of the plane.

—*I want to go home to Noah, but it's hard to leave Bali. I'm not ready to die. But I'm ready to consider the prospect.*

Bill reached for Connie's hand, found it, and drew it across Jeanette's shoulder. They held her more tightly between them and Jeanette smiled.

—*I smashed a table, you know*, she said.

'How did you do that?' Connie asked.

—After I came home from the hospital. After the operation when they couldn't do what they planned. I saw the glass coffee table we used to have. Smooth and whole. And I couldn't see why a table should be like that, and not me. I smashed it to pieces. Pounded it with a paperweight.

'I never liked that table,' Bill said.

—You were shocked.

'Yes, that's true. It was so unlike you.'

—Dying was unlike me.

Not is, Connie noted. She was finding it hard to keep back her tears.

'Did smashing it make you feel better?' she asked.

—No. Not at all. I was shocked at myself. But you know what? Bali has helped me. Your green wave, that was beautiful. The smell in the village of earth, rain, incense. The bodies burning, the party. It was apt. Just life and death. It made me think of Mum and Dad. Us three. Even Noah, some day. Only bones. And then the spirit set free. Maybe. You never know.

Her face split suddenly into a pumpkin-lantern smile.

—You could say, Bali has helped me see the bigger picture.

'That's the best recommendation for the island I've ever heard,' Connie replied.

Jeanette yawned. *—Have I got long enough for a nap?* she asked.

Connie looked at her watch. 'Maybe half an hour?'

They released her and she curled up on her side, sighing with satisfaction as she pillowed her cheek on her folded hands.

Bill shook himself and sat up. 'I'm going to have a swim,' he said.

Jeanette seemed already to be dozing.

'I'll come with you,' Connie said.

They walked down to the water's edge and waded in. Bill stared out to sea. Abruptly he said, 'Has Jeanette ever talked to you about afterwards? About what is supposed to happen when she's gone?'

Connie kept her eyes fixed on the horizon. 'Only at the beginning, the first day I came down to Surrey. She told me then that she loves you and you love her, and I agreed that there's never been any doubt of that.'

'Did you?'

'It's true, isn't it?' Connie heard herself say. 'And I've been able to share the weeks since then with the two of you. I've been included in her dying, even though the three of us made it impossible to share life. And I am grateful for it,' she truthfully concluded.

'Yes,' Bill agreed. 'I understand.'

He stripped off his shirt and threw it onto the sand, then dived under the water. Connie stood and watched him swimming powerfully out to sea as if he would go on and on, and never turn back again.

The telephone used to ring in the flat in Belsize Park and she would hear Bill's low voice.

'I could see you for an hour, this evening.'

And without a thought even taking shape in her head she would answer, 'Yes.'

From their first evening together after the Docklands party, they both knew that there was no hope of a happy ending. It was even true that to be stalked by the twin threats of imminent discovery and impending pain gave an extra edge to their temporary ecstasy.

Most of the time they spent together, in the fourteen months before the end came, was snatched in brief hours after work when Bill could plausibly have been with clients. They retreated to Connie's apartment and set about constructing a miniature universe together.

'I know this isn't real,' she said once, sadly. 'We long for each other so much, and every meeting is like drinking champagne. We never see each other on irritable weekday mornings, or when one of us has flu.'

'It's real to me. The bench mark of reality isn't necessarily sharing the breakfast cornflakes.'

'What would it be like, if we were married?'

As soon as she asked, she wished she had resisted the temptation.

But Bill didn't hesitate. 'It would be wonderful. To be together every day, to see you in the instant before I fall asleep and as soon as I open my eyes. But I can't leave Jeanette and Noah, you know. I won't ever do that.'

'Have I ever asked you to? Even hinted at it?'

'No, you haven't,' he said humbly. 'What we have now isn't enough for either of us, but it's all there can be. Will you forgive me?'

'No. Because there's nothing to forgive. We made this choice together. And it's good.' Her voice cracked.

'It's not good. It's all wrong, but I love you so, so much.'

A handful of times, when Bill was legitimately away on business, they managed to spend a night together. The few hours that followed contained the essence of happiness.

And while the affair continued, for the first time in her life Connie stopped probing at the riddle of her identity. She defined herself simply as a woman in love and all her being was concentrated in the present.

Just once, they spent three days in Rome.

Bill crammed three days of meetings with an Italian client into a single day. For the rest of the time they walked the streets, drank coffee in tiny bars, and sat in the shadows of baroque churches.

Then, very suddenly, the end came.

Connie and Bill had flown back from Rome, and they were standing at the carousel at Heathrow waiting for their bags. Two whole days and nights with Bill had lulled Connie into a wifely rhythm. She linked her arm through his as streams of luggage circulated on the belt, then stretched up to kiss the corner of his mouth.

An instant afterwards they turned their heads.

The moment froze into horror for ever afterwards.

Cousin Elaine—who was returning with her best friend from a fort-night in Tenerife—was staring at them across the mounds of suitcases.

It was immediately clear to all three of them that a bomb had silently exploded in baggage reclaim and that the fallout was going to affect every corner of their lives.

Within twenty-four hours Elaine had told Jeanette what she had seen.

Jeanette made an unprecedented journey to Belsize Park. She marched into the flat with her coat pulled round her body, and told her adopted sister that she was a despicable adulterer, ungrateful, a liar and a cheat, and not worthy of having been taken out of council care and welcomed into the Thorne family.

Connie stood and silently took it all. In the grip of hurt and fury, Jeanette looked like an avenging angel in a Renaissance painting. With a kind of bleak detachment, Connie had to admire her magnificent passion.

—*You are not my sister. You never were*, Jeanette said.

Connie didn't point out that the biological bare fact was hardly news to her. And if Jeanette now chose to sever the remaining connection, with all its patina of Echo Street, then Connie couldn't really blame her.

—*You will not see my husband again.*

Connie couldn't disagree with that either.

—*I don't want to see you ever again.*

Connie tipped her head in silent acknowledgement. Jeanette wrapped her coat even more tightly round her and swept out of the flat.

After she had gone, Connie stood behind her front door and listened to the silence. She had never felt as lonely as she did then.

Jeanette and Hilda formed an alliance of two. Bill was to be forgiven, eventually, once he had endured enough reproach. But Connie was never to be properly rehabilitated. She tried to forget Bill by immersing herself in work, by travelling far from London, by constructing all the appearances of a happy and productive life.

Over the years, the absolute exclusion from the family softened to the point where she was invited to set-piece events like Jeanette's fortieth birthday and Noah's eighteenth. She knew that this probably had more to do with her being with Seb Bourret, who was glamorous and quite famous, than with Jeanette's or Hilda's reviving affection for herself.

Then Hilda died, and there was one more terrible argument on the day Connie saw the contents of the old cardboard box.

She and Jeanette did not speak again until Jeanette knew that she was going to die.

Connie waded through the water, the soaked hem of her skirt clinging to her legs. At last she saw the dot that was Bill's head dip as he swam in a circle and headed back to the beach.

She waved her arm over her head and pointed to her watch.

Jeanette was lying on her side, but her eyes were open.

'Did you sleep?' Connie asked.

—*No. I just wanted to lie here.*

Connie helped her to sit up, then put her wrap round her shoulders.

Bill sprinted up the beach, and dragged on his trousers.

'Let's get going.' He took Jeanette's hand to lead her.

Connie picked up the folded blanket and the picnic box and they began the slow walk back. Their taxi was parked in the shade of some scrubby bushes, with all four doors open to catch a breeze.

The driver had been asleep on the back seat, but he leapt up as soon as they approached. '*Lapangan terbang.* Airport, quick, quick,' he said, beaming, and they settled Jeanette into her seat.

They had spent longer at the beach than they intended, and the check-in queue had shortened to a handful of people. Connie could see from the sign that the Singapore flight was already boarding. Jeanette stood with her hand tucked under Connie's and her slight weight resting against Connie's arm while Bill checked them in.

—*I wish you were coming home.*

'I'll be there soon,' Connie said with an easiness she didn't feel. She had deliberately chosen not to return with Bill and Jeanette because she thought it would be right for them and Noah to have a few days alone together, without having to work out whether she should be with them.

'We'd better go through,' Bill said.

At the barrier Jeanette turned and held up her arms, like a child.

Connie kissed her, and closed her arms round her sister's shoulders. There was almost nothing left of Jeanette's once luscious body.

—*Thank you. It was wonderful*, Jeanette signed.

'It was,' Connie agreed.

Bill and Connie exchanged the briefest hug. Bill and Jeanette held hands, and walked through the barrier. They turned back just once to wave before they passed out of sight.

Chapter Nine

NOAH WAS DRIVING home from Surrey. He stared at the lines of rush-hour traffic but he couldn't get his mother's changed face out of his mind. In the two weeks since he had last seen her, she had faded and shrunk. Her skin was like stretched tissue paper over knobs of bone. Instead of firing questions at him and demanding to be told the latest details of his life, she had been content to sit quietly and hold his hand.

'Mum? Tell me all about Bali. What was it like?'

She smiled. —*Beautiful*.

'Do you feel rested?'

—*Yes*, she agreed, but he knew that she said it only to please him.

'OK,' Noah murmured. He squeezed her brittle fingers.

—*How is Roxana?*

'She's fine. Still working for Auntie Connie's friend, in the film business.'

Jeanette hadn't asked any more, whereas once she would have wanted to know all about it.

Noah blinked. He couldn't see properly to drive. It was stupid; he had known for months that she was going to die. But it was not until this minute that he properly understood what dying was going to mean.

He pulled over and called Roxana on her mobile.

'Where are you, Rox?'

'Still at work. How is your mother?'

'She's very weak. Not seeing her for two weeks has made me realise how fast she's going.'

'That's bad, Noah. I'm really sorry.'

'What are you doing? I want to see you.' He needed very much to hold her and let some of her life and strength seep into him.

'I was going back to the apartment. But I'll meet you for a drink.'

He smiled, fastening on to the prospect. 'I'll be there in an hour.'

They went to a pub they both liked and had several drinks. Roxana listened to him talk about his mother, but didn't try to offer too much sympathy. She just accepted what was happening, in just the right way. Noah knew that he loved her, and as he looked at the angle of her thigh he was even more strongly aware of how much he wanted her.

He shifted in his chair. His mother's hold on life was loosening, and his response was to feel an overwhelming need for sex? Was that shocking, or was it the normal, selfish response of those who were still healthy?

'Roxana?'

'Yes, Noah?' Her mouth curved. She knew what he was thinking.

The lift doors parted and Noah and Roxana stepped out into the lobby. Roxana took the keys from her bag, and singled out the heavy Chubb. She turned it to the left, expecting the familiar resistance and then a click, but the key refused to turn at all. The door was already unlocked.

When she went to work she must have forgotten to secure the Chubb.

She fitted the Yale without difficulty and the door opened. She turned on the lights and the white walls were flooded with brightness.

Roxana knew that she hadn't forgotten to lock up properly—that was just the explanation she allowed herself to reach for—but at first glance everything seemed as it always did. Relieved, she took a few steps forward into the big room. Noah turned towards the bathroom and she continued down the corridor towards Connie's music room and bedroom.

And then she saw the open doors.

The tidy work area had been turned upside-down. The computer and the keyboard had gone. Filing cabinets and drawers stood open and the floor was a drift of music manuscripts and strewn debris.

A tide of horror swept through Roxana. She wanted to run and bury her head, but she made herself walk on into Connie's bedroom.

Every drawer and cupboard stood open. Clothing, photographs and emptied boxes had been flung everywhere. She pressed the heels of her hands into her eyes, then looked again. The devastation was still there.

She walked back to the big room, although her legs were shaking. Noah was standing by the window.

'What?' he demanded as soon as he saw her face. 'What's happened?'

'A bad thing.' In her anguish, language escaped her. She couldn't remember the English words for burglar or break-in.

In her room, the mess was the same as in Connie's but Roxana had nothing worth stealing. Her savings were in the bank, thanks to Connie. Even her beach postcard was still on the wall beside her bed.

Noah was at her shoulder. 'Shit,' he breathed. 'You've been burgled.'

Cold shock waves were breaking over Roxana.

'It is my fault, it is my fault,' she kept repeating.

Noah put his hands on her arms. 'How did they get in?'

Roxana could see it all. She was standing over there by the kitchen counter, where she had tried to kick Philip in the balls. The evening's silly golden glow of champagne and sumptuous food had already faded into the dull reality of stale old bargains and men wanting sex from her. Philip had muttered that he would use the bathroom before Roxana threw them out, and she had let him go.

While Cesare had soft-soaped her with apologies, Philip must have crept down the corridor and gone swiftly through Connie's belongings. And somewhere in a drawer he must have discovered a set of keys.

'How did they get in?' Noah asked again. 'The front door was locked, wasn't it?'

'Yes,' Roxana said miserably. 'I mean, no. I'm sure the men did it.'

'*What* men?'

'I asked them up here.' She could have tried to lie, but honesty seemed the last thing she had to offer. 'Mr Cesare Antonelli,' she whispered.

Disjointedly, as Noah stared at her, Roxana told him about the evening.

'Nothing happened, Noah. I know I was foolish. I was thinking about movies, about maybe being a model. They said I could be.'

'I thought you were pretty streetwise, Rox, and you brought them up here, to Auntie Con's place? What were you thinking?'

'Nothing. I got rid of them. But I let one of them go to the bathroom.'

Noah let out a long sigh.

'Noah, I am so sorry. I . . . wanted to seem like a London girl. I let them think that this was my place. I wanted to be like your Auntie Con.'

'Well, you aren't.' His voice sounded hard. 'Right. Let's think. We've got to start by calling the police. You'll have to tell them everything.'

Roxana sank down onto a chair. She was afraid of the police. At home, they were not the people you looked to for any help.

'And then we'll have to telephone Auntie Con. We'll have to deal with everything. I don't want to tell my parents. I don't want Dad to have to think about anything except Mum.'

Noah took out his mobile, frowned at it, then tapped out 999.

Bill stood at his kitchen window and watched the sun rise. The branches of the beech trees formed a dark lattice against the dishwater sky, but then a shaft of light suddenly caught them and they glimmered with rainwater. He was holding a mug of tea; when he looked down it was with surprise because he couldn't remember how it had got there.

He listened, straining his ears. The house was silent, and the silence had a massive quality as if the pressure it exerted on the doors and windows might cause them to fly open.

Upstairs, Jeanette lay, seeming to sleep, in the bed where he had finally left her.

The gorge was a ripple of leaves, and from her chair on the verandah Connie could hear the rustle as a quick breeze sprang up.

In the house the telephone began to ring.

She put down her book and padded inside to answer it.

'Connie.' His voice with a break in it.

'I'm here.'

'Jeanette died about three hours ago.'

The words entered her head and she put them together.

'Oh, my darling.'

It wasn't clear to her whether she meant Bill or her sister.

'I've been upstairs with her. I lay there and held her for an hour or so. I didn't want to leave her all alone, Con, but she's dead, you know?

'Last night she was restless and she couldn't find any way to lie that didn't hurt her poor bones. I brought up all the pillows in the house and put them underneath her to make the bed softer. I held her hands, and she smiled at me and signed *good night*.

'Then in the middle of the night I knew she was dying.'

'I wish I had been there.'

Bill said, 'I think she would have preferred it this way. It's as if she left you straight from Bali. She wanted it to come, you know. She probably willed it. That will of hers was still strong, even at the end.'

'Yes.'

'I've got to go now, Connie.'

'Is Noah with you?'

'It's still early. I thought I'd let him finish his night's sleep.'

'I don't want you to be on your own.'

'I'll call him now. Jeanette's nurse will be here in an hour.'

'All right. I'll be there as soon as I can.'

After Bill had said goodbye, Connie went to sit down at her keyboard.

An unexpected phrase of music was running in her head and she picked out the sequence of notes, then repeated them. She frowned in the effort to harness her imagination to a lyrical line. The fingers of her left hand spanned the keys as she reached with her right for a sheet of manuscript paper and scribbled *For Jeanette*.

When the telephone rang beside her she thought it was Bill again.

'I'm here.'

'Connie, this is Roxana. I am calling from London on your telephone, I am very sorry, but my mobile will not—'

'That's all right, Roxana. What's the matter?'

'I have bad news to tell you and Noah said for me to call you at once about it. He has gone home now to his father because, you know . . .'

'Yes,' Connie said gently. 'Just tell me what has happened, please.'

Roxana's fractured English was eloquent of her distress. 'We are broken into, things gone, beautiful things belonging to you and all because I am stupid and I believe what a man says to me when all my life I am knowing better than to think such words are true. You have been so kind to me and I have paid you like this, Connie. I don't ask that you forgive me but I will pay back everything over some time, I promise—'

'Roxana, stop talking. The flat has been burgled, is that right?'

'Yes. I'm trying now to find out all what has gone because the police are here making questions and I don't know—'

'Listen. If the police are there I'll speak to them in a moment. Just tell me how the burglars got into the flat.'

'It was because of me, and I am so sorry for it.'

'How is that?'

Roxana said she had met some men and she had been a fool to trust them, and she had let them into the apartment and this had happened.

'I see,' Connie sighed. 'What have they taken?'

'Your music machines and the computer. And some jewellery.' From the strangled sound of her voice, Roxana was now in tears.

'Oh dear.' Connie couldn't work out what the extent of the damage might be. Nor, at this moment, did she care very much. 'All right,' she said as calmly as she could. 'Let me talk to the police now.'

She discussed with the officer the probability that the thieves had found a spare set of keys in her bureau drawer, and had chosen a convenient time to let themselves in and go through her possessions.

'I understand from your young lady lodger here that she met one of the men through her place of work.'

'Did she? The lap-dancing club?'

'That she didn't mention. No, in her statement she said it was . . .' There was a pause while he consulted his notes. 'Oyster Films.'

Connie put her hand to her head and pinched the bridge of her nose between her fingers. She felt rather as if she were in a novel with a very convoluted plot that wasn't holding her attention.

The policeman advised her to put a stop on all her cards and to change her PIN numbers and passwords immediately.

Connie thanked him, and asked him to put Roxana on again.

'You see, Connie? It is very bad.'

'It's not very good, but we'll deal with it. The first thing to do is get an emergency locksmith to change the locks. Ask the police to help you. I do not want you to trouble Noah or Mr Bunting with any of this.'

'You do not have to tell me such a thing,' Roxana shot back. 'I also have had my family dead. Do you think I do not know what this feels like?'

'Of course you do. I'm sorry.'

'Please. I will make the locks good.'

'Thank you. I'll be home in a day or so, I don't know exactly when. You'll have to be there to let me in.'

'Of course. I dread to see you, Connie, but I will be glad as well.'

Connie smiled, in spite of everything. 'Listen. Whatever the burglars have taken, it's only things. Just stuff. A computer, a few rings and necklaces. No one can break in and steal from us what really matters.'

'I hope so,' Roxana said bleakly. 'And I am very sorry indeed that you have lost your sister.'

Connie booked and paid for a ticket to London. After making sure she had enough cash in dollars to see her home, she made a series of calls to cancel her cards, as the policeman had advised. She found that it was helpful to concentrate on these practical matters. The pressure of grief was steadily gathering inside her skull.

At length, she decided there was nothing more she could do until she reached London again. In Bali it was coming up to midnight.

In her bedroom, the bed was neatly made under its white cover. She sat down where Jeanette had slept, and gently touched the pillow.

Beside the bed stood a wooden cabinet, locally made, with a single drawer. Connie slid the drawer out, unhooked a latch and lifted it out of the way. At the back of the recess was a hidden compartment.

The only item in the secret place was a small box.

She opened the box with a practised twist of her fingers, and tipped the marcasite earring with an old-fashioned screw fastening into the palm of her hand. It glinted in the light of her bedside lamp.

The burglars hadn't got her earring. It was always with her, her talisman. She closed her fist on it now, and began to cry for Jeanette.

In the fourteen months of their love affair, Connie and Bill spent a total of perhaps three hundred hours together.

It was such a brief interval within the drawn-out stretch of the rest of her life that Connie was surprised, once it was all over, by the abject loneliness that descended on her. She ached for Bill, even to hear the sound of his voice, but she didn't see or speak to him.

There was an instinct for survival buried deep in her.

She had work to do, and plenty of friends who were loosely connected with work. She won an industry award, and more commissions came in as a result. Money accumulated in blocks and wedges, but it seemed to hem her in rather than offer greater freedom. As an antidote she began to travel, to India and the Far East and South America, alone or with friends. She visited temples and archaeological sites, made notes and searched for inspiration and wrote music, and all the time she felt as if she was drifting without an anchor.

Once, drinking Thai beer beside the slow brown river in Bangkok and watching the crowds flooding onto an upriver ferry, she realised with a jolt that in this distant place she was searching the faces for any features that bore a resemblance to her own.

Her companion was a dry Australian woman whom she had met on a plane a few days earlier.

'What's up?' the woman asked.

'I don't think I know what I'm doing here,' Connie responded.

The woman raised her eyebrows. 'What you're doing here is what you're doing, having a beer with me and wondering about heading north. What else is there? What do you want to know?'

'All right. I want to know who I am.'

Connie had told her a little about her history. It was easy to confide in a stranger.

'Why don't you try to find out, if it's biting you so hard?'

Connie smiled at the oversimplification of this. But once she was back in England she extracted her birth certificate from a file of papers and studied the shreds of information it contained.

On or about 19 June 1963. Found in garden at 14 Constance Crescent, London E8.

She prickled with renewed desire to trace her real mother. If she only knew her mother's story, however sad it might be, she could then continue her own, like adding chapters to a novel. It was having no beginning, Connie thought, that made it hard to develop a coherent narrative.

She made an appointment, and went back to discuss the circumstances of her adoption with a different social worker. Mrs Palmer had retired. She learned that the social-work file that she had not been allowed even to see would have been kept in a safe place for twenty-five years after her birth, but now it had been removed and destroyed.

'It's a shame, that,' sighed the young woman who interviewed her. 'It's quite a small window, really, for people to apply for the facts. Can't you ask your adoptive mother about the details?'

'No,' Connie said.

She refused to be disheartened. She wrote an advertisement giving the date of her birth and the circumstances of her discovery, asking for anyone who might know any more to contact her, and placed it in a series of newspapers and magazines.

The only response came from a journalist.

Connie agreed to be interviewed for an article, which appeared in the colour supplement of a mass-circulation paper alongside a full-page colour picture of herself looking wistfully out of the window of the Belsize Park flat. The introduction read, 'Connie Thorne is a successful musician and composer. But there is a hollow at the centre of her life.'

The article produced no response except a sharp note from Jeanette to say that its appearance had really upset Hilda, and did Connie never think about the consequences of her actions?

After the interview, the journalist asked Connie if she had searched the national newspaper archive for any press coverage following her rescue. It was quite likely that there would have been several local news items about Baby Constance.

A few days later at a desk in a utilitarian library reading room in a North London suburb, Connie opened up a bound volume of the *Hackney Gazette* for June 1963.

She found herself staring in amazement at a picture of herself as a two-day-old baby. She was loosely swaddled in a blanket, and her tiny, crunched-up face looked surprisingly serene.

> Baby Constance is being cared for by nurses at the Royal London Hospital, who have named her after the street in East London where she was discovered. One-day-old Constance was tucked inside a shopping bag that had been left under a hedge. Police and medical staff are anxious to trace the baby's mother, who may be in need of medical treatment.

Connie studied the picture. A hedge and a shopping bag, she thought. They were antecedents of a kind. Better than knowing nothing at all.

Hunched over the newspaper volumes in the dry library atmosphere, greedily absorbing the smallest details of her history, Connie read the *Gazette*'s interview with a girl named Kathleen Merriwether:

> 'My boyfriend Mike thought it was a cat,' Kathleen reported, 'but I knew straight away it was a baby . . .'

The name jumped out at Connie from the grey mass of newsprint.

Kathleen Merriwether had found her, surely only a matter of minutes or a bare hour since her mother crept along the hedge like a shadow and left her there. If she could find Kathleen, maybe she could cajole her into remembering some tiny detail that would bring her mother closer. Perhaps even close enough to reach.

In her desire not to think about losing Bill, the search began to obsess Connie. How, she wondered, did you go about tracing someone when all you had was their maiden name and their age? She thought of birth records, but that wouldn't give much of a clue to Kathleen's present whereabouts, and of electoral rolls, but that might well mean searching the whole country for someone who in all probability would now be known by her husband's name.

Connie decided she might as well begin close to home. She took down the London telephone directory and counted the listed Merriwethers. There were only a handful with that spelling.

The first four calls led nowhere. Two were picked up by machines and Connie immediately hung up. Another call was answered by an au pair with small children clamouring in the background, who advised her in a strong Spanish accent to call back when Mrs Merriwether was at home. A very old man in response to the fourth call said that he had no relatives by the name of Kathleen, but told her a long anecdote anyway about his daughter, who was now living in Western Australia.

A woman answered the fifth call. Connie's speech was well rehearsed by this time. 'Good evening, I'm sorry to trouble you, I'm trying to contact a Kathleen Merriwether.'

'This is Kathy Merriwether,' the voice said. 'How can I help you?'

Surprise almost took her breath away. It took her a moment before she could say, 'My name is Constance Thorne.'

'It's Baby Constance, isn't it?' the woman replied at once. 'You know, I've always wondered if I'd hear from you.'

To have found her so easily was such a stroke of good luck that it seemed almost inevitable to learn that Kathy Merriwether lived in Kentish Town, only two miles from Connie's flat.

It was a warm spring evening when Connie walked up the street. Kathy's house had stone steps leading up to the front door, net-curtained bay windows, and three doorbells mounted one above the other.

Connie rang the one marked Merriwether, and as she waited she heard the whistling rush and then the buried *thud-thud* of a fast train in a deep cutting. Echo Street might have been just round the next corner.

The woman who opened the door was in her late forties. She was broad, with heavy shoulders and pretty plump arms exposed by a pale-blue T-shirt. She was wearing loose trousers and house slippers.

'So you are Constance.' She smiled. 'Baby Constance, after all this time.'

Connie held out the flowers she had brought. Everything was as she'd expected, yet she felt awkward, and dull with the sudden certainty that this meeting wasn't going to deliver any of the clues she had longed for.

Kathy accepted the flowers and sniffed them appreciatively. 'How lovely. You didn't have to do that.' She shook Connie's hand. 'Come on up. It's the top floor, I'm afraid.'

Kathy puffed slightly as they climbed the steep stairs.

'Dear me. Here we are, then. Make yourself at home.'

The sitting room was over-full with a squashy sofa and a pair of arm-chairs. China ornaments were lined up on the wooden mantelpiece over a gas log fire. Connie sat down in one of the armchairs while Kathy clattered in the kitchen, coming back first of all with the flowers arranged in a jug, which she placed on the coffee table, then with a tray. She poured tea into cups patterned with rosebuds and handed one to Connie.

The window looked down into a garden that sloped to a high wall. Connie had just registered that beyond this was the railway cutting when another train whistled through. Vibrations set the window glass rattling.

'You get so used to them you don't even hear them go by,' Kathy said.

'I know. The house I grew up in was the same.'

Kathy smiled. 'Was it? Where was that?'

'Echo Street, East London.'

'East London? You know, I've thought about you so often over the years. I wondered how life had turned out for you.' She glanced at Connie's shoes and the soft leather bag in which she carried her papers. 'It turned out all right, by the look of it. That's good. Now. What can I tell you?'

Connie hesitated. Now that the moment had come, the only question that properly formed itself in her mind was, *Who am I?*

She tried to put it neutrally. 'What happened when you found me?'

'Well. I was sixteen, and out with my boyfriend. I was supposed to be back home by ten o'clock at the very latest. My dad was quite strict.'

Kathy told her about the empty street, the way the arched plane trees made a dark tunnel of the pavement. In her mind's eye, Connie saw Constance Crescent as it had been on the day she went there with Bill.

'We were behind a hedge in one of the gardens. Mike was trying it on, and maybe I was leading him on a bit. Then I heard a cry. It was a baby, I knew that straight away.'

'What did you do?'

'It was there, under the hedge. I picked it up. Brown plastic shopping bag, with handles. And you were inside.'

'Was there anyone else there? Could someone have been watching?'

'I don't think so,' Kathy said. 'There wasn't so much as a shadow moving anywhere.'

'Perhaps . . .' Connie said, 'perhaps she hid nearby, to make sure someone . . . found me?'

'Perhaps,' Kathy said doubtfully, then continued the story. 'Mike went to the house next door and rang the bell, and the woman who lived there ran out in her dressing gown. We took you inside and the woman's husband rang for the police and ambulance. While we waited, I held you inside my cardigan. Trying to keep you warm against my skin.'

Kathy's voice caught a little. Connie kept her eyes on the patch of sky outside the window.

'And there was the earring.'

'What? What's that?'

'It was a single earring, I can see it now, fastened to the blanket you were wrapped in. One little glittering droplet. The mother, *your* mother, must have kept the other one. A keepsake, one for each of you. Maybe it was all she had to leave. I thought it was the saddest thing I had ever seen. It still makes me cry, thinking of it.'

Kathy reached into the pocket of her loose trousers and extricated a tissue. Connie kept on looking at the sky.

Kathy blew her nose. 'What could have happened to that poor girl? What circumstances was she in, that made her abandon you?'

'I don't know,' Connie managed to say. 'I'd like to find out.'

Longingly, she thought, If only I had even that much of her. Just the keepsake she left me.

It wasn't until after Hilda's death that she learned that her trophy had been there all along, hidden in the attic at Echo Street.

'Of course you would. That's only natural,' Kathy was saying. 'At the hospital they gave you my name. Babies have to have names. Constance, Merriwether, that's who you were.'

Connie looked at her again. Constance *Merriwether*. There was a bond between her and Kathy after all.

'I didn't know that,' she said. 'I never saw the adoption papers.'

'Tell me about the family who adopted you.'

Connie told her about the Thornes.

'So it was a successful adoption?' the other woman asked.

'Yes, I think so,' was all Connie would say.

'And now? What do you do now?'

Connie told her, briefly. Kathy clapped her hands in delight.

'Really? You wrote that? *Boom, boom, baboom ba ba, bababa ba.*'

'What do you do, Kathy?'

'Well. I went into nursing. Because of you, you could say. That night changed things for me.' Kathy's broad face turned solemn. 'Up until then, I was a silly girl. You know . . . boyfriend, clothes, trying not to let my dad find out the half of what I got up to. Then I saw you, dressed in nothing but a little cardigan and a bit of a towel, and left in a bag under a hedge. Once I'd held you, I knew I'd never forget you. I was playing about with Mike—and this was before the pill, remember—and I realised all of a sudden that what all that would inevitably lead to was you—not *you*, of course, but a baby who was a scrap of humanity, full of the potential to be someone and to love and be loved, not just me getting pregnant and having to leave school. It was a big, serious world. I looked at poor Mike a bit differently after that, I can tell you.'

'I can imagine,' Connie said. She was gazing at Kathy's plump, pretty arms that had once held her.

'In the hospital when I visited you, the nurses talked to me about their work. I was impressed because it seemed really important and valuable. My mum and dad were quite pleased when I decided to go for nursing training. I finished with Mike and they didn't mind that, either.'

'Did you marry someone else in the end?' Connie asked. There were no rings on Kathy's fingers.

'I did. It lasted ten years. I was a staff nurse on a paediatric ward, doing a lot of night shifts. What happened was just about what you'd expect.'

'Children?'

'No. I've looked after plenty, though. You were the first, and there must have been hundreds since then. I'm a health visitor now.' She drained her teacup. 'Are you married, Constance?'

'No,' Connie said.

Kathy didn't miss much. 'I see,' she said gently. 'And are you in love?'

'No. Yes. Or I was.'

'Do you want to tell me any more?'

Connie lifted her head. She found that she did want to talk to Kathy Merriwether. She liked her for her warmth and matter-of-factness.

'There's not much to tell. Not now, because it's over. A married man. It's painful, but I've been lucky in many other ways. That's what my life feels like. Luck. A lottery.'

'And you'd rather have facts and tidy explanations?'

Connie thought for a moment. Except with Bill, and the woman she had met on the plane, she wasn't used to discussing these matters.

'I think if you don't have a history, the randomness of life strikes you harder. I also feel that if I knew my real mother, if I could find out what has happened to her, even if it was just enough to know that it wasn't all tragedy, I wouldn't always have this sense of another parallel existence that's waiting for me to step into it. It's partly a sense of foreboding, and partly of something very precious that I lost and need to find again.'

Connie realised that she hadn't heard a train go by for quite a long while. The city's commuters would all be home by now, and it was time she went home herself. She stood up.

Kathy stood too and held out her arms. 'Here,' she said.

Held in a weighty hug, a memory of babyhood and the knowledge of a mother passed over Connie like a shadow from a bird's wing.

'Thank you,' Connie whispered.

Kathy came back down the steep stairs with her and stood on the stone step. 'You keep in touch, Constance Merriwether.'

'I will,' Connie promised. It was a promise she kept.

Connie locked up the Bali house and gave the key to her neighbour Wayan Tupereme. The little man bowed his forehead to the tips of his folded hands and she returned the salute.

'May the *pengabenan* of your sister be blessed, and may her spirit ascend to *suarga*.'

'Thank you, Wayan. You know, funerals in England are not very like Balinese ones.'

'This I have heard.' Wayan sighed in sympathy. 'However, when the rituals are complete, please come back to the village and to your friends.'

Connie had made no plans beyond flying to England for the burial.

'I hope to,' she said.

Chapter Ten

'LET US PRAY.'

Connie bowed her head.

She could see a double row of black-shod feet. Opposite her were Bill's shiny Oxfords, Noah's less well-polished boots, and some Italian loafers sported by a red-faced old man with a wheezy chest who had turned out to be Uncle Geoff, whom Connie had not seen for twenty years.

On Connie's side was a pair of matronly heels, shuddering with the force of Sadie's weeping, two sets of black knee boots, Jackie's and Elaine's, and a shuffled-up line belonging to the cousins' children.

Between the two rows of shoes lay Jeanette's open grave.

There was not a shiver of movement anywhere. Even the rain had stopped. Sadie caught her breath, causing a short break in her sobbing.

Funerals in England are not very like Balinese ones, Connie had told Wayan Tupereme. She thought briefly of the *wadah* and the single swoop of the paper dragon's wings before they were consumed by a sheet of fire, the stench of kerosene and flakes of soot gently drifting in the twilight, and Jeanette's observant admiration of the ceremonies.

Today's event could not have been more different, or more mutedly English and monochromatic by comparison, and yet it was also fitting. Jeanette had expended so much of her formidable energy on living a normal life, and to be conventional in her taste and behaviour—to have chosen a traditional funeral was all of a piece with that.

At the short church service that had preceded the committal, there had been familiar hymns and Psalm 23, and Bill had spoken briefly and movingly about Jeanette's life. Noah had recited from memory 'The Lake Isle of Innisfree', which he described as Jeanette's favourite poem.

Connie could read nothing of Bill himself in any of this. These choices must all have been Jeanette's. She thought how remarkable it was that a man as imposing as Bill could be so self-effacing.

Now Bill's black shoes took a step forward out of the opposite line. The toes were almost at the edge of the grave, where the raw earth walls had been masked with a roll of fake turf. Connie lifted her eyes from the ground but she did not venture a glance at him.

Bill had been holding a tiny bunch of flowers. There were some twigs of rosemary and three frail white roses, picked that morning in Jeanette's garden. He kissed the blooms and then let them fall onto the coffin lid.

But that was you, Connie silently said to him, and the blood in her veins seemed to make a complicated double surge.

Sadie choked into her handkerchief, and one of her daughters placed an arm around her shoulders.

Almost briskly now, Bill took the very clean spade that one of the undertaker's men handed to him. He dug one spadeful of earth from an uncovered corner of the mound piled on boards next to the grave and scattered it over the flowers, then Noah took the spade and did the same thing. Cut off by the grave from his ex-wife and daughters, Uncle Geoff seized the spade from Noah and contributed his own few clods of earth. Connie couldn't see beneath the brim of Auntie Sadie's big black hat, but she sensed a glare that smouldered hot enough to dry the flood of tears.

The vicar closed his prayer book. There was a moment's silence as they each attended to their own thoughts. Then he turned and led the family procession away from the grave. Bill and Noah walked side by side, straight-backed, and the rest of them closed into a black phalanx.

Behind them, Connie supposed, the undertakers would remove their trappings and roll up the turf, and then the gravediggers would come and fill in the earth.

The word *gravedigger* was just about as archaic as *foundling*, she thought. All this black clothing and the line of waiting black cars beyond the Victorian lych-gate, the polished coffin and the artificial grass and *we are gathered here to remember our dear sister Jeanette* seemed in that moment supremely irrelevant.

—*Just bones*, Jeanette had said. —*Just dry bones on the blaze and the spirit set free. I like that.*

Minus the hearse, the cortege took the reverse of the two-mile route back to the house that it had taken on the way out. The lead car, carrying Bill in the front and with Connie between Noah and Auntie Sadie in the back, made just one part-circuit of the roundabout, exactly as on the outward journey.

Connie realised that she was smiling quite broadly at the memory of Jeanette's order—*twice round the roundabout on the way to the cemetery for me.* She adjusted her expression before Auntie Sadie could see her.

There were already cars parked up and down the lane outside the house when the cortege drew up, and the caterers were opening the front door to muted couples and groups. The African violets in the big brass bowl in the hallway looked lush and well watered, and the finger of the long-case barometer indicated RAIN.

Connie moved into the drawing room, which was filling up with dark suits. Uncle Geoff was wedged in the corner beside the fireplace.

'I thought the world of her,' he told Connie, sticking out his chin and squaring his shoulders in a double-breasted suit now much too big for him. 'There was no way I was not going to be here. Whatever *she* might think, or say.' He jutted his chin farther, at Auntie Sadie's turned back.

'Of course you did. Of course you had to be here,' Connie agreed.

Later, when people were beginning to leave, she took some empty glasses out to the kitchen and found Elaine propped against the sink. Connie put down her tray, remembering that other funeral, Tony's.

Elaine stubbed out a cigarette and moved aside to let Connie reach into the dishwasher.

'How are you, Connie?'

'I'm all right, thanks.' A colourless answer, but it was difficult to be any more expressive to cousin Elaine.

'It was nice, that music of yours,' Elaine offered.

'Was it? Thank you.'

Bill had asked Connie if she would play some of her music during the funeral service. 'Jeanette would have wanted this,' he said. They had decided on a version of the tune she had been working on on the day of Jeanette's death, a simple melody into which she had attempted to weave some of the Balinese gong notes and sinuous drumbeats. In the end, however, the piece had sounded to Connie like an awkward hybrid, without proper roots in either tradition, when she would have wished it to be the best music she had ever composed.

Connie tried to listen to what Elaine was saying. She felt all her perceptions distorted and her responses headed off into dead ends and irrelevances by the bulky interposition of grief. Elaine was waiting for an answer to a question.

'Yes, still doing the composing. Commercials, some film work when I can get it,' Connie managed to say. 'What about you?'

'Oh, you know. I work in admin, NHS.'

Connie couldn't even remember the last time she had spoken to Elaine or Jackie. Not at Hilda's funeral, certainly, since that had taken place before she could get home from Tasmania.

Weddings and funerals, when families that were not familial briefly and painfully got together.

Elaine's thoughts must have been following the same path. 'I was thinking about when Uncle Tony died.'

'He wasn't your dad.'

'What do you mean?'

'You're adopted, aren't you?'

'I've been meaning to say this for years, and now I'm going to. I shouldn't have told you about being adopted, that was wrong of me.'

'I suppose it was, yes. But I would have had to find out somehow, in the end. Perhaps you did me a good turn.'

Connie tried to imagine how Hilda might have told her, but couldn't envisage it. Maybe Tony would have done it, if he had lived.

Elaine sighed. 'We were so against anything that was different, back then. It seemed an immense secret, that you weren't born into the family.'

Connie reflected that it was Jeanette who had been truly, dramatically different from all of them.

That was why Bill had loved her. She was a series of contradictions: her luscious appearance against her puritanical spirit, her cloak of conventional behaviour adopted as a protection for her deafness, and her constant denial of deafness itself.

'Do you mind me saying this?' Elaine was asking glassily.

Connie smiled. She had warmed to Elaine. 'No, of course I don't mind.'

The other woman immediately grasped Connie's wrists. 'Friends, then,' she murmured dramatically. 'It's taken long enough, hasn't it?'

This was how Jackie and Sadie found them. Sadie's arm was tucked under Jackie's. She looked older than seventy-five and her face was grained and puffy after all the crying.

'I've been saying to Connie that I'm really sorry,' Elaine told them.

Jackie nodded wisely. 'That's what Jeanette would have wanted.'

Quite a number of things have been grouped under that umbrella today, Connie thought.

'It's been a sad day,' Sadie said, in a voice that startlingly resembled Hilda's. Uncle Geoff had already gone, sunk into his black overcoat. Sadie hadn't spoken a word to her ex-husband. Her ability to bear a grudge was as developed as Hilda's.

Connie said goodbye, kissing all three of them. She watched them go, with Jackie and Elaine supporting their mother on either side.

The last of the friends and neighbours also filtered away and the caterers ferried their equipment out to a waiting van.

Connie emptied ashtrays and loaded the dishwasher. Bill closed the front door. The house was finally empty, except for the three of them.

'Thank you for doing so much to help,' Bill said to her. He spoke with an odd formality. His face was drained of colour; even his mouth looked bloodless. Connie ached to put out her arms and hold him.

Noah had undone his black tie and it hung loose from his collar. He said, 'I'm going upstairs to phone Rox, then I'm just going to chill for a bit. Is that OK, Dad?'

Roxana had insisted that she would not come to the funeral. 'I didn't know Mrs Bunting so much, and all the family and friends will be there, I don't feel it is quite right.'

Bill answered now, 'Of course, that's fine. Are you all right?'

'Yeah, Dad.'

Connie followed Bill into the drawing room. He poured himself a whisky and Connie shook her head to decline one. They sat down facing each other and silence crept round them.

'Do you think that went the way Jeanette would have wanted?' Bill asked abruptly.

'Yes, I do.'

He let his head fall back against the cushions and gave a congested sound that was more a cough than a laugh. Silence fell again.

It's here, Connie thought. Afterwards is now.

'I'm sorry,' Bill said, even more abruptly. He sat up and drained the whisky and then rotated the glass on the sofa arm.

'What for?'

'Let's see. For everything I have done, and also failed to do.'

'Bill, don't *talk*. There's nothing to be said at this minute. It's the day of Jeanette's funeral.'

'So it is,' he said, with a hollowness she had not heard before.

For so many years, even when they hadn't seen each other for months, whenever they spoke the words had been ready and fluent, seeming to spring straight from their hearts. Yet now they found themselves stiffly talking like two actors under a spotlight.

Connie would have gone to him, warmed his hands between hers and tried to offer what comfort she could, but even the way that Bill was sitting told her that he didn't want to be touched. She sat in her place, her ankles together and her hands folded, and let the silence lengthen. Bill was staring out of the window into the dark garden.

'I think', she said carefully, 'I should head back home now.'

'I miss her.' Bill's words cut across hers and they jumped, because this dissonance was new to them.

'I know you do. So do I. I wish it had been me, not Jeanette.' She spoke impulsively, out of the whirl of her thoughts, not thinking she should measure what she said. To Bill, she had always spoken what she felt.

His eyes moved from the window and settled on her face. 'I don't think you do wish that.' There was a thin metal edge in the words.

Connie was lost for a response.

'I'm sorry,' he said again, after a moment.

She got up from her seat and went to stand beside him. The black glass of the window reflected their faces.

'What are you going to do?' she asked.

'This week, I am going to look after Noah, do paperwork, write letters. Next week, go back to work. Next month, probably also work. Next year? The year after that? I don't know, Connie. That's the truth.'

'You're wise not to make too many plans. Or to place yourself under any obligations.'

She saw his reflection incline its head. He was so sad that her heart knocked in her chest with pity.

She touched her hand to Bill's arm, then withdrew it. 'I'll be at the flat if you need me.'

He came out into the hall, handed her her bag and helped her on with her coat.

'If there's anything I can do,' she began again.

'Thanks, Connie.' He leaned forward and kissed her on the forehead, cold-lipped, as if she were one of the neighbours.

He stood in the doorway, his hands at his sides, watching her cross the gravel to her parked car. As she drove out of the gate the door closed behind him and the porch light blinked off.

She navigated the country lanes with furious concentration.

Grief. Everything that was happening to them was a manifestation of grief and it did not have an expiry date, or a set term to run. She was only just beginning to comprehend the pervasiveness of it, but one certainty was growing in her. Jeanette's death was as much of a barrier between Bill and herself as their marriage had ever been.

The apartment was in darkness. Connie glanced out at the diamond grid of the city, then clicked on the lights.

'Roxana?' she called.

Roxana wasn't at home. They had had one difficult encounter on Connie's return from Bali, when Roxana had handed over keys for the new locks and blurted out apologies that Connie was too distracted to process, but since then she had made herself invisible.

Connie went down the corridor to Roxana's room and looked in. The bed was made, the beach postcard was in its usual place and Connie was reassured by the sight, but she would have liked it even better if Roxana had been there in person. In spite of the mushrooming chaos the girl had caused, Connie wished for her company. She didn't work at the Cosmos Club any longer, and she wasn't with Noah because he was with Bill in Surrey. She hoped that Roxana was safe, wherever she was.

In the room that before the burglary had been her office and studio, she studied the place on the desk once occupied by her laptop. The drawers of her cabinets were closed on the ransacked files; she had done that much after the police concluded their cursory investigations.

Connie sighed. She looked at her watch. It was only ten forty. She picked up the phone.

'Ange? You're not in bed, are you?'

'What? It's only just past teatime.' Connie could almost see her I'm-hardcore-me-I-am face, and it made her laugh.

'I hope the funeral went all right.'

'Yes. It was done as these things have to be done.'

'That's good, at least. Con, I'm so sorry about the burglary. I feel responsible. If Roxana hadn't met that man in our office . . .'

'You aren't responsible, Ange. Not even Roxana is, really. Any word on Signor Antonelli?'

'The police interviewed us. Antonelli was just cold-calling, blagged his way to a meeting, came back a second time on a pretext and met Roxana in reception. He's disappeared. No one in Rome knows him.'

'What a surprise. Was Roxana working today?'

'Yep, she was here. Are you unhappy about that? Because—'

'No. I'm glad. I'm worried about her.'

'What about you? How are you going to work without your laptop?'

Connie thought rapidly. 'That's no problem, I've got all my files backed up. I'll go out first thing, buy a new laptop—'

'Er, I thought you'd cancelled all your cards.'

'Oh, yes.' Connie started to panic.

'Listen, come into the office tomorrow. You can borrow a laptop.'

'Thanks, Ange. You're a real friend.'

Connie lay awake until she heard the sound of Roxana's key in the lock, and her soft footsteps on the way to her own bed. Then she turned over and fell asleep.

'I'll come in with you,' Connie said to Roxana in the morning.

Roxana spun round from the sink. 'What? Where to?'

'To Oyster Films. That's where you're going, isn't it?'

'Yes. I still work for them, I do not know how long it will last.'

Roxana's mouth turned down at the corners. Connie noticed that she had discarded her big-buttoned jacket in favour of her old Soviet-style denims, and her crest of blonde hair was showing dark at the roots. All the gleam and bounce had gone out of her.

'Come on then,' Connie said gently. 'We'll get the bus together.'

They found adjacent seats. Roxana stared past Connie at the rush-hour streets and the bobbing heads of people bearing newspapers and Starbucks lattes towards their desks. To Roxana, the city tide seemed to be streaming away from her and leaving her on an uncomfortable shore.

'Roxana?'

'Yes.' The syllable slid out between frozen lips.

'No one's blaming you for anything. I can imagine exactly how it happened. It was a mistake, and you won't make it again.'

Roxana's shoulders twitched. 'I don't know. There are too many things I do not understand. At first it seems a simple business, that you can step into another country and make yourself what you want. But it is not. You and Angela, you would know at once that Mr Antonelli is not a person to trust. All I see is a man with a fine watch, and charming behaviour and a card that tells me he is in the movie business. So I believe what he says to me, and I take him and his friend as guests up to your apartment because

I want to make them think I am someone who matters in this world. Then it turns out that he is not what he says, much more than I am not.' Her lovely mouth twisted. 'I am a stupid girl with stupid ideas about being an English girl. And this is the way I repay you for your kindness.'

'I'm going to show you something, Roxana.'

Connie reached inside the collar of her coat, searching for the thin cord next to her skin. She drew out a tiny silk pouch that hung from the cord and eased it open, then withdrew the marcasite earring. Since the news of the burglary, she had taken to carrying it everywhere with her. She held it cupped in the palm of her hand for Roxana to examine.

'Money, credit cards? None of that matters. What else? Laptop, musical and studio equipment, a few rings and necklaces, a camera, some clothes? All of those I can replace. I am insured. This earring is the only thing, the one and *only* inanimate object, I possess that I truly value and could never replace. And I've still got it. It's safe here, in my hand.' Connie closed her fist over it, and smiled.

A spark lit Roxana's eyes. 'It is pretty, yes, but you have only one?'

Connie craned to see the bus's whereabouts. They would reach their stop in not more than five minutes.

'Long story. I'll tell you quickly.'

Roxana listened. At the end of the brief recounting, she breathed out through parted lips. 'If those men had stolen your mother's earring away from you, I think I would have died.'

They reached their stop. Connie slipped the earring back into its pouch and buried it beneath the layers of her clothes.

At Oyster Films, Roxana made her way to her desk, where her pre-production legwork for the St Petersburg shoot was waiting. Angela was in her office, on the telephone, with the door shut.

Connie left the busy office, then went down the street to a coffee shop.

Sitting on a tall stool, gazing out at the passing crowds, she realised how much she would have liked to talk to Bill. It took a great effort of will not to reach for her mobile. Bill had the broad dimensions of grief to map, and then learn to inhabit. As she did herself.

The impulse to tell Jeanette about the burglary flickered and then snuffed itself out when she recalled—with the same stab of pain that came a hundred times a day—that she couldn't tell Jeanette anything.

Roxana finished her work. Angela had given her some notes, then had hurriedly left for home more than an hour ago, without speaking to anyone. Connie had picked up the spare laptop computer and had gone again before it was even lunchtime. For Roxana, it was the end of a long day. Film pre-production work seemed mostly to consist of trying to persuade local suppliers to offer more of their services for less money, and this was not a system that the Russians were very amenable to.

As she was putting on her coat, Noah called her.

'Where are you?' he wanted to know. When he was at the house in Surrey he was always asking her this, as if he felt trapped there, and feared that she might slip away from him.

'I am still at work,' she said. 'How is your father today?'

'He's quiet. Just . . . very quiet. Are you going back to the apartment?'

'Yes, in a bit,' Roxana admitted.

She didn't want to go back there yet, because she felt she didn't deserve the privilege. When Noah was with his father, she had taken to staying out on her own until it was late enough for her to slip into Limbeck House and go straight to bed.

'Call me, then, when you get there?'

'All right,' she said.

Some evenings, Roxana went to the cinema. It was expensive, though, in the West End. She didn't like sitting alone in pubs or bars, so she went back to the Best Little Internet Cafe on the Planet.

Roxana logged on, and went automatically to the Uzbek language portal. Up came the picture of blue domes against the desert-blue sky. Until this moment Roxana would have denied that she ever felt homesick, but now she felt an unwieldy longing to be in this place again.

She clicked at the keyboard and the picture of Bokhara disappeared. She opened her email inbox, and saw that there was a message from Yakov saying that he needed to speak to her urgently.

Roxana stood up, pushed back her chair and went out into the rain. There was another shop a few yards away. Peeling signs read *Cheap Calls/China/Russia/Asia*. It was late to be making this call, but Roxana could not wait until morning. Yakov didn't sleep much anyway.

He answered within a few seconds, so she knew he had been awake.

She could see him clearly, a shapeless dome of flesh topped with a bald bean of a head. Her mother's old friend, the one-time scholar.

'My daughter. I have some news to tell you,' Yakov gasped.

'**R**oxana?'

Connie had been sitting in the semi-darkness, watching the lights beneath her and the planes on their winking descent.

'Yes.'

'Noah called. He's been trying your mobile. Can you . . . Roxana? What's happened?'

Roxana let her bag and her coat fall to the floor. 'My brother.'

She had held herself together all the way home but now her face was beginning to work out of control.

'My brother did not die in Andijan. He is in prison, but he is not dead.'

It was the same golden-lit bar that had so impressed Roxana when Cesare Antonelli took her there. Connie and Angela strolled in, choosing one of the leather-circled booths as if the place belonged to them. They scanned the drinks menu and told each other that tonight was definitely the night to have the cachaça and absinthe mint cocktail, and when the drinks came they clinked glasses with each other. They told Roxana to remember that friends were what mattered.

'They are *all* that matters,' Angela said. Deliberately she made a face like someone trying to be tragic in a TV comedy show.

Angela smoked constantly and kept taking off her tinted glasses and then putting them on again, but she and Connie both laughed a lot as well, and teased each other and Roxana, and even after all that had happened they made her feel as if she was one of them, one of the confident women who were at home in places like this.

When the second round of cocktails arrived, Connie became serious. She raised her glass again. 'Here's to you, Roxana. I'm so happy for you and your brother. I hope you'll be able to see him soon, and that he'll be out of prison before too long. I know you've got to go back right away to do whatever you can to help him. But I'm really going to miss you.' She took a big gulp of her drink. 'Good luck. *Bon voyage*,' she added.

'You'll miss me, even though I let those men into your home?'

'Those men took the things that don't matter and I've still got everything that does.'

Roxana's eyes went to the thread that held the pouch, just visible in the V of Connie's top.

'Good luck, Roxana,' Angie added, then, without any warning, her eyes filled up with tears. She gave a sob and then tried to cover it up, and Connie gently grasped her wrist.

'Bugger it.' Angela sniffed. 'I am going to give you some advice, Roxy. Don't ever get involved with a married man. Con men, nightclub owners, even ad men if you must. But never ever, take it from me, lose your heart or give your life to a man with a wife and children.'

Roxana felt awkward, because of Connie and Mr Bunting. It came to her that even Angela did not know about this piece of Connie's life, and when she met Connie's dark eyes she saw that this was the case.

'I will remember,' she said carefully.

Connie and Roxana saw Angela into a taxi, and then took another back to Limbeck House.

Roxana's bag was packed, ready to go, and her room was bare except for the postcard. Roxana eased it off the wall, and gave it to Connie.

Connie held out her arms and they hugged each other.

'Maybe some day you will come to visit me and Niki in Uzbekistan,' Roxana said.

Noah took her to the airport. He didn't want her to go, but there was no hope of her staying. Her brother had been delivered back from the dead, and there wasn't a single card in the pack that he could play to trump that. He was happy for her, and bereft for himself.

'Are you sure you will be able to get on the flight? And back into Uzbekistan, on an expired holiday visa?'

She reassured him. The confidence and determination that had temporarily seeped away were back again. 'At Tashkent I will have to pay some fine, for an expired visa, I think. Your people, the British, will be happy to see the back of me.'

'I have never so not wanted to see anyone's back.'

He grasped the lapels of her denim jacket as if he could physically prevent her from leaving. Noah had always hated goodbyes.

'Roxana, you have to promise that you'll call me, and email. I want to know about Niki. I want to know you're safe and well.'

'Yes.' She pressed her warm mouth to his. 'Noah?'

'I'm here.'

'Thank you for all the times we have had. You have been kinder to me than anyone else in my whole life. You and Connie.'

If only we could leave Auntie Con out of this, Noah thought in despair. They were at the Departures line.

'Tell your father I send him my best wishes.'

'I'll do that.'

'It's time for me to go,' she whispered.

They kissed each other, and then very firmly she put her hands on his arms and turned him to face away from the line. She gave him a gentle but definite push.

'Are you coming back?' Noah asked softly.

Roxana grinned. 'Maybe one day.' Then she shrugged, a fatalistic, comical gesture that was more eloquent than any words. 'But . . . I never was an English girl, was I? I don't think I ever will be.'

She stepped back and blew him a kiss. Then she walked towards the departure gate and out of his sight.

Chapter Eleven

CONNIE HAD BEEN travelling for almost a year.

She had been working, writing music and watching the constant flow of the crowds in a series of cities from Berlin to New York. Then she had a call to do some urgent rescue work on the musical score for a Bollywood/Pinewood joint film production, and she had flown out to Mumbai for a month of intense collaboration with people she didn't know well. It had been stimulating but also very hard work. Afterwards she went to China and travelled overland to Kashgar, a remote trading city in the far west that she had always wanted to visit.

It was an interesting trip, although as soon as it was over Connie realised that since Jeanette's death she had been moving constantly from place to place, meeting people, listening and responding with only a part of herself, all the while telling herself that everything was fine and that this was the way her life was lived. But she felt more rootless than she had ever done, and now she was bone-weary as well.

After China, while staying with friends in Singapore, she had a sharp urge to go back to Bali and look at her green wave. She flew down to Denpasar, and took the public *bemo* up to the village.

'Long time, my friend,' Wayan Tupereme said to her.

'Long time,' Connie agreed, bowing over her folded hands.

The view from her verandah pleased Connie as much as ever. But she kept seeing Bill sitting in the old rattan chair or opening drawers in her kitchen. This almost-presence only highlighted the real absence.

She could see Jeanette just as clearly, but Jeanette was a more peaceful memory now.

Then an email arrived from Roxana.

Hello Connie! How are you? I am well. I have been visiting my brother in jail in Tashkent. It is a bad place, but at least I can see him. I miss you and London and Noah, but this is where I must be and where I want to be because Niki is my brother and to me that is the most important thing in this world.

So this is to ask, when can you come to visit me, my friend?

Connie walked out onto her verandah again and studied the silver loops of the river far beneath her. A breeze laden with moisture shivered the leaves. The little house and the village and the view all soothed her, but there was nothing tangible to hold her here. It would be good to see and talk to Roxana.

Travelling on was more than a habit, she reflected. It was becoming a way of life. She wrote back:

I'll look into flights and mail you in a day or so.

Less than a week later she found herself in Bokhara, waiting for Roxana in the shade of the mulberry trees that fringed an ancient pool.

After the mists of her fecund Balinese valley and the air-conditioned voids of Singapore, she was finding it hard to adjust to the desert furnace of central Asia. She felt not unlike one of the dogs that lay panting in the dust beside the outer wall of the mosque.

Connie blinked to clear her eyes of dust and the harsh dazzle of the sun, and saw Roxana striding towards her.

They had met twice since Connie's arrival and Roxana was taking her role as hostess and tour guide seriously. Today she had been at her job. She was still wearing her work clothes—a hotel receptionist's frumpy skirt suit and open-necked blouse, with a pair of mid-heeled court shoes. She was bareheaded even in the baking midafternoon.

'You are here already,' Roxana exclaimed as she reached Connie's table. 'I hope I am not late?'

Connie edged along the bench, making room for her in the mulberry shade. 'I was early,' she said, smiling. 'It's very warm.'

It was almost forty degrees. The light was blinding, flat out of a white sky, striking into the crucible of baked mud walls and dust-coated streets and further concentrating the heat.

Roxana sat down and spoke quickly to the waiter, then turned back to Connie. 'So, tell me, what sights of Bokhara have you seen today?'

'Let's see. I went up the minaret.'

From 150 feet up a slim brown tower there had been a wide view over turquoise-blue domes and tiled archways, and a jumble of smaller brown domes and arches cracked by dog-leg alleyways, away to the city's flat outskirts marked out in Soviet-built apartment blocks, and beyond that to the limitless, colourless extent of the desert that faded into a purple-grey haze on the horizon.

'And then I went to the Ark.'

The ancient fortress and home to the Emirs of Bokhara, massive in shimmering brick, was now mostly given over to a series of museums.

Roxana quickly drained her Coke. 'And now, are you ready for the women's *hammam*?'

'I'm ready,' Connie said equably. She had no idea what to expect. Roxana had told her only that this was a proper Bokharan tradition, for women of the city, not tourists.

Roxana set off, with Connie walking quickly to keep up. Within ten steps sweat glued her shirt to her back.

The low, domed building was buried deep in a maze of unmarked streets in the old town. Above the brown doorway, in both Arabic and Cyrillic scripts, the single word *Hammam* was carved in stone.

Inside the doors was a dim, cool passage. Thick walls closed out the sounds of the street. There was the steady drip of water, a faint sulphurous whiff, and the sunless scent of old stone. Connie followed Roxana into a room lit from above by skylights.

The first impression was of a mass of female bodies, which resolved itself into a group of women undressing and stowing their clothes in rickety lockers. Copying Roxana and the others, Connie stripped off too. Naked except for the silk pouch containing her earring, she felt conspicuously hairy among such lush expanses of billowy, smooth flesh. All the other women were fully depilated, even the oldest ones.

Connie undid the strings of the pouch. Roxana briskly took it from her, extracted the earring and fixed it to Connie's ear lobe.

She studied the effect. 'Nice,' she said. She tossed the pouch in after the rest of their clothes and shut the tin locker, then gathered up the soap, shampoo and towels that she had brought. 'Now, come.'

Connie hooked her hair behind her ears and meekly followed Roxana down a spiral of hollowed stone steps. The drip of water grew louder, and a thin veil of steam rose to meet them.

There was a circular stone room under the dome, insulated because, except for the dome itself, the building was all underground. Water splashed from ancient piping and ran over the stone slabs. The walls and the stone benches dripped and steam curled lazily through metal grilles. The room was full of pairs of women, coils of hair wound on their heads, their broad backs and buttocks and thighs shining. They were talking and laughing and scrubbing each other.

Connie gazed around her.

A series of smaller, domed alcoves led off the central space. Roxana beckoned. The first was the hot chamber. Steam hissed from the gratings and swirled in dense clouds, and the women lay like basking seals on tiers of stone slabs. Their talk subsided to a low murmur as they gave themselves up to the heat.

As they progressed through the sequence of *hammam* chambers, Connie was thinking of the thousands of women, Bokharans and travellers alike, who had preceded her through these stone arches. The *hammam* itself had stood here, at the heart of its Silk Road oasis, for more than four hundred years.

She felt herself slipping and sliding out of her present self into a place of unexpected comfort. She no longer felt conspicuous among the languid, smooth, fleshy women of the city. Roxana was one of them too, even with her bleach-blonde hair and her dancer's body. They moved slowly, all of them, through the steam and through curtains of tepid water, and into cooler rooms where the talk and laughter broke out afresh.

Roxana reached for the soap and shampoo, and like the other pairs of women they took turns at rubbing each other's skin with a coarse mitt, shampooing one another's hair and bringing buckets of water to sluice over their heads.

Afterwards, with their skin tingling, they sat in a tepid room to rest. Connie fingered her rakish earring.

'It is still there,' Roxana assured her. She leaned back against the stone seat, ready for a talk. 'Tell me, how is Angela?'

'It's taken time, but I think she's forgetting about Rayner.'

'She has fallen in love again?'

'Not that. Not yet.'

'Have you heard any news from Noah?'

'Hardly anything. His father told me he is fine, more or less, although he misses his mother a good deal.'

Roxana waited attentively.

Connie's communications with Bill over the past months had been brief and businesslike, mostly concerned with Jeanette's estate. They were respectful of each other, and concerned not to intrude on one another's private mourning. Or to intrude in any way, Connie thought with a touch of bleakness.

When Connie didn't expand further, Roxana remarked, 'I have had some emails from Noah, you know.'

'What does he say?'

'One thing he said is that he would like me to go back to London.'

'And what do you feel about that?'

'What do I feel about London, or Noah?'

'OK. Noah first.'

Roxana drew up her legs and rested her chin on her knees. 'He is the best boy I ever met. But he is in London and I am here. I want to be in Uzbekistan to be near to Niki, and to work with Yakov and Niki's friends to get him out of prison. So that is also the answer to the other half of your question, about London, isn't it? I dreamed of it, yes, and of being an English girl, and I tried very hard to—what is the word?—integrate myself. I thought that by being a part of Noah's beautiful English family, I could belong even more in England.' She sighed, and her expression was eloquent. 'But as you know, that was not such a success because if I was truly English I would not have been taken in for one moment by Mr Antonelli.'

Connie patted her shoulder. 'That's all in the past. It's finished.'

'I'm glad of that. I learned a very big lesson. You know, Connie, what truly matters is your family. Niki is my family. The first time I went to the prison I was—oh—so happy to see him. Can you imagine what that was like? He had come back from the dead. He is very thin and he had been beaten, and he had spent many days locked up alone, but still he was there, the same smile, the same person. My brother. Now I know what is important. Here I am. In Uzbekistan. This must be my place.'

The passion in her words touched Connie. Her admiration for Roxana renewed itself.

'I understand,' she murmured. 'And you are quite right.'

'I would rather be in this country, and have my brother alive and with some hope in the future, than be in England for ever without him. To be a sister comes from in here.' Roxana pressed her fist to her breastbone.

Connie understood. 'Yes. Niki is lucky to have you for his sister.'

'Mrs Bunting was lucky to have you.'

Connie said quietly, 'Actually, I think it was the other way round.'

There was a burst of laughter from the main chamber. The pairs of glistening, wobbling women passed from the heat to the cooler rooms, gasped as they were deluged with water, or sat and gossiped on the old stone benches.

Roxana beamed. 'You see? You come here with your mother or your sister, and if you are not lucky to have them you are like us, with your good friend, and you talk and talk. You are scrubbed clean and you have opened your heart, and then you go out into the world again.'

Later, they went back up the spiral stone steps. Off the upper corridor was another, grander salon with a marble floor strewn with rugs and cushions, and towel-covered divans against the wall. After their *hammam*, the women lounged and drank tea, their hair tied up in coloured turbans. Naked fat babies lay on blankets and brown-skinned toddlers ran between them. Connie thought it was like walking into a Victorian academician's painting of a seraglio. Roxana delivered her to an enormous, towelled Russian woman with a wide slash of gold tombstone teeth.

'Massage, *da?*'

'Um, yes. Thank you,' Connie murmured, as she was stretched out like a sacrifice on one of the divans.

The Russian masseuse was strong as well as big. Under her vigorous hands Connie's joints creaked and snapped and the women within earshot all laughed appreciatively. At the end, when her muscles were unknotted and her limbs felt like jelly, the woman scooped her up like a rag doll and cradled Connie's head against her immense bosom.

It was like being held by Mother Earth herself.

Fingers massaged Connie's scalp and her neck, even her ears, with as much love and tenderness as if she were a baby.

And without the slightest warning, Connie began to cry.

The tears poured out of her eyes. She wept like a baby in its mother's arms, hiding her face against the massive breasts as the woman hummed and crooned to her. She stroked Connie's hair and patted her hands, waiting until she was done with crying and began to regain possession of herself. When the flood finally stopped, the woman dried her face for her and gently set her upright once more.

'Oh dear. I am so sorry,' Connie gulped. Then she realised that she didn't feel sorry at all.

She felt light, and calm and peaceful. A small, hard knob of anger that she had carried within her for too long had detached itself from the place beneath her breastbone, and it had floated clean away.

She wasn't going to know the woman who had given birth to her, and she would never learn why—in all the years since then—she hadn't tried to find her lost daughter.

She would have her reasons, whatever they were, whoever she was.

That was all there was to know. The difference was that now, among all these women in this strangest of places, Connie thought truthfully, for the first time, that she could forgive her.

Outside the *hammam* it was still stiflingly hot. They walked slowly, scuffing up the dust, and Connie's feet and head felt light with happiness.

'Where are we going?' she murmured to Roxana.

'We will go and have a cold drink. There is a place near here.'

They threaded their way to a low concrete cube of a building with faded awnings offering some shade from the sun. They passed inside to a line of metal-topped café tables beside a tall counter. Connie glanced to the back of the room and saw three computer terminals with keyboards cased in plastic to protect them from the all-pervading dust.

'Maybe I will check my mail while we are here,' Roxana said casually.

'This is the Bokhara Internet café?'

'Why not?' Roxana countered. 'I used to go in London, when I lived there, to somewhere calling itself the Best Little Internet Café on the Planet, which is quite funny, but I think personally this place is better.' She glanced round at the bare walls, the dog panting on the threshold, the chest freezer humming and shuddering in the corner.

A boy of about ten brought their drinks and they settled at one of the terminals. Roxana peered and tapped at the plastic-shrouded keyboard.

'And here is an email from Noah. Hm. Hm. Would you like to read it, Connie?'

'Isn't it private?' Connie asked curiously.

'Not so much that you should not see it.'

Connie changed the angle of her chair so that she could see the screen more clearly. Roxana took a long gulp of her drink. Connie read,

Hi Roxy, how's it going?

I miss you, babe. Life still seems so quiet without you.

Strange to think it's nearly a year since my mum died. I think of her every day, and sometimes I still go, 'must tell her about this or that', and then remember that I can't—but I don't have to tell you what that feels like, do I? But time is doing its thing. She was such a great mother and such a good person to know, and I feel lucky to have had all that.

Been spending quite a lot of time with my dad. He's pretty good, considering. Time's doing its thing for him as well. He's lonely, though. I asked him this weekend if he could imagine being with someone else some day and he gave a smile and said yes, he imagined it regularly.

Have you heard from Connie? I know Dad hasn't, and neither have I. Did anything come of that plan for her to come and visit you?

What's the latest news on Niki?

Connie read on down to the end of the message. Then she looked at the date. The message was several days old. Of course Roxana had been intending all along for her to read it.

Roxana had got up and was standing at the entrance, gazing out into the baking street. Then she looked back to where Connie was sitting, and gave her a brilliant smile of expectation and encouragement.

Connie's mind was spinning.

She had been running away: constructing defences and then racing behind them whenever a breach was threatened.

She had started to put up the barriers long ago, years before she met Bill, even before the day of Tony's funeral and Elaine's blurted truth, *He wasn't your dad . . . you're adopted, aren't you?* That had only been putting into words what troubled her already and the trouble had started before she could even articulate the word *different*.

Connie thought, I rejected *them*, Hilda and Jeanette, just as much as the other way round.

That one word—adopted—and all the longing, and mystery and opportunities for disappointment and betrayal that crowded with it, had always stood between them. What chance did we have, in the face of that? she asked herself.

As the realisation dawned on her, she braced herself for the sadness and regret that might have followed it.

But all that happened was the joy and lightness that had been with her in the *hammam* lifted her to her feet. She floated to the door where Roxana was waiting for her.

'Thank you for letting me see Noah's email. You wanted me to read about his dad being lonely and the implication that I could change that, didn't you?'

Roxana said softly, 'Do you want to know what I think?'

'Go on.'

'I think you should go back to England. I think you should go to see Mr Bunting, and tell him that you love him.'

'Do you? Why?'

'Because it is the *truth*.'

By the time Connie reached England, it was summer.

The trees in the parks were in full leaf and at lunchtimes girls with bare arms poured into the streets. From her apartment, which seemed empty without Roxana, she telephoned Bill.

'It's Connie,' she said.

'Connie. Are you in London?'

Bill's warm voice was very close, as if it came from somewhere within her own head.

'Yes. How are you? You sound different.'

There was a silence while they listened to each other.

'It's you who sounds different,' he said at length.

Connie took a breath. 'I've been bouncing around the world like a ping-pong ball. I want to stop now.'

'That's good.'

'Can I see you? I want to so much, but maybe it's too early, or you may feel that it wouldn't be right?'

'I want to see you too,' Bill answered. 'Just lately, you're in my head more than ever. I wasn't even surprised to hear your voice just now.'

Connie looked out at the cranes angled over the city's building sites.
'Shall I come up to London?' Bill asked.

Connie thought quickly. London's streets were mapped out by the past. Nowhere came to mind that was not touched in some way either by the years of being painfully apart from him, or by the snatched intervals of their love affair.

'No, not London,' she said hastily. 'Somewhere else.'

'Where?'

She knew why he sounded different. The ripple in his voice that had faded years ago was there again.

'I know. Let's go to the seaside. Let's go to . . . Devon.'

Connie couldn't recall ever having been there. And an English shingle beach with mild, greyish breakers would be far enough removed from the last beach they had visited, back in Bali.

'Devon?' Bill was laughing openly now. But he understood what she was thinking, and he entered into the idea with her. There would be an unmarked page for both of them. 'I will meet you in Devon in . . . let's see. Forty-eight hours from now. Look at your watch. It's three o'clock. Take your mobile with you. I'll call you at eleven a.m. the day after tomorrow, and tell you where.'

Connie laughed too, although her heart was thumping.

'Forty-eight hours,' she repeated.

The spell of fine weather continued. In the early-morning sunshine before she set out to meet Bill, Connie put on a bright red cotton dress and stared at herself in the mirror. There were deep lines bracketing her mouth and at the corners of her eyes, but at the same time she felt stripped of all the armour of experience, as if inside her skin she was sixteen again.

At 11 a.m. precisely her mobile rang. His voice in her ear stilled the roar of motorway traffic.

'Where are you now?'

'I am at the service station just before the M5 junction.'

He gave her the exact details of where he was waiting.

'I'll be there,' she promised. She drove carefully, like the mature woman she was, but at the same time she was thinking that this was the most erotically charged moment of her life.

It was a weekday, but the car park of the little seaside town was almost full. As Connie searched for a space, men with bare, sun-reddened chests padded towards the seafront laden with body boards and heavy cold-boxes and children chased between the cars. It was a few minutes before three o'clock. She parked at the end of a row and sat with her hands still resting on the steering wheel. The hot smell of the car merged with salt and sun cream and frying fish, and a pair of kites tugged towards freedom in the blue space between earth and sea. All her senses were sharpened.

I am alive.

A swell of amazed gratitude and happiness lifted her.

I am alive, she repeated. *And I wish you were alive and here with me. With us. I miss you, Jeanette, every day.*

Connie let her hands slip into her lap.

Afterwards was now.

She loved Bill and had always loved him, and whereas that had once been wrong she didn't believe it was wrong any longer.

I love you just as much, she added to Jeanette. *Forgive me now, if there is anything still to forgive.*

Connie walked across the road to the seafront. Outlined against the glitter of the water a man was standing against the railings with his back turned, his arms spread and his hands resting on the top rail. He was the only person in the world.

She ran forward and put her hands over his, fitting her body against him. They hung there for a moment, their faces hidden from each other, waiting for the future.

Then Bill spun round and caught her face between his hands. He kissed her, blotting out the sun-dazzle and the twirling kites. Without lifting his mouth from hers he murmured, 'It felt like making an assignation with a stranger. Driving down here, waiting for you to arrive. It was extremely exciting.'

'I know. I felt that too.'

'But now I see you and touch you, you're the opposite of a stranger. You fit me, Connie.' His voice was very low. As he had done many times before, he drew her closer to him so that her head rested at the angle of his jaw. She let herself melt against him and the easiness of it surprised her. There had always been a thin layer separating them, she realised now. It had been her own guilt interleaved with his, and her old, wary defensiveness. The barriers felt stale and constricting now, and she wriggled to free herself like a snake shedding its skin. His body felt very warm and solid.

'Is it less exciting, me turning out not to be a stranger?'

'No,' he said roughly. 'I want you to know that I have booked a room. I want you to come back there with me. Will you do that?'

'I will,' she said.

Her composure suddenly struck both of them as very funny. They laughed, and a teenaged couple glanced back at them as if they were wondering what two middle-aged people could find so comical.

They linked hands and began to walk along the seafront. A wall projected out into the waves, enclosing a little harbour where fishing boats and sailing dinghies were moored.

'How have you been, Bill?'

He said, 'Grief is a strange commodity, don't you think? I thought it was something you dealt with. I thought you either coped well or not, depending on who you were and the particular circumstances, but that you handled it in some way. But I have found that it doesn't make much difference what you do. You can go out and be with friends or strangers, or you can go to a film or look at art. You can stay in with a book or a bottle of whisky, or just yourself and silence. You can square up to it, saying, "Come on, wash right over me, do your worst because I'm ready for you." Or you can try to ignore it. Whatever you do doesn't matter, because grief is still just *there*. What happens, of course, is that as time passes the presence becomes less constant. Now I can see how its absence begins to take shape.' He looked down at her, his mouth curling in the way it always did. 'That's how I've been. What about you?'

Connie nodded. 'Similar, only I didn't handle it as well as you. I miss her so much, so I tried to escape the loss by running away. True to form, you might say. It wasn't until Roxana took me to the *hammam* in Bokhara that I broke up and cried properly, from right inside myself.'

Bill gazed at her. 'Noah's Roxana, is that? *Bokhara*?'

'I have been bouncing around the world . . .'

'Are you ready to stop now, or are you still my wild, wandering girl?'

'I am ready to stop,' Connie said soberly. 'I've been thinking a lot. About Jeanette and me when we were girls, about Echo Street, and when Noah was born and when Hilda died. All those years.' With the hand that wasn't linked in Bill's she lightly touched the silk pouch that still hung at her throat. 'And I have been making peace, with Jeanette and my real mother and with myself.'

They were walking out along the harbour wall now, where waves slapped against slippery stone steps. They reached a line of bollards at the far end, and a stone bench set into an angle of the wall. They sat down and Bill's arm circled her shoulders while they watched the gulls at their feet and the kite-flyers out on the beach. Connie told him about Roxana and the email from Noah, and Roxana's words of advice.

'And what exactly was her advice?' Bill murmured.

Connie turned to face him. 'She said that I should come back to

England, see Mr Bunting, and tell him that I love him.'

'I see. You know what? I'd say that was very, *very* sound advice.'

Their mouths were almost touching now.

'Yes,' Connie agreed. 'And so I am acting on it.'

Arm in arm, as if they had been together for ever, they retraced their steps along the harbour wall. The wind had strengthened and the rigging of the dinghies tapped out a metallic rhythm. There were families picnicking on the shingle, light glinting off the cars crawling along the seafront road, the distant tinkle of music from a child's fairground ride. To both of them, the world looked new and fresh and completely enticing.

Bill said suddenly, 'I'd like an ice cream, wouldn't you?'

There was a kiosk directly across the road from the harbour wall and they hurried to it, dodging cyclists and pensioners out with their dogs. Behind a sheet of glass, square metal tubs were full of fondant colours.

'Look, coconut ice,' Bill exulted. 'One scoop or two?'

Connie made a face that Angela herself might have been proud of.

'Coconut? I *loathe* coconut. Don't you know that?'

He admitted that he did not.

As trivial as an ice cream or as important as happiness, they still had as much to learn about each other as the wealth they already knew.

With Bill's double coconut scoop and Connie's single chocolate in hand, they turned away from the kiosk and joined the afternoon strollers.

'Can I ask you something?' Connie smiled.

'Anything.'

'How far is it, to this room you booked?'

'About . . . ten minutes.'

'*That far?*' she whispered.

She shaded her eyes so that the sunny afternoon was squared down to contain nothing but Bill's face. He caught her raised wrists and held them.

'Much less if we run,' he said.

'Race you,' she countered.

Holding their melting ice creams aloft, they chased each other through the gentle crowds.

Rosie Thomas

Is it true that after your divorce you 'de-cluttered' your life?

Yes, I did. Over ten years ago I moved from a large Victorian house into a small flat and I got rid of lots of baggage. I still find that I keep possessions to a minimum. I no longer hoard books and CDs, I don't have many clothes. Like Constance in the novel, I enjoy a minimalist lifestyle.

Why did you set part of this novel in Bali?

I was invited to a wedding in Bali—otherwise I don't think it's a place I would have visited, as it's a little too 'touristy' for me. But there are lots of off-the-beaten-track areas to explore where most tourists never venture. As I love mountaineering I climbed the sacred volcano, Mount Agung, which is 9,000 feet high, overnight just to see the sunrise. When I was writing *Constance* and wanted an exotic location, my experiences in Bali fitted the bill perfectly.

Did you listen to gamelan music in Bali?

Yes, I heard it there for the first time. The instruments are tuned fractions of a tone apart and you get this extraordinary tonal shimmer, which is wonderful to listen to in that climate, as the humidity in the air makes for a plangent sound.

Did you visit Roxana's native Uzbekistan as part of your research?

I love travelling to unusual, fascinating places and I had been to Uzbekistan before I started writing *Constance*. I wasn't researching, but places and people just get embedded in my memory and then they pop up when I'm writing and I think: I'll use that. The story in the novel about the *hammam* was actually straight out of my own experience as I went to the women's *hammam* in Bokhara and had a Russian masseuse. It was a moment of maternal connection for me and so that part of Connie's experience was lifted straight from my life. I went to the *hammam* on my own and was befriended by a local woman, a medical student. It is all very intimate, with everyone naked, and I felt very skinny and gawky and hairy among all the plump, depilated women. The young girl who befriended me spoke very good English and when I asked her what her ambition in life was she replied, 'To see the sea.' Uzbekistan is land-locked and I used this in the novel for Roxana.

How did you research the pole dancing?

I went to a lap-dancing club in London. That was a pretty depressing experience, I can tell you. I paid for an hour's conversation with a young woman called Scarlet, whose job it was to try to persuade me to buy another bottle of something masquerading as champagne for £90. She showed me some of the moves and told me that most of the girls working in the clubs are funding a habit of some kind. Many of them are here illegally. It's definitely a dark underbelly of London life.

There are a number of issues in *Constance*. What was the key one for you?

My original intention was to write about identity, and how we define ourselves. Is it by our background, or our genes, or our present identity? I wanted to play with the notion of whether or not we can decide to be someone different, as Roxana tries to do. Connie never feels as though she has found her real identity, except through her love for Bill.

Why did you make Jeanette deaf?

It's a metaphor for the silence within dysfunctional families, and to show the double failure of fifties' families, like the Thornes, to talk about anything emotional—such repressed Englishness. Many children at that time did not know that they were adopted until they reached adulthood: my ex-husband actually experienced this.

What's happening next in your life?

I've got a couple of mountaineering trips coming up this summer but my next big trip is sailing the Atlantic in January. I'm not a sailor but will be with friends who are. I will be doing the cooking and I'm apparently in charge of the log and the blog.

Jane Eastgate

STARBURST
Robin Pilcher

The Edinburgh International Festival, with its
promise of stardom for a few, and dawn to dusk
entertainment for many, is about to begin.
Comedienne Rene will be making her debut;
young French violinist Angélique will be starring
in sell-out concerts; Leonard has been given a
chance to make one last film, and Roger is planning a glittering finale to a long career.
After the next three weeks, their lives will never
be the same again.

One

THE CONFETTI WAS A BIT of a mystery. Two weeks after the wedding and the multicoloured flakes still kept appearing in every room of the flat. Sometimes they materialised in force under the new king-sized bed or piled up in small drifts behind the television in the sitting room; other times no more than a single fragment floated delicately on toaster thermals around the kitchen. At first, its presence had given Tess a warming sense of fulfilment, a reminder of everything that had happened on her Big Day. But now, as she pulled the polo-necked jersey from her wardrobe and a fresh flurry drifted down onto the polished floorboards of the bedroom, she felt it was all becoming a bit of an inconvenience.

Tess had a sneaking suspicion that it was Allan who was to blame. She had visions of him tiptoeing about the flat, sprinkling the tissue petals around like love dust to keep the spirit of their wedding day alive. But when she had broached the subject on the previous morning, as he stood shaving in front of the bathroom mirror, he had rather disappointingly denied the whole idea. 'Nice thought, angel'—mouth to the left as he scraped away at the right cheek—'but I'm afraid it's not been me'.

Seated on the edge of the bed, Tess pulled on her brown leather calf-length boots, wrestled the legs of her jeans over them, and then got up and walked over to open the wooden shutters on one of the room's tall sash-framed windows. Her spirits, which had been flying since the wedding, sank a little when she looked out onto another grey day in the Scottish capital. It was the beginning of May and it could as well be February. An icy draught sought out a space at the side of the ancient window frame, surrounding her with a chill that made her shiver. Having to leave her cosy little flat in West College Street and move here to Allan's great barn of a place in the infinitely smarter New Town was the one thing she regretted about getting married.

Tess picked up her mobile from the bedside table and thumbed a couple of buttons. She held it to her ear as she pulled on her jacket and shouldered the strap of her laptop case. When eventually Allan answered, his greeting was unintelligible through a mouthful of food.

'It's me,' Tess said, picking up her keys from the table in the hallway.

'I know. Your name came up. Sex Maniac.'

'It does not say that!'

'No, you're right. It says Mrs Goodwin.'

The name change was something else Tess was having difficulty getting used to. 'That's nice,' she said with a smile, as she locked the door of the flat and began descending the stone steps. 'So, where are you?'

'In a traffic jam on the M8, twenty kilometres from Glasgow.'

'What time did you leave this morning?'

'Six thirty. You were out for the count, so I just gazed hungrily at you and left. Are you still in bed?'

'No, I'm on my way out.'

'My word, that's a bit keen, isn't it? It's only just gone seven thirty.'

'I know, but I've got to be up at the Hub early. Alasdair's calling in from Budapest at eight. He's sounding out some dance company he thinks might fill an empty slot.'

'I thought Sarah liked hogging the morning phone calls with the great Sir Alasdair Dreyfuss.'

Tess smiled wryly as she pulled shut the heavy entrance door. Allan was right. Sarah Atkinson, the marketing director of the Edinburgh International Festival, and her own immediate boss, liked to be the one who liaised with the director.

'She's down in England, having a meeting with the Royal Shakespeare Company,' she replied, glancing down Dundas Street to see if there was a bus in sight. A double-decker, in the corporation colours of maroon and dirty-white, stood at the traffic lights. 'What time do you think you'll be home?'

'Sevenish.'

'Fancy something to eat out?'

'No, I fancy you.'

Tess felt a warm glow. 'I know. But that doesn't answer my question.'

'OK, we'll eat out. Hey, the traffic's starting to move. See ya, angel.'

Tess slipped her mobile into the pocket of her jacket and boarded the bus. She climbed to the upper deck and jolted into a window seat. It hadn't been the best time to get married, with Allan just getting a promotion and her working all hours at the Festival office, but then again it had almost come down to a 'make or break' situation. Their relationship had always blown hot and cold, for a four-month period two years ago they had taken a complete break from each other. During that time, they slalomed into affairs and crashed out of them, coming back together to lick their wounds.

Those flings were easy to forgive. The one Tess had the following year was not, yet even though it rocked their boat it never capsized it. And that was the danger. It was Allan who said that neither was doing the other any favours by continuing without any form of commitment. So he'd proposed to her, and Tess had agreed. It had seemed the most natural thing to do. It was just they'd never got round to it.

In the same way that they'd never got round to organising a honeymoon. Maybe she would get onto the Internet this morning and see if she couldn't book a couple of weeks in September after the festival. Right now she fancied somewhere sunny, exotic, with white sandy beaches and palm trees and a blue sea that merged into the sky. Barbados would just fit the bill nicely, thank you very much.

Tess gazed out at Edinburgh's citizens walking to work. Men and women in formal, colourless clothes, adding to the general drabness of the day. It never ceased to amaze her that a city that seemed to wallow in such stolid lugubriousness should, for three weeks in August, suddenly behave as if its water supply had been spiked with amphetamine. Even though the festival was now regarded as one of the world's foremost cultural gatherings, it had been only in the past ten years that local opinion had changed towards the event. Until then, it had been viewed as a yearly inconvenience. There was no doubt in the minds of everyone who worked in the International office that the change of opinion was due to the present director, Sir Alasdair Dreyfuss. Prior to his arrival little had been made of the kudos the festival brought, nor of the revenue generated.

Tess got off the bus and began to walk up Lawnmarket, the uppermost stretch of the Royal Mile. This was her old stamping ground and the place where she felt comfortable: the Old Town, with its cobbled streets and its small-windowed buildings of ancient stone. Crossing the street, she entered the aromatic interior of a Starbucks café, one of the few insurgent establishments in the street. As she took her place in the queue, two away from being served, the entrance door crashed shut behind her. Everyone in the chrome-strewn place looked up or spun round, the stares focused on the young man with frenzied curly hair that spilled onto the shoulders of his too-large overcoat. He stood in front of the door, his eyes closed and a pained expression on his face.

'Sorry . . . sorry . . . sorry.' He opened up one eye.

Tess decided to help him out. 'That was some entrance, Lewis,' she said with a smile. Lewis Jones was in the marketing team of the Fringe, one of the independently organised festivals run under the title of the Edinburgh Festival. 'Why the rush?'

Lewis shrugged. 'I was just about to go into the Fringe office when I saw you. I just wanted to ask how married life was treating you?'

'It's . . . very exciting,' Tess replied with a nod of affirmation. 'I strongly recommend it.'

Lewis sighed. 'No one on the horizon for me, I'm afraid. Let me buy you a coffee and we can have a chat.'

'I can't, Lewis, sorry. I've got to be in the office in less than five minutes for a telephone call.' Tess turned to the girl behind the counter. 'A cappuccino to go, please.'

'Oh, well, never mind,' Lewis said dourly. As soon as the girl put the paper cup on the counter, he picked it up and gave it to Tess. 'Here you are, this one's on me. You'd better get going.'

Tess shot him a smile. 'Thanks, Lewis. See you around.'

She left the coffee house and ran up Lawnmarket towards the offices and headquarters of Edinburgh International Festival, which were housed in a converted church at the top of the Royal Mile, 'rechristened' the Hub. Pushing her way through two sets of swing-glass doors, Tess hurried along the central passage, at one time the aisle of the church, taking the staircase two at a time. As she reached the upper landing, she heard the telephone ringing in her office. She ran in and reached across the desk for the receiver, simultaneously ridding herself of her coffee cup and allowing her laptop case to fall from her shoulder.

'Good morning, Tess. It's Alasdair.'

'Morning, Alasdair.' Tess walked round the desk to her seat. 'How're things in Budapest?'

'All right. The dance company is good, but I don't think the choreography is up to scratch. I'm not going to risk booking them.'

'Nothing you want me to do from this end?' Tess asked.

'Not for this project,' the director replied. 'But listen, I noticed in the newspaper that Angélique Pascal is playing at the Barbican in London this Thursday. It's a bit early for publicity, but seeing she's going to be the star turn this year, try organising an interview and then give Harry Wills a call at the Sunday Times. There's every probability you'll get stalled by Albert Dessuin, her manager, but give it a go.'

Tess jotted the names down on her pad. 'Anything else?' she asked.

'Yes, I want you to ring up Jeff Banyon at the Scottish Chamber Orchestra and ask him if it's definitely Tchaikovsky they're going to be doing for the fireworks at the end of the Festival. Now, do you have anything else for me?'

Tess searched the top of her desk for messages others might have left. 'No, nothing at all.'

'All right. I'll be back in the office tomorrow late afternoon, if all goes well with Air Paperclip. When does Sarah get back?'

'This afternoon.'

'OK. I'll speak to her first thing tomorrow morning. Bye, Tess.'

Tess whistled out a breath of relief. She really liked the director but had always felt in awe of him. It was only now, as she started work on her third festival in the International office, that she felt he treated her as an integral part of the team. The story could have been completely different if he'd ever discovered what had happened over the course of the previous two festivals.

Her affair with Peter Hansen had been clandestine, exciting, and fired by the creative energy that thrummed through the city at the time of the festival. Peter was one of Denmark's top artistic directors, brought in on a two-year contract to direct a number of theatrical productions, and it had been Alasdair Dreyfuss himself who had given Tess the job of chaperoning the man. In his mid-forties, Peter was a practised seducer, and Tess, flattered by his attentions, soon accepted their energetic sessions in one of Edinburgh's five-star hotels as part of her duty. She and Allan had been going through one of their 'cool' periods, and there was never a question of him finding out. When the second year came round, she and Peter took up where they had left off, even though Tess knew that their affair was dangerous, not least because Peter Hansen was one of Sir Alasdair Dreyfuss's oldest friends, and that their respective families had joined together for skiing holidays.

It had all come to an abrupt end a week before the end of last year's festival. Tess had arrived at work to find a note on her desk from Sarah Atkinson saying that Peter Hansen had rung to say he had no further need of her services and that he would be leaving for Copenhagen after the final performance of the play he had been directing. Tess had tried to contact him on his mobile, but he had never answered.

Sir Alasdair Dreyfuss had never found out about the affair. If he had done so, there was no doubt in her mind that she would have been thrown out of the International office. But Allan had found out. It was her own fault, really, walking around in a gloomy daze and bursting into tears for no apparent reason. So when he eventually asked her what was wrong, she told him everything, and dear, sweet Allan simply pulled her close to him, heaved out a long, painful breath and said, 'We're going to have to stop doing this to each other, Tess. We can't sustain a relationship when we're constantly ignoring the basic rules of trust and fidelity. Our only chance of survival is to get married. What d'you think?' And she'd accepted without hesitation.

Tess jerked her head to break away from her thoughts, realising she had been staring at the telephone ever since her call with the director. She leaned over and picked up her discarded case from the floor, unzipped it and placed her laptop on the desk. As it was booting up, she glanced at her watch and decided it would be as well to wait until nine o'clock before making any of her telephone calls. Which gave her all of forty-five minutes to look on the Internet for a September booking for a much-delayed honeymoon.

Two

OWING TO AN INADEQUACY of space in the industrial unit on the outskirts of Cheltenham, the offices and storage facilities of the Exploding Sky Company had recently been moved to a block of farm buildings in the Cotswold Hills. Even though the transaction had stretched the relationship with his bank manager to near breaking point, Roger Dent was extremely thankful at that moment that he had undertaken the move, if only for the soothing vista of sheep quietly grazing outside his window. He sat slumped at his desk, open-mouthed with jet lag, hardly aware of the fact that Cathy, his wife and personal assistant, had succeeded in turning the dark and smelly piggery into the company's new office in the two weeks that he had been away. White-painted windows now replaced the open frames, hardboard floors were laid and carpeted, and the walls, now lined with plaster board and resplendently fresh in magnolia paint, were hung with photographs that displayed some of Roger's most triumphant moments. The largest of them all was an aerial shot that showed a night sky emblazoned with trailing meteors that fell in flames of red and gold onto the battlements of Edinburgh Castle: testament to his skills as a master pyrotechnic.

Roger was brought out of his soporific state by a coffee mug being placed on the desk in front of him and a kiss being planted on the side of his bearded face. He turned to watch with heavy eyes as his wife came to lean on the desk beside him.

'You look all in.'

Roger ran a hand over his thinning hair. 'I am,' he replied, mid-yawn. 'There was a problem in Shanghai. We were four hours late boarding.'

'What time did you get back here?'

'Six thirty this morning. I didn't bother coming to bed. Thought I'd just disturb you.'

'That was very considerate of you,' Cathy said with a smile. 'So, tell me, how did the trip go?'

'All in all, really good. We managed to visit the factories in Beihai and Hengyang and they got pretty excited about the new material we've ordered. We spent two days on the test ground with this new lad from the research department in Hengyang. Some of the new multishot batteries he'd come up with were mind-blowing.' Roger took a hefty slurp of black coffee. 'Talking of which, have you seen Phil today? I have to remind him to send an email off to that lad this morning.'

'He's in the storeroom, getting the gear ready for the weekend.'

Roger leaned across his desk and opened his diary. 'Oh, for heaven's sakes, I'd forgotten about Cardiff. Looks like we'll have to be back on the road tomorrow to get that one set up.'

Cathy pushed herself away from the desk. 'Jeff Banyon from the Scottish Chamber Orchestra called this morning to find out how you were getting on with the Tchaikovsky piece for the festival.'

'What did you tell him?'

'I told him that everything was going well.'

Roger snorted out a laugh. 'We haven't even made a start on it.'

Cathy ruffled her husband's hair. 'You always say that some of your best displays are the ones you've left to the last moment.'

As she moved over to the door of the office it opened with force, and a short, well-built man with blond hair and eager blue eyes walked in. He encircled Cathy's waist with powerful forearms, picked her up off the ground and twirled her round. 'Hi there, Cathy. Good to see you, babe,' he bellowed out in a thick Australian accent. He dropped her back to her feet, moved over to the desk and gave Roger a solid slap on the shoulder. 'How're you feeling this morning, Rog?'

Roger fixed his right-hand man with a caustic glare.

'Not very well, actually,' Cathy replied for her husband, 'which makes me slightly wonder why *you're* so chirpy?'

Phil Kenyon planted his sizable backside on top of the desk, covering Roger's diary in the process. 'Oh, I never get jet lag,' he said cockily. 'Comes from all those years of flying back and forth to Oz.'

'Bully for you,' Roger mumbled quietly, giving his diary a sharp tug to free it from captivity.

'Not feeling our best today, are we, Rog, mate?'

'Don't bait him, Phil,' Cathy said warningly. 'Not when he's in this kind of mood. In fact, I think I might just leave you both so I don't have to clean the blood off the new carpet.'

As Cathy closed the door behind her, Phil jumped off the desk with a purposeful clap of his hands. 'So, what's on the cards today?'

'The Tchaikovsky piece for the Edinburgh Festival. We've got to start programming it.'

Phil's smile changed to a joyless grimace. 'Oh, well, we'd better give it a go, I suppose. Where d'you put the CD they sent us?'

Roger's energy levels were sufficient only for a finger to be pointed towards the row of filing cabinets against the wall. Phil walked over to them, retrieved the CD from a drawer and placed the disc in one of the players to one side of the desk. 'Right,' he said, sitting down and pulling forward a thick block of lined paper. 'Ready to make a start?'

Roger shook his head slowly. 'You know, Phil, with all those quiet passages, I just don't see how it's going to come together.'

Phil wrote, 'Tchaikovsky, Edinburgh' at the top of the page, and then dropped the pen on the desk and turned to his boss. 'Listen, mate, you've been doing the fireworks concert in Edinburgh for over twenty years now, and every year is more spectacular than the one before. Why should this one be an exception to the rule?' He picked up the remote and pressed the PLAY button for the CD machine. 'So what d'you say we just chill out and get on with the job in hand?'

When the telephone rang, Lewis Jones made no immediate attempt to answer it. At this time of the year, it was almost certain to be a theatre company or comedy act leaving it to the last to book into the Fringe. There were other people in the office whose jobs it was to handle such calls. However, when the ringing continued, he got to his feet and looked over the partition that gave him a little privacy in the cluttered, open-plan space. The eight others in the Fringe office were all engaged in other telephone calls. With a resigned shrug, Lewis sat down again and picked up the receiver. 'Good morning, Fringe office.'

The man on the other end of the line spoke with a distinct Yorkshire twang, his words flowing at a speed only matched by their inaudibility.

'All right, one thing at a time,' Lewis interjected as the man avalanched him with information. He had to push a finger into his uncovered ear to be able to hear. 'What was the name of the performer again . . . ? Rene Brownlow . . . Yes . . . look, could you just hang on and I'll see if I can find her on the database.' He typed in the name, 'Right, I've got Rene Brownlow, care of Andersons Westbourne Social Club, Hartlepool . . . Well, it looks like you've paid the registration fee of twelve pounds, but nothing else.'

That set the man off like a train on a downhill stretch. Lewis managed to ascertain that a venue had been booked in West Richmond Street, that money was coming from different sources and that it had all been very complicated to coordinate. 'I can understand all that,' Lewis cut in loudly, 'but in the bulletins we sent out, it does say that to secure your place and get your name in the programme you have to pay three hundred quid before the end of April—and now it's two weeks into May.'

The man stuttered out some excuses and then careered off sideways into a non sequitur about someone being 'very hard done by' and 'life dealing her a cruel blow'.

'Could you just hold a moment?' Lewis asked. Hearing the man still speaking when he pressed the hold button, Lewis got to his feet and once more peered over the partition. 'Gail, give us a help here, will you?' he whispered loudly.

Gail asked her caller to hold. 'What is it?'

'I've got some fellow from Hartlepool here who hasn't paid up the three hundred pounds.'

'Has he got a venue and has he got the money?' Gail asked.

'Apparently.'

'Well, tell him to get the money here by tomorrow, along with his act description. We won't be finalising the programme for two weeks.'

Lewis gave Gail a solid thumbs-up, sat down at his desk and put the receiver to his ear. 'Hello? Right, if you get a cheque and an act description to us by tomorrow, then you'll be all right . . . no, I'm not Indian, I'm Welsh . . . that's all right, don't give it another thought . . . goodbye.'

Standing at the bar in Andersons Westbourne Social Club, known in Hartlepool as Andy's, Stan Morris replaced the receiver on the payphone and shovelled the remainder of the change into his cupped hand. He let it cascade with a jangle into his trouser pocket, then turned to smile at the four men that were eyeing him expectantly.

'Well?' the smallest of them asked, his face wrinkled up to stop his bottle glasses from falling off the end of his nose. 'What did she say?'

'It was an 'e,' Stan replied importantly, clearing a path for himself by holding the palms of his hands together like an old-fashioned diver. Everyone fell into step behind him as he headed back to the table in the corner of the sparsely furnished bar, where several pints of beer awaited them. Wooden chairs were shifted back noisily on the linoleum floor as they resumed their seats. 'I thought 'e was Indian,' said Stan, taking a sip from his glass, 'but 'e was Welsh.'

'Bugger 'is nationality,' exclaimed the little man with the glasses, 'what did 'e say about Rene?'

Stan shot a haughty look at the man. 'I was telling you that, Skittle, as a point of interest.' A universal groan went round the table. 'All right. The man said we were in time if we got a cheque in the post by tonight.'

A murmur of relief greeted the news. 'For a moment, I thought ye'd blown it,' said Derek Marsham, whose down-turned mouth gave the impression that he suffered constant and immeasurable unhappiness.

'I beg your pardon, Derek,' Stan retorted. 'What d'ye mean by that?'

'Well, ye prattle on so. It was a bloody wonder the man understood one word of what ye were saying to 'im.'

Stan pulled himself upright in his chair. 'I'll have ye know, Derek my friend, that at one time I was an accomplished after-dinner speaker. Sought after the length and breadth of Yorkshire, I was—'

'Come on, lads, this is getting us no place.' Four faces turned to look at a man sporting a short denim jacket with a turned-up collar. Terry Crosland, in his mid-fifties, would have been younger than his companions by at least ten years, yet his long dark sideburns and Teddy-boy quiff seemed to put him in a bygone era.

Stan Morris composed himself once more. 'I quite agree with ye, Terry. Well spoken, that man.'

Terry rubbed his hands nervously on the legs of his jeans. 'OK, we've got the money together, but don't you think it's time we told Rene what we've been planning?' The suggestion brought about a rumble of agreement. 'Also, there's another three months before the festival, so 'ow's about we put the motion before the committee that we keep raising the money for 'er, because we can't send 'er off up to Edinburgh flat broke.'

Norman Brown cleared his throat and leaned forward to enter the discussion. 'That's a good point,' he said. 'Our Maisie lives up Clavering way and 'er kids go to the same school as the Brownlow kids, and she says that the Brownlows took out a mortgage just before Gary Brownlow lost 'is job, so they're skint . . .'

Norman tailed off, silenced by the hardened stare on Stan Morris's face. 'Thank you, Norman. I think we know that, otherwise we wouldn't be bothering to do all this for Rene.'

'I don't mind going up to see Rene and telling 'er what's been planned.' It was Terry who spoke, just after he had shot a wink at disheartened Norman to give his fragile confidence a bit of a boost. 'I 'ave to 'ead up towards Clavering any road this evening to do a paint job.'

Stan Morris knocked a fist on the table. 'Very good idea. Much better to break the news to 'er in 'er own home, rather than when she's pulling pints behind the bar 'ere. Everybody in agreement that Terry should take this on?' The assembled company nodded their approval. 'Right, then,' Stan sang out, taking a ballpoint pen and a notebook from his jacket. 'So what we 'ave to do now is come up with a forty-word description of Rene's act.' He creased open his notebook with the side of his hand. 'I'll start the creative ball rolling. What about "'Ilarious comedienne from 'Artlepool?"'

'That's only four words,' droned Derek Marsham.

Raising an eyebrow, Stan threw the pen down on the table and crossed his arms. 'Ooh, I can tell this is going to be a long afternoon.'

Three

IN THE SMALL SUBS' OFFICE of the *Sunday Times* in Edinburgh, Harry Wills popped a stick of Nicorette chewing gum into his mouth. At the same time, receiver jammed against chin and shoulder, he continued to write his own form of shorthand on the spiralled notepad, sometimes interspersing the text with longhand words for which, in his thirty-odd years in journalism, he had never worked out abbreviations.

He dropped the ballpoint pen on the desk. 'Thank you, Monsieur Dessuin, for your time. I think that's all I need to ask. You said you were going to be at the Tower Hotel until tomorrow, is that right? . . . just in case there's anything else I need to know . . . good . . . well . . . goodbye.' Harry thumped the receiver down on its cradle in frustration and then briefly read through his spidery jottings before lobbing the notebook onto the desk with an angry groan.

There wasn't a story there at all. He had been trying to get a personal interview with Angélique Pascal for two years now, ever since she had become the 'great new discovery' after winning the coveted Prix du Concours Long-Tibaud at the Conservatoire, but never had he been able to get beyond speaking to her manager, Albert Dessuin. He shook his head resignedly. Well, at least he knew he wasn't alone in his failure. It was well known among his colleagues that Dessuin kept the young French violinist under such a tight rein that her existence could be described, at best, as reclusive.

Heaving himself out of the chair, Harry walked over to the window and gazed down onto the sun-striped lawns of Princes Street Gardens. This year, he thought to himself, right here in Edinburgh. With Pascal in the city for more than a week when she performed at the festival, there would never be a better chance to get that interview.

On the fifteenth floor of the Tower Hotel in London, Albert Dessuin also stood gazing out of the window. Small cutters and sightseeing barges plied the murky waters of the Thames, appearing and disappearing under the majestic span of Tower Bridge. His mind, however, was not focused on the view. He stood with an elbow resting in one hand, the other playing with the collar of his cashmere polo-necked sweater. His eyes twitched rhythmically behind the gold-framed spectacles seated firmly on his long, thin nose. He was listening intently to the strains of the violin that drifted in from the adjoining room, as it played the first movement of the Violin Concerto in D Minor by Sibelius. Then, suddenly, he strode over to the door and pulled it open. 'Angélique, what are you doing?'

The girl stopped playing instantly. She turned to look at him, her large brown eyes eyeing him with uncertainty. She dropped the violin from her shoulder. 'What do you mean?' she asked hesitantly.

'I can tell you are not concentrating. You are missing so many beats.'

The girl's full mouth broadened into a wide smile. 'I know. I was looking out of the window. It is so beautiful out there with the sun on the river. Oh, Albert, I love London. I am going to live here one day.'

'Pfoo!' Dessuin snapped. 'Paris has better shops, better restaurants, nicer people. You are mad to even think about it.'

A sparkle of excitement glinted in her eyes. 'Maybe one has to do mad things at some time or other.'

'Of course, but not at *this* time. You are twenty-one years old and very fortunate that together we are able to cut out an excellent career for you, and that is what you should be concentrating on right now.' He put a hand under her violin and guided it back under her chin.

Angélique lifted her bow to the strings and with a gentle dip to her head, began to play. After the opening three bars, she stopped abruptly. 'I heard you talking on the telephone. Who was it?'

Dessuin shrugged. 'Some *journaliste* from Scotland. Keep playing.'

Angélique tapped her bow on the strings of the violin. 'Why don't you allow me to talk to the press? I'm quite capable.'

Dessuin narrowed his eyes before fixing the girl with an insincere smile. He draped an arm round the shoulders of his protégée. 'Of course you are, but it is so much better for you to do what you are best at, and I will do likewise.'

'Your mother has been on the telephone,' she said quietly.

Dessuin dropped his arm from her shoulder. 'When was this?'

'About an hour ago. You were away from your room at the time.'

Dessuin nodded slowly. 'And what did she say?'

Angélique played a trill on her violin. 'She thinks she is suffering from flu again,' she said lightly. 'She wants you to call her.'

Dessuin strutted over to the door of his bedroom, opened it, then turned to glare angrily at Angélique. 'My mother has been good to you. You should not be so mean about her *fragilité*.' His rebuke was met with a blank stare. 'I think you are a very cold person sometimes, Angélique. I am going to call her now, and then I am going to get some fresh air.'

'Oh, may I come too, Albert?' Angélique asked breathlessly. She placed the violin hurriedly on her bed and moved towards him. 'I know I should not have been so *flippante* about your mother. I am sorry. Please tell her I was asking after her.'

Dessuin flicked his head huffily to the side. 'I suppose you could come . . . if you are sure you are ready for the concert tonight.'

'Albert, you know I can play Sibelius with one hand behind my back.'

'Five minutes ago, it sounded to me that you were. If you play it like that tonight, you will make yourself a laughing stock.' Dessuin could tell he had succeeded in casting doubt in her mind. He decided to push her a little further. 'And what about Mozart in two days' time? Your reputation will be shot down in flames if you screw up in Vienna.'

Angélique's enthusiasm drained visibly from her. 'Maybe I should stay and do a bit more practice.'

He smiled. 'A good idea. Anyway, it's cold outside. We don't want *you* getting a chill like my mother, now, do we?'

Angélique stood watching as Dessuin closed the door behind him, then turned to pick up the violin from the bed. She closed her arms round it, holding it hard to her chest. It was her comfort, almost her only friend these days. Since leaving the Conservatoire, she had hardly seen any of her old acquaintances. For two years, the routine had been constant. One hotel room, one concert hall after another. She wanted a break from it all. She wanted to go out once more to the cinemas and to the bars in Paris with her friends from the Conservatoire, and she wanted to go home to Clermont Ferrand to visit her family and spend time with Madame Lafitte. Oh, how she missed that wonderful woman!

Angélique sat down on the bed and blew out a long breath to steady the wave of nausea that flooded up from her stomach. Over the past two months this had been brought on by the unthinkable realisation that she, Angélique Pascal, was beginning to feel bored of playing this wonderful instrument. How could she ever entertain such an idea when people clamoured at the box offices to hear her play? How could she tell the man who had nurtured her through her days at the Conservatoire, who had given up everything to become her manager and counsellor? What would she say to Madame Lafitte? As she sat there, a tear slowly trickled down her cheek.

'**H**ello?' The voice on the telephone sounded weak.

'Hello, Maman. It's Albert.'

'*Mon cher*, why have you not called me before now?' A pathetic cough followed.

'I am sorry, Maman. I did not know you *had* called until a moment ago.'

'You mean the girl never gave you the message?' Suddenly there seemed to be strength in the voice.

Dessuin pressed his hand against his forehead. For eight years, Angélique had been living with him and his mother in their capacious apartment in the *quinzième* district of Paris, and still she could hardly bring herself to call her son's protégée by name. 'I have been away from my room, Maman, and Angélique has been practising for the concert tonight.'

'I am not feeling at all well, Albert.' The voice was weak again.

'Have you called the doctor?'

'The doctor knows nothing. When are you coming home, Albert?'

'Friday, Maman.'

'Ah, *mon Dieu*! I may be on my deathbed by then.'

'Maman,' Dessuin said irritably, 'you are as strong as an ox.'

'How would you know?' Again the strength in the voice returned. 'You have never considered how I am feeling. If that had been so, you would never have left your job at the Conservatoire to fly around the world with that girl.'

'Maman, I have talked to you countless times about this.'

'You were never able to make the grade, were you, Albert? You are only doing this because you see in her the talent you lacked.'

'That is most unfair, Maman.'

'Pah! What age are you now? Thirty-seven? Are you going to follow this girl around the world like a lapdog for the rest of your life?'

Dessuin wound the telephone cord tightly around his fingers. 'Isn't it strange how you always seem to sound better when you are angry?'

There was a moment's silence. 'Albert,'—the suffering in the voice had returned—'I am sorry to say such things to you. It must be the fever. I do feel quite delirious. You are a good boy, Albert. I know that. *Mon seul fils, et je t'aime beaucoup.*'

'*Et je t'aime aussi, Maman.* I must go now. I will call you tonight.'

Dessuin replaced the receiver and sat for a moment, then he leaned forward and clenched his hair with both hands. Why was it so much part of her nature to belittle those who were closest to her? She had acted the same way with his father, so that the man had often been driven to vent all his pent-up emotions in a rage that had left neither Albert nor his mother physically untouched. He had vivid memories of his puny young arms braced against his bedroom door.

When, in his last year at school, he returned home one day to find an ambulance and two police cars outside the house and was told that Guillaume Dessuin had taken his own life with the revolver he kept as a souvenir from the last war, Albert's desolation was tempered by relief.

But as his mother's silent chagrin lifted from her embittered being, Albert found himself becoming the target for her verbal abuse, now more vitriolic than ever before. And it soon came to him that Guillaume Dessuin had succeeded in something at which Albert himself was forever destined to fail, to rid himself of the cause of misery in his life.

Abruptly, Albert stood up and strode over to the minibar. He poured two small bottles of whisky into a glass and drained it in two gulps, feeling his body give out an involuntary shiver at the impact of the alcohol. In that moment, he became aware that no sound was coming from the next-door room. He moved across to the adjoining door and opened it quietly. Angélique was lying fast asleep on the bed, her violin clutched like a comforting teddy in her arms. It was a sight that made Albert smile. He had watched that girl grow up, becoming more attached to her than she would ever realise, and he knew only too well what that particular instrument meant to her. It was her fairy-tale world to which she used to escape from the uncultured lifestyle of her family in Clermont Ferrand. And, over the years he had witnessed it coaxing

194 | Robin Pilcher

from her a most remarkable talent. Oh, how easy life would be if one needed only to take one's solace from a shapely piece of wood with a few strings attached to it.

Dessuin pulled the door closed and turned once more to raid the minibar of its anaesthetising contents.

The shutters in the drawing room of the house in Clermont Ferrand were kept closed during the summer to protect the antique furniture from the sun, especially the lacquered top of the grand piano, which stood in the large bow window, squatting like a giant toad on its turned-out legs. It was covered with a white lace cloth upon which sat a stack of music scores and the blue Limoges terrine in which Madame Lafitte kept a supply of Nestlé's plain chocolate.

So efficient were the shutters that it was always impossible to see anything in that room, even at ten o'clock on a summer's morning. If one took care not to bump into anything it was possible to *smell* one's way around the room. The fireplace came first with its reek of unswept chimney; next the long bookshelves, which gave off a heady whiff of leather; round past the grand piano to Dr Lafitte's high-sided armchair with the rich aroma of hair oil on its linen head cloth; then along the smooth-fronted sideboard, which gave off the fading bouquet of pot pourri; and then journey's end came by the small Louis XV chair beside the door, which ponged of Madame Lafitte's two elderly Pekineses.

It was during one of these sojourns, when the perpetrator had decided to widen the search for new discoveries behind the grand piano, that a foot came into contact with some form of solid object, causing it to sound off a muffled reverberation in protest. After a moment of thumping heartbeat, ten little fingers sought to break the sacrosanct spell of darkness, gripping hard at the edge of one of the tall shutters and pulling it open to allow the narrowest sliver of light to fall upon a box. The little girl in the shapeless cotton dress and dirty plimsolls knelt down and slowly undid the three spring catches on the lid, and then oh, so carefully, she opened the box up. She gazed at the contents, mesmerised by what she saw.

Then the door to the drawing room was opened and a light turned on. 'Angélique? Are you in here?'

The woman, tall, upright and elegantly turned out, her grey hair pinned in a circular plait to the back of her head, was puzzled by the light that showed through the shutters. She walked over to the window and let out a cry of surprise when she came across the little girl huddled behind the piano. 'Oh, Angélique, what a fright you gave me,' she said.

The child looked up at the old lady, her face radiant. 'What is this?' she asked, pointing at her discovery.

The woman was so warmed by the child's expression that any thought of reprimand melted from her mind. 'That, Angélique, is a violin.'

'Is it very special?'

The old lady smiled. 'That one is, yes.' She held a finger up. 'Wait. I must tell your mother I found you.' She walked over to the door and called out, 'She is here in the drawing room, Marie, calm yourself.'

Madame Lafitte walked back to the window and pushed an armchair on squeaky castors to where Angélique remained. She sat down and lightly moved a thumb over the violin strings. 'It was given to me by my father many years ago,' Madame Lafitte said. 'I had not long started playing the violin when he came home with it one evening. Of course, it is only a small one because I was very young at the time.'

'How old were you?' the little girl asked, briefly taking her eyes off the violin to look up at Madame Lafitte's kindly face.

Madame Lafitte laughed. 'Oh, not as young as you. How old are you now? Six or seven?'

'Six and a half.'

'Well, I think I was probably about ten, and—' Madame Lafitte was interrupted by the arrival of a heavy tread and an unhealthy wheezing. In the doorway stood a large woman with a tangle of brown curls adorning a round red face. Her figure was encased in a floral overall.

'Oh, madame,' she gasped, as she rocked her way over to the piano. 'I am so sorry. She knows this room is *interdite*.' She placed her fists on her hips and frowned angrily at her daughter. 'Angélique,' she boomed, 'come out from behind that piano and apologise to madame.'

Madame Lafitte held up a hand. 'It's all right, Marie,' she said in a calming voice, 'it is good for little girls to be so inquisitive.'

'But not here, madame. It is unforgivable, here at my work.'

'And how much more work do you have to do this morning?' Madame Lafitte asked, trying to steer matters away from Angélique.

'I have yet to finish off the polishing in Dr Lafitte's study, madame, and then if I might leave the dining room until tomorrow, I would be grateful. I have to be home to make lunch for all my family.'

'What?' Madame Lafitte asked quizzically, knowing that the three Pascal sons and elder daughter laboured alongside their father in a furniture factory. Marie Pascal had been working as a cleaner in the house for nearly eight years and consequently Madame Lafitte knew that Angélique's birth had been a mistake, remembering the woman's shock on discovering that she was pregnant fourteen years after her previous confinement. 'Why would they be home for lunch on a Wednesday?'

Angélique's mother flicked back her head. 'They are all on strike.'

Madame Lafitte clicked her tongue. 'Oh, not another strike . . . Well, Marie, you get yourself off home when you have finished the study, and while you are doing that, I shall keep Angélique here with me so that she does not feel the need to carry out any more of her explorations. We are going to have a little talk about the violin.'

With a shake of her head, Angélique's mother headed towards the door, running a yellow duster along the full length of the sideboard before departing the room.

Madame Lafitte smiled conspiratorially at the little girl, who had waited for her mother to leave before sinking to her knees in front of the violin once more. Angélique stared as the violin was taken from its case and the bow unclipped from the lid. Madame Lafitte placed the violin under her chin and plucked at each of the strings, turning the wooden pegs at the end of the fingerboard to tune the instrument.

'Oh, my word, it has been so long since I have played. My fingers are not so nimble nowadays and also the violin is quite small for me, so you must be ready to excuse a great many mistakes, Angélique.'

The little girl watched with wide eyes as the old lady straightened her back, held the bow lightly against the strings, and began to play.

Immediately the room was warmed by the sweetest sound Angélique had ever heard. She stared at the hand that moved effortlessly over the strings, at the fingers that quivered to make every note resound more beautifully, and at Madame Lafitte's face, which suddenly seemed to have become so much younger than before. It's like magic, Angélique thought to herself, the most special thing I have ever discovered.

When Madame Lafitte finished playing, she laid the violin and bow across her knees and smiled. 'Well, not so many mistakes after all.'

'Do you always have to pretend you're sleeping when you play?' Angélique asked.

Madame Lafitte laughed. 'No, my dear, I close my eyes to concentrate.'

'If I closed my eyes, would I be able to play?'

'I don't know. Would you like to have a try?'

Angélique jumped to her feet. 'Am I allowed to?'

'Of course you are. Let's see if we can't play a note or two.'

When the violin was placed under the little girl's chin, her face was at such an angle that she had to squint sideways to look at the strings. Madame Lafitte bit her lip. 'That does not look very comfortable.'

'Oh, it's very comfortable,' exclaimed the little girl, terrified the old lady would take the violin away from her.

'All right, then.' She put the bow in Angélique's free hand and raised the girl's arm so that the bow rested on the fourth string of the violin. 'We are only going to use this string, so that is the one the fingers of your other hand need to press, *tu comprends?*'

'*Oui.*'

'*Bon.* So let us start with that finger, which we call your fourth finger, and now gently move the bow across the string.'

The violin emitted an ear-piercing screech. The girl let out a shrill laugh. 'That sounds like the noise our cat makes when Papa stands on its tail by mistake!'

Madame Lafitte smiled. 'We must immediately stop the suffering of your poor cat! Come on, we shall try *encore une fois.*' This time the note came out almost perfect. 'That was wonderful, Angélique. Well done, you. Now what I want—'

But Angélique had already begun to play again, her eyes screwed tightly closed, and when she repeated the note, she mirrored the technique of the quivering finger she had seen Madame Lafitte use. It resounded exactly as the old lady's had done. So Angélique pressed her third finger to the string and pulled the bow back across it, and again the lower note came out as pure as the last. And then she moved to the second finger, and after an initial screech, she readjusted her wrist and the note once more came out perfect.

The old lady watched the girl's tenacity with fascination. 'All right, now let's try the next string over.'

The bow and fingers moved together to the next string, and following one false start, three perfect notes were sounded, the playing hand arched just as it should be to avoid coming into contact with the fourth string, and then, without prompting, Angélique moved back to that string and played the three original notes again.

'Do you want to try the second string now?'

Angélique did not reply, her fingers feeling instinctively for the next string. Madame Lafitte could tell from the girl's face that this was an effort with fingers as short as hers. She managed almost immediately one clear note before the moment was broken by the sound of the drawing room door being forcefully opened.

'That's the study finished, madame. Again, I am sorry about my daughter's behaviour. I can assure you that it will not happen again.'

Madame Lafitte, with a gentle smile, took the violin from the little girl. She saw the longing in Angélique's eyes as the instrument was replaced in its case. 'Marie, why is Angélique not at school?'

'There was a holiday today, madame. In future, I will—'

'I would like you to bring her here any time you possibly can, schooldays or not.' She turned and looked at the cleaner. 'Would you be able to do that?'

Angélique's mother was perplexed by the request. 'Madame? I'm not sure what you—'

'It's very simple, Marie. Would somebody be able to bring Angélique to my house every day and then fetch her later? I want to teach her to play the violin.'

The housekeeper let out a laugh. 'The violin? Ah, madame, you don't want to bother yourself trying to teach my daughter—'

'Marie, what I do in my own time is my affair. So, can someone bring Angélique to my house every day and then collect her later?'

Angélique's mother shrugged. 'I suppose someone can walk her round, but it would depend on the shifts the others work.'

'It doesn't matter. Any time. I am always here.'

'Very well, madame.'

Madame Lafitte put her arms round Angélique and planted a kiss on the side of her dark hair, before whispering in her ear, 'I think, Angélique, my dear, that one day you will become an exceptional violinist.'

And so it was that Madame Lafitte became the most important person in Angélique Pascal's young life. It was she who gave Angélique her lessons until the ability of the ten-year-old outshone her own. It was she who arranged and paid for the teacher who continued to nurture her extraordinary talent, and together with whom Madame Lafitte put out a search for a full-sized violin that had the same resonance as the one Angélique had been using, eventually tracking one down in a backstreet shop in Munich and purchasing it despite its enormous price tag; it was Madame Lafitte who set up the audition for the thirteen-year-old at Le Conservatoire National Supérieur de Musique et de Danse de Paris; and it was she who persuaded the Pascal family that Angélique's attendance there would have no detrimental impact on their finances, and that the girl's future promised much more than working in a factory.

It was Madame Lafitte who accompanied Angélique to Paris for the first time, the girl holding tight to her hand as they travelled on the Métro below the streets of the city before emerging in front of the inspirational white structure of the Conservatoire. Then, having watched Angélique being taken off for her audition, the old lady had sat alone in the echoing foyer, drinking a cup of coffee while keeping the fingers of her free hand tightly crossed. It was a full hour and a half before Angélique eventually returned to the foyer, accompanied by a tall bespectacled young man wearing a dark green corduroy suit. When they reached the perimeter of the seating area, he put a hand on Angélique's shoulder and spoke to her. The girl smiled at Madame Lafitte and pointed a finger in her direction. Settling Angélique in a chair, the man bought her a bottle of orange juice and gave it to her along with a reassuring smile, then approached the old lady.

'Madame Lafitte?'

'*Oui, c'est moi*,' she replied, struggling to rise from her chair.

'Please, don't get up,' he said. 'I am sorry we have taken so long with Angélique. My name is Albert Dessuin and I am a violin teacher here.'

Madame Lafitte watched the young man lower himself into a chair on the opposite side of the table. She could not bear to wait for news of the audition. 'Monsieur Dessuin, may I ask how Angélique got on?'

Dessuin leaned forward in the chair, resting his elbows on his knees and linking his hands together in front of his chin. 'Madame Lafitte, all I can say is thank you for bringing Angélique to the Conservatoire.'

Tears immediately sprang to the old lady's eyes. 'Oh, I am so pleased you said that. She has a wonderful talent, *n'est-ce pas?*'

'I certainly believe it, and that is why we felt the need to discuss at length her future here.' The young man dropped his hands from his chin. 'Madame, I truly feel that I can make something wonderful out of this talent. But I feel that one so young, and one who has not had a great deal of experience of the outside world, should not be staying by herself in a students' residence.'

Madame Lafitte nodded. 'This has been one of my worries, also.'

'Good, so I hope that the suggestion that I am going to make, which has been approved wholeheartedly by the *directeur*, will be acceptable to yourself as well. Madame, I live with my mother in a very large apartment here in the *quinzième*, and we have customarily lodged some of the younger students. The girl who is with us at present is now of an age to move into the students' residence, which means that Angélique could take over her room. It would facilitate my supervision of both her music tuition and the educational studies that she will receive here.'

'Monsieur Dessuin, that would seem the most perfect idea. Of course, I will recompense you and Madame Dessuin for this.'

Dessuin held up a hand. 'Well, let us see what I can first arrange. For a girl from Angélique's background, I am sure that there are grants available to cover such costs.'

Madame Lafitte tilted her head to the side. 'My husband and I were never fortunate enough to be blessed with any children, monsieur. Maybe it was the plan of some greater being that I should wait until my eighties before being called upon to nurture a child as I now do

Angélique. She need never worry about money, *comprenez-vous?*'

'Of course, madame. I can assure you that I will keep in close contact with you regarding all financial matters relating to Angélique.'

'I am very grateful, Monsieur Dessuin. So when are you thinking that she might start?'

'Next month, in September.'

Madame Lafitte nodded thoughtfully. 'I must first talk to Angélique's parents, monsieur. I am sure I will be able to persuade them by then.' She glanced over to where Angélique sat, holding the violin case. 'Now, I think, would be a good time to give Angélique the news.'

Every week for the next six years, Madame Lafitte received a letter from Angélique, telling her everything about the music she was playing, about the friends she had made, and about the walks along the banks of the River Seine and the visits to museums and art galleries she had made with Albert Dessuin. In turn, Madame Lafitte would read these aloud to Angélique's mother.

Happiness seemed to radiate from these dispatches, so much so that it never occurred to Madame Lafitte that not once had Angélique mentioned her home life with Albert Dessuin and his mother. If she had but known about the tirades, the selfish hypochondria and the cold unfriendliness of the dreadful woman, the clinking of bottle against glass that sounded from Dessuin's bedroom as Angélique passed by late at night to go to the bathroom, then Madame Lafitte would have taken the first train to Paris to make other arrangements. But Angélique never included a word of this, frightened that such a disclosure might end her time at the Conservatoire.

It was two days before her eighty-eighth birthday that Madame Lafitte received the news from Angélique that she had won the Prix du Concours Long-Tibaud. In another letter from Albert Dessuin, which arrived on the same day, he announced that he had decided to give up his position at the Conservatoire in order to continue to teach Angélique and manage her affairs. She was already being inundated with requests from concert halls around Europe and Dessuin felt that there was no way she could cope alone with such pressure.

Madame Lafitte did not read either of the letters herself. That was left to a young male nurse who sat on a chair close to the stroke victim's bedside in hospital. When he had finished, he looked closely at her face and nodded. Good news, he thought to himself, for both her and for the doctors. The smile was the first sign of understanding she had given since being brought there.

Four

THE BATTERED TRANSIT van drove slowly through the streets, every one of them lined with identical stark-fronted houses, before coming to a halt at the entrance to a cul-de-sac. Terry Crosland rolled down the window and just made out the letters of Bolingbroke Close beneath a swirl of black graffiti. He swung the nose of the van round and reversed down the street to a point where he wouldn't interrupt a game of three-a-side football, but, as he opened the door, a deafening bang resounded around the tinny confines of the van and he saw the football dribble past him. Thumping the door closed, he pulled the ball towards him with his foot and deftly flicked it up into his hands.

A boy came running down the street. 'Sorry 'bout that, mister.'

'No 'arm done, lad,' Terry smiled and lobbed him the ball. 'Any idea which is the Brownlows' 'ouse?'

'Number seventeen,' the boy replied, pointing to a house. 'That's Robbie Brownlow playing in goal.'

Terry cast an eye towards the small figure in front of the goal-chalked wall at the end of the cul-de-sac. He was gazing up into the sky, more interested in the vapour trail of a plane than in getting on with the game.

'Good, is he?' Terry asked.

'Nah,' the boy replied. 'That's why we put 'im against the wall.'

Terry walked across the road and entered the Brownlow property through a paint-starved gate. The path to the front door was blocked by a pile of large stones so Terry walked down the narrow passage that divided the twelve-foot gap to the adjacent house. He knocked twice on the back door, then turned away to smooth his greased hair and give his quiff a quick remodel. By the time the door opened, he was standing with his hands pushed into the pockets of his jeans.

The woman who stood at the door was dumpy, wearing black leggings with a pair of scuffed white trainers, her large hips and big bottom well hidden beneath a man's shirt. Her face, however, was smooth-skinned, her cheeks rosy, and her mouth and eyes radiated humour. 'Well, if it isn't Elvis 'imself,' she said with a laugh, and then began to move her fat little body in the twist, singing the refrain of

'Return to Sender' in a deep, sexy voice. When she stopped she stretched her hand up the side of the door, pouting provocatively. 'If I'd known ye were coming round, I'd 'ave put on me see-through negligée.'

Terry smiled. 'I take it that Gary's not home, then?'

Crossing her arms beneath her bosom, Rene Brownlow raised her eyebrows. ''E's where 'e normally is. In the sitting room, watching telly. I doubt 'e'd notice if we had a *bonk* in front of 'im.' She dropped her hand from the side of the door. 'Nor would 'e probably mind, come to that.'

Terry cleared his throat uncomfortably. He liked Rene, but he could never quite cope with her frankness. Still, that was why she was the best comedienne on the Hartlepool circuit, and heroine of Andy's Social Club, where she worked part-time behind the bar. Terry also knew her domestic relationship had been under strain since her husband had lost his job, but he certainly hadn't come round to get mixed up in all that. Rene sensed his unease. 'So what can I do for ye, Terry me lad?'

'I need to 'ave a word.'

Rene leaned her back against the open door. 'In that case, ye'd better come in.'

Terry walked past her into a kitchen still cluttered with dirty pans from the evening meal. ''Ave a seat there.' She pointed to a small plastic-covered stool. 'Like a cuppa?'

'Milk and two sugars, please.'

Rene let out a low growl. 'Ooh, I like a man with a sweet tooth.' She shook her head. 'I'm only joking, ye know, Terry. I can't 'elp it. It's the way God made me. And bloody 'ell, it's 'ard enough trying to keep joking round 'ere.'

Rene pulled a stool away from the table and sat down. Terry wondered if its thin wooden legs were going to be able to take the strain. He turned his eyes away before Rene had a chance to notice and, as a form of diversion, pulled a pepper pot across the table and began spinning it.

Rene leaned over and pushed it to the far end of the table. 'Ye're worse than the kids, y'are. Always find something to fiddle with when they're going to tell me something . . . bad.' Rene emphasised the last word and watched closely for Terry's reaction.

'No, it ain't bad, Rene. Far from it . . . I think. The lads down at the club 'ave been 'aving a whip-round. We've arranged for ye to go up to Edinburgh in August.'

'Edinburgh? Why on earth would I want to go up to Edinburgh?'

'It's for the Edinburgh Festival—the Fringe.'

'The Fringe?' Rene shook her head. 'I'm sorry, Terry, ye've lost me.'

'The Fringe, Rene, is part of the Edinburgh Festival. A whole load of different acts all round the city. Plays and reviews and comedy shows. We think ye should go up there and put on a show.'

Rene stared incredulously at Terry. 'Ye're joking!'

'Far from it.' He leaned forward on the table. 'Listen, Rene, the lads down at Andy's think ye could make it big, and the Fringe is a really good launching pad for people like you.'

'People like me?' Rene exclaimed. 'People like me don't do that kind of thing. We live in 'ouses with unemployed 'usbands. We can't afford to have pipe dreams, Terry, about making it big. It don't work that way.'

'Who says it don't? What about people like Jim Davidson and Jimmy Tarbuck and the like? They both came from pretty 'umble rootings.'

'I know that, Terry, but they are them and I am me.' She let out a sigh. 'Ye know, I'm really touched you and the lads 'ave done this for me, but spend the money on something more worthwhile.'

Terry shook his head. 'No, it's you going to Edinburgh or nowt. We've paid the money and booked the venue. If you don't go, we'll all be out of pocket.'

'But why the 'ell did ye pay before telling me about it?'

Terry simply smiled at her, a knowing look on his face.

Rene flicked back her head, understanding everything. 'You knew there wasn't a chance of me considering it otherwise, isn't that right?' She leaned her elbows on the table and rested her forehead in the palms of her hands. ''Ow long's it for? A couple of nights?'

'Three weeks.'

Rene shot upright. 'Three weeks! Terry, I can't go up to Edinburgh for three weeks. For a kick-off, I couldn't afford it!'

'That's all been taken care of.'

'Oh, bloody 'ell, Terry! I couldn't just 'ead off and leave the kids to fend for themselves. What about Gary? 'E's not working.'

'Rene, don't find excuses for this one. We can work around it. You 'ave a real gift, lass, for making people laugh. Why keep it for 'Artlepool when ye could make yerself some decent money? If you let this chance slip, ye could go regretting it for the rest of your life.'

The door leading from the kitchen into the front of the house opened and a tall skinny man appeared. 'What's going on in 'ere, then?' he asked, exhaling cigarette smoke through his hawk-like nose.

Rene smiled at the man. 'Ye know Terry, don't ye, Gary? Ye've met him at Andy's.'

The man nodded his head briefly in greeting. 'Terry.'

'Nice seeing you, Gary.'

Gary walked over to the sink, ran water onto the stub of his cigarette and threw it into the bin. He turned round, leaned his bottom against the kitchen sink and folded his arms. 'So what gives 'ere?'

'Nowt, really,' Rene replied, narrowing her eyes at Terry in a bid to stop him from even starting on an explanation. Terry chose to ignore it.

'What d'ye think of Rene as a comedienne, Gary?'

'She's damned good,' Gary replied.

Terry shot a look at Rene. 'Aye, that's what I was telling 'er.'

'So that's what ye've come round to tell 'er, is it? That she's funny?'

'No, not exactly.'

'So, what's yer explanation for being 'ere, then?'

Rene took a deep breath. 'Right, then. I'll do the explaining. Some of the lads down at the club 'ave put money in a kitty to send me up to Edinburgh in August to do me act at something called the Fringe. I've told 'im that I can't make a decision right now.'

'What would ye 'ave to do?'

'Just do me act.'

Gary shrugged. 'Why not, then? Ye could take the train up and get back next day.'

Rene looked at her husband. 'It would be for three weeks, Gary.'

'Three weeks? No way! Ye can't abandon yer family for three weeks, especially not in August! That's when Robbie and Karen'll be getting ready to go back to school.' Gary shook his head.

'Excuse me,' Rene exclaimed, her voice rising in volume, 'but is there any good reason why *you* shouldn't look after Robbie and Karen?'

Gary leaned over, centimetres away from Rene's face, his eyes pierced with anger. 'What would 'appen if I got a job while ye were away? Who'd look after the kids then?'

'*I* don't know, Gary. I haven't given it that much thought yet!'

Terry got slowly to his feet. 'Look, I'll leave you two alone to talk about it.' He eased his way between them, and, with a pensive scratch to his cheek, turned back and smiled at Rene's husband. 'Listen, Gary, I know it's 'ard for ye right now. I appreciate it all, mate. I got laid off at the shipyard back in '92, and it took me an age to get back on me feet. But you 'ave a wife with an amazing talent, and to 'ave that locked away here is a real waste. I mean, she could make a whole load of money.'

'And are ye trying to tell me I'm not capable of making the money then?' Gary replied irately, taking a step towards Terry.

Terry held up his hands defensively. 'I'm sorry, it was never meant to sound that way, 'onest, lad.' He gave Rene a sad smile. 'I'll let meself out.' He opened the door and closed it behind him, and as he stood on the step he blew out a long breath of both regret and relief. He walked round the side of the house, past the pile of stones and out through the gate. He was just about to pull the van away from the curb when again he was made to jump at the sound of something heavy hitting the side. He glanced in his wing mirror only to find Rene standing beside him on the pavement. He rolled down the window.

'All right, lass?' he asked concernedly.

She nodded. 'Aye, I'm fine.'

He flicked his thumb over his shoulder. 'Sorry about that in there—'

'I'll do it. I'll go to Edinburgh for the whole bloody three weeks. For once in me life, Terry, I'm not even going to think about Gary. This is my chance, and I want to give it a go. It'll never come round again.'

'Ye can still think about it, if ye like.'

'I don't 'ave to. I've made up me mind this is what I want to do.'

Terry gave her a wink. 'And, by God, you'll show 'em, lass.'

Saturday night at Andersons Westbourne Social Club was always busy, but on that particular occasion, there was hardly room to move, due to the much publicised visit of Danielle Vine, a young singer who had recently been a finalist on the television show *Stars in your Eyes*, thanks to her impersonation of Celine Dion.

Harold Prendergast, manager and licensee, decided to come out front so that he could watch with eagle eyes as the money flowed in and out of the three cash tills spaced evenly along the shelf at the back of the long bar. Two weeks before he'd had to sack one of his bar staff for having 'light fingers'. OK, truth be told, he'd had to pay her off just to keep her mouth shut about what happened, or more to the point, what *hadn't* happen behind the closed doors of his office. He'd always considered it a perk of the job, having a bit of fun with the girls, and he wasn't used to having his advances spurned in such a forceful manner.

He eyed the new girl at work. Her size certainly outweighed her beauty, but there was something sexy about her. A girl could be as pretty as paint, but still exude as much sexual attraction as a cross-eyed donkey. Talking of which, he thought to himself, as he glanced over to the permanently reserved table next to the stage where his wife sat, chatting away primly with her friends from Thursday night bingo. With a shake of his head, he turned to look himself over in the mirror that backed the bar. He adjusted the striped bow tie and smoothed his well-trimmed moustache from centre outwards. Out of the side of his eye he caught sight of the reflection of the new girl, wrestling to control head on a pint of Guinness. He shot a look over to where his wife was seated, before gliding over to the girl and putting his hand on top of hers on the tap. 'Come on, Rene, lass,' he said kindly. 'Ye should 'ave mastered the Guinness tap by now.'

Rene looked round and smiled. 'Sorry, Mr Prendergast. I think it's because Joe's just changed the barrel.'

'Never mind, we'll do this one together. Just pour the head off into the waste tray and we'll try it again.' He pushed up the tap and then eased it down, moving his hand gently against Rene's. 'I think ye'll manage that now, won't ye?'

'I think so. Thanks for the help, Mr Prendergast,' Rene replied.

'That's what I'm here for,' he said soothingly. He started to move away, then turned back and put a pensive finger to his lips. 'Actually, Rene, maybe ye could spare me a moment in me office after ye've finished that round of drinks. Just a few things I need to say.'

Rene looked anxiously at him. 'I can do them most times, Mr Prendergast. It was just the new—'

'No, no,' he cut in with a smile and a shake of his head. 'Nothing serious, lass. Just a couple of words.'

Five minutes later Harold was seated behind his desk watching the close-circuit television that relayed front-of-house proceedings to his office, when there was a knock on the door. He ran a hand either side of his parted hair before moving over to the door and opening it. 'Come in, Rene.' He stood aside and ushered her in. 'Take a seat over there,' he said, indicating the chair in front of his desk. Rene smoothed her black skirt over her large bottom and sat down.

He walked over to an ornate-fronted cabinet that hung on the wall, unscrewed a bottle of malt whisky and poured a large shot into a crystal tumbler before seating himself on the edge of the desk beside Rene. He took a sip from the glass. 'So, tell me, how are ye finding the work?'

Rene shrugged. 'Fine, I suppose.'

'Not too much of a strain?'

'No.' She snorted out a laugh. 'Not when the heaviest thing you have to lift is a pint of beer.'

Harold threw back his head in mirth. 'That's not what I meant, lass, but it's very funny.' His face became serious. 'No, what I really wanted to say to ye, Rene, is that if ever there comes a time when ye *do* feel stressed, then ye must know that the door of my office is always open.'

'That's very kind of ye, Mr Prendergast.'

'Not at all, Rene,' he said, putting his glass down on the desk and moving around behind her, 'because, ye see, I know all about tension, Rene. It just happens to be my speciality.' He placed his hands on Rene's shoulders and began to knead the back of her neck rhythmically with his thumbs. He leaned over close and whispered in her right ear. 'I am a man who has been gifted with 'ealing 'ands.'

'Oh? That's summat, in't it?' Rene replied brightly, darting her eyes from side to side in an attempt to work out why he was doing all this. Surely Mr Prendergast wasn't trying to come on to her?

She jumped to her feet and circled her arms, easing out her shoulders. 'Ooh, that was lovely, Mr Prendergast. Just set me up right for the rest of the night.' She turned to him and smiled. 'I think I should be getting back to the bar now.'

'No, no, there's no hurry, lass,' he sang out, taking her by the arm and trying to guide her back to the chair. 'I've got to work on yer spine yet.'

Rene pulled her arm away from his grip. 'No, let's make it another time, Mr Prendergast. I shouldn't keep the punters waiting, should I?'

Rene saw the hand moving back towards her, but then a knock on the door made the manager retract it and he moved swiftly round the back of his desk and sat down, his face composed. 'Come in,' he called.

Joe, the assistant manager, put his head round the door. 'We've got a no-show, Harold. Danielle Vine's come down with tonsillitis.'

Harold slapped a hand to his forehead. 'Oh, bloody 'ell! That's all I need. What about our reserve act?'

'Eddie's away in York doing a show tonight.'

Harold scratched the fingers of both hands hard at the back of his head. 'Right, then, ye'd better leave me, you two. I've got some thinking to do to come up with an act in the next 'alf an 'our.'

With relief, Rene followed Joe out of the office and closed the door behind her. She took in a deep breath and let it out slowly to compose herself before walking along the passage and out into the bar.

'Be a lass, Rene, and give us a pint of ale.'

Rene turned to see Terry Crosland smiling over the counter at her. She hadn't been working in Andy's long enough to put a name to all the regulars, but she knew Terry because there had been a couple of quiet nights when he'd come in by himself and they'd had a chinwag.

'Coming up,' she replied quietly, still distracted by what had just happened in the office. She put his pint on the bar, rang his money up on the till, placed his change in front of him and turned away.

'What's the matter with you tonight, lass? Cat got yer tongue?'

Rene smiled. 'No. Sorry, Terry, I'm feeling a bit . . . strange right now.'

Terry raised his eyebrows. 'Right. Well, that were a tenner I gave ye just then,' he said, knocking a finger on the bar next to his change, 'so ye owe me another fiver.'

'Oh, I'm sorry, lad.' She opened up the till and found the ten-pound note slid into the compartment that held the fivers. She moved it over, then took out Terry's additional change and shut the drawer. 'There y'are,' she said, placing the note on the bar. 'Sorry about that.'

'So what's wrong?'

Rene shook her head. 'Nowt, really.'

'Well, there must be summat up, ye haven't come out with any of yer jokes. Ye've just been in the office with 'Arold Prendergast, haven't ye? 'E's tried to come on to ye, 'asn't he?'

Rene stared at him, then leaned forward on the bar. ''Ow d'ye know that?' she asked quietly. 'I mean, 'as 'e done it before?'

'Aye, 'e's done it before . . . countless times.'

'Who knows about it, then?'

'You, me, and the other girls who have had to leave because they told 'im to get lost!'

''Ow come you know?'

'Because I found out about it from the first girl that it 'appened to. Met 'er outside in tears just after she'd been given the sack. She was still 'olding the money 'e'd given her to keep 'er mouth shut.'

'And ye've done nowt about it?'

Terry shook his head. 'I know, it doesn't sound right, does it? The man's got it coming to 'im, but the opportunity's never come up.'

Rene looked at him questioningly. 'I don't understand.'

Terry turned round, his eyes looking towards the table by the stage. 'You see that group of women over there? Third one from the left is 'Arold's wife.'

Rene stared with wide eyes in the direction of the stage. 'I don't believe it. D'you mean to say 'e'd try it on with . . . with 'is *wife* here? What a bloody *scumbag*!'

'Exactly,' said Terry, turning back to face her. 'So that's what I mean about the opportunity not coming up yet, but it soon will, Rene my girl, you mark my words.'

Rene did not say anything for a moment, but stood eyeing the stage, her eyes deep-set with hostility. 'I think, Terry, old fruit, that our opportunity has just presented itself. There's a no-show tonight. Danielle What's-'er-face has got tonsillitis, and the reserve act's in York.'

'Oh, bugger me!' Terry exclaimed, looking round at the hundreds of people in the packed club. He let out a high-pitched chuckle. 'Oh, my word, 'Arold's for the 'igh-jump!'

With that, the lights on the stage were brought up to full power and Harold Prendergast came out of the side wing, squinting blindly into the room. He was greeted by a thunderous hand clap. He approached the microphone too fast, making it screech with feedback. 'Ladies and gentlemen, I'm afraid that I 'ave some bad news for ye.' This brought about an immediate and complete silence. 'I'm sorry to inform ye that our star performer, Danielle Vine, 'as been taken unexpectedly ill—'

He got no further. The audience erupted with angry jeers and a chorus of 'We want our money back!' and Harold soon gave up and reversed away to the sanctuary of the side wing.

'Right, go up and introduce me, Terry,' Rene shouted above the din.

Terry turned and stared at her. 'What? I can't go up there.'

'Terry, this is our opportunity. All ye've got to say is something about the club being lucky enough to have some in-house entertainment.'

'And what are *you* going to say?'

Rene burst out laughing. 'I don't know yet.'

Terry made his way reluctantly through the tables. Nobody noticed him until he jumped up onto the stage and walked over to the microphone. The noise abated to a questioning hum, then silence.

'Ladies and gentlemen, we might not be getting what we came for—'

A voice yelled out: 'Too bloody right, we're not!'

'—but I know this girl who is funnier than anyone *I've* ever seen up on this stage, and what's more, she works right 'ere in Andy's. So I ask ye now, ladies and gentlemen, to welcome 'er up 'ere by giving our own Rene Brownlow a big round of applause.'

There was a smatter of clapping and all eyes turned to watch Rene duck under the bar lid and make her way towards the stage. As she passed Terry, she reached out and gave his hand a squeeze.

The first laugh came before Rene had even got onto the stage. There being no steps at the front, Rene tried to get up by swinging one leg first and then the other before turning turned round and pulling two well-built lads out of their chairs to give her a heave-up. Rene's feet hardly made contact with the ground until she was centre stage and she had to grab hold of the backdrop curtain to stop herself from falling. 'Thanks, lads,' she said, smiling down at the two men. 'I'll take your numbers later in case I ever want to get shot into space!' The remark brought some chuckles and she watched as the two guys had their backs slapped by those around them.

'Right. First I'd like to thank Elvis for that kind introduction.' More laughter as people turned to look at Terry run both hands over his quiffed hair. 'Not every girl who gets her act announced by the King himself.' That continued the laugh for a moment, sufficient time for Rene to work out what she was going to say next. 'OK, my name's Rene Brownlow. I'm the short fat one who works over there.' She pointed to the bar. 'Of course, anyone who's the same 'ight as me 'as probably never clapped eyes on me before. Either that, or ye've thought I was just a disembodied 'ead rolling backwards and forwards along the bar.'

That gave her another thirty seconds. Her eye was caught by a shadowy figure in the side wing. Harold Prendergast. 'And,' she said, moving her wide hips provocatively from side to side, 'I'm no Marilyn Monroe, but I'll 'ave ye know there are some who find me *most attractive!*' There was a loud cry of agreement that Rene didn't allow to end. 'OK, 'ands up, all you sexy gentlemen out there,' she yelled above the noise, 'who finds me outrageously attractive?'

It was working. She looked out onto a sea of hands, laughed and then turned towards the side wing. ''Ang on a moment!' she said, frowning theatrically. 'There's a man over 'ere who 'asn't put 'is 'and up.' She moved quickly over to the side wing and grabbed his arm.

'What the *'ell* are ye playing at?' Harold Prendergast hissed angrily at her. 'Don't ye realise my *wife's* out there?'

Rene turned back to the audience. 'Oh, he says 'is *wife's* out 'ere. Stop hiding yerself in there, 'Arold, and come and point 'er out to us all.'

The laughter in the club was growing louder, but it was never as strong as the chorus of 'Come out, 'Ar-old!'

With a sneer of fury, Harold allowed Rene to drag him onto the stage and the audience applauded his arrival. Rene held up her hand and there was immediate silence. She knew she had the audience totally with her. 'So, go on, 'Arold, tell us all where yer good wife is sitting.'

Harold pointed down to the table in front of the stage and flashed an uneasy smile at his wife.

'That's no use, 'Arold,' Rene exclaimed, shaking her head from side to side in time with her words. 'I can see at least eight beautiful ladies sitting at that table. Which one is she, 'Arold?'

'That one,' Harold said quietly, pointing again to his wife.

Rene shielded her eyes against the lights as she made a show of appraising the manager's wife. 'Wow, 'Arold, you've got a real stunner there! Tell me, 'ow long 'ave you two been married?'

'Twenty-four years,' he replied meekly.

Rene drilled a finger into her left ear. 'I'm sorry, 'Arold, my 'earing doesn't seem to be too good tonight. 'Ow long did you say?'

'Twenty-four years,' he repeated, only a fraction louder.

'Twenty-four years!' Rene exclaimed, jamming the microphone under her armpit as she joined in with the audience's applause. 'Well, that is what I call a wonderful achievement!' She moved close to Harold and leaned her head against his chest, anguish written all over her face.

'I can see now why ye never put yer 'and up. How could I *ever* compare with someone as beautiful as that?'

There was a cry from the back of the hall. 'Put yer bloody 'and up!'

Others began to join in the refrain and very slowly, Harold Prendergast raised his hand. Rene pulled his face towards her and planted a lingering kiss on his cheek, and the club was filled with the beating of pint glasses on the tables.

Rene knew what was coming. As the manager made to speak, she leaned her hand against his right shoulder. He was so distracted with anger and humiliation that he did not realise that that was the hand in which she held the microphone.

'I want to see you in my office afterwards, d'ye understand?'

He had meant it to be a whisper, but his words rang round the club. Rene turned towards her audience with a knowing grin on her face, giving a slow continuous nod. To begin with, the audience burst out laughing, but then, as 400 eyes focused on Mrs Prendergast to witness her reaction, the volume faded away to an uneasy silence. Glaring with hostility at her husband's drooping form onstage, she grabbed her jacket from the back of her chair and, with her head bowed, started to make her way towards the exit.

By the time the door had closed behind her, Harold had disappeared from the stage, quickly making for the fire door in order to catch up with his wife. Having recaptured her audience's attention with a quick-fire remark, Rene kept them engrossed for the next hour, never giving the manager another thought.

After the show, she went to his office. A weak voice answered to her forceful knock. Ten minutes later she bounced back along the corridor and out behind the bar, where the bar staff were having a hard time keeping up with the orders. Rene could do nothing to help out, as those who thronged the bar greeted her with cries of congratulations and thrust out hands for her to shake. Rene said her thanks while scanning the bar for Terry. She eventually caught sight of him in the corner, watching her every move. She walked along to the end, ducked under the bar lid, and hardly had the chance to straighten up before she found herself enveloped in a tight hug.

'You were bloody fantastic, lass. Spot on.'

'D'ye think so?'

Terry pushed her away and eyed her suspiciously. 'Ye know fine well it was, don't ye? I don't think ye've left 'Arold Prendergast much of an 'eart to try out his old tricks again, that's for sure. Did ye go to his office to see him? What 'appened?'

Rene smiled. 'We threw insults across his desk and then negotiated.'
'Right. So, what did ye come away with?'

Rene's face broke into an excited grin and she reached up and grabbed hold of the lapels of Terry's denim jacket. 'A bloody raise and an 'alf 'our comedy spot up on that stage every Thursday night!'

Terry grabbed her by the shoulders and gave her a shake. 'That's the best news I've 'eard for a long time. Ye'll show 'em 'ow it's done, lass.'

Five

HAVING SHOWN the affluent-looking man into her sitting room, the elderly woman excused herself, closed the door and walked past the dark-varnished staircase to the kitchen. She put the kettle on to boil, then slid open one of the double-glazed doors that led out into the small garden allowing the noise of the traffic on the Kingston bypass to fill the room. 'Leonard,' she called out, 'are you there?'

No reply. She crossed the grass and made her way round the curved flower bed where she found her husband kneeling on a plastic sheet, digging with a hand fork. Leonard Hartson turned to look at her, shielding his eyes against the sun with an earthy glove. 'Coffee time, is it?'

'No, dear. It's Nick Springer. You remember, he said he was going to pop in today.'

'Oh, goodness!' her husband exclaimed, getting laboriously to his feet. 'I forgot he was coming. You should have reminded me, Gracie.'

'I did, dear, this morning at breakfast.'

'Oh, bother me, did you?' he said, pulling off his gardening gloves. He cast an eye over his corduroys and ragged jersey. 'Do you think I should change my clothes before I see him? I do look rather scruffy.'

'I don't think he'll mind. He seems very nice.'

Leonard smiled at his wife. 'Nick always was a charmer.' Putting a hand on her elbow, he guided her back towards the house. 'Where is he, then?'

'In the front room,' she replied as she ran her hand either side of his straggling grey hair to make him look slightly more presentable. 'I'll bring through coffee and biscuits.'

Leonard opened the door of the sitting room. Nick Springer turned from the mantelpiece where he had been studying some photographs. 'Leonard!' He approached the elderly man with his hand outstretched. 'How wonderful to see you!'

Leonard winced a smile as the grip sent an arthritic jolt up his arm. 'Nice to see you too, Nick. It's very rare I see anyone from the old days.'

Nick gave a sharp pull at the creases of his navy-blue suit trousers before sitting down in the armchair Leonard indicated to him. 'It's been a long time. I reckon it's all of twenty-eight years.'

Leonard shook his head slowly. 'Oh, well, time stops for no man, as they say.' He observed the younger man as he brushed a hand across his thick dark hair. Nick had been one of his better camera assistants, a quick learner with a good sense of humour. Whatever he had done with his life, Leonard could tell that he had accomplished it with some success. 'So, are you still behind the camera?' he asked.

Nick shook his head. 'No, I run my own production company now.'

The door handle of the sitting room rattled. Jumping up from the chair, Nick was there in two strides, taking the tray from Grace Hartson's hands before she had even the chance to enter the room.

'Nick, you've met my wife, Grace, haven't you?' Leonard asked.

'Of course. I met Mrs Hartson many years ago, when I picked you up here once on the way down to Portsmouth for a shoot. I was just saying to Leonard, Mrs Hartson, that it was twenty-eight years ago.'

'My word,' she said quietly, already making her way out. 'Well, I'll leave you two to have your chat in peace.' She closed the door soundlessly behind her.

'Shall I do the honours?' Nick asked, squatting down and picking up the coffee pot from the tray. 'How d'you like it?'

'Just milk, please.'

'What? No sugar, Leonard? I remember you put so much sugar in your coffee that you could practically stand a spoon up in it.'

Leonard laughed. 'I'm afraid I can't get away with that any more.' He patted his heart. 'Doctor's orders, you know.'

'Really?' Nick handed Leonard the cup of coffee and then sat back down. He took a sip from his cup, then leaned back in the armchair. 'So, is that the reason you gave up work? The heart?'

Leonard shook his head. 'Oh, no. That's only been a slight problem for the past five years.'

'So why did you give up? It took everyone in the industry by surprise.'

'Now, I know you're over-exaggerating on that account, Nick. I never did quite make *that* kind of a mark.'

Nick pushed himself forward in his chair. 'You always were a self-deprecating devil, Leonard. I went up to Sammie's in Cricklewood Broadway to pick up some hire equipment about three months after you retired, and I was informed that they'd received endless correspondence from the likes of David Watkin asking why you'd retired.'

'You're not being serious?'

'I certainly am. Come on, Leonard, I know for a fact that you were only a stone's throw from being made a member of the British Society of Cinematographers. So, why did you choose to give it all up?'

Leonard took a sip from his coffee cup and let out a long sigh. 'I was becoming disillusioned with all the changes in the industry. I really had no time for all the new video technology. I hated the way one was supposed to just blast a set with lights. There was no delicacy any more, no artistry. I thought it to be the death knell of the industry as I had known it. I even believed features would end up being shot on video.'

'But they haven't. The quality of video production has improved in leaps and bounds, you know, especially now with High Def Digital.'

Leonard laughed. 'I'm afraid you've lost me on that one, which really only goes to confirm my belief that if I'd stayed on I would have just become an old dinosaur.'

'So what did you do? You could only have been in your mid-forties.'

Leonard let out a short laugh. 'It was a difficult one. I had no training to do anything else. I'd left school at the age of sixteen with no qualifications and went straight to work at Ealing Studios as a general dogsbody. I'm close on seventy-three now, so, yes, you're right. I would have been in my mid-forties . . . I became a taxi driver.'

Nick started with amazement. 'What? A London cabbie?'

'No, just a private hire company here in Kingston. Actually, I found it quite a relief. I'd spent so much time away from home, and from Grace.'

Nick drained his coffee, then leaned forward and placed the cup on the tray. 'Do you have any regrets now? About leaving the film industry.'

Leonard pulled at his earlobe thoughtfully. 'I would say that I *did* have regrets but they have faded with time. I never quite came to terms with the fact that, in my mind, I had never accomplished what I would have considered to be my definitive film. If you really want to know the truth, Nick, I did harbour a deep frustration for a number of years.'

Nick nodded. 'Do you still remember much about how you worked?'

Leonard smiled. 'You don't forget how to ride a bicycle, do you?' He knocked a finger at the side of his head. 'It's all still up here. I don't know what I'd be like at operating a camera now. My hands may be a bit shaky, but no doubt equipment will have improved and someone will have invented a tripod that's even superior to the great Miller fluid head. And I'm sure film stock will have changed for the better too.' He let out a nostalgic laugh. 'My word, you've got me harking back.'

Nick rested his arms on his knees, his hands clutched together. 'Do you remember a job we did at the Royal Ballet?'

'Of course I do. We shot it all on 7242 Ektachrome with available light. All pretty grainy, but it turned out to be quite effective.' He pointed a finger at Nick in recollection. 'You operated on that job and did a damned good job of it too. It was after that one I was convinced you were going to make the grade.' He let out a sigh. 'But you gave it up too and went into production, right?'

'Yes.' Nick's face became serious. 'And that's the reason I've come down here to talk to you today.' He rubbed his hands together as he gathered his thoughts. 'Leonard, I'll get straight to the point. Would you ever consider coming out of retirement?'

Leonard observed the man for a moment, his eyes and forehead creased in question. 'To do what?'

'I want you to film a Japanese dance company at the Edinburgh Festival in August.'

Leonard continued to stare at Nick, and then, with a disbelieving shake of his head, he turned and fixed his eyes in silence on the fire.

'Look, Leonard, let me explain the situation,' Nick said. 'I received a telephone call last week from an old friend of mine, Alasdair Dreyfuss. I used to play tennis with him on a regular basis before he moved north to become director of the Edinburgh Festival. One of the big Japanese conglomerates is sponsoring this traditional dance company at the festival this year and one of the broadcast companies from Tokyo has been in contact with me, asking if I could arrange the filming of the event. The commissioner has given express instructions it should be shot on film rather than on video, so that, in his words, "the essence of the dance can be captured in its purest and most natural form".'

Nick was becoming uneasy at Leonard's total lack of response to his proposal, but he decided to continue with his explanation.

'Now to be quite honest, Leonard, my line of work is strictly corporate, and we have always centred our business on video production, but the moment that Alasdair told me about this project, my mind was taken back to that job we did with the Royal Ballet—'

'That was all of thirty years ago, Nick,' Leonard cut in quietly.

'I know it was, but you said yourself that the knowledge is still there.'

'Maybe so, but that doesn't mean I could suddenly take on a job like this. For heaven's sakes, I'm seventy-two years old, Nick!'

'So? There are plenty of DOPs still working at your age, and if I'm not very much mistaken, the great Freddie Young was still making films way into his nineties! I'd get you a full working crew, Leonard. You wouldn't have to lift a finger other than just light the set and shoot it.'

Leonard shook his head. 'My word, what an extraordinary proposal.'

'Three weeks of shooting in August, Leonard. Three weeks and you just make your own time.'

'You said I would have to light the set,' Leonard said. 'Surely the company would be performing in a theatre with fixed lighting?'

'I'm going to send a location scout up to Edinburgh to see if he can't find an unused warehouse with a three-phase supply. I would suggest that some you shoot under theatre light during the performance to get the atmosphere and the rest you shoot in the warehouse.'

'How would that edit?' Leonard's eyebrows arched with worry. 'And what about film stock? I wouldn't have the first idea what to use now.'

'We have three months before the festival, Leonard,' Nick said quietly. 'I'll make sure you know as much about the equipment, the film stock and the lighting as you did thirty years ago.' He paused. 'This could turn out to be your definitive film, you know. Why not take the chance to achieve it?'

Leonard rubbed his forehead. 'I would have to speak to Grace.'

'Of course,' Nick said, knowing he had managed to sow the seed of acceptance. 'I'll give you a call in the next couple of days and you can let me know your answer. If it's yes, then we'll start the ball rolling.' He glanced at the Rolex watch on his wrist. 'I must be on my way. I have a lunch meeting in the West End at one.' He sprang to his feet and stood waiting as Leonard raised himself stiffly from the sofa.

'It was good of you to remember me, Nick,' Leonard said, undoing the lock on the front door. He held out a hand and when Nick grasped it with his own, Leonard wrapped his other hand over it and gave it an affectionate squeeze. 'I'll have an answer for you when you call.'

Leonard followed the tall man out onto the gravelled path and stood watching as he slid himself into a dark green Jaguar. As the car sped away, he turned to find Grace leaning over an azalea bush, plucking away some of its withered leaves.

'This doesn't seem to be doing very well here, Leonard. I think we should move it.' She straightened up and turned her gaze to the vanishing Jaguar. 'What a nice man he is. He has a very loud voice, though.' She turned to look at her husband and her face broke into a broad grin when she witnessed a sparkle in his eyes absent for so many years.

'What?' he asked, perplexed.

Grace planted a long kiss on his cheek. 'Are you going to do it, then?'

He took hold of both her hands and gave them a squeeze. 'I don't know. The idea fills me with fear, but at the same time I am honoured he should have asked me. What do you think, Gracie?'

His wife was silent for a moment before replying. 'I could give many reasons why you should *not* do it, my dear,' she said. 'I would worry about you, about your physical ability to take on a project such as this. But you have been given an opportunity to counter all those lost years away from the industry that you loved.' She gave his hands a shake. 'So I would suggest you go for it.'

Six

FRED BROWNLOW GAVE himself the once-over in the mirror in the narrow hallway of the council house in Wilson Street, Hartlepool, admiring his turnout just as he had done three decades before when serving as a company sergeant major with the Durham Light Infantry.

'Ready to go?'

He turned to see his wife come along the passage from the kitchen.

'Aye, Agnes,' he said, taking the white cap down from the hook on the hallstand and fitting it snugly onto his head. 'Ready for action.' He took a bunch of keys from the stand and scooped up the bag that contained his bowls from the floor. 'I'll not be late the night.'

'Right. Well, play well and don't get all moody if ye get beaten.'

Fred rolled his eyes. 'As if I ever do,' he scoffed.

As he left the house, Agnes gave a shake of her head. She knew that one followed the other more often than he cared to admit.

Fred closed the latch on the iron gate and began to walk up Wilson Street. As he hit his stride, he caught sight of the man with the two children walking towards him, seemingly unaware of his presence. He quickly sidestepped off the pavement and crouched down by a parked car, but he had hardly time to complete his act of concealment before the slap-slapping of feet came running up the pavement towards him.

'We know ye're there, Grandpa!' he heard the voice of his grandson call out. 'We saw you 'iding!'

Fred stood up just as Robbie came to stand beside the car, a beaming smile on his face. 'Rats! I thought I'd managed to outsmart ye that time.' He turned just as Karen reached him and launched herself into his arms. 'Oh, my word!' he cried out, dropping his bowling bag with a clatter to the ground and swinging her round in a full circle. 'Ye nearly had your old grandpa off his feet.' He gave his son a welcoming flick of his head as he approached. "Ow ye're doin', Gary? All well?'

'Aye, good enough,' Gary replied sullenly. 'Looks like ye're off out.'

'Aye, I've got the semifinals of the district league.' He cocked his head back towards the house. 'Yer mother's in. Go pay her a visit.'

'Ah'll do that.'

'No luck yet, then, with the job-'unting?'

Gary shook his head. 'There's nowt much doing.'

Fred gave his son's arm an encouraging squeeze. 'Summat'll turn up, lad.' He picked up his bag. 'Best be off. Can't keep the boys waiting.'

'Aye, play well,' Gary replied, raising a hand in farewell as he turned to follow the children who had already disappeared into the house.

The television in the front room was on at full volume when Gary shut the front door behind him. He glanced into the room in passing and saw Robbie and Karen squeezed together into one of the maroon velour armchairs, their eyes transfixed on the screen.

'What d'ye think ye're doing?' Gary asked. 'Ye're here to see yer nan.'

'I said they could,' Agnes soothed as she came past, carrying two glasses of orange juice. She placed them on the lace mat she had arranged on the small table next to the children's armchair. 'Fancy a cup of tea, luv?' she asked, giving her son's arm a loving rub. 'We'll go through to the kitchen and leave these two to their programme.'

Gary followed the small figure with her neat grey curls along the narrow passage to the kitchen.

'Rene working today?' Agnes asked, freshening up the brew in the china teapot with boiling water.

'Aye, she was asked to do the afternoon shift down at Andy's. Probably just as well. She's not in the best mood with me.'

"Ow's that, luv?' Agnes asked as she poured out two mugs of tea.

Gary let out a long sigh. 'This lad from Andy's came round the other day, said they'd been raising money to send Rene off to Scotland for this Edinburgh Festival thing, you know, to do her comedy turn, and she wants to do it—only I've sort of put a dampener on the whole idea.'

'Oh? Why's that?' Agnes asked, concentrating on carrying the brimming mugs over to the table.

'It was for three weeks, Mum, that's why! She can't go for that length of time. It's when the kids will be getting ready to go back to school.'

Agnes sat down. 'And that makes a difference, does it?'

'Of course it makes a difference! 'Ere, I thought you'd support my point of view on this one.'

'Oh, luv, I am supportive of you, and the lads at Andy's must be pretty supportive of Rene as well if they're willing to send 'er all the way up to Scotland. They must think she's really good.'

'Oh, there's no question about that,' Gary replied with enthusiasm. 'It's just that . . .' Agnes noticed his shoulders slump with dejection. 'I was 'oping I might 'ave found meself a job by then.'

Agnes reached out and patted her son's hand. 'And I'm sure ye will, Gary, but even when that happens, we can still manage. I can do my bit with the kids and so can yer dad. It's a pleasure for us, ye know.' She gave a thoughtful shake of her head. 'She's a brave one, is our Rene.'

''Ow d'ye mean?'

'Well, she's considering taking off from 'Artlepool, a place she's 'ardly left in her life, and spending three weeks away from 'er family in a place where she'll know nobody. She must feel she can make a success of 'erself at this festival. Why not give 'er the encouragement she needs?'

Gary nodded slowly. 'Ye reckon she should go then?'

'Absolutely, and if ye want to show how much ye love her, then ye'll be waving her off up to Scotland with flags unfurled.'

On a cloudless early August morning, Jeff Banyon strode along Princes Street, feeling a bead of sweat break out from under his shirt collar and trickle slowly down his back. Still one week to go before the Fringe started, two weeks before the International, but already there was an increase of tourists. He quickened to a run as he turned down Waverley Bridge, seeing the dark-blue-and-red GNER engine appearing from the tunnel below the castle.

It was his fourth season working with the Scottish Chamber Orchestra and dealing with the organisation of the fireworks concert, yet experience did not seem to make it any easier. Over the last three months he had managed to speak to Roger Dent, owner of the Exploding Sky Company, on just four occasions, and only today had it been confirmed to him they had succeeded in scoring the Tchaikovsky piece and begun to stockpile the equipment and hardware for the show.

Dealing with Roger always meant high-octane stress. The man was totally unorthodox in the way he conducted his business, but at the end of the day always produced a display that left the audience open-mouthed, something he'd succeeded in doing for twenty-odd years.

Jeff flashed his ticket at the barrier and made his way to the front of the train. Acquiring a first-class ticket off the Internet at a much-reduced rate gave him an hour and a half of tranquillity to gather his thoughts before meeting Sir Raymond Garston, the man charged with conducting the Scottish Chamber Orchestra when it accompanied the fireworks display on the final Saturday night of the festival.

At the rear section of the crowded train, Leonard Hartson eventually managed to squeeze his suitcase into a luggage rack, half a carriage away from his reserved seat. He edged his way back along the central aisle, found his seat and sat down.

Despite Gracie's encouragement, he had taken his time to agree to Nick Springer's request. In the cold light of day, he had begun to doubt his ability to take on the Edinburgh job and to question Nick's judgment in not using a cameraman who had both age and technical knowledge on his side. Nick, however, was not to be swayed and arranged for Leonard to study the work of a freelance cameraman for a week, saying that Leonard could give him an answer after that period.

The cameraman, who was young, nevertheless knew well of Leonard's reputation and had appeared more nervous at the prospect of working with the cinematographer than Leonard was of starting from scratch. Leonard had stood aside as the young man set his lights, watching in fascination, and it wasn't until he had touched the redesigned body of the Arriflex 16SR3 camera that he'd felt back where he belonged. The young cameraman watched his action closely, and then changed the static lens for a Canon 10:1 zoom, inviting him to try it out. Leonard pressed the button on the automatic zoom, marvelling at its smooth action. With the zoom tight in, he focused on a book that lay on a table in the centre of the set, and then returning to wide angle, ending up close in on the book, perfectly focused. Nothing had changed, and he knew he had the ability to accept Nick's commission.

Now, having carried out his recce in Edinburgh, and having seen the Edinburgh warehouse that the location scout had found, Leonard knew what he required. He had made out the list the night before and faxed it to Nick's production manager. In two weeks' time, he would be back here in Edinburgh to meet up with his assistant cameraman and two electricians who would be bringing the equipment from London.

Three kilometres north of Waverley Station, over the New Town's genteel crescents, a surge of wind blew through the concrete council flats on Pilton Mains before losing its force over the Firth of Forth.

In Thomas Keene's bedroom, on the third floor of one of the blocks, an empty baked beans tin on the edge of the broken-backed chair by his bed fell victim to the gust that blew in through the uncurtained window. It clattered to the ground and rolled across the floorboards, adding to the detritus covering the room. The figure on the bed stirred under the uncovered duvet and a leg shot out in a stretch, revealing a dirty green undersheet too short for the grubby mattress. After a moment, the duvet was thrown back and Thomas Keene, known as T.K., greeted the new day with a rub at his stinging eyes and a string of expletives.

Swinging his legs over the side of the bed, T.K. sat in his T-shirt and shorts, dragging fingers with difficulty through his tangle of greasy hair. He stood up and pulled on a pair of jeans then pushed his bare feet into dirty trainers, their laces already tied. Pulling a hooded sweatshirt off the bare screw in the wall, he walked into the sitting room where his father slumped vacantly eyeing the television.

'Whit's there tae eat?' T.K. asked, rubbing a hand down the unshaven stubble on his pockmarked cheek.

His father answered with a negative flick of his head.

'Could ye gie's some money, then?'

'Awa' tae hell,' his father replied, without taking his eyes off the television. 'D'yae think ah'm daft or summat?'

T.K. shook his head slowly at his father's mistrust. 'It's fi food. Ah havnae touched the stuff fi twa months. Gie's some credit fi tha'.' Thomas Keene senior turned, a sneer on his face, and began to slow-handclap his son in strong, aggressive beats. He turned back to the television. 'Try getting yersel' a joab then, if yuv stopped fryin' yer brains.'

'There's naine aboot.'

'Well then, dae wha ye did last year. Awa' an' tak' photies of a' thae tourists aw aboot the toon.'

'Ah cannie,' T.K. replied morosely. 'Ah've flogged the camera.'

His father turned and glared at him. 'Fi a fix?'

'Na, fi cash!' T.K. replied angrily. 'Ah told ya before, ah'm clean!'

His father shook his head. 'Then, get yersel' uptoon and see wha gives.'

'I've nae change fi the bus.'

His father let out a long sigh. 'God gae ye legs, lad. Awa' an' use 'em.'

T.K. shambled over to the door of the flat and opened it with force. He turned and gave his father a middle-finger salute before slamming the door behind him. He always used the stairs, because the lift never worked, and if it did, there was more likelihood of being roughed up inside it. He took the concrete steps two at a time, trying to hold his breath so he didn't have to take in the odour of disinfectant and urine.

He burst out into the sunlight at the bottom, heaved in fresh air and made his way across the estate to the cul-de-sac where the dustbins were kept, the entrance to the shortcut uptown.

As he turned into it, he quickly pulled back against the wall, then edged his head round the corner of the building and eyed the two policemen who were walking around a dark blue Ford Mondeo. The police car was drawn up alongside the stolen vehicle.

He had no option now other than to go the long way round. If he was seen anywhere near a stolen car, he knew he'd be roped in for it. He hadn't nicked a car for the past few months, ever since he had given up on the hard stuff. It had been hard graft but he owed it to his solicitor, Mr Anderson, for somehow getting him a two-month probationary order with compulsory rehab instead of the expected spell in Borstal.

T.K. ran out to the front of the estate and turned eastwards onto the main road towards Leith Docks. Not that he didn't miss it, though. The joy-riding, that is, not the drugs. He was determined not to go back on the hard stuff, but the joy-riding was a different matter. First time he'd done it was when he was fourteen years old. A Ford Fiesta, parked up for the night. The boy he was with got into the car and hot-wired it within 100 seconds, and with a burn of rubber they'd headed off on an exhilarating trip, eventually ending the evening triumphantly when they abandoned the car with its front wheels on the top step of the war memorial in the centre of the gravel sweep at Fettes College.

After that, T.K. had been hooked. He became an artist at his craft, able to break into the most sophisticated German car, disabling its alarm, hot-wiring its supposedly foolproof ignition system, all within the space of two and a half minutes. He did get caught once in his early years, and that's when he'd first met Mr Anderson, who'd managed to get him off on the grounds of it being his first-time offence.

And then he had done the contract theft of the BMW for the man in Craigmillar and he suddenly found himself with £200. Word got around the estate that T.K. had money and the dealer came knocking on the door of the flat. After that, he never again had the concentration nor the ability to carry out his craft. And so he had come to rely on petty theft to feed his habit, hanging around the coffee shops uptown, watching out for an open handbag or a jacket slung casually across the back of a chair.

Then three months ago, impulse had made him jump into a Vauxhall Vectra left outside a newsagent with its engine running. T.K. only managed to drive it a mile before sideswiping a parked car at speed. The impact slewed him across the road and the car ended up with the driver's door caved in against a tree. It was following the resultant court case that T.K. decided to take Mr Anderson's advice to heart.

After an hour and a half's walk, T.K. found himself heading towards the top of Leith Walk. He stopped for a rest and glanced across the street at a small coffee shop, its stone surround painted in pastel green with the words *The Grainstore* in looping italics above the door. T.K. could smell the aroma of ground coffee beans and warm bread drifting out through the open door, and his stomach began to ache with hunger. Ignoring the orderly queue inside, he approached the girl operating the till at the counter.

'If you want something, you'll have to join the queue,' she said.

'Ah'm no' aifter some' in' tae eat or drink. Ah'm aifter a joab.'

The girl let out a short laugh of disbelief. 'Oh, you are, are you?'

'Yeah, ah'll dae onythin'. Waash dishes, whativver ye waant.'

The girl turned to catch the eye of a tall thin man.

'Can I help you?' he asked, taking in T.K.'s dishevelled state.

'Ah've just said tae the girl here that ah'm needing a joab.'

'I'm afraid we're fully staffed,' the man said curtly.

T.K. shrugged his shoulders. 'Aye, cheers onyway, mate.' He turned and made his way over to the door. The queue now stretched out onto the pavement, causing a bottleneck in the entrance. As T.K. joined the throng, he was pushed hard against the back of a chair, and he shot an apologetic smile at its elderly occupant. And then he saw the open bag and the silver glint of the camera inside. One of the new compact JVC digital video cameras. His father's words of 'Awa' an' tak' photies of the tourists' spun round his head, merging with Mr Anderson's 'I can't help you any more, T.K.' And then the crush of the bottleneck started again, and he was pushed along with the crowd and out onto the street.

He walked swiftly until he had cleared the corner of the coffee shop, and then, tucking the camera into the front pocket of his sweatshirt, he pulled up the hood and took off as fast as his tired legs would carry him, convinced that some fleet-footed coffee drinker was giving chase. There was no lessening in his pace as he raced round the corner into London Street. At that point, he felt he had to look back to see if there was need for him to jettison the camera and make a break for it, so he did not see a young man walking towards him carrying two paint cans. As T.K. turned again with relief, he veered to the same side of the pavement as the paint carrier and their shoulders came into heavy contact, sending the cans clattering to the ground.

T.K. heard a yell of anger behind him, but he didn't stop running until he thought he would be safe from any pursuit.

Jamie Stratton watched with annoyance as the hooded figure with the sagging jeans disappeared round the corner. 'Effing junkie,' he said quietly and then stepped down into the gutter where the two paint cans had come to rest. Somehow they were still intact. He picked them up, then switched them to one hand in order to take a bunch of keys from the pocket of his jeans. He walked towards a set of wide stone steps leading up to a heavy black entrance door. Once inside, he took the stairs two at a time to his third-floor flat.

Stooping to pick up the mail, he walked through to the large kitchen, depositing the keys, the paint cans and the mail on the table. He moved across to the sink and filled the kettle, then flicked the switch and leaned back against the worktop.

He had bought the high-ceilinged, four-bedroomed Georgian flat at the beginning of his second year at Edinburgh University. His father had lent Jamie the deposit for the mortgage, saying that it would be a good investment and that he could pay off the monthly instalments by renting out the three other bedrooms to fellow students. Over the next three years the place had endlessly thumped with the sound of music and laughter, to such an extent that he had been more than relieved at the end of his university career, two months before, to walk away with a 2:2 Honours Degree.

And now his three flatmates had left and he had been offered a September placement with a publishing company in London. His father had persuaded him it was time to sell the flat and roll his capital over into a small property in London. The place would go on the market in mid-September and Jamie was to ready it for sale over the summer months, covering the intervening mortgage payments by renting out the empty bedrooms during the hectic weeks of the festival.

Jamie let out a nostalgic sigh and turned to shake a dollop of Nescafé into a mug before pouring in the boiling water. He sifted through the mail, lobbing the circulars directly into the bin by the cooker. Two letters remained, one a heavy, buff-coloured A4 envelope from the *Edinburgh Fringe Review* and the other from the accommodation agency renting out his flat. The envelope from the newspaper enclosed a Fringe programme, a heap of flyers on the forthcoming acts and the treasured yellow ticket that would allow him free passage into any of the shows. He read through the accompanying letter, confirming they were pleased he would once again be joining their team of reviewers.

Jamie spun the letter onto the table and set to opening the smaller envelope. '*Shit!*' he yelled out. 'What the *hell* do I do now?' He ran his hands over his thick blond hair as he tried to work out what options were open to him. With a further loud expletive, he strode into the hallway and dialled a number.

'Good afternoon, R. and J. L. Mackintosh, Solicitors,' a female voice sang out in a refined Edinburgh accent.

'Yeah, can I speak to Gavin Mackintosh, please? It's Jamie Stratton.'

The line went onto hold and Jamie drummed his fingers irascibly.

'Hello, Jamie, Gavin here. How's that father of yours? Still chasing sheep over the Lammermuirs, is he?'

'Nothing changes,' Jamie replied with a chuckle. His father and Gavin Mackintosh had been friends since their time together at school, and subsequently Gavin had become his father's solicitor almost from the moment he'd joined the family firm.

'So you've finished with university. Did you get what you wanted?'

'Yeah, a 2:2, a drinking degree.' Jamie laughed. 'I was hoping to squeeze a 2:1, but what the hell, I've still managed to get a job with a publishing company in London, starting September.'

'Good for you. Now, how can I be of help?'

'I wanted a bit of advice about the London Street flat. I had the flat rented out for the festival through an agency and they've written to say the theatre company involved has cancelled. I really need the money to cover my last mortgage payments, and the agency say they won't be able to find anyone else so close to the start of the festival. Maybe we should think about bringing the date of the sale forward?'

Jamie heard Gavin hum thoughtfully on the other end of the line.

'My first instinct, Jamie, is that even if you sold the flat immediately, I wouldn't think you could expect payment for a good couple of months, which doesn't help your predicament, does it?'

'Not really,' Jamie replied despondently. 'So what d'you suggest I do?'

'Well, there are notices in shops and newsagents all over the place advertising rooms to let, so why don't you do the same? I can't believe there aren't people out there still looking for somewhere to stay.'

'Yeah, that's not such a bad idea. Certainly worth a shot.'

'And drop a couple of flyers into the Fringe office too.'

Jamie twisted his fingers round the telephone cord. 'But if nothing comes of all that, how the hell am I going to pay the mortgage?'

'We'll get you fixed up with a short-term bank loan to cover the payments. You'll have to pay a bit of interest, but you'll no doubt recoup it by allowing the flat to be on the market for a good competitive period.'

'D'you reckon I'd get the loan, though? I'm near flat broke.'

'Don't worry about that, Jamie. That flat of yours will have appreciated in value considerably over the past few years.' He laughed. 'I'm sure you'll find the banks falling over themselves to get your business.'

'Well, that's good news. Cheers, Gavin.'

'Not at all, Jamie. Keep in touch and let me know how you get on.'

Gavin Mackintosh made a note of his telephone call with Jamie, picked up the cup of now-lukewarm coffee and sat back in his chair. He hadn't really given much thought to the fact that it was festival time again until he had spoken with Jamie. Although every year he had great intentions of going out and enjoying some of the events, unfailingly his workload seemed to increase and the whole three weeks came and went. His wife, however, persevered, booking tickets for concerts and operas, but she usually ended up having to take a friend.

Pushing himself out of his chair, Gavin went over to the tall window and looked out across Heriot Row onto the tranquil shrub-lined paths of Queen Street Gardens, then he turned and walked over to the stack of brown folders on the refectory table beside the door. He selected one and returned to his desk. Maybe this year would be different, he thought to himself. There was one event he did especially want to attend. It was a reception for the brilliant young French violinist Angélique Pascal. He was going to make every effort to attend the party at the Sheraton Grand, just to get a glimpse of her.

Opening the folder, Gavin pulled his chair in close to the desk and began reading through the Last Will and Testament of Mrs Annie Dalgety. He had just begun to note down a few observations, when there was a loud knock on the door. John Anderson, one of the firm's junior partners, stuck his head round. 'Have you got a moment, Gavin?'

'Certainly, John.' He pointed to the chair at the other side of the desk.

The solicitor moved in an ungainly lope across the room, placing the large pile of folders he had been carrying on the desk.

Gavin eyed them suspiciously. 'What have we got here?'

John Anderson sat down. 'Ah, I *thought* you might have forgotten,' he murmured. 'I'm off on holiday for two weeks on Monday.'

'Och, of course you are!' Gavin exclaimed, hitting the palm of his hand hard against his forehead. 'It had completely slipped my mind.'

'I'm sorry. Maybe I should have reminded you earlier.'

Gavin waved a dismissive hand at him. 'It's been in my diary for at least three months, and I should know by now. This is about the third year I've been covering for you on the legal aid cases, is it not?'

'Fourth, actually,' John replied with an apologetic smile. 'But I promise it's not as bad as it looks. I'm in the magistrates' court for the next couple of days and hope to clear up two of them.'

'Depends what comes up when you're away, though, doesn't it?' Gavin slapped his hands down on the desk. 'Never mind. You go away and enjoy yourself, John. Where are you off to this year?'

John picked up the folders. 'Majorca again,' he replied, his tone lighter now that he had accomplished his mission. 'It suits the kids.' The solicitor made his way to the door. 'I'll leave those cases I haven't cleared with your secretary on Friday afternoon, if that's OK with you?'

'That'll be fine, John. I'll read them up sometime over the weekend.'

As the door closed, Gavin rubbed his fingers over his balding pate. Oh, well, he thought to himself, looks like another few weeks of uncultured bliss. One thing is for certain, though. You'll be getting yourself to that reception at the Sheraton Grand come hell or high water.

Robbie, quit doing that and come over and stand by me!' Rene Brownlow's yell was barely audible above the cacophony of Newcastle railway station, dominated by an announcement heralding the arrival of the Intercity service to Edinburgh. Robbie pushed the luggage trolley at speed along the platform, giving it a final spin to extract one more squeal of delight from his sister.

'They're doing no 'arm,' Gary Brownlow said quietly.

'What d'ye mean? They could go under the train.'

Gary smiled at his wife. 'Feeling a bit nervous?'

Rene sighed. 'As if I was 'eading off to me own execution.'

Gary laughed and put his arm around his wife's shoulder. 'You'll be fine, girl, I know it.'

Rene gazed up at her husband. 'Are ye sure ye're all right about me doing this, Gary? I can't 'elp remembering yer reaction when Terry—'

'Oh, forget that, lass,' Gary cut in with a wave of his hand. 'That was me own frustration. I should've kept me big mouth shut. What I want you to do is get yerself up to Edinburgh and knock 'em all dead.'

Rene smiled fondly at her husband. 'Listen, if something comes up while I'm away or ye find ye can't cope with the kids—'

'Between me and me parents, we'll cope.'

'Aye, I reckon ye will.' Rene turned her head and looked past Gary. 'I feel like the bloody Queen,' she said out of the side of her mouth.

''Ow d'ye mean?'

She flicked her head sideways. 'My entourage.'

Gary glanced round at the five committee members of Andersons Westbourne Social Club smiling at them from a distance of twenty feet.

'D'ye think we could get a photo now, Rene, seeing that the train's approaching?' Stan Morris asked, taking an opportune moment.

Rene laughed. 'Aye, why not, Stan?' she called over to him.

The committee members rushed forward and gathered themselves round the Brownlow family. Stan squinted through the eyepiece. 'All squeeze in a bit. Right, one, two, three . . . OK, that's done.' The group broke up as the first of the carriage doors started opening.

'Ye're in the one down 'ere, Rene,' Terry Crosland said as he scooped up her suitcase and hurried off down the platform, the farewell committee following on his heel like ducklings.

Rene ambled along, holding hard to Gary's hand. 'I'll call ye every night.' Reaching up, she pulled his head down towards her and gave him a long kiss on the lips. Then she broke away and gave each of her children a hug. 'Ye look after yer dad now, you two.'

Robbie and Karen both replied with a nod.

'Come on,' Gary said, grasping her arm. 'Let's get ye on board.'

Leaning out of the window as the train pulled out of the station, Rene watched the cluster of waving hands until the bend in the train hid them from sight. Well, she thought, ye're on your own now, girl.

T.K. had worked up a tidy little business for himself over the week. Having discovered how to take digital stills with the video camera, he had set himself up on the junction of Princes and Hanover streets and started waylaying tourists, offering to take their photograph with Edinburgh Castle as the backdrop. It was a success from the start.

Once he had at least ten different customers on record, he would whip out the memory card, take it up to the Kwikflick shop and have the prints back on Princes Street within the hour, catching the punters on their return. Today, however, had not been the best for trade. He pulled his meagre takings from his pocket, then headed along the street to get himself a burger.

The cardboard cup and polystyrene container were discarded over the railings of a basement flat at the bottom of Dundas Street just before he started out on one of the short cuts he knew to get back home. He zigzagged through narrow cobbled alleys, climbed walls, squeezed his narrow frame through loose wooden fence panels and swung himself over arrow-tipped railings. He jumped up onto the precipitous wall that ran above Glenogle Road and walked along its length, jumping the last six feet to the ground.

As he turned the corner to cut down the next street, he stopped and drew himself back against the end gable of a row of houses. He peered round the corner and watched the two boys who were ambling along the road in his direction. One was positioned on the pavement, looking nonchalantly about him, while the other walked parallel to him on the street, looking for the nod from his mate. T.K. laughed to himself. They were about to attempt a car theft in broad daylight. He noticed them spending time over one particular car, an old Ford.

It was at that moment that T.K. remembered the video camera. He pulled it out of the pocket of his sweatshirt. Right, he thought, let's see how fast you two can pull this off. He stuck the lens around the corner of the building, adjusting the viewing screen so that he could see what was going on. His timing was perfect. He started the camera running the moment the boy on the street ducked below the level of the car roof and wrenched the driver's door open. Then the accomplice jumped in, and TK watched as the driver struggled to hot-wire the car. Suddenly the engine roared to life and with a squeal of tyres the car shot out of the parking space and sped down the street towards the T-junction, where it veered right onto the main road and headed away.

T.K. kept the camera rolling until the Ford disappeared, then, putting his hand over the screen to shield it from the evening sunlight, he read the length of the recorded scene on the time code. Four minutes twenty seconds. He laughed out loud. Lousy, lads! he thought.

Closing up the screen, T.K. stuck the camera back in his sweatshirt pocket and swaggered off down the street in the knowledge that he, Thomas Keene, was still one of the unbeaten artists at the job.

Seven

WHEN RENE BROWNLOW arrived the following evening at the Corinthian Bar, half an hour early for her first show, the last thing she felt like doing was standing up on a stage and being funny. The first wave of homesickness had engulfed her the moment she got off the train, and thereafter events conspired to reduce her fragile confidence to rubble. She had dragged the heavy Samsonite suitcase, bought for her by Terry Crosland at a car-boot sale, the two kilometres to her digs in Morningside.

The woman who eventually opened the front door of the unspectacular bungalow in Greendykes Terrace eyed the plump figure with the bright red face with suspicion. 'You'll be Rene Brownlow,' she stated.

Rene had simply nodded, not having breath left to answer her.

'Right, I'm Mrs Learmonth. I'll show you to your room.' Ignoring Rene's load, the woman turned and walked back into the house.

As Rene used her last ounce of energy to carry the suitcase up the steep staircase, Mrs Learmonth stood at the top barraging her with the rules of the house. Breakfast at nine o'clock on the dot; no visitors; no use of the house telephone and the room vacated between eleven o'clock and three o'clock for cleaning. When Rene cast a spirit-sapping eye around the sparsely furnished bedroom built into the low roof of the bungalow, she couldn't quite work out why Mrs Learmonth needed five hours to clean such a minute area. Later on that evening, after she had picked at a near-inedible meal in Mrs Learmonth's dingy dining room, Rene had stood in the littered telephone box 300 metres from the house desperately trying to maintain her self-control when Gary's voice had sounded at the other end of the line.

At precisely eleven o'clock the next morning, Rene had left the house, eager to get away from the place. She had walked all the way back to the High Street to locate the Fringe office and then tagged on to a small gathering around a young man shaping a dog out of balloons for a toddler, while she washed a ham sandwich down with a can of Coke. When the sky had clouded over she'd sought out the warmth of a crowded pub, where she sat at a corner table trying to eke out her shandy.

Taking in a steadying breath, Rene pushed open the heavy glass door of her venue and entered. The Corinthian Bar was obviously a new establishment, equipped with all things chrome. The tables, chairs, handrails, footrests below the bar all sparkled, reflecting myriad small low-voltage lights suspended from wires cobwebbing the ceiling. The whole wall at the back of the stairs down to the toilets—and, as indicated by a temporary sign, to the theatre—was covered with posters, all larger versions of the leaflets describing the acts. Rene took one of her own from a rack on the counter and glanced through it as she walked along the wide ceramic-tiled passage to the bar.

There were only about ten people in the place. Two couples were eating at tables, while the rest sat on stools or stood leaning on the dark granite surface of the bar. As Rene approached it, a young barman with gelled spiky hair came over to her. 'Hi there, what can I get ye?'

'Oh, nothing, thanks,' Rene replied. 'I'm here to do a show.'

'Oh, right. Just hang on a minute then. Hey, Andrea!' he called to a girl coming up the stairs. 'This is the woman doing the show tonight.'

Rene turned to watch Andrea approach, a blonde in a pair of tight-fitting black jeans and polo-neck jersey.

'Hi, you must be Rene,' she said, offering out a hand that gushed blood-red nails. She spoke in a twanging English voice.

'That's right,' Rene replied with a smile.

'Good. Well, look, I think the best thing is for me to take you straight downstairs and show you where everything is.' She turned on the stiletto-toed heels of her boots and Rene followed on behind.

The 'theatre' turned out to be nothing more than the pub cellar, hastily converted by a black backdrop strung across its ceiling. About ten plastic tables with matching chairs were crammed into the small auditorium, some sloping at weird angles because of the uneven flag-stoned floor. The place was damp and stank of stale beer, and Rene was only thankful that it was brightly lit by two spotlights positioned on stands against the back wall, their beams focused on the microphone.

''Ow many people d'ye expect will be coming?' Rene asked flatly.

Andrea crossed her arms over her neat little bosom. 'It depends, really. If the word gets round there's a good show going on it can really fill up. We've had as many as thirty people in here.'

The girl shot her such an enthusiastic smile that Rene felt she had to muster up some sort of jovial response. 'Oh my, that's summat, in't it?' she said. Any hope of her 'making it big' in Edinburgh had just sponta-neously combusted.

'Of course,' Andrea continued, 'it depends on how well you've been able to publicise the show yourself.'

''Ow am I meant to do that?'

Andrea's smile faded. 'You should have been handing out leaflets all day up on the High Street.' She raised her eyebrows. 'How else do you expect anyone to come? That's where all the punters are during the day. You've got to go up there and attract them. Otherwise you could find yourself well out of pocket when the show comes to an end.'

Rene swallowed hard. ''Ow's that, then?'

Andrea let out a sigh. 'Don't you know about the conditions?'

'No, I don't,' Rene replied quite forcefully, becoming irked by the girl's attitude. 'I didn't arrange this 'ole thing. It was done for me.'

'All right,' Andrea countered defensively, holding up a hand to steady Rene's mood. 'I'll explain then. We rent out the theatre to you for a fixed sum over the three weeks. If you don't manage to cover that figure through box-office takings, then you are liable for the shortfall.'

'And 'ow much does the theatre cost?'

'Seventeen hundred pounds.'

Rene stared at the girl. 'Bloody Aunt Ada,' she exclaimed, as the figure flashed in her mind like a neon warning light. She looked round the room, counting the seats. 'Bloody Aunt Ada, that's damned near impossible!'

The voice of the barman rang down the stairs. 'Andrea, there's a couple of people waitin' here tae buy tickets.'

Andrea glanced at her wristwatch and walked over to the door. 'On my way!' She turned back to Rene. 'If you could be ready to start in about ten minutes . . . I hope it goes well.' And she swung round on her sharp-heeled boots and left the comedienne to her fate.

Rene's first show was played to a grand audience of five, at least three of them foreigners. She struggled to raise one good laugh and called an end to her suffering fifteen minutes early, waiting behind the backdrop until her audience made their exit. Then she came out and sat down at one of the tables in the deserted theatre.

'How did it go?' Rene turned to see Andrea's smiling face pop round the door. Rene slowly shook her head. 'Don't worry,' Andrea said as she flicked off the switch of one of the spotlights. 'Once you've got used to the intimacy of the theatre, you'll find it much easier.'

'Maybe,' Rene replied, getting to her feet and wondering how Andrea could possibly describe this subterranean torture chamber as 'intimate'.

'It's a bit of a pity, though,' Andrea said, turning off the other light and plunging the place into coal-mine darkness. 'There was a reviewer from Radio Scotland in the audience.' She turned and gave Rene a thin smile. 'Never mind, he might not bother saying anything about it at all.'

Rene kept staring up the stairwell long after Andrea's tight little bottom had disappeared from view, and then, putting a steadying hand on the chrome banister rail, lowered herself slowly onto the bottom step, clutched her handbag to her chest, and burst into tears.

Harry Wills sat in front of the Costa coffee stall at Edinburgh Airport, toying with a cup of espresso as he kept an eye on the two photographers who were chatting at the entrance through which the arrivals on the BA flight from London flooded into the baggage reclaim area. He saw them separate, their movements suddenly more animated, and when a series of blinding flashes went off, Harry began to make his way towards them. The two photographers were now moving backwards away from the entrance, focusing their lenses on a tall bespectacled man who accompanied a dark-haired girl with a violin case in her hand. The man paid little attention to the photographers as he approached the cluster of uniformed drivers. He spoke to one, who immediately lowered the sign he had been holding up, and guided them with outstretched hand over to the luggage carousel.

As the two photographers hurried away towards the exit, their assignments completed, Harry pushed through the mass of people gathering around the carousel and approached the man from behind. 'Monsieur Dessuin, Mademoiselle Pascal, welcome to Edinburgh.'

The man turned round, a questioning frown creasing his high angular forehead, and slowly put out a hand to the one Harry offered in greeting. 'I'm sorry, I'm not sure if we have—'

'Harry Wills, the *Sunday Times Scotland*.'

'Ah, of course,' Albert Dessuin murmured.

'I thought I'd come along today just to introduce myself in person. We've spoken often enough on the telephone.' Harry switched his attention to the young girl. 'However, I haven't had the pleasure of speaking to you before, mademoiselle.'

'Mr Wills,' Albert Dessuin cut in, 'we arrived early this morning in London after an all-night flight from New York, and after a long delay at Heathrow we have now made it here to Edinburgh. Tonight we have to attend a reception and tomorrow Mademoiselle Pascal must start rehearsing for a concert the next evening. I would suggest, therefore, that this is the wrong time and the wrong place to try for an interview.'

'Of course, I understand that. I was just hoping to fix—'

'I seem to remember also, Mr Wills,' Dessuin continued, clicking his fingers at the driver and pointing to a large brown suitcase on the carousel, 'that it was only a few months ago that I gave a great deal of time for an interview with you. I would not think, so soon afterwards, there would be much I could add.'

Harry Wills decided to go for broke. 'Monsieur Dessuin, what I really want is to write a story from Mademoiselle Pascal's point of view. I want to write about her influences, about her background, about her interests . . . and about being Angélique Pascal. She is becoming one of the most famous violinists in the world and everyone, including the young people, wants to know about her.' Harry turned to Angélique, who, having just pointed out another suitcase to the driver, now stood watching him. 'Mademoiselle Pascal, would there be any time over this next week when you would be willing to do an interview with me?'

'Mr Wills,' Albert Dessuin exclaimed irately as he grabbed the full luggage trolley from the driver and put a hand against Angélique's back. 'From now on, I will not consider one further interview with you, and please remember it was your own dogged stupidity that led to this.'

Harry stood watching as the driver escorted his charges towards the exit, Dessuin guiding Angélique Pascal almost forcefully with a hand on her arm. Letting out a derisory grunt, Harry ambled off to his car.

In the office of the International Festival, Tess Goodwin ran through her checklist for the reception that night in the Sheraton Grand. The hotel's events manager had confirmed that the function room had been set up. The PR agency had already hung the two large posters of the Italian baritone, Guiseppe Montarino, and the French violinist, Angélique Pascal, in whose joint honours the reception was being held. All that was left for her to do was to make a few courtesy calls to sponsors of International events remiss in replying to the invitation. As she reached for the telephone, she saw the director's intercom light flash. She picked up the receiver, noticing the outside call he kept on hold.

'Yes, Alasdair?'

'Are we all set for tonight, Tess?'

'Yes, everything's ready. I'm about to call up some of those sponsors.'

'OK, but before you do that, I've got an old friend of yours wants to have a word with you.'

'Who is it?' But the director had already put down his receiver.

'What do you mean, "who is it?"' a male voice replied with a laugh. 'Did your boss not tell you?'

Tess felt her face flush with panic, recognising the smooth-spoken voice with its precise foreign accent. It was one she had hoped never to hear again. 'Is that you, Peter?'

'Of course it's me. I'm sure you did not really need to ask.'

Tess felt the skin on her back tingle with nervous apprehension. 'Peter, I think—'

Tess heard Peter Hansen sigh. 'Listen, I thought it would be a good time to make amends for the way I behaved. If we could meet up—'

'What do you mean? Where are you?'

'In Edinburgh. I came for the festival . . . and to see you, of course.'

Tess gave a cry of disbelief. '*What*? Are you being serious?' She shook her head at the gall of the man. 'Peter, I really am too busy to meet up.'

'In that case, I could be round in your office in five minutes. It would be good to see Alasdair as well.'

'You will do no such thing,' Tess exclaimed, knowing the director's intuitive nature would pick up on her uneasy vibes.

'OK, then. Why not invite me to the reception tonight?'

'No!' She realised he was leaving her with little alternative other than to meet up with him there and then. 'Right, where are you?'

'About two hundred metres away. There is a church on the right-hand side of the High Street. I am standing on the steps.'

'I warn you, I haven't got long.'

'I'll be looking out for you—and, Tess? I'm longing to seeing you.'

By the time Tess had made arrangements to cover for her short absence from the office fifteen minutes had elapsed before she reached the small square where the church was situated. Peter Hansen was instantly recognisable. Tall, lean, with a shock of Viking-blonde hair, he possessed an almost visible aura of self-admiration. He lifted his hand in a brief wave, then threaded his way through the pedestrians.

'Tess, it is so good to see you.' He enveloped her in a hug, then pushed her away a little. 'You look fantastic. Life is good, yes?'

Tess gave him a brief smile. 'Never been better.'

He put an arm round her shoulders. 'Let's go and get a cup of coffee.'

Tess pulled herself from his hold. 'Five minutes, Peter, that's all.'

'I think we can down a cup of coffee in that time,' he said, already starting to make his way across the High Street to a small café.

Having ordered a cappuccino for Tess and a herbal tea for himself, Peter leaned his elbows on the table and smiled affectionately at her. When she met his gaze with an ice-cold stare, he reached across the table, but she avoided contact by sitting back in her chair.

'I think you are still very angry with me,' he said. 'It was wrong of me to leave last year without talking to you. I had to get back to Copenhagen urgently.'

'So your note said.'

'It was just that my wife . . . well . . . she had not been in good spirits.'

'I hope she's better now.'

Peter paused for a moment, eyeing Tess, unsettled by her quick-fire remarks. 'Yes, thank you, she is. But she is very . . . untrusting of me—'

'With every reason, too,' Tess interjected sharply. 'What are you doing back here, Peter?'

The question disarmed him. 'I have missed you. I don't think a day has passed when I have not thought of you.'

Tess nodded. 'Right, so let me get this straight. You just want to take up where we left off.'

'Of course not. But maybe I thought we could meet for dinner and remember the good times . . . because they were good times, Tess.'

'To be quite honest, I haven't given them another thought. And I'll tell you why, Peter. You see, I'm not free now, for you or anyone else, because I'm married.'

Peter shrugged. 'I know. Alasdair told me on the telephone. You married Allan, didn't you? If I remember right, you had been going out with him ever since we first became . . . involved. So, if that is the case, then nothing has changed. An innocent dinner, that is all I am asking. You could treat it as part of your routine entertainment at the festival.'

He paused to take a sip of his coffee. 'To make it legitimate, maybe I could speak with Alasdair.'

Tess swallowed hard. 'No, I don't want you to do that.'

'Ah, yes, of course. We don't want the director to find out about our little affair. Alasdair knows the way I am, but maybe he would think it rather unprofessional of you. If I have to take more formal action to arrange a dinner date with you, well then, it might put you in a bit of a predicament, don't you think?'

Tess stared at him. 'That's as good as blackmail.'

Peter frowned. 'Oh, nothing so serious as that, surely? But I think it does prove how much I want to see you again.'

Needing time to consider her options, Tess turned her head and fixed her eyes on a young female street performer juggling with three blazing torches. God, Tess thought, the girl's not the only one playing with fire here. She had brought it upon herself. There was really only one option open to her.

Have dinner with the man and finish it for good, and then neither Allan nor Sir Alasdair need ever be the wiser. She turned back to Peter. 'All right, we'll have dinner.'

Peter's face registered victory. 'I'm so glad to hear it. When, then?'

Tess took her diary from her handbag and flipped through the pages. 'It'll have to be either next Tuesday or Wednesday.'

Peter nodded. 'OK, I'll call you.'

'No, I'll do the calling.'

'You still have my number?'

'If you haven't changed it.'

Peter shot her a knowing wink. 'No, it's exactly the same.'

Tess glanced at her watch. 'Dammit, I'm so late.' She pushed back her chair. 'The dinner next week will be the last, Peter.'

'In that case, we will have to celebrate it in style.'

As soon as Angélique Pascal entered the vast function room of the Sheraton Grand, she was sure she would not be wanting to leave Albert Dessuin's side. As she descended the wide carpeted steps to the crowded floor, she felt 300 pairs of eyes turn to look at her and reacted to it by putting out a hand to grasp her manager's arm. Shyly, she returned the smiles beamed her way as Albert led her through the crowd to a small group gathered by the window. A thin, studious man detached himself and came towards Albert and Angélique with his hand outstretched. 'Albert, welcome to Edinburgh.' He shook Albert's hand, and then turned to his charge. 'Angélique, what a pleasure it is to meet you at last. I'm Alasdair Dreyfuss, director of the International Festival.' He gave her a light kiss on the cheek. 'Come with me and I'll introduce you to some of my colleagues . . .'

The man spoke English too fast, a trend that seemed to be set thereafter. After three-quarters of an hour of listening to unintelligible words, she felt very tired. Squeezing Albert's arm and gesturing with a finger for him to lean over, she whispered in his ear that she was going to look out of the window. He nodded his approval.

The recess by the window was much deeper than she had imagined: a twenty-foot carpeted passage that ended at a wall on which a large gilt-framed mirror was hung. Angélique crossed her arms and leaned against the window frame, looking down onto the bustling crowds in the street below. As she gazed, she let out a long, lingering yawn.

'You must be exhausted,' a female voice said.

Angélique turned to see a young woman approaching her tentatively along the passage. She was carrying two glasses of champagne. 'I saw you didn't have anything to drink,' she said, handing Angélique a glass.

'Thank you,' the violinist said, smiling. She had noticed her at the back of the group when Albert had greeted the festival director, and it had occurred to Angélique that they must have been about the two youngest people in the room. Her close-cropped brown hair framed an honest, happy face, and she was dressed quite informally in a red wraparound dress over a black polo-neck.

'I'm sorry, we weren't introduced,' the young woman said. 'I'm Tess Goodwin. I work in the International office.'

'I am pleased to meet you, Tess,' Angélique said, shaking her hand.

'You speak English very well.'

'But I find it difficult when there are many people,' Angélique said. She took a sip from her glass. 'Edinburgh is very beautiful, I think. Do you come from here?'

'No, I'm from Aberdeen, much further north, but I live here now.' Tess stepped closer to the window. 'Do you see the church spire there?'

Angélique nodded.

'I was married there five months ago.'

'How wonderful for you!' Angélique exclaimed with genuine excitement. 'What is your husband's name?'

'Allan.'

'I like the name *Alain*,' Angélique remarked decisively. 'Does *Alain* work in Edinburgh, too?'

Tess studied the interest in Angélique's face. She was really beginning to warm to the open friendliness of this young celebrity. 'Yes, here and in Glasgow. He's recently been promoted, so he's having to work very long hours.' She gazed out of the window, her mind caught up with the clandestine arrangement she had made with Peter Hansen only hours before. 'We don't see much of each other at the moment.'

Angélique wrinkled her nose. 'That is hard for you both, *n'est-ce pas*?'

Tess smiled. 'Very. We didn't even have time to go on honeymoon.'

'*Oh, ça c'est triste!* But you will go eventually, will you not?'

'Yes, once the festival is over I think we will go to Barbados.'

'Ah, it is one place I have never been,' Angélique said.

'It must be one of the *only* places you've never been.'

Angélique gave a short laugh. 'You are right, but unfortunately, my life means I am never in one place long enough to enjoy it.'

'I'm sure constant jetting around the world isn't as glamorous as it sounds.' Tess put down her glass on the low windowsill and opened the zip on her suede shoulder bag. 'Listen,' she said, taking out a business card and handing it to Angélique, 'maybe you'd like to come out one night with Allan and me? We could show you round Edinburgh.'

Tess noticed sadness in Angélique's eyes as the violinist studied the card. 'That is very kind of you, Tess. I don't think I will have the time.'

Tess shrugged her shoulders. 'Well, keep the card anyway. If you do find you have a spare moment, or even if you just want to have a chat, you can always contact me on my mobile phone.'

Angélique's eyes never lifted from the card. 'Thank you very much.'

'Excuse me, I hope I'm not breaking into a private conversation.'

Both women turned to look at the middle-aged man who stood peering round the corner of the recess at them. He was smartly dressed in a dark grey pinstriped suit with a striped shirt and yellow silk tie, but his most striking feature was the smile beamed in their direction.

'I just wanted to have the opportunity of saying to Mademoiselle Pascal how much I enjoy her playing,' the man said as he came along the passage towards them.

Tess turned to Angélique. 'I'll leave you with your fan,' she said.

The young violinist gave Tess a kiss on both cheeks. 'I have enjoyed meeting you, Tess.'

'Me, too,' Tess replied, making her way along the corridor.

'I'm sorry, I didn't mean to cut in,' the man said, seemingly flustered about having invaded Angélique's privacy, 'but I really did not want to leave without saying to you in person how I admire your playing.'

'Thank you very much,' Angélique replied, accepting the compliment with a small bow of her head. 'That is a nice thing to say.'

The man put out a hand to her. 'My name is Gavin Mackintosh,

Mademoiselle Pascal, and I am most honoured to meet you.'

'It is also an honour to meet you, too, Mr Mackintosh,' Angélique replied with a laugh as she took his hand.

'Please, you must call me Gavin.'

'And you must call me Angélique.'

'I would like that,' Gavin said. 'So, you've just arrived?'

'Yes. I was in New York last night.'

Gavin let out a sigh. 'You must be tired. How long are you staying?'

'I think seven nights. I am rehearsing tomorrow and then I will be playing in concerts the following two evenings in the . . . Ush . . .'

'Usher Hall.' Gavin pointed to the large round ornate stone building on the opposite side of the road. 'That's it over there.'

'After that I think there are some late-night concerts when I am to be playing some of the Bach violin sonatas. And then on to Singapore.'

Gavin shook his head. 'I don't know how you do it.'

Angélique laughed. 'It is quite hard. Do you live here in Edinburgh?'

'Yes, all my life. I am a solicitor.'

'And do you have a family?'

'I do. I have a wife, two daughters and four grandchildren.'

'Four grandchildren! But you do not look old enough for that.'

Gavin bit at his lip and slowly nodded his head. 'You know, that's probably the nicest thing anyone has ever said to me.'

'*Mais, c'est vrai!*' Angélique stepped away from the window. 'I think maybe I have been hiding in here too long,' she said, threading her hand through his arm. 'Will you take me to meet your wife, Gavin?'

Gavin put his hand on hers. 'Nothing would give me more pleasure.'

They had taken a couple of steps towards the function room when Albert Dessuin suddenly appeared. Gavin could see his eyes focus on the hand nestled under his arm. 'Angélique? What are you doing? There were so many people whom you should have met, but they have left already.' He spoke his French very fast.

'Albert, I have been speaking to Tess and Gavin, who are both new friends of mine,' Angélique replied in English, 'and I am now going to be introduced to Gavin's wife.'

Gavin felt Dessuin's glare of distrust. 'I am sorry, but there is no time,' he replied, this time in English. 'Our plans have changed. We are now having dinner with Sir Alasdair Dreyfuss in a restaurant and already he has left.' He came over and took hold of her free arm. 'I am sorry, but we have wasted enough time. I apologise, monsieur.'

'Of course,' Gavin replied. Unfolding Angélique's hand from his arm, he gave her a kiss on either cheek. 'It's been my pleasure, Angélique.'

He watched them as they walked away, thinking how much he liked her, and how much he disliked him. He put his hands into the pockets of his suit jacket and began to walk slowly back to the function room.

Just at that point, Angélique appeared again. 'Two tickets for the concert.' She turned away. '*Albert, je viens!*' She looked back at Gavin. 'I shall leave them at the concierge desk. Please come.' She blew him a kiss and disappeared.

Eight

THE ELDERLY MAN cast an eye round the lobby, then made his way over to the receptionist. 'I wonder if you could tell me where I might find a telephone.'

'Certainly, sir, there's a payphone in the corner over there,' she replied, pointing to a glass door beside the lifts. 'May I ask if you are staying in the hotel?'

'Yes, I am. Hartson, room 215.'

'Ah, Mr Hartson, a gentleman has been trying to contact you quite urgently.' She turned and took an envelope from one of the cubbyholes. 'He asked that you ring this number as soon as you returned to the hotel. I was going to suggest you might like to use the telephone in the seating area over there and I'll just add it to your bill.'

Leonard Hartson made his way to the seating area and pulled the chair away from the small telephone desk. Flustered, he dialled the number. 'I would like to speak to Nick Springer, please.'

'Who's calling, please?'

'Leonard Hartson.'

'Oh, Mr Hartson, we've been trying to get in touch with you all day. I'll put you straight through.'

'Hello, Leonard?' It was Nick's voice. 'I have been trying to get in touch. It's a pity you don't have a mobile phone.'

'I've never had need of one . . . what's the matter, Nick?'

'This is all very difficult, Leonard. I know how much of a disappointment it's going to be to you . . . I had an email today from the Japanese broadcast company that commissioned the film. They're shedding jobs like crazy and a freeze has been put on all recently commissioned works. Unfortunately, your job just happens to be one of them.'

'Oh my word,' Leonard said. 'Is there nothing we can do?'

'I'd never be able to find another broadcast company to take on the commission at such short notice. We've got to cut our losses now and get the equipment back to London as soon as possible, Leonard.'

'Nothing more to be done, then,' the old cameraman murmured.

'I really am sorry about this, Leonard.'

'Not your fault, Nick.'

'Listen, the boys are heading back tomorrow with the vans, but there's no reason for you to return straight away. Why not stay up there for a day or two and I'll foot your hotel bill? That's the least I can do.'

'No, I think I'll just get back home.'

'All right. I quite understand.'

'It would have been a wonderful film to make, Nick, and I can't thank you enough for entrusting it to me.'

'If there was anything I could do at this stage to continue with the project, then I would. But keep in touch, and I promise I'll call in to see you next time I'm on my way down the A3.'

'You do that, Nick. Look after yourself.'

The old cameraman reached forward and put down the telephone. He sat for a moment staring at the wall in front of him, and then, with a sigh, made his way slowly back to the reception desk.

'All right, sir?' the young receptionist asked him with a smile. 'Did you manage to contact the gentleman?'

'Yes, thank you, I did. I'm going to be checking out tomorrow.'

'Oh, I'm sorry to hear that, sir.' She looked down at her computer monitor and typed quickly on the keyboard. 'Your bill is going directly to Springtime Productions.'

'Thank you for all your help.'

'Good night, sir, and I hope we have the pleasure of having you to stay with us again very soon.'

In room 215, Leonard emptied out the pockets of his tweed jacket and placed everything on the dressing table. He sat down on the edge of the bed and eyed the telephone, wondering how on earth he was going to break the news to Gracie. He felt aged with disappointment, so he couldn't imagine how she, who had encouraged him to take the job, would react to the news. He dialled the number.

'Hello?' Grace answered. Leonard could sense an air of excited expectancy in her voice. 'I've been longing to hear from you. How's everything going? Has all the equipment arrived safely?'

'Yes, about an hour ago.'

'Oh, how exciting! So when do you think you will start shooting?'

Leonard closed his eyes tight and clenched his fist.

'Leonard?' Gracie asked quietly. 'Is everything all right, dear?'

'We're not going to be shooting, Gracie,' Leonard replied. He cleared his throat. 'The job's fallen through. The funding's been withdrawn, and Nick says there's no time to find it elsewhere.'

'Oh, Leonard, I can't believe this. Such a waste of time and effort.'

'I know. I had such ideas about how I was going to film it. I really do believe, Gracie, that I could have done a wonderful job here.'

'Your definitive film,' Gracie replied in a voice heavy with chagrin. 'So what happens now?'

'I should be back home some time tomorrow evening.'

'And what will happen to us, Leonard?'

Leonard smiled. 'Nothing will happen to us, my dear. We will continue as we have done for the past seven years.'

'With nothing to look forward to except our eventual demise.'

Leonard let out a surprised laugh. 'I don't think we need to be considering that *just* yet, Gracie.'

'Well, then, why don't you and I take some risks?'

'How do you mean?'

'Leonard, we have no children nor grandchildren to bless with an inheritance. We just have each other, and time is running out for us. Have you any idea what the budget for this film was?'

'Probably around a hundred thousand pounds.'

'In that case, I think you and I should fund it ourselves.'

'*What?*'

'Leonard, when we thought about moving two years ago, the estate agent valued this house at two hundred and seventy thousand pounds. Now it must be worth much nearer three hundred thousand. We don't have a mortgage, so why don't we just use it as collateral against a loan for the film?'

'Gracie, my dear, have you gone quite bonkers?'

'I have never been more serious in my life, neither have I ever come up with such a sound idea. Leonard, you know yourself you have rued the day you gave up work in the film industry, and you were heading into the twilight days of your life feeling dissatisfied and unfulfilled. Living with you over the past few months has been a complete joy for me. I have the man I knew thirty years ago, and I love it, and I love you. If you came back now, everything would change, and with nothing to look forward to, I doubt much time would pass before one of us would just fade away. Leonard, we are only talking about a third of the capital value of the house, but in all honesty I would rather risk losing everything we own than to lose you, the way you are right now.'

Grace's impassioned monologue brought tears to Leonard's eyes. 'Gracie, you are a remarkable woman.'

'Shall we do it, then? Take the risk? Think how rejuvenating for us both it will be.'

Leonard laughed. 'In that case, why not? Cast our fates to the wind.'

'And no regrets, my dear, whatever the outcome. You get a good night's sleep and don't go mulling it over. We've made the decision and you will be needing all your energies over the next weeks for making the most wonderful film.'

'Good night, Gracie. I love you, my girl.'

'I know you do.'

Leonard got to his feet and sought out Nick Springer's mobile number. 'Nick, it's Leonard Hartson.'

'Oh, hello, Leonard. Give me a moment while I pull the car over.' Leonard heard the rev of an engine and then quiet. 'Are you all right?'

'Yes, fine. Nick, I wonder if you might be able to tell me what the approximate budget for the film was?'

'Well, off the top of my head, I think it was about one hundred and fifty thousand pounds, perhaps a bit less.'

'Right. Nick, could you cancel the return of all the equipment? Gracie and I have decided we're going to fund the film ourselves.'

'*What?*'

'We're going to take out a loan against the value of our house and make the film ourselves. We've decided.'

'No, I can't allow you to do that. You and Grace can't put your security at risk like that, Leonard.'

'Yes, we can. Anyway, if you say the full budget is around a hundred and fifty thousand pounds, then we would only have to take out a loan on about half the value of the house, and I have a few ideas already on how to reduce the costs further.'

'By doing what?'

'By sending the electricians and the assistant cameraman back to London. I'll find someone local to give me a hand. I'll move out of this hotel, of course, and look for somewhere cheaper.'

'Leonard, are you really being serious about all this?'

'Never more so in my life.'

'Then I have to come in on the deal.'

'Nick, you don't need to—'

'No, I insist. I simply cannot allow you to take on such a financial risk alone. I shall put up fifty thousand pounds and you, Grace and I will produce it as equal partners under the umbrella of Springtime Productions. I'll give you back-up for whatever you need and arrange for all processing and post-production work to be done in London.'

'Are you sure, Nick?'

'In your words, Leonard, never more so in my life. I'm just so delighted you're still going to be able to make the film. If I wasn't so busy, I'd come up and assist you myself! You won't try going it alone, will you? You have to consider your health.'

'Nick, I know my limitations.'

'I sincerely hope so. Have you been in touch with the dance company yet?'

'Yes. They have a young Scottish girl acting as an interpreter, and together we spoke with Mr Kayamoto, the director. He never mentioned any changes to the schedule, so I doubt he knew at that time. I'll give the girl a call now and arrange another meeting for tomorrow. I'm sure Mr Kayamoto will be willing to continue as planned.'

'One problem has just occurred to me, Leonard. You have two vanloads of equipment up there. How are you going to manage to drive both? And what will you do with all the equipment overnight?'

Leonard pondered for a moment. 'I think having seen the warehouse, that I can afford to glean off some of the equipment, so I'll just keep hold of one of the vans and get the boys to drive the other back to London with what I don't need. And you don't have to worry about security. I can lock the van and the equipment in the warehouse.'

'That's good, then, and listen, my contribution to this venture is accessible now, so if you're in need of any money short-term, just get in touch. Is that understood?'

'Thank you, Nick . . . for everything. I can't tell you how happy I am this is going to go ahead after all.'

The following morning, Leonard took a taxi over to the lodgings where the rest of the crew was staying. He found them in a gruff mood, having had the night to mull over the fact that they had lost out on three weeks' work, but Leonard managed to mollify them by telling them that he would ask Nick to seek some form of compensation from the Japanese company. By the time they set off back to London in the spare van, having helped Leonard to sort through the equipment at the warehouse, any ill feeling had dissipated.

However, the day did not continue in such a positive vein. Having booked himself out of the Sheraton Grand the previous evening, Leonard spent the lunch hour and the early part of the afternoon on the telephone in the hotel lobby, vainly trying to track down somewhere to stay. By three o'clock, he realised that it was to no avail. He approached the reception desk to ask if he might have his room back for one more night, only to be told it had been taken. The receptionist could only suggest he try the offices of the International festival.

A taxi took Leonard the short distance up past the castle and dropped him outside the old church at the top of the Lawnmarket. He entered the building towing his suitcase behind him and made his way along the passageway to the ticket office, where he approached a young man wearing a festival logo-ed sweatshirt.

'Can I help you, sir?' the young man asked with a cheery grin.

'Yes. I wonder if it would be possible to speak to someone in the International office?'

'Do you have an appointment?'

'No, I'm afraid I don't, but my name is Leonard Hartson, and I'm up here to film the Japanese dance company that's performing this year.'

'Ah, right.' He picked up the receiver on the telephone and pressed an intercom button. 'Hello, Tess, there's a Mr Hartson here in the ticket office who's needing to speak to someone . . . no, he doesn't, but he's filming the Japanese dance company . . . All right, I'll tell him.' The young man put down the receiver. 'Mr Hartson, Tess Goodwin will be down to see you in about five minutes. If you go across to the Hub café on the other side of the corridor, Tess will meet you there.'

Leonard walked the few steps across the corridor and pushed open the coffee shop door. Ten minutes later, as he drained the last drops of his lukewarm coffee, a young woman came in, holding in her hand a spiral notepad. She scanned the tables before catching sight of Leonard, who had risen to his feet on her entrance.

'Mr Hartson? Tess Goodwin,' the young woman said, offering a hand to Leonard. 'I work in the International marketing department.'

'Miss Goodwin . . .' Leonard began, shaking her hand. 'Thank you for sparing time to meet me. I know you must be very busy right now.'

'Up to the eyeballs, actually.' She pulled out a chair for herself and opened her notebook. 'How can I be of help.'

Leonard resumed his seat and started his explanation immediately. 'Tess, this might not be part of your remit, but I have to find lodgings for the festival. I've been staying at the Sheraton Grand, but there have been changes to the budget and I can't afford to stay there.'

Tess tapped the end of her pencil on the notebook. 'I can't promise you anything,' she said, picking up her mobile, 'but I'll try the Fringe office.' She keyed a number and held the mobile to her ear. 'Hello, may I speak to Lewis Jones, please? It's Tess Goodwin at International.' She smiled reassuringly at Leonard as she waited to be connected. 'Lewis, good afternoon, it's Tess . . . Listen, Lewis, I am with a Mr Hartson who is in Edinburgh to film one of our events and he needs to change his accommodation arrangements . . . you don't know of anything available, do you? . . . Oh, right. Yes, I can hold.'

She took the mobile away from her ear. 'He says someone came in a couple of weeks ago who had rooms to let, due to a cancellation. He's just trying to find the piece of paper now.' She raised her eyebrows hopefully at Leonard as she began writing on the notebook. 'Jamie Stratton . . . OK . . . number seven London Street? . . . Right, and telephone number? . . . that's brilliant, thanks, Lewis.' She punched the end button on the mobile.

'Well, let's give this Mr Stratton a call.' She bit at a fingernail as she listened for the telephone to be answered. 'Hello, Mr Stratton? I believe you had some rooms to let . . . oh, that's wonderful . . . just the one, it's for a Mr Hartson . . . Right, are you going to be in for an hour or so? . . . Good . . . bye.' She ended the call with a smile. 'You're in luck,' she said, tearing a sheet from her notepad and handed it to Leonard. 'London Street is quite central, so you should be able to find it easily enough.'

'I can't thank you enough, Tess,' Leonard said, tucking the piece of paper into the top pocket of his tweed jacket.

'I'm glad we managed to sort something out for you,' Tess said, rising from her chair and picking up her notebook and mobile. Giving him a brief wave, she turned and hurried towards the glass door.

Walking out onto the Lawnmarket, Leonard felt the late-afternoon sun warming his back as he began to walk towards the High Street where the street theatre was in full swing. He never noticed the small dumpy woman who kept abreast of him on the other side of the street, trying to keep the large Samsonite suitcase she dragged behind her from keeling over on the uneven paving slabs.

Rene Brownlow bumped the suitcase uncaringly up the two stone steps and pushed open the door to the Fringe office. She towed the suitcase into a corner where it wouldn't be in anyone's way and approached the long counter.

A girl left her computer screen and approached her. 'Can I help you?'

'My name's Rene Brownlow. I've been doing a show in the Corinthian Bar, but I want to—' She never got any further, feeling the tears bubble in her eyes, just as they had done for the past twelve hours.

The girl smiled at her. 'I know exactly who you need to talk to.' She came round and put a hand on Rene's shoulder. 'Come on, Lewis Jones'll sort everything out.'

These were the first kindly words since Rene had arrived in Edinburgh a week and a half before, so by the time she took her seat at the desk in front of the young man with the mop of curly hair, she was snivelling uncontrollably. Lewis leaned forward on the desk, a huge grin spread across his face. 'Come on, things can't be going that badly, can they?' he said in a lilting Welsh voice. He took a handful of tissues from a box at the side of the desk and passed them over.

'They couldn't go any worse,' Rene sobbed. 'I've 'ardly 'ad anyone come to the show, and no one understands me 'umour and I'm never going to be able to cover the theatre cost. I just want to go 'ome.'

'Rene, would you believe you are the fifth person I've had in today, saying exactly the same thing?'

Rene wiped at her eyes, her sobs slowing down as his words sank in.

'Look, it's early days,' Lewis said. 'A number of the performers get a bit despondent about this time. My advice to you is to stick it out.'

At that point a dark-haired girl put her head over the partition that separated Lewis's desk from the rest of the office. 'Lewis? Is that Rene Brownlow you've got with you? I thought you might like to see this.' She handed over a folded newspaper before disappearing behind the partition. Lewis scanned through the piece Gail had highlighted.

'There you are, you see,' he said, spinning the newspaper onto the desk in front of Rene. 'You are being a bit hasty. That's in *The Scotsman*. Everybody reads that in Edinburgh.'

Rene stared at the black and white photograph of herself. She glanced quickly through the words underneath. 'Rene Brownlow . . . an original wit . . . splitting my sides at her characterisation of the members of Andersons Westbourne Social Club in her home town of Hartlepool . . . this act is definitely worth a visit.' Rene placed the newspaper back on the desk and let out a short laugh.

'Not bad, eh?' Lewis said.

Rene smiled at him. 'I'd better get on with it, then.'

'You wait until tonight. I bet you'll find the place packed.'

Rene lowered her head and began wiping at her eyes again.

'What's up now?' Lewis asked in a baffled voice.

'I don't want to go on living where I am now,' Rene sobbed. 'I'm in this 'orrible 'ouse with this dreadful woman, and I 'ave to be out every day at eleven o'clock and I just 'ave to walk the streets all day.'

Lewis puffed out his cheeks in disbelief. 'OK. It sounds like that particular lady deserves to lose your custom. Hang on a minute.' He ducked out of sight and came up brandishing a scrumpled piece of paper. 'Here.' He smoothed out the paper before dialling a number. 'Let's just keep our fingers crossed,' he said, shooting a wink at Rene. 'Hello, is that Jamie Stratton? . . . Lewis Jones at the Fringe office. I've just given your name to a colleague of mine . . . yes, that's right . . . ah, so do you have any more rooms available? . . . Yes, Rene Brownlow . . . ah, well, there you go then. I've just given it to her to read . . . Right, so she can come round any time, then? Good, thank you, Jamie.'

Lewis smiled at Rene. 'There you are, you're famous already. Your new landlord has just read your review. You're going to be in London Street, just down the road a bit from the top of Leith Walk, so it's a good place to stay. He says you can go round any time you want.'

Getting to her feet, Rene reached up and threw her arms round the lanky Welshman's neck. 'Lewis, you're a real star.' She gave him a big kiss on the cheek. 'And sorry about all that blubbing.'

Jamie Stratton punched the air and let out a loud whoop of relief. Thank God things were looking up at last. His bank balance was just about at its limit. Now, in the space of twenty minutes, he had rented out two of the rooms. He probably had enough time to get a celebratory cup of coffee from The Grainstore.

Jamie bought more cups of coffee per day at The Grainstore than was probably good for him, but he had an ulterior motive. It was his considered opinion that, underneath her red-striped apron, Martha had a body to die for, an uncommon asset for a girl who edged him in height by as much as three notches over his own six feet. Her attraction went deeper than a mere clawing at his carnal senses. Humour constantly simmered in Martha's blue-green eyes, her face radiated so much health that make-up was a non-essential, and her zaniness was marked by the pointless black plastic hairband that adorned her short blonde hair. Jamie considered her his ultimate woman. The only problem was that, during their many brief encounters, he had found out she had six years on him and had been in a steady relationship for three of them. But inaccessibility only made the crush grow deeper.

The coffee shop was enjoying good custom that afternoon, but there was no queue at the counter. Martha caught his entry and immediately turned to one of her colleagues, slumping her shoulders and raising a long-suffering eyebrow. Undeterred, Jamie approached her with a broad grin. 'Hi, there, Martha.'

When she turned at his greeting, Martha gave him only the briefest of smiles. 'Well, James, what is it you're wanting this afternoon?'

'Black coffee to go, please.'

Martha turned to the espresso machine. 'Still home alone, are you?'

'Not any more. I've managed to get two of the bedrooms rented out.'

Martha glanced over her shoulder. 'That'll please the bank manager.'

'Too right.' He dug in the pocket of his trousers for some change. 'And what about you? Busy as ever?'

Martha placed the Styrofoam cup on the counter and pushed on a lid. 'Didn't close up until midnight last night.'

Jamie handed her the exact change. 'No more cameras going missing?' he said with a laugh.

Martha shut the drawer of the till with force. 'It's not good for business, having people come in here and nicking things.'

'No, I reckon not.' He picked up the cup from the counter. 'I'd better be getting back in case one of my punters arrives. I'll see you later.'

'Nothing in life could be more certain,' Martha replied quietly through clenched teeth as she turned to another customer.

Seeing the taxi pulling away from outside his flat, Jamie ran the last thirty metres along London Street. An elderly man in a tweed jacket and cavalry-twill trousers was pressing one of the bells on the brass panel.

'Are you Mr Hartson?' Jamie asked. 'Hi, I'm Jamie Stratton. Sorry I wasn't here. I was getting myself a cup of coffee.'

'No need to apologise,' Leonard Hartson replied with a shake of his head. 'I have only just this moment arrived.'

Jamie pulled a bunch of keys from the pocket of his shorts and unlocked the door. Holding it open with a foot, he reached out his un-coffee-ed hand and grabbed the handle of the man's suitcase.

'Oh, I can manage that,' Leonard said, making a move to take the suitcase from Jamie's grasp.

'It's no bother,' Jamie replied. 'The flat's on the third floor, so I'm afraid you've got a bit of a climb.'

Leonard laughed. 'In that case, I am grateful for a fit young landlord.'

By the time the man had made the stairs, Jamie had opened the shutters on the large windows and given the bedroom a quick visual appraisal.

'Oh, my word, that is some climb,' Leonard said, entering the flat.

'Yeah, sorry about that. Better to take it in stages.' Jamie held out a hand to guide Leonard towards the bedroom. 'You're in here, Mr Hartson. It's on the quiet side of the building, so you won't hear the traffic. The bathroom is on the left, just outside your bedroom door—I hope you won't mind sharing it with me. The kitchen is down the hall on the right, and there's a large sitting room at the other end with satellite television, which you're welcome to use whenever you like.' He looked round the room. 'Does this seem all right for you?'

Leonard nodded his approval. 'Perfect.' He walked across to the window and looked out onto the gardens enclosed by the surrounding buildings. 'Very pleasant.' He turned back. 'And what about cost?'

'Well, erm . . .' Jamie had given this some thought. 'How about fifty pounds per night?'

Leonard nodded. 'Would you consider sixty pounds a night and allow me use of your telephone? For UK calls only, of course.'

Jamie raised his eyebrows thoughtfully. 'Yeah, sounds good to me.' He leaned his back against the wall. 'So, are you going to be here for the whole of the festival?'

'Yes, I am. I'm going to be working.'

Jamie wondered what type of work a man well past retirement age would be undertaking. 'And what is it you do?'

'I'm a lighting cameraman.'

'Is that right?' Jamie replied, suitably impressed. 'What type of films do you make?'

'I've worked on every kind of film in my time, but I'm up here to do a documentary.'

'So you've done features as well? Would I know any of them?'

'The last feature I worked on was made long before you were born,' Leonard chortled.

'I'll bet my father would know it. He's a complete movie buff.'

Leonard nodded slowly. 'I wouldn't suppose your father has any contacts up here in the film industry?'

Jamie laughed. 'No. Dad's a farmer. Why do you ask?'

'I'm looking for someone to assist me, and I'm not sure where to begin.' He scratched a finger down the side of his lined face. 'I don't suppose you know of anyone who might be looking for a job for the next three weeks? Experience isn't really necessary. I just need someone who has a bit of muscle and common sense about them.'

Jamie shrugged his shoulders. 'I'm afraid not. All my university friends are on summer vacation. I'll have a think about it, though.'

'That would be most kind,' Leonard replied.

Jamie pushed himself away from the wall when he heard the front-door buzzer sounding in the hall. He excused himself from Leonard and picked up the receiver.

'Jamie Stratton? This is Rene Brownlow. I'm outside your front door.'

'Right. When you hear the buzzer going, push the door open. I'm on the third floor.'

'What? I can't get this suitcase one inch further. My arms have stretched that much in length, ye'd think my dad was an ape!'

Jamie chuckled. 'All right, I'll be down in a sec.' He headed down the stairs at his customary speed and opened the door. A woman swathed in a loose-folded coat that appeared to have been manufactured from a couple of multicoloured rag rugs jumped back with surprise.

'My, that was quick! You must 'ave wings!'

'I'm used to those stairs,' Jamie said, picking up her suitcase. 'By the way, I read your review this morning. Pretty good.'

Rene stared open-mouthed at the ease with which he had lifted her enormous Samsonite burden. 'Nice of you to say so,' she replied.

Jamie cocked his ear, catching the sound of a telephone ringing up the stairwell. 'Dammit, that's my phone. Just make your own way up.' He turned and began taking the stairs two at a time. Dropping the suitcase with a thump on the flagstone floor at the door, Jamie crossed the hall and made a dive for the telephone. 'Hello?'

'Good afternoon, Jamie. It's Gavin Mackintosh here. I was just ringing to see if you'd managed to find any tenants for the festival.'

'Well, funny you should ask that now,' Jamie replied, glancing around to see that Mr Hartson's bedroom door was closed and Rene Brownlow was yet to make it to the top of the stairs. 'Two have just arrived today.'

'Oh, excellent. So does that mean you'll be all right for your mortgage payments?'

'Yeah, I should be OK until the end of September.'

'I take it your tenants will be there for the whole of the festival?'

'Probably not both of them. One is doing a show on the Fringe, so she could well leave before the final week. The other guy's a cameraman who'll be around for the duration. Talking of which, Gavin, you don't have any contacts in the film industry up here, do you?'

'No, Jamie. Why do you ask?'

'Well, this cameraman is in need of an assistant, so he asked me if I knew of anyone. He said he'd take someone with no experience.'

'No one springs to mind but I'll keep my thinking cap on.'

'That'd be great. Cheers, Gavin.' Jamie waved a greeting to Rene as she entered the flat and sat down with a flump on her suitcase. 'By the way, did Dad get hold of you?'

'No. What would that have been about?'

'A game of golf at Muirfield tomorrow evening, I think.'

'Ah I won't be able to make it. Jenny and I are going to a concert to hear Angélique Pascal.'

'She's the French violinist, isn't she? There was a photograph of her on the front page of the newspaper this morning. Pretty fit-looking.'

Gavin laughed. 'You're not wrong there. I had the pleasure of her company at a reception yesterday evening and she is captivating.'

'Sounds as if you're a bit hooked there, Gavin. Maybe you should consider ditching Jenny tomorrow evening and going it alone.'

'Ah, Jamie, I think maybe this would be an apt time to finish this call before you come up with any other suggestions and I'm tempted to charge you for my time. We'll keep in touch, though.'

'Right you are. Thanks, Gavin.' Jamie turned to his new tenant, who was still catching her breath. 'Sorry about that.'

Rene held up a hand. 'Not at all. I'm not used to all this exercise. Living in Edinburgh is like being at a bloody 'ealth farm.' She got slowly to her feet.

Jamie smiled at her as he picked up the suitcase. 'Come on, I'll show to your room and you can recover in comfort.'

Nine

THE PANDA CAR was sitting at traffic lights in Stockbridge when the report of suspicious behaviour came through from the control room. WPC Heather Lennox took the call while her colleague switched on the blue light and swerved out of the queue. As they approached, the driver killed the blue light and drove slowly round the corner, hoping for an element of surprise. He flicked the headlights onto full beam, illuminating the two youths who turned with panic on their faces, stepping away from the car into which they were only a moment away from gaining entry. As the panda car accelerated towards them, the boys took to their heels like frightened gazelles, finally scrambling up and over a seven-foot wall before disappearing from sight.

The driver threw open the car door, ready to give chase, but was stopped by WPC Lennox. 'Dinnae bother, Jim. We'll never catch 'em.' She stared out of the back window. 'Did ye see onything odd back there when we turned intae the street? I'm sure there was some'dy standing in that end doorway wi' something like a pair of binoculars.' She unslotted the radio handset. 'I think it's worth checking it.'

The driver drove to the end of the street and stopped at the junction with the road. 'Which way?' he asked.

WPC Lennox glanced up and down the street. There seemed to be only one person walking alone. 'That could be him up there. Wait for a couple of cars, then drive past at a speed where I can tak' a look at him.'

Sixty metres away, T.K. was still chuckling to himself. It had been the third time he had videoed those two boys attempting to nick a car, but that one really had to take the Oscar. He had had the zoom set right in to record every detail of the theft and had seen the expressions of horror on the boys' faces when they turned to look up the street. Then he had zoomed out, catching the police car approaching, and he had kept the camera switched on until the lads disappeared over the wall. He could not resist reviewing the whole hilarious scene then and there. He rewound the tape and pressed playback, studying the screen as he walked, oblivious to the cars that passed him on the street.

'Well, speak o' the devil,' WPC Lennox breathed.

'D'ye know him?' her colleague asked.

'That, Jim, is Thomas Keene, who has mair stolen cars to his name than the Queen of England has jewels.'

'Ye'd think he'd notice us, then. What was he doing?'

'I don't know. He was holding something in his hand, but I couldn't work out what it was. We'll just ask the lad a few questions, shall we?'

T.K. was so distracted by his masterpiece that he missed the step at the end of the pavement and landed awkwardly on his foot. Wincing with pain, he bent down, put his camera on the ground and started to rub at his ankle, suddenly becoming aware of the two shadows darkening the area around him. He slowly lifted his head. The bloody polis. He glanced down at the camera by his right foot.

'Would you stand up so that we can ask you a few questions, Keene?' the policewoman asked, taking a step towards him.

T.K. put his hand on the camera and manoeuvred his feet into a position as near as possible to that of a hundred-metre sprinter about to push off from his blocks. The policeman sensed the lad's intentions and reached down to grab his shoulder, but his hand closed on thin air.

'Bring the car. I'll get him,' the policeman called out as he ran off in pursuit, the gap between him and the wee bastard increasing.

T.K. shot a quick glance behind him. He was putting welcome distance between himself and his pursuer, but he had to get out of sight.

He knew from the moment he turned into the small mews street that he had made a mistake. The cobbled lane came to an abrupt end at an eighteen-foot high wall topped with a spiral of razor wire. T.K. looked frantically around. A cluster of dustbins were tucked away into the corner of the wall. He dragged one of them out, pulled off the top and pushed the camera down deep among the plastic bags. Then a spur-of-the-moment decision made him retrieve it. He was damned if he was going to lose his precious videotape. He ejected the cassette and rammed the camera back into its hiding place. Then, squatting down behind the dustbin, he slid the cassette down the side of his battered trainer, just seconds before a torch beam hit him full in the face.

Gavin Mackintosh rose to his feet along with the rest of the audience in the Usher Hall to give tumultuous applause to the performance of Mozart's Violin Concerto No. 3 in G Major. With outstretched hand, the conductor directed the acclaim towards the young soloist, then gave her a short Germanic bow. Angélique Pascal, dressed in a black strapless cocktail dress reciprocated by blowing him a kiss before continuing in similar style to the packed auditorium.

Gavin's clap was the last to echo round the vast concert hall, his eyes fixed on the departing orchestra. His wife touched his arm to draw his attention to those others in their row who were waiting to get past him. Gavin held up a hand in apology, slipped the programme into the inside pocket of his jacket and followed her up the staircase to the exit.

Outside, a cool wind swerved around the curved walls of the Usher Hall. Fastening his suit jacket, Gavin took hold of Jenny's arm and manoeuvred through the crowds, at the same time taking his mobile phone from his breast pocket. He had felt it reverberate halfway through the concert. Now, he listened to the message.

'Don't say you have a call-out,' Jenny said in a long-suffering voice.

'One of John Anderson's legal aid cases. The lad's been taken into Gayfield Square Police Station.' He held up a hand to hail a taxi. 'I'll have to stop in at the office to see if I can unearth some files on the boy. You take this taxi home and I'll be back as soon as I can.' As the black cab pulled up alongside them, Gavin gave his wife a kiss on the cheek. 'At least this year we managed to get to see the concert.'

Jenny smiled knowingly at him. 'I think you might have been in a bit of a grump if you'd missed out on both Mademoiselle Pascal's musical *and* physical attributes this evening.'

Gavin laughed. 'Nothing more than a boyish infatuation.' He closed the door and headed off towards Princes Street.

T.K sat slumped in the windowless interview room. He hated the stink of these places, the sour aroma of disinfectant doing little to cover the ingrown stench of fear. His agitation was exacerbated by the fact that he was beginning to break out in a cold and clammy sweat, being a good hour overdue with the methadone.

He glanced at the pair of battered trainers on the table. Why had he kept the tape? He should have known they would give him a thorough search. There was enough evidence on that tape to put at least nine lads in front of the juvenile court, and it wouldn't take long before everyone on the Pilton Mains estate knew exactly who was responsible for sup-plying the evidence. He leaned back in the chair, clasping his hands behind his head. Where the hell had that damned Mr Anderson got to? The polis must have put the call through a good hour and a half ago.

The door of the interview room opened and WPC Lennox entered. 'Your solicitor is here, Keene.'

A large man in a dark blue pinstriped suit walked in and thumped a buff-coloured file down on the table. T.K. stared at him in alarm. 'Where's Mr Anderson?' he asked, panic in his voice.

'On holiday, I'm afraid, Thomas. I'm Mr Mackintosh. You're going to have to make do with me.'

T.K. let out a groan of hopelessness on hearing the gruff tones of his new solicitor. This is it, he thought. No way ye're goin' tae escape time.

Gavin turned to the policewoman. 'Constable Lennox, would you be good enough to allow me two minutes with my client?'

The policewoman flicked her head uncertainly. 'We should really just get on wi' it, Mr Mackintosh, but I'll give ye a couple of minutes, as long as ye don't hold back on anything during the interview.'

Gavin nodded. 'You have my assurance.'

As the door closed, Gavin pulled out one of the chairs opposite T.K. and sat down. He took out a pair of half-moon reading glasses from his pocket and spent a moment scanning through the reports on the first few pages. Pushing the file to one side, he eyed the young man over his spectacles. 'Well, it doesn't look too good, does it, Thomas?'

'Ah didnae dae onything,' T.K. mumbled disgruntledly.

Gavin found it difficult to suppress a laugh. 'You seem to have sup-plied the police with enough evidence to cut car crime in Edinburgh by half overnight. What happened to the camera?'

'Ah dropped it in the chase.'

'Why did you take the tape out, then?'

T.K. managed to pause only fractionally before replying. ''Cause I'd just loaded it wi' a new one.'

'You know Constable Lennox's colleague went back to look for the camera. There was no trace of it.'

'Some thievin' gypsy must hae picked it up, then.'

'What model was it, Thomas?'

'A JVC digi'al compact.'

Gavin nodded. He had a half inkling to believe the boy. His experience was that those who stole cameras were usually only interested in what money they could raise from its sale. 'You seem to be bit uncomfortable, Thomas. Are you back on the hard stuff?'

'No, I'm just sweatin' 'cos ah'm due ma "script".'

'Could you tell me why you've been filming people stealing cars?'

T.K. eyed the solicitor distrustfully before shrugging a silent reply.

'It would help your cause if you gave me some sort of answer, Thomas. How did you know who was going off to steal cars?'

T.K. sighed and stared up at the bare ceiling light. 'They meet uvvy night on the estate. They talk aboot how they nick the different cars, some o' them learn themselves, others learn fi' the boys they meet in detention centres. That's how it works.'

'It's like a club, then?'

'Aye, s'pose.'

'And you were in this club, then?'

'No!' T.K. replied with vehemence. 'If ye want proof o' that, tak' a look at the film. I never went near 'em.'

Gavin leaned over and leafed through the pages in the file. 'Car theft does seem to be your speciality. Your knowledge is probably infinitely greater than the lads you've been filming.'

T.K. scoffed out a laugh. 'Ah dinnae wanna steal cars onymair, d'ya unnerstand that, ah wanna film stuff. Whit else is there tae shoot when ye live in a shitehole like Pilton Mains?'

Gavin studied the gaunt, loose-lipped face of the young man. 'Is that the truth, Thomas?'

'Aye, it is,' T.K. replied quietly, as if embarrassed by what Gavin had just drawn out of him. 'Ah'm tryin' ti go straight, eh.'

Gavin drew the buff file towards him. He replaced the rubber bands with a twang and got to his feet. 'I think it's time we started the interview, don't you, Thomas?'

T.K. held his arms across his chest to stop the developing shakes. 'Honest, Mr Mackintosh, I didnae dae onything. Ye've gotti believe me.'

Gavin shot him a wink. 'Just stay cool, Thomas, and answer the questions. I'm on your side, lad.'

Fifteen minutes past midnight, Gavin walked into the cool night air and stood listening to the breeze rustling the leaves on the trees that stood in the centre of Gayfield Square. A moment later, he heard the door of the police station open and he sensed someone come to stand beside him. He turned to see T.K. stick his hands into the pockets of his baggy jeans and pull in a long breath of relief.

'Cheers fae that, Mr Mackintosh,' he said, nodding his appreciation at the solicitor. 'I'm no' sure what ye said in there aifter the interview, but . . . cheers onyway.'

'I did stick my neck on the block for you in there, Thomas, and judging from your notes, Mr Anderson has done likewise in the past. I was willing to take the risk because I think you probably are making an effort to keep out of trouble. Just don't disappoint me.'

T.K. answered him with a shake of his head before casting a glance up the street. He wasn't out of the shit yet. He now had to go back to the flat in Pilton Mains. The police would have been knocking on doors already, which meant it would be unlikely he'd get through the night without getting knifed or having a broken bottle slice open some part of his body.

He shot Gavin a sad smile. 'Mr Mackintosh, is there any chance you could gie's some cash tae get hame? Ah'm skint.'

Gavin sucked his teeth. 'Where'd you keep your methadone, Thomas?'

T.K. frowned. 'In ma bedroom in the flat.'

'Well,' said Gavin with a pensive nod. 'I suggest we take a taxi back to my house, pick up my car and you can show me where you live. Once I've fetched the methadone from your bedroom, I'm going to bring you back uptown and take you to a hostel for the night.' Gavin gestured for T.K. to walk with him up the road towards Leith Walk. 'I don't do this for all my clients, you know, Thomas, but in your case, I have an ulterior motive.' He fixed the lad with a stern glare. 'I shall come and pick you up at the hostel at nine thirty sharp. Is that clear?'

T.K. nodded dolefully.

'Because then I'm going to try out an idea which might hopefully result in my never having to encounter you in a police station again.'

Albert Dessuin arrived just over three-quarters of an hour late for the post-concert reception in the Sheraton Grand. His mobile had rung the moment he had walked out of the Usher Hall. He had listened, reasoned and accepted responsibility for gross negligence, and finally he had abruptly ended his mother's call with a stab of his finger. Now, as he entered the function suite, he could sense the black cloud of irritation that resulted from such a call.

He swept a glass of champagne from the waitress's tray, downed it in one gulp and took another before skirting the outside of the room. His eyes eventually fixed on the cluster of men who were gathered around the unused bar in the corner of the room. In the midst of them, Angélique and another girl, who he recognised as Tess Goodwin, the marketing assistant from the International office, sat on the high counter, chatting and laughing.

Ever since the concert in Munich two weeks ago, he had begun to notice unwelcome changes in Angélique. This new, grown-up Angélique Pascal was beginning to show too much independence. He watched as she placed her hand on the shoulders of one of the men, drew him towards her and kissed him on his forehead. She then threw back her head in laughter and pushed him away, flicking her hands as if dismissing him from her presence. It was indicative of yet another unwelcome change in Angélique. If that was the way she wished to behave, then it was obvious to Albert that now was the time to educate her in ways other than simply playing the violin. Wiping beads of perspiration from his forehead, he made his way towards the group.

'Albert?'

He found a smiling Sir Alasdair Dreyfuss standing beside him.

'I'm sorry, I've been rather negligent of you this evening,' the director said, putting a hand on his arm. 'I'm afraid Signor Montarino has rather commandeered my attention up until this point.'

Albert managed to flicker a smile at the director. 'Please do not worry. I have also been engaged in numerous conversations.'

'About the concert tonight, I am sure.' Alasdair Dreyfuss glanced in the direction of Angélique. 'Quite startling. She seems to be becoming ever more accomplished. You really are to be congratulated, Albert.'

'Thank you,' Albert replied distractedly.

Alasdair eyed him concernedly. 'Are you all right, Albert? You're looking a bit pale.'

Albert shook his head. 'Only a bit of a headache, but I was thinking I might slip away to lie down in my room for a while.'

'I'd be grateful if you might just spare me a moment before you go,' the director said, guiding him away from the young violinist's admiring group. 'I want to have a quick word with you about the late concerts Angélique will be performing. Let's head over to the recess by the window so we won't be disturbed.'

And as Sir Alasdair led him across the room, Albert heard Angélique's laughter sound out once more and he turned with fury in his eyes as the distance grew between them.

As Tess stood thanking the departing guests for their attendance, she heard her phone ringing in her handbag. 'What are you doing?' she whispered angrily into her mobile. 'I said I'd be the one to make contact.'

'I know,' Peter Hansen replied, 'but I wanted to let you know I've booked a table for a week today in La Hirondelle at eight thirty. Our favourite restaurant should be a good place to renew our friendship.'

'It's not going to happen, Peter. The only reason I agreed to have dinner with you is because I love my husband and I love my job and I am certainly not going to lose either because of you.'

'Tess, there's no reason to be like that. I have made it my plan not to leave Edinburgh without mending all our differences.' Tess heard one of his slow, seductive laughs. 'I thought you might wear that blue dress I bought for you? You always looked very beautiful in it.'

'I chucked that ages ago.'

There was a brief silence. 'OK, no matter, then,' he said, the tone of disappointment in his voice satisfying Tess. 'I am sure you will look wonderful in whatever you wear.'

'I have to go, Peter. Our guests are leaving.'

'All right. A week today, then, eight thirty at La Hirondelle.'

Still dressed in the cocktail dress she had worn for the concert, Angélique Pascal lay huddled on the bed in her hotel bedroom, staring at the distorted image of her violin case on the Regency-style chair.

She had never before had such a row with Albert. She had played her heart out at the concert, and had felt unusually buoyant during the reception afterwards, dissipating the smog of exhaustion that had enveloped her over the past month. But it had only lasted until the moment she had returned, or had *been* returned, to her hotel bedroom by Albert, who had caused a scene at the crowded reception by extricating her from the room like a naughty schoolchild.

In the privacy of her room, he had set about berating her for the sloppiness of her performance and the way she had acted at the reception. And then he had ordered her to start practising. She had retaliated. She told him in a quiet, controlled voice that she'd had enough. When Edinburgh was finished, she wanted to take a complete break.

'Albert, you must understand that I cannot go on like this, playing night after night. It affects the way I feel about the music. You are probably right to criticise me, although tonight I made a great effort to play well. But it does not make me happy, Albert, to have to *make* that effort. I need a rest. I want to return to Clermont Ferrand to stay with Madame Lafitte. She will help me regain my enthusiasm for music.'

'*Pah*, that ancient old crow could give you *nothing* now. You will not go back. You will continue to play. There is no way you can back out of your obligations at this stage. It would spell the end of your career.'

'Could we not just say that I am sick?'

'But you are not sick. And I am not going to be party to such subterfuge. Now, change out of that dress, which makes you look like a tart, and get on with your practising.'

Angélique shook her head slowly. 'Oh, Albert, sometimes you are so like your mother.'

'How *dare* you say such a thing!' Dessuin screamed at her, raising his hand as if to strike her across the face. Falling back onto the bed to avoid the blow, Angélique crawled away from him, pushing herself against the headboard. He turned on his heel and stormed out of the room, slamming shut the door that connected their bedrooms.

Sitting up now, she glanced across at the radio alarm on her bedside table. It was a quarter past midnight. Two hours had passed since Dessuin had left the room. Intending to have a shower, she slipped out of her dress as she walked across to the bathroom, her nakedness spared only by a black lace thong.

She turned with a start at the sound of the connecting door being thrown open, her immediate reaction to cover her breasts with her hands and push her legs together.

'Albert, what the *hell* are you doing?' she said to Dessuin, who stood framed in the doorway, one hand against the doorpost. In the other, he clutched a bottle of whisky. 'I am naked, so please get out of here *now*.'

Dessuin gave a short, scornful laugh. 'Oh, look at you, Miss Modesty,' he said in a slurring voice, 'trying to cover yourself up.'

Angélique turned to get into the bathroom, but drunk as he was, Dessuin made it across the room, blocking her path. She backed away into the centre of the room, shaking with uncertainty and fear.

'Come on, Angélique,' he laughed derisively. 'You would have loved to have given one of those young men tonight the chance to see you as I am now seeing you.'

Angélique squatted down, covering her breasts as best she could with her elbows. 'Albert,' she sobbed quietly, 'please leave me alone.'

'Leave you alone?' he whined. 'Why should I leave you alone?' He came and leaned over her, and she could smell the alcohol. 'I *own* you—you will never get rid of me.'

Angélique stared up at him, her eyes afire with hatred. 'My God, you are a screwed-up *bastard*, Albert Dessuin. You are nothing more than a worthless, drunken *cochon*!'

The force of the blow knocked Angélique onto her side and rolled her across the floor. She lay with her head spinning, trying to work out how she could avoid the next blow, when he yanked her to her feet. She let out a cry of pain as he dug his fingernails into her arm, dragging her across to the desk so that he could rid himself of the bottle of whisky. Then, with both hands free, he threw her spreadeagled onto the bed.

'Right, Mademoiselle Pascal, world-famous musician, if you choose to call me that name, I will show you exactly what a *cochon* excels at!'

He clumsily unbuttoned his trousers and pushed them to the floor, but as he pulled his legs up to step out of them, the cuffs caught on his shoes and he fell heavily to the ground. Angélique, seeing her moment, jumped off the bed and grabbed her dress from the floor. As she ran towards the door, a hand grasped at her ankle and she fell forward onto the desk, knocking over the whisky bottle in the process. It toppled over onto a metal wastepaper basket, shattering its neck. Putting his near-spent energy into one final heave, Dessuin brought Angélique crashing to the ground, but even in his drunken stupor, the ensuing scream cut through to his senses and he released his grip.

All thoughts of protecting her modesty now long gone, Angélique sat on the floor staring at her hand and at the blood that flowed down her arm from the wound.

'Oh, *mon Dieu*, what have you done?' she cried out, her desolate sobs shaking every part of her body. 'You have just ruined my *life!*'

'Oh, Angélique,' Dessuin said, his voice slurring heavier than before. 'I'm so sorry, *ma chérie*, I did not mean . . .' He tried to make a move towards her, but the struggle and the alcohol coursing through his body took its toll and he toppled over unconscious.

Never taking her eyes off her hand, Angélique got slowly to her feet and stepped over Dessuin's prostrate form. She went into the bathroom and turned on the cold tap, wincing with pain as she held her palm upturned under the gushing stream. She held her hand up to the light to see if there was any glass embedded in the wound. The gash was long and deep, but as far as she could tell, clean. Taking a white towel from the rack, she bound it tight out around her hand and viewed her frightened face in the mirror above the sink.

Oh, Angélique, you cannot stay here with this man who has betrayed your trust. But maybe everyone will believe it was your fault . . . He will certainly do everything to manipulate the story for it to appear so. You have no alternative but to leave, and leave everything behind you.

She peered round the door of the bathroom. Dessuin lay snoring gently, his glasses pressed awkwardly into the side of his face. She noticed two small patches of blood on the carpet beside the desk and decided there and then to cover her tracks, removing as much evidence as she could of the struggle.

Moving guardedly around Dessuin, Angélique wiped away the blood from the carpet and soaked up the whisky with the help of half a roll of lavatory paper, before flushing it away. She took the bottle and its broken neck through to Dessuin's bedroom and put it in his wastepaper basket. Returning to her room, she picked up her dress from the floor and stepped into it. Taking a jacket from the wardrobe, she pulled it awkwardly round her shoulders and kicked her feet into a pair of flats.

She took one last fleeting look at those things that were now useless to her—Albert Dessuin, and the black violin case on the cream Regency-style chair. For a moment, Angélique eyed the room key but decided she would not take it. She would never return here again. She hurried along the corridor and pressed the button for the lift. As she waited for it to make its journey from the ground floor, her face crumpled and tears streamed unchecked down her cheeks, in the full realisation of all that she was leaving behind and the terrifying uncertainty of what she would face in her future and much-changed life.

Ten

DURING THE THREE WEEKS of the Edinburgh Festival, the city rarely succumbs to rest. Every hour of the day each street corner becomes a venue for some aspiring entertainer, attracting an ever-shifting audience from the crowds that throng the streets, creating a cacophony of sound that drowns out even the constant traffic. In the small hours of the morning, an ambling pedestrian on Princes Street might find himself striding out in military style to the skirl of the bagpipes before gliding past a string quartet playing a Strauss waltz; and then staggering away in laughter from the comedian whose act had been conducted from the confines of a council wheelie bin. He might then be reduced to tears of compassion by a couple of teenage actors, performing the death scene from *Romeo and Juliet* with as much passion as one might witness in the splendour of the Old Vic. Intensifying this atmosphere are the blazing lights from every misty-windowed restaurant, crammed public house, queued-up café and buzzing street stall, each staying open until the last of their customers adjourns to their smart hotels and homely boarding houses, sparse lodgings and shared bedrooms.

It was against such a backdrop that Jamie Stratton, having spent the evening reviewing Fringe shows, made his way back to the London Street flat. A distant bell rang out two o'clock as he walked briskly down Broughton Street. He noticed the lights of The Grainstore coffee shop still ablaze further down the road but the coffee shop appeared to be completely deserted and there was no sign of Martha. Suspicion gripped at his stomach as he pushed down on the door handle. It was locked. Maybe Martha was in need of his help. 'Martha, are you in there?' he yelled. 'Martha? Can you hear me? Are you all right?'

He pressed his face to the glass, squinting through The Grainstore logo, and then, with relief, he caught sight of her, looking up over the counter from her seated position behind it. Getting to her feet, she approached the door, opening it a fraction. 'What do you want, Jamie?'

'You had me worried. I thought something had happened to you. I saw all the lights on, and I thought, well . . .'

'You thought what?'

'That you'd been robbed or something.'

Martha laughed mockingly. 'Ah, and I suppose you were going to do your "Sir Galahad" bit and rescue me?'

'Well, no, but I was just . . .' He scratched self-consciously at the back of his head. 'Why *are* you open so late, then?'

Taking a quick glance behind her, Martha came out onto the doorstep. 'Listen, Jamie,' she said in a quiet voice. 'Do you really want to be a help to me?'

Jamie shrugged. 'Yeah, sure. What d'you want?'

Martha jabbed a thumb over her shoulder. 'There's a girl in there who won't leave. Every time I think she's about to finish up, she orders another cup of coffee. And I'm knackered and I want to get to bed.'

'Well, why don't you just tell her to leave?'

Martha raised her eyebrows. 'Because I think she's French and I don't know what to say to her.'

'So you want me to tell her to leave—in French.' Jamie tried to recall his sparse GSCE French vocabulary. 'Well, I could give it a go.'

Martha put two hands on his back and pushed him into the coffee shop. 'I'll go to the loo and get my things while you get rid of her.'

As he approached the counter, Jamie saw for the first time the dark-haired girl who sat at a table in the far corner, slowly spinning her empty coffee cup around in its saucer. He walked across and leaned his hands on the back of the chair opposite her. '*Excusez-moi, mademoiselle? Êtes-vous française?*'

From the moment she turned to face him, Jamie knew there was something very wrong. Her eyes were swimming with tears and an ugly bruise spread purple across her right cheekbone. She sat awkwardly, one hand hidden in the·folds of something bulky inside her linen jacket. '*Tout est bien, n'est-ce pas?*' Jamie asked.

'*Oui,*' the girl replied unconvincingly.

There was something familiar about her, but he could not work out what it was. '*L'heure est très tarde, mademoiselle, et mon amie veut fermer le café.*'

The girl nodded slowly, smiling apologetically at him. 'Yes, of course. I am sorry to have stayed so long.' Her grasp of English far outmatched Jamie's stuttering attempt at her own native tongue. 'I will leave.'

'Ah, I'm sorry, I didn't realise you spoke English. I'm sure Martha would have talked to you if she'd known.'

'Please don't worry,' the girl said, dismissing his remark with a wave of her exposed hand. As she pushed herself to her feet, Jamie noticed her screwing up her eyes, as if she had suffered a stab of pain. 'Maybe you would be kind enough to give me some advice before I leave? Would you know if there is a hotel·close by where I might get a room?'

Jamie began to explain that there·was little chance of her finding anywhere to stay, never mentioning the fact that he himself had a spare room in his flat. And then suddenly, out of nowhere, the image on the front page of the newspaper came to him and he clicked his fingers in recognition. 'You're Angélique Pascal, aren't you?'

The girl's eyes widened in alarm. She lowered her head and walked past him towards the door. 'I must leave now, but thank you for your kindness.'

'Hang on a minute,' Jamie said with such force that the young violinist froze in her tracks. 'Listen, it may be none of my business, but you, of all people, must have somewhere to stay tonight. You have to be booked into one of the big hotels.' Jamie paused, giving her time to answer, then took a step towards her.

'Something's happened, hasn't it? What's gone wrong? What have you done to your hand?'

Renewed tears welled in Angélique's eyes. 'I have cut it,' she sobbed. 'Very badly, I think.'

Jamie put an arm on her shoulder. 'Come on, you're not in any fit state to leave.' He guided her back to the table, and once she had resumed her seat, he pulled round a chair and sat down next to her. 'Right,' he said, 'let me have a look at it.'

Angélique undid her jacket and slowly pulled out her hand wrapped in the bloodstained towel.

At that point, the door of the ladies banged shut and Jamie turned to see Martha staring at him. *What are you doing?* she mouthed.

'Martha, just come here for a sec.'

Throwing her eyes heavenwards, Martha walked over to the table.

'Right,' Jamie said gently to the violinist, 'just lean your elbow on the table. I'm going to remove the towel really slowly, OK?' He carefully unwrapped it and handed it to Martha. As Jamie slowly unclenched Angélique's hand with his fingers, blood dripped from the wound and the young violinist let out a cry of pain. 'Martha, get me some paper towels to wipe this up and also something really clean to cover it with.'

With a sigh of impatience, Martha clumped off behind the counter. Jamie studied the uneven gash that ran across the violinist's now-swollen palm. 'Ow, that looks quite deep. How on earth did you do it?'

'I fell over onto broken glass,' Angélique answered in a faltering voice.

'Where, in the street?'

'No, in my hotel bedroom . . .' Her voice trailed off to silence as she cast a worried glance between Jamie and Martha, who had returned with a large kitchen roll and two clean white tea towels.

Jamie studied the violinist's face. 'Well, first, we need to get this cleaned up and stitched. You'll probably need a tetanus jab as well.' He began to rebind the wound with one of Martha's tea towels, then rose to his feet. 'Right, Martha, we'd better get Angélique to A and E and—'

'What do you mean, "we"?' Martha cut in.

Jamie turned fully in his chair. 'You've got a car, Martha, and I don't.'

'I've got to get this place opened up at half past eight tomorrow morning. Can't you take a taxi?'

'For God's sakes, just do us a favour and drop us off,' Jamie hissed at her. 'We'll get a taxi back once the girl has been treated.'

Martha was taken aback by the vehemence of his reply. 'All right, you don't have to get on your high horse. You'll have to give me time to get her table cleared and the till locked up.'

'OK.' Jamie gave her a short nod. As he watched her sweep away the coffee cup from in front of Angélique, he knew that the next time he set foot in The Grainstore, it would be for coffee and nothing else.

'Angélique, I'm trying to work things out. Who else knows you've cut your hand?'

Angélique shook her head. 'Nobody.'

'Right,' Jamie said, rubbing his forehead. 'I know for a fact you were playing in a concert in the Usher Hall this evening, and I'm pretty sure you've got another one tomorrow. I think it's quite obvious to both of us you won't be able to play with your hand.' He paused, catching the violinist's unease. 'We should tell someone you're going to be out of action. What about that man in the photograph with you? Your manager? Do you think we should let him know?'

'No! Don't do that!' Angélique cried out, fear in her eyes.

Jamie held up his hands to calm her. 'All right, all right, we won't do that.' He shook his head. 'Angélique, I haven't got a bloody clue what's gone on this evening, but if you're trying to hide from someone there's a spare bedroom in my flat. But if you don't turn up for your next concert, I'm afraid the press will come looking for you.' He leaned forward. 'So, what do you want me to do?'

The violinist studied the face of this well-built young man who was being so kind. 'Listen, maybe,' she said eventually. 'For an hour or so?'

Jamie nodded. 'OK, I'd be happy to.' He glanced round as Martha came out from behind the counter and scooped up her bag. 'Let's leave it for now,' he said quietly, giving Martha a nod.

She walked over to the entrance door and pulled it open. 'Come on, then,' she said resignedly. 'Let's get you to the hospital.'

Cathy Dent and Phil Kenyon were deep in conversation when they walked into the office of the Exploding Sky Company as the clock that hung on the far wall clicked onto nine o'clock. Both stopped talking when they realised that Roger was already there, sitting with his feet up on the desk, a mug of coffee in his hand, staring out of the rain-lashed window at the dark Cotswold landscape.

Taking it that the boss was in one of his morning moods, Phil pulled a long face at Cathy before giving Roger a slap on the shoulder. 'How're things this morning, mate?' he asked jovially. 'Raring to go?' He went through to the small kitchen to make coffee for himself and Cathy.

Cathy pulled out the chair next to Roger and booted up her computer. 'You all right, love?' she asked. 'I never heard you get up.'

'I'm fine. I've been here since six o'clock.'

'What have you been doing?'

'Just thinking about this and that.'

Phil came through from the kitchen carrying two mugs of coffee. Handing one to Cathy and placing the other on the desk, he pulled up a chair and opened the schedule diary at the 17th of August. 'Right, so it looks like we're getting gear ready for Edinburgh today.'

Sliding his feet off the desk, Roger leaned forward and put his own mug on the desk. 'We're doing a bit more than that, Phil.' Roger picked up the pile of papers in front of him and handed them to his colleague.

Phil glanced through them quickly. 'This is the firing plan for Edinburgh. You've gone and added stuff.' He blew out a long breath of frustration. 'Mate, this is going to screw up all the timings.'

'No, it's not. All the new firings will be simultaneous with those already programmed.'

Phil tossed the papers onto the desk. 'But we're completely full up on the slave units, Rog. There's no room.'

'I'm going to increase the number of units to forty. That should do it.'

'Jeez, mate, this isn't going to be easy to set up.'

'I know. That's why I'm rescheduling our departure from here for the 26th of August. That'll give us a day extra.'

Phil flipped through the pages of the diary. 'That's nine days' time!'

'Yes, so we've got a bit of work to do.'

'And how! Are the crew going to be able to make it?'

'Not sure yet. If not, then we'll just start rigging without them.'

Cathy had sat watching her husband during the interchange between the two men. Getting up from her chair, she went to stand behind him, encircling his neck with her arms. 'Is this what I think it is?' she asked.

'Yeah, love, this is it.'

Phil let out a short laugh and shook his head. 'I'm obviously being kept in the dark about something.'

Roger held hard to his wife's hands as he looked across at his colleague. 'My swan song, old friend. Edinburgh's going to be my last show.'

Phil stared at his boss, open-mouthed. 'You're joking, Rog.'

'No, I'm not.' Roger unwrapped his wife's hands from around his neck and rose stiffly to his feet. 'I'm just . . . dog-tired of it all. This is a young man's game, Phil. This constant shifting around the country, the intensity of the workload, it's all getting too much for me. I want to spend time with Cathy and maybe do something completely different.'

'Like what?'

Roger chuckled. 'I've always fancied the idea of breeding pigs.'

Phil threw back his head in laughter. 'What the hell do you know about breeding pigs?'

'About as much as I did about putting on a firework display when I first started out.'

'He's been reading up on it for the past year,' Cathy interjected.

Phil shook his head in disbelief. 'God, is that how long you've been planning all this?'

'Maybe a bit longer,' Roger replied. 'It was one of the reasons I bought this place. The thirty acres included in the sale are all I'm going to need.'

Discarding the diary Phil scratched the back of his head. 'So, that's it, then. The end of the Exploding Sky Company.'

'Doesn't have to be,' Roger replied, picking up a lengthy typewritten document from the desk and handing it to the tough little Australian.

'What's this?'

'A partnership agreement. Saying that I keep a vested interest in the company, but hand over forty-nine per cent to my new partner. The business is doing well, so he should be able to pay for his shareholding over a ten-year period on a no-interest loan basis.'

Phil's eyes never left the page. 'My name's on this.'

'Of course it is,' Roger replied with a laugh. 'I wouldn't take anyone else on as a partner. You, Cathy and I have built up the Exploding Sky Company together, Phil, and if you're not going to take it on, then I'd rather close the whole damned shooting match.' He flicked his head to the side. 'But it'd be a pity, seeing we're at the top of our profession.'

Phil stood biting his bottom lip as he flicked through the pages of the agreement. 'It's a bit of a no-win situation for you and Cathy, ain't it?'

'Not at all. We have a company that keeps going and we retain a controlling shareholding.' He eyed his colleague. 'So what d'you think?'

Phil shrugged his shoulders. 'I'll go for it, mate.'

Roger put out his hand and the Australian grabbed it and shook it forcefully. 'Only thing is,' Roger said, holding up a finger, 'part of the payment is this.' He pointed at the new firing plan for Edinburgh. 'I want to put together a display that's just going to knock 'em all dead.'

Phil laughed. 'You wanna go out with a bang, mate.'

Roger slid an arm round Cathy. 'Quite literally, old friend.'

While Gavin Mackintosh retrieved a parking ticket from the machine on the street corner, T.K. stood next to the solicitor's Volvo, wondering if there might be some ominous reason behind Mr Mackintosh's choosing to park his car in the exact location where, just over two weeks ago, T.K. had bid a hasty retreat with the stolen video camera.

Sticking the ticket onto the windscreen of the car, Gavin shut the door and glanced across at T.K., taking the boy's unease solely as an attack of nerves at the thought of the imminent meeting. Gavin gave him a reassuring slap on the back. 'Come on, then.'

They climbed the three wide stone steps that led up to one of the many entrance doors in the row of smooth-stoned, tall-windowed Georgian buildings. Running his finger down the list of names on the polished brass panel, Gavin pressed one of the buttons. 'This is the residence of Mr James Stratton,' a woman's voice crackled from the speaker, affecting a smart upper-class accent quite unconvincingly. 'How can I be of assistance?'

Gavin chuckled to himself and pressed the button. 'Is Jamie there?'

'I 'aven't seen him this morning,' the voice replied, now in a strong Yorkshire accent. ''E's probably still in his bed.'

'I see. Well, I'm Gavin Mackintosh, Jamie's solicitor, and I do need to see him urgently, so I would be most grateful if you would let me in.'

Immediately there was a long buzzing sound and Gavin pushed open the heavy entrance door. With T.K. at his heels, he made his way up the three flights of stairs to Jamie's flat, where a small plump woman with short streaked hair was waiting to greet them at the door.

'Good morning,' Gavin said, holding out a hand to the woman. 'You must be one of Jamie's new tenants. I'm Gavin Mackintosh.'

'Rene Brownlow,' the woman replied, giving his hand one strong brief shake. 'Pleased to meet ye.'

Gavin revealed his companion, who was lurking behind him. 'And this young man is Thomas Keene.'

Rene nodded at the boy before stepping back into the flat. 'Well, you'd better both come in, then.' She shut the door with a bang when Gavin and T.K. had entered. 'As I said, I 'aven't seen Jamie this morning. D'you want me to knock on his bedroom door?'

'Not necessarily,' Gavin replied thoughtfully, 'You wouldn't happen to know Jamie's other tenant, would you?'

Rene shook her head. 'We've passed once or twice in the corridor, but we haven't got as far as a formal introduction yet.'

'Not to worry. Would you have any idea if he's here or not?'

She pointed to a door at the end of the corridor. 'I saw 'im go into the sitting room about ten minutes ago.'

'Right,' Gavin replied with a slow nod as he eyed the door, 'but you can't help me with his name?'

'I'm pretty sure Jamie's written it on the wall chart in the kitchen.' She walked into the first room on the left. 'Aye, 'ere it is. Leonard 'Artson.' She reappeared seconds later. 'Leonard 'Artson's 'is name.'

Gavin smiled broadly at her. 'Thank you.' He pointed at the sitting-room door. 'What I'm going to do then is just pop in there to see Mr Hartson with Thomas, and hopefully by the time we finish, Jamie might have surfaced from his bedroom.'

Rene shrugged. 'Fine by me. Do you want a cup of coffee or summat to take in with ye? I've just put the kettle on.'

Gavin shook his head. 'I think we'll give it a miss. Thomas and I have something we need to discuss with Mr Hartson.'

Rene stood and watched as Jamie's solicitor, shadowed by the strange young man, knocked on the door of the sitting room. 'Mr Hartson?' she heard him ask, 'might I come in for a moment?'

Half an hour later, seated at the kitchen table, Rene looked up from the aged copy of *Hello* she had been leafing through to see Jamie enter the room dressed in nothing but a bath towel round his waist. Seemingly oblivious to Rene's presence, he made his way over to the sideboard and switched on the kettle. Rene smiled as she cradled her cup of tea in her hands. 'Ye shouldn't go walking round the place like that, Jamie, when ye've got impressionable ladies as your 'ouse guests.'

Turning with a start, Jamie peered at Rene through bleary eyes. 'Bit of a late night. Not really with it yet.'

'Out on the booze, were ye?'

'I wish,' he replied. 'I had to take someone to the hospital.'

Rene's expression turned to one of concern. 'Nothing serious, I 'ope.'

'Not really. Three stitches in a cut hand.' Jamie replied, rubbing at the gritty tiredness in his eyes. 'But that turned out to be only half the story. It's all a bit secret, really.'

Rene nodded. 'OK, but let me know if there's anything I can do.'

'Yeah, I will. Thanks.' He glanced at his watch. 'Listen, I've just got to make a phone call.'

At that point, a door slamming at the far end of the corridor jogged Rene's memory. 'Damn, I almost forgot to tell ye. Yer solicitor called in about 'alf an 'our ago, along with some dozy-looking young lad. They're in the sitting room right now with that gentleman who's staying 'ere.'

Jamie frowned at Rene. 'Gavin Mackintosh? He's here in the flat?'

'That's right,' a voice said from behind him, and Jamie turned to see the solicitor's portly frame standing in the kitchen doorway.

Jamie gave his head a quick disbelieving shake. 'How weird is that? I was just about to call you. What on *earth* are you doing here?'

'Just a bit of worthwhile networking. I've managed to find someone to give your Mr Hartson a hand.'

'What?' Jamie asked, still baffled.

Gavin flumped himself down on the sagging sofa that was pushed hard against the wall next to the fridge. 'A young man called Thomas Keene. I doubt you'd know him, Jamie.' He let out a short laugh. 'Not quite in the university scene, this one.'

'And what did Mr Hartson think?'

'He reckons Thomas will suit his needs extremely well, and I hope to hell he's right.' Gavin stretched his hands along the back of the sofa. 'I was pretty amazed just how well the lad managed the interview. I doubt he's ever undergone one like that before in his life.'

'So what's he been doing up until now?'

Gavin wagged a finger at Jamie. 'Ah, that's between myself, Thomas and Mr Hartson for now. Let's just say we're in a probationary period.'

Rene laughed. 'I think I understand. I've known a lot of lads like that in my time.' She got up from her chair. ''Ow's about I make ye a nice cup of tea or coffee now, then, Mr Mackintosh?'

'A black coffee would go down a treat, Rene. Thank you.' Gavin turned to Jamie. 'So what were you going to call me about?'

Jamie glanced in Rene's direction. 'Well, it's a bit . . . delicate.'

'Don't worry,' Rene said. 'I can take a hint. I'll make myself scarce.' She made up the mug of coffee and handed it to Gavin. 'I've got to come up with some more funnies for my show tonight, any road.'

As she closed the door behind her, Jamie walked to the table, pulled out a chair, spun it round to face Gavin and sat down. 'Well,' he said. 'Gavin, you are *not* going to believe who I've got sleeping in the free bedroom. Angélique Pascal.'

Gavin almost choked on his coffee. 'I think you're having your leg pulled, lad,' he laughed, wiping his mouth.

'It's no joke, Gavin. I met her in a café last night, and me and this other girl ended up taking her to hospital, and then afterwards . . .'

'You had to take her to *hospital*? Why?'

'She'd cut her hand quite badly.'

'Her hand?' Gavin's eyes suddenly clouded over with concern and he shook his head slowly. 'Oh, no, not her hand.'

Jamie bit his bottom lip. 'Yeah that's why she was so terrified to go to the hospital. She really thought she was going to be told she'd never be able to play the violin again. However it wasn't nearly as bad as it looked. The doctor said no tendons had been touched and that the swelling in her fingers would soon go, so I reckon she won't be out of action for too long . . .'

'*You* reckon, Jamie? I'd be more interested in hearing the doctor's considered opinion.'

Jamie paused for a moment, caught in the solicitor's steely glare. 'Actually, Gavin, we never mentioned to the doctor that Angélique was a violinist. In fact, I did something that's probably against the law. I gave her a false name when we registered her at the hospital.'

'You did *what*?'

'She insisted on it. She said she didn't want anyone to know who she was, because she was frightened the press would find out about her injury, and . . . she didn't want her whereabouts to be known, either.'

'Jamie . . . Jamie,' Gavin stuttered, trying to steady his thought process. 'Could you please just start at the beginning and tell me everything that happened last night?'

'OK, but it could take some time. I was up until five o'clock this morning listening to the whole saga.'

Gavin nodded. 'Right,' he said, pushing himself up from the sofa. 'I'd better cancel all my appointments for this morning.' He thumped at the pockets of his suit jacket. 'Hell, I must have left my mobile in the car. Can I use your telephone?'

Jamie pointed at the door. 'It's out there on the sideboard.'

When Gavin had left the kitchen, Jamie got up and went to make another coffee. As he poured water into the mug, he turned to see Leonard Hartson standing outside in the hall with a tall, straggly-haired youth peering over his shoulder. 'I thought I'd let you know I have found myself an assistant,' Leonard said. 'Thank you for putting the word around so promptly.'

'Glad it all worked out, Mr Hartson,' Jamie replied, carrying his coffee over to the door and leaning a shoulder on the doorpost. 'Hope all goes well for you. Are you going to start filming today?'

'No, not yet. My immediate plan is to give young Thomas here a crash course on the equipment.' The cameraman turned and smiled up at the youth. 'I am counting on my new assistant to be a fast learner.'

Jamie gave Thomas a friendly smile which went unreciprocated. Studying the gormless expression on the assistant's face, it struck him that Thomas looked anything *but* a fast learner. 'Well, best of luck.'

As he watched the two move off to the front door, Jamie was taken by the incongruity of this new partnership, the lanky figure of the assistant, with his threadbare hooded sweatshirt and baggy jeans worn at half mast, towering menacingly over the diminutive, dapperly dressed figure of the elderly cameraman. He found himself searching his mind for some glimmer of identification, knowing that there was something familiar about the boy—especially, for some reason, the back view.

'Right,' said Gavin Mackintosh, as he pushed purposefully past Jamie into the kitchen. 'The rest of the morning is yours, Jamie my lad, so shut the door behind you and let's be having the story.' An hour later Jamie welcomed the chance to rest his voice as Gavin, with brow furrowed, sat leafing through the copious notes he had written in the back of his diary. 'And that's about it, is it?' the solicitor asked eventually, studying Jamie over his spectacles. 'She told you nothing else?'

'Near enough.' Jamie began drumming his fingers on the table. 'So what do you think we should do?'

Gavin stared thoughtfully out of the window, then let out a long sigh. 'I don't think anything can be done until I've spoken with Angélique myself and ascertained exactly what course of action she wants to take.'

Jamie pushed himself to his feet. 'I'll go and wake her, then.'

'That would be the best idea,' Gavin replied, 'and if you wouldn't mind, I think I should speak to her myself. There could be some complicated legal procedures involved in this whole affair, and consequently it should remain as confidential as possible.'

'OK,' Jamie replied. 'Do you want me to do anything?'

'I'd suggest you get yourself showered and dressed. I could well be in need of your assistance after I've spoken to her.'

Five minutes later, Jamie ushered Angélique into the kitchen. Her eyes were drowsy and the oversized dressing gown she was wearing trailed behind her across the floor. 'She's a bit out of it, I'm afraid,' he said. 'The doctor gave her some pretty strong painkillers last night.'

As Jamie settled her on a chair, Gavin smiled kindly at the violinist, but his eyes were registering deep anger at the sight of the purply-black bruise that spread down one side of her face and the white elastic bandage bound round the palm of her left hand. He waited for Jamie to leave the kitchen before he sat down opposite her. 'Angélique, I don't know if you remember me, but my name is Gavin Mackintosh. We met the other night at the reception at the Sheraton Grand.'

'*Bien sûr*,' she replied woozily. 'You are the lawman.' Angélique gazed foggily around the kitchen before fixing Gavin with a look of bewilderment. 'You do not live in this place as well, do you?'

Gavin laughed. 'No, I don't.'

The drowsiness faded from the violinist's face and she stared at him, wide-eyed with panic. 'Then who told you I was here?' she exclaimed, pushing herself clumsily to her feet. 'How did you find out?'

'It's all right, Angélique,' Gavin said in a calming voice. 'Nobody knows you are here, except Jamie and myself.'

She studied his face to try to detect any sign of deception, and then, very slowly, she sat back down on her chair.

'Let me explain,' Gavin said, leaning forward and interlocking his fingers. 'It just happens that I am Jamie's solicitor. I have been a friend of his father for years, and have always handled the family's legal affairs. Now, Jamie, quite rightly, was going to call me to ask advice about your . . . predicament, but it just happened that I had to visit this morning for a different reason.'

The violinist took in a faltering breath. 'So now Jamie has told you the whole story,' she said quietly. 'He is very kind.'

Gavin nodded. 'You were lucky to bump into him last night.'

'I know that,' Angélique breathed out almost indiscernibly. 'Martha was very kind also, because she kept the café open for me and drove us to the hospital.'

'But Martha wasn't present when you told your story to Jamie?'

'No, she had gone home, but when she dropped us at the hospital, Jamie made her promise not to say a word about me to anyone.'

Gavin let out a long sigh. 'My dear, I am so sorry this has happened to you. How does your hand feel today?'

Angélique lowered her eyes. 'It is quite sore.'

Gavin stroked a finger thoughtfully across his mouth. 'I'm afraid this is a difficult question, but what action do you wish to take against your manager, Mr Dessuin?'

Angélique jerked her head up. 'What do you mean?'

'Well, I know that he has been your tutor and manager for many years, but I think his immediate actions suggest that he could well pose a real threat to you, Angélique, and accordingly my advice would be that we seek a restraining order against him as soon as possible.'

'How would you do that?'

'You and I would have to go to the court here in Edinburgh to ask for what is called an interim interdict.'

'I would then be in the newspapers?'

'It's not unusual for the press to be at a hearing, especially when the case involves someone who is as much in the public eye as yourself.'

'Then I cannot let it happen.'

Leaning back in his chair, Gavin folded his arms and puffed out his cheeks. 'May I ask you why not, Angélique?'

Angélique shook her head. 'You do not understand Albert Dessuin. He is very . . . complex? If something bad was to be written about him in the newspapers, I know he would do something very stupid.'

'You mean he would attempt suicide?'

Angélique shrugged. 'It is very possible. I found out that his own father killed himself. So, even though he treated me so badly last night, I cannot do anything to hurt him. It would always then be my fault.'

Gavin scratched frustratedly at his forehead. 'But you must understand I cannot allow you to leave Edinburgh with him. It would then be *my* fault if something were to happen to *you.*'

The violinist shook her head. 'It is all finished between us. I decided that even before I left my hotel bedroom.'

'And what will you do? Tour the world by yourself?'

'I suppose I will have to find another manager.'

'But what about Dessuin, Angélique? You are a famous person. It wouldn't be difficult for him to find out where you are at any time.'

Angélique looked up at the solicitor with sad eyes. 'I can never be the reason for him doing harm to himself.'

Gavin got up from the table and began to pace the floor.

'OK, I shall reluctantly leave that issue aside for now. What we have to do, as a matter of urgency, is break the news that you won't be playing for the rest of the festival. We must do it in such a way that nobody need know what really happened, and we certainly should not reveal your whereabouts.' He waved his hands as he thought. 'We could just say you've cut your hand in an unfortunate accident and had to return to France to recover.' He pondered this for a moment. 'Actually, that's not such a bad idea. It might even act as a false trail. It'll get Dessuin away from the hotel and, at best, out of the country. The only problem is your clothes. Jamie said you left everything in the hotel bedroom.'

'And my violin.'

'And the key to your room?'

'I left it there too,' Angélique replied sheepishly.

Gavin shook his head. 'Not to worry. We'll just have to find a way of getting everything out of your room while Dessuin is not about.' He blew out an anxious breath. 'My word, the plot thickens, doesn't it?'

'Gavin, will I really be returning to France?'

'Well, it's entirely up to you, Angélique, but I would suggest it would be better if, for now, you just stayed here in Edinburgh and kept a very low profile. It'll give you time to recover, and at the same time it'll give me the chance to monitor Dessuin.'

'But where would I stay?'

'No better place than where you are right now. Nobody else is using that bedroom you slept in last night, and Jamie's going to be around until the end of September.'

'But he might not want me to stay.'

Gavin smiled at her. 'I'm sure he'd be delighted.'

'I could pay him, of course.'

Gavin clicked the fingers of both hands simultaneously.

'Jumping Jupiter, there's a problem.' He sat back down on the chair, clenching his fists. 'Angélique, does Dessuin handle your finances?'

The violinist shook her head. 'No, everything is managed by the lawyers of Madame Lafitte in Clermont Ferrand. They give me an allowance each month and pay Albert his salary.'

Gavin heaved a sigh of relief. 'We'll have to notify them in due course.' He pushed himself to his feet once more. 'So what about this story we've concocted for the press? I'm quite seriously bending the rules of my profession with all this subterfuge, but would you agree to it?'

'Yes, I think it would be a good idea.'

'Right,' Gavin said, walking over to the window and gazing down at the bustling activity in London Street. 'So, all that remains for me to do is to find a journalist with a bit of integrity.'

Angélique sat in silence for a moment, her brow creased in thought. 'I know of a journalist, here in Edinburgh. He has been trying to interview me for many years. Maybe we could ask for his help? Will, I think is his surname. No, Wills. He is called Harry Wills. He seems to be a nice man, although I know that he does not care much for Albert.'

Gavin nodded. 'Sounds like the perfect contact.' He wrote down the name in his diary. 'I'll see if I can arrange a meeting with him straight away, because it's imperative that we get this story into the *Evening News* tonight. I will also ask Mr Wills to liaise with the International office. They'll need to arrange for another soloist for the concert tonight.'

A sudden pinpoint of clarity shone in Angélique's eyes. 'Of course, he must speak with Tess Goodwin. Do you remember her? She was the person I was speaking to at the reception when you came to talk to me. She works at the International office and she has become a friend of mine. I was going to call her last night, but I was frightened the true story would then be put in the newspapers.'

Gavin wrote down the second name. 'You were probably wise not to call her. We won't involve Tess right now.' He slipped both the diary and the pen into the inside pocket of his jacket. 'The only other person I am going to tell about this incident is my doctor, who is a trusted friend of mine. He'll be able to keep an eye on that very special hand of yours.' He smiled at the young violinist. 'Now, take yourself back to bed and rest well, and don't worry about a thing. If you want to contact me just speak to Jamie. I'll make sure he looks after you.'

Angélique got up from her chair and moved across the room towards him, putting a hand on his arm. 'I was very lucky to meet you at the reception the other night. Thank you for being such a kind friend.'

Gavin grinned at her. 'My dear,' he said, 'the circumstances are not what I would wish for, but it is indeed a pleasure to be of assistance.'

Albert Dessuin sat slumped forward, his head cradled in shaking hands, trying to trawl through his memory for some recollection of what had taken place the previous night. He had found himself on the floor of Angélique's bedroom, but his recollection of the events that had led to him being there had been completely wiped out. He always drank in private so maybe he had come into her room last night just to check on her. But if that was the case, where was she now? No, it was more likely that Angélique had risen early and left the room before he had come in. But she had not slept in her bed—unless she had made it up herself. And why would she do that in a hotel?

He got to his feet and moved slowly across the room to the bathroom, clutching his arms around his shivering body. A cold shower was what he needed. It always helped to clear his head.

Tess Goodwin sat at her desk in the International Festival office, listening, opened-mouthed with disbelief, to the gravelly male voice at the other end of the telephone line. When she ended the call she was too shocked to speak. She hurried over to the door to Sir Alasdair Dreyfuss's office. His meeting with Sarah Atkinson and the morose director of the Estonian National Symphony Orchestra was scheduled to run for another half-hour, but this was something that definitely could not wait. She gave one cursory knock on the door and walked in.

Both Alasdair and Sarah looked up at her, enquiry and annoyance in their eyes. 'I think you might have your time wrong, Tess,' Alasdair Dreyfuss said pointedly. 'I said we wouldn't be free until midday.'

'I'm sorry to interrupt, Alasdair, but something extremely important has come up, and I wonder if I might just have a couple of minutes with you and Sarah.'

'Can't it wait, Tess?' Sarah asked tersely, but she was stopped by a hand on her arm from the director, who could tell from the expression on his marketing assistant's face that something was seriously amiss.

'Valdek, would you please excuse us for two minutes,' he said, getting to his feet. 'I do apologise for this.'

The Estonian gave his consent with a flick of his pawlike hand, and Alasdair and Sarah followed Tess out.

'I've just had a journalist on the phone who says that Angélique Pascal had an accident last night. She's cut her hand pretty badly and she's heading back to France.'

'What?' her two superiors exclaimed in unison.

'He said the story's going to be on the front page of the *Evening News* tonight and that he was only telephoning the International office so we could find another soloist for tonight's concert.'

'Who was the journalist, Tess?' Sarah Atkinson asked.

'He didn't give his name, and I'm afraid I didn't recognise his voice.'

Tess shook her head. 'I can't believe this. I spent much of the evening at the reception with her last night, before her manager spirited her away.'

'Maybe it's some kind of hoax, then,' Sarah Atkinson said.

'We've got to take it as being true,' Alasdair Dreyfuss said. He turned to his marketing director. 'Sarah, head back to my office and give my apologies to our Estonian friend, finish off the meeting with him, and then get hold of Julia Parfitt and put her on standby for tonight.'

'What are you going to do, Alasdair?' Sarah Atkinson asked.

'First off, I'm calling the *Evening News* to see if they're going to run with this story, and if so, I want to get hold of Albert Dessuin and ask him what the hell is going on and why he hasn't let me know about this sooner.' He took off his spectacles and rubbed a hand across his face. 'Dammit, I thought everything was going too smoothly.'

Albert Dessuin stood in the middle of the hotel dining room and scanned the few tables still occupied for breakfast. Apprehension gripped at his stomach when he realised Angélique was not there, and he hurried out to the reception area. There was a queue but he bypassed them and went straight up to the desk.

'Excuse me,' he said ungraciously to the young female receptionist who was trying unsuccessfully to swipe a credit card.

'I'm sorry, sir,' she replied, 'but you'll have to wait your turn.'

'I have no time to wait. You must tell me, have you seen Angélique Pascal this morning?'

The girl looked questioningly at him. 'Do you mean the violinist, sir?'

'Of course I mean the violinist.'

'I'm sorry, sir, I've only just come on duty, and I certainly haven't seen her this morning.'

Dessuin snorted angrily. 'Well, then, who *was* on duty? I need to speak to them immediately.'

'I'll see if I can find out, sir.' She smiled apologetically at the couple with whom she was dealing and walked off to the door at the side of the desk. She turned back to Dessuin. 'May I ask who you are, sir?'

'I'm her manager, Albert Dessuin. Now go and find out if anyone knows where she is. This could be very serious.'

'Excuse me, Mr Dessuin,' a voice said from the far end of the reception desk. 'There's a telephone call for you.'

Albert turned to the other receptionist, who stood with her hand cupped over the mouthpiece of a telephone. The guests in the queue were now regarding him with increasing impatience.

'*Enfin!*' Dessuin exclaimed, striding along the desk. 'Thank you,' he said to the receptionist, jerking the receiver from her hand. 'Angélique, where the hell are you?' he hissed into the receiver.

'Oh, so *you* obviously don't know what's happened, then, do you?' a man's voice replied.

'Who is this?' Dessuin demanded.

'It's Alasdair Dreyfuss, Albert.'

Dessuin stood speechless. 'Ah, Alasdair—I apologise,' he stuttered out eventually. 'I did not mean to be so abrupt.'

'What on earth is going on, Albert? I have just been on the telephone to the *Evening News* and they are about to run a front-page piece about Angélique Pascal. Seemingly Angélique had an accident last night. She cut her hand quite badly and is flying back to Paris as we speak, which of course means she'll be unable to fulfil her commitments here at the festival. Albert . . . Albert? . . . are you still there?'

The words of the director of the International Festival were enough to start clearing the fog of alcoholic amnesia from Dessuin's brain. Angélique's naked form flashed into his mind, the raised hand coming down with force on the side of her face. He clenched his fist. 'Oh, no,' he murmured, dropping the receiver by his side. 'What have I done?'

'Albert, for God's sake, are you still there?' Alasdair Dreyfuss's distant voice asked again.

Dessuin slowly brought the receiver back to his ear. 'Yes,' he replied.

'This has put me in an extremely difficult position, you know. Trying to find another soloist at the eleventh hour for the concert tonight . . .'

As if in a trance, Dessuin reached across the desk and dropped the receiver back onto its cradle. He turned and walked to one of the chairs grouped around a coffee table and sat down. Covering his face with his hands, he began to piece together what had taken place the previous night, and then tears of remorse and shame began to flow. 'Oh, Angélique,' he sobbed to himself, 'I never wished to hurt you. Please do not tell anyone I have done this terrible thing. *Please* do not tell.'

He felt a hand press lightly on his shoulder. 'Are you all right, sir?' a female voice asked.

Dessuin looked up at the young receptionist who had left to find out about Angélique's whereabouts.

'I am fine, thank you,' he replied in a quavering voice.

'I'm afraid I can't get hold of any of the receptionists on duty last night.'

Dessuin shook his head. 'It does not matter now.' He reached for the girl's hand. 'Would you do something else for me, please?'

'Of course, sir,' the girl replied in an uncertain voice.

'Can you find out for me what flights leave for Paris today?'

'Yes, sir. I'll get onto the Internet straight away.'

'Thank you very much,' Dessuin said, releasing her hand. 'I will go to my room now.' Pushing himself to his feet, he made his way across to the stairs and began to climb them, moving like an old man, every tread an effort. Halfway up, his mobile rang and he eagerly glanced at the screen, hoping it would be Angélique.

It was not. He continued to climb the stairs, only answering when he reached the next floor. '*Bonjour, maman. Ça va?*' He listened with an empty expression on his face.

When he reached the door of his room he spoke for the first time. 'Listen to me, you spoilt old woman. When will you ever consider how I am feeling? You never do. Never, *never!*' He punched the button to end the call and as he turned the key in the lock, he felt the weight of hopelessness and despair bear down upon him, realising that he had succeeded in alienating himself from the only two people who played any part in his pathetic life. Just as his father had done.

Eleven

IN THE MIDDLE of the empty warehouse, deep in Leith's docklands, Thomas Keene sat uneasily on the silver camera box, a look of concentration on his face as he attempted to load the dummy roll of film into the camera magazine for about the twentieth time. He glanced at the wristwatch Leonard Hartson had left hanging on a light stand for him to time his progress, but it only served to remind him that it was nearly three o'clock in the afternoon and his stomach was aching with hunger.

He shut his eyes, trying to envisage what his fingers were doing inside the changing bag as he threaded the film into the pick-up chamber of the magazine and doubled over the end so that it sat tight in the spool before clicking the spring catch closed. When he thought all was in place, he pulled his arms free from the constraints of the elasticated armholes, just as the warehouse door opened. T.K. watched Leonard Hartson pick his way over the electric cables, ducking to avoid the lights that they had set up earlier that day.

'There you are,' the cameraman said, handing T.K. a paper bag and a can of Sprite. 'Two ham and cheese rolls. How did you get on?'

'I think ah've go' it,' T.K. replied, putting the black bag to one side and making to flick back the ring pull on the can.

'Don't do that yet,' Leonard said sharply. 'Never handle food or drink while you're loading a film magazine. If one single foreign body gets into that changing bag, it could gum up the whole roll of film.'

'Ah've finished loadin', onyways.'

'No, you haven't. What did I tell you? Magazine out of the bag, check it's secure, tape it up and write on it the stock number and film roll.'

T.K. let out a disgruntled sigh. He put down the can and picked up the black bag, then pulled out the magazine. As he placed it on his knee, the cover on the load reel fell off in his hand. 'Aw, *shite!*' He glanced apprehensively at Leonard. 'Ah mean, sorry.'

Leonard raised an admonishing eyebrow.' 'Don't worry. It's only an end-roll, but remember, you must check the cover plate is fitted securely into its grooves before you lock it. If you'd just loaded that magazine with an unexposed roll, we would've had to throw it away.'

'Ah'm no 'goin' tae get a-haud o' this,' T.K. murmured solemnly.

Leonard tried to judge the meaning of T.K.'s last sentence by the expression on his face. Eventually, he just shook his head. 'Thomas, if our partnership is to work successfully over the next couple of weeks, I think it's going to be of paramount importance that we understand each other. I'm not saying anything derogatory about the Scottish accent and it is probably my fault that I have never taken the time to study the colloquial intricacies . . .' He stopped mid-sentence when he saw a broad grin stretch across T.K.'s face. 'What's the smile for?'

'Are ye saying ye cannot understand what I am sayin'?' T.K. asked, mouthing out the words in laborious fashion.

Leonard nodded. 'That is exactly what I'm saying.'

'That's good, 'cos I wis goin' tae say the same thing tae you.'

They eyed each other for a moment before both burst out laughing. 'Well,' Leonard said eventually, wiping a trickling tear from his cheek. 'I think we might have just had a breakthrough there, Thomas.'

Still smiling, T.K. carefully pulled the film out of the magazine and placed everything back in the changing bag. 'You can call me T.K.,' he mumbled as he refastened the zip and pressed down the Velcro flap.

'What was that?' Leonard asked.

'T.K.' His cheeks flushed with embarrassment as he once more pushed his hands through the elasticated armholes. 'My friends call me tha'.'

In that instant, Leonard realised there had been more than just a breakthrough in their language barrier. 'In that case, I would be delighted to call you T.K.'

'Ah think ah've got the hang o' this now.'

'All right,' Leonard said, reaching out to take his wristwatch from the light stand. 'I'll time you.'

Just under two minutes later, T.K. pulled his hands free of the changing bag, opened it up and held the loaded film magazine out.

'Perfect. Couldn't have done better myself,' Leonard said, handing the magazine back to T.K.

While Thomas Keene had found gainful employment that day, the case was not the same for Rene Brownlow's husband, Gary. He had spent the day sitting in the Employment Exchange. Then, when his long-awaited interview eventually did take place, he had to leave halfway through to get back to the school to pick up the kids.

When he entered Andersons Westbourne Social Club, his impression was that the lounge bar was deserted. It was only when he heard the clink of dominoes from the table near the stage at the far end of the room that he surmised that some of Rene's 'Fringe committee' were there.

He walked over to the bar and shot a wink at the elder of the two women manning it. 'Hi, Mags. I 'ope ye don't mind me bringing the kids in. I just wanted to see Terry Crosland for a moment.'

'Aye, they'll be fine,' Mags replied. 'Was it just Terry ye wanted to see?'

Gary turned round to find that the five domino players had gathered around him, their faces alight with enquiry.

''Ave ye 'eard 'ow Rene's doing?' Stan Morris, the self-appointed chairman of the committee, asked.

'All right,' Gary replied noncommittally, catching Terry's eye and greeting him with a brief nod.

''As she been on telly yet?' Skittle asked, squinting up at Gary through his bottle glasses.

'Give 'er a chance!' Stan Morris said, glaring at Skittle. 'It takes time to build up fame.' He pushed his hands into the pockets of his tweed jacket. 'Now, I remember the time I appeared on the television—'

'All right, lads,' Terry Crosland cut in. 'Ye're wanting a word with me, mate,' he said to Rene's husband.

'Aye, if you can spare me a couple of minutes,' Gary replied.

Terry turned to his fellow domino players and waved his hands towards their table. 'Go on, lads, just get on with the game. I'll be over once I'm through talking with Gary.'

'But I am the chairman—' Stan blustered out.

'I know y'are, Stan,' Terry interjected in a diplomatic tone, 'and if any part of our discussion might have some relevance to those business matters over which you 'ave jurisdiction, then I will inform you.'

'Right,' Stan said, shrugging up his tweedy shoulders importantly. 'Fair enough. Right, lads, let's allow Terry time to converse with Gary.'

'Sorry about that,' Terry said to Gary once he had seen the four members of the committee settle themselves back at the table. 'Fancy a pint?'

'Just a Coke would do me, thanks.'

'And what about you lot?' Terry asked, looking down at Gary's children. 'Shall we make it four rounds of Coca-Cola?' Robbie and Karen nodded. Terry turned to the bar girl. 'Four glasses of Coca-Cola and give the kids a set of those darts ye keep behind the bar. They can knock 'ell out of the dartboard while Gary and I have a chat.'

The two men carried their glasses over to the furthest corner away from where the dominoes had resumed and sat down.

'So, any luck yet on the job front?' Terry asked.

Gary shook his head. 'Not yet.' He looked round the interior of Andy's, as if embarrassed to make eye contact with Terry. 'Listen, mate, I never said owt that day we put Rene on the train, but I want to apologise for being bloody rude that time ye came round to see 'er.'

Terry waved his hand dismissively. 'No need to worry, lad. As I said then, I understand your situation.'

'Aye, maybe, but ye shouldn't 'ave been the one to cop the flak for my frustration.'

'Enough said,' replied Terry, taking a drink from his glass. 'So, 'ow's she getting on?'

'Not too good.'

'Oh?' Terry leaned forward, concern on his face. 'What's gone wrong?'

'She's not getting the punters coming to 'er show and she's dead worried she's going to end up 'aving to foot the bill at the end of the run.'

'She don't 'ave to worry about that!' Terry said. 'That's taken care of!'

'I tell you, Terry, it took all me limited powers of persuasion to stop 'er from packing 'er bags and coming 'ome.'

'Oh, bloody 'ell,' Terry murmured, running a hand lightly over his Teddy boy quiff. 'Mind you, there's another week and an 'alf to go. If she can stick it out, things could change.'

Gary shrugged. 'Aye, they could, but what she could do with is a bit of encouragement from the 'ome crowd.'

'What are ye saying?'

'Well, it's the last thing I can afford to do, but I'm going to take the kids up to Edinburgh at the weekend to see Rene's show. Give 'er a bit of moral support. I was wondering if ye might like to come with us.'

Terry contemplated Gary's suggestion. 'Mate, I don't think there's any way I can make it this weekend. I've got that much work on. I don't suppose you could leave it until the following one?'

Gary's laugh had a cynical edge to it. 'Terry, I could make it any weekend. The only thing about that is we'd only be there for Rene's last show, but I don't suppose it would matter . . . OK, let's make it next weekend.'

Terry flicked his head towards the domino players at the far end of the room. 'What about that lot? I don't think I'd make myself that popular if I 'eld back on telling them our plans.'

'Tell 'em, then. I don't mind if they all come. They deserve it, really, 'aving raised all that money for Rene. Anyway, it'll help swell 'er audience, even if it is only for the last night.' He drained his glass and got to his feet. 'Well, I'd better take the kids back to do their 'omework.'

''Ow're you planning on getting up to Edinburgh?' Terry asked.

'Probably by train.'

'I suppose we could take me van. Strictly illegal, but I'll risk it.'

'D'ye reckon it would make it?'

Terry laughed. 'Aye, I reckon. I'll do a bit of tinkering with the engine beforehand and get a new exhaust stuck on. It's long overdue.'

'We'll be needing somewhere to stay as well, won't we?'

'That's true,' Terry replied, rubbing thoughtfully at his chin. 'I'll 'ave a word with Stan Morris. 'E's always going on about 'is great contacts.'

Gary stuck out a hand to Terry. 'I appreciate yer 'elp, mate.'

Terry stood up and shook it. 'Don't think anything of it.' He looked over to where the four other committee members were staring at them expectantly. 'I'd better give me report.'

The world had suddenly become a brighter place for T.K. He made his way across town to the hostel, a purposeful spring in his step. He had found himself a job and he had also received praise from his new boss in the way he had picked up so much technical information during the course of the day. 'I called it a steep learning curve,' the old cameraman had said to him in the taxi, 'but, so far, you seem to have diminished it to a gentle incline.' As he walked, T.K. went over in his head all the skills he had learned. When he turned into the street where the hostel was situated, he was so preoccupied with his thoughts that he never clocked on to the two boys leaning against the railings on the opposite side of the street. As soon as they saw him, they began to make their move. They crossed over to meet him at a diagonal, keeping their faces turned away to avoid recognition.

T.K. only became aware of their presence behind him when he had begun to climb the stone steps leading up to the hostel door. A hand grabbed his arm, another his shoulder and he was slammed against the railings with such force that he let out a scream of pain. One of the boys took hold of the neck of his sweatshirt and twisted it in his hand, and T.K. found himself choking for breath as it tightened like a noose.

'Whit the fuck hae *you* been dain', ye bloody toe rag?' the boy said, his face contorted with hatred.

'Jeez, Lenny, let go,' T.K. gasped out in a high-pitched voice, his face beginning to turn puce. 'Ah cannae breathe.'

'Tha's the whole idea, ye wee bastard. Ma younger brither wis takin' aff by the polis this mornin', and guess wha the cause o' that wis?'

''Onest, Lenny, it wisnae—'

The other boy stepped forward and backhanded T.K. hard across the cheek. 'Dinnae ye try tae fuckin' well deny it, mon. The word's a-roond the estate, a' aboot you takin' videos o' the lads nickin' the cars.'

T.K.'s legs gave way. 'It wis a mistake, Rab. Ye gotta believe me.'

Lenny eased off the pressure on T.K.'s neck. He didn't want him to black out just yet. 'Ah fuckin' mistake!' He let go of T.K.'s sweatshirt and aimed a violent kick at his side. T.K. let out another cry of agony.

Lenny squatted down on his haunches, his face only centimetres away from T.K.'s. 'So ye thocht ye could hide awa' frae us, did ye? Jist yer luck, then, that auld Peesy McGill from ma block decided tae get guttered last night and ended up in yer dosshoose. It wis him wha' telt me.' He gave T.K. a knowing wink. 'As Rab said, Thomas Keene, the word's oot. A'body's efter ye. Ye're bloody done fer, pal.'

The door of the hostel was suddenly flung open and a huge man appeared on the doorstep, wearing a vast pair of jogging pants and a dirty white T-shirt. 'Whit the hell's goin' on here?'

'It's naine of yer business, fatty,' Rab said.

The man seized the lapel of Rab's denim jacket with one hand, lifting him almost clear of the ground. 'A'thing that happens on these steps is ma business, ye wee tosser,' he said through clenched teeth, glancing momentarily at T.K.'s sprawled form on the step, 'especially if it's tae dae wi' wan of ma lads.' He jerked the youth closer to him. 'And whit's mair, ah dinnae like bein' called "fatty", so if ah wis you, ah'd git the hell oot o' here afore I call the polis, is that understood?'

He let go his grip on the lad, giving him a push that made him stumble down the steps. Lenny backed away to join his colleague on the pavement. He balled his fist and flicked out a thumb, affecting the action of a switchblade. 'Ye'll be gettin' it comin' tae ye, Thomas Keene.'

'Get awa' wi' ye!' the caretaker yelled out with an angry wave of his hand. He looked down at T.K. 'Ye'd better get yersel' inside and ah'll hae a look-see whit damage they've done tae ye.'

'Ah'm fine,' T.K. replied dolefully. 'Ah'll jist stay here fer a minnit and catch ma breath.'

The caretaker gave a brief nod of his head. 'A'right. Come in when ye're ready,' he said as he turned and walked back into the house.

Casting a quick glance up the street to make sure the two boys had gone, T.K. descended the steps and headed away in the opposite direction, clutching a hand to his side.

He kept walking until well after midnight, never being too sure that the two boys weren't following him. Eventually, he took the risk of ducking down a dimly lit alleyway where he squatted behind a refuse bin for half an hour, waiting to see if his fears were justified. Then he quit his hiding place and began to make his way back along the narrow street, walking unexpectedly into the blast of air coming from a heating duct set into the side of one of the buildings that fronted onto Princes Street. He realised then that he would be unlikely to find a more comfortable place to pass the night than right there on that spot. He pulled up the hood of his sweatshirt, then he sat down, propping his back against the wall and focused on the cool starlit sky. Please, he thought to himself, if there's onybody up there, please gi' us a break.

Albert Dessuin stood in the queue at the British Airways desk at Edinburgh Airport, his face lowered as he looked over the top of his dark glasses, not wishing to draw attention to himself. As the queue inched forward, he pushed the two suitcases along the ground, making sure the violin case remained hidden between them. He could hardly bear to look at it. It was only when he had returned to Angélique's bedroom that he had realised how serious a situation had arisen. To abandon her most treasured possession, the violin, was beyond comprehension. Oh, Angélique, he thought, please let me find you.

He did not mean to look round, but he found himself looking directly at a man with a large camera slung round his neck, who was idly scanning the queues at the check-in desks. The man did a double take. He pushed himself away from the pillar and made his way over.

'It is Mr Dessuin, isn't it?' the man asked, adjusting the dials on his camera and taking the cap off the lens.

Albert did not reply, but then the camera flashed and Albert reacted instinctively, holding up his hand to shield his face. It was all the verification the photographer needed.

'Mr Dessuin, where is Angélique Pascal?'

Other people had begun to take interest in what was going on, turning to look. Leaving his bags on the floor, Albert walked quickly away from the queue and then turned to confront the photographer, who had followed, hot on his heels.

'I have no comment to make about anything,' Albert hissed. 'I'm sure your newspapers have said it all.'

'It's all a bit airy-fairy, though, Mr Dessuin. All that's been reported is that Angélique Pascal had an accident and was returning to France.'

Dessuin contemplated what the photographer was telling him. Maybe Angélique had not disclosed the true facts after all. There was, then, hope of reconciliation. He made a mental effort not to display the elation he was feeling to the photographer. 'And that is all that happened. Mademoiselle Pascal has returned to Paris, and I am about to catch a plane to join her, so if you will now please excuse me . . .'

The photographer put a hand on his arm as Albert prepared to return to the queue. 'I can tell you Angélique Pascal has definitely not returned to Paris. Over the past twenty-four hours my colleague and I have been doing shifts here and there hasn't been one person who even vaguely resembles her booking in for anywhere in France.'

Albert shook his head. 'You are mistaken.'

'I've even had an acquaintance of mine check the passenger lists. Angélique Pascal has not left from this airport.'

Albert looked around at the queue. 'She has obviously then been directed to a flight from another airport.'

The photographer let out a short, disbelieving laugh. 'Mr Dessuin, the whole story about her returning to France is a sham, for some reason or other. Have you any idea why that might be, Mr Dessuin?'

Albert stood looking at the man, working through the logic of his reasoning. He realised he had to remain in Edinburgh, but first he had to throw this photographer off the scent.

Albert smiled and shook his head. 'The story is not a sham. I spoke with both her *and* my mother on the telephone last night. They are together in my house in Paris.' He cocked his head at the man. 'Mademoiselle Pascal must, therefore, have eluded you. So, if you will excuse me.'

He walked back to the queue, watching the photographer out of the corner of his eye as he talked on his mobile. When the man had finished, he walked quickly over to the revolving doors and left the terminal. Albert glanced at his watch. He would give the photographer five minutes' grace, and then he himself would take a taxi back to the city.

Jamie Stratton sat cross-legged on a large threadbare Turkish carpet that covered a fraction of the floor space of his cavernous sitting room, scratching perplexedly at his thick mop of blond hair as he stared at the backgammon board on the coffee table. 'You can't tell *me* you haven't played this game before,' he said, eyeing his opponent with suspicion.

Angélique grinned at him. 'Not very often.'

'Hah! I knew it! You're nothing more than a damned hustler.'

Angélique laughed. 'Of course,' she said. 'There is no other way to be.'

Jamie pushed himself away from the table and leaned his back against an armchair. 'OK, so you'd better tell me about your other hidden talents, just so as I don't get duped again,' he said, smiling.

Angélique got to her feet, pulled the large towelling dressing gown around her and flopped back onto the sofa. 'Well, I could tell you the names of the French rugby fullbacks all the way back to Serge Blanco.'

'You're joking.'

'My brothers thought it was necessary for their little sister to know. Shall I tell you the names?'

'No, I'll believe you,' Jamie laughed, holding up his hands as if to defend himself from what was to come. He watched her closely as she ruffled her short dark hair, still wet from the shower, with the fingers of her unbandaged hand. It was funny, he thought to himself, how he had always been drawn to tall, shapely blonde girls with sparkling blue eyes. But having spent two days in the company of Angélique Pascal, he realised that this preference had been narrowing the field quite unnecessarily. He studied the mischievous brown eyes and the small dark-lipped mouth that challenged him with its smile. He was beginning to see this young French violinist as one of the most mysteriously attractive members of the opposite sex he had ever clapped eyes on.

'Anything else?' he asked.

Angélique rocked her head from side to side in consideration. 'I suppose I am quite good at playing the violin as well.'

'Maybe you should take it up professionally then.'

'I suppose it's a consideration,' she replied quietly, the smile on her face fading away.

Jamie realised immediately his joke had been crass and badly timed. 'Sorry, that was a stupid thing to say. How's the hand feeling today?'

Angélique flexed her fingers. 'I do not have so much pain now.'

'In that case, I've got something for you,' he said, clambering to his feet. He turned and lobbed something small and black to Angélique. She caught it and then turned the object around in her fingers.

'I think this is a ball for playing squash,' she said.

He took the ball from her hand and began squeezing it repeatedly in his fist. 'Last year, this rugby prop forward from one of the Borders teams decided it would be fun to grind his studs into my hand during a game. I used this squash ball to get my fingers working again, and I was back on the rugby pitch in two weeks.' He put the ball back in her bandaged hand and gently folded her fingers over it. 'How does that feel?'

Angélique's mouth screwed to one side, as if she was trying hard to suppress a laugh. 'Very nice. Quite sensual, actually.'

Jamie smiled at her in surprise. 'Just keep squeezing it. It does help.' He straightened up. 'Listen, I've got to get on with writing some of these reviews. I have a deadline for this afternoon, so I hope you don't mind if I leave you to fend for yourself for an hour or two.'

Angélique swung her legs off the sofa. 'Jamie, have you heard yet from Gavin?' she asked concernedly.

'No, I haven't.'

'So we don't know what Albert is doing?'

'I'm afraid not.'

Angélique nodded. 'It's just that I would really like to have my violin. I feel . . . lost without it.'

Jamie scratched thoughtfully at his head. 'If I don't hear from him by midday, I'll give Gavin a call.' He walked over to the door and opened it. 'In the meantime,' he said, turning back to her, '*work the ball*!'

An hour later the telephone began to ring shrilly in the hall. Pushing his chair away from his computer, he made a dive for the telephone.

'Jamie, it's Gavin here. How's Angélique this morning?'

'Doing OK. She's not in so much pain now.'

'A good sign, then. Listen, I think our little plan about getting her luggage back from the hotel might have backfired. Dessuin didn't leave the Sheraton Grand yesterday, which is why I never called you about collecting Angélique's belongings. Now it would appear that he checked out of the hotel at about eight o'clock this morning and took a taxi to the airport. I can only deduce that he's following her to Paris.'

'He hasn't taken Angélique's stuff with him, has he?'

'That I can't tell you, but I'm afraid it's highly likely.'

'So, what happens now? Angélique was just saying she was desperate to get her violin back.'

'Well, I suggest you go round to the Sheraton and see what's what.'

'All right. I'll call you when I get back.' Jamie replaced the receiver and turned to see Angélique leaning against the door of the sitting room, silently watching him. 'You probably gathered I'm going to try to pick up your things this morning.'

'If they are still there.'

'Yeah, that's right,' he replied, moving off towards his bedroom door. 'I'll go as soon as I've finished writing that review.'

'Jamie?' She was following him with her dark brown eyes. 'Do you want me to leave?' she asked quietly.

'No. Why do you ask?'

'Because I am causing you a lot of problems. It would be easier for you if I was not here.'

Jamie grinned at her. 'But life would be a helluva lot more boring.'

'Do you mean that?'

'Course I do. Anyway, you can't go. You're not leaving here until I've beaten you at backgammon.'

The shadow of worry evaporated from Angélique's face as she contemplated this challenge. 'I cannot be here for ever, you know.'

Jamie jabbed a finger in her direction. 'Tonight, Mademoiselle Pascal, you are history.'

Leonard Hartson adjusted the 1K Redhead to balance the contrast of light hitting the chalk-white face of one of the Japanese dancers and the reflective gold thread woven through the silk of her deep-red kimono. He scanned her with his light meter before returning to the row of canvas chairs T.K. had set up, two of which were occupied by the dance company director, Mr Kayamoto, and Claire, his young interpreter.

'Right, I think we're about ready to shoot.' He smiled reassuringly at Kayamoto as Claire translated his words. 'And I suggest after we've finished this scene, the company breaks for lunch. That'll give me time to reset the lights.' He glanced towards the unlit area of the warehouse behind the camera. 'Right, T.K., if you could start the music and then mark the scene.' He stepped up onto the camera box he had positioned behind the tripod legs and waited for the music to start. Nothing happened. 'T.K., when you're ready.' Again, nothing happened. The director and his interpreter turned to see why the music hadn't started. Leonard stepped stiffly off the camera box and walked away from the dazzling pool of light. He placed a hand on the shoulder of the boy's slumped form and gave it a gentle shake. 'Are you all right, lad?'

T.K. jumped to his feet too quickly and fell hard against one of the large loudspeakers. It toppled over with a low resonant thump. 'Sorry about tha',' T.K. said, gingerly returning the speaker to its position. 'Ah think ah drapped aff.'

Leonard stared hard at the boy. Because T.K. had not turned up that morning until well after the dance company had arrived, Leonard had decided to hold back from saying anything to him about his appearance and his sloppy, wordless demeanour during the morning's shoot, but he certainly would have to address it during the lunch break. T.K. was wearing the same clothes he had worn the day before, his hair was greasy and dishevelled, and he emanated a sour smell of body odour.

'Yes, well,' Leonard said curtly, 'if you're ready now, maybe you would turn on the music and then come and mark the scene.'

It took three takes before Leonard managed to put the shot in the can but the third worked beautifully. He watched as the little ensemble in their bright, out-of-place clothes filed through the fire door at the side of the warehouse and closed it behind them.

'Shall ah turn the lights aff?' T.K. asked, his voice tentative.

Leonard pressed his hand to the slight pain he felt at the left side of his ribcage. Maybe it had been foolhardy to take on this young lad who knew little about what he was doing and who could hardly keep his eyes open. It was certainly going to test his fading stamina to the full. Leonard let out a despondent sigh. 'Yes, you can do that.'

T.K. came to stand beside him. 'If ye're goin' tae check the gate, ah've already dunnit,' he said quietly. 'It's clean.' Leonard smiled at the young lad. He was trying his best. 'Well done. I had forgotten to do it.'

T.K. stuck his hands deep into the pockets of his jeans. 'Ah'm sorry ah dozed aff, Leonard. Ah'll no dae it again.'

Leonard shook his head. 'Listen, I do understand you're being thrown in at the deep end here, but before we go any further, there are a few things we've got to get straight.'

'It wis jist that—'

'I know,' Leonard said, holding up his hand to curtail T.K.'s further excuses. 'Just hear me out, if you would. When one is making a film, T.K., it is important that you are seen to be totally professional in everything you do, because that is what impresses the client. Tomorrow I want you not only to turn up for work on time, but also having smartened up your appearance quite considerably.' Leonard paused, seeing the lad dip his head in embarrassment. 'Now, I don't want you to get disheartened. You had one slip-up today—that was all. Other than that, I thought you worked pretty well.' He put a hand on the boy's shoulder. 'Appearances are crucial, T.K., so when you finish up this afternoon, I want you to go home, get yourself cleaned up, look out some clean clothes and then have an early night. Is that understood?'

The young man nodded dolefully in reply.

'Right, enough said,' Leonard said, turning to check the footage in the film magazine. 'I want to do some close-ups on the faces, so if . . .'

'Leonard?'

Leonard turned back to the boy. 'Yes?'

T.K. stood with his head still lowered. 'Ah don' like tae ask ye this, because ah know ah havna earned it yet, but could ye lend us some money so ah can get ma claithes washed?'

'Do you not have a washing machine at home?'

T.K. scratched the back of his greasy head. 'Ah'm no' livin' at haim at the minnit.'

'Oh, right, there's no washing machine in the place you're staying now, is that it?'

T.K. moved over to the camera, swung it round and locked off the tripod head. 'Ah'm no' stayin' onyplace,' he said quietly.

'What do you mean, you're not staying anyplace? Where did you spend last night?'

T.K. shrugged his shoulders. 'Doon the back o' Marks and Spencer's. There's a hot air duct comin' oot the back o' the building, so it's good an' warm, but people kept walking past so ah didna get much sleep.'

Leonard let out a long sigh, understanding now exactly what the boy was saying to him. 'How long have you been doing this?'

'Jist the once. Mr Mackintosh had paid fer me to stay in a hostel fer a week, so's I could get started wi' you. But ah didna want tae go there.'

Leonard sat down on one of the lighting boxes. 'Why would that be?'

''Cos there's folk wha are efter me. They know ah wis staying there.'

Leonard nodded, realising the boy did not wish to elaborate. 'So, in a nutshell, you have nowhere to stay and you have no clothes other than those you're standing up in?' Leonard leaned forward and covered his face with his hands. 'Oh dear, oh dear, oh dear,' he stated rhythmically. He felt the lid of the lighting box sink as T.K. came to sit beside him.

'Ah'm sorry, Leonard. I wis hopin' you widna find oot. Ah could always sleep here, if ye'd allow me tae. Naebody wid find me here.'

The old cameraman reached across and patted the boy's knee. 'No, that would not work. You'd be no better off.' He looked across at his assistant. 'T.K., do you really want to work with me?'

'Aye, ah do, Leonard. Ah promise ah won't be late again, and ah'll get masel' sorted oot, honest ah will.'

'I can't have you sleeping rough.'

'Ah willna dae it,' he replied, his voice rising in agitation at the thought of losing his one big chance.

'No, what I mean is, if you work for me then you are part of my crew and it is up to me to find you lodgings.' Leonard rubbed his hands on the knees of his cavalry twill trousers. 'Trouble is I can't afford to pay for your accommodation and I doubt I'd be able to find anywhere for you stay right now.' He paused. 'Which leaves only one option.'

T.K. got to his feet and took a couple of paces towards the lighting stage. 'Ye're goin' tae say ah canna work fer ye, aren't ye?' he sniffed.

'No, I am not. I offered you a job and I'll stick by that.'

'So, whit did ye mean aboot the wan option?'

Leonard clambered wearily to his feet. 'Well, I'll have to clear it with my landlord, but there are two beds in my room, and—'

'Are ye sayin' that ah can come and stay wi' you?' T.K. stared at Leonard, wondering if he had misunderstood the old cameraman.

'I don't think there's much alternative, is there?'

T.K. eagerly approached Leonard. 'If ah did that, I widna be a nuisance tae ye, ah promise, and ah dinna snore or a'thing, and—'

Leonard smiled and held up a hand to halt T.K.'s exuberant outburst. 'One thing at a time, lad. After we've finished shooting I suggest we get you kitted out with a few things, including a pair of jeans with a decent belt. I don't want you to continue exposing half your backside to our assembled company every time you bend down to unplug a light.'

T.K. pulled up his trousers and ran a hand round the waistband to tuck in his grimy T-shirt. They immediately slipped to their original position when he launched himself at the cameraman and grabbed hold of his hand. 'Cheers, Leonard. I willna let ye doon, ah promise.'

Leonard pulled his hand free from the boy's grip and took a few paces back to escape an unsavoury cloud of body odour. 'The first thing you do when we get back to the flat is have a long hot shower.'

T.K. grinned broadly at him. 'Aye, ah will.'

Shrugging on a corduroy jacket, Jamie descended the stairs and flung open the front door. He managed to swerve in time to avoid a thumping collision with the small solid figure.

'Is there ever a time when ye slow up?' Rene Brownlow asked.

'Yeah, waking up in the mornings is a pretty slow affair, as you've witnessed,' Jamie laughed.

Rene glanced about her. 'More's a pity there's no one about to 'ear you say that,' she said, stretching out a street map in front of her.

'Where are you off to?'

'I thought I'd try to find a quicker route uptown than the one I've been taking the last couple of days.'

'Come with me, if you like. I'm heading up there now. I'll let you set the pace,' Jamie replied with a smile.

'That'll do me,' Rene said, as they headed off along the street. 'So, did ye manage to get it all sorted out with your lawyer chap yesterday?'

'We're getting there.'

'Don't think I'm prying, like, but has it got something to do with that nice French violinist who's staying in yer flat?'

Jamie looked at her in amazement. 'How come you know about *her*?'

'Well, yer flat is large, but it's not Buckingham Palace.' She shifted her bag up onto her shoulder. 'We bumped into each other this morning. I asked what she'd done to 'er 'and and she told me she'd cut it on glass and 'ow sad she was because she wasn't going to be able to play the violin for a bit.' Rene slowed her pace as they started up Dublin Street. 'And then when I got back to my bedroom I was leafing through some festival brochures and there she was, staring out of the pages at me. Angélique Pascal, world-famous violinist.'

'Listen, Rene, if I tell you something about Angélique, will you swear you won't mention it to anyone else, most of all the press?'

'Jamie, I don't reckon the press will be queuing up to ask Rene Brownlow, small-time comedienne from 'Artlepool, for her views.'

'If they discover you're living in the same flat as Angélique Pascal, they'll find what you have to say pretty important, I can tell you.'

Rene nodded. 'Right,' she said, realising now her landlord was seriously concerned. 'In that case, of course I promise.'

So Jamie told Rene about his chance meeting with Angélique in the coffee shop. By the time they turned into George Street and he had told her of the assault, Rene was so captivated she forgot all about her lack of fitness, even breaking into a trot to avoid missing a word.

'So, this is where they were staying, is it?' Rene wheezed when they eventually came to a halt, looking across Festival Square at the glass-fronted rectangle of the Sheraton Grand.

'Yeah, it is,' Jamie replied distractedly as he looked around.

'Do ye think 'er manager is still somewhere abouts?'

'No, I'm pretty sure he's headed back to Paris.'

'So what're ye going to do?'

Jamie exhaled a deep breath. 'Just go in, I suppose.'

'D'ye want me to come in with ye? I've got nowt pressing.'

Jamie smiled at Rene. 'All right. Maybe you could stay here, just in case I am followed out of the hotel.'

'Consider it done. I'll get a seat in that café and keep me eyes peeled.'

As Jamie hurried across to the steps and entered through the swing doors of the hotel, Rene walked across to the café, put her bag on an empty table and flumped down facing the hotel entrance so that she had an unhindered view of Festival Square.

And had she not been so attentive while waiting for her cappuccino to arrive, she would never have noticed the woman with the mass of red hair and the pink scarf wrapped round her neck get up from the table beside her, nor the brown leather purse left beneath her chair.

'Excuse me!' Rene called out, pushing herself to her feet. She leaned over awkwardly and picked up the purse.

The woman had not heard her, walking off in the direction Jamie had taken five minutes before. Rene bustled off across the square after her.

'Excuse me!' she called out again, this time much louder. The woman turned and looked back at her, a querying frown on her freckled face. 'Ye dropped yer purse,' Rene said, as she approached her.

The woman's mouth opened in horror. 'Oh my God!' she said, taking the purse from Rene's outstretched hand. 'How can I ever thank ye?'

Rene smiled at her. The woman spoke with a northern accent, although Rene could tell she didn't hail from Yorkshire.

'Think nowt of it,' Rene replied with a shrug of her shoulders.

'Well, let me at least buy you a coffee.' The woman flicked a thumb towards the Sheraton Grand. 'I'm going into that 'otel there.'

Rene shook her head. 'Thanks, but ah'm waiting for someone. Ah've just ordered a cappuccino back there at the café.'

'Right, well, in that case, what can ah say other than thanks.' A quizzical frown came over the woman's face. ''Ave we met before? You look quite familiar.'

'Maybe you've seen my double in *Vogue* or summat like that.'

The woman laughed. 'Aye, maybe that's it.'

Rene turned to see the waiter put her cappuccino on the table. 'Ah'd better get back, then,' she said, pointing a finger.

'Aye, ye'd better. Thanks again. That was a real lifesaver.'

Giving her a brief wave of farewell, Rene turned and walked back to her table. She was savouring every sip of her cappuccino when she saw Jamie appear through the doors of the hotel and cast a searching look around the square. When he caught sight of Rene, he beckoned. She showered some coins onto the table and hurried over to the steps.

'What's up?' she asked.

'Bloody Dessuin's standing in the queue right now at reception. He was meant to have gone back to Paris. He's got her blue suitcase and the violin with him.'

'But I thought yer lawyer had said he'd checked out.'

'He must have come back, which means . . . somehow he's worked out Angélique is still here in Edinburgh.'

Rene blew out a long breath. 'So what should we do?'

'Only one thing for it. I've got to get her suitcase and violin now. There's never going to be another opportunity. If the worse comes to the worst, you'll have to set up some kind of diversion.'

Rene pushed through the swing doors in pursuit of Jamie and scurried along the corridor to catch up with him. "Ow do I do that?'

'I have no idea,' Jamie said as he descended the wide black banistered staircase leading down to the reception area. 'You'll just have to use your imagination, if need be.'

'We're not going to break the law, are we?' But Rene got no answer to her question. She stood transfixed on the final landing of the stairs, watching Jamie as he made his way over to the reception where a tall thin man in a macintosh was in debate with a young receptionist.

Rene slowly descended the remaining few steps in a trance of panic, her eyes never leaving Jamie as he reached down nonchalantly to pick up the blue suitcase and the violin that stood in the row of luggage behind the man. This is not going to work, she thought to herself.

'Oh, I've suddenly come over all faint,' she said shrilly to no one in particular, theatrically grabbing hold of the large square banister knob and weaving her body in a circular motion. She delivered her line with such volume that she attracted the attention of all those in the hotel lobby including the person whom Jamie was so far doing a very good job of evading. There was a brief moment when he glanced over to her with an agonised look on his face before he made a furtive dart for the back entrance of the hotel, clutching Angélique's suitcase and violin. Through her oscillating vision, Rene watched as the Frenchman's unsympathetic glare turned from her to Jamie, a boy in quick retreat, and his expression changed to open-mouthed horror.

'Hey, you, come back with those!' he yelled as he began to take off in pursuit of Jamie. Rene glanced down at the floor, measuring her distance, and with a desperate prayer that the carpet was indeed top-of-the-range with a deep spongy underlay, fell poleaxed to the ground on the very spot where Dessuin was about to plant his black, highly polished shoe. His foot caught the side of Rene's body with such force she momentarily opened her eyes wide, muffling a cry of pain, as Dessuin's legs flew over her in a horizontal arc. As she heard the thump of his body coming to rest, she closed her eyes and feigned serene unconsciousness. She sensed people gathering round her and then, rather alarmingly, hands started to undo the top buttons of her shirt.

And then she heard a female voice say, 'I'll call the police, sir.'

'No, don't do that,' came the immediate reply. 'I do not want to involve the police.'

'But, sir, you've just had some luggage stolen.'

'I said I do not want you to call the police. It is all a misunderstanding. I know who has taken the cases. I will get them back from him.'

There was a pause, during which someone raised Rene's head off the floor and slipped a soft cushion underneath it. Then she heard the man's soft tread skirt her supine body. 'Does anyone know who this woman might be?' he asked.

Oh, no, Rene thought. I wonder 'ow I'll 'old up under interrogation.

'She's a friend of mine,' a female voice replied, very close to Rene's head. 'We were about to have tea together when she said she was feeling faint and headed off to the ladies' toilet.'

There was another pause before the Frenchman's voice replied, 'Very well,' and then Rene heard him walk away. She flickered one eye, trying to see who it was that had come to her rescue. Through the diffusion of her eyelid, she could make out the curly red hair and pink scarf.

'That's about five minutes now,' the woman's voice whispered to her. 'I reckon that's sufficient. Just flutter your eyelids like you're seducing Brad Pitt and let out a bit of a moan.'

Rene smiled, her eyes still tightly shut. 'I'm 'oping those were your 'ands that were getting dangerously close to my cleavage.'

'No such luck, pet. That was Brad Pitt.'

Rene fought to suppress a giggle, but it spluttered out nevertheless.

'I said moan, you daft cow, not laugh!'

Rene did as requested, and with a flicker of eyelids looked up into the face of the woman whose purse she had returned. It wore such an expression of hilarity that Rene had a strong urge to burst out laughing. Not that it would have mattered. The woman was now the only person who was paying any attention to her. 'Ye're Lancashire, aren't ye?' Rene said, seeing no reason to speak in hushed tones. 'I've just worked it out.'

'Aye, and you're Yorkshire. I remembered where I recognised you from. Ye're Rene Brownlow, aren't ye? I've seen yer show.'

Rene raised her eyebrows in astonishment. 'Fame at last.'

'That fainting bit,' the woman said, giving Rene's arm a light shove with her hand, 'was one of the funniest things I've seen in years.'

Rene grinned at the woman. 'Thanks for stepping in just then.'

The woman shrugged. 'Us comediennes had better stick together.'

'Oh my word, is that what ye do too?'

'Aye, every day, every night.' The woman stuck out her hand. 'Matti Fullbright.'

Rene took the hand. ''Ello, Matti Fullbright. Listen, d'ye think you could 'eave me back up onto me pins?'

'Aye, but make it look as if you're still a bit unsteady, OK?'

Rene accomplished the upward movement and held hard to Matti's hand as she weaved her body round once more.

'You can stop that now,' Matti said, glancing around. 'No one's taking a blind bit of notice. Listen, how d'ye fancy a nice cup of tea?'

Rene flicked her head to the side. 'I'd really like that but I'd better get back to me flat. I've got to make sure of a few things.'

'Like if your young friend made it back there with the suitcase and violin? What the hell was all that about?'

Rene bent down and picked up her handbag. 'Believe me, we were both doing someone a good turn.'

'Aye, I'm sure you were,' Matti replied. 'I didn't like the look of that man. He gave me the once-over as he walked past, and from the expression on his face ye'd think he'd just stepped in dog's mess.' She took hold of Rene's arm. 'Come on, let's get out of here.'

They turned and made their way up the staircase, unaware of a certain tall, thin gentleman in a belted macintosh, who had been sitting out of sight on the other side of it.

Halfway across Festival Square, Rene stopped and looked back at the imposing hotel. 'So what were *you* doing in that posh place?'

'I had a meeting with my agent.'

Rene looked impressed. 'Really? You must be at the top of the game.'

Matti stuck her hand into her blue canvas bag and handed a leaflet to Rene. 'Come and see the show. It's a freebie.'

Rene glanced at the leaflet. ''You're on at the Smirnoff Underbelly! That's one of the top venues, in't it?'

Matti shrugged her shoulders. 'I've been lucky. I was there last year and they asked me to come back.'

'You must be damned good, then.'

Matti squeezed Rene's arm. 'Come and see for yourself.'

'I will,' she replied, pushing the leaflet into her handbag, 'and thanks again for yer 'elp back there.'

'And likewise, thanks for my purse. See you around, I 'ope.'

As Matti Fullbright strode off, Rene let out a long, satisfied breath, realising that her lonely existence in Edinburgh had taken a change for the better over the past hour or two. Jamie had needed her help that morning, and she liked nothing better than to feel needed. And then in meeting Matti, with her sense of humour, Rene realised that, for the first time ever, she had come across a person who was *just like her*.

She smiled to herself as she saw her new friend disappear out of sight. 'Aye, see you around,' she murmured.

Twelve

ALBERT DESSUIN FLICKED back the net curtain of his new room, now on the fourth floor but still with the same panoramic view over Festival Square. It had been easy enough to single out the bumbling little figure with the loose-fitting multicoloured coat that threaded its way through the crowds and then turned towards Princes Street. Things could not have turned out much better.

He had been in a blistering mood when he had arrived back at the hotel an hour earlier. But it had slowly begun to dawn on him that, from the start, Angélique had orchestrated the whole affair, displaying her naked body in front of him like that, knowing that he had already admonished her for her sluttish behaviour. His fury was totally natural, a reaction that came from a deep sense of protection for his protégée. And this story about having cut her hand was just to put him off the scent, to blackmail him into keeping away from her. Well, she would not get rid of him that easily.

There was no chance of him being able to recognise the young man who had taken the suitcase and the violin, save for the fact that he had blond hair. He was undoubtedly one of those who had clustered around Angélique, tongues hanging out, at the reception. He knew she had never before laid eyes on the fat little woman who had foiled his pursuit of the young man. That's why he had decided to hang around and listen after the mêlée had died down. He hadn't been able to decipher everything she had said to that red-headed woman, but he had heard enough.

He picked up the copy of the Fringe show guide that he'd found on the display stand next to the reception desk. He spotted what he was looking for halfway down the index. He memorised the venue reference number and leafed through the guide until he came to the correct page. 'Hilarious Comedienne from Hartlepool' was the strapline above the photograph of the woman whose face he had first seen as she lay flat out on the carpeted floor of the hotel lobby. Creasing the guide open at the page, he took out a miniature of Scotch and a bottle of mineral water from the minibar. He raised his glass. 'Here's to you, Rene Brownlow. I'm sure that in time you will prove very useful to me.'

Jamie had bundled Angélique's luggage into a taxi and slumped down into the seat beneath the level of the rear window, expecting to hear a police siren threading its way towards them at any moment. He knew Dessuin had caught sight of him. Under normal circumstances he could have outpaced the man quite easily, but burdened with the suit-case and violin, he thought the Frenchman would have been breathing down his neck before he reached the street. Maybe Rene had managed to set up some kind of diversion, but he couldn't imagine how. There had only been a moment for her to react.

By the time the taxi dropped him outside his flat, Jamie was begin-ning to have serious concerns about the comedienne, realising now that it had been unfair to have involved her. He was convinced she was clos-eted in some back office at the hotel being interviewed by the police and a very interested Albert Dessuin. She might be forced to identify Jamie as the 'mastermind' behind the bag snatch, and also Angélique's whereabouts. Having paid off the taxi, he let himself in through the entrance door, his heart in his mouth as he tried to work out his next move. Maybe he should ring Gavin straight away and tell him what had happened. Or maybe he should hang fire for twenty minutes or so, just in case Rene came back by herself.

He hurried over to the telephone. He couldn't risk waiting for her. He began to dial the number of Gavin's law firm, but just before he hit the fourth digit, he stopped, and stood listening to the low reverbera-tion of voices coming from the sitting room. Jamie let out a sigh of relief, realising it could only be his solicitor, and walked quickly along the hall passage to the door of the sitting room and threw it open. 'Gavin, thank goodness you're—'

Angélique and a heavily built middle-aged man were sitting on one of the sofas, their mouths frozen in mid-conversation as both looked round in surprise at his sudden entry.

'What's going on?' Jamie demanded, his eyes ablaze with concern for Angélique and distrust for the man. 'Who are you?'

Angélique quickly uncurled her feet from underneath her and stood up. 'It's all right, Jamie. Harry Wills is a journalist who is an acquain-tance of mine. It was he—'

Jamie shook his head, never taking his eyes off the man. 'I told you not to let anyone into the flat. What the hell's the point of me trying to hide you away if you allow any Tom, Dick or Harry in?'

He knew as soon as he had said it, it was the wrong metaphor to use. Angélique frowned at him. 'Who is Tom and Dick?'

Harry Wills stood up. 'I'm sorry, this is my fault. You are right. I should never have come round without giving you both some warning.'

'How did you find out she was here, anyway?' Jamie asked abruptly.

'If you will listen to me, Jamie, I'll tell you,' Angélique said, her voice rising in frustration. 'Harry wrote the story about me having cut my hand and leaving the country. I suggested his name to Gavin, and they both met to work out what should be written in the newspapers.'

Jamie glanced from one to the other. 'Well, maybe it would have been an idea to let *me* know about all this as well.'

Angélique walked over to him and gave the sleeve of his jacket a tug. 'I am very sorry. I promise I will not overlook such a thing again.'

'I'm being quite serious, actually,' Jamie mumbled.

Angélique pulled a long face, stood to attention and gave him a brisk salute. 'I quite agree, and I am now taking it very seriously.'

Jamie smiled reluctantly. 'Oh, get lost,' he said, waving a hand in the general direction of the hall. 'Your suitcase and violin are out there.'

'*Oh, ce n'est pas vrai!*' Angélique exclaimed. She gave him a quick peck on the cheek before rushing out into the hall.

Jamie turned to the journalist. 'Sorry about the misunderstanding.'

'No bother. You were quite right to question my presence here. You're obviously doing a good job of looking after her.'

Jamie shrugged off the compliment. 'Were you doing an interview?'

'Not about immediate events, I can assure you, and anyway, nothing will get printed until this whole situation has rectified itself.'

'We've a long way to go before that happens,' Jamie murmured.

'What makes you say that?'

Jamie took a backward step to glance along the hall, just in time to see Angélique disappear into her bedroom with the suitcase and violin. He closed the door of the sitting room and turned to the journalist. 'Dessuin knows she's still in Edinburgh. By now he could very well know she's here in this flat.'

Harry Wills's expression showed immediate concern. 'Why do you think that?'

'I've just seen him booking himself back into the Sheraton Grand. He saw me take Angélique's cases.'

'You took the cases from in front of his eyes?' the journalist asked incredulously.

'No, they were actually sitting behind him. I reckon I would have got away with it . . . well, let's just say he turned round at the wrong time.'

'But he didn't follow you?'

'No, for definite.'

'Then why do you think he might find his way here?'

Jamie told him briefly of Rene's involvement in the suitcase snatch and his uncertainty as to what had happened to her.

When he had finished, Harry Wills stood in silence. 'Well,' he said eventually, 'this poses a bit of a problem.'

'Especially for me! I could get arrested.'

Harry waved a hand at him. 'Dessuin will do his utmost to avoid involving the police. Would there be any reason for him to think Rene *might* have been helping you?'

Jamie blew out a derisive laugh. 'She would have been as well having a notice hanging round her neck saying, "*I am the thief's number-one accomplice*"!'

While Harry looked thoughtful over this new predicament, Jamie heard Angélique in her bedroom play a cautious scale on her violin. The notes were clear and resonant, but the speed at which she played them seemed faltering.

'Is there any place you and Angélique could lie low for a couple of days?' the journalist asked. 'Preferably away from the city.'

Jamie looked dubious. 'I'm not sure. I'm meant to be writing Fringe reviews, but I could get out of that. What about my tenants, though?'

'I'm sure they could fend for themselves for a few days.' He paused, seeing Jamie still vacillate. 'I'd strongly recommend the idea.'

Jamie shrugged his shoulders. 'I suppose we could go to my parents' place in East Lothian.'

'That would be good,' Harry said, nodding his approval of the idea, 'and while you're away, I'll stick myself outside your flat and keep an eye out for Dessuin turning up here.'

'Really? Would you mind doing that?'

Harry laughed. 'I was an investigative journalist for a number of years, Jamie, so I'm used to sitting in my car outside people's houses.'

Jamie stared at the man for a moment. 'May I ask you a question? Why are you willing to give us so much help? Surely you've a hundred better things to be doing with your time?'

Harry sat his sizable bottom down on the arm of a sofa. 'Because Albert Dessuin happens to be one of the most discourteous human beings I've ever had the displeasure of meeting.'

'You *know* him?'

'There have been numerous occasions over the past few years when I've been party to the more unpleasant side of his nature. Ever since Angélique left the Conservatoire, I have been trying to get a personal interview with her and Dessuin has always been there to thwart me. Does that answer your question?'

'I suppose it does,' Jamie replied with a smile.

'OK, so I suggest if there's been neither sight nor sound of the man over the next few days, then I'll give the all-clear for you both to return to the flat. Do you have a number I could contact you on?'

The journalist wrote down Jamie's mobile number before getting to his feet. 'You and Angélique should get yourselves ready to go.'

'Another problem,' Jamie said tentatively. 'I don't have wheels.'

Harry delved into a trouser pocket. 'In that case,' he said, taking out his own mobile, 'it's time we involved Gavin Mackintosh.'

The sound of the front door slamming shut had both men looking questioningly at each other. Jamie squinted down the hall. 'Oh, hell! It could be too late!' he exclaimed quietly. 'It's Rene.' He opened the door to see the comedienne staggering along the passage towards him.

'Glad to see ye made it back,' she said, dumping her coat along with her handbag onto a chair. 'I am dead beat,' she puffed out. 'That's far too much excitement for one day.' She glanced up at Jamie and Harry, who had come to stand side by side in front of the fireplace, observing her closely. 'So, aren't you going to introduce me to yer friend, Jamie?'

'Oh, sorry; this is Harry Wills. Rene, what happened?' Jamie went on, eager to ply her for information. 'Why didn't Dessuin follow me?'

'Because I set up a diversion, like ye asked me. I pretended to faint right in 'is path.'

Jamie pulled his hands across his head in desperation. 'Oh God. What did he do?'

'He gave me a kick in the ribs, then fell with a thump to the floor.'

'Were the police called? Were you questioned at all?'

'It was all a bit odd, really. I was lying on the floor with me eyes closed, when some girl—probably the receptionist—asked if she should call the police. The Frenchman went all panicky and said he didn't want them involved. He said he knew who ye were and 'e'd sort it all out later.'

'That's exactly what I thought he'd do,' Harry said, 'and he was just bluffing when he said he knew you, Jamie.'

'But he must have known you were helping me, Rene. Weren't you asked any questions at all?'

'No. Mind you, I've little doubt I would 'ave been, if it 'adn't been for this woman coming to my rescue. I was still flat out on the floor when the Frenchman asked whether anybody knew me, and this woman said I was a friend of 'ers, and we were going to have a cup of tea together when I'd come over all faint.'

'And Dessuin believed her?' Harry asked.

'I'm certain of it. 'E just stormed away after that.'

Harry and Jamie glanced at each other, relief on their faces.

'So, there's no chance Dessuin could have followed you back here?' Jamie asked.

'I had to stop off in a pub on the way back to go to the loo, and when I came out I certainly didn't see anyone lurking about.' She stood up. 'Now, unless you've got some more furtive action planned, I think I might just get back to the normal pace of my life.'

Jamie planted a kiss on Rene's hot round cheek. 'Thanks for being a real star. I could have ended up in deep shit if it hadn't been for you.'

When she had left the room, Jamie turned round to the journalist. 'Looks like we're in the clear, then,' he remarked hopefully.

'We might be,' Harry replied. 'Let's just say Dessuin is no fool. I think we should continue with the plan for you and Angélique to leave Edinburgh. If he doesn't show up here over the next two days, I reckon then, and only then, we can probably say we're in the clear.'

Leonard Hartson had a smile on his face as he climbed the steps to the London Street flat. It had been there ever since T.K. had appeared out of the barber's, where, on his own insistence, he'd had his greasy mane reduced to a very presentable fuzz of hair. It had transformed his features. But the most extraordinary by-product of the barber's clippers had been to unlock the floodgates. T.K. had questioned Leonard incessantly on all aspects of film-making, hardly waiting for a reply before he was on to the next query.

Even now, while Leonard extracted the door keys from his jacket, T.K. stood beside him eager to find out how long it had taken Leonard to be considered proficient enough to operate a camera. While the cameraman cast his mind back in an attempt to come up with an accurate answer, the entrance door flew open and his young landlord appeared.

'I'm glad I've caught you, Mr Hartson,' Jamie said, as he came down onto the steps, shouldering a rucksack. 'I have to head off for a couple of days, so just use the flat as your own. My mobile number is on the hall table if you need to contact me.'

Leonard was about to speak when Gavin Mackintosh, the solicitor who had introduced him to T.K., appeared at the entrance door carrying a canvas overnight bag and a violin case. 'Ah, Mr Hartson, I do hope everything's going well for you both,' he said, before catching sight of T.K. 'My word, Thomas! You've changed into a dapper-looking fellow.' He gave T.K. a pat on the arm before hurrying off down the steps, closely followed by a young woman wearing a large pair of sunglasses.

Gavin opened the back passenger door of a Volvo estate car and waited for the girl to get in before walking round to the back to put her luggage in the boot. While this operation was in progress, Leonard noticed Jamie casting searching glances up and down the street.

'Could I just have a moment of your time?' Leonard asked quickly, realising there seemed to be a degree of urgency in their departure. 'I'll be as brief as possible. T.K. here has found himself temporarily without lodgings, and I wondered, therefore, if you might have any objections to him making use of the other bed in my room.'

'Yeah, that's fine by me.'

'Of course, I shall pay a bit more for the rent of the room.'

'Oh, don't bother about that,' Jamie replied, with a shake of his head.

'No, I insist. What would you say to eighty pounds per night?'

'Seventy-five,' Jamie said in reply as he opened the front passenger door of the Volvo. 'That's my final offer.'

Leonard smiled at him. 'That's very kind.' He turned and raised an eyebrow at his crop-haired assistant. 'Looks like we're in business.'

While T.K. went off to have his much-needed shower, Leonard telephoned Nick Springer in London, telling him of the progress he had made during the initial day's shooting and the name of the courier service that would be delivering the exposed film stock to his office. Nick sounded busy so Leonard kept the call short then rang Grace with a more in-depth account, including news of the sleeping arrangement he now had with his young assistant. He did not, however, mention the facts that led to this happening. Neither did he mention the pain that had begun to nag at the left side of his chest.

When he replaced the receiver, Leonard turned to find a young man standing in front of him he hardly recognised. T.K.'s face immediately broke into a broad grin. 'What d'ya think, then?' he said, arms outstretched as he gave himself the once-over.

Leonard nodded approvingly as he appraised the new-look T.K., with his clean white T-shirt, new Levi's and a virginal-white pair of Adidas trainers. Slung over his shoulder was the new Timberland jacket at which T.K. had gawped longingly while Leonard was paying the bill for two pairs of jeans, six T-shirts, boxer shorts, a six-pack of white socks, a cotton sweatshirt, a belt, and a pair of Adidas trainers. 'And I think we'd better take that jacket as well,' Leonard had said quietly.

'Well?' T.K. asked again.

Leonard laughed. 'I really am very impressed, T.K. And I think it's only right that we should celebrate your new appearance by searching out a suitable eating establishment that can provide us with some well-earned sustenance.'

'Eh?' T.K. remarked, reverting too easily to his imbecilic look, his mouth curled up at one side.

'How would a very large steak and a glass of beer suit you?'

'Oh, aye, tha' sounds great,' T.K. replied enthusiastically.

A door opening at the far end of the hall made them both turn, and their fellow tenant appeared, her attention caught up with trying to find something in her large handbag. Rene looked up and saw them. 'My word!' she said, her eyes fixed on T.K. as she came along the passage. 'What 'appened to you?'

Leonard held out a hand as she approached them. 'We've not yet introduced ourselves. My name's Leonard Hartson.'

Rene shook his hand. 'Nice to meet you, Leonard. Rene Brownlow.'

'Are you just on your way out?'

'Aye, I am.'

'In that case, you wouldn't care to join us for something to eat?'

Rene sucked her teeth disappointedly. 'Oh, what a grand thought, but I can't, luv. I've got to do a show in 'alf an 'our.'

'Maybe another time.'

Leonard stood aside to allow her to leave the flat first. 'Well, consider it a firm invitation, then.'

'I'll tell you what, though,' Rene said as she walked past him. 'Seeing as Jamie's left us 'ome alone, what about me cooking us all a meal tomorrow night? After me show, about nine o'clock?'

'I think that would suit us both very well,' Leonard replied with a nod. 'We shall look forward to it.'

During the journey to East Lothian, what little conversation there was in the car was between the two men in the front, although Jamie would occasionally ask Angélique if she was all right. She was not, however, in a great mind to talk. At first, when the car was travelling slowly through the colourless Edinburgh suburbs, her mood had been rock-bottom. But then, as the dual carriageway left the city behind, her spirits improved, and her troubled thoughts subsided as she looked out of the window, shielding her eyes against the early-evening sun on the rolling wheat fields. When the car breasted the hill above the village of East Linton, Angélique could not help but wonder as she looked out across the Lammermuir Hills shouldering in the velvet-green coastline.

Gavin swung the car to the right and took a narrow high-banked road that wound its way up towards the hills, then turned left past a number of low livestock sheds. A hundred metres on, they passed through a stone-pillared gateway leading onto a gravelled driveway bordered by well-tended lawns. A tall white house with a steep slated roof came into view, standing proudly defensive of a circular sweep.

As the Volvo came to a halt in front of the house, a couple of sheep-dogs appeared from nowhere and started biting ineffectually at the front tyres with snarling teeth. Jamie gave them a yell as he got out, but it was only when a voice like thunder rang out around the grounds that the dogs slunk off to lie on the lawn, their eyes fixed on the quad bike that came at a breakneck speed up the drive, spurting up gravel that landed dangerously short of the back of the car.

'Hey, quit that, Stratton!' Gavin shouted angrily. 'If there's so much as a scratch, I'll have you foot the bill for a complete respray.'

Angélique smiled at the grinning man who sat astride the mud-spattered quad. He was dressed in a heavy cotton lumberjack shirt and waterproof trousers pulled over wellington boots, a battered baseball cap jammed back to front on his head. He put a dirt-ingrained hand up to his ear. 'I'm sorry,' the man said, looking at Gavin with a bemused expression. 'Did you say anything of interest just then, Mackintosh?'

'God, he's such a lad,' Angélique heard Jamie mutter as he came to stand beside her. 'Come on, I'll introduce you to my father.'

They walked over to where the two men were already engaged in sparring banter. 'Dad, this is Angélique Pascal.'

The man swung a leg over the handlebars of the bike. 'Good to meet you, Angélique,' he said, flipping off his cap and landing a bristly kiss on both her cheeks. 'I understand you're a bit of a violinist.'

'A bit of a violinist!' Gavin exclaimed. 'You really are an uneducated heathen, Stratton.'

Rory laughed, encircling his son's shoulders with a pair of wiry arms and giving him a welcoming hug. 'Just because our tastes in music differ.' He took Angélique's bag and her violin case from the car. 'Come on, then,' he said. 'Time for a drink.'

'Count me out, Rory,' Gavin said, closing the boot. 'I have to be get-ting back to Edinburgh. I have a mountain of work to get through.'

Jamie's father turned with a disappointed frown. 'How boring of you.'

Gavin smiled at his old school friend. 'Maybe another time, but tell Prue I'm sorry to have missed her.' He waved to Angélique as she fol-lowed Rory towards the house, then turned back to Jamie. 'How have you left things with Harry Wills?'

'He's going to call me in a couple of days' time if all's well.'

'Right, well, give me a call if you need anything.'

'Will do, and cheers, Gavin, for bringing us out here.'

'My pleasure,' the solicitor said as he got into the car. 'Let's hope this whole business resolves itself soon.'

Jamie found his father standing in jeans and stockinged feet in front of the unlit fire in the sitting room, a large glass of whisky in his hand.

'Where's Angélique?' Jamie asked.

'Your mother's showing her to her bedroom.' Rory took a healthy swallow of whisky and cocked his head to the side. 'Nice-looking girl, that. *Very* nice-looking, in fact,' Rory continued, as he eyed his son.

Jamie shook his head. 'Leave it out, Dad.'

Rory laughed and sat down in an armchair. 'Oh, by the way, I bumped into Gordon McLaren in Dunbar today. He said there's a pre-season warm-up game tomorrow evening at the club if you wanted to play.'

Jamie shrugged. 'I'm not that fit.'

'Do you some good, then, wouldn't it? Give him a call, anyway, and in the meantime you can start your fitness training tomorrow morning by going up onto the hill and looking round the sheep for me. I've got some lambs going through the ring at Kelso, so I won't be able to do it.'

'Thanks for that, Dad,' Jamie replied morosely.

'Well, you may as well do some work! Take Angélique with you. I'm sure she'd appreciate a taste of the Scottish wilderness.'

The door of the sitting room opened and Angélique entered with a small blonde woman dressed in a long denim skirt and white cotton shirt. She came over to Jamie arms outstretched. 'Darling, how are you?' she said, giving him a kiss that left traces of her pale lipstick.

'I'm good, Mum,' Jamie replied, 'except Dad's giving me grief as usual.'

Jamie's mother looked over at her husband, her expression turning to one of horror. 'Rory!' She hurried over to where he was sitting and delivered a resounding thwack to one of his knees. 'I'll give *you* grief, you dreadful man. Get out of that chair!' Rory leaped to his feet and Jamie's mother dusted off the vacated seat with her hand. 'I've told you before, you are *not* to sit on these new covers in your filthy jeans.'

Rory pulled a schoolboy face at Angélique. 'I hope you've been treated a bit better by my wife.'

'Prue could not have been kinder,' Angélique replied.

'You wait. After two days in this house you'll be bossed around like the rest of us.'

'Oh, you talk such rubbish!' Prue scoffed, taking hold of his arm. 'Come on, you can give me a hand to get supper ready.'

'See what I mean,' Rory said over his shoulder as his wife led him to the door. 'Boss, boss, boss.'

'They are lovely people, your parents,' Angélique said to Jamie when they were alone. 'They are very happy, I think. A good mixture.'

'Probably. Talking of mixtures, what can I get you to drink?'

'A Coca-Cola, if you have one.'

While Jamie searched the drinks tray, Angélique walked around running her fingers over the furniture. 'I love your house, Jamie. It is filled with so many old things.'

Jamie clinked ice into a glass and poured in the contents of the can. 'Well, I think about four or five generations of Strattons have lived with this furniture.'

'It reminds me of Madame Lafitte's house in Clermont Ferrand.'

'Who's she?'

Angélique traced a finger around the diamond-shaped pane of glass in a tall display cabinet. 'She is the lady who started me playing the violin. She is very old now, but she is the most wonderful person.'

'Is she a relation of yours?' Jamie asked, handing her the Coca-Cola.

'No, but she is as close to me as any of my family. It was Madame Lafitte who paid for me to go to the Conservatoire.' Angélique walked over to the sofa and sat down. 'My mother worked as her cleaner.'

Jamie could not help but stare at Angélique. 'Oh, I see. Have you seen her recently?'

The expression on Angélique's face changed to one of deep sadness. 'No. My schedule has never allowed me the time. She suffered a stroke just before I finished at the Conservatoire and she is now confined to a wheelchair in her house. It is my greatest regret that she has never been able to come to one of my concerts.'

'Are you still in touch with her?'

'Oh, yes, every week. She talks very slowly because of the stroke, but her brain is as sharp as ever, even though she is in her ninetieth year. I long to see her again.' She paused. 'It was one of the reasons why Albert Dessuin got so angry on that night.'

Jamie nodded. 'You wanted to go back to France to see her.'

'I did not think it was so much to ask.' She lowered her face. 'I just have this feeling that I will not be seeing her again.'

Jamie sat on the stool in front of her. 'Hey, don't think that,' he said, giving her knee a couple of gentle thumps with his hand. 'Of course you'll see her again.'

Angélique forced a smile onto her face. 'Why is it, Jamie, that you always manage to say the things I most want to hear?'

'Well, maybe because . . .' His forehead creased in thought. '. . . no, sorry, I've no idea.'

Angélique smiled. 'I think it is because inside that tough exterior of a rugby player you are covering up the heart of a *romantique*.'

'Oh yeah?' Jamie said with a distasteful look. 'That sounds like me.'

'Hah! You are not prepared to admit it, are you? You are very fortunate to have such a perfect balance in you. For me, playing a violin is not just a physical process. I must make my violin take me to a different level of understanding to achieve the balance between the emotional and the physical. It is like . . . how do you say . . . an "out-of-body" experience.'

Jamie scratched the back of his head. 'Yeah, I can understand that, but you can't compare it with playing rugby. If I walked out onto a pitch and was confronted by fifteen socking great lads who knew I had "the heart of a romantic", I'd be subjected to an "out-of-body" experience within the first five minutes of the game! By the way, I heard you playing this morning.' He pointed to her strapped hand. 'How does it feel?'

'It is feeling much better. Look'—she delved into the pocket of her jeans—'I still have the squash ball.' She began squeezing it in her hand.

'That's good, but you should be trying to increase the pressure a bit.' He wrapped his hand round hers and gently closed his fist until he could feel the ball flatten against the palm of her hand. 'Is that OK?'

'I don't feel any pain,' Angélique replied.

He opened up her hand and inspected each of her fingers. 'Bruising's almost gone and so has the swelling.' He scowled seriously at her. 'It is my considered opinion, mademoiselle, that you will very shortly be resuming your career.'

Angélique grinned at him. 'It would never have been possible, *monsieur*, without your inventive cure. How can I ever repay you?'

'Don't worry, I shall be sending you a bill which should keep me in squash balls for forty years.'

'In that case, I had better start to play my violin as soon as possible.'

Their faces had been edging closer, so when the sitting-room door burst open they sprang apart.

'Oh, sorry,' Jamie's father said, glancing from one to the other. 'Hope I wasn't interrupting anything.'

'No,' Jamie replied, fixing his father with a challenging stare, daring him to say anything. Rory answered with a raising of his eyebrows.

'Well, in that case,' he said, 'if you would care to follow me, I shall show you to the kitchen where your evening meal awaits you.'

T.K. lay in bed, a contented grin on his face, staring up at the shaft of orange light that shone through the gap in the curtains. All was quiet except for Leonard's breathing in the bed next to his. He moved his feet back and forth over the clean undersheet, feeling the weighty warmth of the duvet moulding itself round his body.

Three days . . . seventy-two hours . . . In seventy-two hours, everything in his life had changed. Out of nowhere he had, by some extraordinary turn of fate, got the break he'd longed for. And across from him was the decent old bloke who had given him that break, who treated him . . . like he was worth something.

'Leonard, are ye awake?' he whispered.

The cameraman let out a sleepy groan. 'Did you say something, T.K.?'

'Aye, ah asked if ye wis awake. I wis just thinkin' aboot whit we did today. Will we get the chance tae see the stuff we shot?'

'Not until it's finished. Once it's gone through the laboratory, it'll go straight to the cutting room in London.'

'That's the master copy and the black-and-white cutting copy, is it?'

'Good for you,' Leonard said sleepily. 'You were obviously listening.'

T.K. linked his hands behind his head on the pillow. 'Dae ye no' get worried that nothing's goin' tae come out on the film?'

'No matter how long one is in the business, T.K., one constantly worries. Sleeping is enough of a problem without . . .'

T.K. listened for Leonard to finish the sentence, then swivelled his head and looked over at the old cameraman. 'Leonard?'

'Yes, T.K.,' Leonard replied with drowsy impatience.

'Are ye all right? It's just that ah saw ye kept haudin' on to yer side a' day. Have ye got a pain there or somethin'?'

'Just old age, T.K. Just old age.'

'Aye, but ye're fit, Leonard, aren't ye? Ye're fitter than ma dad and he's only fifty-twa, but that's no' surprisin' 'cos he does bugger all except sit in his chair watchin' TV and gettin' through fifty fags a day.'

'Good night, T.K.'

T.K. stretched out his legs and once more smiled contentedly to himself. 'Good night, Leonard. See you in the morning.'

The quad bike ascended the hill at speed, brushing before it the tall grass that grew in the centre of the deep-rutted track. Angélique stifled a yawn as she sat behind Jamie, her arms tightly encircling his waist. The sun promised warmth for the day, but as it had yet to appear above the top of the hill, she shielded her face from the wind by pressing her cheek against Jamie's back. The high-revving engine cut out any possibility of conversation, but Angélique was happy to watch the view unfold before her and feel the comforting warmth of Jamie's body.

Finally, they came out into the sun at the head of a long deep gully that frothed with clear fast water tumbling down the hillside. Jamie left the track, turned the quad to face out over the view and cut the engine.

'What d'you think of that?' Jamie said, sweeping his gaze around. Angélique rested her chin against his shoulder. She took in a deep inhalation of air, the sweet smell of the damp vegetation on the moor mingling with the faint aroma of shaving cream on the side of Jamie's face. Without moving, she focused her eyes on the mass of blond hair, pushed back behind his ear and curling down to his shirt collar, and she wanted, there and then, to reach up and push it to one side so that she could press her mouth against his warm downy neck. 'That is one of the most beautiful sights I have ever seen,' she replied eventually to his question, without averting her gaze.

'That's the North Berwick Law over there,' Jamie said, pointing to a conical-shaped rock that jutted out of the sea beyond the coastline. 'It's a carboniferous volcanic plug, composed of phonolytic trachyte and formed over three hundred and thirty-five million years ago. It's about the only thing I remember from my geography lessons at school.'

'There are some extinct volcanoes where I come from, too. Les Monts Dôme, les Monts de Cantal.'

Jamie shot a quizzical frown at her. 'Where on earth are they?'

'In the Massif Central. Clermont Ferrand lies in the heart of one of the most beautiful mountain ranges in Europe.'

'Right,' Jamie said with a nod. 'In that case, the good old North Berwick Law is just a bit of a bump to you.' He let out a sigh. 'I'm beginning to wonder why I bothered bringing you up here in the first place.'

Angélique laughed and tightened her grip around his stomach. 'I would not have missed it for all the world.'

Jamie gave her hands a light slap. 'Come on, let's check these sheep out.' Swinging a leg over the handlebars, he took a duffle bag from the front pannier rack on the quad.

'What's in there?' Angélique asked as she clambered off the bike.

'The usual veterinary stuff, a Thermos flask filled with undrinkable coffee and a couple of tepid bacon rolls.'

'Ah, breakfast on the moor. That is a wonderful idea.'

'Actually, it was the old man's. I think he's taken a bit of a shine to you.'

'A man of impeccable taste,' Angélique remarked airily.

'I think you should leave off judgment until you've tried his coffee.'

Three-quarters of an hour later they sat in the morning sun, their backs against a large smooth-sided boulder, looking out over a small loch that was surrounded by grazing sheep. Pouring out two cups of coffee from the Thermos, Jamie handed one to Angélique and waited for her to take her first mouthful.

'Your verdict, then?'

'It's'—she swilled the liquid round in her mouth and then licked her lips—'quite disgusting, actually.'

'I told you it would be.' He laughed, taking the bacon rolls from their wrappers and passing one to her. 'Not really Parisian café quality, is it?'

Angélique smiled at him. 'No, it is not,' she answered quietly.

Jamie took a bite of his roll. 'You miss Paris, don't you? Will you head back there after all this is over?'

She took a small piece from her roll and began rolling it between her thumb and forefinger. 'I don't think so. I have commitments to fulfil.'

'Where?'

'All over the world.'

'D'you reckon you'll be able to do them by yourself?'

'I don't think I have any other choice.'

'What about getting a new manager?'

She turned her head away from him. 'I actually don't know how to start to find one I will be able to trust.'

'I can understand that,' Jamie said, taking a mouthful of coffee. 'Dessuin's really succeeded in messing up your life, hasn't he?'

Angélique turned and looked at him with glistening eyes. 'It is very difficult when someone shatters your illusions.'

Jamie could only nod his head in reply. He felt a hand settle on his knee. 'And what about you, Jamie?' Angélique asked, a brave smile on her face. 'Are you going to stay in Edinburgh?'

'No, I'm heading down to London in September to start a job.'

'That will be good fun. I would very much like to live in London.' She paused, toying once more with her bacon roll. 'Maybe we could meet up if I have a concert there?'

'I'd like that.'

'I would too.' She handed him the roll. 'You have this. I'm not hungry.' She lay down, resting her head on his lap. 'I hope you don't mind.'

'What? Eating your fingered bacon roll?'

She hit him playfully on the leg. 'You know what I mean.'

Jamie watched a flight of ducks coast down onto the loch, breaking the dark water in parallel wakes.

'You know, last night was the best fun I have had for a long time,' Angélique said. 'Being with you and your parents, I sensed what it would be like to be part of a close and contented family. When I was a little girl in Clermont Ferrand, there was always something wrong in my home. Either my father had drunk too much, or he and my brothers were arguing; and then my mother was *always* complaining. That's why last night will become a very special memory for me.' She paused before letting out a long, sad sigh. '*En fait*, I really don't want it to end.'

Jamie looked down at the side of her face. 'What don't you want to end?' he asked, putting the last of the roll into his mouth.

She turned her body and looked up at him. 'Any of it. Being up here alone with you. Being so far away from all the travelling.' She smiled wistfully at him. 'With all this happening, I don't know if I will ever be able to return to the normal things again. I feel . . . very lost, Jamie.'

Jamie took hold of her bandaged hand and rubbed a finger against the strapping. 'Listen, you'll do OK,' he said, smiling down at her. 'You've got a lot of healing to do, not just this hand here but . . . well, in yourself as well. When all that's happened, you'll find yourself playing your violin better than ever. Your life will no longer be ruled by that creep Dessuin, and I know you have the courage and the talent to go it alone.'

Pulling her hand free from Jamie's grip, Angélique reached up and pressed a finger to his chin. 'There goes that heart of yours saying all the right things again.' She pushed herself upright and, leaning back against his chest, she pulled his arms round her. 'I think that I will have to tell all your rugby-playing friends about it this afternoon.'

'For Chrissakes, lads, what the hell are you doing?' the coach of the Dunbar First XV yelled as he stood at half-time in the middle of the semicircle of sweating, heaving bodies. 'You're letting them walk all over you! Right, Billy,' he said, addressing a giant of a man, 'I want you to contest every line-out. Get up in the air, spoil their tactics.' He pointed at a player who leaned forward, hands on knees, revealing a neck as thick as a bullock's. 'Callum, you're letting that tight-head prop control the scrum. You've got to get on top of him, otherwise there's no way we can get good ball to the three-quarters, is that clear?' The player nodded. 'And you, Jamie,' the coach continued, staring fixedly at his stand-off half, who was tipping the contents of a water bottle down his throat, 'their backs are lying flat, so I want you to break the gainline by running every ball, is that understood?' Jamie nodded, wiping a dirt-streaked arm across his mouth. 'Right, just go out there, you lot, and start working as a team.'

As the coach stomped off the field, the players sloped off to their positions to wait the few minutes until the referee restarted the game.

'There's someone over there trying to attract your attention, Jamie,' the inside centre said as he stretched a leg up behind him.

Jamie looked over to where Angélique was waving at him frantically.

'You'd better go,' the inside centre said with a teasing smile. 'I don't think she can wait until after the game.'

Jamie raised a finger at him as he ran over to the touchline.

'Yeah? What is it?' he asked Angélique.

'How fast is your left wing?'

Jamie turned and looked across to the far side of the pitch. 'Andy? He's fast. Beats me by about two seconds over a hundred metres.' He turned back to her. 'Why do you ask?'

'Their three-quarter line is lying very flat.'

Jamie eyed her with amusement. 'That's what the coach has just said.'

'Well, I was just thinking that if Michalak was playing in your position and he had a very fast player like Dominici on his left wing and he saw a gap behind the three-quarter line of the opposition, he would put the ball there for Dominici to chase.'

Jamie smiled at her. 'You do know about this game, don't you? But I'm afraid our coach wants us to run every ball.'

Angélique shrugged. 'In that case, you will lose.'

Jamie crossed his arms. 'Glad you're so confident. Anything else you want to say?'

'No, but if you do not try it, I shall embarrass you,' she said with a wicked smile.

Jamie pulled his mouth guard from the pocket of his shorts.

'Watch your step, Mademoiselle Pascal,' he said before running back to his position as the referee readied himself to start the second half.

Five minutes later, after Jamie had started a number of abortive three-quarter-line movements, a scrum was called in front of Angélique. She found herself standing next to the coach, who had been patrolling the touchline yelling orders at his players.

Angélique glanced over to the opposition's three-quarters and saw that their fullback had joined in the line as it edged forward to cover their opposing backs. 'Try it now, Jamie,' she yelled.

As the scrum half waited for the ball to be released from between the number eight's feet, the coach turned to Angélique, a querying look on his face. 'Try what, love?'

The scrum half picked up the ball from the base of the scrum and spun it at speed out to Jamie.

'Now move it down the line!' the coach yelled. 'Oh, no! What the effing hell are you doing?' He clapped both hands to his head as he watched Jamie kick a lobbing cross-field ball over the heads of the gawping opposition. Jamie's left wing was indeed a flyer. Timing his run to perfection, he scooped up the awkward-bouncing ball in one hand and tucked it under his arm, swerving to avoid his opposing wing. Once he had a clear path to the try line, he changed his running angle towards the centre of the posts and touched the ball down unchallenged.

At the end of the game Jamie ran across the pitch to Angélique, pulling a sweatshirt over his head. 'I owe you one,' he laughed. 'That tactic of yours really screwed them.'

She took hold of the neck of his sweatshirt and pulled his head down towards her and gave him a kiss on the cheek. 'You played well. In fact it is a pity you were not born a Frenchman.'

Thirteen

ALBERT DESSUIN THREW a pound into the cardboard box of the young juggler in the doorway of Marks & Spencer on Princes Street, then turned to look into the brightly lit store, wondering if he shouldn't go in and try to find the woman. The place was packed with shoppers and there was a possibility she could slip out of the back entrance, but nevertheless he decided to wait. It had been four days since he had first encountered her on the floor of the reception area in the Sheraton Grand, and so far he had done a good job of keeping himself out of sight. He wasn't going to risk ruining his chances at this stage. He moved away from the doorway, pulling up the collar of his mackintosh. The wind was getting up and there was rain in the air.

He saw her coming out of the store, weighed down by two bulging plastic bags. He quickly turned towards the castle, watching her out of the side of his eye. She moved away from him, westbound on Princes Street, lumbering along with her shoulders hunched. It was easier than he could ever have imagined. As she laboured her way up Hanover Street he decided to make it more interesting for himself and hurried his pace so that he was no more than twenty feet behind her, close enough to hear her gasping breath, stopping when she stopped and starting again when she continued her plodding ascent.

And then, as she reached George Street, the handle on one of her overloaded shopping bags gave way and the contents fell with a clatter onto the pavement. He stood frozen as he watched a tin can roll down the street towards him and then she turned to face him, bending down to retrieve her goods. He moved over to the side of the pavement and pretended to study the window display of a photographic shop.

'Oh, bugger, bugger, bugger!' said Rene as she watched the oxtail soup roll off down the road and disappear over the edge of the pavement. 'That's all I need.' She put the shopping bag on the ground and bent down to try to fashion a makeshift loop out of the broken handle. 'Right, should get me 'ome. Now where on earth did that soup get to?'

She had taken no more than two steps down the street when her attention was caught by a man in a mackintosh, twenty feet away from her, studying the window display of a small photographic shop. She saw the high cock's comb of hair and knew instantly who it was.

'Oh, bloody 'ell!' she murmured to herself and, without bothering to retrieve the lost can of soup, she took off across the street and scurried away as fast as her tired legs would carry her.

Albert Dessuin snatched a glance in the woman's direction, then spun round when he realised she had gone. After a quick appraisal of Hanover Street, he ran up to the junction with George Street. The full length of the street was heaving with pedestrians competing for space on pavements narrowed by queues awaiting entry into show venues. There was no sign of her. Albert smiled to himself. Maybe she had seen him, maybe not, but it did not matter. There was always another night.

Rene peered round the side of the shop doorway and looked along the length of George Street. A momentary gap opened up in the mass of people and she caught sight of the Frenchman at the junction, leaning his head one way and then the other as he searched the street.

'Oh, 'eck, it is me 'e's after,' Rene murmured to herself as she hurried off, weaving her way in and out of the crowds to keep herself hidden. 'You've got to get yourself off the street, lass.' She passed by a long queue formed outside a wide, glass-doored entrance and veered off towards the brightly lit haven, only to feel a hand grasp her shoulder.

'Hang on, love, you need a pass or a ticket to get in here.'

Rene looked up into the faces of two black-shirted bouncers.

'What kind of pass do I need?' Rene asked in desperation. She delved into the folds of her coat, pulling out the Fringe pass. 'Is this any use?'

'That's all we need,' one of the bouncers said, pushing open the door.

Rene bustled across the pillared, stone-floored hall and entered the double doors at the far end. The bar was crammed with people—on sofas, chairs, even on the tables. She set her shopping bags down on the floor, blowing out a long breath of nervous exhaustion.

'Rene!'

To her relief, the caller's tone was distinctly female. She scanned the room, seeing no one she knew, then spotted a bobbing mass of red hair threading its way towards her.

'Hi, there, girl. How're you doing?'

'Matti Fullbright, am I pleased to see you!' Rene exclaimed.

'You look all in. Let me get you a drink.'

'Aye, I'm needing one bad, luv,' Rene said, leaning heavy-elbowed on the bar. 'Bacardi and Coke would go down a treat.'

With a click of her fingers, Matti attracted the attention of the barman and ordered up two drinks. 'So what's been going on?'

'Ye won't believe who I've just seen out there in the street. The bloody Frenchman. I think 'e might 'ave been following me.'

The barman put two drinks down on the bar and Matti handed Rene her Bacardi and Coke. 'I doubt there's any way he could have been doing that. It's just a coincidence, that's all.'

'Some bloody coincidence!' Rene exclaimed, taking a hefty slug from her glass. 'Edinburgh's a big place just to go bumping into someone.'

'It happens all the time during the festival. I'm forever meeting people I know on the street.'

'Well, I suppose ye could be right,' Rene said. 'After all, 'ere's you and me meeting up again. That's pretty extraordinary, in't it?'

'Haven't you been here before?'

Rene gazed around the bar. 'No, never. Why should I?'

'All the Fringe acts congregate here at the end of the day.'

Rene shook her head in disbelief. 'Would you credit that? I'd no idea.'

Matti laughed. 'In that case, you didn't read all that bumph you were given. Anyway, how did the act go this evening?'

'Same as ever. Three foreigners and a drunk.'

Matti nodded. 'It's not been brilliant for me, neither. I think I'll have to do a major overhaul of my act quite soon, but I'm not sure how.'

'Maybe you should try doing it in the nude.'

Matti almost choked on her mouthful of gin and tonic. 'For God's sake, I don't want my audience to run screaming for the exits!'

The two women's laughter was so loud it made those around them turn to stare. Matti blew out a deep breath to control herself. 'Oh, my word, it does you good, don't it?'

'Tell that to the audience,' Rene replied with a giggle.

'Aye, maybe we should.' Matti took a drink from her glass and then turned to Rene, her eyes narrowed in thought. 'Listen, what're you doing tomorrow afternoon?'

Rene shrugged. 'Nowt at all.'

'Right, d'ye know the Royal Scottish Academy on Princes Street?'

'No, but I s'pose I could find it.'

'Good. Meet me there at one thirty.'

'Why?'

'I want you to come to see my new show.'

'What? Ye've worked something out already?'

'I think I might have just done that very thing, Rene my girl,' Matti replied. 'Come on, let's set up another round.'

Rene shook her head. 'I can't, thanks, lass,' she said, bending down to pick up her shopping bags. 'I've sort of taken on the evening cooking duties for these two lads in the flat.'

'Right,' Matti said disappointedly. 'Oh, well, see you tomorrow, then, and watch out for skulking Frenchmen.'

Why this evening? Tess Goodwin thought to herself as she leaned over in her seat hoping to see what had caused the bus to remain stationary for the past ten minutes. There had to be some sort of blockage up ahead. It was half past seven. The last thing she wanted to do was to arrive at the restaurant in a fluster.

Getting to her feet, she slung the strap of her laptop case onto her shoulder and walked down the aisle to stand by the driver. 'Are we going to be moving soon?' she asked, peering up the street.

'Nae idea,' the driver replied. 'Looks like an accident. Ah've just seen a police car head down past the roundabout on George Street.' He turned to her. 'How far are ye goin'?'

'Dundas Street.'

'D'yae want tae walk, then? Ye'd be better tae.' The doors opened with a swish and Tess jumped down onto the pavement.

This had to be the most imperfect climax to a gruelling week. The dinner with Peter Hansen had been permanently at the forefront of her mind. She was distracted at work, forgetting to organise press calls that would normally have been second nature to her, and then, because Peter had kept calling her she had become paranoid about her mobile phone ringing. She considered turning it off altogether, only she knew it was her lifeline during the festival.

But the worst had always been when her day's work was over and she had gone home to Allan. She had tried to act naturally with him, but everything she said or did seemed so deceiving. Eventually she resolved to plead utter exhaustion and keep all conversation between them to a minimum, hoping he would not question the sudden change in her mood and character. Every night she would lie beside him in bed, her eyes fixed on the television, while he would give up on his nightly attempts to make love to her and fall asleep with his head against her shoulder. She dreaded the day when she would have to meet Peter Hansen at the restaurant, yet she also longed for it so that she could put an end to this appalling charade and get her life with Allan back.

Just before arriving at the flat, she put her mobile to her ear. Her call was answered at once. 'Yes, it's Tess,' she said. 'I'm going to be late . . . I don't know, maybe half an hour . . . I'm on my way home now. I want to have a shower first . . . no, Peter, you read nothing into that.' Angrily, she put the mobile back into her handbag as she shouldered open the entrance door. She ascended the stairs quickly, praying she still had time to get changed and away before Allan came back from the office.

Her heart sank as soon as she walked into the flat. She could hear the television from the bedroom. Allan was lying propped up on the bed drinking a mug of tea, still in his suit trousers but with stockinged feet. An open newspaper lay beside him. His eyes momentarily left the television screen and she saw immediately the sadness in his eyes.

'Allan?' she asked quietly, feeling her heart give a jolt of apprehension. 'What's happened?'

He smiled at her. 'Nothing.' He zapped the television with the remote. 'Just been watching the end of some stupid romantic film. Got to me a bit.' He dropped the remote on the bed beside him. 'I came home early 'cos I thought we could go out to dinner.'

Tess bit her bottom lip. 'I can't, Allan. I've got to attend another reception tonight. I've just come home to change.' Feeling her face colour, she walked back over to the door. 'I'm just going to have a quick shower.' She returned five minutes later wrapped in a towel, her skin tingling from the scalding she had given herself in the hope it would purge her guilt. Allan was still sitting on the bed, still looking at her. She smiled at him as she walked over to the wardrobe and took out a dark red silk cocktail dress on a hanger.

'We need to talk,' Allan said.

Tess glanced round at him. 'What about?'

Allan shrugged. 'Anything you want. We haven't communicated for about a week, or maybe you haven't noticed.'

Tess placed the dress on a chair and walked across to the bed and sat down next to him. 'I know and I'm sorry. After tonight, things will be different, Allan, I promise.'

Allan shrugged and picked up the newspaper. 'Have you any idea what happened to Angélique Pascal?' he asked.

'No,' she said, walking over to a chest of drawers and taking out a pair of pants and a bra, 'other than she's returned to France.'

Allan let out a hollow laugh. 'You're really a strange one, Tess. A week ago you were beside yourself with worry about her, and now you're acting as if you couldn't give a damn.'

Dropping the towel to the ground, Tess slipped on her pants and her bra, and then stood for a moment staring at her reflection in the mirror on top of the chest. He was right, of course. She hadn't given Angélique another thought ever since she'd left. She was too preoccupied with her own damned problems. 'I *am* concerned about her,' she said, picking up the dress from the chair. 'It's just that—'

'*How* concerned are you?' he cut in. 'It's been over a week since she left Edinburgh and there's been no follow-up story, no progress report, not even a photograph. Don't you think that's a bit weird?'

Again, he was right. Even though she'd had her nose buried in the newspapers looking for reviews on artistes, it had not occurred to her there hadn't been a mention of Angélique.

'Maybe she's asked for some privacy during her convalescence,' she offered hopefully. 'She is quite a private person.'

'Come on, you know as well as I do the paparazzi don't give a damn about the privacy of *any* celebrity. It's all just money to them. And don't you think it's quite odd she hasn't been in touch with you? You became pretty chummy with her and she did have your mobile number.' He closed the newspaper. 'I think you should try to find out more about her because *I'm* concerned even if no one else appears to be.'

Tess gazed at him. 'You're right.' Pulling on her dress, she walked over to the door and left the room. She returned a few moments later with her mobile phone and address book. She sat down on the bed next to Allan, flicked through the pages and then began dialling a number.

'Who are you calling?' Allan asked.

'A reporter called Harry Wills,' Tess said, putting the phone to her ear.

Allan got to his feet. 'D'you want a cup of tea?'

'Hello? Harry Wills?' Tess asked, shaking her head at Allan's offer.

Five minutes later, Allan returned to the bedroom, mug of tea in hand, to find Tess staring out of the window. 'How did you get on?' he asked.

'He's coming round here now.'

'Why? What did he say?'

'Well, to begin with, he seemed quite adamant that Angélique had gone back to Paris, but then when I told him she was a friend of mine and that I couldn't understand why I hadn't heard from her, his attitude changed. He asked me how I'd met her and when was the last time I'd seen her, and then when I told him I worked in the International office, he said it would be best if he came round to see me.' She laid her mobile and address book down on the bedside table. 'Funny thing is, I recognise his voice. I'm sure it was Harry Wills who called the International office to break the news about Angélique's accident.'

'Sounds as if I was right, then,' Allan said, sitting down on the edge of the bed. 'My word, there seems to be a hell of a lot of cloak-and-dagger stuff going on at the festival this year.'

Tess shot him a worried glance out of the corner of her eye.

Forty minutes later, Tess closed the door of the flat behind Harry Wills and walked back to the bedroom. Allan was pulling on his suit jacket, studying the page the reporter had ripped out of his notebook.

'Where are you going?' she asked.

'Out to East Lothian. Someone's got to go and see Angélique.'

Tess bit her lip. This was decision time, but already, in her heart, she knew where she had to go. 'I'm coming too.'

'Don't bother,' he said, studying her face intently. 'You'd better go to your reception.'

She glanced at her wristwatch. A quarter to nine. It was all too late now, anyway. She didn't know what Peter Hansen's next step would be, but she was prepared to face the consequences. She picked up her handbag from the chest of drawers. 'No, I want to come.' She walked towards the door. 'I'll just make a quick phone call to Sarah Atkinson to say I won't make the reception.'

It was not a good time to be attempting to cross over to the other side of Edinburgh. The streets were clogged with traffic and pedestrians and for the greater part of the journey through the city Allan drove in silence, only breaking it to mutter some oath as the traffic lights changed to red each time he approached them. Tess didn't care. Her mind was completely set on the inevitable confrontation between herself and Sir Alasdair Dreyfuss. She kept trying to work out what she would say when he questioned her about her affair with Peter Hansen, knowing that whatever she said would make little difference. Her future as an employee of the International festival would be untenable.

When she had spoken to Peter Hansen on the phone before leaving the flat, he had been surprisingly understanding. 'How disappointing,' he had said. 'We must make it another night.' And she had replied, 'Maybe.' Now she thought to herself how much more self-preserving it would have been to have answered, 'Yes, of course,' but she knew she had made the right decision not to continue with this stupid damaging game any longer. Her job was expendable, but not her husband. This was the man she loved, and this was the man she did not want to lose.

She switched her mind to Angélique and wondered if she should ring her at the house in East Lothian to warn her they were on their way. She took her mobile from her handbag and picked up the slip of paper next to the gear stick on which Harry Wills had written the address and the mobile number of Angélique's friend, Jamie Stratton. She read his name again, trying to work out why it seemed familiar, and then her mind registered the meeting she had had in the Hub café with the elderly cameraman who had been desperate to find somewhere to stay. Distractedly she put her mobile back beside the gear stick and leaned her head against the window, thinking how extraordinary it was that she'd already spoken to Jamie Stratton.

The next thing she knew she was jolting herself awake, blinking her eyes at the glare of the oncoming headlights. The car was now travelling at speed along a dual carriageway. She reached across and squeezed Allan's hand. 'Sorry about that. I dropped off.'

'You must be exhausted,' he said. 'Too many late nights, burning the candle at both ends.'

Tess frowned. There was a frenetic edge to his voice. 'Not really.'

'Are you sleeping with him again, then?'

Tess felt her face go on fire. '*What?*'

'Peter bloody Hansen. You just can't stop yourself, can you? I saw him this evening. He was round at our flat knocking on the door. He recognised me and scuttled off like the rat he is.'

Tess shook her head. 'Allan, I—'

'Don't even start to tell me you didn't know he was here. Who was it you called just before you left the flat? Wasn't Sarah Atkinson, was it?' He picked up her mobile from beside the gear stick and punched at the buttons. 'Look,' he said, holding the screen centimetres from her face. 'Lo and behold, if that isn't the name of Peter Hansen. Now, are you going to tell me that's just coincidence?'

Tess closed her eyes tight. 'Stop the car.'

'Why? Do you want to get out here and walk all the way back to his loving arms? Is that what you want?'

'Please, just stop the car.'

Allan swerved into a lay-by at speed and slammed his foot on the brake and turned off the engine. The silence was absolute. Tess heard him let out a deep, quivering groan and turned to see him slump forward on the steering wheel, his head in his hands.

'I really didn't know he was going to turn up, Allan. He just did and the arrogant bastard expected everything to be exactly as it was before.'

Allan raised his head and looked at her. 'And was it?'

'No, of course it wasn't. I'm married to you now. I don't want anyone else in my life, least of all him.'

'But you were going to go out with him tonight, weren't you?'

Tess paused, realising at that moment how badly she had handled this whole situation. 'Yes, I was. I was going to have dinner with him.'

'Jesus!' Allan muttered angrily.

'Let me finish—please! I agreed to have dinner with him only because he threatened to tell Alasdair Dreyfuss about our'—the word stuck in Tess's throat—'"relationship". I didn't want to lose my job and I certainly didn't want to lose you. I was going to have dinner with him and that was going to be the end of it. I decided not to tell you about him being here, because . . . well, I thought I could handle it myself.'

'Why? Did it never occur to you that this involves me as well? If you screw up your life, you screw up mine as well.'

Tess looked down into her lap, feeling tears of stupidity and hopelessness begin to well up in her eyes. 'I know, and I'm really sorry. I should have told you.' She opened the glove box in front of her and took out a box of tissues. She pulled out a wodge and wiped her eyes. 'I have hated this week more than any week in my whole life. I've felt I've been betraying you every moment of it.'

There was a long silence before Allan broke it. 'I don't know what to say, Tess. I thought we'd made an agreement we would never hold back secrets from each other. And now you've just blown the whole thing out of the window, as if all those endless talks on trust and reconciliation were totally expendable. And yes, that's exactly how you always end up making *me* feel—utterly expendable.'

Tess laid a hand on his arm. 'Please, you must never, ever think that. I know I've made a hash of things but you have to remember that nothing happened, Allan, and nothing similar will ever happen again in the future, because you are the only person I want in my life.'

With a shake of his head, Allan turned the key in the ignition, pumping his foot on the accelerator, making the engine roar angrily to life. 'We'd better go and find Angélique.'

'Can't we call a truce first?' Tess asked quietly

Allan turned to her, letting out a long breath of consideration. 'OK, but for your friend's sake only, because, Tess, you think back on what you've just said about nothing similar happening again. You used almost exactly the same words last year.'

'I know what is going to occur next,' Angélique said as she and Jamie lay on the sofa in the sitting room, the only source of the light coming from the television. 'The man with the beard has followed her home and got into the house.'

'How?'

'Through an open window, maybe?'

'Wrong.'

Angélique lifted her head from his chest and turned to look at him. 'Why do you think that?'

'Could be intuition.' He smiled at her. 'Or could be because I've seen the film before.'

'Oh, you are such a cheat!' she exclaimed, reaching for a cushion. The imminent blow never struck its target, as her arm stopped mid-arc when the door of the drawing-room opened and the lights were turned on. Both she and Jamie turned to see Rory Stratton standing there.

'Hi, Dad,' Jamie said. 'I thought you'd turned in.'

'Yes, well, I was on my way upstairs when I heard a car arriving. You've got visitors.'

The news brought them straight to their feet. Jamie stared in bewilderment at the young couple that entered the room, having never set eyes on either of them before. Both were dressed as if they had been to a party, the man in a suit, the young woman in a dark red cocktail dress. He spun round when he heard Angélique let out a gasp of astonishment.

'Tess!' She crossed the room and flung her arms round the woman.

'Oh, Angélique, how are you?' the young woman said, giving her a kiss on both cheeks. 'We've only just found out what happened to you.'

Angélique pushed herself away. 'But how did you know I was here?'

'Yeah, good question,' Jamie said, looking suspiciously at the couple.

'Well, then, find out over a drink, Jamie,' his father retorted, still standing by the door as he shot a steely glare of disapproval at his son's lack of welcome. 'I'm off to my bed, so I'll bid everyone good night.' He was about to leave the room when he glanced back at Jamie. 'If you want to talk into the small hours, Allan and Tess can stay the night if they want. The double bed's usually made up in the top spare room.'

Jamie nodded. 'Thanks.'

As Rory shut the door behind him, the two women walked to the sofa and sat down, engrossed in a deep private conversation. Jamie forced a smile on his face as he approached the man, his hand outstretched. 'Hi, we haven't met. Jamie Stratton.'

The man shook his hand. 'Allan Goodwin. And that's Tess—my wife.'

'Right . . . so, what can I get you to drink?'

'A beer would do me fine.'

'And for Tess?'

Allan shrugged. 'Just something soft. She's driving home.'

'Where exactly is home?' Jamie asked as he walked over to the drinks tray, not yet willing to extend his father's offer of a bed until he had found out more about the couple.

'Edinburgh,' Allan replied, following him across the room. 'In fact, Tess says she knows you. She spoke to you on the telephone.'

'Concerning what?'

'Renting a room to a Mr Hartson? She said he was a cameraman.'

Jamie stared hard at the man. 'I seem to remember that call came from the International Festival office.'

'It would have done. Tess works there.'

'Oh, I see,' Jamie replied. 'But it couldn't have been Mr Hartson told you we were here. He had no idea where we were going.'

'No, that information came from a reporter called Harry Wills.'

'*Harry Wills?*' Jamie exclaimed incredulously, just stopping short of overflowing a glass of Coca-Cola over the floor. 'Excuse me for asking this, but why did he think it necessary to tell your wife?'

'Because Tess hadn't heard from Angélique since she left for France. She called Harry because she knew he'd had contact with Angélique.'

'And Harry . . . told you everything?'

'Yes, he thought it would be safe enough now. He said he'd stopped his vigil outside your flat about three nights ago.'

'Yes, I know that. He phoned me. But I didn't expect him to start telling people we were here.'

'Don't worry, neither Tess nor I will be breathing a word to anyone.' Allan studied the look of distrust on Jamie's face as the young man handed the glass of Coca-Cola to Tess. 'I think, quite honestly,' Allan continued quietly when Jamie had returned to pour him his beer, 'that the more allies you have in your camp, the better. Tess has become a good friend of Angélique, and she would never do anything to jeopardise either her safety or her privacy.'

Jamie handed Allan his beer, and then looked over to where Angélique and Tess were chatting. He gave a shrug. 'I wonder why Angélique never mentioned her friendship with Tess to me.'

Allan shot a withering look at Tess and shook his head. 'I'm afraid that's the female mind for you,' he said, raising his glass of beer in salute. 'They have a bloody awful habit of keeping secrets from us men.'

Jamie raised his glass to the man. 'I'm sorry about being a bit . . . well, unfriendly towards you. I was completely thrown into this whole game and I suppose it has made me quite . . . protective towards her.'

'Yes, I can see that,' Allan replied, glancing briefly at Angélique before turning back with a grin, 'and I think I can understand why.'

Jamie felt his face colour. 'So, how about it?' he asked, deciding to change tack to avoid further discussion on the subject. 'Do you want to stay the night? As my father said, the bed's made up.'

'Thank you, that's very kind. We wouldn't want to impose on you.'

'No imposition at all,' Jamie replied, walking over to the drinks tray. 'In that case, we have no excuse now not to hit the hard stuff.'

'**H**ang on, lass, stop kicking around,' Rory Stratton muttered, squeezing his legs tighter around the body of the ewe to stop her from making a break for freedom. 'Right, let's see if we can't get you back into shape.'

He turned to pick up an aerosol antibiotic from the ground and started when he saw the figure standing behind him. 'You're up bright and early,' Rory said to the young man he had welcomed to the house the previous evening. He gave the aerosol a shake as he appraised the man's attire. 'Not wearing the ideal clothes for a visit to a sheep pen.'

Allan glanced down at his dark blue suit and black shoes, and smiled. 'You're right, but I just felt like a walk.' He leaned on the wooden railing. 'Do you always talk to them like that?'

Rory laughed. 'A bit mad, eh?' He bent down and gave the ewe's hoof a spray. 'My wife accuses me of speaking more to my sheep than I do to her. She calls them the other women in my life.'

Allan pushed his hands into the pockets of his trousers. 'At least your wife only has to compete with a load of woolly animals.'

Rory detected the melancholy in his voice. He eased the ewe forward onto her front hooves and let her go, then watched as she ran to the far side of the pen. He walked over to the railing and put the aerosol can in a bag that hung on one of the posts. 'Have you been married long?'

Allan stared at him. 'Why do you ask?'

'Well, it's probably none of my business, but I just saw that shiny new ring on your finger and wondered why someone would prefer to trudge round a muddy farmyard at this time in the morning, rather than choosing to be tucked up in bed with a beautiful young wife.'

'Sometimes things aren't how they seem, if you get my meaning.'

Rory laughed. 'I know exactly what you mean! I'm afraid, my friend, that's just one of the anomalies of marriage. You'd think after twenty-seven years of being wedded to my wife, there'd be a Zen-like plane of understanding between us and we'd avoid the pitfalls we know put us at loggerheads—but no.' He flashed a wicked smile at the young man before walking across the pen to release the ewe into the paddock. 'I think it's healthy to have a bit of fire in a marriage.'

'And what about trust?' Allan asked.

'That's fundamental.'

'So there should be no secrets, nothing hidden?'

'That depends on their context, whether they're being deployed for deception or protection. One represents total breakdown in communication, the other love.' Rory climbed over the railings and he smiled at the young man. 'Don't think marriage is always going to be a bed of roses, but it's infinitely better than sitting on a dung heap by yourself.'

Allan smiled. 'That's a good quote. I might use it sometime.'

'Remember where you heard it first. A Stratton original.' He nodded his head in the direction of the house. 'I think you might have company.'

Allan turned to see Tess coming towards them. He glanced back at Rory. 'We'll be heading back to Edinburgh soon, so if we don't see you, many thanks for letting us stay the night, and, erm . . . for the advice.'

'My pleasure,' Rory said. 'Have a good journey back.' He made his way to the lambing shed, hung up the bag on a nail inside the door and then walked over to the grain store to turn on the drying plant. Ten minutes later he was astride the quad bike in the lambing shed. He fired up the engine and drove it outside. A hundred metres away, he spotted the young couple still standing in the middle of the road talking, and then he witnessed the man drawing his wife to him and kissing her long on the mouth. Rory grinned with satisfaction at the sight and then set off at speed up the dirt track road.

Fourteen

SIR ALASDAIR DREYFUSS placed the cup of coffee on his desk and sat down, rubbing at the fatigue that was smarting in his eyes. For the past ten days, the earliest he had been to his bed was two o'clock in the morning and it was really beginning to tell. Almost immediately, the telephone began to ring.

'Oh, where the hell is everyone?' he exclaimed, grabbing the receiver on its sixth ring. 'Hello, International Festival.'

'Alasdair?' a woman's voice asked.

'Yes,' the director answered, a quizzical frown on his face.

'It's Birgitte Hansen.'

'Birgitte!' Alasdair exclaimed, leaning back in his chair, relaxing immediately in the knowledge it was to be a social call. 'How are you?'

'I am good.'

'And the family?'

'Busy doing different things. We are all very much looking forward to our holiday with you, Paula and the kids in Lillehammer next April.'

Alasdair laughed. 'That goes for me too. We're bang in the middle of the festival here and it's chaos in the office. How's Peter getting on?'

There was a long silence. 'I'm sorry,' Birgitte said. 'What did you say?'

'I wondered how Peter was?'

'But you should know how Peter is. He is with you in Edinburgh. He is directing some plays for you.' Alasdair began to note a rising level of desperation in her voice. 'I am sending him something in the post today as a surprise, but I do not know the address of his hotel and I don't want to contact him on his mobile phone, so I wondered if you might be able to tell me.'

Alasdair rubbed his brow. 'Birgitte, I'm sorry, but if he's here in Edinburgh I haven't seen him and he isn't directing anything for me.'

He heard her mutter something forcefully in Danish.

'Birgitte, are you all right?' he asked concernedly.

There was a long sigh. 'Yes, I'm all right,' she replied in a resigned, almost sad voice. 'Tell me, Alasdair, do you know of a girl called Tess?'

'Well, I suppose you'll be referring to Tess Goodwin. She works in the office here.'

'Ah, she still works there? I found out she was quite a friend of Peter's.'

'I suppose she was. She looked after him a couple of years ago, when he first came here to direct.'

'And she did a very good job, not just for one year, but for two.'

Alasdair frowned. 'I'm not sure quite what you mean, Birgitte.'

'Peter had an affair with this girl. It went on for the two years he was in Edinburgh and I found out about it last year.'

Alasdair stared with shock at the door of his office. 'Are you sure?'

'I heard it from Peter himself. He is like a little boy, Alasdair. He has to tell me everything to . . . to exonerate himself.'

Alasdair ran a hand over his head. 'Birgitte, I had no idea. Why on earth do you stand for it?'

'Because of the children and because—this may sound stupid to you—but because he is honest about his indiscretions.' She sighed again. 'However, it looks like his affair with this Tess has continued, so maybe this time I have to make a decision.'

'I really don't think you're right on this one, Birgitte. Tess got married earlier this year. I just can't see her jeopardising that relationship.'

'Do you know how long she went out with her husband before they got married?'

'Yes, quite some time. I think about three—' Alasdair stopped abruptly when he realised what he was saying. He closed his eyes. 'Oh, Birgitte, I really don't know what to say.'

'It's all right. It is my problem. I shall find out the truth.' She laughed quietly. 'He will no doubt tell me. Goodbye, Alasdair.'

He returned the farewell and thumped the receiver back on its cradle. A moment later the phone rang again; this time it was an internal extension that flashed.

'Good morning, Alasdair.' It was Sarah Atkinson. 'I've got Peter Hansen holding for you on line one. Do you want to speak to him?'

'Well, speak of the devil. Yes, I most certainly do. Sarah, would you send Tess into my office as soon as I've finished this call?'

'Will do.'

As soon as she had hung up, Alasdair heard the smooth voice of Peter Hansen greeting him with his usual self-confident charm.

'Peter,' Alasdair cut in vehemently, 'I've just spoken to Birgitte, and if I were you, you stupid bastard, I'd zip up your trousers and get back to her as fast as you bloody well can.'

He slammed down the receiver and jumped to his feet, then walked over to the window, trying to gather his thoughts before Tess came in. There was a knock on the door.

'Come in!'

He turned as Tess walked in and he could tell from the apprehensive expression on her face that Sarah had warned her some kind of confrontation was imminent.

'Take a seat, Tess,' he said, gesturing towards the armchair at the other side of the desk. He watched as she sat down, nervously smoothing her skirt over her knees. 'Are you all right?'

'Yes, fine. Ready for what the world has to throw at me.'

'Right.' He cleared his throat. 'Tess, there's no easy way to ask this, but did you . . . have you been having an affair with Peter Hansen?'

She nodded slowly. 'You've obviously spoken to him.'

'Very briefly, but it was his wife who's just broken the news to me.'

Tess closed her eyes and lowered her head. 'I had no idea she knew.'

'So it's been going on for three years?'

She jolted up her head. 'No, it all finished last year. I had no idea he was going to turn up again. About a week and a half ago, he rang you out of the blue, don't you remember? You put him through to me.'

'He was here in Edinburgh at that time?'

'Yes, and he literally forced me into meeting with him.'

'How did he do that?'

'By implying that he would tell you about our affair if I first didn't see him, and then later, go out for dinner with him.'

Alasdair rubbed his fingers across his brow. 'For heaven's sake, that's as good as blackmail. But, Tess, you didn't, er, succumb to him this time, did you?'

Tess could not help but smile at his formality. 'No, of course I didn't. I'm happily married now, Alasdair, and I certainly wouldn't put that at risk. I agreed to have dinner with him last night. I've no doubt he viewed it as the necessary stepping stone in order to rekindle the affair, but it was going to be my opportunity to tell him to get out of my life.'

'And did you say that to him?'

'No. For one reason or another, I didn't turn up.'

Alasdair nodded slowly. 'So that's obviously why he called me this morning . . . to let the cat out of the bag.'

'I'm sure.' Tess leaned forward, resting a hand on the desk. 'I don't even know how to start apologising to you, Alasdair. I know he's a great friend of yours and I can't imagine what his wife is thinking—'

'She's thinking it is all still going on.'

'I promise you that's not true. It ended pretty acrimoniously last year, but I still feel so guilty for allowing it all to happen and for letting you down so badly.'

Alasdair gave a dismissive wave of his hand. 'Tess, you've no reason to feel that way. *I'm* the one that's guilty.'

She stared at him, perplexed. 'I'm sorry?'

'I didn't admit it to his wife, but I've known for years that Peter is a philanderer. He's had girls in every country he's worked in. I should *never* have put you in charge of him for that first year. It was as good as sending a lamb to slaughter. It's me who owes *you* the apology.'

Tess remained silent for a moment. 'Thank you,' she said quietly. 'I can't tell you how good that makes me feel.'

Alasdair smiled at her. 'And how bloody awful it makes me feel.'

Tess rubbed nervously at the palm of her hand. 'And . . . what about my job? Do you want me to continue?'

The director stared incredulously at her. 'Of course I do. You have become an extremely important part of the team here, Tess. I think, quite honestly, you could not have handled this appalling situation with Peter Hansen any better.'

'Yes, I could. I told Allan last year about the affair and that was the main reason we spurred on the marriage, but I never told him about Peter Hansen returning again and he found out.'

'Oh, my word, no,' Alasdair replied. 'Has it caused great difficulties?'

'I thought I'd blown it completely, but we eventually managed to reason it out. If there's any upside to this whole stupid situation, it has to be that it's made me appreciate just what a special person Allan is.'

'Well, what a lucky girl you are to have hooked him.'

Tess grinned. 'Yes, I know.'

Following hard on Matti Fullbright's heels, Rene entered the Smirnoff Underbelly at the top door beneath a narrow archway from which a sign of an upside-down cow with gravity-defying teats was suspended, and descended the steps into a small, brightly painted reception area.

'Is this it?' Rene asked as she looked around, wondering why so much hype surrounded this Hobbit-sized venue.

'Just you wait,' Matti replied. 'Don't make a judgment until you've seen the whole place.' She led the way down a circular stone staircase, each step worn by centuries of use. Spotlights played on the thick dark walls, plastered from top to bottom with posters. At the bottom of the flight it opened out into a small but crowded space, off which led two doors hung with signs reading QUIET PLEASE, SHOW IN PROGRESS.

'Come on, keep up,' Matti said as she led on down another identical flight of stairs.

'I don't know if I'm enjoying this very much,' Rene said, putting her hands against the dank walls to steady her descent. 'It's like going into the bowels of the earth. What is this place?'

'Old bank vaults,' Matti's disembodied voice echoed up the stairwell. 'They're supposed to be haunted.'

'Oh, bloody 'ell,' Rene mumbled, hurrying to catch up with her guide. They eventually ran out of staircases, coming out into a large bar that was filled to bursting point.

'This is the famous Beer Belly,' Matti said as she pushed her way through to the blue-fronted bar. 'I'll get us some drinks up and meet you outside in the yard.' She pointed a finger towards an entrance at the far end of the room.

Rene threaded her way through the crowd and walked out through the lower entrance door into a narrow cobbled alleyway, its fifty-metre length strung with a dazzle of lighted bulbs. Small, open-doored rooms and arched alcoves lined the street, each set up as a temporary coffee stall or fast-food kitchen. Rene stopped in front of a huge board that showed the full programme of events, smiling at the puns that gave names to each of the venues—Belly Button, Belly Dancer, Delhi Belly. She scanned the list of acts, eventually finding Matti's name under a column headed Belly Laugh.

'Here y'are,' Matti said as she handed her an enormous glass brimming with spitting bubbles. 'A very large Bacardi and Coke.'

''Eavens, lass, I'm not used to drinking in the middle of the day.'

'You're going to need it,' she said, grabbing Rene by the arm. 'Come on, I'm running late.'

The musty-smelling changing room was as sparsely furnished as a nun's cell, yet it was a hundred times more salubrious than the Corinthian Bar. 'Take off your coat and sling it on a chair,' Matti said as she hurried to get herself ready, 'and then go out on stage and have a squint through the curtains. I need to know if there's anyone out there.'

Shrugging off her coat, Rene walked round the side wing and out onto the stage. She pulled the curtain aside a fraction, catching her breath when she saw that the auditorium was jam-packed. She scuttled back to the changing room.

'It doesn't look as if there's a spare seat in the place!' she said to Matti, who was trying to fix a red rose in her hair with a kirby grip.

'Fantastic!' she exclaimed, picking up the plastic bag she had brought with her. 'Just what I wanted.' She extracted a white rose and another kirby grip from the bag and handed it to Rene.

'Stick that in your hair, girl.'

'What for?'

'Don't ask, just do it.'

Moving over to the mirror, Rene arranged the rose above her right ear and secured it with the grip. She stood back, swinging from side to side as she admired herself. 'A touch of Carmen, don't ye think?'

'You look perfect,' Matti said, pulling Rene by the arm out towards the stage as the announcer began his rambling introduction.

'I'd better go and try to find a seat out there,' Rene said, trying to wrest her arm free from Matti's grip.

'Leave it to the last minute, would you? I'm feeling dead nervous about my act today.'

'. . . so, ladies and gentlemen,' the announcer's voice crescendoed through the sound system, 'will you please welcome that red-haired lady from Lancashire, MATTI-I-I-I FULLBRIGHT!'

As the curtains drew back and the audience burst into applause and loud whistles, Rene tried once more to free herself from Matti's vicelike hand. 'I'd better get off now,' she said.

'Too late. We're on.' Matti gave Rene an almighty heave and the next thing she knew she was standing in the middle of the stage in front of the largest audience she had faced since being in Edinburgh.

'Good evening, everybody, good evening!' Matti yelled out, waving her hands in the air in acknowledgment of the thundering applause. 'OK, calm down, calm down.'

She turned to Rene and eyed her in a strangely hostile way as the noise abated. 'I decided tonight to bring along a friend with me. Well, not really a friend, actually. How could she be?' She nodded knowingly. 'She's from Yorkshire.' She turned and walked towards Rene, giving her a wink as she approached. 'Ladies and gentlemen,' she said, putting her arm round Rene's shoulders, 'this is Rene Brownlow, one of the funniest women I know, but unfortunately'—she patted Rene's stomach— 'coming from Hartlepool, she's too fond of her fish suppers.'

As the audience burst out laughing, Rene looked up at Matti, aghast. Her fellow comedienne smiled and leaned over and whispered in her ear, 'Come on, defend your rose.'

And then Rene understood. The red rose of Lancashire, the white rose of Yorkshire. Matti was setting up a double act. No rehearsals, no scripts. She wanted a duel of head-to-head ad-libbing, one bouncing off the other. The audience was silent, waiting for the riposte. She slowly unwound Matti's arm from her shoulders and stood her distance from her, appraising her from head to foot. 'You're a fine one to talk, ye red-'aired tramp. Bad breeding, that's what it is'—she held out her hands to the audience—'but what can ye expect, coming from Lancashire.' And with that, the partisan spirit of the audience was unleashed with whoops of support and cries of umbrage.

It was the perfect ice-breaker, but neither Matti nor Rene could keep up the animosity during the performance, and they settled into an off-the-cuff routine that had both the audience and themselves in fits of laughter. At the end of the show the audience clapped and banged their feet for ten minutes before the curtain finally fell on the two performers.

'**R**ead that!' Matti exclaimed, striding across the Assembly Rooms bar and throwing a copy of the *Evening News* at Rene.

'What is it?' she asked, putting her drink on the table.

'Just read it and see,' Matti said, her face aflame with excitement.

Rene scanned the newsprint, trying to find what she was meant to be looking for, and then her own name bounced out at her. She moved quickly to the start of the small article, entitled 'War of the Roses'.

> This had to be written today. It couldn't wait. At two o'clock this afternoon, the Belly Laugh venue lived up to its name when two comediennes took to the stage for a raucous side-splitting, hour-long ad-lib session.
>
> Wacky-haired Lancastrian Matti Fullbright, a favourite with audiences at the Underbelly for the past three years, teamed up with feisty little Yorkshire lass Rene Brownlow (currently appearing at the Corinthian Bar in West Richmond Street) to produce one of the most pulsating double acts seen so far on the Fringe this year. And rumour has it that it's not going to be a one-off either, so go beg, steal or kill your best friend for a ticket. It's just a pity they hadn't pooled their considerable talents before now, because there's no doubt they would have been up there with the front-runners contesting the Perrier Comedy Award for this year.

'Did you find it?' Matti asked, placing two glasses on the table before applying all her strength to prising the cork out of a bottle of Cava.

Rene could not reply. She read through the article again, taking in every accolade, every nuance of what the reviewer was implying. 'What have we done?' she asked, her eyes registering total incomprehension.

'We've cracked it, Rene, that's what we've done.'

'But what's all this about the show continuing? We never said that.'

Matti grinned as she filled the glasses with frothing liquid. 'I did.'

Rene stared at Matti in disbelief.

'Why not? We're electric, Rene. I've never had a reaction to any of my shows like that. Have you?'

Rene looked at Matti open-mouthed. 'Are ye saying that . . . we should team up, like?'

'Of course I am!' The grin slid from her face, taking Rene's blank expression as one of rejection to the idea. 'Don't you want to?'

Rene slowly shook her head. 'Matti, ye're successful. Ye've been working the Fringe for years. For God's sakes, ye've even got an agent! Ye don't want to be saddled with me.'

'What d'you mean, "saddled with you"? Rene, it's vice versa! I told you I had to change my act. I need you. The question is do you need me?'

'But what about my own show in the Corinthian? What about that?'

'Ditch it! You said yourself you weren't getting the punters in. We'll go fifty-fifty on everything. That'll cover all your costs and more.'

Rene bit her bottom lip to stop her face from crumpling into tears. It didn't work. She got up from the sofa, walked around the table and put her arms round Matti's neck. 'Thanks, lass, thanks so much.'

Matti chuckled. 'Do I take that as a yes, then?' she asked, pushing Rene away from her.

Rene snuffled out a laugh. 'Aye, why not? Let's go for it.'

'Oh, that is great, girl!' Matti said, punching her fists in the air. She picked up the two glasses from the table and handed one to Rene. 'Here's to us, my love, here's to the War of the bloody Roses!'

On the Thursday, two days before the last acts of the Festival Fringe were to be staged and nine days before the final curtain was brought down on the International Festival, four white trucks, emblazoned with the Exploding Sky Company logo drove slowly across the castle esplanade through a chevron of tourists. Once the leading truck was parked in the Castle's inner courtyard, Roger Dent jumped down from the cab and stretched his arms above his head, ridding himself of the stiffness in his body after the ten-hour drive. He walked over to the battlements and looked out across the New Town while the other trucks came through the tunnel and drew in close to his own. Roger pushed himself up onto the wall and sat watching as the drivers made their way over to him. Every one of his crew had at least two years' experience of this job, each choosing to spend his two-week summer holiday helping him put the show together. They were a crazy bunch of misfits—Dave Panton, a weapons expert for the Ministry of Defence; Graham Slattery, a computer programmer with IBM; and Annie Beardsley, an air traffic controller at Gatwick Airport—but they seemed to gel as a team.

And it was just as well he had an experienced group with him this year. The programme he and Phil Kenyon had devised for the climax of the Festival was to be the most work-intensive his company had ever dared stage, the intricately timed detonation of over five tonnes of fireworks in thirty minutes. Even now, the thought of the logistics was enough to make his stomach knot tight in trepidation.

'Right, before we adjourn to the pub,' Roger began, a remark that received an immediate cry of approval from his attentive audience, 'I'm afraid there's a good bit of work to be done. We'll start by unloading all the workshop equipment and get it set up under the stairs in the master gunner's office. Lay it out exactly as we've done in previous years. If we get all that done this afternoon, we'll start loading the shells first thing tomorrow.' He pushed himself off the wall. 'OK, make a move.'

As the crew headed back to their vans, Phil Kenyon appeared from one end of the narrow terrace and made his way across to Roger. 'All looks good,' the Australian remarked, handing Roger a clipboard with pad attached. 'The riggers are due to arrive first thing on Saturday morning. The briefing will take most of the day, so we'll start getting the multicore cabling laid out on Sunday morning.'

'And when are you due to meet up with the score reader?'

Phil shot him a wink. 'The beautiful Helen? She's coming across from Glasgow tomorrow afternoon, so we'll start then on the timing plan.'

'It could take quite a while. A lot of those new cues will be completely alien to her.'

'We'll make it, as long as we don't have too many interruptions.'

As Phil said this, a young woman in a suit came through the castle tunnel and strutted meaningfully towards them. 'Oh-oh, I spoke too soon,' Phil said. 'You deal with her and I'll go and help the others.'

He headed off to the vans and Roger leaned back against the wall as Pauline McCann, PR coordinator for the Scottish Bank, the main sponsor of the fireworks display, approached. 'Hi, there, Pauline, how're things with you?' He gave her a welcoming peck on the cheek.

'Working away, Roger,' the woman replied jovially. She dug a hand into her shoulder bag and extracted a moleskin notebook. 'Right, first off, I have a few messages for you. Jeff Banyon wants to meet you at the Scottish Chamber Orchestra office tomorrow evening, so he asked if you'd give him a call. And Sir Raymond Garston, the conductor, would like to meet up around lunchtime on Tuesday at the Balmoral Hotel.' She flicked over a page of her book. 'Now, the International office has scheduled the press call this year for Monday morning at ten o'clock. Does that sound all right for you?'

Roger shrugged. 'As long as you keep it as brief as possible.'

Pauline smiled at him. 'I'll do my best.' She put the notebook back in her bag. 'I'll send out a blanket email to all the papers, so is there anything you can tell me about what you've got planned this year?'

'It's going to be the largest and the most complicated display I've ever staged. I'm throwing every bit of caution to the wind.'

'Any reason for that?'

Roger nodded slowly. 'It's to be my last show.'

'*What*?' Pauline exclaimed, eyes wide in disbelief. 'But you can't . . . you've been doing it for . . .'

'This is the twenty-third year,' Roger offered.

'So . . . does this mean it's the last year the Exploding Sky Company will be doing the Fireworks Display?'

'I hope not. Phil Kenyon is taking on the business, so I suppose it'll be up to him and the Scottish Bank as the sponsors. You'd be doing me a favour in letting them know before the story hits the press. You can entitle your press release "Going out with a bang!"'

Pauline laughed. 'That's not such a bad idea, actually. Maybe you should think about starting a second career as a journalist.'

About the same time as the clientele of the Queen's Head in Grassmarket was swelled by the ranks of the Exploding Sky Company, a mud-spattered Land Rover was pulling up outside a flat in London Street. Rory Stratton clambered out and walked round to open up the back door.

'Thanks for the lift, Dad,' Jamie said, hoisting the straps of the two bags onto his shoulder and taking the violin case in his hand. 'Do you want to come up for a drink?'

Rory shook his head. 'No, I'll head home. I half promised your mother to take her out for a meal in the pub this evening.'

'You should do that. It'll give her a break. I don't think she realised she was going to have to put up with us for a whole week.'

Rory put a hand on his son's shoulder. 'It was a great time. We both loved it.' He walked over to Angélique and gave her a kiss on either cheek. 'And what a bonus meeting you, my beautiful French girl. Keep in touch with Jamie's old fogies now, won't you?'

'Of course I will,' Angélique replied, giving him a long hug. 'Thank you so much for having me to stay, Rory. It has been wonderful.'

Rory smiled, then turned back to Jamie. 'Look after yourself, boy, and keep in touch.'

'Will do, Dad.' They waited until the Land Rover had pulled away from the kerb before Jamie put the key in the door and they both entered the building. No more than twenty seconds after the door had closed behind them, a dishevelled figure hurried across the street and up the steps and pressed his hands against the door, as if willing it to open. Albert Dessuin turned away and slowly slid his back down the door to sit on the cold stone step, feeling the damp seep through the fabric of his raincoat. He cared little for that, or for the general grubbiness of his appearance, because now he had found Angélique Pascal.

Five days had passed since he had followed the fat little comedienne back to this address. How his whole life had changed in that time. At first, he thought the refusal of his credit card at a restaurant had been a fault of the electronic banking system, but then when he tried it in four automatic machines without success, he knew something was amiss.

Returning to his hotel, he had phoned his bank in Paris and was informed that his monthly cheque had not been paid in. He had instantly rung the lawyers in Clermont Ferrand, demanding to know why his salary had not been paid. A Monsieur Chambert introduced himself in a frosty voice as the recently appointed secretary of the trust set up by Madame Lafitte for Angélique Pascal. Albert could do nothing but listen in mute horror as the man recounted to him in a controlled, precise manner, every detail of what took place between himself and Angélique on the night of the 16th of August in the Sheraton Grand, as a result of which it was considered by the trustees that he, Albert Dessuin, was an unsuitable chaperone for Angélique Pascal and that his contract of employment was to be terminated with immediate effect. No consideration should be given to financial compensation. At that point Albert Dessuin could hear the change in the lawyer's voice as he spat out his closing line: 'And if you ever go near Mademoiselle Pascal again, I will make sure every police force in the world has knowledge of what you have done. Goodbye, Dessuin.'

He had booked himself out of the hotel immediately and had eventually ended up staying in a grubby room above a pub in Tollcross, where he had spent many a lonely hour, his mind increasingly embroiled with hatred and revenge. Monsieur Chambert had confirmed to him that Angélique had been divulging what had happened that night. He could now sense a thousand pairs of judging eyes upon him, watching his every move with distrust and loathing.

He pulled out a half-bottle of whisky from the inside pocket of his mackintosh and got to his feet, steadying himself on the cast-iron handrail as he left. The waiting was over. A few more hours, even a few more days would make no difference. Eventually he would be able to confront Angélique Pascal and ask her why, after all those years he had sacrificed for her, she had chosen to ruin him.

The delicious aroma of roast chicken was floating around the hallway when Jamie and Angélique entered the flat. Rene Brownlow, Leonard Hartson and his young assistant, T.K., were seated at the kitchen table, in the throes of eating, a glass of red wine in front of each. When he and Angélique walked in his three tenants turned to look their way. 'Well, if it's not our absentee landlord,' Rene said with a smile.

'Yeah, sorry about that,' Jamie replied. 'We stayed a bit longer than expected.' He eyed the plates piled with food on the table. 'You seem to have been coping all right, though.'

'Aye, well, someone had to play mother for these poor starving lads.' She pushed herself to her feet. ''Ow about some for yourselves? There's masses left over.' Grabbing a cloth from the sideboard, Rene opened the door of the oven and took out an enormous roast chicken, one side of it still untouched. 'Come on, join the party.'

'Are you sure?' Jamie asked.

'Of course you must,' Leonard Hartson cut in, pulling an unoccupied chair away from the table. 'Move yourself round the table, T.K., and allow the young lady a bit of space beside you.'

'Hello,' Angélique said, reaching across the table to shake hands with the two men. 'My name is Angélique Pascal.'

'What a pleasure!' Leonard said, bowing his head as he took her hand. 'I have long been an admirer of your wonderful playing.' He introduced both himself and T.K. to Angélique.

Rene placed two plates brimming with chicken, vegetables and potatoes on the table. 'Right, get stuck in.' She took two wineglasses from the cupboard above the worktop and put them next to the plates. 'And I'm sure Leonard wouldn't mind if you had some of 'is wine.'

Sitting down next to T.K., Angélique took a sip from her glass. 'It is delicious. You are obviously knowledgeable about wines, Leonard.'

'Leonard knows a lot aboot everythin',' T.K. stated with pride.

The cameraman laughed. 'Flattery will get you everywhere, T.K.'

As Jamie took his seat, he looked across the table. The old man seemed to have aged visibly. His eyes were twinkling, but they were set deep into a chalky-white face lined with either worry or pain.

'So, how's it going with the filming?' Jamie asked.

'A little bit behind in our schedule,' Leonard replied. 'But hopefully we'll be able to complete everything in the next nine days.'

'The stuff we've shot so far's been great, isn't that right, Leonard?' T.K. said, looking eagerly at the cameraman.

'The reports from London have been encouraging.' He shot a clandestine wink at Jamie. 'My assistant is a constant boost to my morale.'

Jamie swallowed a mouthful of food. 'Well, I'm glad all's been going so well while we've been away.'

'Aye, an' for Rene, too,' T.K. said.

Jamie turned to the comedienne. 'Really?'

'Go on, Rene, tell 'em whit's happened tae you's,' T.K. prompted.

Rene's face flushed to a colour similar to that of the wine. 'I've . . . erm . . . started a new show. In the Underbelly.'

Jamie stared at her. 'You're kidding! How did you manage that?'

'I teamed up with another girl who was doing a show there. A lass from Lancashire, Matti Fullbright. We're now on as a double act.'

Jamie's jaw dropped. 'Matti Fullbright! Rene, she's fantastic! I reviewed her show last year when she was short-listed for the Perrier.'

It was Rene's turn to gawp. 'Ye're kidding! She never told me that!'

'Well, all I can say is that you've got yourself teamed up with one of the funniest women I've ever seen. Is this a permanent partnership?'

Rene shrugged. 'I reckon it could be. We've been playing to packed audiences every day. They've even shifted our act on to twice daily.'

'How did they organise that?'

'They found an act who was 'appy to move to my old venue.'

Jamie flicked his head to the side. 'You've got it made, Rene. That's great news. What do the folks back home in Hartlepool think about it?'

Rene grimaced. 'I 'aven't actually told them, yet.' She turned to Angélique. 'So, 'ow's your 'and getting on, luv?'

Angélique held up her injured hand, showing no sign of a strapping, only a small pink scar across the palm. 'It is back to normal, I think.'

'Oh, that looks brilliant,' Rene said, scrutinising the healed wound. 'You'll be playing the violin in the blink of an eye.'

'Angélique reckons she's ready to play in public again,' Jamie said. 'We're hoping the International office can arrange for her to do one of the late concerts next week, just before the close of the festival.' He thumped his hands down on the table. 'So, I think all occupants of number seven London Street have got quite a bit to celebrate, so how's about we adjourn to the local pub and have a drink?'

All except Leonard jumped to their feet and started to clear away the plates. 'If you don't mind,' he said, 'I think I might just give it a miss.'

'Whit's up, Leonard?' T.K. asked concernedly.

Leonard held up a hand. 'Nothing a good night's rest won't cure.'

'Ah'll gie ye a hand tae the bedroom,' T.K. said, putting a supporting hand under Leonard's elbow.

Leonard smiled at the rest of the party. 'Quite an assistant, is he not?'

'**D**o you think he's all right?' Jamie asked, pulling on his jacket as he came down the steps to join Rene and Angélique on the pavement.

'To be quite 'onest, I think 'e's bitten off more than 'e can chew,' Rene replied as they began walking. ''E told me this is the first job 'e's done for twenty years. 'E was meant to have a whole load of people 'elping 'im, and now it's just 'im and the young lad.'

'Maybe we should ask that nice doctor who treated my hand to come round to see him,' Angélique suggested.

'Good idea,' Jamie replied. 'We'll see how the old boy's getting on in the morning and make a decision then.' They turned the corner and began walking up Broughton Street. 'Come on, let's take a short cut,' he said, turning down a narrow cobbled street.

'I'm glad I'm in the presence of a tough young man,' Rene said, wrapping her coat round her. 'I wouldn't fancy walking down 'ere by myself.'

'Do you think T.K. will know where we are?' Angélique asked.

'I told him the name of the pub before we left. He'll find it.' There was the sound of footsteps running up the street behind them. Jamie turned. 'Speak of the dev—'

The force of the blow to his shoulder was so great that it made him spin round. He put out his hands to try to grab hold of something that would keep him on his feet, but he knew it was a lost cause. The side of his head hit the cold stone of the building and his knees gave way, his eyes swimming in and out of focus as he slowly sank down the wall. He heard Angélique scream and Rene shout, their voices sounding as if both were standing in an echo chamber. The words 'Let go of 'er!' resonated through his brain, followed by a hollow slap like a fish being thrown down onto a wooden chopping board. Through blurred vision he saw Rene lying in front of him, clutching at the side of her face. 'Albert, stop this! Please, stop this!' he heard Angélique cry out.

The name rammed into Jamie's brain. He levered his body up the wall and staggered towards Dessuin, who had Angélique by the wrists. The Frenchman turned to see him approach and let go of Angélique. 'You filthy bastard!' he spat out, as he came towards Jamie. 'You think you can turn her against me?' He grabbed hold of Jamie's hair and yanked his head down, at the same time bringing his knee up into the pit of Jamie's stomach. Jamie keeled over, fighting for breath, but still Dessuin was not finished. He pulled Jamie's head up by the hair and slammed him against the building, clutching him by the lapel of his jacket. Jamie saw the fist being drawn back and knew he was without the energy either to duck or to parry the blow. His only act of resilience was to keep his eyes open while the finishing blow was administered.

But it never came. He suddenly saw Dessuin spin round in front of him and sink to his knees, blood spurting out between his fingers. Gulping in air, Jamie tried to focus on the figure that stood before him.

'Jeez,' T.K. groaned as he rubbed hard at his forehead. 'Ah never got the hang o' the head butt.'

Jamie shook his head. 'You did bloody well, mate. I owe you one.' He looked past T.K. to see Angélique enveloped in Harry Wills's arms. 'God, the cavalry arrived in the nick of time, didn't it?'

Jamie stumbled round Dessuin's hunched form and squatted down beside the little comedienne's supine body. 'Rene,' he said gently, taking hold of her hand, 'are you all right?'

Rene opened one eye. 'Aye, I'm fine. I just decided to play dead until that bloody French madman had gone.'

Jamie smiled at her. 'Well, you're safe enough now,' he said, pulling her to her feet. 'Sorry about that. I'm afraid I wasn't much good.'

He felt an arm slip round his waist and turned to find Angélique looking up at him, her face stained with tears. 'Are you badly hurt?' she sobbed.

'No, I'm fine. Just aching a bit,' he replied, putting an arm round her shoulders. 'Don't worry. It's all over and done with now.'

'I'm sorry about all this, Jamie,' Harry Wills said, looking down at Dessuin. 'I never caught sight nor sound of him while I was outside your flat. I really had no idea he knew where you lived.'

'No matter. Where did you spring from, anyway?'

'I came by the flat just after you'd left to go to the pub. I was coming round with T.K. to join you for a drink.'

'Just as well,' Jamie replied. He nodded towards Dessuin. 'So what are we going to do with him?'

Harry Wills heaved Dessuin to his feet. He put a hand into his pocket and pulled out his mobile phone. 'I think this game we've been playing has run its course. It's time to call in the police.'

As he began punching in a number, Angélique glanced at Albert. He still clutched at his nose, covering his face with his hands. 'Please wait, Harry. Don't do it just yet.' Walking over to Dessuin, she reached up and took a hand away from his face and held it in hers. 'Albert, you must understand it's all over. Please, will you go home now? You are such a talented man and you must use that talent to help others as you once helped me. And, Albert, you must find someone else to look after your mother because she will continue to make your life a misery and you do not deserve that. So, please, Albert, go back to Paris.'

Dessuin's body suddenly heaved with sobs. 'I'm so sorry, Angélique.'

Angélique planted a gentle kiss on his cheek. 'Will you go?'

Harry Wills slipped the mobile back into his pocket. 'I'll take him back to Paris. It's the least I can do. Anyway, I'm not so forgiving as Angélique and I'll not rest easy until I've seen this chap out of the country. He can stay with me tonight then we'll get a flight out tomorrow.' He gripped Dessuin firmly by the arm. 'Come on, let's make a move.'

'Harry?'

The reporter turned round to Jamie. 'Yes?'

'Could you give me a call tomorrow before you leave? There's something I want to discuss with you.'

Harry nodded. 'Sure.'

Having watched Harry guide Albert Dessuin down the street, Jamie leaned over, resting his hands on his knees, and took in a couple of deep breaths. 'Angélique, would you head back to the flat with Rene?'

'Why? What are you going to do?' she asked.

'Just recover for a moment. T.K. and I will be along soon.'

Angélique took the comedienne by the arm and they walked off in the direction of London Street.

'Hell, I didn't want to let on,' he said to T.K. once they were out of earshot, 'but that bloody man's really managed to hurt me. Just give me a minute.' He looked up. 'T.K., have we met before . . . I mean, before you came round with Gavin Mackintosh?'

T.K. grinned at him. 'Aye, we coulda done. I think it wis you I bumped intae roond the corner there.'

Jamie nodded as the picture of the paint cans rolling off the pavement came to mind. 'Of course. You went haring up London Street.'

T.K. laughed. 'Aye, I thocht someone wis efter me.'

Jamie scrutinised him. 'It wouldn't have had anything to do with a stolen video camera from the coffee shop, would it?'

T.K. scratched at the back of his head. 'Aye, well, sort of.'

Jamie had a sudden fit of coughing and gripped his side in agony.

'Whit's the matter?' T.K. asked. 'Are ye all right?'

Jamie lifted his head. 'Yeah, I'm just laughing and it bloody hurts.'

'Whit's so funny?'

'Nothing, really,' he said, pushing himself upright and giving T.K. a thump on the shoulder. 'Only that both you and I have damned good reasons not to set foot inside that coffee shop again.' He began to walk slowly down the street. 'I could kill for a pint of beer. What about you?'

T.K. hurried to catch up with Jamie. 'Aye, why not?'

Jamie felt the relieving effects of the two power-plus painkillers, swallowed with the aid of a large malt whisky, drift over his body like healing hands as he lay in the darkness of his room. He was only a moment away from deep, restful unconsciousness when it happened, so he could not tell whether it was a dream of unrequited desire rather than sublime reality. It started with a beam of light falling across his face for a brief second before darkness enveloped him once more. A sliver of cold air hit him as the duvet was lifted away and he felt the form of a female body melt its contours into the arch of his back. He lay there without moving, sensing the push of her breasts against his spine, then smiled to himself in total contentment and turned to her.

'Hi,' Angélique whispered.

'Hi,' he replied, reaching out a hand to the silk-soft skin of her face.

'Did you know it was me?'

Jamie grinned into the darkness. 'Well, I was hoping it wasn't Rene.'

Angélique muffled a laugh into the duvet. 'How is your head?'

'Throbbing.'

'And your body?'

'Aching.'

'Shall I make you feel better?'

'How do you plan to do that?'

He sensed Angélique raise her head from the pillow and then felt the pressure of her lips against his mouth. 'I don't think you really need to ask,' she breathed out.

Fifteen

GAVIN MACKINTOSH SAT in the Hub café toying with his empty coffee cup as he watched a group of Japanese tourists at the next table discussing with incomprehensible excitement their plan for the day.

'Gavin?'

He turned to find the young woman he had first seen talking with Angélique at the reception at the Sheraton Grand. He stood and offered a hand. 'Tess, how good to meet you at last.' He pulled out a chair for her and sat down next to her. 'I just felt I should come in person to say how grateful I am for all your help during the past week. The support you have shown Angélique has been invaluable.' Gavin stopped talking when a waiter came and hovered beside him. 'What can I get you?'

'A cappuccino, please.'

Gavin ordered and then leaned forward on the table. 'No doubt you've been in touch with Angélique?'

Tess nodded. 'I had a long chat with her this morning. It seems your fears over Dessuin were justified.'

'I think we were very lucky it didn't all turn out a great deal worse.'

'How's Jamie? I hear Dessuin gave him quite a beating.'

Gavin smiled at her. 'He's a tough lad. He'll make a speedy recovery.'

'And Angélique?'

'Despite what happened, she seems a different person this morning. I think a weight has lifted off her shoulders with Dessuin's departure.'

Tess raised her eyebrows. 'I can well believe that, and I—' The waiter approached and placed cappuccinos in front of them. She waited for him to leave before continuing. 'I'm just so glad it's all over for her.'

Gavin took a sip from his cup. 'She feels ready to play again.'

'She told me. I'm going to see Alasdair Dreyfuss this afternoon.'

'What will you say to him?'

'Just that Angélique's hand has healed much faster than expected, and she's decided to return here from France so that she can at least fulfil a small part of her commitment.'

Gavin nodded. 'You're right to keep it simple.'

Tess blew out a breath. 'I have to. One way and another, I've been keeping too many secrets from Alasdair this year. Anyway, once we've rescheduled one of the concerts, we can publicise it.'

Gavin drained his cup of coffee. 'I'm sure it will be a sell-out within hours.' He glanced at his watch. 'Now, I really must fly,' he said, getting to his feet. He placed a five-pound note on the table. 'It's been good meeting you properly, Tess.'

They stood and shook hands. 'And you too, Gavin. I know how much you've done for Angélique.'

'It's been nothing but a pleasure.' He held onto her hand. 'Actually, Tess, there is one other thing. Would you be able to reserve two tickets for me for this concert before the word gets out?'

'Consider it done.' Tess laughed. 'And seeing you've paid for the coffee, I think we can put the tickets on the house.'

Jamie and T.K. stood up from the kitchen table as the tweed-suited doctor walked into the room, slipping his stethoscope away.

'How is he?' Jamie asked.

The doctor gazed seriously at them both over the top of his spectacles. 'Mr Hartson, I'm afraid, has quite a serious heart problem and the mental strain of making this film has certainly exacerbated it.'

'Are ye saying he's gotta stop makin' the film?' T.K. exclaimed.

'I don't think anything I may suggest will stop him from doing that. The making of this particular film obviously means a great deal to him, but my advice would be that he should take a couple of days off.' He studied Jamie's face. 'That's a nasty-looking bruise.'

Jamie smiled at the old man. 'I'm fine, honestly.'

'Right, well, all I'd advise you to do is to take a couple of Arnica pills.'

'I'll get some. Thanks.'

While Jamie showed the doctor out of the flat, T.K. pushed open the door to his and Leonard's bedroom. The old cameraman was sitting on the edge of his bed, leaning over with effort to tie up his shoelaces.

'Whit are ye daen', Leonard?' T.K. asked as he entered the room. 'The doctor said—'

The cameraman cut him short. 'Oh, the doctor says! I've had this condition for five years, T.K., and I know my limitations.' He pushed himself to his feet. 'So let's get on with the work.'

As the old man opened the door, T.K. did not move, but stood there, a worried expression on his face. 'Leonard? This is no' a good idea.'

Leonard smiled reassuringly at the boy. 'I really am all right, T.K. I decided myself last night that I should try to take things easier, and my plan for today is that you should take over the role of camera operator.'

T.K. stared open-mouthed at Leonard. 'D'ye mean that?'

'I've thrown you in at the deep end all the way through this shoot, so I don't see why that should stop. I can concentrate on the lighting.'

'What are we waiting for?' T.K. said, bounding towards the door.

The lights shimmered and flared on the bright silk kimonos of the Japanese performers as they dipped and turned and rolled with liquid precision through the ancient ritual of their dance. Leonard sat in the canvas-backed chair watching every move T.K. made with the camera as he followed the action exactly as he had been directed. There was no doubt in Leonard's mind that the boy had the knack.

Oh, to be able to get the chance to live my life again, Leonard thought to himself as he slipped a hand inside his jacket to press against the pain that was once more building in his side. Why did I ever give up this kind of work? Why did I allow myself to be cast out into the wilderness for all those years, to turn my back on so many potential opportunities to make films such as this? He took a handkerchief from his pocket and dabbed at his watering eyes as he turned his attention to the lighting.

'Shall ah stop rolling, Leonard?' T.K. asked, taking his eye away from the viewfinder of the camera.

'Are you quite happy with it?'

'Ah think so.'

'Good lad. In that case, cut it.'

The battered van was sitting so low on its suspension that Terry Crosland could hear the new exhaust scrape the ground at every bump as he drove into Edinburgh. The journey had taken a good hour longer than he had envisaged, owing to the half-hourly pit stops requested by the committee members, who proved incapable of synchronising their needs. It was the two youngest members of the party, Robbie and Karen

Brownlow, who had endured the bum-numbing discomfort the best, hardly opening their mouths as they sat on the makeshift seats.

'Where do we go from 'ere?' Terry asked as he approached the round-about on Leith Walk.

Gary Brownlow studied the Streetfinder they had bought. 'Left and then straight on at the next roundabout.' He turned the map round and counted off the roads with his finger. 'West Richmond Street is about fifth on the left after that. I reckon we'll make it by a good ten minutes.'

Stan Morris walked quickly to the front of the party as they hurried towards the Corinthian Bar, eager to resume his role as spokesman. He pushed open the heavy glass door, letting it swing back on Terry's face, and approached the tall blonde girl in the black T-shirt who stood behind the ticket-office desk.

'Good evening, lass,' he said importantly. 'Would ye be so kind as to supply us with eight tickets for tonight's performance, please? And I don't suppose,' Stan continued, giving her the benefit of his most per-suasive smile, 'that ye might see fit to give a reduction for juniors?'

The girl frowned at him. 'Juniors? What age are they?'

Stan turned and pointed at Gary's children in turn. 'That there is Robbie and he's ten and his sister, Karen, is . . . how old are ye, lass?'

'Eight,' Karen breathed out, embarrassed.

Stan turned back to the girl, who was staring concernedly at the two children. 'Are you sure you want to take them to this show?'

Stan laughed. 'Of course we do, lass! It's their mother who's perform-ing. They especially want to see her!'

The girl looked even more bemused, her mouth dropping open as she glanced back and forth between Stan and the children. 'So, which of the Fruit Sundaes is their mother, then?'

It was Stan's turn to frown. 'Fruit Sundaes? What do you mean?' he said impatiently. 'Their mother is Rene Brownlow, "the 'ilarious comedi-enne from 'Artlepool",' he finished with a flourish.

The girl slapped her hand to her mouth. 'But Rene isn't on here any more. She swapped venues with the Fruit Sundaes.'

Stan felt the rest of the committee pressing up behind him, eager to hear what was going on.

'Where's she on, then?' Gary demanded.

'At the Underbelly.' The girl rummaged behind her desk, coming up with a programme. 'Hang on a minute,' she said, flicking through it. 'Here . . . she's on at the Belly Laugh. There's a show at eight o'clock.'

Terry looked at his watch. They had twenty minutes before it began.

'I don't know if you'll get in, though,' the girl continued. 'Her new show's been a sell-out for the last week. She's been the talk of the town.'

Gary looked down at his children and gave them a proud wink. 'D'ye 'ear that, kids? Yer mam's the talk of the town.'

'Come on, lads, we'd better get going,' Terry said, ushering the party out into the street.

I'm sorry. It's the final show and it's a sell-out. Has been for the past week,' the red-T-shirted boy at the Underbelly ticket office explained.

'Oh, 'ell, no!' Terry exclaimed, running an exasperated hand over his quiff. 'Are ye saying there's no chance at all of seeing it?'

'I'm afraid not.'

'But we've come all the way up from 'Artlepool to see 'er. We've got 'er 'usband and kids with us an' all!' Terry indicated the group of friends and family that stood waiting silently behind him.

'Hang on a minute,' the boy said, getting to his feet and grabbing the arm of a woman who was hurrying past him. They talked together in low voices before the woman approached Terry.

'We can let you all in, but I'm afraid you'll have to stand at the back of the auditorium.'

'That'll do us fine,' Terry said as he began to count out the money.

'Don't worry about that, sir,' the woman said with a smile. 'Seeing you're all from Rene's home town, I think we can let you in for free. You'd better hurry, though. It's just about to start.'

The theatre door was opened by a girl who pressed a finger to her lips. 'Are you the party from Hartlepool?' she whispered.

Terry nodded.

'Right, follow me, but be very quiet. The show's started.'

The auditorium was already echoing with laughter as the girl led them along the back aisle. On the stage, Rene stood close to one of the side wings with a white rose behind her left ear, while on the opposite side a woman was passing comment on the red rose she wore in her entanglement of carrot-coloured hair.

Karen Brownlow tugged on her father's jacket and Gary bent down so that she could whisper in his ear. Gary nodded and straightened up.

'Kids can't see, Terry. Can you stick Karen on yer shoulders and I'll take Robbie?'

Terry gave the young Brownlow boy a hand to clamber onto his dad's shoulders before hefting Karen onto his own. 'Who's the other woman with Rene?' he said to Gary.

'Never seen 'er before in me life.'

As they spoke, Rene walked across the stage and put a hand on the redhead's arm, cutting her off in mid-sentence. Rene turned and looked up into the obscurity of the auditorium to where Gary and Terry and the rest of the Hartlepool crew were standing.

'I've got great 'earing, you know,' she called out. 'Matti and me are dying for a rest, so seeing as you lot at the back seem to be in a talkative mood, we'd much appreciate it if you came down 'ere and did the show for us, so's we can get off to our beds.'

The audience tittered, and to a man turned round and looked towards the back. The committee members cast embarrassed glances from one to the other. 'Oh, shurrup, girl, and just get on with it,' Gary called out at the top of his voice.

Rene walked to the front of the stage, shielding her eyes with her hand as she sought out the location of the heckler. 'Gary?' she said.

Terry took over the shout. 'Aye, get on with the show, lass.'

Rene started to laugh. 'You 'n all, Terry?'

The red-haired girl put her hands on her hips and scowled impatiently at her partner. 'Here, Yorkie, are you just going to gawp at the audience all night? They've paid good money, you know.'

'Oh, keep yer 'air on,' Rene replied as she returned to stand beside her fellow comedienne. She pensively scrutinised the untidy mass of red curls that tumbled around Matti's face. 'On second thoughts . . .' And with that they slipped back into their routine, the slanging match between them turning, as it had done over the past eighteen shows, into a warm-hearted ad-lib session that had both performers and audience falling over one another in laughter. An hour and a half later, after Rene and Matti had taken more curtain calls than at any of their previous performances, the lights brightened, and the audience rose from their seats in a hum of good humour.

'Bloody marvellous!' Terry said, lifting Karen from his shoulders and putting her down on the floor. 'What d'ye think of yer mam, lass?'

'Can we go and see 'er now?' was all that Karen had to say.

Terry rubbed a hand gently on her head. 'Aye, I'm sure we can.'

The girl who had shown them in led the Hartlepool party round the back of the stage to Rene and Matti's dressing room.

'Oh, my Go-o-o-od!' Rene cried out, jumping to her feet when Robbie and Karen rushed towards her. She held them tight against her, raining kisses on their heads. 'Oh, 'ow I've missed you lot.'

'My word, Rene, you've got a real fan club here, haven't you?' Matti remarked as she surveyed the six faces peering round the doorway.

Rene glanced towards the door. 'Oh, for goodness' sakes, you're all 'ere,' she laughed, hurrying over to give each of the committee members a kiss on the cheek. 'Whose bright idea was this?'

'Gary thought you needed some moral support, but obviously 'e got the wrong end of the stick,' Terry replied.

Rene grinned at her husband. 'Oh, come 'ere,' she said, dragging him round the side wing and out onto the stage. She reached up and pulled his face down to hers and gave him a long kiss on the lips, then took hold of his hand. 'So, tell me, 'ow's it been?'

'No problems. We managed fine, but we 'aven't 'alf missed ye.'

Rene squeezed his hand. 'And I've missed you lot so much as well. Dare I ask 'ow the job 'unting's going?'

Gary smiled and gave her a wink. 'Don't let's talk about that. Tonight's your night,' he said, leading her back, 'so let's get celebrating.'

As they squeezed into the dressing room, Matti popped the cork on the second of the two bottles of Cava she and Rene had bought to celebrate their last night. 'You're the only two without,' she said, handing two frothing paper cups to Gary and Rene.

'Gary, this is Matti,' Rene said, grinning. 'She's my new partner.'

Gary gave Matti a kiss on the cheek. 'Pleased to meet you, lass. I was just saying to Rene you two were just tops tonight.'

Matti gave Rene a nudge on the arm. 'Has he got a brother?'

'If I could 'ave yer attention for a moment, please,' Stan Morris called out above the laughter. 'I would like ye all to drink a toast to the success of these two girls, and I am pleased that it was due to my efforts—'

'Oh, shut up, Stan,' Terry cut in with a laugh, holding his paper cup in the air. ''Ere's to ye both. Ye really showed them out there tonight.'

'I couldn't agree more,' a softly spoken American voice interjected. Everyone turned, their cups halfway to their mouths, as they stared at the smartly dressed woman who stood leaning against the doorpost. 'I apologise. I didn't mean to interrupt.'

'Not at all. Come in and join us,' Rene said, picking up a spare cup of sparkling wine from the dressing table and carrying it over to her. The woman took the cup and held out her hand to Rene.

'It's Rene, isn't it? My name's Mary Steinhouse. I just wanted to say how much I've enjoyed your show. You and Matti have one of the most original acts I've seen in a long time.'

'Thanks for that,' Rene replied, glancing round at Matti.

'And I'm sorry that I had to cut in on your celebrations,' the woman continued, 'only I'm heading back to the States first thing tomorrow morning, and I really wanted to see you both before leaving.'

'Oh aye?' Rene said, a questioning frown on her face.

'You see, my husband and I sponsor a large cultural festival held annually in Boston. I come over each year and invite the best acts on the Fringe over to take part, and I was very much hoping you and Matti might consider coming.'

Rene's jaw dropped. She turned to Matti, seeing her face register similar disbelief. 'When would this be?'

'The week after next. I'm returning here for the Saturday-night fireworks concert, which I adore, and then those acts I have chosen will fly back with me on the Sunday.' She paused. 'That is why, I'm afraid, I need an answer as soon as possible.'

Gary cleared his throat. 'As far as Rene is concerned, she can do it.'

Rene looked at her husband, emotion pricking her eyes. 'Gary?' she said quietly.

'What about it, Matti?' Gary said, pressing her for an answer.

'Oh God, yes!' Matti exclaimed, coming over to Rene and throwing her arms round her. 'Yes, yes, yes!'

'I'm so glad,' Mary said with a clap of her hands. 'So, if we could meet next Saturday afternoon at the Balmoral Hotel in Princes Street. I have a half-dozen rooms booked and you are invited to stay with me there. We'll have an early-evening reception, during which I will brief you as to what will be happening the following week, and then we can go watch the fireworks together. How does that sound?'

Rene drew a hand across her damp cheeks. 'I can't go.' A rumble of concern swept round the room. 'Not without my family. I've been away from them for three weeks and I need to spend time with them.'

Gary put a hand on his wife's shoulder. 'Come on, Rene, we'll be—'

'No, Gary,' she cut in. 'I've made up me mind.' She smiled apologetically at the woman. 'I can only go if me family comes too.'

Mary glanced at the strange little group in the room. 'What, *all* of them?' she asked in a surprised voice.

Rene spluttered out a laugh. 'No, just me husband and the kids.'

Mary shrugged. 'I'm sure we can find somewhere for you all to stay.'

Rene grinned at her. 'In that case, ye're on. America, 'ere we come.'

'Wonderful,' Mary said, pushing herself away from the doorpost. 'Until next Saturday, then, and enjoy your celebrations. You really deserve it, both of you.'

After she had left there was a momentary silence in the room before Matti let out a whoop of joy, and, grabbing Derek Marsham, began dancing around the room. Rene leaned her head against Gary's chest. 'Is this really all 'appening?' she said quietly.

Gary gave his wife a kiss on the top of the head. 'I think it is, lass.'

Sixteen

THE RAIN CAME to Edinburgh on the Wednesday evening, eight hours later than predicted. The torrential downpour had every street awash with water, yet the energy and enthusiasm of the festival continued unabated. The tourists, punters and office workers still filled the streets under a mass of umbrellas, while high on the castle battlements, where the wind threw the rain in violent blasts against the pitted walls, Roger Dent held hard to the hood of his waterproof jacket as he raced across the courtyard, jumping over lines of multicore cabling already connected up to the slave units that would power his explosions. Hurrying down the store steps, he threw open the door. 'Bloody hell!' he exclaimed, shaking the water from his arms. 'It's filthy out there.'

'Jeez, mate, you look like a drowned rat,' Phil Kenyon said, getting up from the table and taking a pair of earphones off his head. 'How's about a cup of coffee?'

'Not just yet,' he replied, hanging his jacket on the wall. 'I'd rather find out what stage we're all at. How did you get on with Helen?'

'Really good. The score's written up and we met Sir Raymond today and went through the piece. He listened to the recording we used to set up the programme, and he reckons he'll be able to stick close to that.'

Roger let out a nervous sigh. 'Well, as long as he doesn't tense up on the night and rocket through the whole thing. We don't have the leeway for it to under-run.' Roger turned his attention to the bespectacled figure of Graham Slattery, the IBM computer programmer. 'Gray, what's the story with the bell wire?'

'Annie and I have got about six hundred metres laid out. The tunnel, the gardens and the ground under the gun are all wired, which just leaves the rock face.'

Roger stared at the man. 'What do you mean, the rock face has to be done? The riggers were supposed to have completed that today.'

Graham's face fell. 'They said the rain made it too dangerous, Rog.'

'Jesus, I pay them to risk their sodding necks. What happens if it rains tomorrow? Are they expecting to sit around drinking tea?'

Graham cleared his throat nervously. 'They don't like the idea of doing the rock face, Rog. The fact is it's never been done before.'

'I couldn't give a damn. It's bloody well going to be done.'

'We'll get it done tomorrow, mate,' Phil cut in, realising Graham was in need of moral support.

'We don't have time tomorrow, Phil,' Roger exclaimed, grabbing a web harness and karabiner off a hook on the wall. 'If this isn't done tonight, there's no hope of us being ready.'

'Hell, Rog, you're not thinking of doing it now? It's bloody near dark! You'll kill yourself.'

Roger threw him a climbing rope. 'Not as long as you're holding on to the other end of this.' Taking his jacket from the wall, he picked up a large drum of bell wire from the corner of the store. 'Are you coming?'

Phil glanced at the concerned faces of the crew and shook his head as he picked up his jacket. 'You're mad as a bull with ticks, mate.'

Roger beamed a smile. 'Of course I am. It's why I'm in this business.'

Fifteen metres below the castle parapet, Roger flattened himself against the rock face as the wind tore the jacket hood off his head, the incessant rain soaking his hair before he had managed to search out his next handhold on the slippery rock. He was getting into a routine now. Handhold first, then foothold, then uncoil the bell wire from the drum suspended from his waist. He was working so fast he felt the rope above him go slack and he realised Phil wasn't keeping up with him. 'Phil?' he yelled out as loud as he could.

'You all right, mate?' he heard Phil's faint voice shout out from above.

'Keep the rope taut.' Roger felt the rope once more reassuringly take his weight. 'How many of you have got hold of it?' he called up.

'All of us,' came the reply.

Roger smiled to himself as he felt for the next cleft in the rock. Only a few metres more and he could start making his way back up to the safety of the terrace. He pushed his fingers deep into a crevice and swung his leg out, but his hands were beginning to cramp up and as he did so he lost his grip. He let out a cry as he spun round in open air before the rope jerked taut, pulling the harness deep into his groin. His back slammed painfully against the solid wall and he swung against the rock face, looking down the sixty-metre drop to Princes Street Gardens below. 'Shit!' he murmured as he gulped in air.

'Rog?' Phil's worried voice yelled out from above. 'You all right?'

Roger took in a steadying breath. 'Yeah, I lost my grip. Is the rope safe?'

'As houses. We've wound it round a bollard. Take your time.'

Roger stretched his arms to the side to relieve his knotted muscles as he looked out across the lights of Princes Street and over the roofs of the New Town, and it suddenly dawned on him that, as he hung there, high and isolated above the streets of Edinburgh, he felt strangely like the statue of Christ the Redeemer on the pinnacle of Corcovado above Rio de Janeiro, enfolding its inhabitants in the benevolent protection of his arms. He felt neither sacrilegious nor irreverent to think such a thing. For twenty-three years, this had been his city, and he felt a sudden burst of love for the people who each year had thronged to watch the spectacle that he had conjured up from his exalted position on the castle walls. 'Bless you all,' he murmured, 'and thank you for those years. And when that final starburst lights up the sky, may your paths run true and your lives be filled with peace from then on.'

He broke away from his meditation, feeling along the rock face to find a new hold and heaving himself round so that he was facing the wall. That really was a weird thing to say, he thought.

'Phil?' he called. 'Take the strain again, will you? I'm on my way up.'

Leonard Hartson stood on top of the stepladder adjusting the spotlight so that it fell onto the face of the dancer he had called to the location that afternoon. There were only a couple of small insert shots to do, so he had decided not to involve the director of the dance company or his young interpreter. After three weeks of energy-sapping work, there were two things prevalent in Leonard's mind: first, that what he had just completed was indeed his masterpiece; and second, that it had come at a drastic cost to his health. He glanced across to the other side of the lighting stage, where T.K. was shifting the camera to its new position. When he was sure the lad wasn't watching, he climbed slowly down the ladder, clutching hard at the lighting stand for support, and then dragged his feet back to the canvas chair, his face grimacing with pain. As T.K. left the camera and came towards him, Leonard forced an excited smile onto his face, hoping to make his voice sound normal. 'We've just about done it, T.K.,' he said.

His assistant smiled. 'Aye, looks like you and I are goin' tae get tae see the fireworks this evening, efter a'.'

'You could be right,' Leonard replied, clandestinely slipping a hand inside his tweed jacket as he felt the tightness in his ribcage building. 'Are you ready to shoot?'

T.K. scribbled a new scene number on the clapperboard beside Leonard's chair. He handed it to Leonard.

The board felt a dead weight in his hand and he let it fall onto his lap. 'Let's not bother with that,' he said with a shake of his head. 'It's only an insert, so just roll the camera when you're ready.'

Leonard watched as T.K. held Leonard's own Weston light meter up to the dancer's face to check the skin-tone exposure. He returned to the camera. 'Right, Leonard,' he called out.

'In your own time, my boy, in your own time.'

T.K. watched the flickering image of the girl's face through the viewfinder. He pressed the zoom and let the camera run for a further fifteen seconds. 'I've got it, Leonard,' he called out. 'D'ye want me tae cut?' The camera ran on as T.K. waited for a reply, never taking his eye away from the viewfinder. 'Leonard? Shall ah cut it?' he said again.

The sound of the clapperboard clattering to the ground made T.K. glance round at the old cameraman. Leonard lay slumped to one side of his chair, his head lolling against his shoulder, his right arm dangling.

'Leonard!' T.K. cried out, turning off the camera and running across to his mentor. He gently pulled Leonard upright and placed a hand either side of the cameraman's ashen cheeks. There seemed to be no sign of life. T.K. heard a gasp and glanced round to find the young dancer beside him, her tiny hands clasped to her mouth. 'Jesus, whit d'we dae? Whit d'we have tae dae?' he yelled out in a panicked voice.

The young girl held out her hands hopelessly, unable to understand. T.K. grabbed his jacket from where it lay on one of the lighting boxes. He rummaged in the pocket for the mobile phone he had made Leonard buy so that they could be in constant touch with Springtime Productions in London, and with shaking hands pressed in the number for the emergency services. 'I need an ambulance doon at Leith Docks right now,' he yelled into the phone. 'Address? There isna one!' He scratched impatiently at the back of his head. 'In that case, jist get the ambulance doon tae Commercial Street and ah'll stand and wait fer it.' He glanced over at Leonard. 'Ah think it could be his hert.' He ended the call and then walked back to Leonard's side. He reached over and pressed his fingers against the cameraman's neck, feeling for a pulse as he had once been instructed. There seemed only the faintest sign of life.

'Leonard, ah'm jist goin' tae get the ambulance,' he said quietly, tears beginning to blur his eyes as he covered the old man with the jacket that had been bought for him, tucking it in carefully around his still body. 'Ye'll be all right, mon. Just sit nice and easy, an' ah'll be back wi' help. Jist haud on, Leonard.'

He turned to the young dancer. 'Ye have to stay here,' he said to her, his speech slow and distinct in the hope she would understand him.

He ran and opened the fire door and stood there a moment, bathed in a beam of sunlight. 'I'm no' going far, Leonard,' he called back to the unconscious figure. 'I promise ah'll be back with ye in no time.'

When Tess Goodwin entered through one of the back doors of the Usher Hall, the curving passage was already resounding to a cacophony of instruments warming up. She followed the passage round, stopping outside a dark-panelled door on which a small brass slide bore the name of Angélique Pascal. She stood listening to the strains of a single violin going through a scale before she knocked. The sound ceased and a voice called out for her to enter. Angélique was standing in the centre of the room, dressed in the figure-hugging black dress she had worn for the opening-night concert, her violin and bow held loosely in her hands. She hurried over to give Tess a kiss on either cheek.

'How are you feeling?' Tess asked, placing her coat on a chair.

Angélique blew out a long breath. 'Nervous. It feels like a long time since I have done this.'

Tess folded her arms. 'I still feel bad about you having to perform at this final concert, but there was such a response to the announcement of your return we felt we couldn't just schedule one of the 'lates' for you.'

Angélique shook her head. 'You must not worry. I have always loved the Brahms concerto, so all I have to do now is play it properly.' She laid her violin and bow down carefully. 'How is Allan today?'

Tess laughed. 'Not too good. He was called in early to the office this morning, so he decided to walk it, to clear his head.'

'That was good fun last night,' Angélique said with a grin. 'I have not danced like that for so long.' She applied lipstick lightly to her mouth in the mirror. 'By the way, have you seen Jamie?'

'Yes, I saw him in the foyer—oh, and he asked me to say he's sitting in the third row back in the central block and he wants you to look out for him when you get up on the stage.'

Angélique turned to Tess with a quizzical frown. 'For what reason?'

'I can't tell you. It's a surprise.'

'Ah, so you know what it is?'

Tess laughed. 'I said I can't tell you.'

There was a knock and an elderly woman put her head round the door. 'Mademoiselle Pascal, the orchestra is ready.'

'Thank you,' Angélique replied, turning to pick her violin up. 'Well, this is it, then.'

Tess gave her a hug. 'Believe me, you're going to have a wonderful time. Just enjoy every moment of it.'

As Angélique walked onto the stage the orchestra rose to its feet along with every member of the audience, and the huge domed building rang with the sound of applause. Angélique walked over to the conductor and beckoned for him to lower his head towards her so that she could plant a kiss on both his cheeks. The applause increased in volume, the audience charmed by the gesture, as she moved to her position on the stage. She bowed first to the side galleries, then to the front, scanning the nearest rows for Jamie. She caught sight of him and gave him a broad smile, and then noticed that Harry Wills, the reporter, was beside him. She watched as Harry turned to his left and her eyes followed, and there, next to him in a wheelchair in the aisle, was an old lady with white hair, her hands clasped together in her lap, her pale blue eyes fixed on where Angélique stood on the stage.

'Oh, *mon Dieu! Mon Dieu!*' Angélique murmured, clasping a hand to her mouth. She moved back towards the conductor's plinth, never taking her eyes off the old lady, until she bumped into the brass rail that surrounded it. 'Please,' she said, turning to the conductor, 'can we wait for a moment? I have to see someone. It is very important.'

The conductor beamed and reached down to take the violin and bow from her. 'Of course, my dear. Take your time. I had a warning this might happen.'

As Angélique walked over to the side of the stage and descended the stage steps, the audience went so quiet that her footsteps echoed round the concert hall. She approached the old lady, tears streaming down her cheeks. '*Oh, je ne le crois pas!*' She got down on her knees and gently took hold of the limp wrinkled hands. 'Madame Lafitte, you are truly here!' She kissed the hands and held them against her hot wet cheeks.

'I . . . have . . . been brought . . . by Mr Wills . . . to hear you play,' Madame Lafitte said in a weak faltering voice.

Angélique got to her feet and flung her arms round Harry's neck. 'Thank you, Harry, thank you so much.'

'Not my idea,' he replied, his face pumping with embarrassment. 'Jamie thought that since I was going to Paris, I might do a detour via Clermont Ferrand on the way home.'

For a moment Angélique stared open-mouthed at Jamie before she pushed past Harry's legs and pressed her lips against his for so long that by the time she broke away he was left gasping for air. The audience loved it, and reacted with wolf whistles and loud yells of approval.

Leaving Jamie with a whispered message in his ear, Angélique stood once more beside Madame Lafitte, looking down into her eyes. 'I shall play for you now,' she said, brushing the back of her hand gently against the old lady's cheek.

'I . . . have waited . . . too long . . . for this moment,' she replied.

Angélique bent down and kissed her lightly on the forehead. 'And you will wait no longer.' And as she walked back onto the stage the conductor raised his hands in the air to bring the orchestra once more to its feet to greet the second entrance of the young French maestra.

Never before had Lillian Lafitte heard her young protégée play as she did this evening. There was a powerful intensity, a newly discovered emotion in her delivery, every note striking at her own inner being, making her feel that her passing years had been scrolled back in time, and she was a young girl once more, walking amid a carpet of spring flowers in a mountain meadow high in the Massif Central, clutching hard to the hand of her companion, the dashing Dr Jean-Pierre Lafitte.

And then she realised what it was that made Angélique play in such a way. The girl had found love. It was the missing part of the jigsaw, completing her understanding of the music, a part that could only be found through the explosion of longing, and then belonging, in the heart. She turned her head and looked along the row at the young man with the blond hair. He was watching Angélique with a fascination, a boundlessness that would make it seem that he was the only person in this vast hall. Lillian smiled to herself. She doubted very much he was listening to one note. How wonderful it is, she thought to herself, that the feeling between these two should be so entirely mutual.

Age has struck your body, Lillian, but your mind is still sharp. So now use it, for Angélique's sake, while you still have the time.

Roger Dent pulled back the sleeve of the new jacket that his wife had had made up for him for the final show, a black windcheater with the ESC logo embroidered on the back in gold thread, studded with sparkling diamante buttons. Ten minutes and the display would begin. There was nothing more he could do now. Everything had been checked a hundred times. It just remained for Phil to call the show.

He walked quickly across the courtyard to the firing position under the one-o'clock gun. Annie Beardsley gave the thumbs-up when she saw him and slipped on her earphones. Returning the gesture, Roger ran off to do a last check with Dave Panton and Graham Slattery, who were manning the other two firing positions in the tunnel and in the gardens. Five minutes later he entered the glass-fronted box where Phil Kenyon and Helen, his score reader, sat next to each other, looking down onto the huge white-shrouded stage in Princes Street Gardens where members of the Scottish Chamber Orchestra sat waiting.

'Are we ready to go, Phil?'

The Australian turned to him with a broad grin. 'Yeah, mate, we're just about to hit it.'

Roger simply nodded in reply, letting out a long nervous breath.

Phil laughed. 'Jeez, Rog, it's going to be fine.' He pulled out the chair next to his. 'Sit down and enjoy your finest hour.'

Roger shook his head. 'Not this time.'

Phil looked at him. 'What d'you mean? You always sit here.'

Roger flicked a thumb towards the door. 'I'm going to be out there. I want to watch the people in Princes Street. I want to watch those hundred thousand faces look up and marvel at what we've created.' He shot his colleague a knowing wink. 'That's what it's all about, Phil. Sheer, unadulterated entertainment.'

Phil shook his head. 'Get outta here, you've finally flipped.'

A loud roar went up from the crowds below and Phil turned to look down onto the stage. 'That's our conductor on,' he said, picking up the earphones and putting them on his head, 'so let's get ready to roll.'

Four hundred kilometres to the south, in an office block overlooking London's Victoria Station, Nick Springer sat with his feet up on his desk as he reran the video that had been delivered to his office late that afternoon. He let out a long contented yawn before pulling back the cuff of his Turnbull and Asser shirt and looking at his watch. It was nearly nine o'clock. Time to call it a day.

He swung his feet off the desk, got up and took his jacket from the back of the chair. Pulling it on, he switched the television off and made his way to the door. As he opened it, the telephone on his desk began to ring. He stared at it for a moment, thinking about letting it go onto the answering machine, but then returned to pick it up.

'Nick Springer . . . Oh, hi, T.K.? I've just been watching the footage you sent down yesterday. Fantastic. Leonard and you have done one hell of a job . . . I'm sorry, T.K., I was talking over you. What did you just say?' As he listened he sat down heavily on the side of his desk.

'When did this happen?' he asked in a quavering voice. 'Oh my God. And where is he now? . . . and were you with him?'

He felt his eyes prick with tears of emotion as the boy talked on. 'Oh, T.K., I know exactly what you mean. If it's any comfort, I think he saw you a bit like a grandson as well . . . yes, I know, lad . . . no, don't you worry yourself about that. I'll drive straight down to Kingston and break the news to her.' He took in a deep sad breath. 'So where are you now? Are you still in the hospital? . . . why on earth have you gone back to the warehouse? . . . have you really? . . . Well, you're a great lad, T.K., Leonard would be very proud of you. I'll see if I can fly up tomorrow with Grace and I'll arrange for someone to pick up all the equipment. You say the remainder of the exposed stock is in the camera case . . .?

Right, and will the place be locked . . .?' He began scribbling on a pad of paper. 'Under the brick below the rubbish skip outside the door . . . OK, I've got that, T.K., and you have the mobile if I need to get in touch with you . . . T.K.? . . . T.K., I didn't understand what you just said. Your voice sounds a bit slurred . . . T.K., are you there, lad?'

Nick hung up the telephone and put his hands to his face, pressing his fingers against his eyes. 'What I have done?' he murmured to himself. 'What the hell have I done?' He pulled his hands down the sides of his face. 'And how on earth am I going to tell Grace?'

T.K. sat in the darkness of the empty warehouse, the packed camera and lighting cases clustered about him. He pushed the mobile phone into the pocket of his jacket and bent down to pick up the half-empty bottle of vodka from the cold concrete floor. He took a swig, coughing as the neat alcohol ran down the back of his throat, then got to his feet and began to stagger unsteadily towards the door. Suddenly, he stopped and turned to walk back to pick up something that lay on top of the camera case. He cradled Leonard's Weston light meter in his hand, and then brought it to his nose for a moment to inhale the smell of its time-worn leather case before putting it into his pocket.

He opened the door, seeing the dark night sky above the buildings opposite light up in blues and greens. The fireworks had started. He turned the key in the padlock and placed it under the brick next to the rubbish skip. He straightened up and realised that the street, usually empty save for the film company van, was lined with cars. He nodded. The fireworks. People would have had to park this far away.

He began to make his way along the street, and then stopped, casting an admiring eye over a brand-new BMW parked there, its body reflecting the light of yet another firework that hit the sky. He stood weaving back and forth as he eyed its plush interior and leather-covered steering wheel. He let out a drunken laugh and walked back to the rubbish skip, and ten seconds later returned to the car with a heavy metal rod he had found buried in it. T.K., the master car thief, he thought to himself. That's all that's left for ye now. You know how tae handle this joab.

Walking round to the front of the BMW, he brought the metal rod crashing down against the front bumper, caving it in. The effect was immediate. The airbags ballooned out from the steering wheel and from the dashboard in front of the passenger seat, and the doors sprang open. Approaching the driver's door, T.K. took a last swig from the vodka bottle before shattering it against the warehouse wall. He pulled open the door, slashing at the airbags with the broken glass, and clambered into the driver's seat, not caring about the powder now covering his clothes.

TK threw the broken bottle out onto the pavement, then reached for the metal rod and wedged it between the spokes of the steering wheel. Using every bit of his strength, he yanked it downwards until the steering lock gave way. He freed the rod, jammed it into the plastic covering below the steering wheel and removed it with a flick of his wrist, exposing multicoloured wiring. He dropped the rod into the gutter and rubbed his hands on his jeans. Right, T.K., he thought, this is where the fun starts. If ye can get past the immobiliser on this beast then ye truly are a bloody master at yer craft.

Lillian Lafitte sat in her wheelchair at one side of the crowded lobby of the Caledonian Hotel, listening to the thunderous booms of the fireworks and the appreciative roar of the crowd outside in Princes Street. She lifted her hand with immense effort and brought it down on top of Angélique's. 'You must . . . go . . . to watch . . . them,' she said, smiling.

Angélique glanced across at Jamie, who sat next to the old lady. 'I would prefer to stay here and talk to you,' Angélique said.

'I insist,' the old lady continued, 'but first . . . I tell you something.' She looked at Angélique. 'You are twenty-one . . . and you can handle your own affairs. . . I am therefore . . . instructing my lawyers . . . to buy you a house . . . in London. It will be . . . a good base . . . for you.'

Angélique clasped her hands to her mouth in amazement. 'Oh, Madame Lafitte, that is . . . that is what I've always wanted!' She made to put her arms around the old lady's neck, but again Madame Lafitte raised her hand a fraction to stop her. 'And I have . . . spoken to someone . . . who I hope will become your . . . new manager.'

'Who is this person?' Angélique asked.

'I cannot say yet . . . the . . . answer will be given . . . tomorrow.' She let out a tired sigh. 'Now . . . I cannot talk more . . . so . . . go!'

Madame Lafitte slumped in her wheelchair at the sheer effort of speaking. Angélique gave her a kiss on either cheek. 'I love you so much, madame,' she said quietly to her. 'You have been so good to me.'

The old lady raised her eyebrows. 'Go . . . Angélique.'

Taking this as the cue to leave, Jamie got to his feet and began to pull Angélique towards the door. 'Come on, those were our marching orders.'

'You will still be here when it is finished?' Angélique called back as Jamie hurriedly dragged her away.

Lillian Lafitte smiled her reply and watched as they entwined their arms round each other and left the hotel, talking excitedly together.

Five hundred metres along Princes Street from the Caledonian Hotel, high above the mass of spectators, Gavin and Jenny Mackintosh stood on the balcony of the New Club, gazing up at the streams of light that showered down upon the castle. They waited with anticipation as the orchestra in the gardens below built up to a crescendo, and then, at the precise moment when the kettle drums pounded and the cymbals crashed, the whole of the rock face below the castle exploded into colour, cascading downwards, never losing its blazing flare until it hit the ground sixty metres below.

'Oh, my word,' Gavin murmured in astonishment. 'I don't think I've ever seen that done before.'

Jenny turned and smiled at her husband. 'When was the last time you saw the fireworks display?'

Gavin laughed and gave her a squeeze. 'True, very true.'

'Well, you certainly got yourself involved this year, didn't you?' she said, leaning her head against his shoulder.

'Yes, I can quite honestly say that, for myself it's been a very satisfactory three weeks'—he let out a relieved sigh—'but I am extremely glad it's all over.'

Jenny looked up at him, her eyebrows raised questioningly. 'You won't go pining after your young girl too much?'

Gavin leaned over and gave her a kiss on the top of the head. 'There's only one young girl in my life and she's standing next to me.'

Across the roofs of Waverley Station, in a building adjacent to the North Bridge, Harry Wills sat in his office, oblivious to the noise and celebration outside as he typed away. He watched the final word of the article come up on his screen and then thumped the full-stop button with a flourish. He began to read it through. It was headed 'The Inquisitive Little Girl who became a Worldwide Star' and opened with the line 'Once, long ago, in the darkened drawing room of a house in Clermont Ferrand . . .'

It had been Madame Lafitte's suggestion that they should wait until they were on the plane before he started to ask her questions about Angélique, so as soon as they were climbing high above the peaks of the Massif Central Harry had taken his tape recorder from his briefcase and switched it on. During the course of the two-hour flight he gleaned from the old lady all the information he had been seeking over the past three years. He saved the document and as the flash of a firework lit the dingy interior of his office he pressed the button on his mouse, sending the article off for inclusion in the next day's edition of the *Sunday Times*.

Tess Goodwin climbed the final staircase of the tall Georgian block in Dundas Street and blew out a long breath of exhaustion and trepidation, before putting the key in the front door of her flat. 'Allan?' she called out when she saw the lights in the hall were on. 'Where are you?'

'In the sitting room.'

She made her way along the stone-flagged passage and pushed open the door. Allan was standing to the side of one of the large windows, looking out at an angle.

'I thought you might have gone to the fireworks,' she said, walking over to him and slipping herself under his arm.

'No, I didn't feel like the crush in Princes Street,' he replied. 'I thought I'd just watch the high ones go off from here.' He gave her a kiss on the top of the head. 'Why aren't you there?'

Tess shook her head. 'I had to meet up with Lewis Jones for our end-of-festival drink, and then I just felt like getting back here.' She smiled up at her husband. 'I'm glad everything's over, and I'm just longing for our honeymoon.'

He looked at her thoughtfully. 'Yeah, roll on the honeymoon,' he replied with little enthusiasm.

'What's the matter?' Tess queried, pulling herself away from his arm.

Allan looked down. 'You know I had to be in the office early today?'

'Yes,' Tess replied, her face frowned with worry.

He looked up at her. 'Well, I've been offered a new job in London.'

Tess stared at him, stunned. 'I don't believe this.'

'It's a hell of an opportunity, Tess,' Allan continued immediately, wanting to get out the explanation he had been conjuring up for her all day. 'The salary is twice what I'm getting up here, so it means we can sell this flat and buy a bigger house, which will be great when we come to have kids—which, OK, won't be for a bit, because this job at the outset involves a fair amount of overseas travel, and, well . . .' He studied her closely for her reaction. 'What d'you think?'

With a laugh, Tess reached up and kissed him on the cheek. 'It's wonderful and I'm very proud of you.'

'You mean, you'd be happy to move down to London?'

'Yes. It's exactly what we both need, a new beginning to our lives.'

Allan shook his head in disbelief. 'Wow, it's almost as if you'd been considering it as well.'

'Oh, I have. I've been offered a job too—in London.'

Allan stared at her, aghast. 'You're kidding me. What is the job?'

'Working for Angélique Pascal as her new manager and chaperone.'

'You never are!'

'I am.' She shook her head. 'And to think I've been trying to work out how to break the news to you.' She reached up and brushed a kiss onto his lips. 'So now we both seem to have got our lives in order, why don't you fetch that bottle of champagne from the fridge and we'll celebrate?'

Allan laughed and looked at his watch. 'You obviously haven't been reading your *Scotsman*. Let's give it ten minutes.'

'I have, actually. What have I missed?'

'It's this fireworks chap's last show.' He positioned Tess in front of him and put his arms round her waist. 'The finale's expected to be awesome.'

'**W**oooooo,' said WPC Heather Lennox as she leaned out the window of the unmarked police car to watch a meteor arc down from the sky.

'Whit wis that?' her young male colleague asked through a mouthful of egg roll.

'I jist said "woooo" at that firework,' she replied, still craning her neck out of the window.

'Ah, right.' He wiped his hands on his trousers. 'Here, d'ya think we should get on the move? We're meant tae be driving aroond.'

'Och, dinnae bother yersel',' Heather replied, knowing that his keenness came from his recent qualification as a police driver. 'Just relax and watch the show. There has tae be some compensation for being seconded tae traffic division for the night.'

With a sigh, the police constable turned to look at the queue of traffic forming at the red lights at the top of Leith Walk. He followed each car down, glancing at the number plates, and then turned to the dark-coloured BMW next to him. 'Nice car, that,' he mumbled. He glanced across at the driver of the BMW. 'Here, d'ya fancy nicking a driver wha's no' wearing a seat belt and using a mobile phone on the move?'

Heather turned to him. 'Whit is it with you tonight?'

The police constable jabbed a finger in the direction of the BMW. 'Look for yerself. A lad, a' dressed in white. No seat belt, mobile phone.'

Heather leaned forward to look past him. 'Jeez, Willie,' she said, pulling the radio handset out of its holder. 'That lad's no' dressed in white. He's got powder a' over his face and hands. We've got oorselves a ghost runner.' Heather peered through the window of the BMW just as it was taking off. 'I know exactly who that is. Get after that car, Willie, and don't let him know ye're following him.' As the Vauxhall powered away from the kerb, Heather called in to the control room.

'OK, can ye tell me now?' the police constable asked, as Heather replaced the handset in its holder. 'Whit's a ghost runner?'

'It's someone wha's broken intae a car by activating the airbags. Ye canna get behind the wheel unless ye burst the bags and they're filled wi' white powder, so that's why that lad's covered wi' the stuff.'

The police constable powered the car into the central lane of Queen's Street desperate to keep the BMW only two cars in front of him. 'But he's drivin' a new BMW. How the hell did he get past the immobiliser?'

Heather shook her head. 'If anyone's going tae dae it, he is.' She slammed her fist against the dashboard, just as another burst of fireworks flooded the night sky. 'Dammit, I thocht he wis going straight. His solicitor rang me up the ither day to tell me a' aboot him working wi' some film company.' She took her mobile from her pocket and started to press buttons.

'Whit are ye dain'?' the police constable asked.

'I'll hae his number here in 'received calls'. Aye, here it is, a mobile.' She held the phone to her ear. 'Hello, Mr Mackintosh. This is WPC Lennox from Gayfield Police Station. Mr Mackintosh, I'm presently in pursuit of a stolen vehicle being driven by one Thomas Keene. Do you know whit—?' She stopped speaking when the solicitor cut into her question, and for the next minute she listened intently to every word he said, every now and again grimacing at what she was hearing. Eventually, she pressed the end button, letting out a long sigh. 'All right, you can tak' it easy now, Willie. We know where he's goin'.'

'Whit d'ya mean?' the police constable asked, making no effort to lessen his speed.

'The lad must have been on the phone to his solicitor at those traffic lights back there. Mr Mackintosh has arranged to meet him at his own home in Ravelston Road in half an hour. He's on his way back from Princes Street right now. It seems the old cameraman Keene wis working fer died this efternoon in the Royal, and the lad's real cut up about it. Mr Mackintosh reckons he's in a pretty fragile mood, no' helped by the fact that he's been drinking to drown his sorrows.'

'He's drunk!' the police constable exclaimed as he swung the Vauxhall into Randolph Crescent. 'Had we no' better tak' him, then?'

Heather glanced at the dashboard clock. Twenty-six minutes past nine. 'No, he's no' driving dangerously. We'll have him in five minutes.'

The police constable turned into Queensferry Street and saw the BMW accelerate to take the next set of lights on orange. He gunned the engine of the Vauxhall and, on instinct, flicked on the switches for the siren and the row of blue lights set into the grille of the car.

'For Chrissakes', Willie, whit the *hell* are ye daen'!' Heather screamed at him. 'We know where he's goin'! Turn the bloody things aff!'

The noise of the siren broke through the hopeless mist of T.K.'s drunken misery. He glanced in the rear-view mirror with tear-filled eyes, seeing the blurry outline of the blue lights veering round a car that had pulled over to the side of the road. 'Oh, *shit!*' he yelled out, pressing his foot down on the accelerator, feeling the power of the car press his back into the soft leather upholstery.

'Oh, no, that's it. He's bloody well seen us now,' Heather moaned as she suddenly saw the gap between the two cars increase.

The police constable pressed his foot down to the floor. 'Dinnae worry, I'll keep up wi' him.'

'Hold on! It's against regulations tae give chase now.'

'I'm no' gi'in' chase! I'm jist keepin' him in front o' me.'

As T.K. drove fast along Queensferry Road, he saw the police car was gaining on him. There were no blue lights now, only headlights fast approaching. He had never been chased before, and a sudden terror gripped at his stomach, panic boiling up its sour taste into his mouth. He pushed the accelerator to the floor, glancing down at the speedometer to see the needle move effortlessly through the 100-kilometres-per-hour mark. He closed his eyes and braced his body for impact as he approached some red lights, and then opened them as he heard the screech of a crossing vehicle being left far behind. He looked in the mirror. The headlights that were following him disappeared for a second, then reappeared and continued the chase.

T.K. wasn't the only one who was frightened. Heather glanced across at the police constable and saw the steely intent burning in his eyes. She reached across and thumped him on the arm. 'If ye dinnae pull over right this minute, Constable, I'm goin' tae put ye on report.'

But the driver was in no mood to reply. He saw the BMW rock over onto its springs as it took a hard left at the roundabout on Queensferry Terrace, and ten seconds later he was actioning the same manoeuvre.

As the BMW slid broadside across the road, T.K. spun the wheel to the right, glancing over to his left through the rear passenger seat window to see the police car turn the corner at the roundabout. He pressed his foot down to the floor once more. The powerful BMW almost left the road as it hit the crest of the hill and he accelerated down Belford Road towards the sharp left-hand bend at the bottom.

'Oh, no. Please, God, no,' Heather murmured as she saw the BMW go across the corner and head down a narrow lane. 'Stop the car, Willie. For Chrissakes, stop the bloody car!' she screamed, as she watched the BMW career onwards with no sign of its brake lights coming on.

'Whit the hell's up wi' you?' the police constable exclaimed, bringing the car to a juddering halt.

'He's jist gone down a cul-de-sac,' Heather cried out, her eyes wide with horror, 'and he's no' got any airbags or seat belt!' She covered her ears with her hands, anticipating the appalling sound of the impact.

The muffled explosion was so powerful that the police car shook. Heather shielded her eyes with a hand against the glare of light blazing in the sky, so powerful that it was as if night had turned to day. Open-mouthed with shock and amazement, she turned and looked towards the narrow lane down which the BMW had disappeared, and in the brief seconds of flickering darkness between the starbursts that lit up the street, she saw that all was quiet, all was safe.

'Oh, thank God! Thank God!' she cried out with relief as she threw open the door of the car. She began to run as fast as her legs would take her down the road.

T.K. had never lessened the power of the car as he drove at break-neck speed down the lane, his hands clutching hard at the wheel as he steered it through the narrow gap between the parked vehicles on either side of him. He had no knowledge of this part of the city, no idea where this was going to take him. A resounding bang had made him jerk his body towards the gear shift and he glanced at the dangling wing mirror, taking his eyes momentarily away from the direction in which he was travelling. And then, suddenly, a dazzling flash of light had fallen upon the street, making him turn to see, in its glaring brilliance, the wall that was looming up in front of him. He let out a scream of panic, bracing his arms against the steering wheel as he slammed the brake pedal to the floor. The car had screeched angrily at the sudden transference of command, its sophisticated anti-lock brake system keeping it to a straight path through the parked vehicles, and it came to a tyre-burning halt three feet away from the end of the cul-de-sac.

T.K. sat shaking as he stared at the solid stone wall, catching his breath in gulps of fear and relief, wondering what kind of phenomenon had just saved his life. And then it dawned on him that it could only be that someone didn't want this to happen, someone who really cared for him was watching over him, and he bent forward, resting his head on the steering wheel, and began to cry once more. Another blaze of light shone out and he looked up, knowing it was a sign from Leonard. He staggered out and leaned on the car roof, tears streaming down his face as he stared up at the gigantic starburst high in the night sky, stretching its flaming tentacles towards heaven and, as only he knew, carrying with it the spirit of the man he had come to admire and love.

He raised a hand. 'See ya, Leonard,' he murmured. 'See ya, mon.'

He began to walk away from the car, his body shaking with grief and adrenaline, and then he saw the figure, wearing a luminous yellow vest, running towards him. The woman police constable slowed to a walk the moment she caught sight of him. T.K. focused his bleary vision on the uniform and, in that moment, was hit by the forgotten reality of his situation. He looked around, trying to find some way to escape.

'It's a'right, Thomas,' Heather called out. 'It's Constable Lennox. I know aboot Mr Hartson, Thomas. I know aboot everything that's happened.' She held out her arms to the side, only to show she had no means of restraint about her person. 'Come on here, lad, ye'll be a' right.'

She saw him start to run towards her, and as he got nearer she opened her mouth to yell out for support from her colleague, but her breath was forced from her body when T.K. flung himself into her arms, clutching tight to her as he sobbed inconsolably.

She stood there until she could no longer support the full, sad weight of his body against hers. 'Come on, Thomas,' she said quietly, giving him a pat on the back. 'Let's get you away from here.' And linking a steadying arm through his, Heather Lennox began walking him back up the lane.

Two kilometres away in the Balmoral Hotel, Gary and Rene Brownlow lay in bed in the dark, propped up against soft pillows and gazing out of the open window at the fireworks as they sipped their champagne.

'I bet the kids are enjoying all this,' Rene said as she cuddled herself against her husband's naked body.

'Aye, I bet they are,' Gary replied, too mesmerised by what was going on outside even to look at his wife. 'It was good of Matti to take them.'

Rene let out a contented sigh. 'America tomorrow. Are ye looking forward to it?'

'Bloody 'ell!' Gary exclaimed as a blinding incandescence of light filled the room. He threw back the duvet and ran over to the window.

'Gary!' Rene screamed in hilarity. 'Ye're stark-bollock naked!'

'Don't be stupid! No one's remotely interested in seeing me tadger,' he said as a second explosion lit up the outline of his lean body. 'They're all looking up at the castle.'

A sudden roar rose from the crowd in the street and Gary pressed his hands against the windowpane to see if he could work out what had caused it. 'My God, Rene!' He turned and beckoned urgently to his wife. 'Come over 'ere quick, lass. You've got to see this.'

Clambering out of bed, Rene grabbed a towel off a chair and wrapped it round her as she walked towards the window.

'Look up there on the battlements of the castle,' he said, putting an arm round her shoulders and guiding her line of sight with his hand.

Rene followed his direction, and beneath the giant palm-tree spread of shimmering light she saw a tiny figure standing on the castle wall, his legs apart and his arms raised towards the sky as if commanding the multicoloured tempest taking place in the firmament above to cease.

'What d'ye suppose 'e's doing?' Rene asked.

'No idea. It's a powerful sight, though. Quite . . . well, biblical, like.'

Rene crossed her arms and looked disappointedly at her husband. ''Ere, I thought we were meant to be doing something during all this?'

Gary glanced round at her. 'D'ye want me to ask them to do it over?'

'No, don't bother,' she laughed, her attention caught by the largest starburst of all, illuminating the thousands of people below and showering its trailing beams down on them. She put her hands up and let her towel fall to the ground. 'But the show's not over yet, you know.'

Gary smiled at her, his eyes twinkling. 'No, it's not, is it!'

And, together, they ran across the room and dived onto the bed.

Epilogue

IT WAS MID-NOVEMBER the following year, another festival had come and gone, and already the ticket hall at Waverley Station was being decked out for Christmas. A large tinsel-covered tree brightened up the seating area, while paper streamers were jauntily looped along the length of the glass-fronted ticket desk. Gavin Mackintosh took off his leather gloves and approached one of the two clerks manning the desk and purchased a return ticket to London King's Cross, only because it was better value than buying a single. There was no doubt in his mind that the return leg would never be used. Slipping his credit card back into his wallet, he took out two twenty-pound notes before returning the wallet to the inside pocket of his suit jacket.

He turned to the young man who stood behind him carrying a large rucksack on his back, the straps cutting deep into his brown Timberland jacket. 'There you are, Thomas,' he said, handing the ticket to T.K. before glancing up at the departures monitor. 'Your train is the ten thirty from platform one, but it looks to be running five minutes late. Do you know what you're doing when you get to London?'

'Aye,' T.K.replied, putting his hand into his pocket and handing a well-thumbed letter to Gavin. 'Mr Springer's written it a' doon there.'

Gavin read through the letter, the offer of a job at Springtime Productions, the plans made for T.K. at Christmas, and the directions he was to give the taxi driver on his arrival in London, then handed the letter back to him. 'I see you're going down to Kingston for Christmas?'

T.K. nodded. 'Aye, ah'm spending it wi' Grace.'

'That'll be good for you both. No doubt you'll be looking forward to seeing the award Leonard's film received at this year's film festival.'

'Ah've seen it, 'cos Grace sent me a photo of it. She'd written on the back, "This is yours as well".'

Gavin smiled. 'Nothing could be truer, T.K. Leonard couldn't have made that film without you.' He reached out for T.K.'s hand and pressed the two twenty-pound notes into his palm. 'This is just to wish you on your way.'

T.K. glanced down at his hand. 'Cheers, Mr Mackintosh.'

'Best of luck with your future, Thomas,' Gavin said, giving the lad a pat on the shoulder. 'You've served your time, so now you can just put all that behind you.' He laughed briefly. 'And for goodness' sakes, don't go driving any cars unless they belong to you, is that understood?'

T.K. looked up with an embarrassed smirk on his face and glanced across at the woman police constable who stood next to them.

Gavin consulted his wristwatch. 'Well, I must be getting back to the office,' he said, holding a hand out to T.K. 'Keep in touch now.'

'Aye, ah will,' T.K. replied, shaking his hand.

Heather Lennox gave T.K. a hug. 'Cheerio, Thomas. Look after yersel'.'

'Aye, and thanks for pickin' us up this mornin'.'

Heather smiled, raising a stern finger to him. 'Well, you mak' sure that's the last time *you* ever get tae ride in a police car again, right?' She gave a short wave of farewell and turned and walked with Gavin towards the doors of the ticket office, leaving T.K. with a broad grin.

'Well, Constable Lennox,' Gavin said as he stood on the pavement pulling on his gloves. 'It looks like things have turned out all right for that young man.'

Heather rubbed her hands together to stave off the chill of the freezing morning mist that hung over the city. 'Aye. He's the lucky one.'

'Very true,' Gavin replied, 'and consequently I doubt very much this will be the last time you and *I* will be meeting up.'

He left her with a smile, crossed over the taxi sweep and, setting a brisk pace, began making his way back up towards Princes Street.

Robin Pilcher

I managed to catch up with Robin early one morning at a pretty west London house where he had been enjoying a brief stay before flying out to his farm in Andalucia in Spain. As he set a steaming cup of coffee before me, and began to chat, the first thing that struck me was his ebullience. But I shouldn't have been surprised. Novel-writing is just one of many interests and ventures that Robin has pursued over the years. Before publishing his first novel, *An Ocean Apart*, in 1999, among other things he'd worked as a cameraman for a documentary film company, written scripts, spent time in public relations and taken over his grandfather's farm in Dundee. He had also set up a recording studio in a disused barn, and helped his wife, Kirsty (pictured above), whom he married in 1973 when he was twenty-two, to run a burgeoning mail-order business.

Was there anything he'd enjoyed more than any other? 'I think I've enjoyed doing everything. I can honestly say that I never came out of doing something because I made a mess of it, but because the time had come to move on.'

So when did he decide to try his hand at a novel? 'It happened by chance really. I'd started writing screenplays and songs as a hobby in the eighties, and then in 1985 we'd had a really bad year on the farm and I said to Kirsty, "I think we should go to Australia for the winter." To my surprise she thought it was a very good idea, so we took off with our children and had the time of our lives. While we were there I took on a few gardening jobs, and this was what gave me the idea for the central character in *An Ocean Apart*.'

The idea didn't immediately bloom into a novel, but was fed into a screenplay written for his mother, author Rosamunde Pilcher, who was busy writing a novel when a film company asked her for a treatment for a new screenplay. With no time available to write it, she turned to Robin for help. 'I said, "OK, but I'll have to think in your terms—families, relationships, something like that." I stuck the gardener figure in America, rather than Australia, and set the story in the malt whisky industry, which I'd worked in and knew a lot about, and that was it.'

Thereafter the project was dropped, so the draught languished inside Robin's computer for six years before he decided to 'pull it out' and turn it into a novel.

'It was very hard. I was used to putting in camera directions like "grouse flies left to right screen" but now I had to describe that and I didn't know if I could.' Did he think of asking Rosamunde for help? 'Yes. I wrote the first few pages and took it up to her—she lives with my father about a mile away from us in a village in Scotland—and I said, "What do you think?" She looked through it and said, "No, Robin, this is not right." And I kicked the furniture and sulked a bit and said, "Why not?" She said, "Well, you're a scriptwriter. You write dialogue. Write the novel in dialogue." So I went home, and after a bit I thought, She's right. There is no reason why I shouldn't write this book as if it's a screenplay. So I just cut the thing in my mind like a film. And because I did that it started motoring. Since then Ros has never read any of my books until they are finished and I give her a copy. But it's marvellous to have someone actually in the family who understands how you feel about writing, understands the mood you're in.'

I wondered if Robin had any reservations about being described as a 'romantic novelist'? 'I think it's sad that books are categorised into Horror, Thriller, Romance and so on. In *Starburst* one of the strongest relationships is between the old cameraman and a young no-hoper. There is love in their friendship, but it's not romantic love, it's respect for each other, that's much more what it boils down to. But I wouldn't want to change my genre.'

Did the large cast of characters in *Starburst* present a challenge? 'You *must* give yourself a new challenge each time you write. This was the first time that I'd written a multi-charactered book and it was a fantastic experience. You have to find a hook to hang your characters on, and the Edinburgh Festival worked perfectly for that. I do admit to being a total voyeur. I've observed and eavesdropped on so many people like those in *Starburst* . . . but then of course it's a matter of being able to transfer what you see and what you hear onto paper.'

Is he happy with the end result? 'I've read through *Starburst* six times now and I still really love every one of those characters. Writing is probably the most self-centred occupation I have ever taken up. It's all about having an affair with about fifteen different people all at the same time and then if you get into trouble with any of them, you go straight to your wife and ask her for help and advice. And Kirsty is blessed with phenomenal lateral thought and never fails to come up with the answers.'

Anne Jenkins

GARDEN SPELLS

SARAH
ADDISON
ALLEN

The fruit and vegetables grown in the Waverley garden have long been famed and feared for their curious, almost magical effects. The garden's secrets have been handed down from generation to generation and now it is Claire's turn to tend the enchanted soil. But Claire knows that change is in the air . . .

1

EVERY SMILEY MOON, without fail, Claire dreamed of her childhood. She always tried to stay awake those nights when the stars winked and the moon was just a cresting sliver smiling provocatively down at the world, the way pretty women on vintage billboards used to smile as they sold cigarettes and limeade. On those nights in the summer, Claire would garden by the light of the footpath lamps, weeding and trimming the night bloomers—the moon vine and the angel's trumpet, the night jasmine and the flowering tobacco. These weren't a part of the Waverley legacy of edible flowers, but sleepless as she often was, Claire had added flowers to the garden to give her something to do at night when she was so wound up that frustration singed the edge of her nightgown and she set tiny fires with her fingertips.

What she dreamed of was always the same. Long roads like snakes with no tails. Sleeping in the car at night while Lorelei, her mother, met men in bars and honky-tonks. Being a lookout while her mother stole shampoo and deodorant and lipstick and sometimes a candy bar for Claire at Shop-and-Gos around the Midwest. Then, just before she woke up, her sister, Sydney, always appeared in a halo of light. Lorelei held Sydney and ran to the Waverley home in Bascom, North Carolina, and the only reason Claire was able to go with them was because she was holding tight to her mother's leg and wouldn't let go.

That morning, when Claire woke up in the back-yard garden, she tasted regret in her mouth. With a frown, she spat it out. She was sorry for the way she'd treated her sister as a child. But the six years of Claire's life before Sydney's arrival had been fraught with the constant fear of being caught, of being hurt, of not having enough food or warm clothes for the winter. Her mother always came through, but always at the last minute. Ultimately, they were never caught, and Claire was never hurt, but while life on the run had been good enough for Claire, Lorelei obviously thought Sydney deserved better, that Sydney deserved to be born with roots. And the small scared child in Claire hadn't been able to forgive her.

Picking up the clippers and the trowel from the ground beside her, Claire stood stiffly and walked in the dawning fog towards the shed. She suddenly stopped, frowning. She turned and looked around. The garden was quiet and damp, the temperamental apple tree at the back of the lot shivering slightly as if dreaming. Generations of Waverleys had tended this garden. Their history was in the soil, but so was their future. Something was about to happen, something the garden wasn't ready to tell her yet. She would have to keep a sharp eye out.

She went to the shed and carefully wiped the dew off the old tools and hung them on the wall. She closed and locked the heavy gate to the garden, then crossed the driveway at the back of the ostentatious Queen Anne-style home she'd inherited from her grandmother.

Claire entered the house through the back, stopping in the sunroom that had been turned into a drying room for herbs and flowers. It smelt strongly of lavender and peppermint, like walking into a Christmas memory that didn't belong to her. She drew her dirty white nightgown over her head, balled it up, and walked naked into the house. It was going to be a busy day. She had a dinner party to cater that night, and it was the last Tuesday in May, so she had to deliver her mint and rose-petal jellies and nasturtium and chive-blossom vinegars to the farmers' market and to the gourmet grocery store on the square.

There was a knock at the front door as Claire was in her bedroom, pulling her hair back with combs. She went downstairs in a white eyelet sundress, still barefoot. When she opened the door, she smiled at the old lady standing on the porch.

Evanelle Franklin was seventy-nine years old, looked like she was one hundred and twenty, yet still managed to walk a mile round the track at Orion College five days a week. Evanelle was a second or third cousin, and the only other Waverley still living in Bascom. Claire stuck to her like static, needing to feel a connection to family after Sydney took off when she was eighteen and their grandmother died the same year.

When Claire was young, Evanelle would stop by to give her a Band-Aid hours before she scraped her knee, quarters for her and Sydney long before the ice-cream truck arrived, and a flashlight to put under her pillow a full two weeks before lightning struck a tree down the street and the entire neighbourhood was without power all night. When Evanelle brought you something, you were usually going to need it sooner or later.

'Well, don't you look eye-talian with your dark hair and Sophia Loren dress,' Evanelle said. She was in her green velours running suit, and slung over her shoulder was a rather large tote bag full of quarters and stamps and egg timers and soap, all things she might feel the need to give someone at some point.

'I was just about to make some coffee,' Claire said, stepping back. 'Come in.'

'Don't mind if I do.' Evanelle entered and followed Claire to the kitchen, where she sat at the table while Claire made the coffee. 'You know what I hate? I hate summer.'

Claire laughed. She loved having Evanelle around. Claire had tried for years to get the old lady to move into the Waverley house so she could take care of her. 'Why on earth would you hate summer? Summer is wonderful. Fresh air, open windows, picking tomatoes and eating them while they're still warm from the sun.'

'I hate summer because most of them college kids leave town, so there aren't as many runners, and I don't have any nice male backsides to look at when I walk the track.'

'You're a dirty old lady, Evanelle,' Claire said, setting a coffee cup on the table in front of her.

Evanelle peered into the cup. 'You didn't put anything in it, did you?'

'You know I didn't.'

'Because your side of the Waverleys always wants to put something in everything. I like things plain and simple. Which reminds me, I brought you something.' Evanelle grabbed her tote bag and brought out a yellow Bic lighter.

'Thank you, Evanelle,' Claire said as she took the lighter and put it in her pocket. 'I'm sure this will come in handy.'

'Or maybe it won't. I just knew I had to give it to you.' Evanelle, who had twenty-eight sweet teeth, all of them false, picked up her coffee and looked over at the covered cake plate on the stainless-steel island. 'What have you made over there?'

'White cake. I stirred violet petals into the batter. It's for a dinner party I'm catering tonight.' Claire picked up a Tupperware container beside it. 'This white cake, I made for you. Nothing weird in it, I promise.' She set it on the table next to Evanelle.

'You are the sweetest girl. When are you going to get married? When I'm gone, who will take care of you?'

'You're not going anywhere. And this is a perfect house for a spinster to live in. I'll grow old in this house, and neighbourhood children will try to get to the apple tree in the back yard, and I'll chase them away with a broom.'

Evanelle shook her head. 'Your problem is you like your routine too much. You get that from your grandmother. You're too attached to this place, just like her.'

Claire smiled because she liked being compared to her grandmother. She'd had no idea about the security of having a name until her mother brought her here, to this house where her grandmother lived. They'd been in Bascom maybe three weeks, Sydney had just been born, and Claire had been sitting in the front yard while people came to see Lorelei and her new baby. A couple came out of the house after visiting, and they watched Claire quietly build tiny log cabins with twigs. 'She's a Waverley, all right,' the woman said. 'In her own world.'

Claire didn't look up, didn't say a word, but she grabbed the grass before her body floated up. *She was a Waverley*. She didn't tell anyone, not a soul, for fear of someone taking her happiness away, but from that day on she would follow her grandmother out into the garden every morning, studying her, wanting to be like her, wanting to do all the things a true Waverley did to prove that, even though she wasn't born here, *she was a Waverley too*.

'I have to pack some boxes of jelly and vinegar to deliver,' she said to Evanelle. 'If you'll wait here for a minute, I'll drive you home.'

'Are you making a delivery to Fred's?' Evanelle asked.

'Yes.'

'Then I'll just go with you. I need Cola. And some Goo-Goo Clusters. And maybe I'll pick up some tomatoes. You made me crave tomatoes.'

Claire took four corrugated boxes out of the storeroom and packed up the jelly and the vinegar. When she was done, Evanelle followed her outside to her white minivan with WAVERLEY'S CATERING written on the side. Evanelle got in the passenger seat while Claire put her boxes in the back. Then Claire handed Evanelle the container with her plain white cake in it, and a brown paper bag.

'What's this?' Evanelle said, looking in the brown bag as Claire got behind the wheel.

'A special order.'

'It's for Fred,' Evanelle said knowingly.

Claire laughed and pulled out of the drive.

Business was doing well, because all the locals knew that dishes made from the flowers that grew around the apple tree in the Waverley garden could affect the eater in curious ways. Fried dandelion buds over marigold-petal rice ensured that your company would notice only the beauty of your home, never the flaws. Anise hyssop honey butter on toast made children thoughtful. Honeysuckle wine gave you the ability to see in the dark, and the salads made with chicory and mint had you believing that something good was about to happen, whether it was true or not.

The dinner Claire was catering that night was being hosted by Anna Chapel, the head of the art department at Orion College, who gave a dinner party at the end of every spring semester for her department. Claire had catered these parties for the past five years. It was good exposure to get her name out among the university crowd.

Claire took the jelly and vinegar to the farmers' market first. Then she went into town and parked in front of Fred's Gourmet Grocery, formerly Fred's Foods, as it had been called for two generations, before a posher crowd started shopping there.

She and Evanelle walked into the grocery store with its creaking hardwood floors. Evanelle headed for the tomatoes, while Claire went to the back to Fred's office.

She knocked once, then opened the door. 'Hello, Fred.'

Sitting at his desk, he had invoices in front of him, but judging by the way he jumped when Claire opened the door, his mind had been on other things. He immediately stood. 'Claire. Good to see you.'

'I have those two boxes you ordered.'

'Good, good.' He grabbed the white blazer hanging on the back of his chair and put it on over his short-sleeved black shirt. He walked out to her van with her and helped her bring the boxes in. 'Did, um, did you bring that other thing we talked about?' he asked as they walked to the stockroom.

She smiled slightly and went back outside. A minute later, she came back in and handed him the paper bag with a bottle of rose geranium wine in it.

Fred took it, looking embarrassed; then he handed her an envelope with a cheque. The act was completely innocuous, because he always gave her a cheque when she delivered her jelly and vinegar, but this cheque was a full ten times what his normal cheque to her was. And the envelope was brighter, as if filled with lightning bugs, lit by his hope.

'Thank you, Fred. I'll see you next month.'

'Right. Bye, Claire.'

Fred Walker watched Claire wait by the door for Evanelle to pay the cashier. Claire was a pretty woman, all dark hair and eyes and olive complexion. People treated Claire politely, but they thought of her as stand-offish. She was a Waverley, and Waverleys were an odd bunch, each in his or her own way. Claire's mother had been a troublemaker who left her children to be raised by their grandmother and then died in a car pile-up in Chattanooga a few years later; her grandmother had rarely left the house; her distant cousin Evanelle was forever giving people strange gifts. That was just how the Waverleys were. But Claire kept the Waverley house in good shape, and it was one of the oldest homes around, and tourists liked to drive by it, which was good for the town. And most importantly, Claire was there when someone in town needed a solution to a problem that could be solved only by the flowers grown around that apple tree in the Waverley back yard.

Fred clutched the bag containing the bottle and walked into his office. He took off his blazer and sat at the desk, staring again at the small framed photo of a handsome man in his mid-fifties. Fred and his partner, James, had been together for over thirty years. But he and James had grown apart lately, and little seeds of anxiousness were starting to take root. Over the past few months, James had been staying overnight in Hickory, where he worked, a few nights a week, saying he was working so late that commuting back to Bascom didn't make sense. This left Fred at home alone far too often, and he didn't know what to do with himself. James was the one who always said, 'You make wonderful pot stickers; let's have that for dinner tonight.' Or, 'There's a movie I want us to see on television.' James was always right, and Fred questioned every little thing when he wasn't there. What should he have for dinner? Should he set the things he needed to take to the dry-cleaner out at night or wait for the morning?

All his life Fred had heard things about the Waverleys' rose geranium wine. It signalled in the drinker a return to happiness, remembering the good, and Fred wanted back the good thing he and James had. Claire made only one bottle a year, and it was expensive, but it was a sure thing.

He reached for the phone and dialled James's work number. He needed to ask him what he should make for dinner.

And what meat did you serve with magic wine?

Claire arrived at Anna Chapel's home late that afternoon. Anna lived in a cul-de-sac neighbourhood just outside the Orion College campus.

'Welcome,' Anna said when she opened the front door to find Claire on her porch, carrying a cooler of things that needed to be refrigerated immediately. She stepped aside and let Claire enter. 'You know the way. Do you need help?'

'No, thank you. I'm fine,' Claire said, though summer was her busiest season and the time when she had the least help. She usually hired first-year culinary students at the college to help her during the school year. The only questions they asked were culinary ones. She'd learned the hard way to avoid hiring anyone local if she could help it. Most of them expected to learn something magic or, at the very least, get to the apple tree in the back yard, hoping to find out if the local legend was true, that its apples would tell them what the biggest event in their lives would be.

Claire went to the kitchen and put away the things in the cooler; then she opened the kitchen door and brought in the rest of the things through the back entrance. Soon the kitchen was alive with the steamy warmth and crafty scents that eventually flowed through the house, welcoming Anna's guests like a kiss on the cheek.

Claire was ready to serve when everyone was seated. The menu tonight was salad, yucca soup, pork tenderloins stuffed with nasturtiums and chives and goat's cheese, lemon-verbena sorbet between dishes, and the violet white cake for dessert. Claire was kept busy, monitoring the food at the stove, arranging the food on the plates, serving and then deftly and quietly taking plates away when the guests had finished a course. This was as formal as any affair she catered. When she had to work alone, she didn't focus on the people, just on what she had to do, which was painfully exhausting that evening considering she had slept the night before on the hard ground of her garden. But it had its positive side. She was never very good with people.

She was aware of *him*, though. He was seated two places down from Anna, who was at the head of the table. Everyone else watched the food as it was placed in front of them. But *he* watched her. His dark hair almost touched his shoulders, his arms and fingers were long, and his lips full. He was . . . trouble.

As she was serving dessert, she felt something almost like anticipation the closer she got to sliding his plate in front of him. She wasn't quite sure if it was his anticipation or hers.

'Have we met?' he asked when she finally made it to his place as she was serving dessert. He was smiling such a nice, open smile that she almost smiled back.

She put his plate in front of him, the piece of cake so perfect, the crystallised violets spilling over it like frosted jewels. It screamed, *Look at me!* But his eyes were on her. 'I don't think so,' she replied.

'This is Claire Waverley, the caterer,' Anna said, happy with wine, her cheeks pink. 'I hire her for every department gathering. Claire, this is Tyler Hughes. This is his first year with us.'

Claire nodded, extremely uncomfortable that all eyes were on her now.

'Waverley,' Tyler said thoughtfully. She started to move away, but his long fingers wrapped gently around her arm. 'Of course!' he said, laughing. 'You're my neighbour! I live beside you. Pendland Street, right? You live in that large Queen Anne?'

She was so surprised he'd actually touched her that all she could do was give a jerky nod.

As if aware that she'd gone stiff, he let go of her. 'I bought that blue house next to you,' he said. 'I moved in a few weeks ago.'

Claire just looked at him.

'Well, it's nice to finally meet you,' he said.

She nodded again and left the room. She washed up and packed away her things, leaving the last of the salad and cake for Anna in the refrigerator. As she worked, she kept running her fingers unconsciously along her arm where Tyler had touched her, as if trying to brush something off her skin.

As she took her last box out to her van, she felt a strange gust of wind. She turned to see a figure standing under the oak tree in Anna's front yard. She couldn't make him out clearly, but there were tiny pinpricks of purple light hovering around him, like electrical snaps.

He pushed himself away from the tree, and she could feel him stare at her. 'Wait,' Tyler called. 'Do you have a light?'

Claire set the box down and reached into her dress pocket and brought out the yellow Bic lighter Evanelle had given her earlier that day. *This* was what she was meant to do with it?

She felt like she had water against her back, pushing her towards the deep end, as she walked towards him and extended the lighter. She stopped a few feet away, digging her heels in as whatever force it was tried to take her closer.

He was smiling, easy-going, and interested. He had an unlit cigarette between his lips, and he took it from his mouth. 'Do you smoke?'

'No.' She still had the lighter in her outstretched hand. He didn't take it.

'I shouldn't, I know. I'm down to two a day. It's not a very social habit any more.' When she didn't respond, he shifted from one foot to the other. 'It was a wonderful meal,' Tyler said, still trying.

'Thank you.'

'Maybe I'll see you again?'

Claire's heart started to race. She didn't need anything more than she already had. The moment she let something else into her life, she would get hurt. 'Keep the lighter,' she said, handing it to him and walking away.

When Claire pulled into her driveway, there was someone sitting on the top step of the front porch. Leaving her headlights on and the car door open, she jogged across the yard, all her earlier fatigue gone in a panic. 'Evanelle, what's wrong?'

Evanelle stood stiffly, the glow from the streetlights causing her to look frail and ghostly. She was holding two packages of new bed linen and a box of strawberry Pop-Tarts. 'I couldn't sleep until I brought you these. Here, take them and let me sleep.'

Claire hurried up the steps and took the things, then she wrapped an arm around Evanelle. 'How long have you been waiting?'

'About an hour. I was in bed when it hit me. You needed fresh sheets and Pop-Tarts.'

'Why didn't you call me on my cellphone? I could have picked these things up.'

'It doesn't work like that. I don't know why. And I don't know what they're for! I never know what they're for!' Evanelle took a deep breath, then said in a whisper, 'I want to go home.'

Claire patted Evanelle gently, reassuringly. 'It's OK. I'll take you home.' She set the sheets and Pop-Tarts on the wicker rocker by the front door. 'Come on, honey,' she said, leading the sleepy old woman down the steps and to the van.

When Tyler Hughes got home, Claire's house was dark. He parked his Jeep on the street and got out, but then he stopped on the walkway to his house. He didn't want to go in yet.

Tyler was teaching classes that summer, but there were a couple of weeks between the spring and summer semesters, and he always got restless when he didn't have a routine. He took a lot of comfort in structure. Sometimes he wondered if he was made that way. His parents were potters, and they had encouraged his artistic streak. It wasn't until he started elementary school that he realised it was wrong to draw on walls. It had been such a *relief*. School gave him structure, rules, direction, and he didn't like the thought of leaving it. So he decided to teach.

His first position after getting his Master's degree was at a high school in Florida. After a year or so, he also started teaching night art classes at the local university. A few years later, during a restless summer break, he found out about an opening in the art department at Orion College, and he interviewed for and got the position.

He heard a thud now from round the side of his house, so he headed to the back yard. The light from the porch illuminated the small yard, not nearly as large as the one next door. The Waverleys' metal fence, covered with honeysuckle, separated the two yards. Twice since he'd moved in, Tyler had pulled kids off the fence. They were trying to get to the apple tree, they said. That apple tree was special.

He walked along the fence, taking deep breaths of sweet honeysuckle. His foot hit something, and he looked down to see he had kicked an apple. His eyes then followed a trail of apples to a small pile of them close to the fence. Another one hit the ground with a thud. This was the first time he'd ever had apples fall on his side of the fence. Hell, he couldn't even see the tree from his yard.

He picked up a small pink apple, rubbed it to a shine on his shirt, then took a bite.

He slowly walked back to his house, deciding that he would put the apples in a box tomorrow and take them to Claire, tell her what happened. It would be a good excuse to see her again.

The last thing he remembered was putting his foot on the bottom step of the back porch.

Then he had the most amazing dream.

2

Seattle, Washington – ten days earlier

SYDNEY WALKED OVER to her daughter's bed. 'Wake up, honey.'

When Bay opened her eyes, Sydney put her finger to the little girl's lips. 'We're going to leave, and we don't want Susan to hear, so let's be quiet. Remember? Like we planned.'

Bay got up without a word and went to the bathroom and remembered not to flush, because the two town houses shared a wall and Susan would be able to hear. Bay then put on her shoes with the soft, quiet soles and dressed in the clothes Sydney had set out for her.

Sydney paced while Bay dressed. David had gone to Los Angeles on business, and he always had the older lady in the town house next door keep an eye on Sydney and Bay. For the past week, Sydney had been taking clothes and food and other items out of the house in her tote bag, not deviating from the routine David held her to, the one Susan kept watch over. She was allowed to take Bay to the park on Mondays, Tuesdays and Thursdays, and to go to the grocery store on Fridays. Two months ago, she'd met Greta, a mother at the park who'd had the nerve to ask what the other mothers couldn't. Why so many bruises? Why so jumpy? She helped Sydney buy an old Subaru for three hundred dollars, a good chunk of the money Sydney had managed to save in the past two years by removing bills from David's wallet every so often. She'd been taking the food and clothes to Greta in the park, to be put in the car. Sydney hoped to God that Greta had parked the car where they'd agreed. David would be back that night.

Every two or three months, David would fly to LA to check in person how the restaurant he'd bought into was running. He always stayed to party with his partners. He'd come home happy, still a little buzzed, and that would last until he wanted sex because she wouldn't compare with the girls he'd been with in LA. She used to be like those girls, long ago. And dangerous men had been her speciality, just as she always imagined it had been for her mother—one of the many reasons Sydney had left Bascom with nothing but a backpack and a few photos of her mother as a travelling companion.

'I'm ready,' Bay whispered.

Sydney went to her knees and hugged her daughter. Bay was five already, old enough to realise what was going on. Sydney tried to keep David from having any influence on her, and by unspoken agreement he didn't hurt Bay as long as Sydney did what he said.

She used to be good at leaving. She used to do it all the time before she met David. Now the fear of it was making it hard to breathe.

When she first left North Carolina, Sydney had gone straight to New York. She moved in with some actors, who used her to perfect their Southern accents while she worked on getting rid of hers. After a year she went to Chicago with a man who stole cars for a living. When he was caught, she took his money and moved to San Francisco. She changed her name then, so he wouldn't find her, and she became Cindy Watkins, the name of one of her old friends from New York. After the money was gone, she went to Seattle and got a job at a restaurant called David's on the Bay.

Sydney had been wildly attracted to David, the owner. He was powerful, and powerful men were thrilling, until the point that they turned frightening. That was when she always left. Things with David started to get scary about six months after she started seeing him. She made plans to leave him, but then she found out she was pregnant.

Bay arrived seven months later, named by David after his restaurant. The first year of Bay's life, Sydney resented the baby for everything that had gone wrong. David disgusted her now, frightened her well beyond the limit she thought there was to being scared. And he sensed it and hit her more. This hadn't been part of her plan. She'd never counted on staying with any of the men she met. Now she had to stay because of Bay.

One day, everything changed. Bay, barely a year old, was playing quietly with the clean laundry in the basket on the floor. Suddenly Sydney saw herself, playing alone while her mother wrung her hands and paced the floor at the Waverley house in Bascom, before her mother left without a word. A powerful feeling surged through her, and her skin prickled. That was the moment she let go of trying to be her mother. Her mother had tried to be a decent person, but she had never been a good mother. She had left her daughters with no explanation, and she never came back. Sydney was going to be a good mother, and good mothers protected their children. It had taken her a year, but she finally realised that she didn't have to stay because she had Bay. *She could take Bay with her.*

She'd been so good at running in the past that she'd been lulled into a false sense of security. She actually made it through beauty school before walking out of the salon in Boise where she'd got her first job and finding David in the parking lot. Before she noticed him standing there by his car, she remembered turning her face into the wind and smelling lavender and thinking she hadn't smelled that since Bascom. He hit her with his fists so many times she lost consciousness. They later went to pick up Bay at the day-care centre, where David had discovered Bay was enrolled, which was how he found them. He was charming, and the teachers believed him when he said Sydney had been in a car accident.

For the past two years, ever since he'd dragged her back from Boise, Sydney would wake up and smell honeysuckle in the air. The scent always seemed to be coming from a window or a doorway, a way out. Suddenly it made sense. She'd been smelling home. They had to go home.

She and Bay walked silently downstairs in the predawn dark. Susan next door could see both the front and back doors, so they went to the window in the living room that overlooked the small strip of side yard that Susan couldn't see. Sydney had earlier popped out the screen, so all she had to do was quietly open the window and lower Bay out first. Next she tossed down her tote bag, a suitcase and Bay's small backpack.

Sydney crawled out and led Bay through the hydrangea bushes.

Greta had said she was going to leave the Subaru in front of the 100 block of town houses one street over. She was going to put the keys above the visor. No insurance, but that didn't matter. All that mattered was that it would get them away.

It was drizzling as Sydney and Bay jogged along the sidewalk, and Sydney's hair was dripping into her eyes when they finally stopped at the 100 block of town houses. Her eyes darted around. Where was it?

She left Bay and checked one street over, just to be sure. It wasn't there.

She ran back to Bay, out of breath, appalled that her panic made her leave her daughter even for a minute. She sat on the kerb and buried her face in her hands. All that courage wasted. How could she take Bay back to the way things were? Sydney couldn't, wouldn't, be Cindy Watkins anymore.

Bay came to sit close beside her, and Sydney wrapped an arm around her. 'It will be OK, Mommy.'

Sydney heard a car. The lights slowly approached, as if searching for something. Then the car stopped, and a door slammed. 'Cindy?'

She looked up to see Greta, a short, blonde woman who always wore cowboy boots and two large turquoise rings.

'Oh God,' Sydney whispered.

'I'm so sorry,' Greta said, kneeling in front of her. 'I tried parking here, but the guy living over there caught me and told me he was calling a tow truck. I've been driving by every half-hour, waiting for you.'

'Oh God.'

'It's OK.' Greta pulled Sydney to her feet and led her and Bay to a Subaru wagon with plastic over a broken window and rust spots from fender to fender. 'Be safe. Go as far as you can.'

'Thank you.'

Greta nodded and got into the passenger seat of the Jeep that had followed her into the parking lot.

'See, Mommy?' Bay said. 'I knew it was going to be OK.'

'Me, too,' Sydney lied.

The morning after Anna Chapel's party, Claire went to the garden for a basket of mint. She was going to start on the food for the Amateur Botanists' Association annual luncheon in Hickory on Friday. Being botanists, they liked the idea of edible flowers. Being a bunch of rich, eccentric old ladies, they paid well and could give a lot of referrals. It was a coup to get the job, but she was going to have to hire someone to help her serve.

The garden was enclosed by heavy metal fencing, like a Gothic cemetery, and the honeysuckle clinging to it was almost two feet thick in places. Even the gate was covered with honeysuckle vines, and the keyhole was a secret pocket only a few could find.

When she entered, she noticed it right away.

Tiny leaves of ivy were sprouting.

Ivy in the garden.

Overnight.

The garden was saying that something was trying to get in, something that was pretty and looked harmless but would take over if given the chance.

She quickly pulled the ivy out, then dug deep for the roots. In her haste, she hadn't closed the garden gate behind her, and she jerked her head round in surprise when she heard the crunch of footsteps on the gravel pathway that snaked round the flowers.

It was Tyler, carrying a cardboard box and looking round as if he'd entered someplace enchanted. Everything bloomed here at once, even at a time of year when it wasn't supposed to. He stopped suddenly when his eyes found Claire on her knees, digging up the roots of the ivy under the lilac bush.

'It's Tyler Hughes,' he said, as if she wouldn't recognise him, 'from next door.'

She nodded. 'I remember.'

He walked over to her. 'Apples,' he said, crouching beside her and putting the box on the ground. 'They fell over the fence. I didn't know if you used them for your catering, so I thought I'd bring them over. I tried your door, but no one answered.'

'I don't use them. But thank you. You don't like apples?'

He shook his head. 'Just occasionally. I can't figure out for the life of me how they got in my yard. The tree is too far away.'

He didn't mention a vision, which relieved her. He must not have eaten one. 'Must have been the wind,' she said.

'You know, the trees on campus don't have mature apples on them at this time of year.'

'This tree blooms in the winter and produces apples all spring and summer.'

Tyler stood and stared at the tree. 'Impressive.'

The tree was situated towards the back of the lot. Its limbs stretched out like a dancer's arms, and the apples grew at the very ends, as if holding the fruit in its palms. It was a beautiful old tree, the grey bark wrinkled and moulting in places.

Claire didn't know why, but every once in a while the tree would actually throw apples, as if bored. She gave the tree a stern look. Occasionally that worked, making it behave. 'It's just a tree,' she said, and resumed pulling at the roots of the ivy.

Tyler put his hands in his pockets and watched her work. She'd been working alone in the garden for so many years that she realised she missed having someone there. It reminded her of gardening with her grandmother. It was never meant to be a solitary job. 'So, have you lived in Bascom long?' Tyler finally asked.

'Almost all my life.'

'Almost?'

'My family is from here. My mother was born here. She left but moved back when I was six. I've been here ever since.'

'So you *are* from here.'

Claire froze. How could he do that? How could he do that with just five little words? He just said the very thing she'd always wanted to hear. He was getting in without even knowing how he did it. He was the ivy, wasn't he? She very slowly turned her head and looked up at him, his lanky body, his awkward features, his beautiful brown eyes. 'Yes,' she said breathlessly.

'So, who are your guests?' he asked.

It took a moment for the words to penetrate. 'I don't have any guests.'

'As I was coming round the front of the house, someone pulled up to the kerb with a car full of boxes and bags. I thought they were moving in.'

'That's strange.' Claire stood and took off her gloves. She turned and walked out of the garden, making sure Tyler was following her. She didn't trust the tree alone with him, even if he didn't eat apples.

She walked along the driveway beside the house, but then she came to a sudden stop in the front yard. Tyler came up behind her, close, and put his hands on her arms, as if aware that her legs had turned boneless.

More ivy.

There was a little girl, about five years old, running around the yard with her arms stretched wide like an airplane. A woman was leaning against an old Subaru wagon parked on the street, her arms crossed tightly over her chest, watching the little girl. She looked small, frail, with unwashed light brown hair, and she seemed to be holding herself to keep from trembling.

Finally making her legs move, Claire crossed the yard, leaving Tyler behind.

'Sydney?'

Sydney pushed herself away from the car quickly, startled. Her eyes went all over Claire before she smiled, that insecure woman with her arms wrapped round her gone, replaced by the old Sydney, the one who always looked down her nose at her family name. 'Hi, Claire.'

Claire stopped on the sidewalk, a few feet away from her. The Sydney Claire knew would never let her hair look like that and wouldn't be caught dead wearing a T-shirt with food stains on it. She used to be so meticulous, so put together. She always tried hard not to look like a Waverley. 'Where have you been?'

'Everywhere.' Sydney smiled that spectacular smile of hers, and suddenly it didn't matter what she looked like. Yes, this was Sydney.

The little girl ran up to Sydney and stood close to her. Sydney put her arm round her. 'This is my daughter, Bay.'

Claire looked at the child and managed to smile. She had dark hair, as dark as Claire's, but Sydney's blue eyes. 'Hello, Bay.'

'And this is . . .?' Sydney asked suggestively.

'Tyler Hughes,' he said, extending a hand past Claire. She hadn't realised he'd come up behind her again. 'I live next door.'

Sydney shook Tyler's hand and nodded. 'I'm Sydney Waverley, Claire's sister.'

'Nice to meet you. I'll just be going. Claire, if you need me for anything . . .' He squeezed Claire's shoulder, then left.

Sydney wagged her eyebrows. 'He's hot.'

'Waverley,' Claire said.

'What?'

'You said your last name was Waverley. I thought you hated the name.'

Sydney shrugged noncommittally.

'What about Bay?'

'Her name is Waverley, too. Go play some more, honey,' Sydney said, and Bay ran back to the yard. 'I can't believe how great the house looks. New paint, new windows, new roof. I never imagined it could look so good.'

'I used Grandma Waverley's life-insurance money to remodel.'

Sydney turned away for a moment. She had stiffened, and it occurred to Claire that this was shocking news to Sydney. Had she really expected to find their grandmother here, alive and well? 'When did she die?' Sydney asked.

'Ten years ago. Christmas Eve, the year you left. I had no way to contact you. We didn't know where you went.'

'Grandma knew. I told her. Say, do you mind if I pull this clunker behind the house?' Sydney knocked on the hood with her fist. 'It's sort of an embarrassment.'

'What happened to Grandma's old car, the one she gave you?'

'I sold it in New York.'

'So that's where you've been, New York?'

'No, I only stayed there for a year. I've been around. Just like Mom.'

They locked eyes, and suddenly everything was quiet. 'What are you doing here, Sydney?'

'I need a place to stay.'

'For how long?'

Sydney took a deep breath. 'I don't know.'

'You can't leave Bay here.'

'*What?*'

'Like Mom left us here. You can't leave her here.'

'I would never leave my daughter!' Sydney exclaimed, a touch of hysteria tingeing her words, and Claire was suddenly aware of all that wasn't being said. Something big had to have happened to bring Sydney back here. 'What do you want me to do, Claire, beg?'

'No, I don't want you to beg.'

'I don't have anywhere else to go,' Sydney said, forcing the words out.

What was Claire supposed to do? Sydney was family. Claire had learned the hard way that you weren't supposed to take them for granted. She'd also learned they could hurt you more than anyone else in the world. 'Have you had breakfast yet?'

'No.'

'I'll meet you in the kitchen.'

'Come on, Bay. I'm pulling the car around back,' Sydney called, and Bay ran to her mother.

'Bay, do you like strawberry Pop-Tarts?' Claire asked.

Bay smiled, and it was Sydney's smile made over. It almost hurt Claire to look at, remembering all the things she wished she could take back from when Sydney was a child, like chasing Sydney out of the garden when she wanted to see what Claire and their grandmother were doing, and hiding recipes on high shelves so Sydney would never know their secrets. Claire had always wondered if she was the one who made Sydney hate everything Waverley. Was this child going to hate everything Waverley too?

In mere minutes, Claire's life had changed. Her grandmother had taken Claire and Sydney in. Claire would do the same for Sydney and Bay. No questions asked. It's what a true Waverley did.

'Pop-Tarts are my favourite!' Bay said.

Sydney looked startled. 'How did you know?'

'I didn't,' Claire said, turning towards the house. 'Evanelle did.'

Sydney parked the Subaru beside a white minivan at the back of the house, in front of the detached garage. Bay hopped out, but Sydney got out a little more slowly. She took her tote bag and Bay's backpack, then she went round to the back of the car and unscrewed the Washington State licence plate. She stuffed it into her bag. There. No clues as to where they'd been.

Bay was standing in the driveway. 'This is really where we're going to live?' she asked, for about the sixteenth time since they'd pulled in front of the house that morning.

Sydney took a deep breath. 'Yes.'

'It's a princess house.' She turned and pointed to the open gate. 'Can I go see the flowers?'

'No. Those are Claire's flowers.' She heard a thud and watched an apple roll out of the garden and stop at her feet. She stared at it for a moment. 'And stay away from the apple tree.'

'I don't like apples.'

Sydney went to her knees in front of Bay. She pushed the little girl's hair behind her ears. 'OK, what's your name?'

'Bay Waverley.'

'And where were you born?'

'On a Greyhound bus.'

'Who is your father?'

'I don't know who he is.'

'Where are you from?'

'Everywhere.'

She took her daughter's hands. 'You understand why you have to say these things, don't you?'

'Because we're different here. We're not who we were.'

'You amaze me.'

They walked into the kitchen through the sunroom, and Sydney looked around in awe. The kitchen had been remodelled. It was all stainless steel and efficiency, and there were two commercial refrigerators and two ovens.

They wordlessly went to the kitchen table and sat, watching Claire put on coffee and then slide two Pop-Tarts into the toaster. Claire had changed, not in big ways, but small ones, like the way light changed throughout the day. A different slant, a different hue. She seemed comfortable, the way their grandmother used to seem comfortable. Don't-move-me-and-I'll-be-fine comfortable.

Watching her, it suddenly occurred to Sydney that Claire was beautiful. The man next door thought so, too. He was clearly attracted to her. And Bay was captivated by her, not taking her eyes off her even when Claire put warm Pop-Tarts and a glass of milk on the table in front of her.

'So, you run a catering company?' Sydney finally asked when Claire handed her a cup of coffee. 'I saw the van.'

'Yes,' Claire said, turning away in a swish of mint and lilac. Her hair was longer than it used to be, and it veiled her shoulders like a shawl. She used it for protection. If there was one thing Sydney knew, it was hair. She loved beauty school and working in the salon in Boise. Hair said more about people than they knew, and Sydney understood the language naturally. Some girls at beauty school thought it was hard. To Sydney, it was second nature.

She didn't have the energy to keep talking to Claire when Claire was making it so difficult, so she took a sip of the coffee and found it had cinnamon in it, just like Grandma Waverley used to make it. When was the last time she'd slept? She wasn't sure she could last much longer before she broke down in tears.

'Come on, Bay,' Sydney said the moment Bay finished her breakfast. 'Let's go upstairs.'

'I left new sheets from Evanelle on the beds,' Claire said.

'Which room?'

'Your room is still your room. Bay can sleep in my old room. I sleep in Grandma's now,' she said.

Sydney led Bay straight to the staircase, not looking around because she was disorientated enough and didn't want to discover what else had changed. Bay ran up the stairs ahead of her and waited, smiling. It was all worth it, just to see her child like this.

Sydney led her to Claire's old room first, and Bay ran to the window. 'I like this room.'

'Your aunt Claire used to spend hours at that window, staring out at the garden. I'm going to start bringing in our things. Come with me.'

Bay looked at her hopefully. 'Can I stay up here?'

She was too tired to argue. 'Don't leave this room. If you want to go exploring, we'll do it together.'

Sydney left Bay, but instead of going downstairs to the car, she walked to her old room. When she was young, she spent a lot of time by herself in her room, sometimes imagining that she was trapped there by her evil sister, like in a fairy tale. For two years after her mother left, Sydney even slept with sheets tied into a rope under her bed so she could crawl out of the window when her mother came back to save her. But then she grew older and realised her mother wasn't coming back.

She also realised that her mother had the right idea by leaving in the first place. Sydney couldn't wait to leave, to follow her boyfriend Hunter John Matteson to college, because they were going to be in love for ever.

She took a deep breath and entered the room reverently, a church of old memories. Her bed and dresser were still there. The full-length mirror still had some of her old stickers on it. There wasn't any dust, and the room smelt familiar, like cloves and cedar. Claire had taken care of it, hadn't turned it into a sitting room or taken Sydney's old furniture out.

That did it.

Sydney went to the bed and sat. She put a hand over her mouth as she cried so that Bay, singing quietly in the next room, wouldn't hear. So much had changed, but her room was exactly as she'd left it.

She crawled to the pillow at the top of the bed and curled into a small ball. She was asleep seconds later.

3

ON THURSDAY MORNING, instead of going to the track, Evanelle decided to walk downtown before the shops opened. When she came to Fred's Gourmet Grocery, she happened to look in the window. It was well before he normally showed up for work, but there was Fred, in his stocking feet, getting a container of yoghurt out of the dairy section. His rumpled clothing was an obvious indication that he'd spent the night there.

She decided to wait for a moment to see if her gift of anticipation would kick in. She stared at him, but nothing occurred to her. She had nothing to give him but advice, and most people weren't inclined to take that too seriously.

Evanelle watched Fred go to the picnic-supply aisle and open a box of plastic utensils. He took out a spoon and opened his yoghurt. She suddenly realised that Fred had stopped short, the plastic spoon in his mouth, and he was looking back at her through the window. She smiled and gave him a little wave.

He walked to the door and unlocked it. 'Can I help you with something, Evanelle?' he said, stepping outside.

'Nope. I was just passing by when I saw you.'

'Is there something you want to give me?' he asked.

'Nope.'

'Oh,' he said, as if he really wanted something, something that would make everything all better. He looked around to see if anyone on the street had seen them, then he leaned forward and whispered, 'I've asked him to be home early for the past two nights, and the past two nights he hasn't come home at all. I don't know what to do when he's not there, Evanelle. He's always so good at making the decisions. Last night I ended up falling asleep on the couch in my office. I don't know what I'm doing.'

Evanelle shook her head. 'You're putting it off is what you're doing. When you have to do something, you have to do it. Putting it off only makes it worse. Believe me, I know.'

'I'm trying,' Fred said. 'I bought rose geranium wine from Claire.'

'What I'm saying is you have to talk to him. Don't wait for him to come home. Call him and ask the serious questions. Stop putting it off.' Fred got a stubborn look to him, and Evanelle laughed. 'OK. You're not ready for that. Maybe the wine will work, if you can get him to drink it. But no matter what you decide to do, you should probably do it with shoes on.'

Fred looked down at his stocking feet, horrified, and hurried back into the store.

With a sigh, Evanelle walked up the sidewalk, looking in windows. Maybe she would just go home and clean up before she went to visit Sydney. Claire had called last night to tell her about Sydney's arrival.

Evanelle passed the White Door Salon, where women with too much time on their hands and too much money in their purses paid way too much for haircuts and hot-stone massages. Then she stopped in front of Maxine's next door, the posh clothing shop that the women from the White Door liked to shop in after their hair was done. There in the window was a button-down silk shirt.

She walked in, even though they hadn't put out the OPEN sign yet. Her gift was like an itch that wouldn't go away until she did what it demanded. And it suddenly, insistently, demanded that she buy Sydney that shirt.

Sydney woke with a start and checked her watch. She hadn't meant to fall asleep. She stumbled to the bathroom and drank water from the sink, then she splashed her face.

She left the bathroom and stopped to check on Bay, but Bay wasn't in her room. Her bed was made, though, and some of her favourite stuffed animals were sitting on the pillows. She checked all the rooms upstairs, then jogged downstairs, trying to stave off panic. Where had she gone?

Sydney walked into the kitchen and froze.

She'd just walked into heaven. And her grandmother was right there, in every scent—sugary and sweet, herby and sharp, yeasty and fresh. Grandma Waverley used to cook like this.

There were two big bowls, one full of lavender and one full of dandelion greens, on the stainless-steel island. Loaves of warm bread sat steaming on the counters. Bay stood on a chair by Claire at the far counter, and she was using a wooden-handled artist's brush to carefully paint pansy flowers with egg whites. One by one, Claire then took the flower heads and delicately dipped them in extra-fine sugar before setting them on a cookie sheet.

'How did you manage this in just a couple of hours?' Sydney said incredulously, and Claire and Bay both turned.

'Hi,' Claire said, looking at her warily. 'How do you feel?'

'I'm fine. I just needed a little nap.'

Bay jumped down from her chair and ran to Sydney and hugged her. She was wearing a blue apron that dragged on the ground and had WAVERLEY'S CATERING written on it in white. 'I'm helping Claire crystallise pansies to put on top of custard cups. Come look.' She ran back to her chair by the counter.

'Maybe later, honey. Let's go get our things from the car and let Claire do her work.'

'Bay and I brought everything in yesterday,' Claire said.

Sydney looked at her watch again. 'What're you talking about? I was only asleep two hours.'

'You've been asleep for the past twenty-six hours.'

Sydney stumbled to the kitchen table and sat. She'd left her daughter alone for twenty-six hours? Did Bay say anything to Claire about David? Had Bay been afraid and lonely in her room all night in a strange house? 'Bay . . .'

'Has been helping me,' Claire said. 'She's a fast learner. We cooked all day yesterday, she had a bubble bath last night, then I put her to bed. We started cooking again this morning.'

Did Claire think she was a bad mother? The one thing Sydney could be proud of, and she was already messing it up.

'Have some coffee,' Claire said. 'Evanelle said she was stopping by today to see you.'

Sydney went to the coffeepot and poured a cup. 'How is she?'

'She's fine. She's anxious to see you. Have some lavender bread. There's some herb butter too.'

Was Claire concerned about her? She'd thought a lot about Claire over the years. Mostly they were thoughts of how adventurous Sydney was being and how poor, pitiful Claire could do nothing but stay at home in stupid Bascom. It was cruel, but it made her feel better because she'd always been jealous of Claire's comfort with who she was. After her third slice of bread, Sydney started walking around the big kitchen. 'This is impressive. I didn't know you could do this. Are these Grandma's recipes?'

'Some of them. The dandelion quiche and the lavender bread were hers.'

'You never let me see them when I was little.'

Claire turned from the counter and wiped her hands on her apron. 'Listen, this is for a job in Hickory tomorrow. I've called two teenage girls who sometimes help me in the summer, but if you need some money, you can help me with it instead. Are you still going to be here tomorrow?'

'Of course I am,' Sydney said.

'While you're here, I could use your help.'

'I guess it's pretty obvious I need the money.'

Claire smiled slightly and Sydney liked that, the small connection it formed. Encouraged, she said, 'So, tell me about that Tyler guy.'

Claire lowered her eyes and turned round. 'What about him?'

'Has he come by today?'

'He doesn't come by every day. Yesterday was the first time. He was bringing some apples that fell on his side of the fence.'

'Did you bury them?'

'We always bury the apples that fall off the tree,' Claire said, and Bay looked at Claire curiously.

'So, Tyler,' Sydney said before Bay could start asking questions. 'Are you interested in him?'

'No,' Claire answered vehemently, like a middle-school girl.

'He belongs here,' Bay said.

Claire turned to her.

'It's this thing she does,' Sydney said. 'She has very firm opinions on where things belong.'

'So that explains it. I asked her to get me a fork and she went right to the drawer. When I asked her how she knew it was there, she said because that's where it belonged.' Claire looked at Bay thoughtfully.

'No,' Sydney said. 'It's not that. Don't force that on her.'

'I wasn't,' Claire said, and she seemed hurt. 'And no one forced it on you. In fact, you ran as far away as you could from it, and no one stopped you.'

'The whole town forced it on me! I tried to be normal and no one would let me.' The pots hanging on the rack above the kitchen island began to sway anxiously, like an old woman wringing her hands. Sydney had forgotten how sensitive the house could be, how floorboards vibrated when people got mad, how windows opened when everyone laughed at once. 'I'm sorry. I don't want to argue. What can I do to help?'

'Nothing right now. Bay, you can go, too.' Claire untied Bay's apron and took it off her. 'Do you have a black skirt and white blouse to wear to help me serve tomorrow?' she asked Sydney.

'I have a white blouse,' Sydney said.

'You can borrow one of my skirts. Have you ever served before?'

'Yes.'

'Is that what you did after you left? Waitressed?'

Sydney wasn't going to tell Claire about her past. Not yet, anyway. 'It was one of the things I did.'

Later that afternoon, Sydney sat on the front porch while Bay did cartwheels in the yard. She saw Evanelle come down the sidewalk and smiled. Evanelle was in a blue running suit, that familiar large tote bag over her shoulder. Sydney used to love to guess what was in it. She hoped Bay would love that, too. There weren't many high points to being a Waverley, but Evanelle was definitely one of them.

Evanelle stopped to talk with Tyler next door, who was in his front yard, contemplating a big clump of grass clippings. He was bored; Sydney recognised the signs. His hair was longish, obviously to hold down the natural curl. That meant he had a creative nature he tried to control, and he was trying to control it by spending most of his day raking a big pile of cut grass from one side of his yard to the other.

As soon as Evanelle left Tyler, Sydney hurried down the steps to meet her. 'Evanelle!' she said as she embraced the old lady. 'It's good to see you. You look exactly the same.'

'Still old.'

'Still beautiful. What were you doing over there with Tyler?'

'Is that his name? He looked like he needed some lawn bags. Lucky I had some on me. Here's his phone number.' She handed Sydney a small piece of notebook paper.

Sydney looked at the paper uncomfortably. 'Evanelle, I don't want . . .'

Evanelle patted Sydney's hand. 'Oh, honey, I don't know what you're supposed to do with it. I just knew I had to give it to you. I'm not trying to set you up.'

Sydney laughed. What a relief.

'I have something else for you.' Evanelle rooted around in her tote for a moment and then handed Sydney a shopping bag from Maxine's. Sydney opened the bag and took out a beautiful blue silk shirt. It was about three sizes too big, but she hadn't had something so decadent in a long time. Sydney sat on the steps. 'It's beautiful.'

Evanelle lowered herself to the step beside Sydney and rummaged through her bag again. 'I know it's too big. Here's the receipt. I was walking downtown this morning, and there was Maxine's. I thought of you, and I knew I had to get you this. This shirt. This size.'

Bay had approached and was shyly fingering the soft shirt in Sydney's hands. 'Evanelle, this is my daughter, Bay.'

Evanelle chucked her chin and Bay giggled. 'She looks just like your grandmother when she was young. Dark hair, blue eyes. She's got Waverley in her, that's for sure.'

Sydney put an arm round Bay protectively. *No, she doesn't.* 'Strawberry Pop-Tarts are her favourite. Thank you for them.'

'Nice to know when things find a good purpose.' She patted Sydney's knee. 'Where is Claire?'

'Busy in the kitchen, preparing for a luncheon.'

'Keep this in mind about Claire. She hates to ask for anything.' Some time passed before Evanelle added, 'It's not an easy thing to do, ask for help. You were brave to come here. I'm proud of you.'

Sydney met the old woman's eyes, and knew that she knew.

It was nearly five o'clock in the afternoon on Friday when Claire, Sydney and Bay arrived home from catering the luncheon in Hickory. Bay had fallen asleep in the van. Sydney thought Claire might be peeved at having to take Bay along, but she didn't argue at all when Sydney said she didn't want to leave Bay with Evanelle just yet. They'd only been in town three days. She wasn't leaving her daughter alone in a strange place. Claire had said, 'Of course not. She'll come with us.' Just like that.

Bay had enjoyed herself. Every time Claire and Sydney came back from collecting plates or refreshing drinks, Bay had cleaned up the area or organised the coolers, instinctively knowing where things were supposed to be.

Sydney carried Bay upstairs and put her on her bed. Then she changed into shorts and a T-shirt, thinking Claire was going to do the same before unloading the things from the van. But when Sydney went back downstairs, Claire had, in that short time, brought everything into the kitchen and was loading the dishwasher and filling the carafes with baking soda and hot water to soak.

'I was going to help you,' Sydney said.

Claire looked surprised to find her there. 'I can do this. When I hire people, it's only to help serve. You can relax. I didn't know if you'd prefer a cheque or cash, so I went with cash. The envelope is there.' She pointed to the kitchen table.

Sydney paused a moment. She didn't understand. Didn't they work well together? What was she supposed to do? She would go crazy if she couldn't do more than just help Claire out every once in a while. Claire didn't even let her do housework. 'Can't I help you with anything?'

'I've got this covered. This is my routine.'

Without another word, Sydney picked up the envelope and walked outside through the back to her Subaru. She leaned against it as she counted the money in the envelope. Claire had been generous.

Folding the envelope, she put it in the back pocket of her cut-offs. She didn't want to go back into the house and watch Claire work, so she walked to the front yard. Tyler's Jeep was parked at the kerb. Impulsively, she crossed the yard and walked up his front steps. She knocked on his door and waited.

When he opened the door, he was wearing paint-splattered jeans and a T-shirt, looking rumpled and forgetful.

'Hi,' she said after he stared at her a few moments, confused. 'I'm Sydney Waverley, from next door.'

He finally smiled. 'Oh, right. I remember.'

His eyes drifted behind her, then to her side. Sydney knew what he was doing, and she wondered how Claire had managed to make this guy so smitten. Maybe he had a thing for control freaks.

'Claire's not with me.'

He looked chagrined. 'I'm sorry,' he said, stepping back. 'Please, come in.'

She'd been in the house a few times when she was young. A lot had been done to the place. It was brighter, and there was a nice red couch in the living room. Rows of unframed paintings were propped against the walls, and cardboard boxes were everywhere. 'I didn't realise you'd just moved in.'

He ran a hand through his hair. 'About a month ago. I've been meaning to unpack. I was just painting in the kitchen.'

'What colour are you painting it?'

He shook his head and laughed. 'No, no. I paint in the kitchen. That's where my easel is set up.'

'Oh, you're a *painter* painter.'

'I teach art at Orion.' He moved some newspapers from a chair and set them on the floor. 'Sit, please.'

'How long have you been in Bascom?' she asked as she went to the chair.

'About a year.' He looked around for another place to sit, running his hand through his hair again, pushing it off his forehead.

'You know, I could trim your hair, if you want me to.'

He turned to her with that chagrined look again. 'I keep forgetting to get it cut. You could do it?'

'You're looking at a bona fide beauty-school graduate.'

'OK. Sure. Thank you.' He moved a box off the couch and sat. 'I'm glad you came by. I don't really know any of my neighbours yet.'

'I'll bring my case over tomorrow to give you a trim. Do you mind if my daughter comes along?'

'Not at all.'

Sydney studied him a moment. 'So, you like my sister.'

She'd caught him off guard, but it didn't seem to occur to him not to answer. 'You cut to the chase, don't you? I don't know your sister very well. But I . . . yes, I like her. She fascinates me.' He smiled and leaned forward. 'I had this dream about her. It was like nothing I've ever dreamed before. Her hair was short, and she was wearing this head-band—' He stopped and leaned back. 'I'm going to stop now before I sound any more ridiculous.'

He didn't sound ridiculous. He sounded nice, so nice it made her a little envious of Claire. 'My daughter likes her, too.'

'You don't sound happy about that.'

'No, I didn't mean it to sound that way.' Sydney sighed. 'It's just not what I expected. Claire and I fought a lot as kids. I think we were both thrilled when I left town. She didn't like me very much. I didn't think she'd like Bay.'

'How long were you gone?'

'Ten years. I never thought I'd be back.' She shook her head, as if to shake away the thoughts. 'Do you mind my coming over? I just need to get out of that house sometimes.'

'You can come by any time you want, but ten years is a long time to be away. There aren't any old friends you want to see?'

She almost laughed. Two-faced backstabbers, yes. Old friends, no. 'No. It's part of that never-thinking-I-was-ever-coming-back thing.'

'Burnt bridges?' Tyler asked astutely.

'Something like that.'

4

THAT NIGHT, ACROSS TOWN, Emma Clark had no idea her world was about to turn upside down as she got ready for the fundraiser ball. She was, in fact, looking forward to the evening because of the attention she always received. Clark women craved the spotlight. They loved attention from men, particularly.

Emma Clark's husband, Hunter John Matteson, was the biggest catch in town. He was handsome, athletic, and heir to his family's mobile home manufacturing empire. Emma's mother, shrewd woman that she was, had positioned Emma to be his wife since Emma and Hunter John were toddlers. Their families mingled and travelled in the same circles, so it wasn't hard to plant suggestions and nudge them together. Their families had even spent a month together on Cape May one summer when Emma and Hunter John were ten years old. 'Look how cute they are together,' her mother said every chance she got.

The only problem was, despite her mother's manoeuvring, despite Emma's beauty and social position, despite the fact that any sane man would want her, all throughout high school Hunter John had been hopelessly in love with Sydney Waverley.

Oh, he knew he shouldn't have anything to do with her. People of their calibre didn't socialise with Waverleys. But when he turned sixteen, in his one and only act of rebellion, he finally asked Sydney out. To everyone's surprise, his parents let him go. 'Let the boy have some fun,' his father said. 'She's the pretty Waverley, and she doesn't seem to have their touch, so she's harmless. My boy knows what's expected of him when he leaves school.'

It was the second worst day of Emma's life.

For the next two years, Hunter John's clique in school had no choice but to accept Sydney into their fold, because she and Hunter John were inseparable. Emma's mother said to keep her mouth shut and her enemies close, so, even though it killed her, Emma made friends with Sydney. Sydney was just a Waverley, but she was smart and fun and had the best taste in hairstyles. Emma would never forget when she let Sydney style her hair once, and then everything went right that day, like magic.

Hunter John had even commented on how pretty she looked. Emma could never replicate it herself. There was a time when Emma actually liked Sydney.

Sydney left town after Hunter John broke up with her at graduation. She'd been devastated to know that school was just a bubble, that she and Hunter John couldn't be together for ever, that the friends she'd made couldn't be her friends after they all graduated. They had to step out into Bascom society and do what their parents expected of them. And Sydney was, in the end, just a Waverley. She'd been so hurt and angry. No one realised that she hadn't known the rules.

Emma would have felt sorry for Sydney if it hadn't been obvious that Hunter John was hurting just as much. It took so much effort that summer to get him to come round, and he still talked of leaving for college. He didn't need this town. So Emma did the only thing she thought she could. She got pregnant.

Hunter John stayed home and married her, and he never complained. They even decided, together this time, that they should have a second child a few years later. He worked for his father, then took over the mobile home construction plants when his father retired. When his parents moved to Florida, Emma and Hunter John moved into his family's mansion. Everything seemed perfect, but she was never really sure where Hunter John's heart was, and that always bothered her.

Which brings us to the worst day in Emma Clark's life.

That Friday night, Emma still didn't realise something big was about to happen. When she and Hunter John arrived at the ball, everything seemed fine. Perfect, in fact. The hospital-fundraiser ball was always held at Harold Manor, a Civil War-era home and *the* place for social gatherings. She'd been there countless times. It was a wonderful, fantasy-like setting, and Emma was immediately the centre of attention, as she always was. But it felt different, as if people were talking about her, wanting to be near her, for all the wrong reasons.

Hunter John didn't notice, but then he never did, so she looked for her mother. Her mother would tell her that everything was all right, even though all the clues were there. Her hair wouldn't curl. Then a pimple popped up on her chin.

She ran into Eliza Beaufort while searching for her mother. Eliza had been one of her best friends in high school. 'Keep the Beauforts as friends,' Emma's mother always said, 'and you'll always know what people are saying about you.'

'Oh my Lord, I couldn't wait for you to get here,' Eliza said. 'I want to know all about how you heard.'

Emma smiled slightly, distracted. 'How I heard what?' she asked, looking over Eliza's shoulder.

'You don't know? *Sydney Waverley is back in town.*' She almost hissed the words.

Emma's eyes darted to meet Eliza's, but she didn't move a muscle. Was that why everyone was acting strangely tonight?

'She came back Wednesday and she's staying with her sister,' Eliza continued. 'You really didn't know?'

'No. So she's back. So what?'

Eliza raised her brows. 'I didn't think you'd take it this well.'

'She was never anything to us, anyway. And Hunter John is very happy. I have no worries. We'll do lunch next week, yes?'

She finally found her mother seated at one of the tables, sipping champagne and entertaining people who stopped by to see her. Ariel looked queenly and elegant and ten years younger than her real age. Like Emma, her hair was blonde and her breasts were big. She drove a convertible, wore diamonds with denim, and was so Southern that she always smelt faintly of cottonwood and peaches.

Her mother looked up as Emma approached, and Emma knew right away that she knew. And she wasn't happy about it.

'Let's take a stroll out to the verandah,' Ariel said, hooking her arm in Emma's and firmly leading her outside. They smiled as they passed some small groups of people who had come out to smoke. Once in a far corner, Ariel said, 'No doubt you've heard about Sydney Waverley. Don't worry. Everything will be all right.'

'I'm not worried, Mama.'

Ariel ignored her. 'I'm going to throw you a party at your house next weekend. Invite all your closest friends. Everyone will see how wonderful you are. Hunter John will see how envied you are. We'll go shopping on Monday and buy you a dress. Red is your best colour, and Hunter John loves you in red.'

'Mama, I'm not worried about Sydney being back.'

Ariel cupped Emma's face with both her hands. 'Oh, sugar, you *should* be worried. First loves are powerful. But if you keep reminding your husband why he chose you, you won't have a problem.'

On Monday afternoon, Claire hung up the phone at her work desk in the storeroom, but she kept her hand resting on the receiver. When you know something's wrong, but you don't know exactly what it is, the air around you changes. Claire felt it. If she went out to the garden, she knew she'd find the morning glory blooming in the middle of the day.

'Claire?'

She turned to find Sydney in the doorway to the storeroom. 'Oh, hi,' Claire said. 'When did you get back?' Sydney and Bay had been to visit Tyler again, the fourth day in a row.

'A few minutes ago. What's wrong?'

'I don't know.' Claire took her hand off the phone. 'I just got a call to cater a party at Mr and Mrs Matteson's house this weekend.'

Sydney hesitated before asking, 'The Mattesons who live in that large Tudor home on Willow Springs Road?'

'Yes.'

'Short notice,' Sydney said cautiously, curiously.

'Yes. And she said she'd double my normal fee because of it, but only if I had enough help for the night.'

'I always liked Mrs Matteson,' Sydney said. 'Are you taking the job? I'll help you.'

'Are you sure?' Claire asked, because things still seemed wrong. Sydney used to have a relationship with Hunter John, and she used to be friends with Emma. If she'd wanted to see them again, she would have gone to see them before now.

'Of course I'm sure.'

Claire shrugged. 'OK, then. Thank you.'

Sydney smiled and turned on her heel. 'No problem.'

Claire followed her into the kitchen. There were some things that hadn't changed about Sydney, like her light brown hair that had just enough natural curl to make it look like waves of caramel icing on a cake. She'd lost weight but still had a stunning figure.

The rest of Sydney was a mystery. She'd been here almost a week now and Claire was still trying to figure her out. She was a terrific mother, that much was clear. But she was jumpy, and she never used to be jumpy. Sydney would get up several times every night to make sure everything downstairs was locked up tight. What was she running from? It did no good to ask her questions; Sydney only changed the subject when asked about the last ten years. She left and went to New York. That was all Claire knew. And Bay wasn't giving up any secrets. According to her, she was born on a Greyhound bus and she and her mother had lived everywhere.

Claire watched Sydney walk to the pot of soup steaming on the stove. 'Oh, I invited Tyler over for dinner,' Sydney said, taking a whiff of the camomile chicken soup. 'That's OK, isn't it?'

Claire gaped at her. 'You did what?'

'Come on,' Sydney said, laughing. 'Give the man a break. Tyler's nice.'

'Is that why you're spending so much time over there? You want Tyler?'

'No. But why don't you?' Claire was saved from answering by a knock at the front door. 'It's for you,' Sydney said.

'He's *your* guest.'

As Sydney went to the door, Claire strained to hear Tyler's voice. 'Thanks for the invitation,' she heard him say. 'Great house.'

'Want a tour?' Sydney asked, which made Claire anxious. She didn't want Sydney showing Tyler the house. She didn't want Tyler knowing her secrets.

'Sure.'

Claire closed her eyes for a moment. *Think, think, think.* What would make Tyler forget her, make him less interested? What dish would turn his attention elsewhere? She had to try to dissuade him in any way she could. Rudely, if necessary. There just wasn't any room for him. She was letting too many people in as it was.

Bay ran into the kitchen ahead of Sydney and Tyler. She hugged Claire, like it was the most natural thing in the world to give a hug for no discernible reason, and Claire held her tightly for a moment. Bay pulled away and ran to the kitchen table and sat.

Sydney walked in and Tyler followed. Claire noticed right away that he'd had his hair cut. It suited him, made him seem more focused. That, she decided when his eyes focused on her, was not a good thing. She turned away.

'It must have been amazing, growing up in this house,' Tyler said.

'It was interesting, all right,' Sydney said. 'There's a step on the staircase, three steps up, that squeaks. When we were young, every time someone stepped on it, a mouse would stick his head out of the knothole on the step above to see what made the sound.'

Claire looked at her sister, surprised. 'You knew about that?'

'I'm not much of a Waverley, but I grew up here, too.'

'Were the two of you very close growing up?' Tyler asked.

'No,' Sydney said, before Claire could.

Claire filled three bowls with soup and set them on the table with a plate of almond butter and ginger jelly sandwiches. 'Enjoy,' she said, and left the kitchen and went out to the garden, Tyler, Sydney and Bay watching her go.

About forty-five minutes later, Claire had finished digging a hole by the fence and was gathering up the apples that had fallen round the tree. It was humid, carrying a hint of the summer to come.

'Stop it,' Claire kept saying as the tree dropped apples round her, trying to vex her. 'The more you drop, the more I bury.'

It dropped a small apple on her head.

'Is that your secret?'

She turned to see Tyler standing on the grass. How long had he been there? She hadn't even heard him approach. The tree had been distracting her. Damn tree.

'My secret?' she asked warily.

'Your secret to this garden. You talk to the plants.'

'Oh.' She gathered more apples in her arms. 'Yes, that's it.'

'Dinner was great.'

'I'm glad you enjoyed it.' When he didn't move, she said, 'I'm a little busy.'

'That's what Sydney said you'd say. And she said to come out anyway.'

'Her confidence is attractive, I know, but I think she just needs a friend right now,' Claire said, shocking herself. She never meant to say that. It sounded as if she *cared*. Sure, she wanted Tyler to turn his attention elsewhere. But not to Sydney. Claire closed her eyes. She thought she was past all that jealousy.

'What about you? Do you need a friend?'

She glanced over at him. He was so comfortable with himself, standing there in his jeans, his button-down shirt. Just for a moment, she wanted to walk into his arms and let that sense of calm envelop her. What was the matter with her? 'I don't need friends.'

'Do you need something more?'

She didn't have a lot of experience with men, but she understood what he meant. 'I like what I have.'

'I do, too, Claire. You're beautiful,' he said. 'There, I said it. I couldn't keep it in any longer.'

He wasn't afraid of getting hurt. He seemed to *welcome* it. One of them had to be sensible. 'That thing about me being busy: I meant it.'

'That thing about you being beautiful, I meant it, too.'

She walked over to the hole by the fence and dropped the apples in. 'I'm going to be busy for a long, long time.'

When she turned back round, Tyler was grinning. 'Well, I'm not.'

She watched him as he walked away, feeling uneasy. Was he trying to tell her something? Was it a warning of some sort?

I have all the time in the world to wiggle my way in.

The Matteson mansion looked the same as Sydney remembered. She could walk up to Hunter John's bedroom with her eyes closed, even now. When they spent time alone in the house, she used to pretend they lived there together. But when he broke up with her at graduation, he said, 'I thought you understood.'

She didn't understand then, but she did now. She understood now that she'd loved him, and he was probably the only man she'd ever loved like that, with such hope. She understood now that she would always have left Bascom, whether or not it was with him.

There was a small, remembered thrill to being somewhere Sydney knew she shouldn't be as Claire pulled round to the service entrance and they entered the kitchen. The housekeeper met them and introduced herself as Joanne. She was in her forties, and her black hair was so shiny and straight that it barely moved, which meant she hated mistakes.

'I was told to wait to arrange the flowers until you arrived,' Joanne said. 'When you finish unloading, I'll be on the patio.' She disappeared through the swinging door of the butler's pantry.

Soon everything was in, and the necessary things refrigerated. On the patio, a warm summer breeze carried the scent of roses and chlorine. There were circular cast-iron tables and chairs set up round the pool, and an elaborate bar had been erected in a corner. Longer tables for the food were skirting the walls, and that's where Joanne was standing, surrounded by empty vases and buckets of flowers.

Sydney felt light-headed. It was the fantasy of it all, the white linens on the buffet tables flapping in the wind, the lights in the pool sending watery shadows over the area, the starlights in the shrubbery. She had wanted this so much when she was young, this prosperity, this dream.

She listened as Claire told Joanne where the roses, fuchsia and gladioli should be placed on the tables. 'Gladioli here,' she said, 'where the nutmeg stuffing in the squash blossoms and the fennel chicken will be. Roses here, where the rose-petal scones will go.' It was all so intricate, a manipulative plan to make the guests feel something they might not feel otherwise. It didn't seem at all like Mrs Matteson. Yet Claire had spent the better part of the evening on Monday discussing the menu on the phone with her. Sydney had overheard her saying things like, 'If it's love you want to portray, then roses.' And, 'Cinnamon and nutmeg mean prosperity.'

After Claire had taken care of the nonedible-flower placement with Joanne, she started to walk back into the house but stopped when she realised Sydney wasn't following her. 'Are you all right?' Claire asked.

Sydney turned. 'It's beautiful, isn't it?' she said, as if proud of it, as if it belonged to her. It did, for a while.

'It's very . . .' Claire hesitated a moment. 'Deliberate. Come on, we don't want to get behind schedule.'

Parties made Emma feel enchanted, like a little girl playing dressing-up. Her mother had been the same way. 'Leave the magic to the Waverleys,' she used to say when Emma was little and she would watch her mother try on dress after dress before parties. 'We have something better. We have fantasy.'

Emma was standing by the bar because that's where Hunter John was. She'd never had a party feel quite like this one, when every other sentence out of everyone's mouth was a compliment to her or an envious remark. It was wonderful.

Ariel walked over to her and kissed Emma's cheek. 'Darling, that red dress is perfect on you. Just perfect.'

'This was a grand idea, Mama. Thank you for doing it all. Who is the caterer? I'm getting compliments on the food.'

Ariel turned Emma so that she faced the patio doors across the pool. 'That, sugar, is my biggest gift to you this evening.'

'What do you mean?'

'Wait. Watch. I'll show you.'

Emma didn't understand, but she laughed with anticipation. 'Mama, what did you do? Did you buy me something?'

'In a sense. Ah, there it is,' Ariel said, pointing with a glass of champagne in her hand.

'Where?' Emma said excitedly. Her eyes focused on two women coming out of the house, carrying trays. They were servers, obviously. Then she realised who one of the servers was. 'Is that Claire Waverley? You hired *her* to cater my party?' It suddenly occurred to her in one terrible moment what her mother had done, and her eyes darted to the other woman with Claire. 'Oh my God.'

Ariel leaned in close and hissed, 'Stop being a fool and go over there. Show her she doesn't belong here, that there's no chance of getting what she had back. And show your husband that you're the belle of the ball, and she's just the caterer. Now go.'

It was the longest walk Emma had ever taken. Hunter John had already made his way over to Sydney and was staring at her while she arranged the new trays on the buffet tables. She hadn't looked up yet. Emma had nearly reached him when Hunter John finally cleared his throat and said, 'Sydney Waverley, is that you?'

Several things happened at once. Sydney's head shot up and she locked eyes with Hunter John. Eliza Beaufort, who was standing at the next table, swivelled on her heel. Claire stopped what she was doing to watch. And Carrie Hartman, one of the old gang from high school, came forward. 'Sydney Waverley,' she said in a singsongy voice.

Sydney looked cornered. Emma felt a rush of embarrassment for her.

'We all heard you were back in town,' Eliza said. 'You were away a while. Where did you go?'

Sydney wiped her hands on her apron, then tucked her hair behind her ears. 'I went everywhere,' she said, her voice quivering slightly.

'Did you go to New York?' Hunter John asked. 'You always talked of going to New York.'

'I lived there a year.' Sydney's eyes darted around. 'Um, where are your parents?'

'They moved to Florida two years ago. I took over the business.'

'So *you* live here?'

'We live here,' Emma said, hooking her arm in Hunter John's and leaning in to press her cleavage against him.

'Emma? You and Hunter John are . . . married?' Sydney said, and her shock was unsettling to Emma. How dare Sydney be shocked that Hunter John chose her?

'We married the year we graduated. Right after you left. Sydney,' she said, 'I see two empty trays here.' Emma tried to tell herself that Sydney had set herself up for this, that her humiliation was all her own doing. But it didn't make Emma feel any better. She didn't like making Sydney feel bad. Emma had won, after all. Right? But this is what Emma's mother would do, would say. And look how long she'd kept Emma's father.

Hunter John looked from Emma to Sydney and back. 'I need to speak with you in private,' he said, and led Emma through the crowd of guests into the house, Sydney's eyes following them.

'What's the matter, honey?' Emma asked when Hunter John led her into his study and closed the door. Emma had decorated this room for him, the butter-and-cocoa-coloured walls, the framed photos of Hunter John's glory days on the high-school football field, the potted plants, and the huge walnut leather-top desk. She leaned against the desk provocatively.

Hunter John stood by the door, his glare as dark as charcoal. 'You did this on purpose. You're humiliating Sydney on purpose.'

'Since when do you care?'

'I care about how this looks. Why bring her into our home?'

'Shh, honey. Calm down. I had nothing to do with it, I swear.' She walked over to him, reached up and patted his lapels. Her hands slid down his jacket to his trousers.

His hands circled her wrists. 'Emma, no,' he said for the first time in ten years, and he stepped away.

Claire felt nervous, and she hated the feeling. She hated when she didn't know what to do.

Sydney's face was tight and her steps were sharp as Claire followed her back into the kitchen. As soon as the door swung closed, Sydney dropped her empty trays on the counter and said, 'Why didn't you tell me Mr and Mrs Matteson were Hunter John and Emma Clark?'

Claire gathered Sydney's trays and stacked them on her own. 'It didn't occur to me that you would think it was anyone else. Who did you think it was?'

'I thought it was Hunter John's parents! How on earth was I supposed to know Hunter John and Emma got married?'

'Because when you broke up with him, he and Emma started dating,' Claire said, trying to keep her stomach from jumping.

'How was I supposed to know that? I wasn't here!' Sydney said. 'And I didn't break up with him. He broke up with me. Why do you think I left?'

Claire hesitated. 'I thought you left because of me. I thought you left because I kept you from learning things, because I made you hate being a Waverley.'

'You didn't make me hate being a Waverley. This whole town did,' Sydney said impatiently. She shook her head like she was disappointed in Claire. 'But if it makes you feel better, I'm leaving because of you now.'

'Wait, Sydney, please.'

'This was a set-up! Didn't you see it? Emma Clark set me up to look like a . . . like a servant in front of Hunter John and all my old high-school friends.' Sydney stared at Claire for a few long moments, her eyes shining with tears. 'Why did you let me do this? Didn't you think it was unusual for Emma to be calling you to cater something meant to flaunt a lifestyle everyone else already knew about? She did this so I would see it.'

'She didn't arrange this, her mother did. I never even spoke to Emma. Maybe this was just a coincidence. Maybe it doesn't mean anything.'

'How can you, of all people, say that? To a Waverley, there's a meaning to everything! And how can you defend them? Are you actually this comfortable with people thinking the way they do about us? I saw you when we were kids, how no boys were ever interested in you. I thought that's why you retreated into all of this'—Sydney waved widely at the food and flowers on the countertops—'because you thought the house and Grandma were all you needed. I wanted more than that. I was devastated when Hunter John broke up with me, but you didn't even notice. And this hurt me tonight, Claire. Doesn't it matter at all to you?'

Claire didn't know what to say, which seemed to make Sydney even more upset. Sydney turned and went to the handbag she'd set by the door. She took out a small piece of notebook paper and then went to the wall phone and dialled the number on the paper.

'Tyler?' Sydney said into the receiver. 'It's Sydney Waverley. I'm stuck someplace and I need a ride.' Pause. 'Willow Springs Road, number thirty-two, a large Tudor home. Drive around back. Thank you so much.'

Sydney took off her apron, dropped it to the floor. She grabbed her bag and walked out of the door.

Claire helplessly watched her go. She couldn't lose what was left of her family, not so soon. She couldn't be the reason Sydney left again.

Those people out there on the patio, they had done this on purpose. Sydney was right. There was a meaning to everything, and Claire had ignored all the warning signs. She took a deep breath, then straightened. She would fix this.

She went to the phone and pushed the REDIAL button.

It took a few moments, but Tyler's voice finally came on the line, slightly breathless. 'Hello?'

'Tyler? This is Claire Waverley.'

There was a definite pause of surprise. 'Claire. This is strange. I just got a call from your sister. She sounded upset.'

'She is. I need to . . . ask you for a favour.'

'Anything,' he said.

'I need you to go next door to my house before you pick Sydney up here. Will you bring me some things from the house and garden? I'll tell you where the keys are hidden.'

While waiting for Tyler to bring the things she needed, Claire lined up the food and flowers. Then she wrote ingredient descriptions and a list of the flowers outside on index cards so she wouldn't confuse a recipe and cause mixed signals. This was too important. They wanted roses tonight to represent their love, but when you added sadness to love it caused regret. They wanted nutmeg because it represented their wealth, but when you added guilt to wealth it caused embarrassment.

She hoped Tyler wouldn't ask what his errand was for. But why would he? He wasn't from here. He didn't know the subversive nature of what she could do.

When Claire got home, Sydney and Bay were already in bed. Sydney had obviously asked Tyler to pick Bay up at Evanelle's house on their way home. At least they were going to stay the night, long enough for some things to be made right.

Claire stayed up late to make her regular order of six dozen cinnamon buns, which she delivered to the Coffee House on the square every Sunday morning.

Around midnight, she sleepily made her way towards her room. She was walking down the hall when Sydney called out, 'I had a lot of calls before you came home tonight.'

Claire backed up a step and peered into Sydney's room. Sydney was lying in bed with her arms behind her head. 'Eliza Beaufort, Carrie, people at the party I didn't even know. They all said the same thing. That they were sorry. Eliza and Carrie even said they really liked me in high school and they wished things were different. What did you say to them?'

'I didn't say a word.'

Sydney paused, and Claire knew by her next question that she was beginning to understand. 'What did you give them?'

'I gave them lemon-balm sorbet in tulip cups. I put dandelion petals in the fruit salad, and mint leaves in the chocolate mousse.'

'That wasn't on the dessert menu,' Sydney said.

'I know.'

'I noticed Emma Clark and her mother never called.'

Claire leaned against the doorjamb. 'They caught on to what I was doing. They wouldn't eat dessert. And I was ordered to leave.'

'Did they pay you the remainder of your fee?'

'No. And I've had two cancellations tonight from acquaintances of theirs.'

A rustle of sheets. Sydney turned in bed to face Claire. 'I'm sorry.'

'They officially cancelled, but they'll call again when they need something. They'll just want me to keep it a secret.'

'I've messed things up. I'm sorry.'

'You didn't mess anything up,' Claire said. 'Please don't leave, Sydney. I want you here. I may not act like it sometimes, but I do.'

'I'm not leaving. I can't.' Sydney sighed. 'As crazy as this place is, the way people think, the sameness, is what makes it safe. Bay needs that. I'm her mother, I have to give that to her.'

The words were left hanging in the air, and Claire could tell immediately that Sydney wanted to take them back. 'Did you leave someplace that wasn't safe?' Claire had to ask.

But she should have known Sydney wouldn't answer. She shifted in her bed again, turning away. She punched her pillow a few times. 'Wake me and I'll help you deliver the cinnamon buns in the morning,' she said as she flopped back down.

'No, I can—' Claire stopped. 'Thank you.'

5

ON TUESDAY AFTERNOON, Claire announced she was going to the grocery store, and Sydney asked if she and Bay could ride along. Sydney wanted to get a newspaper to check out the want ads and, though it pained her to do so, she had to return the shirt Evanelle had given her. And Bay needed kid food. Claire was a great cook, but she'd looked at Bay blankly yesterday when Bay asked if she had any pizza rolls.

When they reached Fred's, Claire and Bay went into the grocery store and Sydney walked up the sidewalk to Maxine's. She returned the shirt, and on her way back to the grocery store she passed the White Door Salon. A patron came out, and with her the scent of chemicals cushioned by the fragrance of sweet shampoo. It was a smell that could almost lift Sydney up and make her float. Oh, how she missed that.

She'd gone to beauty school under her real name, a name David didn't know, so she reminded herself that he wouldn't find them here. The only reason David had found her in Boise was because she'd registered Bay under her real name, thinking she had no choice when the day-care centre asked for Bay's birth certificate. She'd thought David would only be looking for Cindy Watkins, not Bay. She wasn't making that mistake again. Bay was a Waverley here.

She patted her hair, glad that she'd trimmed her fringe that morning. Then she straightened her shoulders and walked in.

Sydney was giddy when she met Claire and Bay at the van. She grinned as she helped them load the bags of groceries.

'Guess what?'

Claire smiled, obviously amused by Sydney's mood. 'What?'

'I got a job! I told you I was staying.'

Claire looked genuinely perplexed. 'But you already have a job.'

'Claire, you do the work of three people. And you only need help occasionally. I'll still work when you need me.'

'Where did you get the job?'

'I rented a booth at the White Door.' It was going to take all her money, including the refund from the shirt she'd just returned, to rent the booth, but she had a wonderful feeling. She would soon make money, and people in Bascom would see that she was actually skilled at something. They would come to *her* like they came to Claire, because of what she could do.

'You're a hairstylist?' Claire asked.

'Yep.'

'I didn't know that.'

Claire was getting too close to asking again about where she and Bay had been, but Sydney still wasn't ready to tell her about the past ten years. As they loaded the groceries, Sydney looked in a bag and asked, 'What is all this stuff? Blueberries? Water chestnuts?'

'I'm going to make a few dishes for Tyler,' Claire said.

'Are you, now? I thought you didn't want anything to do with him.'

'I don't. These are special dishes.'

'You're not going to poison him, are you?'

'Of course not,' Claire said. 'But maybe I can make him less interested.'

Sydney laughed but didn't say a word. She knew a lot about men, but making them less interested had never been her speciality. Leave it to Claire to make it hers.

Bay stretched out on the grass, the sun on her face. Things that had happened even a week ago were fading in her mind. What colour were her father's eyes? How many steps were there from their old house to the sidewalk? She couldn't remember.

Bay had known all along that they were going to leave Seattle. They just didn't belong there, and Bay knew where things belonged. Sometimes, when her mother would put things away at their old house, Bay would sneak in later and put the things where she knew her father wanted them to be. But his desires changed so quickly that sometimes Bay couldn't keep up with them, and he'd yell and do bad things to her mother. It had been exhausting, and she was glad to be someplace it was clear where things belonged. Utensils were always in the drawer to the left of the sink. Linen was always put in the closet at the top of the stairs. Claire never changed her mind about where things went.

Bay had dreamed of this place a long time ago. In the dream she was stretched out on the soft grass in this garden by this apple tree. But in her dream there were rainbows and tiny specks of light on her face, like something sparkling above her. And there was the sound of something like paper flapping in the wind, but the only sound now was the rustling of the leaves on the apple tree.

An apple hit her leg, and Bay opened one eye to look up at the tree. It kept dropping apples on her, almost like it wanted to play.

She sat up suddenly when she heard Claire call her name. This was Sydney's first day at work, and Claire was watching Bay. 'I'm right here,' Bay called as she stood up.

Claire was standing at the other end of the garden by the gate, holding a casserole dish covered with aluminium foil. 'I'm going over to Tyler's to take him this. Come with me.'

Bay ran down the gravel pathway to Claire, glad that she was going to see Tyler again. When she and her mother had visited last time, he'd let her draw on an easel, and when she showed him what she'd drawn, he'd hung it on his refrigerator.

Claire closed and locked the gate behind them, and they walked round the house to Tyler's yard. 'Aunt Claire, why does the apple tree keep dropping apples on me?'

'It wants you to eat one,' Claire said.

'But I don't like apples.'

'It knows that.'

'Why do you bury the apples?'

'So no one else will eat them.'

'Why don't you want people to eat them?'

Claire hesitated a moment. 'Because if you eat an apple from that tree, you'll see what the biggest event in your life will be. If it's good, you'll suddenly know that everything else you do will never make you as happy. And if it's bad, you'll have to live the rest of your life knowing something bad is going to happen. It's something no one should know.'

'But some people want to know?'

'Yes. But as long as the tree is in our yard, we get a say-so.'

They reached Tyler's steps. 'You mean it's my yard, too?'

'It's very definitely your yard, too,' Claire said, smiling.

'This is a pleasant surprise,' Tyler said when he opened the door. Claire had taken a deep breath before she knocked, and when she saw him she forgot to let it out. He was in a paint-splattered T-shirt and jeans. Sometimes her very skin felt so jumpy that she wanted to crawl out of her body. She wondered what a kiss from him would do. Help? Make it worse?

'I made you a casserole,' she said as she handed it to him.

'It smells delicious. Please, come in.' He stood back for them to enter, which was the last thing Claire wanted to do.

Bay looked at her curiously. She thought something was wrong.

Claire smiled at her and entered so she wouldn't worry.

Tyler led them through the living room into a white kitchen with glass-fronted cabinets. There was a very large breakfast nook off the kitchen, with floor-to-ceiling windows. The floor of the nook was covered with a tarp, and two easels were set up.

'That's the reason I bought this house. All that beautiful light,' Tyler said as he put the casserole dish on the kitchen counter.

'Can I draw, Tyler?' Bay asked.

'Sure. Your easel is right over there. Let me put some paper on it.'

While Tyler adjusted the easel to her height, Bay went to the refrigerator and pointed to a coloured drawing of an apple tree. 'Look, Claire, I did that.'

It wasn't that Tyler put Bay's drawing on his refrigerator that Claire appreciated; it was that he'd left it there. 'It's beautiful.'

As soon as Bay was settled, Tyler walked back to Claire, smiling.

Claire's eyes went to the dish worriedly. It was a chicken and water chestnut casserole made with the oil from snapdragon seeds. Snapdragons were meant to ward off the undue influences of others, and Tyler needed to free himself of her influence over him. 'Aren't you going to eat it?' she prompted.

'Right now?'

'Yes.'

He shrugged. 'Well, OK. Why not? Will you join me?'

'No, thank you. I've already eaten.'

'Then sit while I eat.' He took a plate from a cabinet and spooned some of the casserole onto it. He led Claire to two stools at the counter. 'So, how are you and Bay getting along with Sydney at work?' he asked as they took their seats. 'She stopped by yesterday and told me about her new job. She has a gift with hair.'

'We're doing fine,' Claire said, watching Tyler as he brought a forkful of the casserole to his mouth.

He chewed and swallowed, and she thought for a moment that maybe she shouldn't be watching. It was almost sensual, his full lips, the bob of his Adam's apple. She shouldn't feel this way about a man who was going to be free of her in a few seconds.

He pointed to his plate with his fork. 'This is wonderful. I don't think I've ever eaten as well as I have since I met you.'

Maybe it just took a few minutes to kick in. 'Next you're going to tell me I remind you of your mother.'

'No, you're nothing like my mother. Her free spirit doesn't include anything to do with the kitchen.' She raised her brows at this bit of information. He smiled at her and took another bite. 'Go on, you know you want to ask.'

She hesitated a moment, then gave in, 'How is she a free spirit?'

'They're potters, my parents. I grew up in an artists' colony in Connecticut. It wasn't for me. I can't help my artistic nature, but security and routine mean more to me than to my parents. I just wish I was better at it.'

You're looking at an expert, she thought, but didn't say it out loud. He would probably like that about her.

Two more bites and he'd cleaned his plate.

She looked at him expectantly. 'How do you feel?'

He met her eyes, and she almost fell off her stool from the force of his desire. It was like a hard gust of autumn wind that blew fallen leaves around so fast they could cut you. Desire was dangerous to thin-skinned people. 'Like I want to ask you on a date,' he answered. 'There's music on the quad at Orion every Saturday night in the summer. Come with me this Saturday.'

'No, I'll be busy.'

'Doing what?'

'Making you another casserole.'

Sydney's third day at work was the third day she went without a single walk-in wanting a haircut. The other stylists were a nice bunch, and they were encouraging, telling Sydney it would get better. But Sydney had to find some way to get how good she was out there, to start bringing people in.

Since she didn't have anything else to do, Sydney started sweeping around a station at the other end of the salon.

'Thanks, Sydney,' the stylist said as she highlighted blonde hair.

The client's head shot up, and Sydney saw that it was Ariel Clark.

Sydney managed a polite smile, even though she was choking the broom handle. If she was going to make a success out of this venture, she couldn't whack White Door clients over the head with a broom, no matter how much they deserved it. 'Hello, Mrs Clark. How are you? I'm sorry we didn't get to say hello at the party.'

'Understandable, sugar. You were working. It would have been inappropriate.' Her eyes slid down the broom to the sad pile of hair Sydney had swept up. 'You're working here, I gather.'

'Yes.'

'You don't actually . . . cut hair, do you?' she asked, as if appalled by the thought.

'Yes, I do actually cut hair.'

'Don't you need some sort of degree to do that, sugar?'

Sydney's fingertips were going numb and turning white from gripping the broom handle so tightly. 'Yes.'

'Hmm,' Ariel said. 'So I hear you have a daughter. And who is her father?'

'No one you know.'

'Oh, I'm certain of that.'

'Anything else, Mrs Clark?'

'My daughter is very happy. She makes her husband very happy. I don't know what you hoped, coming back here. But you can't have him.'

That's what this was all about? 'I know this is going to come as a surprise, but I didn't come back to get him.'

'So you say. You Waverleys have your tricks. Don't think I don't know.' She flipped her cellphone out of her handbag and started dialling. 'Emma darling, I have the most delicious news,' she said.

At about five o'clock that afternoon, Sydney was going to give up for the day and leave. That's when she saw a man in a nice grey suit at the reception desk, and she got a sinking feeling.

Hunter John asked the receptionist something, and she turned and pointed at Sydney.

He walked across the salon towards her. At twenty-eight, his sandy hair was thinning. A better cut would hide it.

'I heard you were working here,' Hunter John said when he reached her.

'Yes, I imagine you did.' She crossed her arms over her chest. 'So you took over your family's business.'

'Yes.'

Matteson Enterprises was a group of mobile-home manufacturing plants about twenty minutes outside of Bascom. Sydney had worked as a receptionist in the front office the same summers Hunter John had interned there. They used to meet in his father's office when he went to lunch, and they'd make out.

'Can I have a seat?' Hunter John asked.

'Do you want me to cut your hair? I'm great at it.'

'No, I just don't want it to look like I only stopped by to talk,' he said as he sat.

She rolled her eyes. 'Heaven forbid.'

'I wanted to clear the air. It's the right thing to do.' Hunter John always did the right thing. The golden boy. The good son. 'That night at the party, I didn't know you'd be there. And neither did Emma. We were as surprised as you, but it was for the best. As you saw, I'm happily married now.'

'Good Lord,' Sydney said, 'does everyone think I came back just for you?'

Hunter John sighed. 'I did love you once, Sydney. Breaking up with you was one of the hardest things I've ever done.'

'So hard that you sought comfort in marrying Emma?'

'Emma and I just grew close after you left. She's the best thing that ever happened to me.'

'Did you go to Notre Dame? Did you travel around Europe like you wanted to?'

'No. Those are old dreams.'

'Seems to me you gave up a lot of dreams.'

'I'm a Matteson. I had to do what's best for my name.'

'And I'm a Waverley, so I get to curse you for it.'

He gave a little start, like she meant it, but then Hunter John smiled. 'Come on, you hate being a Waverley.'

'You should go,' Sydney said. Hunter John stood and reached for his wallet. 'And don't you dare leave money for a pretend haircut.'

'I'm sorry, Sydney. I can't help who I am. Neither can you.'

As he walked away, she thought what a sad thing it was that she'd only ever loved one man. And it had to be that man.

She wished she really did know a curse.

'I was getting worried,' Claire said when Sydney came into the kitchen that evening. 'Bay's upstairs.'

Sydney opened the refrigerator and took out a bottle of water. 'I stayed late.' She walked over to the sink where Claire was washing blueberries. 'So, what are you making? Something to take to Tyler again?'

'Yes. I'm going to sprinkle blueberry tarts with the petals from these bachelor's-buttons.'

'And what do they mean?'

'Bachelor's-buttons make people see sharper, helpful for finding things like misplaced keys and hidden agendas,' Claire said easily.

'So you're trying to make Tyler realise you're not what he's looking for?'

Claire smiled slightly. 'No comment.'

Sydney watched Claire work for a while. 'I wonder why I didn't inherit it,' she said absently.

'Inherit what?'

'That mysterious Waverley sensibility you and Evanelle have. Grandma had it, too. Did Mom?'

Claire turned off the spigot and reached for a hand towel to dry her hands. 'It was hard to tell. She hated the garden, I remember that much. She wouldn't go near it.'

'I don't mind the garden, but I guess I'm more like Mom than anyone in the family. She moved back here so you would have a stable place to live and go to school, just like I did for Bay.'

'Mom didn't move back because of me,' Claire said, surprised Sydney thought that. 'She moved back so you could be born here.'

'She left when I was six,' Sydney said. 'If it weren't for those photographs of Mom that Grandma gave me, I wouldn't even remember what she looked like. If I'd meant something to her, she wouldn't have left.'

'What did you do with those photos?' Claire asked. 'I'd forgotten about them.'

Sydney was transported back to Seattle, to the living room of the town house. There under the couch was an envelope marked *Mom*. She'd forgotten it was there. Inside were photos of Lorelei's life on the road, a life Sydney had tried to emulate for so long. One photo was of her mother, maybe eighteen years old, standing in front of the Alamo. She was smiling and holding a handmade sign that read NO MORE BASCOM! NORTH CAROLINA STINKS!

What if David found the envelope? What if he figured it out?

'Sydney?' Claire was shaking her arm.

'I forgot to take the photos with me,' Sydney said. 'I left them.'

'Are you all right?'

Sydney nodded, trying to get a hold of herself. 'I'm fine. I was thinking of Mom.' She shrugged, trying to get rid of the tension in her shoulders. David didn't know where the photos were. He wouldn't find them.

That evening, Evanelle put on a robe over her nightgown and walked into her kitchen. She had to step round boxes full of matches, rubber bands and Christmas ornaments. Once in the kitchen, she went searching among the boxes for microwave popcorn.

She didn't want any of this stuff, but one day someone was going to need it, so it was better to have it around than to go looking for it at three in the morning at the all-night Wal-Mart.

She turned when she heard a knock. Someone was at her door. Now this was a surprise. She didn't get many visitors.

She turned on the porch light, then opened the door. A short, middle-aged man stood there, a small suitcase at his feet. 'Fred!'

'Hello, Evanelle.'

'What on earth are you doing here?'

His face was drawn, but he tried to smile. 'I . . . need a place to stay. You were the first person I thought of.'

'Well, come in.'

Fred picked up his suitcase and entered, then stood in the living room looking like a little boy who had run away from home. 'Shelly, my assistant manager, came in early today. She caught me in my pyjamas in my office. It's been easier just to stay at work. I know what to do there.'

'Have you talked with James at all?'

'I tried. Like you said. After that first night I slept at the store, I called him at work. He said he didn't want to talk about it, that just because I finally noticed something was wrong didn't mean I could make it right now. I don't understand what happened. It's like he's been leaving me by degrees, and I didn't even notice. How does a person not notice that?'

'Well, you can stay here as long as you like. But if anyone asks, I get to say my undeniable womanliness turned you straight.'

'I make terrific Belgian waffles, with a wonderful peach compote. Just tell me what you want me to cook, and I'll cook it.'

She patted his cheek. 'Not that anyone will believe me.'

She showed him to the guest bedroom down the hall. After Fred put his suitcase on the bed, Evanelle said, 'I was going to make some popcorn and watch the news. Want to join me?'

'Sure.' Fred followed her, as if glad to be told what to do.

Well, isn't this nice, Evanelle thought as they sat on the couch with a bowl of popcorn, watching the eleven o'clock news together.

'Is it true that you once gave my father a spoon when you were kids?' Fred asked. 'And that he used it to dig a quarter out of the dirt when he saw something shiny? And he used the quarter to go to the movies? And that's where he met my mother?'

'It's true that I gave him a spoon. I don't have the power to make things all better, Fred.'

'Oh, I understand,' he said quickly. 'I was just asking.'

Evanelle suddenly realised the real reason he was there. Fred wanted to be closer, on the off chance she was going to produce something that would make sense out of everything happening with James, that spoon that was going to help him dig out of this.

Sydney, Bay and Claire sat on the porch that Sunday, eating cinnamon buns that Claire had made extra from her regular order for the Coffee House. It was hot and things were out of whack. Doorknobs that everyone swore were on the right side of the doors were actually on the left. Butter melted in the refrigerator. Things weren't being said and were left to stew in the air.

'There's Evanelle,' Sydney said, and Claire turned to see her coming up the sidewalk.

Evanelle walked up the steps, smiling. 'Your mother had two beautiful girls, I'll give her that. But you two don't look so chipper.'

'It's the first heatwave. It makes everyone cranky,' Claire said as she poured Evanelle a glass of iced tea from the pitcher she'd brought outside. 'How have you been? I haven't seen you in a couple of days.'

Evanelle took the glass and sat in the wicker rocker by Claire. 'I've had a guest.'

'Who?'

'Fred Walker is staying with me.'

'Oh,' Claire said, surprised. 'Are you OK with that?'

'I'm fine with it. It's nice to know that you two aren't the only ones who like having me around.' Evanelle put her tea down and rooted through her tote bag. 'I came because I had to give you this,' she said, bringing out a white headband and handing it to Claire. 'Fred tried to talk me out of giving it to you. He said you use combs, not headbands, that headbands are for people with short hair. He doesn't understand. *This* is what I had to give you.' Evanelle turned to Sydney. 'So tell me, how is work?'

Sydney and Bay were sitting on the porch swing, and Sydney was using one bare foot to gently rock them back and forth. 'I have you to thank for it. If you hadn't given me that shirt I returned, I never would have gone into the White Door.'

'Fred said he saw you last week, sweeping up.'

'That's all I'm good for right now.'

'What's the matter?' Claire asked. Sydney had been so excited about her job at first, but as the days wore on she came home earlier and earlier, smiling less and less.

'The clientele at the White Door all seem to know the Clarks and the Mattesons. I had a visit from Hunter John my third day. Apparently, some people, and I'm not naming names, aren't happy with that and spread the word.'

'So . . . so people have been snubbing you?' Claire asked. 'Not even giving you a chance?'

'If this keeps up, I'm not going to be able to keep the booth. But maybe it's just as well,' Sydney said, putting her arm round Bay. 'I'll get to spend more time with Bay. And I'll be free to help you any time you want.'

Claire had been in a hair salon three times in her adult life, only when her hair would get too long to control and she needed a couple of inches taken off. She went to Mavis Adler's Salon of Style on the highway. Mavis used to make special house calls to cut Claire's grandmother's hair, and if Mavis was good enough for her grandmother, she was good enough for Claire.

Claire didn't consider herself unsophisticated, but when she walked into the White Door and found leather couches and original artwork and a gaggle of some of the more wealthy women in town, some of whom she'd catered brunches, lunches and teas for, she suddenly felt frighteningly out of place.

She spotted Sydney in the back, sweeping hair from around another stylist's chair, looking beautiful and self-contained. She looked so alone.

Sydney saw her and immediately walked to the reception area. 'Claire, what's wrong? Where's Bay? Is she OK?'

'She's fine. I asked Evanelle to watch her for an hour or two.'

'Why?'

'Because I want you to cut my hair.'

A crowd of stylists and patrons gathered around, waiting for Sydney to begin. Whispers of Claire's beautiful long hair and Sydney's untested abilities floated around like dust motes.

'Do you trust me?' Sydney asked as she pumped up the chair after she'd washed Claire's hair.

Claire met her sister's eyes in the mirror. 'Yes,' she said.

Sydney turned her round, away from the mirror.

Over the next few minutes, Claire's hair felt lighter and lighter as wet chunks of dark hair fell onto the smock she was wearing, looking like thin strips of molasses candy.

When Sydney finally turned the chair back round, the people around her applauded.

Claire couldn't believe what she saw. Sydney had taken off at least twelve inches. The cut angled down so that it was longer in the front, but high and full at the back. The thin fringe made Claire's eyes look beautiful and sparkling, not flat and judgmental. There in the mirror was someone who looked like Claire had always wanted to be.

Sydney didn't ask her if she liked it. There was no question. It was a transformation performed by an expert. Everyone was looking at Sydney with awe, and Sydney was shining like polished silver.

Claire felt tears come to her eyes, a joy of birth, of redemption. Somewhere deep inside her, Claire had always known. It had been the source of all her jealousy when they were kids. Sydney had been born here.

That was a gift, and this had always been inside Sydney, just waiting for her to embrace it.

'You can't deny it any more,' Claire said.

'Deny what?' Sydney asked.

'*This* is your Waverley magic.'

6

LESTER HOPKINS sat on an aluminium lawn chair under the chestnut tree in his front yard. A ribbon of dust followed a car in the distance, coming up the long driveway to the house next to the dairy.

Lester had come back from his stroke last year with a limp and a corner of his mouth that wouldn't quite turn up, so he kept a handkerchief handy to wipe away the spittle that collected there. Didn't want to offend the ladies. He spent a lot of time sitting these days, which he didn't mind. It gave him time to think. Truth be told, he had always looked forward to retirement.

But there were a few glitches along the way. He had to work harder than he imagined after his father died when Lester was seventeen, which left him to run the dairy by himself. And he and his wife were blessed with only one son. But his son married a hard-working woman and they all lived there in the house, and his son had a son and everything was all right. Then Lester's wife got cancer, and his son died in a car accident two years later. Lost and grieving, his daughter-in-law wanted to move to Tuscaloosa, where her sister lived. But Henry, Lester's grandson, then eleven years old, wanted to stay.

So Lester had known only two things of constant faith: his farm and Henry.

As the car came closer, Lester heard the screen door bang shut. He turned to see that Henry had come out of the house to see who it was. It was too late for business. The sun was nearly set.

Henry called out, 'Are you expecting something, Pap?'

'My ship to come in. But that ain't it.'

Henry walked down to the chestnut tree and stood beside Lester. Lester looked over at him. He was a handsome boy, but, like all

Hopkins men, he was born old and would spend his life waiting for his body to catch up. This was the reason all Hopkins men married older women. Henry was taking his time, though, and Lester had taken to helping him along a little. Lester would tell Henry to lead the elementary-school tours of the dairy if the teachers were the right age and unmarried. And the decorating committee at church consisted of mostly divorced women, so Lester let them come out to collect hay in the fall and holly in the winter, and he always made Henry go out to help them. But nothing ever took. Solid and sure of himself, hard-working and kindhearted, Henry was quite a catch, if only he wasn't so happy with himself.

But that's what happens when you're born old.

The car came to a stop. Lester didn't recognise the driver, but he did recognise the woman getting out of the passenger seat.

He cackled. He always liked for Evanelle Franklin to come by. It was like finding a robin in the winter. 'Looks like Evanelle needs to give us something.'

The driver stayed in the car as Evanelle crossed the yard. 'Lester,' she said, stopping in front of him and putting her hands on her hips, 'you look better every time I see you.'

'They have a cure for cataracts now, you know,' he teased. 'What brings you out this way?'

'I needed to give you this.' She reached into her bag of goodies and handed him a jar of maraschino cherries.

'Well, I haven't had these in a long time. Thank you, Evanelle.'

'You're welcome.'

'Say, who's that who brought you?'

'That's Fred, from the grocery store,' Evanelle said. 'I'll see you at the Fourth of July celebration?'

'We'll be there,' Lester said, and he and Henry watched her walk away.

'She gave me a ball of yarn once,' Henry said. 'I was probably four-teen, and we were on a school field trip downtown. I was so embar-rassed. I threw it away. But the very next week I needed it when I was working on a school project.'

'Men in this town learn their lesson young when it comes to Waverley women,' Lester said. 'Whenever there's one around, best pay attention.'

The next afternoon, Claire heard Sydney's voice upstairs. 'Where is everyone?'

'I'm down here,' Claire called to her.

Soon she heard the creak of the dusty stairs as Sydney walked down to the basement towards the shine of Claire's flashlight. The light bulbs in the basement had all burnt out in 1939, and what had started out as someone too tired to replace them had turned into a family tradition of keeping the basement in the dark.

'Where is Bay?' Sydney asked. 'Isn't she down here with you?'

'No, she likes to stay in the garden most of the time. She's OK. The tree stopped tossing apples at her when she started throwing them back.' Claire handed Sydney the flashlight. 'Help me with this, will you? Shine here.'

'Honeysuckle wine?'

'The Fourth of July celebration is next week. I'm counting the bottles to see how many we have to bring.'

'I saw a bottle on the kitchen table when I came in,' Sydney said as Claire counted.

'That's the rose geranium wine Fred gave back to me,' Claire said, then clapped her hands together to get rid of the dust. 'Thirty-four bottles. I thought I made forty last year. No matter. This should be enough.'

'Are you going to give the rose geranium wine to Tyler?'

'Actually, I was hoping you would take it to him for me.'

'He's teaching his summer-session classes,' Sydney said. 'He won't be around much.'

'Oh,' Claire said, walking away, glad that Sydney couldn't see her confusion. She sometimes thought she was going crazy. Her first thought when she woke up was always how to get him out of her thoughts. And she would keep watch, hoping to see him next door, while plotting ways to never have to see him again. It made no sense.

They reached the kitchen, and Claire closed and locked the basement door behind them. 'He's a good guy, Claire,' Sydney said. 'Imagine that. Men can be good. Who would've thought?'

'He's not a constant,' Claire said. 'The apple tree is a constant. Honeysuckle wine is a constant. This house is a constant. Tyler Hughes is not a constant.'

'I'm not a constant, am I?' Sydney asked, but Claire didn't answer.

Was Sydney a constant? Had she really found her niche in Bascom, or would she leave again? Claire didn't want to think about it. The only thing Claire could control was not being the reason Sydney left, giving her reasons to stay.

'So how's work?' Claire asked brightly.

'So busy, thanks to you. People look at me now like I'm a teacher or something. I don't understand it.'

'You've just learned the secret to my success,' Claire said. 'When people believe you have something to give, something no one else has, they'll go to great lengths and pay a lot of money for it.'

Sydney laughed. 'So you're saying, if we're going to be strange anyway, we might as well get paid for it?'

'Exactly.'

'You have cobwebs in your hair from the basement,' Sydney said, walking over to her and sweeping them away with her fingertips. Territorial about Claire's hair now, Sydney had taken to finger-combing the fringe across her forehead or fluffing up the back.

'Where did you cut hair before?' Claire asked.

Sydney stepped back. 'It's been a few years. But in Boise, for a while.' She turned away, grabbed the rose geranium wine off the table and hurried out of the back door, a curious smell of men's cologne trailing after her. 'I'm going to say hi to Bay, then I'll just take this over to Tyler.'

Ever since that day Sydney mentally returned to the town house in Seattle and remembered she'd left the photos of her mother there, the scent of David's cologne would appear without warning. Sometimes even Claire would smell cologne in the house and wonder aloud where it had come from. The cologne made Sydney realise what kind of danger she'd put her sister in by coming here. Claire was doing so much for her.

When Sydney walked outside, the scent of cologne faded in the garden, pummelled by the fragrance of apples and sage and earth. Sydney sat with Bay under the tree, and they talked about her day and about the Fourth of July celebration. Bay spent several hours every day lying on the grass by the apple tree. When Sydney asked her why, she said she was just trying to figure something out. Sydney didn't press, and so much had happened that it was natural that Bay needed time to figure it out.

After talking to Bay, Sydney walked over to Tyler's. She found him in his back yard, bringing a lawn mower out of his small shed.

'I come bearing a gift from Claire.' She held up the wine bottle.

Tyler hesitated, as if silently squelching the first thing he wanted to say. 'You know, I'm having no luck figuring out your sister. She gives me gifts when she clearly doesn't like me. Is this a Southern thing?'

'Oh, she likes you. That's why she's giving you this stuff. Do you mind if I have some of this? I'm a little shaky right now.'

'Sure, come on.' They walked into his kitchen through the back, and Tyler took two wineglasses out of his cabinet. As soon as he poured her a glass, she took a long drink of it.

'What's wrong?' he asked.

'My mind went somewhere it shouldn't have a while back. It still spooks me.'

'Anything you want to talk about?'

'No.'

He nodded. 'OK. So, what is this?' Tyler poured himself a glass and lifted it to his nose.

'Rose geranium wine. It's supposed to bring back good memories.'

He lifted his glass to her. 'Here's to good memories.'

Before he could drink it, Sydney blurted out, 'She's hoping this will make you remember someone else and forget her. Like the casserole with the snapdragon oil.'

He lowered his glass. 'I don't understand.'

'The flowers grown in our back yard are special. They can affect the eater. You're obviously immune. Or maybe she's trying too hard, maybe that changes the way it works. I don't know.'

Tyler looked at her incredulously. 'She's trying to make me not interested in her?'

'Which means you're in already. Let me tell you something about Claire. She likes things that don't go away. So don't go away.'

Sydney wondered if she should have revealed something so personal about her sister. But then Tyler smiled, and she knew she'd done the right thing. 'I'm not going anywhere,' he said.

'Good.' Sydney looked away. The words of a good man could bring tears to a woman's eyes. She'd known a lot of men after she left Bascom, none of them good. 'Drink up,' she said.

Tyler lifted his glass to his lips and took a sip. 'So what are your good memories?' he asked.

'It's so strange. My good memories are of this week. This week has been the best of my life. You?'

'It's good wine, but I'm not getting anything. I'm just thinking of Claire.'

She smiled and drank some more. 'You're hopeless.'

Bascom's Fourth of July celebration was held every year on the square downtown. On the green by the fountain, families and church groups set up tables and brought food so everyone could sample delicacies before the fireworks display. Waverleys always brought honeysuckle wine so people could see in the dark, but whether or not the town knew it, the wine also brought about a few revelations every Fourth of July. A side effect of being able to see in the dark is being aware of things you weren't aware of before.

The Waverleys had a table off to the side. Bay was over in the supervised children's area, making paper hats and getting her face painted, so it was just Sydney and Claire and the hooch. People would quietly come by for small paper cups of honeysuckle wine, and every once in a while the sheriff would stroll by and ask, 'Now, this is non-alcoholic, right?'

And Claire would answer, straight-faced, as every Waverley had, 'Of course.'

When Sydney was a teenager, the Fourth of July always meant spending the day at a friend's pool, then showing up on the green just in time for the fireworks. She felt older than her old high-school friends now, most of whom had obviously come from back yard barbecues or pool parties and had tans and bathing-suit straps peeking out from under their shirts. Emma was at the Presbyterian church's table, talking with Eliza Beaufort. Knowing what she knew now, Sydney didn't envy that life of privilege any more.

Evanelle walked up and took a cup of wine. 'Whew, I need this,' she said, throwing back the wine like a shot. 'There's so much to do. I need to give something to Bay.' She set the cup down and brought a truly gaudy brooch out of her tote bag. Faintly 1950s, it was made of clear but yellowing crystal in a starburst pattern.

'She's getting her face painted right now,' Sydney said.

'OK, I'll stop by there. Fred is helping me organise my house. I found this in an old jewellery box we came across, and when I saw it I knew I had to give it to Bay.'

Claire leaned forward in her seat. 'Fred has been helping you?'

'He's come up with a system for all the stuff I have. He created something called a spreadsheet.'

'I've been offering to help you do that for years, Evanelle,' Claire said. She seemed hurt.

'I know. I didn't want to bother you with it. But since Fred is living with me—'

'Living with you?' Claire exclaimed. 'I thought he was just staying with you for a while.'

'Well, we figured he might as well be comfortable while he's there. He's turning the attic into his own little apartment and making some improvements around the house.'

'You know if you ever need me, I'm here for you,' Claire said.

'I know. You're a good girl.' She put the brooch back in her tote bag. 'After Bay, I have to take some nails to Reverend McQuail and a mirror to MaryBeth Clancy. See you later.'

'Bye, Evanelle. Call me if you need me!'

A few minutes and another walk-by from the sheriff later, Sydney nudged Claire. 'In case you haven't noticed, Tyler keeps looking at you.'

Claire sneaked a glance, then groaned. 'Damn. You had to go and make eye contact. Now he's coming over.'

'Oh, heaven forbid.'

'Yeah, well, I'm not the only one who's being stared down. You've got one, too.' Claire indicated a canopy across the green with HOPKINS DAIRY written on it. A handsome man, blond and lean and tanned, was scooping ice cream out of electric ice-cream makers to put on paper cones. He was solid, as if made to withstand wind. He kept looking over to the Waverley table.

'That's Henry Hopkins,' Claire said.

'Henry! I'd almost forgotten him. We were . . . friends, I guess. In elementary school. We grew apart after that.'

'Why?' Claire asked, her eyes darting to Tyler as he got closer.

'Because I was a blind ass in high school,' Sydney said.

'You were not.'

'Was so.'

'Hello, ladies. Need a referee?'

'Hi, Tyler,' Sydney said.

'Claire, your hair,' Tyler said, and Claire's hand went to her hair self-consciously. She was wearing the white headband Evanelle had given her. 'It's beautiful. I had a dream . . . I dreamed your hair was like this once. I'm sorry, there was really no way for that not to sound stupid.' He laughed, then rubbed his hands together. 'So, everyone keeps telling me I need to drink some of the Waverleys' honeysuckle wine. Either it's a town tradition, or everyone is in on this Claire-trying-to-make-me-not-interested-in-her game.'

'What?'

'Sydney told me what you were trying to do with the dishes you were giving me.'

Claire turned to Sydney, who tried to look sheepish but felt otherwise unrepentant.

'Honeysuckle wine helps you see in the dark,' Claire said stiffly. 'Have it or don't have it. Walk into a tree when it gets dark. Fall over a kerb. I don't care.'

Tyler picked up a paper cup and drank the wine, not taking his eyes off her as he did so. Sydney just sat back and smiled. It was like watching a dance when only one of the dancers knew the steps.

When Tyler walked away, Claire rounded on her sister. 'You told him?' she asked.

'Why are you so surprised? I'm predictable like that.'

'You are not.'

'I am so.'

'Oh, go socialise and stop feeling your Waverley oats,' Claire said, shaking her head. But there it was, a hint of a smile, the beginning of something new and close between them.

It felt good.

Henry Hopkins could still remember the day he and Sydney Waverley became friends. Sydney was sitting alone inside the dome of the monkey bars during recess. She seemed so sad that he went over to her and started climbing the bars above her.

She watched him a while before asking, 'Henry, do you remember your mother?'

He'd laughed. 'Of course I do. I saw her this morning. Don't you remember yours?'

'She left last year. I'm starting to forget her. When I grow up, I'm never leaving my kids.'

Henry remembered feeling ashamed, a feeling so intense he actually fell off the monkey bars. And from that day forward, he stuck like glue to Sydney at school. For four years, they played and ate lunch together and compared homework answers and buddied up on class projects.

He had no reason to expect that, on their first day of middle school after summer break, things would be any different. But then he walked into their homeroom and there she was. She'd grown in ways that made his pubescent head spin. Every time she tried to speak to him that day, he felt like fainting and ran away. After a while, she stopped trying.

It was so unexpected, that attraction, and it made him miserable. He wanted things back the way they were. He was sure Sydney thought he had abandoned her, like her mother. He felt terrible. In the end, Hunter John Matteson fell hard for her and did what Henry couldn't—he actually told her. Henry watched while Hunter John's friends became her friends and she began to act like them, laughing at people in the hallways, even Henry.

'You're staring so hard you're going to knock her over.'

Henry turned to his grandfather, who was sitting on his aluminium lawn chair behind the table. 'I was staring?'

'For the past thirty minutes,' Lester said. 'You haven't heard a word I've said.'

'Sorry.'

'Heads up. She's on the move.'

Henry turned and saw that Sydney had left the Waverley table and was walking to the children's area. Her hair shone in the sun, bright like honey. She went to her daughter and laughed when her daughter put a paper hat on her head. Sydney said something to her, her daughter nodded, and together they walked towards him.

They were walking towards him.

When they approached the table, Sydney smiled. 'Hi, Henry. Remember me?'

Henry was afraid to move for fear he would explode from the riot going on in his body. He nodded.

'This is my daughter, Bay.'

He nodded again.

Sydney looked disappointed but shrugged it off and discussed the choices of ice cream with her daughter. There was chocolate mint, strawberry rhubarb, caramel peach and vanilla coffee.

'Could we have two chocolate mint, please?' Sydney finally asked.

Henry scooped out balls of ice cream and put them on the paper cones. Sydney studied him as he handed them the cones. Still, he didn't say a word. He couldn't even smile.

'It's nice to see you again, Henry. You look good.' She and her daughter turned and walked away. Halfway across the green, she looked over her shoulder at him.

'That was the most pitiful display I've ever seen,' Lester finally said, cackling.

'I can't believe I didn't say anything,' Henry said.

Evanelle and Fred sat on the rock bench circling the fountain. They waved as Sydney and Bay passed, eating ice cream. Bay had the ugly brooch Evanelle had given her pinned to her pink T-shirt, and Evanelle felt guilty. That wasn't a brooch for a little girl. Why on earth did Evanelle need to give her such a thing? She sighed. She might never know.

'I'm nervous,' Fred finally said, rubbing his hands on his neatly pressed shorts. 'He said he'd be here to talk. In public. What does he think I'm going to do if we're alone, shoot him?'

'Men. You can't live with them, you can't shoot them.' Evanelle patted his knee. It had been nearly a month since Fred had asked for sanctuary in her home, and he had become an unexpected bright spot in her days. The arrangement was supposed to be temporary but slowly, surely, Fred was moving in. He and Evanelle had spent days going through all her old things in the attic and Fred seemed to enjoy the stories she told. He was footing the bill to renovate the attic space.

'It's getting late,' Fred said. 'People are already putting out blankets. Maybe I missed him.'

Evanelle saw James before Fred did. James was a tall, handsome man. Evanelle had never had a bad word to say about James. No one did. He worked for an investment firm in Hickory and kept to himself. Fred had been his only confidant for over thirty years, but suddenly that had changed, and Fred couldn't figure out why.

Fred went still when he finally saw James approaching.

'I'm sorry I'm late.' James was a little out of breath, and a fine sheen of perspiration dotted his forehead. 'I was just at the house. I took a few things, but the rest is yours. I wanted to tell you that I have an apartment in Hickory now.'

Ah, Evanelle thought. That's the reason James wanted Fred to meet him here, so James knew when Fred wasn't going to be in the house and he could take things out without having to discuss it first with Fred. One look at Fred, and Evanelle knew he'd figured that out, too.

'I'm taking early retirement next year, and I'll probably move to Florida. Or maybe Arizona. I haven't decided yet.'

'So, that's it?' Fred asked, and Evanelle could tell there were too many things he wanted to say, all fighting to get out. Ultimately, the only thing that escaped was, 'That's really it?'

'I'm tired of trying to show you the way,' James said. 'I dropped out of school for you. I came here to live with you because you didn't know what to do. I had to plan the meals and what we did with our free time. I thought I was doing the right thing. When your father died and you had to leave college, I was terrified you wouldn't be able to make it on your own. It's taken me a long time to realise that I did you a great disservice, Fred. By trying to make you happy, I prevented you from knowing how to figure it out on your own. By trying to give you happiness, I lost my own.'

'I can do better. Just tell me—' Fred stopped, and in one terrible moment realised that everything James said was true.

James squeezed his eyes shut for a moment. 'I should be going.'

'James, please don't,' Fred whispered, and grabbed his hand.

'I can't do this any more. I can't keep telling you how to live. I've almost forgotten how to do it myself.' James hesitated. 'Listen, that culinary instructor at Orion—Steve, the one who comes into your store and talks recipes with you—you should get to know him better.'

Fred let his hand drop, and he looked as if he'd been punched in the stomach.

Without another word, James walked slowly away.

Sydney watched Bay run around the green with a sparkler, but she turned when she saw someone approach from the right.

Henry Hopkins walked to the edge of her quilt and stopped. He'd grown up to be a handsome man, lots of blond hair cut close and practical, and tight muscles in his arms. He'd been a gangly youth, but he had a quiet dignity that she'd appreciated when they were little kids. They grew apart as they grew up, and she didn't know exactly why. She just knew she'd been horrible to him once she got everything she thought she wanted in high school. She didn't blame him for not wanting to talk to her when she went to the Hopkinses' table that afternoon.

'Hi,' Henry said.

Sydney couldn't help but smile. 'He speaks.'

'Do you mind if I sit here with you?'

'As if I could refuse a man who gives me free ice cream,' Sydney said, and Henry lowered himself beside her.

'I'm sorry about before,' Henry said. 'I was surprised to see you.'

'I thought you were mad at me.'

Henry looked genuinely confused. 'Why would I be mad?'

'I wasn't very nice to you in high school. I'm sorry.'

'I was never mad at you. Even today, I can't pass a set of monkey bars and not think of you.'

'Ah, yes,' Sydney said. 'I've had many men tell me that.'

He laughed. She laughed. All was right. He met her eyes after they'd quieted, then said, 'I'm glad you're back.'

Sydney shook her head. This was an unexpected turn to her day. 'You are, quite possibly, the first person to actually say that to me.'

'Well, the best things are worth waiting for.'

You don't stay for the fireworks?' Tyler asked as Claire was boxing up the empty wine bottles. He'd come up behind her, but she didn't turn round. She was too embarrassed to. If she turned round, she would become that deeply disturbed woman who couldn't handle a man being interested in her.

Her edges were crumbling like border walls, and she was feeling terribly unprotected. The worst possible time to deal with Tyler.

'I've seen this show before,' she said, her back still to him. 'It ends with a bang.'

'Now you've ruined it for me. Can I help you?'

She stacked the boxes and took two of them, planning to get the other two on her second trip. 'No.'

'Right,' Tyler said, picking up the boxes. 'So I'll just grab these.'

He followed her across the green to her van, which she'd parked on the street. She could feel his stare on the back of her neck. She never realised how vulnerable short hair could make a person. It exposed places that were hidden before, her neck, the slope of her shoulders.

'What are you afraid of, Claire?' he asked softly.

'I don't know what you're talking about.'

When they reached the van, she unlocked the back and put her boxes in. Tyler came up beside her and set his boxes beside hers. 'Are you afraid of me?'

'Of course I'm not afraid of you,' she scoffed.

'Are you afraid of love? Are you afraid of a kiss?'

'No one in their right mind is afraid of a kiss.' She closed the back of the van and turned round, finding him closer than she expected. Too close. 'Don't even think about it,' she said, sucking in her breath, her back plastered against the van as he stepped closer still.

'It's just a kiss,' he said, moving in, and she didn't think it was possible for him to be so close and not actually touch her. 'Nothing to be afraid of, right?'

He put one hand on the van, near her shoulder, leaning in. She could leave, of course. Just scoot away and turn her back on him again. But then he lowered his head, and she was done for.

Slowly his lips touched hers and there was a tingling, warm, like cinnamon oil. Then his head tilted slightly and there was this friction. It came out of nowhere, streaking through her body. Her lips parted when she gasped in surprise, and that's when things really got out of control. A million crazy images raced through her mind. Her hands were suddenly everywhere, touching, grabbing, pulling him closer. He was pressing her against the van, the force of his body nearly suspending her in air. It was too much, she was surely going to die, yet the thought of stopping, of actually breaking contact with this man, this beautiful man, was heartbreaking.

The whistles slowly invaded her senses, and she pulled back to see some teenagers walk by on the sidewalk, smiling at them.

'Let go of me,' she said.

'I don't think I can.'

She slid out from between him and the van. He fell forward against the van, as if he had no strength to stand. She understood why when she tried to walk to the driver's side and was so weak she nearly didn't make it.

'All this from one kiss,' he said. 'If we ever make love, I'm going to need a week to recover.'

He talked of the future so easily. But she couldn't start this, because then it would end, and she would spend the rest of her life missing it, hurting from it.

'Leave me alone, Tyler,' she said as he pushed himself away from the van, his chest still rising and falling rapidly. 'This never should have happened. And it's not going to happen again.'

She got in the van and sped away, jumping kerbs and running stop signs all the way home.

7

MORE THAN A CENTURY AGO, Waverleys were wealthy, respected people who built a showy house in Bascom. When they lost their money through a series of bad investments, the Clarks were secretly overjoyed. The Clarks were rich landowners, with acres of the best cotton and the sweetest peaches; the Waverleys weren't nearly as wealthy, but they had always held themselves better than the Clarks thought they should.

When news of the Waverleys' poverty reached them, the Clark women danced a little dance in the secretive light of the half-moon. Then, thinking themselves quite charitable, they brought the Waverleys woollen scarves riddled with moth holes and tasteless cakes made without sugar. They secretly just wanted to see how badly the floor needed polishing without the servants and how empty the rooms looked with most of the furniture gone.

It was Emma Clark's great-great-great-aunt Reecey who took the apples from the back yard, and that started the whole thing. The Waverley women wanted to show the Clarks their flowers, because tending the garden was the only thing they really had any success doing. It made Reecey Clark jealous, because the Clarks' garden could never compare. There were many apples around the garden, shiny and perfect, so she secretly filled her pockets and her reticule. Why should the Waverleys have so many beautiful apples, apples they didn't even eat?

When she got home, she took the apples to their cook and told her to make apple butter. For weeks after, every single one of the Clark women saw such wonderful and erotic things that they began to get up earlier and earlier each morning just for breakfast. The biggest events in the lives of Clark women, it turned out, always involved sex, which could have come as no surprise to their frequently exhausted husbands, who spent and forgave too much because of this.

But then, quite suddenly, all the apple butter was gone and with it the erotic breakfasts. More was made, but it wasn't the same. Reecey knew then that it had been *those* apples. The Waverley apples. She became insanely jealous. It simply wasn't fair that they got to have such a tree and the Clarks didn't.

And that resentment stuck in the Clark family, long after the reason faded away.

The day after the Fourth of July, Emma Clark Matteson tried to use the time-honoured Clark way of getting what she wanted from Hunter John. Afterwards Emma tried to get him to talk about Sydney. She wanted him to think about how sexy Emma was compared to how old Sydney looked in her plaid shorts yesterday, which she had described to him in detail. But Hunter John refused to talk about Sydney at all, saying she had nothing to do with their lives any more. He got up and went to the bathroom to shower.

Emma was distraught, so she did the only thing she could think of. She called her mother and cried.

'Your mistake was in bringing Sydney up with Hunter John this morning,' Ariel told her.

'But you said to make him compare us,' Emma said, lying in bed and hugging a pillow after Hunter John had gone to work. 'How can I do that without bringing her up?'

'You're not paying attention, sugar. I set that up so he could compare Sydney to you when Sydney was serving and you were the hostess. Just that once. Don't keep doing it, for heaven's sake.'

Emma's head was spinning. She'd never doubted her mother's considerable knowledge in the ways of men, but this seemed so complicated.

'You haven't let Hunter John anywhere near her since he went to see her at the White Door, have you? That was another mistake.'

'No, Mama. But I can't keep track of him all the time. When do I trust him? When do I know?'

'Men are untrustworthy creatures. You have to work to keep him,' Ariel said. 'Buy something new and skimpy, just for him. Surprise him.'

'Yes, Mama.'

'Clark women don't lose their men. We keep them happy.'

'Yes, Mama.'

'**W**here is Bay?' Sydney asked, walking into the kitchen on her first Monday off since the Fourth of July. 'I thought she was helping you.'

'She was, but she heard a plane overhead and ran out to the garden. Happens every time.'

Sydney laughed. 'I don't understand it. She was never this crazy about planes before.'

Claire was at the kitchen island making chocolate cupcakes for the Havershams, who lived four doors down. They were hosting their grandson's pirate-themed tenth birthday. Instead of a cake, they wanted six dozen cupcakes with something baked inside, a child-size ring or a coin or a charm. Claire had made candy strips from thin shoots of angelica from the garden and was going to make a tiny x on the frosting of each cupcake, like the sign on a treasure map, then she was going to put tiny cards on toothpicks with riddles as to what was buried within.

Sydney watched Claire with the frosting. 'So when is this gig?'

'The Havershams' birthday party? Tomorrow.'

'I'll be glad to take time off work to help you.'

Claire smiled, touched by Sydney's offer. 'I've got this one covered. Thanks.'

Bay came in at that moment, and Sydney laughed. 'Oh, honey, you don't have to wear that brooch that Evanelle gave you every day. She doesn't expect you to.'

Bay looked down at the brooch she'd pinned to her shirt. 'But I might need it.'

'Ready to go for our walk to see the school?'

'Will you be OK without me, Aunt Claire?' Bay asked.

'You were a great help today, but I think I can finish up,' Claire said. She was going to be sad when Bay started school in the fall.

'We won't be gone long,' Sydney said.

'OK.' Claire suddenly felt prickly, and she looked at the hairs on her arms standing on end. Damn. 'Tyler's about to come to the front door. Please tell him I don't want to see him.'

Sydney laughed as soon as there was a knock. 'How did you know that?'

'I just knew.'

Tyler and Bay waited together on the front-porch swing. As they swung, Bay thought about her dream, the one of her in the garden. Things here weren't going to be perfect until she could replicate it exactly. But she couldn't figure out how to make sparkles on her face in the sun and, even though she'd taken notebooks out to the garden and held paper up to the wind, she could never quite get the sound of paper flapping right, either.

'Tyler?' Bay said.

'Yes?'

'What kinds of things make sparkles on your face? Like if you were lying outside in the sun? Sometimes I see planes go by and they're shiny and sometimes the sun makes sparkles on them, but when I try lying in the yard when planes pass overhead, they don't make sparkles on me.'

'You mean like light reflecting and making sparkles?'

'Yes.'

He thought about it for a moment. 'Well, when a mirror catches the sun, it causes flashes. Metal or crystal wind chimes outside in the sun, when the wind blows, might have reflections coming off them. And water in the sun has sparkles.'

'Those are good ideas! Thank you.'

He smiled. 'You're welcome.'

Sydney walked out at that moment, and Tyler stopped the swing so suddenly that Bay had to hold on to the chain to keep from falling off. Her mother and Aunt Claire had that effect on people.

'Hi, Tyler,' Sydney said, standing in front of the screen door. She looked back into the house, unsure. 'Um, Claire said she didn't want to see you.'

Tyler stood, which set Bay swinging again. 'I knew it. I scared her.'

'What did you do?' Sydney demanded in the voice she had used when Bay tried to cut her own hair once.

Tyler looked down at his feet. 'I kissed her.'

Sydney suddenly laughed, but then covered her mouth with her hand when Tyler's head shot up. 'I'm sorry. But that's all?' Sydney walked over and patted his arm. 'Let me talk to her, OK? If you knock, she won't answer.' Sydney gestured for Bay to get off the swing, and they all walked down the steps together. 'A kiss, huh?'

'It was some kiss.'

'I didn't know she had it in her.'

Tyler said goodbye to them when they reached his house. 'I did.'

'Is Claire upset about something?' Bay asked as they turned the corner. 'She forgot where to put the everyday silverware this morning. I had to show her.'

'She's not upset, honey. She just doesn't like it when she can't control things. Some people don't know how to fall in love, like not knowing how to swim. They panic first when they jump in. Then they figure it out.'

'I've already fallen in love.'

'You have, have you?'

'Yes, with our house.'

'You get more like Claire every day,' Sydney said as they finally stopped in front of a long red-brick building. 'Well, there it is. Aunt Claire and I went here. It's a good place.'

Bay looked at the building. She knew where her classroom was going to be, through the door and down the hall, the third door on the left. She nodded. 'It's the right place.'

'Yes,' Sydney said. 'Yes, it is. So, are you excited about school?'

'It's going to be good. Dakota belongs in my class.'

'Who's Dakota?'

'A boy I met on the Fourth of July.'

'Oh. Well, I'm glad you're making friends.'

'You should make friends, too, Mommy.'

'Don't worry about me, honey.' Sydney put her arm round Bay's shoulder and pulled her close as the scent of David's cologne floated by on the wind. It made Bay afraid for a moment, not for herself, but for her mother. 'We're close to downtown. Let's go by Fred's and get some Pop-Tarts!' Sydney said brightly, in that voice adults always use to try to distract kids from what's really going on.

Bay didn't argue. Pop-Tarts were good, after all. And she liked them better than her father.

When they reached Fred's, they walked in, and Sydney took a basket by the door. They had just passed the produce section when there was a crash, and suddenly there were hundreds of apples rolling everywhere, into the bread section and under people's carts. The culprit was standing by the now-empty apple display, not looking at what he had done, but staring straight at Sydney.

It was Henry Hopkins, the man who'd given them ice cream on the Fourth. Bay liked him. He was still, like Claire. Steadfast.

Not taking his eyes off Sydney, he walked over to her.

'Hi, Sydney. Hi, Bay,' he said.

Sydney pointed to the apples. 'You know, we impress easily. You didn't have to do this to get our attention.'

'Here's a secret about men. Our foolishness is always unintentional. But it's usually for a good reason.'

'Bay and I are on a Pop-Tart run.'

'It must be a sweet tooth kind of day. A couple of weeks ago, Evanelle brought my granddad a jar of maraschino cherries. He saw them yesterday and said, "Why not make more ice cream and have banana splits?"

The only things we were lacking were the bananas, so I took off early today to get them.'

'Sweet stuff is definitely worth the extra trip,' Sydney said.

'Why don't you come out? There'll be plenty of banana splits. And I could show Bay around. She could see the cows.'

Bay's mind cleared, like the sun peeking through clouds. 'Let's go see the cows!' she said enthusiastically. 'Cows are great!'

Sydney looked at her, puzzled. 'First planes and now cows. Since when did you get to be such a cow-lover?'

Bay tugged on her mother's shirt. Didn't she see how calm she was around Henry, how their hearts were beating in rhythm? The pulses at their throats were in sync. 'Please, Mommy?'

Sydney looked from Bay to Henry. 'Looks like I'm outnumbered.'

'Great! I'll meet you at the check-out,' Henry said, and walked away.

'OK, dairy queen, what gives?' Sydney asked.

'Don't you see it?' Bay said, excited. 'He likes you. Like Tyler likes Claire.'

'Maybe not quite that way, honey. He's my friend.'

Bay frowned. This was going to be harder than she thought. Usually, things fell into place a lot easier when Bay pointed out where they belonged. She really had to figure out how to reproduce her dream in real life. Nothing was going to be exactly right until she did.

They met Henry out front, and he showed them to his truck. It was a king cab, and Bay got to sit in the back, which was cool.

The day turned out to be absolutely wonderful. Henry and his grandfather seemed more like brothers, and Bay liked their calm sense of themselves. Old Mr Hopkins, upon first seeing Sydney, asked her when her birthday was. When he discovered that she was five months older than Henry, he laughed and clapped his grandson on his back and said, 'Oh, well, that's all right, then.'

Bay was certain this was the place where her mother belonged.

But Sydney didn't know it. Her mother, she realised, had always had a problem knowing where she went.

Lucky for her, that was Bay's speciality.

Henry drove them home after dark, and Bay fell asleep in the back. When Henry pulled in front of the house, he cut the engine, and they talked. About where they wanted to go with their lives, what they thought the future might be like. Sydney didn't tell Henry anything about the stealing she'd done, or about David. It was almost as if they didn't exist. She liked that feeling.

She talked herself hoarse, sitting there in his truck. Before she knew it, it was midnight.

She'd just entered the house, Bay in her arms, when Claire appeared in her nightgown. 'Where have you been?'

'We met Henry Hopkins at the grocery store. He invited us to his place for banana splits,' Sydney said. She took a good look at Claire, and her heart suddenly lurched in fright. Claire's face was pinched, and her hands were clasped tightly in front of her as if she had terrible news. Oh God. It was David. David had found them. 'What happened? What's wrong?'

'Nothing's wrong.' Claire turned and headed to the kitchen. 'You just should have called me to let me know.'

Sydney followed, clutching Bay to her now. By the time she caught up with her, Claire had already walked through the kitchen and was in the sunroom, putting on some gardening clogs. 'That's all?' Sydney said breathlessly. 'That's it?'

'I was worried. I thought . . .'

'What? What did you think happened?' Sydney asked, scared because she'd never seen Claire like this.

'I thought you left,' Claire said softly.

Sydney couldn't quite get her mind around it. 'You're upset because you thought we left? You mean for good?'

'If you need me, I'll be in the garden.'

'I . . . I'm sorry I worried you. I should have called. Claire, I told you. We're not going anywhere. I'm sorry.'

'It's OK,' Claire said, pushing open the sunroom door and leaving a smouldering brown imprint of her hand on the casing.

Sydney watched Claire cross the driveway and unlock the garden gate. When she disappeared into the garden, Sydney turned and went back into the kitchen. She was thoughtful for a moment. Then she sat down and, with Bay cuddled in her lap, reached for the phone.

Like every person who had ever fallen in love, Tyler Hughes wondered what was wrong with him. Claire had all this energy that surged through him when they kissed. Every time he thought of it now, he had to sit down and put his head between his legs, and when he finally caught his breath he had to drink two full glasses of water to cool his fever.

But what did he really know about her? What did anyone really know about Claire Waverley?

That afternoon, he had been sitting in his office at the college when he saw Anna Chapel, the head of the department, pass by. He called to her, and she popped her head in.

'How well do you know Claire Waverley?' he'd asked.

'Claire?' Anna shrugged and leaned against the doorjamb. 'Let's see. I've known her for about five years. She caters all our department parties.'

'I mean, personally, how well do you know her?'

Anna smiled in understanding. 'Ah. Well, personally, I don't know her well. You've been here a year; I'm sure you've noticed certain . . . peculiarities in this town.'

Tyler leaned forward, curious. 'I've noticed.'

'Local legend is important here, as it is with most small towns. The locals believe that what's grown in the Waverleys' garden has certain powers. And the Waverleys have an apple tree that is talked about in almost mythic proportions around here. But it's just a garden, and it's just an apple tree. Claire is mysterious because all her ancestors were mysterious. She's really just like you and me. She's probably more savvy than the average person. After all, she was smart enough to turn that local legend into a lucrative business.'

There was probably some truth to what Anna was saying.

'I get the feeling this isn't what you wanted to know,' Anna said.

Tyler smiled. 'Not exactly.'

'Well, I know she has a half-sister.'

'*Half*-sister?' Tyler said with interest.

'They have different fathers, from what I've heard. Their mother was a little wild. She left town, had kids, brought the kids here, then left again. I take it you're interested in Claire?'

'Yes,' Tyler said.

'Well, good luck,' Anna said. 'But don't mess it up. I don't want to have to find someone else to work our department parties just because you broke our caterer's heart.'

Later that night, Tyler sat on his couch, trying to focus on the class line-drawing assignments, but he kept thinking about Claire. His cellphone rang, and he reached over to where he'd set it on the coffee table. 'Hello?'

'Tyler, it's Sydney,' she said in a soft voice. 'Claire's out in the garden. The gate is unlocked. You might want to come over.'

'She doesn't want me over there.' He hesitated. 'Does she?'

'But I think she might need you. I've never seen her like this. She's like a live wire. She's actually singeing things.'

He remembered the feeling. 'I'll be right over.'

Tyler walked across the yard and round the Waverley home to the back garden. As Sydney had said, the gate was unlocked, and he pushed it open.

He was immediately met with the scent of mint and rosemary, as if he'd walked into a kitchen with herbs simmering on the stove.

The footpath lamps looked like small runway lights, and they cast a yellowy glow over the garden. The apple tree was a dim figure at the back of the lot. He found Claire in the herb patch, and the image stopped him short. Her short hair was pulled back with that white headband. She was on her knees in a long white nightgown that had straps over the shoulders and a ruffle at the hem, and she was picking at the ground with a hand rake. Taking deep breaths, he slowly walked over to her, not wanting to startle her. She stopped raking, turned her head and looked up at him. Her eyes were red.

Good God, she was crying?

She winced. 'Go away, Tyler.'

'What's wrong?'

'Nothing is wrong,' she said tersely, clawing the dirt with her hand rake again. 'I hit my thumb, and it hurts.'

'Sydney wouldn't have called me if this was just about a sore thumb.'

That pushed a button. Her head jerked round. 'She called you?'

'She said you were upset.'

'I can't believe she called you! Will it ease her conscience if she knows you'll be here for me when she goes? You'll leave, too. Doesn't she know that? No, she doesn't know that, because she always does the leaving. She never gets left.'

'She's leaving?' Tyler asked, confused. 'I'm leaving?'

Claire's lips were trembling. 'You all leave. My mother, my grand-mother, Sydney.'

'First of all, I'm not going anywhere. Second, where is Sydney going?'

Claire turned away again. 'I don't know. I'm just afraid she is.'

She likes things that don't go away, Sydney had told him. This woman had been abandoned too many times to let anyone in again. The epiphany brought him literally to his knees. So many things about her made sense now, and Anna was right about one thing: Claire was like everyone else. She hurt just like everyone else. 'Oh, Claire.'

He was beside her now, both on their knees. 'Don't look at me like that.'

'I can't help it,' he said, reaching out to touch her hair. He expected her to pull away, but to his surprise she leaned into his hand.

He inched forward, lifting his other hand to her hair, now cupping her head. Their knees touched, and she leaned forward to rest her head on his shoulder. Her hair was so soft. He ran his fingers through it, and then he touched her shoulders. She was soft everywhere. He rubbed her back, trying to give her some comfort.

After a moment, Claire pulled back and looked at him. Her eyes were still wet with tears, and he used his thumbs to wipe her cheeks. She lifted her hands to his face, touching him the way he touched her. Her fingers outlined his lips, and he could only watch, as if he were outside himself, as she leaned in to kiss him. This would be a stupid time to faint, he told himself. Then she ended the kiss, and he returned to his body and thought, *No!* He followed her as she pulled back, his lips finding hers.

Minutes passed like this. 'Tell me to stop,' he said.

'Don't stop,' she whispered back, kissing his neck. 'Make it better.'

She hugged him. His skin tightened at the contact.

This was probably going to kill him, he thought drunkenly. But it was a hell of a way to die.

He kissed her again. She pushed, and he fell on his back to the ground, but they never broke the kiss. He was lying on some herb, thyme maybe, and his weight was crushing it, its scent exploding around them. This all was faintly familiar to him somehow, but he couldn't quite place it.

Claire finally pulled up for a breath. Tears were still running down her cheeks.

'Please don't cry. Please. I'll do anything.'

'Anything?' she asked. 'Will you not remember this tomorrow? Will you forget everything tomorrow?'

He hesitated. 'Are you asking me to?'

'Yes.'

'Then, yes.'

Suddenly it was hard to breathe again. He wound his arms around her, rolling her over onto some sage. Again, it was so familiar. Then he remembered. He'd dreamed this all before.

He knew exactly what was going to happen. Everything about Claire screamed fate. And everything that had brought him here to Bascom had led him to this.

To a dream that came true.

The next morning, Claire felt a swish of air and heard a thud echo in her ear, coming from the ground beside her. She opened her eyes, and there was a small apple about six inches from her face. Another thud, and another apple appeared beside it.

She'd fallen asleep outside again. She'd done it so many times before that she didn't even think. She just sat up and automatically reached for her gardening tools.

But something wasn't right. She looked down and gasped.

On the ground beside her was Tyler! His eyes were open, and he was smiling. 'Good morning.'

Everything came back to her. 'Don't say anything,' she said as she stood. 'You promised me you would forget everything. Don't say a word about this.'

He rubbed at his eyes sleepily, still smiling. 'OK.'

Fat raindrops began to fall as she ran out of the garden. By the time she'd reached the house, the sky had opened up and it was pouring.

8

'IF YOU NEED US, Bay and Henry and I are going to be at Lunsford's Reservoir. We'll be back no later than five o'clock,' Sydney said, as if trying to calm Claire down.

Claire closed the lid to the picnic basket, raised the handles and handed it to Sydney. She must have really scared Sydney that night a week ago. But as long as Claire pretended it was all OK, maybe it really was. Sydney and Henry had spent a lot of time together this past week, dinners with Bay, mostly. On Sunday they went to the movies. Claire tried to tell herself that it was a good thing. She used that time alone to can vegetables and weed the garden and catch up on paperwork, all secure and routine things. She needed that.

'Will you be OK there?' Claire asked, following Sydney out of the kitchen.

'Of course. Why wouldn't we be?'

'It's pretty far out, and you'll be all alone.'

Sydney laughed and set the basket by the front door. 'We'll be lucky if we find a place to eat our lunch. The reservoir is always crowded in the summer.'

'Oh,' Claire said, embarrassed. 'I didn't know. I've never been there.'

'So come with us!' Sydney said, grabbing Claire's hands. 'Please? It will be fun. You've lived here most all your life, and you've never been to the reservoir. Come on. Please?'

'I don't think so.'

'I really want you to come,' Sydney said, squeezing Claire's hands hopefully.

Claire felt a familiar anxiousness at the thought of doing something purely social. Work was fine: Claire didn't socialise when she worked. She said what needed to be said, or she didn't say anything at all. Unfortunately, this didn't translate well into a social setting. It made her seem rude and stand-offish, when it was only a sincere and desperate effort not to do or say anything foolish. 'I'm sure you and Henry want this time together.'

'No, we don't,' Sydney said, suddenly serious. 'We're just friends. This is for Bay. You packed the picnic, at least come eat it. Hurry, go change.'

Claire couldn't believe she was actually considering it. She looked down at her white capri pants and sleeveless shirt. 'Change into what?'

'Shorts. Or a swimsuit if you want to go swimming.'

'I don't know how to swim.'

Sydney smiled. 'Want me to teach you?'

'No!' Claire said immediately. 'I mean, no, thank you. I'm not a fan of large bodies of water. Does Bay know how to swim?'

Sydney went into the sitting room, where she'd left two quilts and a beach bag full of towels. She carried them to the hall and set them by the picnic basket. 'Yes, she had lessons in Seattle.'

Claire instantly perked up. 'Seattle?'

Sydney took a deep breath and nodded. That titbit of information hadn't just slipped out. Sydney had told her on purpose. A first step. 'Seattle. That's where Bay was born.'

So far, she'd mentioned New York and Boise and Seattle.

There was a honk outside, and Sydney called, 'Come on, Bay!'

Bay came running down the stairs, wearing a bathing suit under a yellow sundress. 'Finally!' she said as she shot out of the door.

'OK, don't change.' Sydney took a pink canvas sunhat out of her bag and put it on Claire's head. 'Perfect. Let's go.'

She dragged Claire out of the house. Henry took Claire's addition to their party gracefully. Sydney said that they were just friends, but Claire wasn't sure Henry felt the same way. There were times when he looked at her sister and his whole body seemed to go transparent, losing himself in her. He had it bad.

Claire and Bay climbed into the back seat of the king cab, and Sydney was about to lift herself onto the front seat when Claire heard her call, 'Hi, Tyler!'

Claire immediately turned in her seat to see Tyler getting out of his Jeep in front of his house. He was wearing cargo shorts and a crazy

Hawaiian shirt. This was the first time since the garden that she'd seen him, and her breath caught. How did people act after something like that? How on earth did people live and function after intimacy? It was like telling a secret to someone, then immediately regretting that they knew. The thought of actually talking to him now made her face chilli-pepper hot.

'We're going to the reservoir for a picnic. Want to come?' Sydney asked him.

'Sydney, what are you doing?' Claire demanded.

'I'm teaching you to swim,' Sydney answered cryptically.

'I have a class tonight,' Tyler called.

'We'll be back in time.'

'Then sure. I'm in,' Tyler said, and walked towards them.

When Claire saw that Sydney was going to open the back door, she nearly hurt herself climbing over Bay so Bay would be in the middle, a kiddy buffer between her and Tyler. But she felt ridiculous when Tyler started to climb in and saw her.

'Claire!' he said, stopping short. 'I didn't know you were going, too.'

When she finally got the nerve to meet his eyes, she didn't find anything hidden there, no telltale sign that he was thinking of her secret. He was just Tyler. Should that be a relief, or should that make her more worried?

As soon as they were off, Tyler asked Claire, 'So what's this reservoir?'

Claire tried to think of something normal to say. 'I've never been there,' she finally admitted. 'Ask Sydney, our social director.'

Sydney turned in her seat. 'It's a popular swimming hole. Lots of teenagers and families with young kids go there in the summer. And at night it's something of a lovers' lane.'

'And how do *you* know that?' Tyler asked.

Sydney grinned and wagged her eyebrows.

'You went out there at night?' Claire asked. 'Did Grandma know what you were doing?'

'Are you kidding? She said she used to go out there at night all the time when she was a teenager.'

'She never told me that.'

'She probably worried about all the flies zooming into your wide-open mouth.'

Claire snapped her mouth shut. 'I didn't think she did things like that.'

'Everyone does something like that at least once in their lives.' Sydney shrugged. 'She was young once.'

Claire sneaked a look at Tyler. He was smiling. He'd been young once, too.

Claire had always wondered what that felt like.

Lunsford's Reservoir was located in the ninety acres of thick woods passed down through a long line of lazy Lunsfords. It was too much trouble to try to keep people away from the reservoir, and the maintenance would be too much hassle if they turned it into a park. And this was the rural South, so they'd be damned if they sold their family land or, worse, gave it to the government. So they posted NO TRESPASSING signs everyone ignored, and left it at that.

There was a trail about a half-mile long from the gravel parking lot to the reservoir. Tyler walked behind Claire all the way there, and she felt very conscious of her body, of what he knew of it, things no one else knew. She thought she could feel his eyes on her, but when she looked over her shoulder, his eyes were always elsewhere. Maybe she felt them there because she wanted them there. Maybe *this* was how people coped after intimacy. When you tell a secret to someone, embarrassing or not, it forms a connection. That person means something to you simply by virtue of what he knows.

Finally, the path opened and the noise swelled. The reservoir itself was a forest lake with a natural beach on one side and a high promontory on the other side that kids climbed up in order to dive into the water. It was as crowded as Sydney said it would be, but they found a place towards the back of the beach and spread the quilts.

Claire had made avocado and chicken wraps and fried peach pies, and Sydney had packed Cheetos and Coke. They sat and ate and chatted, and a surprising number of people came by to say hello—clients of Sydney's, mostly, who came by to tell Sydney that their new haircuts gave them more confidence, that their husbands noticed them more. Claire was unspeakably proud of her.

As soon as Bay had finished eating, she wanted to go swimming, so Henry and Sydney walked with her to the water. Which left Claire and Tyler alone. Tyler stretched back on a quilt, his hands behind his head. Claire was sitting on a separate quilt beside him. A few minutes later, Tyler sat up on his elbows, his eyes going to the edge of the water where Henry and Sydney were watching Bay. Someone on the beach called to Sydney. Sydney said something to Henry, and he nodded, then she walked to a nearby gathering of women to talk.

Tyler stood up and kicked off his shoes. 'I think I'll go for a swim.'

'But you still have your clothes on.'

'I love a lot of things about you, Claire,' he said, reaching his hands over his head and grabbing his shirt at his shoulders and pulling it off, 'but you think too much.'

He ran to the water and dived in. Wait a minute. Did he mean that? *He loved her?* Or was that just one of those things people said? She wished she understood these games. Maybe she could play if she did. Maybe she could do something with these feelings for Tyler that were so painful and so good at the same time.

Henry was still watching Bay, so Sydney walked back to the quilts and sat beside Claire. 'Was that Tyler?'

'Yes,' Claire said, watching his head emerge from the water. He shook his head, and his dark hair flung around and stuck to his face. Bay was laughing at him, so he swam over to her and splashed her. She splashed back. Henry, at the edge of the water, pulled his shirt over his head and jumped in after them.

'Wow,' Sydney said. 'Milk, it does a body good.'

'There's a reason I am the way I am, you know,' Claire blurted out, because she had to explain it to someone.

Sydney grabbed a can of Coke and turned to her curiously.

'We didn't have a home, Mom and I, the first six years of my life. We slept in cars and homeless shelters. She did a lot of stealing, and a lot of sleeping around. You never knew that, did you?' Claire asked. Sydney slowly shook her head. 'I don't know if she ever intended to stay, but when we came here, I knew I was never going to leave again. The house and Grandma Waverley were permanent things, and that's all I ever dreamed of. But then you were born, and I was so jealous of you. You were given that security from the moment you entered the world. It's my fault, our relationship as kids. I'm sorry I'm not good at being a sister. I'm sorry I'm not good with Tyler. I know you want me to be. But I can't seem to help it. I can't help but think how temporary everything is, and I'm scared of that kind of temporary. I'm scared of people leaving me.'

'Life is about experience, Claire,' Sydney finally said. 'You can't hold on to everything.'

Claire shook her head. 'I think it might be too late for me.'

'No, it's not.' Sydney suddenly slapped the quilt beside her angrily. 'How could Mom ever think that was the kind of life for a child? It's inexcusable. I'm ashamed of myself for envying her, and there are times I think I've turned out just like her, but I'm not leaving you. Never. Look at me, Claire. I'm not leaving.'

'Sometimes I wonder what her reason was. She was a smart woman.

Evanelle told me she was a crackerjack student before she dropped out.
Something had to have happened.'

'Whatever the reason, there's no excuse for her messing up our lives
like she did. We can get past this, Claire. We can't let her win. OK?'

Words were easier said than implemented, so Claire said, 'OK,' but
wondered how in the world she was going to get past something that
had taken her decades to perfect.

They stared at the water for a while. Bay had grown tired of the
splashing game, and she swam back to the beach and walked over to
Claire and Sydney. Henry and Tyler were still splashing at each other,
each trying to make the biggest splash with his hand.

'Look at those two,' Sydney said. 'Boys, the both of them.'

'This is nice,' Claire said.

Sydney put her arm round her. 'Yes, it is.'

'**D**o you know what I heard today from Eliza Beaufort?' Emma Clark
Matteson said brightly at dinner that night. 'Sydney and Claire
Waverley went on a double date to Lunsford's Reservoir. What does
Sydney think she's doing? No one our age goes out there. And Claire!
Can you imagine Claire at the reservoir?'

Hunter John didn't look up from his dessert. It was his favourite
chocolate cake with buttercream frosting. Emma had ordered it especially for him.

Instead of answering her, Hunter John wiped his mouth and put
down his napkin. 'Come on, boys,' he said. 'Let's go toss a football.'

Josh and Payton immediately jumped up. They loved when their dad
played with them, and Hunter John always made time for his boys.

'I'll come with you,' Emma said. 'Wait for me, OK?'

Emma rushed upstairs and changed into her red bikini, the one
Hunter John liked, but when she came back down, they hadn't waited.
The pool was right off the tiled family room, so she walked out and to
the balustrade that looked over the lawn below. Hunter John and the
boys were playing in the yard, their hair already wet with sweat. It was
seven thirty in the evening but still light and still sweltering. Summer
was a lady who didn't give up her spotlight easily. Emma understood
that. She liked summer.

There was no sense in getting her hair wet if Hunter John wasn't
going to watch her swim, so she put on a sarong and cheered on the
boys from the patio. When the sun began to set, Emma brought out a
pitcher of lemonade. Soon, the boys and Hunter John made their way
up to the pool.

'Lemona—' she said, but before she could finish, the boys had jumped in the pool to cool off.

Emma shook her head indulgently. Hunter John was walking towards her. She smiled and held a glass out. 'Lemona—'

She didn't even get the word out before he passed her and walked into the house. She didn't want the boys to know anything was wrong, so she waited for them to play in the water a while, then got them towels and made them get out. She shooed them to their rooms to change and watch television, then she went to find Hunter John.

He was in their steam shower, so Emma lifted herself to sit on the bathroom counter facing the stall and waited for him to come out.

When the door opened and he emerged, her breath caught. He could still do this to her. He was so beautiful. He had just washed his hair, and she could see how much it was thinning, but that didn't matter to her. She loved him so much.

'We need to talk,' she said. 'I need to know why you never want to discuss Sydney.'

He looked up, startled to find her there. He grabbed a towel and dried his hair vigorously. 'I think the more important question is why are you so obsessed with her? Have you noticed that Sydney isn't actually in our lives? Has it escaped your attention that she hasn't actually done anything to us?'

'She's done plenty, just by being back,' she said. 'You won't talk about her. How do I know you're not talking about her because you still have feelings for her? How do I know you didn't take one look at her and remember all the choices you had before I got pregnant? How do I know, if you went back, you would do the same thing? Would you sleep with me? Marry me?'

He slid the towel off his head. His expression was tight as he walked up close to her, which made her heart beat faster with both fear, because he looked so angry, and anticipation, because he was so damn sexy. 'How do you know?' he repeated incredulously, his voice low and vibrating. 'How do you know?'

'She's been places. You always wanted to travel.'

'What have you been thinking these past ten years, Emma? The sex and the boob job and the sexy clothes. The perfect dinners and the football games. Was all of that because you thought I didn't want to be here? Was any of that because you loved me at all? Or have you been competing with Sydney all this time?'

'I don't know, Hunter John. Have I?'

'That was the wrong answer, Emma,' he said, and walked out.

'Claire, are you awake?' Sydney said from the doorway of Claire's bedroom that night.

She wasn't surprised to hear Claire say, 'Yes.'

She walked into Claire's room, the turret bedroom that had once been their grandmother's. The walls were pastel yellow, and the floors were covered with throw rugs. There were stacks of books beside a comfortable window seat.

Sydney went to the bed and looped her arm round one of the bottom posts. 'I need to tell you something.'

Claire sat up on her pillows.

'About the past ten years.'

'OK,' Claire said quietly.

There had been a chance, on the quilt at the beach, to tell Claire this, but she hadn't been able to do it. She didn't know it then, but she was waiting for night, because it was the sort of thing that needed darkness to tell. 'I went to New York first, you know that. But after that, it was Chicago. Then San Francisco . . . then, Seattle. I've known a lot of men. And I did a lot of stealing. I changed my name to Cindy Watkins, an identity I stole.'

'Mom did that, too,' Claire said.

'Do you think she did it for the thrill? Because it was thrilling, but it was exhausting, too. Then Bay came along.' Sydney moved to sit at Claire's feet, just to feel her near. 'Bay's father lives in Seattle. That's where I met him. David Leoni.' She swallowed, frightened by saying his name out loud. 'Leoni is Bay's real last name, but not mine. We never married. David was scary, but I thought I could handle him. I was getting ready to leave him—that's what I always did when things got too intense—but then I found out I was pregnant. I didn't realise how having a baby could make you so vulnerable. David started hitting me, and he got more and more violent. When Bay turned one, I left him. I took her to Boise, went to beauty school, got a job. Everything seemed to be going so well. Then David found us. I lost a tooth and couldn't see out of my left eye for weeks after his payback. What good would I be to Bay dead? So I went back with him, and he made my world more and more hellish. But then I met a woman at the park. She knew what was going on just by looking at me. She got me that car and helped me escape. David doesn't know my real name, and he thinks I'm from New York, so this was the only place I knew to go, the only place he wouldn't find me.'

Claire sat up straighter and straighter the longer Sydney talked.

'So, those are my secrets.' Sydney sighed. 'They don't seem as big as I thought they were.'

'Secrets never are. Do you smell that?' Claire suddenly asked. 'I've smelled it before. It's like cologne.'

'It's him,' Sydney whispered, as if he would hear her. 'I brought that memory with me.'

'Quick, get in bed,' Claire said, and threw back the sheet. Sydney darted in and Claire tucked the sheet around her. It was a humid night and all the upstairs windows were open, but Sydney was suddenly cold and she snuggled against her sister. Claire put her arm round her and held her close. 'It's OK,' Claire whispered. 'Everything's going to be OK.'

'Mommy?'

Sydney turned quickly to see Bay in the doorway. 'Hurry, honey, get in bed with me and Claire,' Sydney said, throwing back the sheet as Claire had done.

They held on tightly to each other as thoughts of David drifted out of the window.

The next morning dawned bright and sweet, like ribbon candy. Claire made breakfast for Sydney and Bay. It was a nice morning, lots of chatter and good feelings, no scent of anything bad in the air. Sydney left for work by the back door, calling over her shoulder as she left, 'There's a whole bunch of apples out here!'

So Claire took a box from the storeroom and she and Bay gathered the apples the tree had thrown at the back door.

'Why did it do this?' Bay asked as they walked to the garden gate in the bright, wavy morning light.

'That tree has a hard time minding its own business,' Claire said as she unlocked the gate. 'We were all together last night, and it wanted to be a part of it.'

'It must be kind of lonely.'

Claire shook her head and went to the shed for a shovel. 'It's cranky and selfish, Bay. Don't forget that. It wants to tell people things they shouldn't know.'

She dug a hole by the fence while Bay stood under the tree and laughed as it shed little green leaves all around her. 'Look, Claire. It's raining!'

Claire had never seen the tree so affectionate. 'It's a good thing you don't like apples.'

'I hate them,' Bay said. 'But I like the tree.'

As soon as Claire had finished, she and Bay went back to the house.

'So,' Claire said, as casually as possible as they walked. 'Does Tyler have a class tonight, like last night?'

'No. Monday and Wednesday are his night classes. Why?'

'Just wondering. You know what we're going to do today? We're going to go through some old photos!' Claire said enthusiastically. 'I want to show you what your great-grandmother looked like. She was a wonderful lady.'

'Do you have any photos of your and Mommy's mother?'

'No, I'm afraid not.' Claire thought about what Sydney had said about leaving the photos of their mother behind. Did she leave them in Seattle? She had seemed so panicked when she remembered that she had left them.

Claire made a mental note to ask Sydney about it.

Was a dress too much? Claire looked at herself in her bedroom mirror. Did it look like she was trying too hard? She'd never tried at all before, so she had no idea. The white dress she was wearing was the same dress she'd worn the night she met Tyler, the one Evanelle said made her look like Sophia Loren. She put a hand to her bare neck. Her hair had been longer then.

Was this stupid? She was thirty-four years old. It wasn't as if she was sixteen, but she certainly felt that way. Probably for the first time in her life.

Claire went down the stairs and out of the front door. She rarely wore heels, but she did that night, sandals with thin heels, so she had to go to the sidewalk instead of across the yards.

When she reached Tyler's front door, she was cheered by the warm light and the soft music undulating from his open windows. He was listening to something lyrical, classical. She straightened her dress and knocked on the door.

He didn't answer.

She frowned and turned to make sure she did see his Jeep parked on the street. She had her back to the door when she felt it open. It stirred the hem of her dress, and she turned around.

'Hi, Tyler.'

He stood there, as if so shocked he couldn't move. If he was going to leave this all up to her, they were both in trouble. Break it down into steps, she told herself, like a recipe. Take one man and one woman, put them in a bowl.

'Can I come in?' she asked.

He hesitated and looked over his shoulder. 'Well, sure. Of course,' he said, stepping back to let her enter. She walked past him, almost touching him, letting him feel the static. This was obviously the last thing he expected, because the first thing he asked was, 'What's wrong?'

'Nothing's wrong,' she said, then she saw her.

There was a woman, a petite redhead, sitting crosslegged on the floor, two bottles of beer on the coffee table next to her. Her shoes were off, and she was leaning forward so that the flowy V neck of her shirt fell away from her chest slightly. She was wearing a peach-coloured bra. It seemed Tyler had two females ready to seduce him that night.

How could she be so stupid? Did she think he was just sitting here *waiting* for her? 'Oh. You have company.' She started backing away and backed right into him. She whirled round. 'I didn't know. I'm so sorry.'

'There's nothing to be sorry about. Rachel is an old friend, passing through on her way to Boston from Florida. She's staying with me for a few days. Rachel, this is Claire, my next-door neighbour. She's a caterer specialising in edible flowers. She's incredible.' Tyler took Claire by the arm and tried to lead her into the living room. After a couple of seconds he had to pull his hand away quickly, flipping it back and forth as if burnt. He met her eyes with a dawning understanding.

'I'm sorry. I really have to go. I didn't mean to bother you.'

'You weren't—' Tyler said, but she was already out of the door.

Claire changed out of her dress and put on her seersucker robe. She was looking for her slippers when her bedroom door opened.

She could only stare, dumbfounded, as Tyler entered and ominously closed the door behind him.

'Why did you come to see me tonight, Claire?'

'Please forget it.'

He shook his head. 'I'm through forgetting. I remember everything about you. I can't help it.'

They stared at each other. Take one man and one foolish woman and put them in a bowl. This wasn't going to work.

'You're thinking too much again,' Tyler said. 'So this is your bedroom. I've wondered which one was yours. I should have guessed it was the turret room.' He walked around, and she had to force herself to stay where she was, not to run to him and take the photo he'd lifted from the bureau, not to tell him to leave the books stacked by the window seat alone, that she had a particular order to them. She'd been about to share her body with this man, and she couldn't even share her room?

'Isn't Rachel waiting for you?' she asked anxiously.

'Rachel is just a friend. We used to be a couple, when I first moved to Florida to teach. It lasted about a year. We didn't work out as lovers, but we remained friends.'

'How is that possible?'

'I don't know. It just is.' He walked towards her. She could have sworn chairs and rugs moved out of his way to make his path easier. 'Did you want to talk? Did you want to ask me to dinner or a movie?'

She was literally backed into a corner. He came up close to her, doing that not-quite-touching thing he was so good at. 'If I have to say it, I will die,' she whispered. 'Right here. I'll fall to the floor, dead from embarrassment.'

'The garden?'

She nodded.

His hands went to her shoulders, and his fingers snaked in under the collar. 'Not so easy to forget, is it?'

'No.'

He kissed her and pulled her away from the corner, devouring her. Take one man, one foolish woman, put them in a bowl and *stir*.

'Give me ten minutes to get rid of Rachel,' he said.

'You can't get rid of Rachel.'

'But she's going to be here three days.' They stared at each other, and he finally took a deep breath. 'Expectation can be nice, too, I guess,' he said. 'Three whole days of expectation.'

'Three whole days,' she repeated.

'What changed your mind?' he said.

She squeezed her eyes shut. How could she want something this much, something she didn't even understand? 'I should let people in. If they leave, they leave. It happens to everyone. Right?'

He looked in her eyes. 'You think I'm going to leave?'

'There can't be this for ever.'

'Why do you think that?'

'No one I know has ever had this for ever.'

'I think of the future all the time. All my life I've chased dreams of what could be. For the first time in my life, I've actually caught one.' He kissed her again. 'I'll give you one day at a time, Claire. But remember, I'm thousands of days ahead already.'

It was Fred's first night in the attic, which had been painted. He had packed up his things and closed his house, and was thinking of renting it out. Evanelle had told him he could stay here as long as he wanted. Now she could hear him moving around. It was nice, knowing someone was upstairs making small busy noises.

All of a sudden, Evanelle sat up.

Damn. She needed to give someone something. She thought about it for a moment. It was Fred. She had to give Fred something.

She turned on the light by her bed and reached for her robe. She walked into the hall and then paused, figuring out where to go. The two other bedrooms downstairs were now neatly organised with filing cabinets and wooden storage shelves for all her things.

She flipped the switch in the second bedroom, went to the filing cabinets and opened the drawer marked G. In the drawer, she found gloves, a grappling iron and a geode neatly categorised under their proper headings. Under the heading GADGET, she found what she needed. It was a gismo still in its store packaging, a kitchen instrument called a mango splitter, purportedly making cutting round the seed of a mango easier.

She wondered how he was going to take this. He had initially moved in because he'd hoped she would give him something that would help him with James. Now, after all this time, she was going to give him something, and it had nothing to do with James. Maybe it was for the best. Maybe he would take it as a sign that he was doing the right thing, moving on.

Or maybe he would think he just needed to eat more mangoes.

She knocked once on the door to the attic, then walked up the stairs. When she got to the top, she saw Fred in his leather chair near the corner cupboard that housed his television. An antiques magazine was on the leather ottoman in front of him. The area still smelt like fresh paint.

He stood. 'What brings you up here? Are you all right? Can't sleep? Do you want me to cook something for you?'

'No, I'm fine.' She held out the package. 'I needed to give this to you.'

9

CLAIRE DISCOVERED that expectation was nice for some things—Christmas, waiting for bread to rise—but it wasn't nice for others. Waiting for certain female guests to leave, for example.

Every morning, just before dawn, Tyler would meet Claire in the garden. They would touch and kiss, and he would say things that made her blush in the middle of the day when she thought of them again. But then, just before the horizon turned pink, he would leave and promise, 'Just three more days.' 'Just two more days.' 'One.'

Claire had Rachel and Tyler over for lunch the day before Rachel was to leave, under the guise of good manners but really because she wanted more time with Tyler and the only way to get it was with Rachel. She set up a table on the front porch and served turkey salad in zucchini blossoms. She knew Tyler was immune to her dishes, but Rachel wouldn't be, and zucchini blossoms aided in understanding. Rachel needed to understand that Tyler was hers. It was as simple as that.

Bay had taken her seat at the table, and Claire had just set out the bread when Tyler and Rachel walked up the steps.

'This looks lovely,' Rachel said. As she sat, she gave Claire a once-over. She was probably a perfectly nice person, but it was clear that she wasn't entirely over Tyler, and her sudden presence in his life was curious. There was a long story to her.

One Claire had absolutely no desire to learn.

'I'm glad the two of you get to spend some time together before you leave tomorrow,' Tyler said to Rachel.

'You know, my schedule is flexible,' Rachel said, and Claire nearly dropped the water pitcher she was holding.

'Try the zucchini,' she said.

It turned out to be a disastrous meal, passion and impatience and resentment clashing like three winds coming from different directions and meeting in the middle of the table. The butter melted. The bread toasted itself. Water glasses overturned.

'It's strange out here,' Bay said from her seat, where she was trying to eat. She picked up a handful of sweet potato chips and left for the garden, where she didn't think anything was strange about the tree. Strange, after all, depended on your personal definition.

'We should go,' Tyler finally said, and Rachel stood immediately.

'Thank you for lunch,' Rachel said. What she didn't say was, He's leaving with me and not staying with you. But Claire heard it anyway.

Claire couldn't sleep that night. In the early-morning hours, she crept to Sydney's room and knelt at the window that overlooked Tyler's house. She stayed there until daybreak, when she saw Tyler walk with Rachel out to her car, carrying her luggage. He kissed her cheek, and Rachel drove away.

Tyler stood there on the sidewalk, looking at the Waverley house. He'd been doing that all summer, watching the house, wanting in to her life. It was time to let him in. She was going to live, or she was going to die. Tyler was going to stay, or he was going to go. She had lived thirty-four years keeping everything inside, and now she was letting everything go, like butterflies released from a box.

Still in her nightgown, Claire went downstairs and out of the door. Tyler's eyes followed her across the yard. He met her halfway and twined his fingers with hers.

They stared at each other, their conversation silent.

Are you sure?

Yes. Do you want this?

More than anything.

Together they walked to his house and made new memories, one in particular would be named Mariah Waverley Hughes and would be born nine months later.

Sydney and Henry walked round the green downtown one afternoon a few days later. Henry had met her after work for what was becoming an almost daily coffee date. Their walks lasted only about twenty minutes because she had to get home to Bay and he to his grandfather, but every day around five o'clock she would start looking towards the reception area for him to appear. As soon as he did, carrying two iced coffees from the Coffee House, she would call out to him, 'Henry, you're a lifesaver!' When Sydney told her coworkers that she and Henry were just friends, they all looked disappointed in her, like they knew something she didn't.

'So, can you and your grandfather come to Claire's dinner party?' Sydney asked as they walked. Inviting people over was something Claire had never done before, but she had Tyler now, and love made her different.

'I put it in my calendar. We'll be there,' Henry said. 'I think it's nice how you and Claire have been getting along. These days I even see you dressing like her.'

Sydney looked down at Claire's sleeveless shirt she was wearing. 'True. And it helped that I didn't bring a lot of clothes with me when I moved back.'

'You left in a hurry?'

'Yes,' she said, not explaining any further. She liked the way things were, the relationship they had, like when they were kids. David was nowhere in that picture. And there was no pressure for anything beyond their friendship, which was a huge relief. 'So did you date a lot back in high school? I don't remember seeing you at any of the date spots,' she said as they sat on the rock bench circling the fountain.

He shrugged. 'Sometimes. My senior year I dated a girl from Western Carolina University.'

'A co-ed, hmm?' She nudged him with her elbow playfully. 'You like older women, I take it.'

'My grandfather is a huge believer in the fact that Hopkins men always marry older women. I do it to make him happy, but there's probably some truth to it, too.'

Sydney laughed. 'So *that's* why your grandfather asked me how old I was when we went to your place for ice cream.'

'That was why,' Henry said.

Sydney had been putting this off because she was so fond of her time with Henry, but she honestly thought she was doing him a favour by finally saying, 'You know Amber, our receptionist, is almost forty. She likes you. Let me set you up with her.'

Henry looked down at the drink in his hands but didn't respond. Sydney hoped she hadn't embarrassed him.

He turned his head and gave her the strangest look, almost sad. 'Do you remember your first love?'

'Oh, yes. Hunter John Matteson. He was the first boy to ever ask me out,' Sydney said ruefully. 'Who was yours?'

'You.'

Sydney laughed, thinking he was joking. 'Me?'

'The first day of sixth grade, it hit me like a rock. I couldn't talk to you after that. I'll always regret it. When I saw you on the Fourth of July, it happened again.'

Sydney couldn't quite get her mind round it. 'What are you saying, Henry?'

'I'm saying I don't want to be set up with your friend Amber.'

The dynamic changed in a flash. She was no longer sitting beside young Henry, her first friend ever.

She was sitting beside the man in love with her.

Emma walked into the living room that afternoon after unsuccessfully trying to make herself feel better by shopping. She had bumped into Evanelle Franklin downtown, and Evanelle had given her two quarters. And, as proof of how bad Emma's day was, taking money from a crazy old woman had actually been the bright spot.

Her big mistake had been in meeting her mother for lunch to show her what she'd bought. Her mother scolded Emma for not buying enough lingerie and immediately sent her off to get something sexy for Hunter John. Not that it would work. She and Hunter John hadn't had sex in more than a week.

She dropped the bags suddenly when she saw Hunter John sitting on the couch, flipping through a large book on the coffee table. He'd taken off the jacket and tie he'd worn to work that morning, and his shirt-sleeves were rolled up.

'Why, Hunter John!' she said, smiling brightly, but at the same time an uneasiness settled in the pit of her stomach. 'What are you doing here at this time of day?'

'I took the afternoon off. I was waiting for you.'

'Where are the boys?' she asked.

'The nanny took them to the movies. I thought we needed to talk.'

'Oh,' she said, fisting her hands at her sides anxiously. She pointed at the book in front of him. 'What are you looking at?'

'Our senior-high yearbook,' he said, and her heart sank. A time he could be proud of, when anything was possible.

A time she took away from him.

The bags and packages left on the floor, she walked to the couch and sat beside him, gently, cautiously, afraid that if she moved too fast he would bolt. The yearbook was turned to a two-page layout of candid photos. Sydney and Emma and Hunter John were in nearly all of them.

'I was in love with Sydney,' Hunter John said, and Emma felt strangely justified. He was admitting it. But then he continued, 'As much as a teenager can feel love. It felt real to me at the time. I look at these photos, and in every single one of them, I'm staring at her. But then I see you, and in every single one, you're staring at her, too. I forgot about her a long time ago, Emma. But you didn't forget, did you? Has Sydney been in this marriage for ten years without my knowing it?'

Emma stared at the images, trying not to cry. 'I don't know. I just know that I've always wondered, if you had to do it all over again, would you still do it? Would you still choose me?'

'Is that what this is all about? You've been trying so hard because you thought I didn't want to be here?'

'I've tried so hard because I love you!' she said desperately. 'But I took away your choices! I made you stay home instead of going off to college. You had children instead of spending a year in Europe. I ruined all your plans. I've been trying to make it up to you every day since.'

'My God, Emma. You didn't take away my choices. I chose you.'

'When you saw Sydney again, didn't you think for just a moment what your life would have been like without me?'

'No, I didn't,' he said, sounding honestly confused. 'I haven't spared her more than a moment's thought in ten years. But *you* keep bringing her up. *You* think that her being back has changed things. But it hasn't changed anything for me.'

'Oh,' she said, turning her face away to wipe under her eyes, where tears were pooling, threatening to fall.

He hooked a finger under her chin and made her look at him. 'I wouldn't change a thing, Emma. I have a great life with you. You are a joy and a wonder to me, every single day. You make me laugh, you make me think, you make me hot. There are times when you confuse the hell out of me, but it's a pleasure to wake up to you in the mornings, to come home to you and the boys in the evenings. I am the luckiest man in the world.'

'Sydney—'

'No!' he said harshly, dropping his hand. 'Don't start that again. What have I ever done to make you think I regretted my choice? I love you. I don't love Sydney. We're not those people any more.' He closed the yearbook in front of him. 'At least, I'm not that person any more.'

'I don't want to be that person, Hunter John. I really don't.'

'Try, Emma. That's all I'm asking.'

Fred sat at his desk in his office, staring at the mango splitter in front of him. What did it mean?

James liked mangoes. This could mean that Fred was supposed to call him and . . . invite him to eat fruit? Why couldn't this have been clearer? How was it supposed to help him get James back?

There was a knock at the door, and Shelly, his assistant manager, poked her head in. 'Fred, there's someone out here who wants to speak to you.'

'I'll be right out.' Fred grabbed his jacket from the back of his chair and put it on.

When he went out, he saw Shelly talking to a man standing by the wine racks. She pointed to Fred, then walked away. The man was Steve Marcus, a culinary instructor from Orion College. They'd had some good talks over the years about food and recipes. It took a moment for Fred to make himself walk. The last thing James had said to him was that he should go out with Steve. This had nothing to do with that, he told himself, but he still found himself hating every step he took. He didn't want to date Steve.

Steve extended his hand. 'Fred, good to see you.'

Fred shook his hand. 'What can I do for you?'

'I wanted to invite you to join a free community class I'm teaching, sponsored by the college,' Steve said affably. He was a stout, good-natured man. 'It's going to be a fun course on making cooking easy with gadgets and short cuts. You'd be a real asset to the class, with your wide knowledge of food and what's available locally.'

This was all too much. It was too soon. 'I don't know . . . my schedule . . .'

'It's tomorrow night. Are you busy?'

'Tomorrow? Well . . .'

'I'm asking everyone to bring any tricks they've learned and gadgets they use that most people wouldn't know about. No pressure, OK? Tomorrow night at six if you can come.' He reached into his back pocket and brought out his wallet. 'Here's my card with my number if you have any questions.'

Fred took the card. 'I'll think about it.'

'Great. See you later.'

Fred walked back to his office and sat down hard in his chair. Bring any tricks and gadgets most people wouldn't know about.

Like a mango splitter.

He'd waited so long for Evanelle to give him something. This was supposed to make everything right. Fred picked up the phone stubbornly. He would call James. He would *make* this the thing that brought them back together, no matter what.

He dialled James's cellphone number. He began to worry after the tenth ring. Then he started saying to himself, after the twentieth ring I'll know this wasn't meant for him. Then the thirtieth. The fortieth.

Bay watched the party preparations from under the apple tree. Everything seemed fine, so she couldn't figure out why she felt so anxious. Maybe because there were tiny vines of thorns starting to sprout along the edge of the garden, so small and hidden that even Claire, who knew everything that happened in the garden, couldn't see them yet. Or maybe she'd decided to ignore them. Claire was happy, after all, and being happy made you forget that there were bad things in the world. Bay wasn't quite happy enough to forget. Nothing was perfect yet.

Maybe it was just the fact that Bay still couldn't figure out how to make the dream she'd had of this place real. Nothing worked. She couldn't find anything that made sparkles on her face, and her mom wouldn't let her take any more crystal from the house outside to experiment. There was no way to replicate the sound of paper flapping in the wind, either. There hadn't even been any wind for days, not until that afternoon when, as soon as Sydney and Claire tried to spread the ivory tablecloth over the table in the garden, out of nowhere the wind suddenly kicked up. The tablecloth snapped out of the sisters' hands and floated across the garden like a child had draped it over his head and was running away with it. They laughed and chased it.

Sydney and Claire were happy. They stirred rose petals into their oat-meal in the mornings, and they stood side by side at the sink as they did the dishes in the evenings, giggling and whispering. Maybe that was all that mattered. Bay shouldn't worry so much.

Big clouds, white and grey like circus elephants, began to lumber across the sky. Bay, on her back by the tree, watched them pass.

'Hey, tree,' she whispered. 'What's going to happen?'

Its leaves shook, and an apple fell to the ground beside her. She ignored it. She guessed she would just have to wait and see.

'Excuse me,' a man said from the other side of the gas pumps.

He appeared in front of Emma suddenly, the elephant thunderheads in the sky haloing him as she looked up into his dark eyes.

Emma was standing beside her mother's convertible, pumping gas for her while Ariel sat in the driver's seat and checked her make-up in the rearview mirror. At the sound of his voice, Ariel turned. She smiled immediately and got out of the car.

'Hello there,' Ariel said, coming to stand beside Emma. They'd been out shopping again that day. Emma and Hunter John were going to Hilton Head for the weekend, just the two of them. Ariel had insisted on buy-ing Emma a new bikini, something Hunter John would like, and Emma went along because it was easier. But no matter what Ariel said now, Emma felt good about where she was with her husband. She didn't blame her mother for her bad advice.

The stranger was handsome, and his smile was megawatt. 'Hello, ladies. I hope I'm not bothering you. I'm looking for someone. Maybe you can help me? Does the name Cindy Watkins sound familiar?'

'Watkins,' Ariel repeated, then shook her head. 'No, I'm afraid not.'

'This is Bascom, North Carolina, isn't it?'

'You've got your toe just over the town limit, but yes.'

He reached into the pocket of his very nice tailored jacket and brought out a small stack of photos. He handed Ariel the one on top. 'Does this woman look familiar to you?'

Emma flipped the tab on the handle of the nozzle to keep it pump-ing, then leaned over to look at the photo with her mother. It was a black and white of a woman standing outside what looked like the Alamo. She was holding a sign that said, very clearly, she didn't care at all for North Carolina. Judging by the style of her clothes, it was taken more than thirty years ago.

'No, I'm sorry,' Ariel said, and started to hand the photo back to the man before suddenly looking at it again. 'Wait. You know, this might be Lorelei Waverley.'

Emma looked more closely at the photo.

'But this was taken a long time ago,' Ariel said. 'She's dead now.'

'Do you have any idea why this woman,' he handed her another photo, a more recent one, 'would have photographs of this Lorelei Waverley?'

Emma could hardly believe what she was looking at. It was a photograph of Sydney standing next to the man. She was wearing a tight evening dress, and his arm was looped round her possessively. She didn't look happy. She looked for all the world like she didn't want to be where she was.

Ariel frowned. 'That's Sydney Waverley,' she said flatly, then handed the photos back to him, almost as if they weren't fit to touch now.

'Sydney?' the man repeated.

'Lorelei was her mother. Lorelei was a ne'er-do-well. Between you and me and the fence post, Sydney's just like her.'

'Sydney Waverley,' he said, as if trying out the name. 'Does she have a child, a little girl?'

'Yes. Bay,' Ariel said.

'Mama,' Emma said, as if in warning. That was something you simply didn't tell strangers.

The man immediately backed off, as if sensing that Emma was growing uncomfortable. 'Thank you for your help. Have a wonderful day, ladies.' He walked to an expensive SUV and got in. The sky grew darker as he drove away, as if he was somehow causing it.

Emma frowned, feeling funny. She took the nozzle from the car and put it back on the pump. There was no love lost between Emma and Sydney, that was for sure. But something was wrong.

'I'll pay for the gas, Mama,' Emma said, hoping to get to her bag in the car, where her cellphone was.

But Ariel already had her credit card out. 'Don't be silly. I'm paying.'

'No, really. I'll get it.'

'Here,' Ariel said, putting the card in Emma's hand and getting back in the convertible. 'Stop arguing and go pay the clerk.'

Emma walked into the convenience store and handed the clerk the card. While waiting, she put her hands in the pockets of her windbreaker and felt something. She brought out two quarters. She'd been wearing this jacket when Evanelle came up to her that day and gave her the money.

'Excuse me,' she said to the clerk. 'Do you have a payphone?'

The wind kept up all afternoon. Sydney and Claire had to tie the ends of the tablecloth to the legs of the table, and they couldn't use candles because the wind blew out the flames. In lieu of candles, Claire brought out sheer bags in amber and raspberry and pale green, and she put battery-powered lanterns in them, which made them look like gifts of light set around the table and tree.

Evanelle was the first to arrive that evening.

'Hi, Evanelle. Where is Fred?' Claire asked when Evanelle walked into the kitchen.

'He couldn't come. He has a date.' Evanelle set her tote bag on the table. 'Mad as a fire ant about it, too.'

'Fred's dating someone?'

'Sort of. A culinary instructor at Orion asked Fred to join a class he was teaching. Fred thinks the class tonight is a date.'

'Why is he mad?'

'Because I gave him something that led him to the instructor instead of back to James. So naturally, Fred thinks he has to spend the rest of his life with that teacher. He cracks me up sometimes. He's soon going to realise that he makes his own decisions. You know, he even asked if I would sneak him an apple from your tree tonight, as if that would tell him what to do.'

Claire shivered. 'You can never know what that tree will tell you.'

'That's true enough. We didn't know what it showed your mother until she died.'

The kitchen went still. Sydney and Claire instinctively moved closer to each other. 'What do you mean?' Claire asked.

'Oh Lord.' Evanelle put her hands to her cheeks. 'I promised your grandmother I would never tell you.'

'Our mother ate an apple?' Sydney asked incredulously. 'One of *our* apples?'

Evanelle looked up at the ceiling. 'I'm sorry, Mary,' she said, as if speaking to a ghost. She pulled out a chair at the kitchen table and sat with a sigh. 'After your grandmother got the call about Lorelei dying in that car pile-up, she figured it out. As close as we can figure, Lorelei ate an apple when she was about ten. The day she ate that apple she probably saw the way she was going to die, and every wild thing she did afterwards was to try to make it not come true, to make something happen that was even bigger than that. Mary said that the night Lorelei disappeared again she found her in the garden, the first time since she was a child. She might have eaten another apple that night. Things seemed to be going well here, so maybe Lorelei thought that her fate had changed. But it hadn't. She left you girls here to be safe. She was supposed to die alone in that huge wreck. Are you girls all right?'

'We're fine,' Claire said, but Sydney was still stunned. Her mother hadn't picked the way she'd lived. But Sydney, in imitating her, had *chosen* to do those things.

'I'll just head outside, then,' Evanelle said.

'Watch out. The tree is cranky today. We're hoping it doesn't freak Tyler and Henry out.'

'If those boys are going to be in your lives, you better tell them everything.' She took her tote bag and walked outside.

'Do you think she's right?' Sydney said. 'About Mom, I mean.'

'It makes sense. Remember, after we got the phone call that Mom had died, Grandma trying to set fire to the tree?'

Sydney nodded. 'I can't believe I left, wanting to be like her, when she left because she saw how she was going to die. How could I have got it so wrong?'

'You're a Waverley. We either know too little or we know too much. There's never an in-between.'

Sydney shook her head sharply. 'I *hate* that tree.'

'There's nothing we can do about it. We're stuck with it.' Claire took a platter over to the stove, where she started taking corn on the cob out of the pot. 'And Evanelle is right. We should probably tell Tyler and Henry.'

'Henry knows. That's one of the good things about someone who has known you your whole life. He already knows how strange we are.'

'We're not strange.'

'Henry told me something the other day,' Sydney said, rubbing at an invisible spot on the countertop. 'Something I didn't know.'

'He told you that he loved you?' Claire said.

'How did you know that?'

Claire just smiled.

'I like having him around,' Sydney said, thinking out loud. 'I should kiss him. See what happens.'

'And Pandora said, "I wonder what's in this box?"' Tyler said as he entered the kitchen. He walked up behind Claire and kissed her neck. Sydney turned her head away, smiling.

Henry had called earlier and said he was running late, so Tyler and Evanelle and Bay were already seated and Sydney and Claire were bringing the last of the dishes out to them when Henry finally knocked at the front door.

Sydney went to the door as Claire took the blackberry corn bread to the garden.

'You're just in time,' Sydney said as she opened the screen door for Henry. He was acting as he always did. She was acting as she always did. So what had changed?

'Sorry I couldn't get here sooner,' he said as he entered.

'It's too bad that your grandfather couldn't come.'

'It was the strangest thing,' Henry said as he followed her to the kitchen. 'Just before we were going to leave, Fred drove Evanelle out to the house. She said she needed to give Pap something. It was a book he's been dying to read. He wanted to stay home with it.'

'Evanelle didn't tell us she went out there.'

'She was in a hurry. She said Fred wanted to get to some class. So,' he said, 'I finally get to see the famous Waverley apple tree.'

'Two things you need to know. One, don't eat the apples. And, two, duck.'

'Duck?'

'You'll see.' She smiled at him. 'You look nice tonight.'

'And you look beautiful.' Sydney had bought a new skirt for the dinner, a pink one with sparkling silver embroidery. 'Did you know I used to sit behind you in eighth grade and touch your hair without you knowing?'

Sydney felt a curious sensation in her chest. Without another thought, she took two steps over to him and kissed him. The force of her body sent him falling back against the refrigerator. She went with him, not losing contact, and colourful paper napkins Claire had stored on the top of the refrigerator fell over the edge and fluttered down around them like confetti.

When she pulled back, Henry looked shell-shocked. He slowly brought his hands up to touch her hair, and she felt goose bumps.

She'd kissed many men who wanted her, but it had been a long time since she'd kissed one who loved her.

Henry asked breathlessly, 'What was that for?'

'I just wanted to make sure.'

'Make sure of what?'

She smiled. 'I'll tell you later.'

'You know, this means that there's no way I'm going out with Amber from the salon now.'

Sydney laughed and lifted a plate with tomatoes and mozzarella with one hand and led Henry out of the back door with the other. The phone rang as they stepped outside. She didn't hear it, or the answering machine as it picked up the call.

'Sydney? This is Emma. I . . . I wanted to call to tell you that there's someone looking for you and your daughter. He doesn't look . . . I mean, there's something about him that . . .' There was a pause on the line. 'I just wanted to tell you to be careful.'

They ate and laughed well into the evening. Claire lifted her glass after everyone had eaten.

'Everyone make a toast. To food and flowers,' she said.

'To love and laughter,' Tyler said.

'To old and new,' Henry said.

'To what's next,' Evanelle said.

'To the apple tree,' Bay said.

'To—' Sydney stopped when she smelled it. No, no, no. Not here. Not now. Why would thoughts of David come to her now?

The tree shivered, and there was a thud as an apple made contact with someone at the front of the garden, near the gate. A male voice cursed, and everyone but Sydney turned.

She felt bruises pop out on her skin like a rash.

'Bay, go behind the tree,' Sydney said curtly. 'Run. Now!'

Bay, who was very aware of who it was, shot up and ran.

'Sydney, what's wrong?' Claire asked as Sydney stood and slowly turned round.

'It's David.'

Claire immediately got to her feet. Tyler and Henry looked at each other, feeling the fear radiating off Sydney and Claire now. They stood simultaneously.

'Who is David?' Henry asked.

'Bay's father,' Claire answered, and Sydney could have cried in relief that she didn't have to say it herself.

From the shadows of the honeysuckle by the gate, David finally materialised.

'You threw a party and I wasn't invited?' he asked, and his shoes made loud exploding sounds on the gravel walkway as he approached. Sydney had to protect Bay and Claire and everyone else there. The simple act of her coming back had placed them in a danger she never thought would follow her here. This was all her fault.

'It's all right, everyone. David and I will leave and talk,' she said. Then she whispered to Claire, 'Take care of Bay.'

'No, no,' David said. As he got closer, Sydney felt her body jerk, like an electric shock. Tears came to her eyes. Oh God. He had a gun. Where did he get a gun? 'Please don't let me interrupt,' he said.

'David, this doesn't have anything to do with them. I'll go with you.'

'What in the hell is going on?' Tyler said when he noticed the gun. 'Put that thing down, man.'

David steadied the gun on Tyler. 'Is he the one, Cindy?'

Sydney knew what Henry was going to do mere seconds before he did it. 'Henry, don't!' Sydney screamed as he lunged for David. A shot burst into the silence like thunder. Henry was suddenly very still. A stain of bright red started to grow over his shirt at his right shoulder.

Henry sank to his knees. After a few moments, he fell onto his back and stared up at the sky, blinking rapidly. Evanelle, as light and small as a leaf, floated over to him unseen by David.

'All right,' David said. 'I guess we know now which one it is.' He lifted a foot, and with one push the table went over, plates breaking, ice skittering into the chicory. Tyler had to jerk Claire back to keep her from getting hit by the falling debris.

'How did you find me?' Sydney asked, to get him to look at her, not Claire and Tyler. Evanelle had taken a scarf out of her tote bag and was wrapping it around Henry's shoulder. There was blood everywhere.

'I found you with these.' He held up a stack of photos. 'This one in particular was of great help. NO MORE BASCOM! NORTH CAROLINA STINKS!' He held up the photograph of her mother at the Alamo. The tree shrugged, as if recognising Lorelei. He tossed the photos at Sydney as she backed away from him, away from the table and everyone she loved there.

'Do you realise how you made me look? I brought Tom home from LA. Imagine my surprise when you and Bay weren't there.' Tom was his business partner. Looking foolish in front of him had driven David to find her with a gun. He hated to look foolish. She knew that. 'Stop backing away, Cindy. I know what you're doing. You don't want me,' he turned and faced Claire, 'to notice her. And who might you be?'

'I'm Claire,' she said fiercely. 'Sydney's *sister*.'

'*Sydney*,' he laughed, shaking his head. 'I still can't get over that. Sister, hmm? You're probably just as stupid as she is or you would have *known* not to take in what was mine.'

Tyler had stepped in front of Claire, but David just smiled. 'Where is Bay? I saw her here. Come out, kitten. Daddy's here. Come give Daddy a hug.'

'Stay where you are, Bay!' Sydney yelled.

'Don't you ever undermine my authority in front of our daughter!' David advanced on her, but then an apple rolled to a stop at his feet. 'Is my Bay behind the apple tree? Does she want Daddy to eat an apple?'

Sydney, Claire and Evanelle all watched, afraid to move, as David picked up the apple. Tyler started to move, to take advantage of David's being distracted, but Claire caught his arm and whispered, 'No, wait.'

David brought the perfectly round pink apple to his lips. The juicy crack of his biting into it echoed throughout the garden, and the flowers twitched and shrank as if in fright.

He chewed for a moment, then he went unnaturally still.

His eyes darted back and forth as if watching something only he could see, a movie projected only for him. He dropped the apple and the gun at the same time.

'What was that?' he said, his voice trembling. When no one answered, he yelled, 'What in the hell was that?'

Sydney looked down at the photos of her mother, scattered around the grass at her feet. She felt a strange sense of calm. 'You just saw your death, didn't you?' she said. 'Was it your biggest fear coming true, David? Was someone actually hurting you this time?'

David went white.

'Years and years of doing it to other people, and finally someone is going to do it to you.' She walked up to him, close, not intimidated now, not scared any more. 'Go as far away as you can, David,' she whispered. 'Maybe you can outrun it. As long as you're here, it will come true. I'll make damn sure it will come true.'

He turned and stumbled a few steps before he ran out of the garden.

As soon as he disappeared, Sydney called out, 'Bay! Bay, where are you?'

Bay came running from the side of the garden, nowhere near the tree. She ran into her mother's arms. Sydney held her tight before they both went to Henry. Sydney went to her knees beside him.

'He's going to be OK,' Evanelle said. 'I'll go call the ambulance.'

'Give the police a description of him,' Tyler yelled after Evanelle, going for the gun and picking it up. 'They might be able to catch that lunatic. What kind of car does he drive, Sydney?'

'He's gone for good,' Sydney said. 'Don't worry.'

'Don't worry? What is the matter with you people?' Tyler was looking at them, suddenly realising they all knew something he didn't. 'Why did he freak out like that? And how in the hell did an apple roll to a stop at his feet if Bay was all the way over there?'

'It's the tree,' Claire said.

'What about the tree? Why am I the only one wigged out about this? Did you see what just happened here? Someone needs to get his licence-plate number.' Tyler started to run towards the street, but Claire grabbed his arm.

'Tyler, listen to me,' she said. 'If you eat an apple from this tree you'll see the biggest event in your life. I know it sounds impossible, but David probably did see how he was going to die. It chased him away. It chased our mother away. To some people, the worst thing to ever happen to them is the biggest thing to ever happen to them. He's not coming back.'

'Oh, come on,' Tyler said. 'I ate one of those apples and I didn't go off screaming into the night.'

'You ate an apple?' Claire asked, aghast.

'The night we met. When I found all those apples on my side of the fence.'

'What did you see?' she demanded.

'All I saw was you,' he said, which made Claire's features go soft as she looked up at him. 'What—' He didn't get to say anything else, because Claire had decided to kiss him.

'Hey,' Bay said. 'Where did all the photographs go?'

10

BAY STRETCHED OUT on the grass under the tree. The wind was blowing slightly, and there was the sound of paper flapping above her. She looked up at the photographs the tree had picked up that night, the black-and-white squares sticking out among the leaves on its highest branches. For six weeks, Claire and Sydney had tried to get the photos, but the tree kept moving its branches defensively, not letting them near. The sun was now beginning to fade the images, and Lorelei was slowly disappearing. Evanelle finally told them to leave it alone. The tree had always loved Lorelei. Let it have her.

School had started, and her friend Dakota was indeed in Bay's class. Things were all right, Bay thought. Maybe only halfway perfect because there still weren't any sparkles and rainbows on her face, but this was good enough. As close to her dream of this place as she was probably going to get.

Claire had planted some baby's-breath in the garden last week, which meant someone was getting married. Claire said it was Sydney. Sydney said maybe in a few years, or at the very least not until Henry regained full use of his hand, which had sustained some nerve damage in the injury to his shoulder. When Henry argued he didn't need his hand to get married, Sydney pointed out that it was his left hand that was injured. If she was going to put a ring on his finger, he was going to feel it. He said he already felt it. They would decide to elope that November. This meant Claire was going to be the one to use the little white flowers in a bouquet; she just didn't know it yet. Bay did, but she wasn't telling.

Evanelle had been in and out, usually arguing about something with Fred, who would never go so far as to admit that he liked his cooking class. But he did like it. A lot. And he treasured the gadget Evanelle had given him. Bay knew that, too.

Wait a minute.

She suddenly thought about the brooch Evanelle had given her, and her stomach jumped. Was that it? Was it really so easy?

She pinched her lips together as she unhooked the brooch from her shirt, where she had worn it every day for two months now, just in case she might need it.

The grass was soft like in her dream. And the scent of herbs and flowers was exactly like in the dream. There was the sound of paper flapping all around her. She lifted the starburst rhinestone pin above her head breathlessly. Her hand was trembling, not wanting to be disappointed. She moved the pin back and forth until suddenly, like a Christmas cracker, the light broke through and multicoloured sparkles rained down on her face. She could actually feel them, the colours so cool they were warm, like flakes of snow.

Bay smiled, and her body relaxed.

Everything was going to be OK.

Perfect, in fact.

Sarah Addison Allen

Sarah Addison Allen grew up in the American South, amid the beautiful mountains of western North Carolina, where her mother still makes cornbread that is out of this world and her father plays old-time banjo, claw-hammer style. Neither of these talents were passed on to Sarah, but she did become 'very good at eating and listening'. The former, she says, made her 'fond of elastic waistbands', the latter turned her into a writer. 'Asheville,' Sarah continues, 'is a strange, artsy, liberal city, birthplace of writer Thomas Wolfe. My dad was in the newspaper business and he worked for the *Asheville Citizen-Times* and became an award-winning columnist.'

Sarah went to college at the University of North Carolina in Asheville, 'where I spent five years trying to figure out what to do', finally graduating with a B.A. in Literature but still uncertain about her future. 'I'd always liked writing—I wrote my first book when I was sixteen, a very embarrassing futuristic romance entitled, *Once from Mood*—so I started again with the goal of being published.' To keep the money coming in while she was concocting stories in her spare time, Sarah did a number of casual jobs—'this period of my life is what I call my Odd Job Years. I've shown merchandise at an auction house. I worked in retail where my job was to stand by the sweater table and look pleasant. I worked for an accountant who liked to sleep on the couch among the clients in the waiting room after lunch. And I was an antiques appraiser's assistant—to name but a few.' In 2003 all that changed when Sarah had her first novel, *Tried and True*, published under the pen name Katie Gallagher. It was nominated by *The Romantic Times* for both Best First Book and Best Duets of 2003. Now Sarah also writes short stories for Southern fiction anthologies.

Growing up in the American South has indelibly shaped Sarah's character and her Southern roots and manners are brilliantly evoked in *Garden Spells*. 'I come from good Southern stock,' Sarah says. 'My mom is from an old Southern family. She wore elbow-length gloves and had a bouffant hairstyle. She married young, had children, and was the perfect wife. Then, when she turned fifty, she dyed her hair red and had her nose pierced. I call her the Disowned Debutante. I have one sister named Sydney, the name of one of the sisters in *Garden Spells*. I'm not married, but Sydney has been married four times, which I think is enough for us both. It was the job of my elegant great-aunt Charlotte to mould me and my sister into something proper. From a very early age we were instructed in the fine art of table place settings and napkin folding. She taught us that handkerchiefs were always embroidered, fingernail polish was always clear, women never pumped their own gas, and you were damned to hell if you didn't send thank-you notes. Sydney and I tried, we really did. But we're the daughters of the Disowned Debutante. We can't help ourselves.'

Jane Eastgate

Mood Food

In *Garden Spells*, Claire Waverley tries to control people's moods with her culinary creations. Pure fantasy, of course. Or is it? Scientists say that some foods do control our attitudes. For instance, the B vitamins in spinach combat sadness, and the tryptophan in turkey helps you relax. Fish high in omega-3 fatty acids, like wild salmon and herring, really are 'brain food', lubricating your nerve connections. The boron in avocados and broccoli keeps you alert. And, best of all, chocolate, with its phenylethylamine, is just what the doctor ordered to induce feelings of love and romance.